My Uncle Napoleon

A Novel by
Iraj Pezeshkzad

Translated from the Persian by
Dick Davis

MAGE PUBLISHERS
WASHINGTON, DC
1996

FIRST EDITION
Printed and manufactured in the United States

Library of Congress Cataloging-in-Publication
Pizishkzād, Iraj. [Dā'i-i Jan Nāpuli'un. English]
My Uncle Napoleon / a novel by Iraj Pezeshkzad;
translated from the Persian by Dick Davis. — 1st ed.
I. Dick Davis, 1945- .
II. Title.
PK6561.P54D313 1996
891'.5533—dc20

Cloth ISBN 0-934211-48-5

Mage books are available through better
bookstores, Baker & Taylor, or directly from the
publisher; toll-free 1-800-962-0922 or 202-342-1642.
Call for catalog or visit Mage online at http://www.mage.com

CONTENTS

PREFACE

THE EXISTENCE in Persian literature of a full-scale, abundantly inventive comic novel that involves a gallery of varied and highly memorable characters, not to mention scenes of hilarious farcical mayhem, may come as a surprise to a Western audience used to associating Iran with all that is in their eyes dour, dire and dreadful. And yet, in Iran itself, this novel is perhaps the most popular and widely known work of fiction to have been written in the country since the Second World War. Its wide acceptance by virtually all strata of society clearly belies the Western stereotype of the country as one that is single-mindedly obsessed, to the exclusion of all else, with religion and revolutionary revenge.

My Uncle Napoleon occupies a unique place in Iranian cultural and literary history, because of both the affection in which it is held by its very large readership, and the self-image of the society which it portrays. In the early 1970s, a few years after its publication, the novel was made into one of the most successful television series ever to have been aired on Iranian television, and it is almost impossible for an Iranian to read the novel without the gestures, voices and faces of the actors who portrayed the characters being present in his or her mind. Certain of these portrayals, especially the actor Parviz Sayad's portrayal of the roué with the heart of gold, Asadollah Mirza, and the late and much lamented Parviz Fanizadeh's portrayal of Dear Uncle Napoleon's servant Mash Qasem, have achieved the status of inviolable icons in popular Iranian culture.

For a foreign reader perhaps the most intriguing question, beyond the enjoyment of the novel simply as the comic masterpiece which it undoubtedly is, must be, How accurate is this portrait of Iranian society? Perhaps the best way of answering this is to make an analogy with a couple of Western comic fictional characters and the novels in which they appear. P. G. Wodehouse's Bertie Wooster seems to his readers—British and non-British—to be quintessentially British in his foibles and absurdity, and there is no doubt that his portrait draws for comic effect on features of social behavior that are or have been highly specific to British society, and yet England is not populated with Bertie Woosters, even though particular English individuals or customs may occasionally evoke a laugh of recognition based on familiarity with the Wodehousian stereotype. In the same way Anita Loos's Lorelei Lee (in *Gentlemen Prefer Blondes)* could only be an American character—her mannerisms and preoccupations tie her irrevocably to American society of the 1920s, and yet she is in her American way as unreal and as fantastic as Bertie Wooster is in his British way. Anita Loos and P. G. Wodehouse have used elements of their own societies and, by presenting them in the distorting mirror of farce, have produced versions of those societies that are recognizably based on features present in reality but are also outrageous exaggerations of those features—exaggerations that have been allowed, in the interests of facetious effect, to obliterate more mundane and less comically fertile aspects of social life. Iraj Pezeshkzad has done the same thing in *My Uncle Napoleon.* Any Iranian, and any foreigner who has more than a nodding acquaintance with Iranian culture, will recognize "real" and very culturally specific elements in the portraits and some of the situations present in the novel, but the Iran of *My Uncle Napoleon* is finally as "real" as Bertie Wooster's England; it is a fictional fantasy that uses isolated features of the author's social background in order to create the distortions and exaggerations of farce. This is not, though, to say that nothing in the novel corresponds with Iranian social reality, at least as it once existed; the book's author has written elsewhere of how after the novel was published various individuals would ask him how he had known so intimately about the speaker's father or grandfather, so convinced were they that this father or grandfather must have been the model for Dear Uncle Napoleon.

My Uncle Napoleon is at least three kinds of novel—a love story, a farce, and a satire on local manners and preoccupations. As regards the first two categories the Western reader should have little trouble following what is going on. The narrator links the love story in which he is involved to both Iranian archetypes (Farhad and Shirin, Amir Arsalan and Farrokh Laqa) and Western ones (Romeo and

Juliet, Paul and Virginie). The only aspect of this element that may give a young Western reader pause is the narrator's insistence that he distinguish his love for Layli from any sexual feelings he may have, and his horror at his uncle Asadollah Mirza's suggestion that he try to sleep with her—but this would have been the case also for many Western heroes created before the 1960s: the Paul of Bernardin de St. Pierre's *Paul et Virginie* is even more determinedly chaste and pure in his intentions toward Virginie than Pezeshkzad's narrator is toward his Layli.

As a farcical comedy the novel has undoubtedly drawn on culturally specific features and phenomena (some of the situations are reminiscent of those used by the Iranian folk comic drama tradition of *ru-hozi* performance), but it also has clear parallels with the Western comic tradition; the authors of *Tom Jones* or *Gargantua and Pantagruel* or *The Good Soldier Schweik* would have had no trouble in responding to what was happening in much of *My Uncle Napoleon*, and anyone acquainted with the Western comic tradition will easily recognize in this novel familiar elements of farce and comic invention. While translating this work, however, I have been made aware of how unsympathetic some presently modish opinions in Western intellectual (more especially academic) circles are to farce; the stereotypical treatments of sexuality and sexual roles that are inherent in the genre, and the anarchic amorality that drives many farcical situations, are neither of them very amenable to sympathetic interpretation by current politically correct standards. This may well be political correctness's loss, but if a Western reader feels uncomfortable with the farcical elements of the novel it is more likely to be for this reason than because the elements are unfamiliar in the Western tradition. Or to put it another way, if the reader can relish the farce in *Tom Jones* and *Gargantua*, the farcical elements in *My Uncle Napoleon* should prove equally accessible.

Satire is the most culturally and temporally specific of all literary genres, and thus it tends to have the shortest shelf life and be the hardest to export. If a satire is to survive the age in and for which it was written, and to appeal to readers from other cultures, it needs to contain substantial elements beyond the satire of local institutions and individuals, as is the case with Swift's *Gulliver's Travels*, for example, a work whose survival is probably due as much to its elements of fantasy and magical realism *avant la lettre* as to its satirical intentions. Certainly *My Uncle Napoleon* contains enough within its pages for it to make a broad appeal to readers quite unfamiliar with the specifics of Iranian cultural history, but equally certainly a knowledge of some features of that history will increase a reader's comprehension and therefore enjoyment of what is happening in the novel.

Much of the immediate historical background of the work can be gleaned from the novel itself, and the few details necessary for an understanding of the plot which the novel does not spell out are easily told. In 1941 the Allies (specifically the British and the Russians) invaded Iran, fearful that its government might declare for the Axis powers or that its oil reserves might fall into Axis hands. The country was occupied after a very brief campaign and the Allied forces stayed in Iran until the end of the war, forcing the abdication of the then shah (king) in favor of his son (who was the shah finally ousted by the Islamic Revolution of 1979). What is not apparent in such a summary outline of events is the cultural resonance of the invasion, and it is this cultural resonance which is the source of one of the chief comic devices of the novel, Dear Uncle Napoleon's obsession with the hidden hand of the English.

Since the early nineteenth century Iran had been an area squabbled over by the British and the Russians. The immediate reason for this was the presence of the British in India, and their desire to protect this jewel in the crown of the empire, and Russian expansion southward into the areas now occupied by the Moslem republics of central Asia. At the opening of the century the British and Russian borders in Asia were over two thousand miles apart; by the close of the century they were in places barely twenty miles apart. The Russians felt that the British had no business being in Asia at all, and the British feared a Russian threat to India. British and Russian agents and envoys both tried vigorously to control the shahs and tribal leaders of Iran and Afghanistan, and to influence them to favor their respective governments. Unfortunately for Iran, during most of the nineteenth century her government was severely strapped for cash and the country was in much need of both fiscal and social reform. Tribal discontent was an easy prey for foreign interference, and the ever-pressing need to raise money meant that successive shahs granted outrageous trading and development concessions to foreign businesses—particularly but not solely British—in return for (often not very much) cash on the table. Iran also went to war briefly with Britain (over Herat, in western Afghanistan), and twice went to war, with disastrous losses of territory as a result, with Russia. In 1907 Britain and Russia concluded an agreement at St. Petersburg by which Iran was to be divided into three "spheres of influence"—British (the southeast), Russian (the north) and neutral (the rest of the country, much of it desert). Iran was not invited to send representatives to the conference which led to this agreement, and naturally felt extremely affronted by its terms. Soon the ex-viceroy of India, Curzon (who was British foreign secretary from 1919-24), was pressing for Iran to be brought even more securely under British control. In the same period, agitation for democratic reform within Iran was at best ambiguously received by England, as one of the main demands of the reformers was the expulsion of foreign economic and political interests from the Iranian scene. The fall of the Qajar dynasty in the 1920s and the rise of Reza Shah (the king deposed by the Allies in World War II) were also seen by many Iranians to have been engineered by the British, and there is still scholarly disagreement as to whether the British were in fact involved in the coup that brought Reza Shah to power, and if so, how far they were implicated. Certainly they were instrumental in removing Reza Shah, and certainly, too, they strongly influenced the American decision to remove, by CIA covert action, the popularly elected prime minister, Mosaddeq, in the 1950s. Iranian suspicion of the power of the British to influence events in Iran, and of their motives and behind-the-scenes methods, has not therefore been—to put it mildly—without foundation.

Given such a background, Dear Uncle Napoleon's obsession with the British becomes more explicable. His (lying) claims to have been active in the Constitutional Movement for democratic reform, and to have fought against insurgents in the south of the country, locate his career in times and places where he could have come into conflict with what were seen as British interests and machinations. The British maintained connections to both sides of the constitutional conflict, and they at the least liaised with tribal factions antagonistic to the central government. Dear Uncle's paranoia is an extreme and comic exaggeration of a common phenomenon in Iranian culture, a conviction that much of the last two centuries of Iranian history, if not every minute detail of it, has been engineered from outside, and probably from Britain and/or (since World War II) the United States. This conviction can lead to what seem, for a Western observer, to be incredibly bizarre claims, including the very commonly held belief among some Iranians that the British organized the Islamic Revolution of 1979, and the almost equally common claim that the United States deliberately provoked the Gulf War against Iraq in order to have an excuse to send war ships to the Persian Gulf so that they could keep a closer eye on Iran. To question these claims is to label oneself either as hopelessly naive or as a sympathizer, open or covert, with those who wish Iran ill.

The brilliance and popularity of Iraj Pezeshkzad's portrait of this desperately paranoid patriot has led to a Persian equivalent of the term "Dear Uncle Napoleon-itis" being adopted as a name for such readiness to see conspiracy theories and the hidden hand of the West behind any and every local Iranian event. And yet there has been a real irony in the popular reception of the novel. In the same way that surveys in the United States have found that some of the audience for the fictional television bigot Archie Bunker in fact identified with his lumpen racist and sexist tirades, rather than finding them ridiculous, many readers of *My Uncle Napoleon* have taken the novel not so much as a lampooning of such paranoia but as a confirmation of the lasting relevance of such attitudes as a way of interpreting Iranian political life.

There is also of course an irony, of which I could not fail to be aware, in the fact that this novel, which bases so much of its comic effect on suspicion of, not to say hatred for, the English is here translated into English, and that the translation has been carried out precisely by a member of the suspected people in question. The ramifications of my own feelings about the matter are perhaps of interest mainly to myself and my family; suffice it to say that the great affection I feel for the novel and for the recently much-maligned culture of Iran, as well as the sheer importance of the novel in Iranian literary and cultural history, have been the impulses that led me to undertake the translation. And these motives have more than made up for the problems involved in this task. Such problems are many: some, like the unfamiliarity of certain customs, will be visible to the reader and need little explanation; I am assuming that the sympathetic reader will not find much difficulty with them. A small example of such a custom might be the wearing of pajamas around the house. What in the West are called (using the Persian word) pajamas are—or were—in Iran the natural informal wear of private life, and it is only the West that has relegated them to the bedroom. Some specific cultural references which may not be familiar, and which may prove to be stumbling blocks, have been explained in the brief glossary. Other problems will be less visible to the English-speaking reader but they remain glaring for the translator and may well be so for any who know the novel in Persian and dip into the translation. Not the least of such problems is the wonderfully rich colloquial and often very culturally embedded language of certain of the characters (particularly Mash Qasem and Aziz al-Saltaneh); such language must be the despair of any translator and I can only say I have tried to do the best that could be managed in finding English equivalents for their comic verbal pyrotechnics.

In carrying out this translation I have incurred many debts and I here record my gratitude to those who have helped me. My first thanks must go to the author, Mr. Iraj Pezeshkzad, who very graciously agreed to my request that I translate his novel, who has read through the completed translation chapter by chapter, and who has made various welcome suggestions.

I must also thank with equal gratitude Mohammad and Najmieh Batmanglij of Mage Publishers, who received my first draft of a translation of the novel's opening chapters with encouraging enthusiasm, and who have been immensely generous with their support while I have been at work on this project.

I should also like to thank Ahmad Hekmat and Helen and Alfred Mananian for providing me with video recordings of the Iranian television series based on the novel. Helen and Alfred are members of the large Iranian community in Columbus, Ohio, where I live, and I am indebted to many other members of this community both for their interest and encouragement and for their explanations of local and slang references and expressions I had failed to appreciate. It would be impossible to name everyone in the community who has helped in this way, and I am forced to ask them to accept my inadequate and collective thanks. I must, however, record my particular gratitude to my friend Mr. Mahmood Karbasi who has made innumerable, very valuable suggestions for improving the translation's accuracy and fluency.

As is the case with all my work on Persian subjects, my translation of this novel owes an immeasurable debt to my wife, Afkham Darbandi. I came to Persian because of her, my deep affection for the culture of Iran is mediated through my love for her, and she has been my inspiration and guide in all my involvements, scholarly and personal, with Iranian culture, including this translation. To Afkham and to everyone else who has helped me in this translation I offer my sincere thanks.

DICK DAVIS

My Uncle Napoleon

PRINCIPAL CHARACTERS

DEAR UNCLE NAPOLEON'S HOUSEHOLD

DEAR UNCLE NAPOLEON........ The patriarch of the family.

LAYLI.................................. Dear Uncle Napoleon's daughter.

MASH QASEM....................... Dear Uncle Napoleon's faithful servant.

NANEH BILQIS...................... Dear Uncle Napoleon's ancient maid.

DEAR UNCLE NAPOLEON'S CLOSE RELATIONS

NARRATOR........................... Dear Uncle Napoleon's unnamed nephew.

NARRATOR'S FATHER.............. Dear Uncle Napoleon's brother in-law.

NARRATOR'S MOTHER............ Dear Uncle Napoleon's sister.

UNCLE COLONEL.................. Dear Uncle Napoleon's brother.

SHAPUR, AKA PURI................ Uncle colonel's son.

DEAR UNCLE NAPOLEON'S DISTANT RELATIONS

ASADOLLAH MIRZA............... An official in the Foreign Ministry and half-brother (by his father's gardener's daughter) of Shamsali Mirza. The "Mirza" of his and his brother's names is an honorific indicating a distant relationship to the Qajar royal family.

SHAMSALI MIRZA.................. Asadollah's half-brother, a retired examining magistrate.

DUSTALI KHAN..................... A favorite of Dear Uncle Napoleon, second husband of Aziz al-Saltaneh, Qamar's stepfather.

MRS. AZIZ AL-SALTANEH........ Dustali Khan's wife and Qamar's mother, a cousin of Asadollah and Shamsali Mirza.

QAMAR.............................. Aziz al-Saltaneh's simpleminded daughter from a previous marriage.

MRS. FARROKH LAQA............. A gossip and a busybody.

NEIGHBORS, TRADESMEN, OFFICIALS AND THEIR RELATIONS

DR. NASER AL-HOKAMA........ The family doctor.

SEYED ABOLQASEM................ A local preacher.

SHIR ALI.............................. The local butcher; the "Shir" of his name means "Lion."

TAHEREH............................. Shir Ali's beautiful wife.

PRINCIPAL CHARACTERS

DEPUTY TAYMUR KHAN.......... A local detective.

CADET OFFICER GHIASABADI.. Deputy Taymur's assistant.

NANEH RAJAB........................ Cadet Officer Ghiasabadi's mother.

AKHTAR................................. Cadet Officer Ghiasabadi's sister.

ASGHAR THE DIESEL.............. Akhtar's boyfriend and protector.

HUSHANG............................. A local cobbler and shoeshine man.

BRIGADIER MAHARAT KHAN ... A Sikh Indian businessman; though not a military man, his honorific Persian title of *Sardar*, which loosely means "commander" has been translated as "Brigadier."

LADY MAHARAT KHAN........ The Brigadier's blonde English wife.

NOTE: The word "Khan," which often follows masculine names, is an honorific used to show respect (particularly from a younger to an older person) or, between equals, affection.

PART ONE

PART ONE CONTENTS

ONE

ONE HOT SUMMER DAY, to be precise one Friday the thirteenth of August, at about a quarter to three in the afternoon, I fell in love. The bitterness and longing I've been through since have often made me wonder whether if it had been the twelfth or the fourteenth of August things would have turned out differently.

That day, as on every day, they had compelled us—meaning me and my sister—by force and threats and a few golden promises for the evening, to go into the cellar in order to sleep. In the savage heat of Tehran an afternoon siesta was compulsory for all the children. But on that day, as on every other afternoon, we were just waiting for my father to fall asleep so that we could go into the yard to play. When my father's snores became audible I stuck my head out from under the coverlet and glanced at the clock on the wall. It was half past two in the afternoon. In waiting for my father to go off, my poor little sister had fallen asleep herself. I'd no choice but to leave her and I tiptoed out alone.

Layli, my uncle's daughter, and her little brother had been waiting in the main garden for us for half an hour. Our two houses had been built within one big enclosure and there was no wall between them. As on every day, we settled down quietly to our games and conversation in the shade of a big walnut tree. And then I happened to catch Layli's eye. A pair of wide black eyes looked back at me. I couldn't tear my gaze away from hers. I've no idea how long we'd been staring at each other when suddenly my mother appeared standing over us with a little multi-thonged whip in her hand. Layli and her brother ran off to their house and my mother drove me into the cellar and under the coverlet, threatening me as she did so. Before my head was completely hidden under the coverlet I looked across at the clock on the wall; it was ten to three in the afternoon. Before she in turn put her head under the coverlet my mother said,

"Thank God your uncle didn't wake up, because if he had, he'd have torn you all to pieces."

My mother was right. Dear Uncle (as we called him) was very particular about the orders he gave. He'd given an order that before five o'clock in the afternoon the children weren't so much as to breathe. Within the four walls of that garden it wasn't only we children who had learned what not sleeping in the afternoon and making a noise during Dear Uncle's siesta meant; the crows and pigeons appeared in the garden much less often because Dear Uncle had taken a hunting rifle to them a few times and effected a general slaughter. The street vendors of our area didn't go through our street, which was named after Dear Uncle, till five o'clock, because three or four times the man who came by on his donkey selling melons and onions had been slapped by Dear Uncle.

But that day my brain was working overtime and the name of Dear Uncle didn't put me in mind of his rages and bad temper. I couldn't get free of the memory of Layli's eyes and of her gaze even for a moment, and no matter how much I tossed and turned and how much I tried to think of something else, I saw her black eyes, brighter than if she were really there in front of me.

That night, underneath the mosquito net, Layli's eyes came after me once more. I hadn't seen her again that evening, but her eyes and her beguiling gaze were there.

I don't know how much time passed. Suddenly a weird thought seized my whole brain, "God forbid, I've fallen in love with Layli!"

I tried to laugh at this idea of mine, but no laughter came. It's possible for someone not to laugh at a stupid idea; that doesn't mean it's not stupid. But is it possible for someone to fall in love, just like that, without any forewarning?

I tried to recall all the information I knew about love. Unfortunately this information didn't amount to much. Although more than thirteen years of my life had passed, up to that moment I'd never seen anyone in love. At that time very few books about love or descriptions of the condition of people in love had been printed. Besides, they wouldn't have let us read any of them. My mother and father and relatives, especially Dear Uncle, the shadow of whose existence and thoughts and ideas enveloped every member of the family, forbade every kind of excursion from the house without a chaperone, and we didn't dare approach the other children who lived on our street. And the radio, which had begun broadcasting only recently, contained nothing in its two or three hours of daily programs which could help illuminate my mind.

In going over the information I had about love, the first thing I came to was Layli and Majnun, whose story I'd heard many times. But however much I dug around in the corners of my brain, I realized that I hadn't heard anything about how Majnun fell in love with Layli; people just said that Majnun fell in love with Layli.

Perhaps it would have been much better if I hadn't brought up Layli and Majnun in my researches, since the identity of names between Layli and Dear Uncle's daughter had an effect on what happened to me later, probably without my being aware of it. But I couldn't help it. The most important lovers I'd heard of were Layli and Majnun. Apart from them, there were Shirin and Farhad, but I didn't know anything special about how they'd fallen in love either. There was a love story published as a newspaper serial that I'd read, but I hadn't read the first few episodes and one of my classmates had described them for me. Consequently I knew nothing about the beginning of the matter.

I heard the clock on the cellar wall strike twelve. O God, half the night was over and I hadn't slept yet. This clock had been in our house for as long as I could remember and this was the first time I'd ever heard it strike twelve midnight. Perhaps this sleeplessness was evidence of my falling in love. From behind the mosquito net, in the half darkness of the yard, the strange, weird silhouettes taken by the shadows of trees and shrubs I saw terrified me—because, before I could reach a conclusion as to whether I'd fallen in love or not, I was terrified by the fate of the lovers I'd gone over in my mind. Almost all of them had suffered a sorrowful fate, ending in death and disaster

Layli and Majnun, death and disaster. Shirin and Farhad, death and disaster. Romeo and Juliet, death and disaster. Paul and Virginie, death and disaster. That love story in the newspaper, death and disaster.

God forbid, I'd really fallen in love and was going to die, too! Especially since at that time death was common among prepubescent children. Sometimes during family gatherings I'd heard them counting the number of children women had given birth to and the number that still remained alive. But then a flash of lightning lit up my mind with hope: we'd heard and read the story of the famous Amir Arsalan many times; only Amir Arsalan had brought his longing to a successful conclusion. Although the story of Amir Arsalan, and its happy conclusion, did on the one hand somewhat allay my terror of romantic adventures, on the other, in answer to my basic question, it weighted the scale in my mind toward the positive answer, that I had fallen in love. How had Amir Arsalan fallen in love? He'd seen a picture of Farrokh Laqa, and in that moment he'd given his heart to her. So, was it possible that I too had fallen in love with a single glance?

I tried to sleep. I squeezed my eyelids together so that sleep would come and I'd be free of these twisting, turning thoughts. Fortunately sleep doesn't let a child stay awake till morning, even if he is in love. Apparently such problems are for grown-ups who are in love.

Morning came. I had no opportunity to think more, because I'd slept longer than usual. I suddenly jumped up from sleep at the sound of my mother's voice, "Get up! Get up! Your uncle wants you."

My whole body trembled as though it had been connected up to an electric outlet. My voice wouldn't come and I wanted to ask which uncle, but the words stuck in my throat.

"Get up! He said you're to go over there!"

I couldn't think. Although it was contrary to all logic and reason, even a child's reason, I was certain that Dear Uncle was aware of my secret and I trembled with fear. The first thing that came into my head to delay my torture was to say that I hadn't eaten breakfast yet.

"Get up and eat quickly and go!"

"You don't know why Dear Uncle wants me?"

My mother's answer calmed me down to some extent, "He said all the children are to go there!"

I breathed again. I was used to Dear Uncle's sessions of advice and moral guidance. Every now and then he would gather all the family children together at once and give them a little advice and at the end of the meeting he'd give each one a candy. So bit by bit I pulled myself together and reckoned that there was no possible way Dear Uncle could have realized my secret.

I ate breakfast fairly calmly and for the first time since I had woken up I once again saw Layli's black eyes, in the steam from the samovar, but I tried with all my strength not to think of her.

As I was going toward Dear Uncle's house I caught sight of Mash Qasem, Dear Uncle's servant, in the yard with his trousers rolled up, watering the flowers.

"Mash Qasem, do you know why Dear Uncle wants us?"

"Well now, m'dear, why should I lie? The Master said I was to call all the children. To be honest I don't know what he wants you for."

Only we, exceptionally, had the right to call Dear Uncle "Dear Uncle," otherwise all our friends and acquaintances and the inhabitants of the area called him "the Master." Dear Uncle Napoleon (as he was called behind his back) was one of those long seven-syllable nicknames. Really seven syllables, in that you had to open and close your mouth seven times in order to have the right to say anything about Dear Uncle's existence. Dear Uncle's father, who for his part had had a six-syllable nickname, was simply "the Master" and little by little people forgot his name. Dear Uncle's father, on his own initiative, so that after he had gone there should be no split in the family unity between his sons and daughters, had had seven houses built in his huge garden and had divided them among his children while he was still alive. Dear Uncle was the oldest of these children and he had inherited the title "the Master" from his father, and, either because of his being the oldest or because of his own character and natural disposition, he considered himself the head of the family after his father's death, and he had made such an issue of this that none of this fairly large family dared so much as to take a drink of water without his permission. Dear Uncle had interfered so much in the private and public lives of his brothers and sisters that most of them had resorted to legal action in order to separate their houses from his and had either built walls or sold up and left.

In the part of the garden still remaining there were us, Dear Uncle, and one other brother of Dear Uncle's whose house was separated from ours by a fence.

Dear Uncle was in the sitting room with French windows, and the children were playing quietly in the inner courtyard of his house.

Layli looked up and came over to greet me. Once again our eyes stayed locked together. I felt my heart beating strangely. It seemed to be making a thumping sound. But I didn't have much opportunity to think about it and draw conclusions. Dear Uncle's tall, skinny, bony body, his leggings clinging to his limbs, appeared from within the room just as he was adjusting his thin cloak of Nain cloth over his shoulders. He was frowning. All the children, even those who were very little, felt that advice and moral guidance were not what was at stake and that something was badly wrong.

Dear Uncle's tall figure stood in front of us and as he looked upwards from behind his usual thick sunglasses he said in a dry, frightening voice, "Which of you has chalked filth on the door of this yard?"

And with a long, skinny finger he pointed behind us at the door of the inner apartments, which his servant Mash Qasem had just closed and beside which he was standing. We all automatically looked in that direction. On the door, in fact on the back of the door that led into the yard, someone had scrawled unevenly in chalk:

"Napoleon is a donkey."

The stares of most of us, of nine or ten children that is, turned toward Siamak, but before Dear Uncle lowered his head we realized our mistake and looked at the ground. For us there was no doubt that Siamak had done it, because we had frequently talked about Dear Uncle's love for and interest in Napoleon, and Siamak, who was more mischievous than the rest of us, had sworn that one day he would write out Napoleon's donkeylike quality on Dear Uncle's door. But a feeling of common humanity prevented us from betraying him.

Dear Uncle, who was standing in front of the line of us like a commanding officer in a prisoner of war camp, started to talk, but in the forceful, frightening, threatening speech he made he mentioned nothing about the insult to Napoleon; the pretext was making the door filthy with chalk.

After a terrifying moment of silence had passed Dear Uncle suddenly yelled out in a voice that seemed quite out of proportion to his skinny body, "I said, who did this?"

Once more surreptitious stares turned toward Siamak. This time Dear Uncle both noticed the stares and fixed his own angry and terrifying gaze on Siamak's face. At this point something happened. (I'm embarrassed to write this but I hope considerations of truthfulness and honesty will excuse such openness.) Siamak was so afraid that he peed in his clothes and began to stammer apologies.

When the punishment for both the crime itself and the crime committed during the search for the guilty one had been carried out, the crying Siamak set off for his house and we children followed him in a silence that was partly the effect of our fear of Dear Uncle, and partly respect and sympathy for Siamak's painful ordeal, since we to a great extent had caused it.

When the weeping Siamak complained to his mother about Dear Uncle, she, though she'd guessed and was in fact certain which Uncle he was talking about, automatically asked, "Which Dear Uncle?"

And her pain-wracked little boy unthinkingly answered, "Dear Uncle Napoleon."

We were all aghast, and stood there rooted to the spot. This was the first time that the nickname which we had given to Dear Uncle among ourselves had been spoken aloud before one of the grown-ups.

Of course this resulted in Siamak being punished once by his parents, too, but we breathed a sigh of relief. We'd repeated this nickname under our breath so often that we felt we were suffocating.

Dear Uncle had been crazy about Napoleon since his youth. Later we knew that he had gathered together in his library whatever books about Napoleon, either in Persian or French (Dear Uncle knew French to some extent), existed in Iran. And in fact a number of his bookcases contained only books about Napoleon. It was impossible for there to be any scientific, literary, historical, legal or philosophical discussion without Dear Uncle interrupting it by quoting some Napoleonic aphorism. Things had gone so far that, under the influence of Dear Uncle's advocacy, most members of the family considered Napoleon Bonaparte to be *the* greatest of all philosophers, mathematicians, statesmen, men of letters and even poets.

It seems that during the reign of Mohammad Ali Shah, Dear Uncle had been in the gendarmerie, with the rank of third lieutenant, and each of us had heard the story of his battles and clashes with bandits and insurgents forty or fifty times.

Among we children each of these incidents was distinguished by a certain name; for example, the story of the Battle of Kazerun, the Battle of Mamasani and so on. In the early years, the basis of each incident was a description of a skirmish that had happened in the little town of Kazerun or Mamasani between Dear Uncle, with five or six gendarmes, and a group of insurgents and vagrant thieves. But as time passed the number of enemies and the bloodiness of the conflicts increased. For example, the Battle of Kazerun had in the beginning been told as a skirmish between a group of insurgents and

Dear Uncle and five gendarmes, and their being cut off by ten or twelve of the insurgents, but after two or three years the Battle of Kazerun had changed to a bloody battle involving about one hundred and fifty gendarmes cut off by four thousand insurgents, egged on by the British, of course.

But what we didn't understand at the time, and which now that we've studied a little history we have understood, was that as Dear Uncle's interest in Napoleon increased, not only did his battles increase astronomically in size but they also began to resemble Napoleon's battles. As he was talking about the Battle of Kazerun he was also describing Napoleon's Battle of Austerlitz, and he didn't even stop himself from having infantry and artillery intervening in the Battle of Kazerun. Something else we only knew later on was that, when the gendarmerie in Iran was reformed and the previous members were given ranks according to their ability and knowledge, Dear Uncle, since he didn't have sufficient skill and knowledge for such affairs, though he claimed to have a genius for them, was retired at a low rank.

The second long night began. Once again Layli's black eyes, once again Layli's beguiling gaze, once again the agitated thoughts of a thirteen-year-old boy and the same questions and the same problems with the addition of one new question:

Perhaps Layli has fallen in love with me, too. O God have mercy! Now if it were only me who was in love there might be hope of some deliverance, but if she too . . .

During the whole time that we'd stood in line in front of Dear Uncle, although we were worried and apprehensive and terrified, and none of us had any confidence that Dear Uncle would find out the truth and administer justice fairly, still I either saw or felt Layli's gaze on my face.

Here was another problem that I had to find the answer to. Was it better for love to be one-sided or mutual?

Who could I ask? Who could I consult? If only Layli were here. No, there can be no doubt that I've fallen in love, otherwise why should I be so keen for Layli to be here? How about if I asked someone? But who?

How about if I asked Layli herself? But that's really ridiculous. For me to ask Layli, "Am I in love with you or not?" But . . . perhaps I could ask Layli . . . what? Ask her if she were in love with me or not? That's ridiculous, too. Besides, it's impossible I'd ever have the nerve to ask her such a question.

I thought about the children of my own age. No, it's impossible . . . Layli's brother, who was younger than me and wasn't very bright, how could I ask Ali? No, he was also a tattletale, he'd go and tell my father or, even worse, he'd go and tell Dear Uncle. Good God, isn't there anyone I can ask whether I'm in love or not?

Suddenly in the midst of my torment and disordered thoughts, a ray of hope appeared: Mash Qasem.

Yes, how about if I asked Mash Qasem? Mash Qasem was a villager who had become Uncle's servant. The whole family always talked about Mash Qasem's goodness and piety. Furthermore, he'd once proved it to me. One day Mash Qasem had seen me when I'd smashed a window in Dear Uncle's house with a ball; he didn't say a word to anyone.

Mash Qasem was always on our side on principle, and he would tell us strange, peculiar stories. The nice thing about him was that he never let any question go unanswered, and every time we asked him a question he would first say, "Why should I lie? To the grave it's ah . . . ah . . . !"

And as he said "Ah . . . ah" he'd show four fingers and later on we realized he meant that since the grave was very close, only the width of four fingers away, one mustn't tell lies. Although we sometimes understood or felt that Mash Qasem did tell lies, nevertheless he never let any question go unanswered; even if it were about something very profound or some astonishing phenomenon, he would find a response to it. It was a wonderful thing to us. When we asked him whether dragons were real or not, he immediately answered, "Well, m'dears, why should I lie? To the grave it's ah . . . ah . . . One day I m'self, with my own eyes, saw a dragon, on the way from Ghiasabad to Qom; I'd just turned a corner when suddenly I saw a dragon jump out and stand there right in front of me. He was an animal—God save you from such a sight!—somewhere between a leopard and a buffalo and an ox and an octopus and an owl. From the slit of his mouth about three yards of flame came leapin' out. I threw caution to the winds and with my spade I smacked him across his slit of a mouth and stopped his breath. He gave such a snort everyone in the town woke up . . . But what was the good of it, m'dears? Not a soul said to me, 'Mash Qasem, thanks for your trouble.'"

Mash Qasem had an explanation for every historical event and every stupendous invention, and if the atomic bomb had been invented at that time, he'd certainly have given a complete explanation of a nuclear explosion. That night the name of Mash Qasem shone like a ray of hope in my mind's darkness, and I slept fairly peacefully.

I woke up early next morning. Fortunately Mash Qasem was an early riser. As soon as he woke up he would busy himself with watering the flowers and attending to the garden. As I went toward him he was standing on a stool tidying the strands of sweetbrier that twisted about Dear Uncle's arbor.

"Can't you sleep, m'dear? How is it you're up so early today?"

"I went to bed early last night. So in the morning I wasn't sleepy."

"Well, go and play, it's not long before school'll be open."

I hesitated a moment, but I thought of the horrors of a third night. I threw caution to the winds and said, "Mash Qasem, I want to ask you something."

"Say on, m'dear!"

"One of my classmates thinks he's in love . . . but, how can I say . . . he's not sure . . . he doesn't have the nerve to ask anyone . . . do you know how a person finds out if he's fallen in love?"

Mash Qasem nearly fell off the stool. In a state close to astonishment he said, "What? How? In love? You mean he's got a crush on someone? One of your classmates?"

Very anxiously I asked, "But, Mash Qasem, is it very dangerous?"

Staring fixedly at his gardening clippers, Mash Qasem said calmly, "Well, m'dear, why should I lie? To the grave it's ah . . . ah . . . me m'self, I've never been in love . . . well, yes, I have, too. To cut a long story short I know what a disaster it is. May God not wish that on any poor devil! God willin' and by all the saints, may God not inflict anyone with the sorrows and sickness of a lover! A grown man can't get through bein' in love except by the skin of his teeth, so what would it be like for a child, m'dear!"

My legs didn't have the strength to hold my body up. I was really scared. I had come to ask Mash Qasem what the symptoms and signs of love were and here he was describing love's terrifying results to me. But no, I mustn't give up! Since Mash Qasem was the only experienced person who could give me the information I needed about love, and the signs of falling in love, I had to be strong.

"But Mash Qasem, this classmate of mine who thinks he's fallen in love wants to know first of all whether he's really fallen in love or not. And then, if he has fallen in love, he wants somehow to soften the pain of it."

"But, m'dear, can love be cured so easily? The damn thing is worse than every pain and unhappiness. God forbid, it's worse than typhoid and stomach cramps."

Bravely I said, "Mash Qasem, this is all very well . . . but how can someone know he's fallen in love?"

"Well, m'dear . . . why should I lie? From what I've seen it's like this, when you're in love with someone . . . when you don't see her you think your heart's frozen over . . . when you see her such a burnin' starts in your heart you think someone's lit a baker's oven in there. You want everythin' in the world, all the wealth in the world, for her, you think you've become the most generous man on earth . . . to cut a long story short, the only thing that's goin' to satisfy you's an engagement party . . . but there's this, too, if, God forbid, they give this girl to some other husband, then oh my Lord . . . There was a man in our town who was in love, and one evenin' there was an engagement party for the girl and another man; in the mornin' that neighbor of mine walked off into the desert, and now twenty years have gone by and still no one knows what happened . . . it's as if he'd turned to smoke and gone up to the heavens."

Mash Qasem wasn't in the mood to stop and he told one story after another about his neighbors and army buddies, and I was in a hurry to end the conversation because I was afraid someone would turn up. I said, "Mash Qasem, I wouldn't want Dear Uncle to know I'd asked you anything . . . because then he'd want to know who this person is or isn't or . . ."

"Would I say anythin' to the Master? Do you think I'm tired of life? If the Master hears anythin' about people bein' in love or sweet on one another he raises cane . . . he's quite likely to kill someone."

Mash Qasem nodded and then said, "God forbid anyone should fall in love with Miss Layli. Because the Master will wipe his family off the face of the earth."

With apparent indifference I asked, "But why would that be, Mash Qasem?"

"Well, I remember once years ago a boy fell in love with the daughter of a friend of the Master's . . ."

"And how did that turn out, Mash Qasem?"

"Well, why should I lie . . . to the grave it's ah . . . ah . . . I m'self with my own eyes didn't see it . . . but that boy suddenly disappeared. As if he'd turned to smoke and gone up to the skies . . . there were many who said the Master shot a bullet into his heart and threw him in a well . . . it was around the time of the Battle of Kazerun . . ." Mash Qasem started describing Dear Uncle's Battle of Kazerun.

We didn't really know when Mash Qasem had become Dear Uncle's servant but what we had gathered was, first, that he'd gone into service after Dear Uncle's duties in the provinces were over and he had returned to Tehran. Secondly, Mash Qasem's character was a little copy of Dear Uncle's. His imagination worked in a very similar way to Dear Uncle's imagination. At first when he backed up Dear Uncle's stories and descriptions of battles, Dear Uncle would yell at him and say, "What are you talking about? You weren't there!" But Mash Qasem took no notice and, because no one would listen to his daydreams independently and believe them, he directed all his attention over the years to becoming Dear Uncle's sidekick. As Dear Uncle little by little felt that his audience wasn't listening with sufficient credulity, particularly to his various stories about battles, perhaps because he needed a witness and perhaps because gradually, under the influence of Mash Qasem's promptings, he actually saw him there on the battlefield, he slowly accepted Mash Qasem's attachment to himself and his presence at the battles. This was especially so because, once Mash Qasem had heard the imaginary details of the battles of Kazerun and Mamasani and so on from Dear Uncle, he remembered them very well, and sometimes during the actual telling of a story he was able to help him out.

But one day, two or three years previously, this acceptance had become official.

That day Dear Uncle was furious. While repairing an irrigation channel Mash Qasem had carelessly, with a pick, cut through the root of Dear Uncle's big sweetbrier bush. Dear Uncle was nearly beside himself with rage and, after hitting Mash Qasem on the neck a few times, he screamed, "Get out of here. You've no longer any place in this house."

And Mash Qasem, bowing his head, said, "Sir, you'll have to have the cops take me out of this house, or have them take my corpse out of this house. Since you saved my life . . . while there's a breath left in my body I have to stay in this house and serve you. When was it that you did the deed you did?"

Then Mash Qasem turned to Dear Uncle's brothers and sisters and their children, who had all gathered there without daring to show any signs of interceding on his behalf, and with emotion in his voice said, "Think of it . . . in the Battle of Kazerun I'd been wounded by a bullet . . . I'd fallen between two boulders . . . bullets were rainin' down on all sides . . . I'd said my last prayers . . . the crows and the vultures were up there in the sky, eyein' me like . . . then suddenly, God bless him, the Master, and may God keep him the great gentleman he is, in the midst of that hail of bullets got himself to me. Like a lion he threw me across his shoulders, and he carried me just like that I don't know how far, till he got back to our foxhole. Do you think a man's goin' to forget something like that?"

All of us, who'd been so moved listening to the story, became aware of Dear Uncle. All signs of rage had disappeared from his face. He was gazing off into the distance. It was as if he really saw the battlefield there. Gently a slight smile formed on his lips.

Mash Qasem had also realized the change in the situation. In a mild voice he said, "If it hadn't been for the Master I'd have been dead and rotten, too, like poor Soltanali Khan."

At this point Dear Uncle repeated under his breath, "Poor Soltanali Khan . . . I wanted to do something for him, too, but it wasn't to be . . . God have mercy on him."

By means of these few words, from that day on, Dear Uncle formally accepted that Mash Qasem had been there in the war, under his command. A man who a little while previously had under no circumstances been ready to acknowledge that he had even known Mash Qasem at that time, after that referred to Mash Qasem as his orderly and he would ask Mash Qasem for the names of certain people and places during the repeated telling of his war stories. After a year or so, during gatherings of friends, he even had Mash Qasem tell the tale of how he, Dear Uncle, had saved his life. In this way

Mash Qasem—though the biggest incident in his life he could come up with while we were small children had been a fight with a few stray dogs in Qom—was also enrolled as one of the brave heroes of the battles of Kazerun and Mamasani.

That day, as usual, Mash Qasem once again started off on his description of the Battle of Kazerun, and while he was talking I quietly stole back to the house.

The conclusion of the involved thoughts that kept going back and forth in my head was that I really had fallen in love with Layli; in particular, the evening of the day when the itinerant ice cream seller had come by and I had happily given half of my ice cream to Layli, the wise words of Mash Qasem came into my mind, "You want everything in the world, all the wealth in the world, for her, you think you've become the most generous man on earth." It had never happened before that I had ever offered someone any of my ice cream.

Little by little I experienced all the signs and signals Mash Qasem had mentioned. When Layli wasn't there I really did feel as though my heart were frozen over, and when I saw her the heat in my heart spread even to my cheeks and ears. When she was with me I never gave a thought to the terrible consequences of love. Only when night came and she had gone back to her house and I was alone did I once again think of the terrible whirlpool of love. After a few nights, little by little, my fear and horror abated. Then, even when alone at night, I wasn't that afraid, because my nights were filled with memories of seeing her during the day. One of our relatives, who was employed in the Ministry of Foreign Affairs, had brought Dear Uncle a few bottles of Russian eau de cologne from Baku. Sometimes Layli's scent, which was that Russian eau de cologne, would stay on my hands and then I didn't want to wash my hands so that the smell wouldn't go. Little by little I felt I was enjoying being in love. After the misfortunes of the first few days I'd become a fortunate person, but I still had one worry in my heart. I wanted to know whether Layli was in love with me or not. I felt she was, but I wanted to be sure.

Despite this uncertainty, the days once more passed in complete happiness. The only times a cloud appeared in the clear sky of my cheerfulness was when I thought—God forbid—Dear Uncle had found out my secret. Sometimes I dreamt that Dear Uncle was standing over me with a gun in his hand, staring at my face with his enraged eyes. In terror I'd start up from sleep, soaked in sweat. Although I tried not to think about the outcome of my love, it was more or less clear to me that Dear Uncle would never accept it. The story of the falling out between Dear Uncle and my father was a very old one. Dear Uncle had been against his sister's marrying my father from the beginning, because he believed his own family was a noble one and he could never accept as suitable the union of an individual who was, in his phrase, an aristocrat, with an ordinary person, and one from the provinces at that. If my father's marriage to Dear Uncle's sister hadn't happened during Dear Uncle's father's lifetime, perhaps it would never have happened.

In addition, my father didn't feel the respect he should have for Napoleon, and in meetings and family gatherings and sometimes in the presence of Dear Uncle, he would disrespectfully refer to Napoleon as an adventurer who'd dragged the French nation through suffering and misfortune. I think this was my father's biggest sin, and the biggest reason for their falling out.

To be sure, the smoldering embers of these differences were normally invisible under the ashes. Just occasionally, for various reasons, especially over backgammon, they would flare up, and then after a few days things would return to normal again through the help of a family member acting as go-between. These skirmishes between Dear Uncle and my father were not very significant to us children because, whatever happened, we were busy with our own games. But after I knew I was in love with Layli, one of my chief worries was a flaring up of the quarrel between Dear Uncle and my father and, as bad luck would have it, one of the biggest skirmishes ever to affect my whole life was lying in wait for me.

The origin of the new hostilities was a party in the house of our uncle colonel. Shapur was uncle colonel's son, and the whole family called him "Puri," following the example of his mother. He had graduated from university and from the beginning of summer there had been talk of the splendid party that uncle colonel was going to give to celebrate his son's graduation.

Puri was a grind and the only member of our large family who'd taken his education beyond the level of a high school diploma. In Dear Uncle's "aristocratic" family, the children usually stopped their education around the third or fourth class of high school, and Puri's graduation from university really was a major event. Everyone in the family talked about his genius. Although the boy was no more than twenty-one, because of his height and the hump he had on his back he looked older than his age, and in my opinion he wasn't an intelligent person, he just had a good memory. He memorized his lessons to the letter and got good grades. Until he was eighteen his mother would take him by the hand and lead him across the road. All in all he wasn't a bad looking person, but when he talked he spluttered a bit. The whole family—especially Dear Uncle—had talked about his genius so much that we had nicknamed him "Puri the Genius." There had been so much talk about the splendid party that uncle colonel intended to give in honor of Puri the great genius's graduation that for the whole holiday half the chatter among us children revolved around it.

Finally the news came that on the evening of Puri's birthday there was also to be a party in celebration of his graduation. This was the first time that I'd spent from noon onwards preparing to go to a party. A bath and a haircut, ironing my suit, ironing my shirt, polishing my shoes, and all the rest of the preening and primping took up a good part of the afternoon. I wanted to show myself off as better than ever in Layli's eyes. I even dabbed a touch from my mother's bottle of "Souvenir de Paris," which was a strong feminine scent, on my head and face.

Uncle colonel's house had also been built in the big garden but uncle colonel had separated it from our house by a wooden fence. Uncle colonel in reality wasn't a colonel, he was a major, what they called then a "Yavar." A few years earlier, however, he had felt he deserved a promotion, and since, coincidentally Dear Uncle Napoleon had suddenly referred to his brother as "colonel," our family considered him a colonel and addressed him as such.

As we went into the inner courtyard behind uncle colonel's house I looked for Layli among the guests who had already arrived. She hadn't come yet. But before I took in the other people, my eyes fell on the great genius Puri. He'd attached a stiff striped collar to his white shirt and there was a tasteless colored tie around his neck.

After the genius's collar and tie, the thing which attracted my attention was the two-man band sitting on chairs beside their instruments (a *tar* and a *zarb*); there was a little table in front of them with some fruit and a few cakes on it. The *tar* player seemed familiar. A moment later I recognized him. He was the mathematics and geometry teacher from our elementary school. Afterwards I discovered that, to eke out his meager teacher's salary, he used to play the *tar* at gatherings and parties. The *zarb* player was a fat blind man who also sang. By eight o' clock the party had really warmed up and at regular intervals the band played a few cheerful songs. In one corner a group was gathered around a table of alcoholic drinks. From time to time I would stretch out my hand to the plates of cakes and fruit and I always took two, one of which I gave to Layli and the other I ate myself. Incandescent lamps flooded the whole area with light, and so I looked at Layli, and offered her cakes and fruit, very circumspectly. Puri the genius kept glancing over at Layli and me in an angry, spiteful way.

The regrettable event happened at about half past ten. Dear uncle colonel was showing off the new hunting rifle which Asadollah Mirza, the official in the Foreign Ministry, had brought him from Baku, and he was going on and on about its good points and waiting for Dear Uncle Napoleon to express his opinion.

Dear Uncle picked it up a few times and held it this way and that and looked at it. The women at the party reminded him a few times not to play with guns, and he answered with a smile that he was an expert on the subject of munitions and knew what he was doing.

While he had the rifle in his hand, little by little he began to think of the brave battles of his past and started to recall his memories of them, "Yes, I had a gun just like this . . . I remember, once in the thick of the Battle of Mamasani, one day . . ."

Seeing the rifle in Dear Uncle's hand and perhaps guessing that there was going to be talk of the wars, Mash Qasem had stationed himself behind Dear Uncle, and at this moment he interrupted the conversation and shouted, "Sir, it was the Battle of Kazerun."

Dear Uncle threw an angry look at him. "Why are you talking rubbish? It was the Battle of Mamasani."

"Well, why should I lie, sir? As far as I remember, it was the Battle of Kazerun." At this moment Dear Uncle realized something everyone had realized and this was that Mash Qasem had expressed an opinion on the name of the battle before he knew what Dear

Uncle was going to say, and that this reflected badly on the genuineness of whatever story he was going to tell. Quietly, but in a voice full of anger, he said, "My good man, I haven't yet said . . ."

"Well, I don't know about that, sir, but it was the Battle of Kazerun."

And he fell silent. Dear Uncle continued, "Yes indeed, it was one day in the thick of the Battle of Mamasani . . . we were in the middle of a valley. On both sides the heights had been taken by armed bandits . . ."

As Dear Uncle went on with his story he would sometimes rise up from his seat and then sink back down into it, and with the rifle under his right arm he made descriptive gestures with his left, "Just imagine a valley three or four times the size of this courtyard . . . now I'm here with forty or fifty infantrymen . . ."

In the midst of the guests' total silence, Mash Qasem once again interrupted, "With your faithful servant Qasem!"

"Yes, Qasem was what they now call my orderly . . ."

"Didn't I say, sir, that it was the Battle of Kazerun?"

"I said don't talk rubbish, it was the Battle of Mamasani, you're getting old, your memory's gone to pieces, you're gaga . . ."

"Sir, I never said a word!"

"Fine! Shut up and it'll be even better! Yes indeed, there I was and forty or fifty infantrymen . . . now those infantrymen were in a wretched state . . . as Napoleon has said, a commander with fifty well-fed soldiers can do much more than with a thousand hungry soldiers . . . and then all at once a hail of bullets started. The first thing I did was throw myself down from my horse. This Qasem here . . . with another fellow that was there . . . was next to me and I grabbed hold of him with my hand and pulled him down from his horse . . ."

Once again Mash Qasem interrupted, "It was me and none other, sir." And, shyly and fearfully, he added, "Not to be pushy like, sir, but I'd like once again to state it was the Battle of Kazerun."

Perhaps for the first time in his life, Dear Uncle regretted having allowed Mash Qasem into the arena of his battles.

"Hell and damnation, wherever it was! Now will you let me speak?"

"Sir, I'm completely dumb. I don't know a thing."

Dear Uncle, in the midst of his rage at Mash Qasem's impertinence—and if people hadn't been sure of his religious principles they'd have been convinced he was drunk—continued, "Yes indeed, I pulled this idiot—and I wish my hand had been smashed and I'd never saved him—down from his horse, and I got myself behind a boulder . . . a boulder about the size of the living-room . . . so what's the situation . . . two or three of our men have bullet wounds . . . and the rest have taken up positions behind rocks. From the way they'd attacked and were firing I immediately realized that I was dealing with Khodadad Khan's lot . . . the famous Khodadad Khan . . . one of the old lackeys of the English."

Under the influence of Dear Uncle's exciting story, Mash Qasem seemed to have taken leave of his senses, and once again jumped into the narrative, "Didn't I say it was the Battle of Kazerun?"

"Shut up! Yes indeed, the first thing I did was I said I've got to trick this Khodadad Khan . . . usually these rebels are pretty daring while their leader's alive, but as soon as he's killed they all run away . . . I crawled my way up the side of the boulder . . . I had a fur hat, I put it on a stick and lifted it up so they would think . . ."

Once again Mash Qasem couldn't contain himself, "Sir, it's like it was yesterday . . . I can see your fur hat before me eyes . . . now, if you remember, you lost your fur hat in the Battle of Kazerun, I mean it was shot through . . . in the Battle of Mamasani you didn't have a fur hat at all."

We were all waiting for Dear Uncle to brain Mash Qasem with the barrel or the butt of the rifle. But contrary to everyone's expectation, he melted a little. Either he wanted to quiet Mash Qasem down and finish his story, or in the world of his imagination he simply changed the site of the episode. He mildly said, "It seems that Mash Qasem's right . . . apparently it was the Battle of Kazerun . . . that is, it was around the beginning of the Battle of Kazerun . . ."

Mash Qasem's eyes lit up with joy. "Didn't I say so, sir? Why should I lie, to the grave it's ah . . . ah . . . it's like it was yesterday."

"Yes, I only had one thought in my head. This was to get Khodadad Khan. When I put my fur hat on that stick, Khodadad Khan, who was a first class shot, lifted his head up from behind a rock . . . now it was me and him . . . I invoked the blessed Ali and took aim."

Dear Uncle's tall body rose up. As if he were taking aim he put the rifle against his right shoulder and even closed his left eye.

"I saw nothing but Khodadad's forehead . . . I had seen him many times . . . those wide eyebrows . . . the scar above the right eyebrow . . . I aimed between the two eyebrows and . . ."

Suddenly, at this moment, in the midst of everyone's complete silence and just as Dear Uncle was aiming right between the eyes of his enemy, an unexpected event happened. From near the area where he was standing, a sound was heard. It was a dubious sort of sound, like the scraping of a chair leg over stone, or the unexpected squeaking of a worn out chair, or . . . but later I realized that most of the guests thought its origin *was* a chair and nothing worse had entered their minds.

For a moment Dear Uncle stood rooted to the spot. Everyone at the party was as if turned to stone; no one stirred. After a moment Dear Uncle's gaze seemed to wake up and move, glaring as if all the blood in his body had rushed into his eyes. He turned toward the nearby area where the sound had come from.

There were only two people there: my father and Qamar, a fat, heavy girl, one of our relatives, who was a bit simple.

For a short moment there was silence. All of a sudden Qamar began to laugh in an idiotic fashion. As a result of her laughter the children and a few of the adults, and even my father, began to laugh. Although I didn't really understand what was going on, I sensed the storm that was about to break and I squeezed Layli's hand hard in mine. For a moment Dear Uncle turned the rifle barrel so that it was pointing at my father's chest. Everyone fell silent. My father looked in a confused way from one side to the other. Dear Uncle suddenly threw the rifle onto a sofa at the side of the courtyard and in a strangled voice said, "As Ferdowsi put it:

> *'To raise up someone vile, to hope that they*
> > *Might then improve themselves in any way,*
> *Is tantamount to cutting your own throat*
> > *And nourishing a snake inside your coat.'"*

And then as he was on his way toward the door, he yelled, "Let's go!"

Dear Uncle's wife set off after him. And Layli, though she hadn't properly understood what was going on, felt its seriousness and withdrew her hand from my fingers' tight grip. With a quick look she said goodbye to me and set off after them.

TWO

IT LOOKED AS THOUGH I had another sleepless night ahead of me. I tossed from side to side beneath the mosquito net but sleep didn't come. It was over an hour since I'd returned from the party in uncle colonel's house. After my father left, immediately on the heels of Dear Uncle's angry departure, the party more or less collapsed. Perhaps a few of the guests were still there but they were talking so quietly that their voices didn't reach beyond Dear Uncle's yard, and I was sure they were discussing the unfortunate incident.

I went over the events of the last few days in my mind: I had suddenly fallen in love with Layli, Dear Uncle Napoleon's daughter. After love's first anxiety-filled days, I'd gradually felt myself to be lucky and I was glad I'd fallen in love, but then this unfortunate incident had destroyed my peace of mind and everyone else's. From the furious protests with which my father had responded to Dear Uncle's irate accusation I'd guessed that my father had had no part in producing the dubious sound. I could still hear the lowered voices of my mother and father coming from their mosquito net. Sometimes my father's voice would be raised and threatening but it was clear that my mother would then put her hand over his mouth. A few times I heard her say, "For goodness sake, dear, make less noise, the children might hear . . . whatever happens, he's my older brother . . . you know I'd do anything for you . . . just let it go!" The last time, before I slept, I clearly heard my father's angry voice again, "I'll give him a Battle of Kazerun he won't forget in a hurry . . . reciting that 'To raise up someone vile' poem at me!"

The next morning I came out from my mosquito net dreading the events which would logically come next. I ate my breakfast in the midst of my mother's and father's silence, and there was complete silence in the garden, too. It seemed that everything, even the trees and flowers, were waiting to see what Dear Uncle would do. Even uncle colonel's servant didn't raise his head while he was bringing back the chairs and plates we had lent for the party. I walked up and down till ten, waiting for Layli to come out of the house. Finally I couldn't stand it any more and I went over to Mash Qasem. "Mash Qasem, why haven't the kids come into the garden today?"

Mash Qasem was rolling a cigarette; he shook his head and said, "Well, m'dear, why should I lie? To tell the truth, I don't know anythin' . . . but it's possible the Master's told them they've no right to put a foot outside the house. You were at the colonel's house last night, weren't you? You saw what happened, didn't you?"

"Is Dear Uncle very angry?"

"Why should I lie? I haven't seen the Master from morning till now. But old Naneh Bilqis, when she took his tea for him, she said you'd think he was a wounded lion . . . and, m'dear, he's got every right to be. For that to happen right in the middle of talkin' about the Battle of Kazerun . . . now, if it'd been the Battle of Mamasani it would've been different, but the Battle of Kazerun's no laughin' matter . . . me m'self, I've seen with these very eyes the things the Master did there . . . if those parts is safe as houses now that's all the Master's doin' . . . God preserve him, I say. When he was on his bay horse swingin' his sword about on the battlefield . . . you'd think a lion was coming . . . me—who was one of us—I was scared to death, never mind the enemy."

"But Mash Qasem, do you think . . . that sound last night . . ."

"Certainly, m'dear, it was that all right . . . of course, why should I lie, I didn't really catch it properly, I mean I heard it but I was thinking about what the Master was sayin' . . . but the Master himself heard it . . . and when we got back to the house with the Master, young master Puri really stirred things up."

"You mean he went back to Dear Uncle's house with you?"

"Certainly, m'dear, he came as far as the door . . . in fact, he came right in. He kept whisperin' in the Master's ear that it was a great insult to the Master."

"But why, Mash Qasem? What will Puri get out of it if Dad and Dear Uncle are at each others' throats?"

I froze when I heard Mash Qasem's answer, the truth of which I only realized later.

"Well, m'dear, if you're askin' me, this young master Puri's really fallen for Miss Layli . . . his mother's already told Naneh Bilqis that she wants to come and ask for Miss Layli's hand like . . . that time last night when you and Miss Layli were foolin' about enjoyin' yourselves, well, it's like he was jealous. Besides, he hasn't figured it out that Miss Layli's thirteen or fourteen years old and can get married, but you, m'dear, can't get married at thirteen or fourteen."

I didn't hear any more of Mash Qasem's explanation. I'd thought of everything to do with love and being in love except a rival. And I should have thought of this before everything else. In every love story I'd ever read there was one person in love, the person he was in love with, and a rival. There were Layli and Majnun and Shirin and Farhad right in front of my eyes and I hadn't thought of a rival.

God, what was I to do about this individual? If I'd been as strong as him I'd have gone and given him a couple of juicy slaps around the head. The long smiling face of Shapur, the great genius, floated before my eyes and he looked far uglier to me than before.

The first straw it occurred to me to cling onto in this stormy sea was once again Mash Qasem; trying to appear completely calm I said, "Mash Qasem, do you think it's possible that Layli could become Puri's wife?"

"Well, m'dear, why should I lie? Layli's a big marriageable girl now. And this master Puri's finished his schoolin' . . . you know what they say, 'A marriage between cousins is arranged in heaven.' It's true he's a bit of a mammy's boy, and stupid with it, but he's a sly one."

Once again the terror of love overwhelmed me. I wanted to find some way to free myself. I was right to have been afraid of love from the beginning. Now I was ready to forget about love, if that were possible. But it was a bit late.

After I'd spent almost till noon struggling with the torments of my tortured heart, I once again went in search of Mash Qasem. "Mash Qasem, can I ask you a favor?"

"Say on, m'dear."

"I have to tell Layli something about some schoolbooks. Would it be possible for you to tell her, this afternoon when Dear Uncle's asleep, to go into the garden, just for a minute?"

Mash Qasem was silent for a moment. Then he raised his eyebrows, looked me up and down, and with a slight smile said, "OK, m'dear . . . we'll manage somethin'."

"Thanks, Mash Qasem, thanks."

That afternoon, as soon as I felt my father was asleep, I went into the garden. I waited almost half an hour. Cautiously, fearfully, Layli opened the door of the inner apartments and stepped into the garden. I came face to face with her under the same tree where, at about a quarter to three on Friday the thirteenth of August, I'd fallen in love with her.

The first thing she said was that she had to get back quickly, because Dear Uncle had said to her that if she set foot in the garden and spoke so much as one word to me or my sister he'd burn the whole house down.

I didn't really know what I wanted to say to her. Why had I wanted her to come? It would seem I had something important to say to her today. But what should I say?

"Layli . . . Layli . . . do you know what Mash Qasem says? He says Puri likes you and wants . . ."

From the look on Layli's face I realized that she knew nothing about this. I suddenly realized what a stupid situation I was in. Before the lover confesses his love to his beloved he becomes the means by which his rival confesses his love.

Layli was quiet for a moment. Like me, she didn't know what to say. We were both as tall as adults but we were still children. After a period of silence in which Layli was perhaps trying to find words, I said, "Puri wants to have his family ask for your hand."

Layli continued to stare at me as if dumbfounded. Finally she blushed and said, "If they do, what will you do?"

If they did, what would I do? What a difficult question she was asking me. I didn't even know what to do now, never mind if this happened! God, how hard it is being a lover! Harder than arithmetic and geometry. I had no idea how to answer. I said, "Well, nothing . . . I mean . . ."

Layli looked into my eyes for a moment, then suddenly burst into tears and ran sobbing toward the door of her house. Before I had time to show any reaction she'd entered the house and closed the door behind her.

Now what was I to do? I wished I could cry, too. But no, I mustn't cry. From the moment our eyes opened on the world, even before we could get our tongues around words or knew what they meant, they'd repeatedly dinned into our ears, "You're a boy, you mustn't cry! Are you a girl to be crying like that? Ha, this isn't a boy crying, it's a girl. Hey, Mr. Barber Man, come and cut his willy off!" When I was back in the basement and had got my head under the coverlet, I realized what I should have said, "I'll kill that Puri like a dog . . . I'll carve his black heart out with a dagger." Bit by bit I got more excited, till I suddenly frightened myself with the sound of my own voice, "You think I'm dead that I'd let that idiot get close to you. You're mine! You're my love . . . no one in the world dare separate you from me."

My father's angry voice returned me to the real world, "You damn fool, what are you shouting about? Can't you see everyone's trying to sleep?"

That night was hard to get through, too. In the morning I once again went in search of Mash Qasem. But Mash Qasem looked extremely angry. With a very serious, even melancholy face, and with a spade in his hand, he was standing by the water channel at the point where it flowed toward our part of the garden.

The layout of our houses in the garden was such that the channel of water coming in from the street entered the garden at the part that belonged to Dear Uncle, then from there it flowed to the part of the garden that belonged to us, and from our house it went to uncle colonel's house; so that in order for the water to get to uncle colonel's house, which was at the end of the garden, it had to go first through Dear Uncle's house and then our house.

I was still looking for a way to ask indirectly how Layli was when uncle colonel arrived with his jacket flung over his shoulders and his long underwear tucked into his socks. In a surprised, expostulating voice he said, "Mash Qasem, our man says that last night you wouldn't let the water through to our storage tank."

Mash Qasem stood there without moving, his spade in his hand, and, without looking at uncle colonel, he said in an expressionless voice, "Well sir, that's how it is."

"What do you mean, that's how it is? What do you mean?"

"Why should I lie? I don't know nothin'!"

"What do you mean 'I don't know nothin'?' You stop the water coming through to us and now you don't know about it?"

"Ask the Master! This is what he told me."

"You mean to say that the Master told you to stop the water coming through to us?"

"Ask the Master, I don't know nothin'."

Uncle colonel, who still couldn't believe that such an order could have been given by his older brother, went up to Mash Qasem to try to get the spade out of his hand and open the water channel, but from the extremely stern face of Mash Qasem, who stuck to his post without moving, like a brave sentry conscious of his duty, he realized that the matter was more serious than he had thought. He suddenly stopped going toward Mash Qasem and set off for the inner apartments of Dear Uncle's house. Mash Qasem, very calmly, said, "If only you knew it, you're payin' for someone else's sins."

Whatever passed between uncle colonel and Dear Uncle Napoleon remained unknown to us. But we soon realized that cutting off our water, and, as a result, cutting off uncle colonel's water, was part of Dear Uncle Napoleon's attempts to be revenged on my father.

And this was the worst revenge that Dear Uncle Napoleon could have taken on us. At that time, when there was no piped water, once each week the man who distributed the water let the water into our street's channel and with this water we had to fill the storage tanks. During the twenty-four hours that the water was flowing we had to fill the tanks or we had no water until it was our turn again.

Two whole days passed in which I didn't see Layli; I even cried at the memory of her tearful eyes, but there was so much coming and going, and the diplomatic discussions aimed at peacefully solving the crisis and restoring the water supply went on for so long, that I'd more or less forgotten about my own troubles. There wasn't even one drop of water left in the storage tank in uncle colonel's house. The flowers and trees had withered completely. My father was acting stubborn and didn't make the slightest objection because we still had a little water in our tank, so he just sat tight, apparently trusting in uncle colonel's efforts, as what happened to him was completely dependent on what happened to us. Every now and then I heard, from behind closed doors, members of the family suggesting to my father that he apologize to Dear Uncle Napoleon, but each time my father raised his voice and got out of it and even said that if Dear Uncle Napoleon didn't apologize to him and still persisted in cutting off the water, he'd get his rights by turning to the courts and the police. The words "courts and the police" made every member of the family tremble and everyone cried out what a calamity it would be if the centuries-old honor of a noble family were thrown to the winds like this. In any case my father felt the strength of his position and not only was he not ready to apologize to Dear Uncle Napoleon, but he firmly expected Dear Uncle, in the presence of everyone else, to apologize to him. Poor me, stuck in the middle of this! And poor little Layli! And poor, hapless uncle colonel!

On Friday I became aware of a great deal of coming and going in uncle colonel's house. I made my way over there, in the hopes of seeing Layli. Layli wasn't there and we children were not allowed into the living room, but, from the people who were arriving, I realized that this wasn't a question of an ordinary friendly visit but that a real family council was in progress. Dear Uncle's two other brothers came. Asadollah Mirza, an official in the Foreign Ministry, came. Dear Uncle's sisters came. Mrs. Aziz al-Saltaneh came. In short, ten or twelve of the senior members of the family were gathered in uncle colonel's sitting room. We children hung around in the corridor and in odd corners.

When we realized that they had sent to inquire a few times for Shamsali Mirza, who hadn't arrived yet, we knew that it was a more serious matter than we'd imagined. Shamsali Mirza was an examining magistrate; for some reason we weren't aware of he'd been relieved of his duties and lived in Tehran.

About an hour after everyone else had come, we realized from the extravagant compliments uncle colonel was making that Shamsali Mirza had also arrived.

"Your excellency, please . . . your excellency, would you be so kind, this way, please . . ."

Although they'd always told us that listening at doors and eavesdropping were disgusting things to do, I was all ears and in fact I'd glued my ear to the sitting room door. In truth I had more right to know what was going on than those who were in there, since they were simply losing their flowers and trees and perhaps their indestructible family unity, whereas I saw my love and perhaps my whole life as being in danger.

Uncle colonel's excited speech about the benefits of a sacred family unity, and the harmful results of the lack of a sacred family unity, didn't last long and ended with these words, "Our late lamented father must be turning in his grave. I have done everything I could to preserve the unity of this ancient family and I've gone on bended knee to both of them but neither my older brother nor my sister's husband will climb down from their high-horses and stop this pigheadedness. Now I'm begging you to do something to preserve the sacred, centuries-old unity of this family and not let the courts and the police set foot in this house."

I couldn't see uncle colonel's face but his excited, bitter tone of voice was testimony to how much he loved his flowers and fruit trees.

After uncle, Shamsali Mirza started to speak. When the new court system had been set up, Shamsali Mirza had been appointed as an examining magistrate and he considered interrogation and cross-examination to be the key to solving all problems—social, familial or of any other kind. In a forceful and logical speech he suggested that before all else it must first be established whether the dubious sound which had caused the argument had a human or a non-human origin; secondly, in the case that it had a human origin, it must be established whether it came from the area where my father was or not; thirdly, in the case that it came from the area where my father was, was it intentional or unintentional.

When Shamsali Mirza saw that the majority of those present objected to going into such details, he did what he usually did; he put his hat on his head and said, "Then, ladies and gentlemen, with your permission your humble servant will take his leave."

Asadollah Mirza, the official of the Foreign Ministry, had a habit, whenever he wanted to suggest that someone consider things for a while and not rush to conclusions, of saying, in English, *moment, moment*, pronouncing the word German-fashion with the second syllable accented. And that day, too, when he saw his brother Shamsali Mirza putting his hat on his head to go, he shouted, "Moment, moment!"

And since everyone had reached a dead end in their attempts to solve the problem, they all joined in and sat Shamsali Mirza down again and submitted to his cross-examination.

Shamsali Mirza's first question, which was whether the dubious sound had had a human or a non-human origin, did not get a proper answer. This was because everyone present had also been at uncle colonel's party that night, and some of them attributed it to a chair while a smaller group considered that it had had a human origin. And there were one or two people who hesitated between a human origin and a chair.

A question that derived from the first and fundamental question was then put: Who had been close to the place where the dubious sound appeared? My father, Dear Uncle Napoleon, Qamar—the girl who was simple—and Mash Qasem. Cross-examination of the first two on this subject was not possible, while Qamar, considering her health and general condition, could not be a good witness. Mash Qasem was the key to solving this riddle.

On Shamsali Mirza's orders Mash Qasem was brought in, and Shamsali Mirza, exactly like an examining magistrate interrogating an accused man, first had him swear that he would tell the truth, the whole truth, and nothing but the truth, and then—after pointing out that his testimony would be instrumental in preserving the sacred unity of a noble family and that he must give his evidence as conscientiously as he could—asked, "Mr. Mash Qasem, did you with your own ears hear the dubious sound which arose while your master was talking?"

After a moment's pause, Mash Qasem answered, "Well now, sir, why should I lie? To the grave it's ah . . . ah . . . God rest his soul, there was a man in our town who used to say . . ."

"Mr. Mash Qasem, you are before a magistrate. I must ask you not to stray from the subject and to answer my questions!"

"Yes sir, you're the boss, you were saying about that duvious sound . . ."

"Dubious!"

"Come again?"

"What do you mean, 'Come again?' You said 'duvious'; I said, say 'dubious'!"

"Well sir, why should I lie? I've not had no schoolin' but what I want to know is, what's the difference?"

"What's the difference?"

"The difference between what I said and what you said?"

Shamsali Mirza lost all patience and yelled, "I said 'dubious' and you said 'duvious'; I said say 'dubious'!"

"And so what's it mean, this duvious and dubious?"

The inappropriate interruption at this point of Asadollah Mirza, the Foreign Ministry official, who always turned everything to a joke, and who explained the "dubious sound" for Mash Qasem by calling a spade a spade, infuriated Shamsali Mirza since one must not joke with the process of the law; once again he placed his hat on his head in order to leave. Everyone jumped up and sat him back down again.

"All right, Mash Qasem, now you've understood what the meaning is, tell us whether you heard this dubious sound with your own ears or not?"

"Well now, sir, why should I lie . . ."

Shamsali Mirza angrily interrupted him, "Yes, yes, we know . . . to the grave it's ah . . . ah . . . we've one foot there already. But answer my question!"

"Well now, sir, why should I . . . do you want the truth or a lie?"

"What do you mean? Are you joking? When I ask a question it's obvious I want the truth!"

"Good, and I'll tell you the truth . . . because why should I lie . . . to the grave it's ah . . . ah . . . Now I heard a sound . . . but whether it was a dubious sound or not a dubious sound . . ."

"My dear sir, I said 'dubious'."

"Isn't that what I said?"

"You said 'duvious'."

"Well, as far as I remember, I said 'dubious'; anyway, I heard a dubious sound . . ."

"Do you consider that this sound came from a chair leg or . . ."

"Or what?"

"Sir, my patience is at an end . . . or what my brother just said."

Hearing himself referred to, Asadollah once again jumped into the conversation, cutting it off with a loud burst of laughter and telling a story about a man from Qazvin and a cloth dealer, which went like this: "Just as the guy from Qazvin was buying some cloth he let out a loud fart, so he started to tear different bits of cloth so that the other guy would think it was the sound of the cloth ripping. The cloth-dealer grabbed him by the wrist and said, 'There's no point ripping the cloth and wasting it; after forty years at this job I can tell the difference between cloth ripping and other sounds.'"

Once again those present sat Shamsali, who was on the point of leaving, in his place, and the cross-examination continued.

"Well, you were saying, Mash Qasem . . . we are waiting for your answer."

There was absolute silence and everyone's eyes were fixed on Mash Qasem's mouth.

"Well sir, why should I lie? It's like it was . . . that, sir."

Shamsali heaved a contented sigh and a satisfied smile spread across his face, exactly as if, after hours of cross-examining a dangerous witness, he had extracted a confession from him. He glanced triumphantly to right and left and then said, "The answer to the first question has been given. Let us proceed to the second question."

In answer to the second question, as to which person the sound had originated from, Mash Qasem paused for a while and then said, "Well, sir, why should I lie . . . to the grave it's ah . . . ah . . . I was listenin' to the Master who was describin' the Battle of Kazerun . . . he was sayin' he'd just taken aim at the middle of Khodadad Khan's forehead, he'd pulled the trigger and the first bullet'd missed and whizzed past Khodadad Khan's ear . . ."

Uncle colonel interrupted, "Mash Qasem, my brother hadn't got that far, he'd only got as far as taking aim at Khodadad Khan's head."

"Yes indeed, sir, but as I've seen it with my own eyes, I was just describin' the rest of it for you."

"That's not necessary. Just answer his excellency's questions."

"Well, sir, why should I lie? When the sound came I was payin' attention to the Master. I turned round and I saw that gentleman was there and also Miss Qamar. Now, was it him or was it her? Why should I lie . . . to the grave it's . . ."

At this point uncle colonel cut Mash Qasem off, "I've thought of something. If Mrs. Aziz al-Saltaneh will agree to it . . . that is, if she could make a small sacrifice for the sacred unity of the family . . ."

"What have I got to do?"

"Be so kind as to agree that we tell my older brother that this trivial thing originated from Miss Qamar."

"I don't follow. What about Qamar?"

"I'm just suggesting that if we tell my older brother that Qamar wasn't feeling very well that night, the business . . ."

It dawned on Mrs. Aziz al-Saltaneh what was being suggested. For a moment she pursed her lips and was silent. Then suddenly a storm of screams and curses directed at uncle colonel and the rest of the family began, "Aren't you ashamed of yourself? Aren't you ashamed to say such things to me, with my white hair? My daughter? My daughter do such a thing?"

She screamed so much that everyone was upset and took great pains to calm her down. Her fury abated but she started to cry, "I've brought that girl up like a flower . . . and now a suitor's appeared for her . . . and it's all ready to be agreed . . . and her own family are ready to throw a spanner in the works . . . they want to drag her name in the mud . . . to think I'd live to see such a thing . . . to hell with their damn family unity . . ."

Everyone was completely silent for a moment, more out of respect for the bad luck of Qamar's future husband and Aziz al-Saltaneh's future son-in-law, than out of regret that the matter still wasn't solved. The first sound to be heard was from Mrs. Farrokh Laqa, one of the family's foul-mouthed, gossiping busybodies. She interfered in everyone's business, and her interpretations of the smallest matters set off arguments and fights. Everyone was surprised that she hadn't said anything until this point. In the complete silence that followed Aziz al-Saltaneh's yelling and crying she suddenly opened her mouth and said, "You're quite right, my dear. These people don't care at all about a girl's reputation or about her future."

Aziz al-Saltaneh didn't let her finish her sentence; wiping her eyes with her handkerchief she said, "Thank you, thank you, dear. They just don't understand how much trouble's involved in bringing up a girl and finding her a husband."

Mrs. Farrokh Laqa, who always wore black and normally only went to religious gatherings, continued in her usual calm, dry voice, "By the way, my dear, how was it that things didn't work out with Qamar's first husband? It seems the wedding was never . . . ?"

"Well, my dear, I've her family to thank for that, too . . . they put a spell on her husband . . . they padlocked him . . . my poor little orphan waited a year . . . and her husband was dying to have her . . . but there it is, dear, when they padlock a man what a terrible thing it is . . ."

Shapur, uncle colonel's son, who was quietly sitting in a corner of the room, started to splutter and asked, "Aunty dear, what does padlocking someone mean?"

It was a stupid question. Even we children had heard the expression so often from Aziz al-Saltaneh, and the women of the family had gossiped about it so much, that we'd realized what was meant. But before anyone involved in the matter could answer, Asadollah Mirza said, "Moment! You, at your age, don't know what padlocking someone means?"

Shapur, a.k.a. Puri, for all his genius, answered, "How should I know?"

Asadollah Mirza winked and with a laugh said, "It means he couldn't manage San Francisco!"

With this explanation even the little children, who were clustered behind the door, realized what was implied. Asadollah Mirza had a habit of shouting out, whenever he or someone else was telling a sexy story and the girl and boy went off together, "And then it was San Francisco time" or "And then off they went to San Francisco."

After his explanation, his loud laugh rang out and he said, "If they'd said before, I could have done something for him . . . whatever happens I've a fine bunch of keys for opening these padlocks . . . as far as the family's concerned, I'm ready to make any kind of sacrifice!"

Everyone burst out laughing at his joke, even the sullen Shamsali Mirza. Mrs. Aziz al-Saltaneh gritted her teeth for a moment and then suddenly hurled a plate with a slice of watermelon on it into the middle of the room and yelled, "Have you no shame? Aren't you ashamed in front of me with my white hair . . . God damn you and your bunch of keys!"

And with no further hesitation she stood up and made for the sitting room door. The next moment the door was flung open and we were able to see very clearly what was going on. Uncle colonel wanted to head her off but Aziz al-Saltaneh struck him on the chest with the flat of her hand and left the sitting room in high dudgeon.

After she had gone everyone blamed Asadollah, either by looks or with sharp words, but he wasn't backing down and said, "Moment, moment . . . don't attack me unfairly . . . I said this out of pure public spiritedness so that if a new suitor should accidentally find himself padlocked, they'll know that when it comes to my own kith and kin, I'm at their service."

And again he roared with laughter.

Uncle colonel quieted him with an angry look and said, "This is no time for joking. Now can you suggest what we should do to get my older brother to climb down from his high horse. Whatever happens, this state of enmity and argument in the family can't go on."

To make up for his levity, Asadollah said in a very serious voice, "Let's get back to the dubious sound. I just want to know how it's so obvious that the dubious sound didn't in fact originate with Qamar. A big fat girl like that who—God bless her and keep her and more power to her elbow—eats three times the amount I do, it's possible . . . it's possible that for once . . ."

Shamsali Mirza flared up again and angrily said, "As this case is now a matter of laughter and tomfoolery, your humble servant, with his friends' permission . . ."

"Moment, moment . . . my dear brother, I beg you not to get angry . . . I'm very seriously looking for a solution. I want to ask the colonel here why, in principle, he has to have Mrs. Aziz al-Saltaneh's agreement? You yourself can tell the Master that it was Qamar who did it."

This suggestion set everyone thinking. Well, yes, really and truly, what reason was there that they should tell Mrs. Aziz al-Saltaneh at all?

After a moment uncle colonel said, "But since I've tried so hard to make peace between my older brother and my sister's husband, he won't believe me. How would it be if we asked Naser al-Hokama to do it?"

This idea pleased everyone and they sent Mash Qasem to find Dr. Naser al-Hokama, who had a house opposite our garden and who had been our family doctor for years. It didn't take long before Naser al-Hokama, with his puffy eyes and many-layered double chin, appeared; his habitual phrase was "Your good health."

To everyone present he bowed his head and said, "Your good health . . . Your good health . . ."

When uncle colonel explained the situation to him, he accepted virtually without any objection and even—for the sake of his own conscience—unhesitatingly considered the poor girl to be the actual perpetrator of the act.

"Yes sir, yes, I've told Mrs. Aziz al-Saltaneh so many times that Miss Qamar should be examined. The girl is overweight, she eats too much, things that cause flatulence . . . and she's not entirely all there. It's natural that, as she's not entirely all there, when there's flatulence in her stomach these unfortunate things will happen."

Dr. Naser al-Hokama, surrounded by expressions of gratitude from uncle colonel and everyone else, and repeating "Your good health," set off for Dear Uncle Napoleon's house.

Half an hour passed with Asadollah's jokes and dirty stories. Dr. Naser al-Hokama's head appeared round the door. He looked very cheerful and satisfied.

"Your good health . . . praise God, the misunderstanding has been cleared up. The Master is very sorry that he judged too hastily. He promised that tomorrow he will make it up to you. Of course I had to work quite hard at it . . . I even swore on the soul of my late father that I myself had heard the sound with my own ears that night and that I had correctly diagnosed its cause."

Everyone, and especially uncle colonel, was indescribably pleased, but I more than anyone felt I was about to burst for joy. I wanted to kiss the doctor's hand. Asadollah started snapping his fingers and with a great guffaw promised he was going to propose the doctor as a member of the League of Nations and I laughed at his fooling around from the bottom of my heart. As he was getting up to go Asadollah Mirza laughingly said, "Moment! The unity of the family has been preserved, but be careful that none of this reaches the ears of Qamar's suitor because this time the padlock will snap shut automatically, and if there's no San Francisco this time, Aziz al-Saltaneh will be out for everyone's key and padlock!"

While those present were busy saying goodbye to uncle colonel, I caught sight of the sad, frowning face of Puri, the great genius. I felt in my bones that he was very upset that the crisis had been resolved. But I was so happy that I paid no attention to his situation and I ran toward our house to tell my father the good news. My father didn't show much pleasure or joy and under his breath he muttered, "It's really true that ignorance is bliss."

My mother started begging and pleading again, "Now that he's calmed down, you calm down, too. God knows I'd die for you, dear, but for your dead father's sake, let it go."

It was night and I'd no hope of seeing Layli now, but thinking of her and hoping to see her in my dreams, I lay peacefully down to sleep.

THREE

I DON'T KNOW how long had passed before I was suddenly awakened by the sound of a distant cry. Some one was shouting out intermittently, as if he were being smothered, "Thief . . . thie . . . thie . . . thief . . ."

I jumped up. My mother and father had also both woken up. We listened attentively. There could be no doubt that it was Dear Uncle Napoleon's voice, calling from the balcony that overlooked the garden. Suddenly the sound stopped and was followed by the noise of running and a general uproar. My mother and father and I and my sister leapt out of our mosquito nets. Our servant grabbed a stake for holding up a mosquito net and ran off toward Dear Uncle's garden and we ran after him in our night clothes.

Mash Qasem, who had just woken up, opened the door of Dear Uncle's inner apartments for us. Layli was standing terrified next to her brother in the doorway of one of the rooms.

"What's happened, Mash Qasem?"

"Well sir, why should I lie . . . I . . ."

"Was it the Master's voice?"

"Looks like it was the Master's voice."

We ran through various rooms toward the balcony where Dear Uncle slept at nights on his great wooden bed. But the door between the verandah and Dear Uncle's room had been locked from the other side. However much they pounded on the door, no answer came, and the door didn't open.

Mash Qasem struck himself on the head, "My God, they've kidnapped the Master."

Layli's mother, who was a relatively young woman, shouted, "Sir . . . sir, where are you? God help us, they've kidnapped him!"

My father tried to calm her down.

Layli's mother was Dear Uncle's second wife. Dear Uncle had divorced his first wife, after they had been together for thirteen years, because she couldn't have children. This divorce had had a profound affect on the whole of Dear Uncle's life, on account of its similarity to the separation of Napoleon Bonaparte and Josephine after thirteen years together as husband and wife. Later we realized that Dear Uncle had foreseen the resemblance between his own fate and the French emperor's largely on the basis of this analogy.

On my father's orders, Mash Qasem brought a ladder and up it quickly climbed first Mash Qasem, behind him my father and, with a rifle in his hand, uncle colonel, who had arrived in a shirt and white longjohns, then Puri and me. On one side of the bed the string holding up the mosquito net had snapped, and the net itself which was only attached by two strings had fallen down at the side. But there was no sign of Dear Uncle Napoleon. In a trembling voice Layli's mother called up from below, "What's happened? Is the Master there? Open that door!"

"Well, ma'am, why should I lie . . . it's like the Master's turned to smoke, he's disappeared into thin air . . ."

At this moment a faint moaning became audible. Everyone looked this way and that. The moaning sound came from beneath the bed. Before everyone else my father bent double and peered under the bed.

"Well, I . . . what are you doing under there, sir?"

Again a voice could be heard but the words were indistinguishable. It was as if Dear Uncle were tongue-tied. My father and Mash Qasem, with everyone else's help, moved the bed a little to one side, got hold of Dear Uncle under the arms, dragged him out from beneath the bed and then laid him on it.

"Sir, why did you go under the bed? Where's the thief?"

But Dear Uncle's eyes were closed and his lips were pale and trembling.

Mash Qasem massaged Dear Uncle's hands. They opened the door between the balcony and the room, and the women and children came out on to the balcony. Seeing her father in such a state Layli started to cry and her mother struck herself on the head and chest.

Mash Qasem muttered, "Looks like a snake's bit the Master."

Layli's mother said, "And you're just standing there? Do something!"

"Mash Qasem, run and fetch Dr. Naser al-Hokama. Tell him to get himself here immediately."

Dr. Naser al-Hokama soon arrived in his nightclothes, clutching his doctor's bag, and set about examining Dear Uncle; after a few moments he said, "Your good health . . . your good health . . . it's nothing important. He's had a bit of a shock," and he trickled a few drops from a phial of medicine into a glass and then poured them down Dear Uncle's throat.

After we had waited a couple of minutes, Dear Uncle opened his eyes. For a while he looked in a confused way from side to side. His astonished gaze came to rest on Dr. Naser al-Hokama's face; suddenly he angrily pushed the doctor's hand off his chest and in a voice choking with anger said, "I'd rather die than set eyes on a lying, treacherous doctor."

"Your good health . . . your good health . . . how's that, sir? We're making a little joke?"

"Indeed not, I'm completely serious."

"I don't understand, sir . . . what's happened?"

Dear Uncle half sat up in the bed and, pointing to the way out, shouted, "Sir, you can go now. You think news of the plot in my brother's house hasn't reached my ears? A doctor who sells his conscience is no longer any doctor of mine and has no place in this family."

"Now don't upset yourself, it's not good for your heart."

"My heart's got nothing to do with you, the same way that the flatulence in Qamar's stomach has nothing to do with you!"

Everyone more or less grasped what was going on. Glances went round looking for the talebearer. I realized Mash Qasem was looking at Puri. Puri was rather uncomfortably looking from side to side so as not to catch anyone's eye.

In a louder voice Dear Uncle said, "I am completely well, I've no need of a doctor. Sir, you can leave now. Go and make another plot to explain your lies!"

To change the subject uncle colonel said, "Brother, what happened? Was there a thief?"

Dear Uncle Napoleon, who had forgotten the matter in hand when he saw the doctor, looked around with a horrified gaze and said, "Yes, it was a thief—I heard the sound of his footsteps, I saw his shadow. Hey there, close all the doors!"

At this moment he suddenly caught sight of my father. He pressed his lips together in anger, stared into space and shouted, "What is this crowd doing here? Is my house some kind of a hotel?"

And then with a long bony finger he pointed to the door, "Out!"

My father threw a furious look at him and, as he was on his way out, muttered, "It's our own fault if we've lost any sleep. The hero of the Battle of Kazerun was having a heart attack under the bed because he was afraid of a thief!"

With a violent movement Dear Uncle stood up and reached out to grab the rifle from uncle colonel's hand, but uncle colonel held it back behind his head, out of Dear Uncle's reach.

The terrified doctor picked up his bag and scuttled toward the door. And I went after my mother, who was on her way out. Just at the last moment I glanced over at Layli and took with me the memory of her tear-filled eyes.

Most of the way back to our house, I could hear Dear Uncle's voice explaining the strategy for searching for a thief.

The search by Dear Uncle and his helpers got nowhere; no sign of any thief was found, and half an hour later the noise and confusion died down.

I was so upset that I couldn't sleep.

There could be no doubt that Puri had ruined the whole family's efforts to settle the quarrel between Dear Uncle and my father. It was clear from his reactions on Dear Uncle's verandah that it was he who had told Dear Uncle about the agreement with Dr. Naser al-Hokama. I wished I could have smashed his buck teeth in. Despicable creep! Tattletale! I just hoped that uncle colonel would realize his son's treachery. If he didn't, I'd have to tell him.

Although I hadn't slept for half the night, in the morning I woke earlier than on any other day. The rest of the household was still not awake. Without making any noise, I went into the garden.

When I saw Mash Qasem, who was watering the flowers, I stood rooted to the spot in astonishment. He had his trousers rolled up to below his knees and Dear Uncle's double-barrelled shotgun on his shoulder; in this state he was deeply absorbed in what he was doing.

"Mash Qasem, what's the gun for?"

Mash Qasem looked around cautiously and said, "M'dear, get back to your own house, quick!"

"Why, Mash Qasem? What's happened?"

"Today's a bad day. Today's Judgment Day. Tell your Mom and Dad not to come over this way either."

"But why? Has something happened, Mash Qasem?"

"Well now, why should I lie . . . today I'm really worried. The Master's given orders that if any one of you crosses over to this side of this walnut tree, I've to shoot him through the heart."

If it weren't for Mash Qasem's serious face and flinty gaze I'd have thought he was joking. Shifting the gun about on his shoulder he said, "Early this morning Abbas—the pigeon-fancier feller—brought in last night's thief, he'd been jumpin' down from the roof of our house."

"What did you do with him?"

"Well now, why should I lie? The Master wanted to kill him on the spot, but I put in a good word for him . . . now we've tied him up with a rope and he's a prisoner in the cellar; I'm his guard."

"In the cellar? Why didn't you turn him over to the police?"

"You don't know the half of it yet . . . the Master's ready to string him up on a gallows in this garden this very day!"

For a moment I stood there, silent and horrified. Mash Qasem once again glanced this way and that and said, "And you mustn't talk to me too much neither . . . if the Master hears I've been talkin' with you he might do away with me, too."

"But Mash Qasem, what has catching the thief got to do with us? Why is Dear Uncle so mad at us?"

Mash Qasem nodded his head and said, "What's it got to do with you, m'dear? If you only knew who the thief was, then you'd realize what a pretty pass things have got to. Oh dear, oh dear, oh dear . . . God help us all . . . God willing, it'll all turn out right."

Extremely worried, I asked him, "Who's the thief, Mash Qasem? What did he steal?"

"Well, why should I lie . . . to the grave it's only ah . . . ah . . . Oh my God, the Master's comin' . . . out of here, quick, off you go . . . you're too young to die, off you go . . . or hide in this boxtree!"

As Mash Qasem saw that there was no opportunity for me to get away, he pushed me toward a huge boxtree, in which it was possible to hide myself among the leaves, while he busied himself with the flowers. When Dear Uncle got close to Mash Qasem I was horrified to see how stern his face was. As soon as he opened his mouth to speak, I realized from his tone of voice that he was extremely angry.

"Qasem, weren't you supposed to stand guard over the thief? Is this the time for this business?"

"Not to worry, sir, I can keep me eyes on him from here."

"How can you keep your eyes on the thief from here when he's in the cellar?"

"Every minute I go and take a peek at him. Now what do you want to do with him, sir? We can't leave him without bread and water, and there's an expense in keeping him. How about we give him to the cops and then we'll all be rid of him?"

"Give him to the police? I'm not letting him go till I get a confession out of him. In particular, my guess is he was put up to it by that fellow!"

As he said "that fellow" Dear Uncle pointed toward our house.

At this moment I felt how uncomfortable Mash Qasem was and I saw him glance over toward the boxtree where I was hidden among its leaves. Dear Uncle continued, "This Hamdullah was his servant for two or three years . . . and he wasn't a thief, either. He was a very upright, God-fearing man, and now this same man comes to my house as a thief! There's no doubt he was put up to it; there's no doubt there's a plot involved."

"Well, sir, why should I lie, to the grave it's ah . . . ah . . . what I say is he's out of work . . . on his uppers, and he came to see if he couldn't improve his prospects a bit . . ."

For a while Dear Uncle stood there silent and deep in thought. Mash Qasem busied himself with his work, but every now and then he glanced over at my hiding place.

Suddenly Dear Uncle said in a hoarse voice, "You know, Mash Qasem, now I'm worried about that malicious fellow's blabbering foul mouth."

"Who, sir?"

Dear Uncle pointed at our house.

"He's already done more than enough dishonorable things for one person—what does he care about someone's honor. I'm afraid he'll go around telling people whatever comes into his head."

Mash Qasem nodded and said, "Well, sir, when people argue, it's no friendly picnic."

And then, as though trying to change the subject because he didn't want the conversation to reach too delicate a stage in front of a witness who, though he was hidden, was there all the same, he observed, "How would it be if you was to forget all about these remarks . . . to kiss and make up and have everything turn out fine for everyone?"

"Me, make up with that fellow?"

There was such violence and anger in Dear Uncle's question that Mash Qasem answered in fear, "Didn't say a word, sir, no, there's no way you could make up . . . he's really acted shameful to you, sir."

"But I'm still afraid he'll go around telling people the first rubbish that comes into his head."

"Well, sir, as far as I know, whatever you wanted to say you've said to each other."

Dear Uncle impatiently said, "Why can't you understand . . . you remember what happened last night . . . I felt a little indisposed, I had a kind of attack . . . you remember what he said while he was leaving?"

"Well, sir, why should I lie? To the grave it's ah . . . ah . . . I don't remember nothin'."

"How can you not remember? He said something that meant I'd been afraid of the thief."

"God forbid! You? Afraid?"

"Exactly! Even if no one else knows, you who've been everywhere in battle with me and on my journeys and different adventures, you know better than anyone that the word 'fear' has no place in my vocabulary."

"Well, sir, why should I lie? To the grave it's ah . . . ah . . . As God's my witness, no one can lay that one on you, sir. I remember Soltanali Khan, God rest his soul, sayin' before the Battle of Kazerun that the Master's so headstrong and fearless it'll land him in trouble. You remember that night when the thieves attacked our tents . . . it's like it was yesterday . . . my God, with one bullet you made three of them thieves bite the dust . . ."

"And they were the savage pitiless thieves of those days . . . compared to them the thieves nowadays are babes still wet round the ears!"

Excitedly Mash Qasem said, "And besides, me who was so brave and wild—well, it's no secret from God, so why should it be a secret from you—I was really afraid that night. That boss of the thieves, how he fell at your feet afterwards all weak and pleading . . . it's like it was yesterday . . . wasn't his name Seyed Morad?"

"Oh yes, I've seen these Seyed Morads, all right."

"May he rot in hell. What a cruel, filthy bastard he was."

Mash Qasem had become so excited that it seemed he'd forgotten I was nearby. Dear Uncle's face was shining, too. From their glowing, rapt faces I felt that neither of them had the slightest doubt as to the truth of what they were saying; it was as if they saw the scenes and people before their eyes with complete clarity.

For a few moments both of them silently gazed into the distance, their faces lit up and smiling. Dear Uncle suddenly came to himself; once again he frowned and said, "But, Mash Qasem, you and I know these things . . . if . . . if that foulmouthed fellow and that simpleminded doctor go around saying so-and-so fainted because he was afraid of a thief, then what's to become of years of my honor and reputation?"

"Who'd believe them, sir? Who in this kingdom doesn't know about your grit and guts?"

"People believe their eyes and ears, and I'm sure that fellow will stop at nothing to harm my status and prestige."

It seems that Mash Qasem once more remembered that I was hidden among the branches of the boxtree. He cast a sidelong glance toward the boxtree and said, "We can talk about it later. Up till now nothing's happened."

"Why are you talking such nonsense? Today they'll be making a song and dance about it everywhere."

"I'll deny it . . . I'll say the Master was unwell."

"Yes, but . . ."

Dear Uncle was deep in thought. Mash Qasem went on, "I could say a snake bit the Master."

"Why are you talking rubbish? If a snake bites someone, he's not up and about the next day!"

"What do you mean he's not up and about? There was a man in our town who . . ."

"All right, all right, there was a man in your town! Anyway, forget about the snake."

Mash Qasem too was sunk in thought. "Aha, I've got it, sir. I'll say the Master'd ate watermelon and honey together and he'd got a stomach cramp."

Dear Uncle gave no answer but it was clear that hadn't paid attention to this suggestion either.

After a few moments' silence Mash Qasem suddenly said, "Sir, you know . . ."

"What do I know?"

"If you ask me it's like it's better we get rid of the thief and let him go."

"We let the thief go? The thief?"

"If it gets around that we've caught the thief . . . then everyone'll be talkin' about the thief . . . and they'll talk about what happened last night, too . . ."

"You're talking nonsense!"

"Well, it's nothin' to do with me, but if you was to let this thief go, it'd be better, then this other bad business will go too. Right now no one except the pigeon fancier knows we've caught the thief . . . meanin' no stranger knows . . . and the pigeon fancier won't say nothin' behind our backs."

Dear Uncle was deep in thought. After a long silence he said, "You are right, Qasem. Forgiveness and magnanimity have always been customary in our family, and it's likely this poor devil did what he did out of the pressure of poverty. For the sake of his children it's better we overlook his sins."

Again Dear Uncle was silent for a moment, and then he said, "Now do a good act and open the floodgates—God will reward you, it's bread upon the waters. Quick, Qasem, free his arms and legs and tell him to make a run for it. Be careful to say to him, 'I'm doing this on my own, and if the Master finds out, he'll skin me alive.'"

Mash Qasem hurried to carry out his master's orders and Dear Uncle started walking up and down, deep in thought.

A few minutes later Mash Qasem, the shotgun still on his shoulder, returned to Dear Uncle, who was sitting on a bench in the arbor formed by the sweetbrier. Mash Qasem had a satisfied smile on his lips. "God keep you in your generosity! You don't know how thankful he was! It's like your blood was made of generosity. If you remember, after Seyed Morad'd begged and pleaded a bit, you let him off, and besides that you gave him enough cash to find his way home."

Dear Uncle was staring at the branches of the walnut tree; in a regretful voice he said, "But Qasem, who knows the value of such things? Perhaps it would have been better if I'd been merciless and cruel like all the others. Perhaps this is the reason I haven't done so well in my life."

"Don't say such things, sir . . . what I know is what everyone knows, it was because of them there foreigners . . . just a couple of days ago in the bazaar they was talkin' about you and I said if the English hadn't been against the Master, there wasn't nothin' he couldn't have done."

"Yes, if it wasn't for the power of the English I could have done many things."

Mash Qasem, who had heard so many times from Dear Uncle's own lips the whole story of the how the English hated him that he knew it by heart, nevertheless asked, "But now, truly, sir, why do them English hate you so much?"

"That hypocritical wolf called England hates everyone who loves the soil and water of his own country. What sin had Napoleon committed that they harried him like that? That they separated him from his wife and children like that? That they broke his spirit like that so that he died of grief? Just that he loved his country. And this for them is a great sin!"

Dear Uncle spoke with vehement passion and Mash Qasem meanwhile was nodding his head and muttering curses, "Now by the sacred Ali, may sweet water never pass down their throats . . ."

"Their enmity for me started when they saw that I love my country . . . I'm a freedom fighter . . . a supporter of the Constitution . . ."

I was getting really tired in my hiding place. My feet had gone to sleep. I tried to shift my position a bit without making any noise but a sudden development stopped me.

It seems that my father had heard the sound of Dear Uncle's and Mash Qasem's conversation and had slowly got himself close to the arbor made by the sweetbrier bush. My heart was in my mouth. O God, what was going to happen now? From where I was, I could see my father but, from where they were behind the clustering sweetbrier branches, Dear Uncle and Mash Qasem couldn't see him. There was no doubt that my father had quietly got himself close to them in order to hear their conversation. God help us all!

Dear Uncle was talking about his own self-sacrifice during the Constitutional Revolution. "Now everyone's a supporter of the Constitution . . . everyone pretends that they struggled for the Constitution . . . but I say nothing, and I'm forgotten."

At this moment an ear-splitting guffaw suddenly burst from my father's throat and, in the midst of his forced laughter, he called out, "So Colonel Liakhoff's Cossaks have become heroes of the Constitutional Revolution now, have they!"

There was a screen of sweetbrier between them. Appalled, I twisted my neck round to see Dear Uncle's reaction. He had gone purple. All the muscles of his face were contracted. For a few moments he didn't move. Suddenly he jumped up and rushed toward Mash Qasem. In a voice half strangled by the intensity of his fury he yelled, "The gun . . . Qasem, the gun!"

And he reached out his hand to grab the gun from Mash Qasem. "I told you, the gun!"

With a shrug of his shoulder Mash Qasem slipped the gun's sling down to his hand. With one hand he held the gun behind his head and placed the other against Dear Uncle's chest so that he couldn't come any closer.

It seems that from the terrifying tone of Dear Uncle's voice my father had seen which way the wind was blowing and he quickly made himself scarce. Again Dear Uncle screamed, "Idiot, traitor, I said give me the gun!"

With a quick movement Mash Qasem got himself free of Dear Uncle's grip and, with the gun in his hand, took to his heels. Like a man possessed Dear Uncle set off after him through the garden trees.

While he was running Mash Qasem shouted, "Sir, for the sake of the blessed Ali, forgive him . . . sir, on the souls of your children . . . he was wrong, he didn't know what he was doing!"

The garden was very big and there was plenty of room to run in. Mash Qasem ran with a weird nimbleness and Dear Uncle ran puffing after him. Suddenly Mash Qasem's foot caught on a dry branch; he fell and the sound of a shot rang out.

"Aggghhh, I'm dead . . . aggghhh, God help me."

The sound of Mash Qasem's voice jolted me out of my bewildered state and I ran quickly toward him. Dear Uncle was standing over the motionless body of Mash Qasem, who had fallen on the shotgun.

"Sir, oh sir, you've killed your Qasem!"

Dear Uncle bent over to lift him but Mash Qasem with a heart-rending cry said, "No . . . no . . . don't touch me, sir . . . I want to die right here."

Dear Uncle pulled his hand back and as he saw me standing nearby shouted, "Dear boy, run and fetch Dr. Naser al-Hokama . . . run, run, boy!"

With a lump in my throat I ran as fast as I could toward Dr. Naser al-Hokama's house. Fortunately at that precise moment he was coming out of his house with his doctor's bag in his hand, as though he was going to pay a house call.

"Doctor, run! Mash Qasem's been shot!"

Uncle colonel's servant was standing at the door to the garden explaining to the curious passersby who had heard the shot that it was nothing, just a firecracker that had gone off in one of the children's hands. We entered the garden and closed the door.

The people who lived in the house were gathered in a circle around Mash Qasem; they were comforting him while Mash Qasem moaned in a low voice, "Aggghhh! It hurts so much . . . aggghhh, the burnin' . . . I'll never get to Mecca now, that's a hope I'll carry to the grave."

When I followed the doctor into the ring of spectators I saw Layli. She was crying and with a handkerchief dabbing water on Mash Qasem's forehead; he lay there with his cheek against the dirt.

"Sir, promise to bury me in the courtyard of the sacred Ma-sumeh's mosque . . ."

The doctor squatted down beside Mash Qasem but when he tried to turn him Mash Qasem screamed out, "Don't touch me!"

"Mash Qasem, it's the doctor!"

Mash Qasem turned his head a little. When he saw the doctor, in that same voice that was half a moan he said, "Good day to you, sir . . . after God, sir, you're my only hope."

"Your good health, your good health. What happened, Mash Qasem? Where's the wound? Who shot you?"

At this moment my father, who was standing nearby, pointed at Dear Uncle and in a loud voice said, "This man! This murderer! God willing, I myself will put the noose around his neck."

But before Dear Uncle could answer, my mother, pleading and pulling, dragged my father away.

"Your good health, your good health. Mash Qasem, tell me where the bullet wound is."

Mash Qasem stayed as he was, lying unmoving on his stomach. With a moan he said, "Why should I lie . . . it hit me in the side."

Dr. Naser al-Hokama signalled with his hand for Dear Uncle to come and help him and tried to turn Mash Qasem over.

"Your good health . . . very slowly . . . slowly a . . . aha . . ."

"Aggghhh, O God . . . all these wars and battles I've been through and I have to die in my Master's garden . . . doctor, sir, please . . . if there's no hope just tell me and I'll say my prayers."

When the doctor opened Mash Qasem's shirt everyone's mouth hung open in surprise since no spot on his body showed any sign of a wound. "So, where did the bullet hit you?"

Mash Qasem answered without looking, "Well, why should I lie . . . I don't rightly know . . . can't you see it?"

"Your good health, your good health. You're healthier than I am."

Breath pent up in people's chests for so long was released and sounds of laughter and joking burst out.

Dear Uncle kicked Mash Qasem in the back as he was getting up. "Get up and get out! Now even you're lying to me, are you, you filthy devil?"

"You mean I wasn't shot . . . then that pain and burnin', what was that about? Then where did the bullet hit?"

"I wish it had hit your head!"

When Dr. Naser al-Hokama saw that he was going to have to speak to Dear Uncle, he closed his bag and, instead of saying goodbye, simply said once "Your good health" and started to leave. Dear Uncle Napoleon ran after him. He said something in his ear for a few moments. It seemed that he was apologizing to the doctor for the previous night. Finally he flung his arm across the doctor's shoulders, they embraced and gave each other a formal peck on the cheek. The doctor left and Dear Uncle returned to the group.

During these relatively safe moments I had gone over toward Layli. Seeing her after the painful incidents of those two days was such a pleasure for me that I was tongue-tied and just stared at her and she too stared back at me with her huge, black eyes.

Before either of us were able to get a word out Dear Uncle became aware of Layli and me. He came over to us, promptly slapped Layli across the ear, gestured toward the inner apartments of their own home, and in a dry tone said, "You, in the house!"

Then, without looking at me, he pointed at our house and in a harsher tone said, "And off with you to your house, too, and don't come this way again!"

Hurt by Dear Uncle's bitter tone and with a lump in my throat, I ran toward our house. I went to a distant room and closed the door on myself. I lay down on a sofa. I was really desperate. I couldn't even think properly. But I was determined to take a definitive decision.

Suddenly loud noises in the yard woke me; it was around noon. Stretched out on the sofa in that quiet room after the exciting events of the morning I had fallen asleep. I quietly left the room. I became aware of an unusual level of activity and found my mother. "What's going on? What's all this noise and coming and going for?"

"How should I know, this morning all of a sudden your father decided to invite the whole family over to supper."

"But why?"

Angrily my mother yelled, "How should I know? How should I know? Go and ask him. He'll be dancing on my grave next . . ."

At that moment my father, who had left the house, came in. I ran to him. "Dad, what's happening tonight?"

With a sly laugh my father said, "Tonight's the anniversary of your mother's and my marriage . . . we're having a party . . . I'm celebrating becoming part of this kind and united family!"

At this moment I realized that my father was speaking louder than usual and was directing his voice particularly toward the garden. I looked to one side of his head and in the distance saw Puri's shadow—apparently he was busy reading a book but it was a good guess that he was eavesdropping on our house.

"Yes . . . I've invited some musicians tonight, too . . . everyone'll be there."

Then he turned to my mother and in the same loud voice asked, "By the way, have you told Shamsali Mirza and Asadollah Mirza . . . and what about Mrs. Aziz al-Saltaneh?"

My father loudly enumerated all the guests and then added, "It'll be a great night tonight! I want to tell our guests some beautiful stories . . . music and songs and beautiful stories."

I saw what was going on. My father wanted to tell everyone the story of Dear Uncle being afraid of a thief and fainting. The description he had given me was really directed at Puri so that he would pass it on to his uncle. Puri slowly made his way over to Dear Uncle's house. After a few moments I threw caution to the winds and set off after him. The door to Dear Uncle's inner apartments was closed and no sound from within the house could be heard.

I was really curious to know Dear Uncle's reaction. I thought for a moment. I listened at the door; there was a distant sound of conversation, but it wasn't comprehensible.

Finally a way occurred to me. The flat roof of one of my aunt's houses ran right next to Dear Uncle's house. With the help of my cousin Siamak, I got myself onto their roof. I carefully lay down at its edge.

Just as I arrived there Puri left Dear Uncle's yard, having completed his job as tattletale. Dear Uncle was irritatedly pacing in his yard and Mash Qasem was standing to one side with a thoughtful look on his face. From Dear Uncle's pallor and face and walk, it was clear that he was extremely preoccupied and upset.

"In fact the only thing we can do is break that fellow's party up so that somehow we'll be able to put things right. I know what his plan is . . . he'll ruin my reputation and your reputation . . . I've known for years what kind of a filthy bastard he is."

"It would be good if we could tell the guests that tonight's the anniversary of your late uncle's death, then they wouldn't go."

"Why are you talking rubbish . . . it's another month before the anniversary of my uncle's death . . ." At this moment it seemed that a thought had occurred to Dear Uncle because he stood still for a moment, and his face brightened. He took Mash Qasem over to the door of his house and said something to him, of which I could only hear the name Seyed Abolqasem. Mash Qasem left quickly. Dear

Uncle walked up and down in his yard talking to himself. I waited a while but there was no sign of Mash Qasem. I'd no choice but to quit the roof and go back to the garden to try to find out the secret from Mash Qasem. Since there was no sign of him I went despondently home. Our servant was bringing big carpets into the garden, with the help of a hired laborer.

My father was involved in a violent counterattack. He even wanted to have his party in the garden so that Dear Uncle could hear it over on his side of the garden.

By about five in the afternoon the scene was set for my father's scheme. Lots of cushions had been placed against trees and on the carpets. In one corner bottles of alcoholic drinks were cooling in a big tub of ice under some sacking.

I kept my eyes fixed on Dear Uncle's shut door the whole time. I was worried about what had happened in his yard, because I knew that Dear Uncle wouldn't take my father's attack lying down, and I felt darkness, thunder and storms were looming on the horizon.

Not long passed before the door to Dear Uncle's inner apartments suddenly opened. Helped by Dear Uncle's maidservant and Puri, Mash Qasem started bringing numerous carpets from the house into the garden, and laying them down about twenty meters from where our party was to be.

I cautiously made my way over to Mash Qasem, but in answer to my question he only said, "Out of the way, m'dear, let us do our job."

As soon as the carpets had been spread out in the area in front of Dear Uncle's house, Mash Qasem and Naneh Bilqis set off for the outer door of the garden, each of them carrying one end of a ladder. Mash Qasem went up the ladder and coolly set up above the garden door the black three-cornered banner which Dear Uncle normally had set up there on evenings when there were ceremonies of religious mourning. The black banner unfurled and the words "Praise Obeidallah Hosayn" appeared on it.

Astonished, I said, "Mash Qasem, what are you doing? Why have you put the black banner up?"

"Well now, why should I lie, m'dear? Tonight we've a mourning ceremony. Very thorough and complete, too . . . seven or eight preachers'll be speaking . . . and we've a group coming to beat their chests and mourn."

"But what night is it tonight?"

"You mean you don't know, m'dear? Tonight is the night of the martyrdom of the blessed Moslem ibn Aghil, and if you don't think so, you go and ask Seyed Abolqasem!"

I heard a choked sound behind me. I turned round and saw my father, his face white as chalk. With his face contorted, and his eyes popping out of their sockets from the intensity of his anger, he was looking at Mash Qasem and the black banner.

My agitated gaze went a few times from my father to Mash Qasem and back. Mash Qasem had realized how extraordinarily angry my father was and out of fear hadn't come down the ladder; he was flicking dust and dirt off the black banner. I was afraid that my father was so angry he would knock the ladder over. Finally, his voice breaking, he said, "Tonight your dad's died, has he, that you've put the black banner up?"

From the top of the ladder Mash Qasem said in his usual calm way, "I wish my dear old dad, God rest his soul, had died on such a holy night. Tonight is the night of the martyrdom of the blessed Moslem ibn Aghil."

"May the blessed Moslem ibn Aghil rot you and your master and every damned liar . . . I suppose when your master was so afraid of the thief he fainted, the angel Gabriel appeared to him and told him that tonight was the anniversary of a martyrdom!"

"Well now, why should I lie, to the grave it's only four fingers . . . I don't know about that . . . but I do know that tonight's the night of the martyrdom of the blessed Moslem ibn Aghil . . . and Seyed Abolqasem knows, too . . . if you want you can ask him."

My father, who was so angry he was trembling, yelled, "I'm going to destroy you and your master and Seyed Abolqasem in such a way that Moslem's own two children will weep for you . . ."

And as he was saying this he started to shake the ladder. Mash Qasem's scream went up to the heavens, "Eh, watch it . . . help, oh blessed Moslem ibn Aghil, help!"

Terrified, I clung on to my father's arm and shouted, "Dad, leave him alone . . . it's not poor Mash Qasem's fault."

When he heard me shouting my father calmed down a little. He flung another angry look at Mash Qasem and hurried back to our house.

Mash Qasem had been very frightened; breathing heavily he came down the ladder, gave me a grateful look and said, "May you live to enjoy your old age, m'dear; you saved my life."

When I got back to the house my father was shouting at my poor mother, "If I'd married into the tribe that lived in Sodom and Gomorrah it'd have been better than this family. Now we'll see whether my party's a success or Napoleon Bonaparte's mourning ceremony!"

It was the first time I'd heard the nickname Napoleon applied to Dear Uncle on my father's lips. Their enmity had gone so far that neither side would hold back from doing anything that would harm the other. One out-of-place squeak from a chair leg, or at most one dubious sound, was not only, in the words of uncle colonel, destroying the family's unity but also shaking the foundations of our whole family life.

My mother clasped my father's arm and in a pleading voice said, "As God's my witness, I'd do anything for you, but let it go! How can you possibly give a party tonight? On that side of the garden people beating their chests and mourning . . . and on this side music and dancing and getting drunk . . . who'd dare to sit at the party . . . those toughs who come to mourning ceremonies from the bazaar would tear you all to pieces."

"But I know this business of the martyrdom of Moslem ibn Aghil is just a fabrication! I know that . . ."

"You know, but people in general don't know! The men beating their chests don't know . . . all our good name in the neighborhood will be destroyed . . . they'll tear you and the children to pieces."

Gradually my father sank into thought. My mother was telling the truth. It was impossible that someone would dare to be living it up on one side of a garden when there was a religious mourning ceremony and chest-beating in progress on the other side. My father would have had to be both the guest and the host all by himself, besides which there was danger involved.

At this moment Mash Qasem, who was carrying the end of the ladder with Naneh Bilqis, passed by the door on the way into the garden and became aware of this conversation. Mildly he said, "If you want the truth, your missus is right . . . you put your party for another night."

My father threw him an angry look, but suddenly his face changed. Trying to give a normal tone to his words, he said, "Yes, yes, you're right . . . it's a holy evening . . . you said it's the martyrdom of the blessed Moslem ibn Aghil?"

"God rest his soul, what he went through . . . God rest his soul, I'd die for him if I could, all innocent he was when those bastards cut his head off from his body . . ."

"Just tell your master that they threw Moslem ibn Aghil off a tower . . . and one of these days another person's going to be thrown off a tower and his bones will be smashed to bits!" And with pretended piety he added, "But when all's said and done, it's a holy evening. Although I'd arranged to have guests over, I've cancelled the party so that I can come to your master's mourning ceremony . . . I'll certainly be there tonight. I couldn't not come on such a holy evening! I'll certainly be there."

Without thinking Mash Qasem said, "Oh yes, sir, do come, it'll do your soul good!"

But as though he'd suddenly become aware of a special motive on my father's part, he set off in a worried way for the inner apartments of Dear Uncle's house.

I waited a few moments, and then I went to find Mash Qasem, who was putting the ladder away in a shed at the corner of the garden. "Mash Qasem, you must know what my father's thinking of."

Mash Qasem looked worriedly around, "M'dear, run along and play. If the Master gets to know I've talked to you, he'll skin me alive."

"Oh, Mash Qasem, we've got to do something to end this argument . . . this quarrel's getting worse every day. I'm afraid of how it's all going to end."

"Well, why should I lie? To the grave it's ah . . . ah . . . I'm really afraid, too . . . and this is nothing compared to every day I've to carry a hundred buckets of water to the colonel master's house to water his flowers."

"But anyway, we've got to do something so that dad doesn't go to the mourning ceremony tonight, or that he doesn't mention last night's thief . . . because I know it'll start another argument that'll end God alone knows how."

"Don't you worry about tonight, m'dear, the Master's already thought about all that. I don't think he'll let your father speak . . . but don't you go telling your father what I've said!"

"No, Mash Qasem, you can rest assured; I've made a vow that if this argument comes to an end I'll light a candle to one of the saints."

"So don't you worry too much about tonight . . . the Master's made an agreement with Seyed Abolqasem that if your father comes he's not to let him speak."

It was clear that Mash Qasem felt I was one of those who really did want the quarrel resolved; he said to me frankly, "And you, m'dear, you do something to stop your father from talkin' too much!"

At this moment Puri's head appeared. Mash Qasem muttered, "Eh, m'dear, watch it, Mr. Puri's come. Now with that muzzle of his that's just like a carthorse's he'll go to the master and say I've been talkin' to you; off with you, m'dear, get back to your own house."

My mother hurriedly sent various messengers to people to say that tonight's party had been cancelled due to its falling on the same night as the mourning ceremony. Of course, after they'd received Dear Uncle Napoleon's invitations to take part in the mourning ceremony, the guests had already guessed my father's party would be cancelled and were not very surprised. Dear Uncle's mourning ceremony got going after sunset. Dear Uncle sat dressed in a black cloak on a cushion near the entrance. On the other side of the arbor a carpet had been spread out for the women. When my father was ready to go to the mourning ceremony I felt very peculiar. On the one hand I was really worried about a confrontation between him and Dear Uncle, and on the other my heart was filled to the brim with happiness and joy at the thought of seeing Layli.

As my father entered the area where the ceremony was being held, Dear Uncle, who was standing up to welcome everyone, didn't move at all and pretended he hadn't seen him. Most of the relatives who lived nearby had already come; only the absence of Aziz al-Saltaneh and her husband was noticeable.

My father sat down next to Asadollah Mirza, who had found the closest place to where the women were sitting. Out of fear of Dear Uncle, I didn't dare get too far away from my father. As soon as he had sat down my father tried to tell Asadollah Mirza about the thief coming and what had happened the previous night, but Asadollah

Mirza was leaning round the sweetbrier arbor, busy quietly laughing and joking with one of the women.

"Yes indeed, your excellency, you really missed something last night, we had quite an adventure . . ."

I couldn't help but look over toward Dear Uncle Napoleon. His whole attention was focused on the movements of my father's lips and anxiety was apparent in every wrinkle of his face. At this moment he turned and looked at Seyed Abolqasem, and Seyed Abolqasem called across at my father and Asadollah Mirza, "Sir, this is a holy evening, give your attention to the ceremony!"

My father tried a few times to start his story, but each time Seyed Abolqasem interrupted him.

The last preacher was Seyed Abolqasem himself. From the moment his sermon started he never took his eyes off my father, and as soon as he saw my father was about to start talking, he would say those catchwords about suffering that are common to such ceremonies and which always produce a wail from the women present, and my father would fling angry looks at him.

Seyed Abolqasem's sermons went on for about half an hour, by which time the poor old man could only get his voice out of his throat with great difficulty. He was silent for a few moments in order to catch his breath. My father, who had been waiting for him to get weak and worn out, said in a fairly loud voice which everyone near him clearly heard, "By the way, did anything happen here last night?"

Dear Uncle had made his way over to where Seyed Abolqasem was sitting; it was as if a skewer had been plunged into his back. The Seyed jumped up and gestured to the group of men who were there ready to beat their chests in ritual mourning; there were about twelve of them and they had bared their chests and were waiting their turn. With his last ounce of strength he started the mourning chant and the ritual of chest beating, "His two poor children . . . his two poor children . . ."

Dear Uncle Napoleon was beating his chest with one hand and chanting with the Seyed and encouraging the group of ritual mourners with the other.

The mourners beat violently and rhythmically against their bare chests, chanting with great enthusiasm at the same time. The guests were not familiar with this kind of mourning, as it wasn't usual to have people beating their chests like this at a mourning ceremony in which sermons were given. For a moment they looked at one another, then when they saw that Dear Uncle had stood up they too stood up and started beating their chests.

My father, who was trembling with rage, didn't move from his place. At this moment Seyed Abolqasem—whether on his own initiative or at a signal from Dear Uncle, I don't know—made his way over to where my father was sitting and shouted, "Sir, if you are not taking part in this mourning ceremony . . . if you have some other religion . . . if you have some quarrel with the faithful, go to your own house, go to your own home, go to your own religion . . ."

My father was beside himself with rage, but since he was aware of hostile looks directed at him by the men who were beating their chests, he stood up and started to beat his chest and, in this way, still beating his chest, he gradually made his way toward his house. A few moments later he slammed the door of his room with such force that I heard it, even at that distance and in the midst of the noise of the chanting.

In spite of all this I breathed a sigh of relief, since once again things had turned out more or less all right. After they had been around the garden a few times the men beating their chests went out of the main door and the guests once again sat down.

The mourners engaged for the ceremony had gone. Only Seyed Abolqasem, who was exhausted and had not a breath left in him, was still there, taking sips from a bowl of mint cordial and wiping the sweat from his face with a handkerchief.

Dear Uncle was worried. I guessed that he was worried that my father might return. But I knew my father very well and was sure he was too angry to return.

FOUR

IN THE MEN'S PART of the gathering there were only four or five very close relatives of ours left and the event was drawing to an end. The women came over and joined the men.

People had more or less forgotten the reason why they'd gathered together and they were busy drinking tea and soft drinks, eating little cakes, chatting and laughing. Just at the moment when Farrokh Laqa was asking why Aziz al-Saltaneh and her husband and daughter hadn't come, and it was clear that she wanted to make something out of this, suddenly, from the direction of the flat roof overlooking the garden, a man's voice was heard calling out for help, "Someone help me . . . come quickly . . . come and save me . . . help!"

We all automatically turned to where the sound was coming from. We saw the outline of a man in a shirt and white longjohns running wildly from one side of the roof to the other.

In the midst of everyone's consternation and amazement uncle colonel said, "It sounds like Dustali Khan's voice . . . yes, it's him." The strong light of the incandescent lamps prevented our seeing the owner of the voice clearly. Everyone present more or less ran in his direction.

It was Dustali Khan, Aziz al-Saltaneh's husband. His house had a common wall with the garden. Horror and extreme fear were apparent in his voice. He shouted continually, "Help me . . . save me!"

Dear Uncle Napoleon shouted, "What's happened, Dustali Khan?"

Dustali Khan answered, "Please, for God's sake . . . bring a ladder . . . help me!"

"Why don't you go down by the stairs?"

"I can't . . . help me . . . a ladder . . . then I'll explain!"

There was such pleading and wailing apparent in his voice that no one asked any more questions. Dear Uncle shouted out, "Qasem, a ladder!"

Mash Qasem had picked the ladder up from its place before Dear Uncle's order was given. Those present didn't for a moment take their eyes off the form of Dustali Khan, which was shaking on the roof like a nocturnal phantom. Mash Qasem leaned the ladder against the wall, and went up it a few rungs to help Dustali Khan come down.

A few moments later Dustali Khan put his feet on the ground and fainted in Mash Qasem's arms. They more or less dragged him over to the carpets and laid him down. Everyone started discussing what had happened and offering opinions as to what it meant.

Dear Uncle Napoleon kept lightly slapping him on the face with the palm of his hand and asking, "Dustali Khan, what is it? What happened?"

But Dustali Khan, with his dishevelled hair, in his shirt and white, mud-stained longjohns, lay there motionless, with only his lips trembling. We were all gathered in a circle around him.

Mash Qasem, who was massaging Dustali Khan's feet, said, "It's like a snake's bit him some place."

Dear Uncle threw an angry look at him, "You're talking rubbish again!"

"Well sir, why should I lie? There was a man in our town who . . ."

"The hell with you and the man in your town. Will you let me see what's happened?" And then once again he gently slapped Dustali across the face.

Dustali Khan opened his eyes. Suddenly he seemed to come back to himself and looked from one side to the other. With a nervous movement he clasped both hands to his groin and shouted, "Cut . . . it's been cut . . ."

"Who's cut? What's been cut?"

Dustali Khan didn't answer Dear Uncle's question but in the same terrified voice repeated, "Cut . . . she wanted to cut it . . . with a knife . . . with a kitchen knife . . . she was going to cut . . ."

"Who cut? Who wanted to cut?"

"Aziz . . . that rotten bitch Aziz . . . my wife . . . that witch of a woman . . . that unnatural bitch of a murderer . . ."

Asadollah Mirza, who had pricked up his ears, came forward, holding back his laughter with some difficulty. "Moment . . .

moment . . . wait . . . wait, let me see . . . God forbid, Mrs. Aziz al-Saltaneh didn't want to cut off your . . ."

"Yes, yes . . . that witch, if I'd jumped a moment later she'd have cut it off."

Asadollah Mirza burst out with a loud guffaw of laughter and said, "Right from the bottom?"

As everyone laughed Dear Uncle Napoleon suddenly remembered that there were women and children present. He stood up and, stretching out his arms wide on each side and so making a curtain with his cloak between Dustali Khan and the children, he shouted, "Women and children over there!"

The women and children went back a little. At this moment Puri, uncle colonel's son, with a stupid expression on his face asked, "What did Mrs. Aziz al-Saltaneh want to cut off?"

Uncle colonel glanced at him angrily and said, "What kind of a question is that to ask, you donkey?"

Mash Qasem calmly answered his question, "M'dear, she wanted to cut his privates off."

Asadollah Mirza laughed and said, "Well, he's brought this on himself . . .

'Someone was chopping the branch off a tree
The lord looked in the garden and happened to see . . .'"

Dear Uncle Napoleon bawled, "Sir, that's enough!"

Then, with a very serious face, and still holding out his cloak as a curtain between Dustali Khan and the women, he said, "Speak properly, Dustali! How is it she wanted to cut it off? Why are you talking such nonsense?"

Dustali Khan, who was still clutching his groin with both hands, wailed, "I saw it myself . . . she'd brought a kitchen knife into the bed . . . she'd got hold of it to cut it . . . I felt the chill of the knife!"

"But why? Had she gone crazy? Had she . . . ?"

"She'd been nagging me all evening . . . she didn't come to your mourning ceremony . . . she said that she'd heard from one of her relatives that I was going with some young woman . . . God damn all such relatives . . . they're all murderers . . . God, if I'd jumped a moment later she'd have cut the whole lot off."

In a choked voice Dear Uncle Napoleon said, "Aha! I understand!"

We all became aware of him. He ground his teeth in fury. In a voice shaking with anger he added, "I know which filthy wretch has done this . . . that fellow who wants to destroy the honor of our family . . . who's made a plot against the honor of our family."

It was very clear that by "that fellow" he meant my father.

Asadollah Mirza, who was trying to be serious, said in an apparently concerned voice, "Well, was any of it cut off?"

Dear Uncle Napoleon ignored everyone's laughter and said through gritted teeth, "I'll destroy him . . . the honor of our family is no joke."

At this moment Shamsali Mirza assumed the extremely serious face of a judge, raised his hands, and said, "Do not rush to judgment . . . first the investigation, then the verdict. Mr. Dustali Khan, please answer my questions carefully and honestly."

The presumed victim of the attack was still lying helplessly on the floor with his hands clutched against his groin. Shamsali Mirza pulled a chair forward and sat down to begin his cross-examination, but uncle colonel interrupted, "Your honor, leave it for tomorrow, this poor devil's been so terrified he hasn't the strength to speak."

Shamsali Mirza glanced at him angrily and answered, "The optimum time for cross-examination and investigation is the moment immediately after the crime has been committed. By tomorrow the factors on which a certain judgment can be based will all have been dispersed."

Mash Qasem, who had been staring at the scene with interest, confirmed his statement, "Oh yes, indeed, sir, by tomorrow who knows who'll be dead and who'll be still alive? There was a man in our town who . . ."

Shamsali Mirza cut him off with a fierce look and once again turned to Dustali Khan, "As I said, answer my questions very carefully and with complete honesty."

Dear Uncle Napoleon, who was staring distractedly into space, said, "There's no doubt it's the work of that filthy fellow . . . he's using Napoleon's own strategy—which he heard from me—against me . . . Napoleon said that in wars you have to attack the enemy at his weakest point . . . this man has realized that my weak point is Dustali Khan. He knows that I've brought Dustali up, that he's like my own son. He's one of my family, his wife's one of my family . . ."

Dear Uncle talked for a while about the special ties which bound Dustali Khan to him. Mind you, he had talked many times about how he had brought Dustali Khan up, and despite the fact that Dustali Khan was over fifty years old, he considered him as his child. Finally he turned toward Dustali Khan and said, "Now, to show your thanks for how I've always looked after you and cared for you, I want you to answer Shamsali Mirza's questions carefully, because we've got to discover the truth tonight, it must be made as clear to everyone as it is to me just who has said all this to Aziz al-Saltaneh. This is a subject of the greatest importance and we are at a most delicate juncture in our family's life . . . we are standing on the edge of ruin . . . in particular we have to make plain to my sister what kind of person she is living with and then she can choose between him and her family."

Dustali Khan's eyes were shut tight and he seemed not to be listening to Dear Uncle's speech but to be in his own fearful, terrifying world, because he suddenly opened his eyes in a very weird way. Pressing his hand against his groin, he cried out in a terrified voice, "Agghhh, she's cut it off . . . help me, she's cut it off with the kitchen knife . . . diamond-sharp it was . . ."

Dear Uncle Napoleon threw a contemptuous look at Dustali Khan. "What times these are . . . here's me who's looked rifles, lances, swords, and shrapnel in the face a thousand times and not for one moment have fear or cowardice ever found a way into my heart, and here's him terrified like this of a kitchen knife."

Mash Qasem took up the theme, "God save him, the Master's got the heart of a lion . . . can you remember how that Jan M'amad Baqameh jumped at you at the Battle of Kahkiloyeh . . . it's like it was yesterday . . . God save you, with one stroke of your sword you sliced him in two from his head to his bellybutton . . . and then this feller's just seen a little vegetable knife and he's ready to give up the ghost . . . and no one's even cut anythin' . . . if they'd cut somethin' then what would he have done . . . ?"

Asadollah Mirza, who out of consideration for Dear Uncle and Shamsali Mirza had suppressed his urge to laugh, said, "Well, have a look, perhaps it really has been cut off!"

Shamsali Mirza glanced at him angrily, "Brother!"

Meanwhile Mash Qasem, at a sign from Dear Uncle, brought a glass of mint cordial to Dustali Khan's lips and made him drink a few drops. Shamsali Mirza wanted to start his cross-examination but Dear Uncle Napoleon raised his hand, "With your permission, your excellency . . . ladies and children, back to the house, just my sister will stay here."

Dear Uncle took my mother's arm and pulled her aside. He wanted her and no one else to be present at the cross-examination. Without making any objection the women went off toward their homes. My longing look followed Layli, who seemed to me to be a thousand times more beautiful beneath her black lace veil. I, too, set off for our house but the confused noise that suddenly blew up excited my curiosity and I quietly and stealthily got myself behind the sweetbrier arbor and sat hidden there. The noise was from Mrs. Farrokh Laqa, who was not going to do as Dear Uncle told her under any circumstances. Harshly Dear Uncle Napoleon said, "My dear lady, this is no place for you, it's time you went!"

"How come it's a place for that woman and not for me?"

"In this matter my sister is an interested party."

It seemed that Dear Uncle had forgotten Mrs. Farrokh Laqa's bad mouth. "Oh, it's like that, is it? Aziz al-Saltaneh wanted to cut off a bit of Dustali Khan's body and your sister's an interested party?"

Asadollah Mirza couldn't contain himself. Under his breath he said, "All the women are interested parties! It's a dangerous matter for the whole female community."

Dear Uncle threw him a fierce look and went ahead as if Farrokh Laqa were not there, "Your excellency, please begin."

Shamsali Mirza began just like a cross-examining magistrate in a court of law, "Are you Dustali Khan, resident . . . excuse me, I mean, explain the details of your case."

With his eyes half closed, Dustali Khan moaned, "What details? She was going to cut it off . . . she was going to cut it off!"

"Now tell us exactly when this happened."

"How should I know, it was tonight, wasn't it? Good God, what questions they're asking!"

"Mr. Dustali Khan, my meaning is, exactly at what time did this occur?"

"Leave me alone, get your hands off me!"

"Mr. Dustali Khan, I will repeat my question. Exactly at what time did this occur?"

"How should I know? I didn't make a note of the time, did I? I just saw she was going to cut it off . . ."

"You don't remember the approximate time?"

Dustali Khan yelled, "How should I know? She was going to cut it off!"

Shamsali Mirza was also getting angry, "My dear sir . . . an attempt has been made against you . . . the crime of deprivation of a member . . . the accused intended to cut off a noble member from your body and you don't know what time this happened?"

Dustali Khan burst out in rage, "For God's sake, I wasn't wearing a watch on the noble member!"

Asadollah Mirza exploded with laughter. He laughed so hard that tears trickled down from his eyes; in answer to the imperious gestures commanding him to be quiet he spluttered, in the midst of his laughter, "Moment . . . moment . . ."

His laughter set uncle colonel and then Mash Qasem off laughing. Shamsali Mirza angrily put his hat on his head. "Then with everyone's permission, your humble servant will take his leave of this joyful and amusing occasion."

With some difficulty they sat him down again. Asadollah Mirza, also with some difficulty, calmed himself down. The cross-examination continued.

"We will leave this question, Mr. Dustali Khan . . . please tell us whether the knife was of the kind that has a sharp edge only or whether it was pointed like a dagger?"

Dustali Khan was once again on the edge of bursting out in rage, but they smothered his first cry of "Agggh, she cut it" in his throat. After gasping for breath for a moment he said, "It was a kitchen knife."

Everyone present listened very carefully, their chairs ranged in a circle around Dustali Khan.

"Which hand was she holding the knife in?"

"How should I know? I wasn't paying attention to such things."

Mash Qasem answered for him, "Well sir, why should I lie? When I've seen them butcher fellers ready to cut up meat, they hold the knife in the right hand."

Shamsali Mirza turned round to say something to Mash Qasem but once again Dustali Khan screamed, "Agghh! Butcher! You said butcher? Butcher?"

Once again uncle colonel put his hand on Dustali Khan's mouth and Shamsali Mirza went on, "So it appears that she was holding the knife in her right hand. Was there anything in her left hand?"

"How should I know . . . how should I know?"

Asadollah Mirza couldn't control himself sufficiently to stay silent, "For sure, the noble member was in her left hand!"

Mrs. Farrokh Laqa became extremely angry and, despite the fact that she was very keen to stay and discover a good slanderous subject for gossiping about, she left the garden in high dudgeon, the reason being that she took the conversation to be an insult to her son-in-law. Her son-in-law's name was Mr. Noble.

Shamsali Mirza continued, "Mr. Dustali Khan, be very careful, this is a question of great importance, at the moment of the attempt on your . . ."

Shamsali Mirza hesitated for a moment and then in a very magisterial manner said, "In order to put this question, I have no choice but to declare a closed court."

Dear Uncle Napoleon objected, "What do you mean closed, your excellency? We aren't strangers. I can tell my sister to go over there a little bit . . . sister dear, go over there for a minute and then come back."

My mother, who usually didn't dare to express an opinion in front of Dear Uncle Napoleon, said in a furious voice, "I am going back to my house. There's a limit to everything. This childish behavior is shameful at our age."

But Dear Uncle gave her a fierce look and said imperiously, "I requested you to be so kind as to step over there for a minute."

My poor mother didn't have the strength to oppose him; she did as he had told her. Shamsali Mirza was silent for a moment and then stood up. He brought his head close to Dustali Khan's ear and asked something. Once again Dustali Khan started whimpering and complaining, "Oh please . . . leave me alone . . . with that ugly old hag . . . haven't you seen how she looks?"

Again Asadollah Mirza couldn't keep quiet, "Now that was a question about San Francisco."

And he guffawed with laughter. Dear Uncle angrily said, "Sir, shame on you!"

Then he turned to Shamsali Mirza. "Your excellency, the problem lies elsewhere. I want you to get this man to confess just who it was who told his wife about his having an affair with a young woman. You're asking about far-fetched, irrelevant . . ."

Shamsali Mirza stood up and placed his hat on his head. "Then would you be so kind as to conduct the cross-examination? I shall humbly take my leave. A magistrate should not stay in a place where there is no respect for judicial authority!"

Everyone was busy persuading Shamsali Mirza to stay where he was when a shout rang out from the roof of Dustali Khan's house, "So the little rat's down there, is he? I'll burn the bugger's beard off . . ."

Everyone looked up. It seems that Mrs. Aziz al-Saltaneh, who had been complacently assuming that her husband had taken refuge somewhere on the roof and would finally have to come down, had gone up to look for him.

Dear Uncle shouted up to her, "My good woman, don't shout like that! What do you think you're doing!"

"Ask that shameless little rat. I know and he . . ."

As she was saying this she disappeared from the roof into the house. Dustali Khan, who was trembling with fear, squeezed his hands into his groin again and screamed, "Now she's coming here, agghh, help me . . . hide me somewhere," and he tried to get up from where he was lying but they held him where he was.

"Calm down, we're all here . . . we have to sort this matter out . . ."

But Dustali Khan struggled wildly to get himself up and run away somewhere. Mash Qasem, at a sign from Dear Uncle, had grabbed him tightly by the shoulders. "Sit down now, there's a good boy . . . the Master's here . . . these little things don't matter so much . . ."

"It's all right for you to talk . . . she was going to kill me, is that a little thing?"

Asadollah Mirza said, "Mash Qasem meant the thing she was going to cut off. He's not lying either. It can't be that big."

Mash Qasem calmly went on where he had stopped, "Now why should I lie? To the grave it's ah . . . ah . . ."

Dear Uncle was about to yell at both of them but he didn't have the chance because there was a sudden violent hammering at the door to the house.

Dustali Khan grabbed at the hem of Dear Uncle's cloak. "Please, on the soul of your father, don't open that door . . . I'm terrified of that witch . . ."

His beseeching tone of voice made everyone stop in their tracks. But the knocking at the door didn't stop for a moment. Finally Dear Uncle said, "Mash Qasem, run and open the door; she's making a laughing stock of us."

The terrified and trembling Dustali Khan was almost hidden under Dear Uncle's cloak by the time the door opened; Mrs. Aziz al-Saltaneh flung herself into the garden, in her housecoat and with a broom in her hand, like a lion that suddenly finds its cage door open, and made for the group of people there.

"That little rat, that fatherless son of a bitch . . . I'll give him what for . . . I'll tear him to shreds . . ."

Dear Uncle Napoleon stood shielding Dustali Khan and said in a commanding voice, "Silence, madam!"

"I will not be silent neither . . . what the hell's it got to do with you? Is he my husband or your husband?"

Everyone tried to calm her down, but Dear Uncle Napoleon raised his hands signalling everyone to be quiet and said, "Madam, the honor and prestige of our family are too important to be stained by these ridiculous feuds. Please explain to us what has happened."

"Ask the smothered little rat himself . . . ask his dirty leering eyes!"

"Is it possible that you tell us just who told you about his relations with a certain young woman?"

"Whoever said it said the truth . . . the shameless dirty bastard, for a year now he's been saying 'I'm tired, I'm sick, I'm worn out, I'm every damn thing' and he's with the wife of Shir Ali the butcher . . . I'll give him what for!"

At this moment a smothered sound came from Dustali Khan's throat, and with all the strength left in his body he moaned, "Blessed Morteza Ali, save me now . . ."

Uncle colonel involuntarily placed his hand over Aziz al-Saltaneh's mouth. The name of Shir Ali the butcher had left everyone thunderstruck.

Shir Ali, the local butcher, was a horrifying man. He was well over six feet tall; his whole body, from head to toe, was covered in tattoos, and there were numerous knife scars visible on his head. His character and temperament fitted his terrifying body exactly. They said that with one blow of a meat cleaver he had sliced through the neck of a man who'd been having an affair with his wife, and since it was obvious that the victim and his wife had been carrying on in a compromising way, he'd only been given six months imprisonment. We couldn't personally remember this incident but we'd heard it referred to many times. But we had repeatedly seen that Shir Ali's shop would be closed for three or four months and people said he was in prison. He wasn't a wicked man but he was extremely jealous and possessive of his wife. In spite of Shir Ali's ferocity, his wife (who everyone—be they big, little, young or old—swore was one of the most beautiful women in the city) went right on with her mischievous behavior.

I'd once asked Mash Qasem about Shir Ali's fights, and he'd answered, "Well, m'dear, why should I lie? To the grave it's ah . . . ah . . . this Shir Ali's a bit deaf and he don't hear people's chatterin' too well . . . he only understands when he sees with his own eyes that his little woman's messin' around with someone . . . then he gets really mad and it's up with his cleaver to make mincemeat of someone . . . they say that these days he's calmed down a lot . . . when he lived in his village they say he chopped four of his wife's friends into little pieces with that cleaver."

That night in my hiding place I well understood Dustali Khan's terror and the shock that everyone felt when they heard the name of Shir Ali the butcher. Once in the bazaar I'd seen him fling his cleaver at the baker's assistant in such a way that if it had hit his head it would certainly have split the skull into two halves. Fortunately it slammed into the bakery door, and went so far in that only the strength of Shir Ali himself was able to get it out again.

The sound of Asadollah Mirza's voice brought the astonished and appalled group back to themselves, "Moment . . . well really, moment . . . this Dustali Khan, with this body of his, has been off to San Francisco with Shir Ali's wife? Wonders will never cease! My congratulations!"

Immediately he turned to Aziz al-Saltaneh, "My dear woman, really and truly it would have been a great pity if you'd cut it off. You should kiss the hem of Dustali's jacket. From the time of the great poet Sa'di until now, butchers have always had evil designs on everyone, even on poor old Sa'di himself. You remember that Sa'di says: 'Better to die for want of meat than that butchers' evil designs . . .' And now that Dustali Khan has taken revenge on a butcher, on poor old Sa'di's behalf, you're reproaching him? If I were in your shoes I'd buy a prize watch for the noble member."

Aziz al-Saltaneh was not in the mood for jokes and sarcasm and shouted, "You shut up, you rotten brat!"

And she took a swipe at Asadollah Mirza with her broom; he ducked his head and skipped back out of danger. When he was a couple of paces away he said, "Moment . . . moment . . . why are you fighting with me? This donkey goes off to San Francisco with Shir Ali's wife and I have to suffer for it . . . he knows and Shir Ali and you . . ."

Then he shouted toward Dustali Khan's house, "Eh, Shir Ali . . . eh, Shir Ali . . . come over here . . ."

Dustali Khan threw himself at Asadollah Mirza and put his hand over his mouth. "Please, your excellency, have pity on me . . . if that polar bear hears, he'll chop me into bits with his cleaver . . ."

Everyone started arguing together. Aziz al-Saltaneh's voice and shouting were louder than everything else. At that moment I realized that our servant was squatting a couple of meters away behind a group of trees and, like me, was listening to the group's conversation. He wasn't a particularly curious man and I made a good guess that he'd been sent by my father, who had heard the uproar and dispatched him to bring back news of what was going on. My father had sent him on these errands a few times before, in order to find out what was happening in Dear Uncle's house.

Seeing my father's spy there really worried me but there was nothing I could do about it. Dear Uncle Napoleon's voice rose above the others', "Mrs. Aziz al-Saltaneh, I ask you, by the sacred name of our family, to tell me who told you that Dustali Khan was having an affair with Shir Ali the butcher's wife."

Dustali Khan interrupted him in a beseeching voice, "Please have mercy and don't say that man's name so much . . . my life's in danger."

Dear Uncle adjusted his language, "Please tell me who told you that this idiot was having an affair with the wife of that ogre in human form?"

Aziz al-Saltaneh had quieted down a little. She said, "I can't say."

"Please! Tell us."

"I said I can't say."

"Madam, I know, I know which malicious individual's started all this but I want to hear it from your own mouth. In the name of the reputation and prestige of a great family, in the name of your husband's honor, I'm requesting you to . . ."

Once again Aziz al-Saltaneh flared up; flinging her broom at her husband who was sitting with his head down next to Dear Uncle, she yelled, "To hell with my husband's honor . . . I don't want a husband for the next seventy years . . . tomorrow morning I'm going to tell Shir Ali the whole thing from soup to nuts and then we'll see if I've a husband left to play these dirty tricks on me!"

Dear Uncle Napoleon calmly said, "That is exactly what you must not do . . . Shir Ali . . . I mean, this individual, if he never realizes his own bad luck until the last minute, it's because no one dares to tell him what's going on. Last year my own servant, Mash Qasem, merely said to him, 'Keep an eye on your wife' . . . and for a week Shir Ali forgot all about his business and sat outside our house with a cleaver while we hid Qasem . . . we had to beg him and plead with him before he'd go back to his sheep carcasses . . . isn't that so, Qasem?"

Mash Qasem found an opportunity to speak, "Well, why should I lie! To the grave it's ah . . . ah . . . just four fingers . . . I'd said this much to him, too . . . I said, 'Don't let your wife go out of the house too much' . . . because a thief had come and pinched their carpet. I wanted to say, 'Tell your wife to be in the house so thieves don't come.' I said it and the godless so-and-so chased me with a cleaver, as God's my witness, from the bazaar to the door of our house. I closed the door and fainted . . . God save him, the Master watched over me for ten or twenty days with a rifle."

Asadollah Mirza found a moment to interrupt; in a serious voice he said, "Ma'am, as God's my witness, if with my own eyes I were to see this Dustali go astray, I wouldn't believe it . . . the poor wretch has hardly got the strength to breathe . . . a mouse could come and eat wheat grains off him . . . how is it possible that he . . ."

Aziz al-Saltaneh suddenly lost all control and yelled, "What's this . . . what's this . . . so Dustali's old and worn out, is he? Dustali can't catch his breath . . . if you'd had enough breath your wife wouldn't have divorced you!"

With some difficulty Dear Uncle Napoleon and uncle colonel quieted down this new argument. Shamsali Mirza said, "If the Master will give his permission, I will put one question to Mrs. Aziz al-Saltaneh which will completely clear up the ambiguities of the case."

But Shamsali Mirza hadn't yet put his question when there was a knocking at the door to the garden. Everyone looked at everyone else.

"Who can it be at this time . . . Qasem, go and open the door."

Everyone stared at the door and Mash Qasem went to open it. Immediately after the sound of the garden door opening we heard Mash Qasem cry out, "God save us all, it's Shir Ali . . ."

There was a short moment's silence and then the muffled sound of Dustali's voice became audible, "Shir Ali . . . Shir Ali . . . Shir . . . Shir . . . sh . . . sh . . ." And he more or less fainted into the cushion he was propped against.

Shir Ali approached the group with heavy footsteps; his head was completely shaved and the old knife scars glittered on it. He greeted everyone and said to Dear Uncle Napoleon, "I saw the light was on and I says to meself, I'll come in and pay me respects . . . you gotta pardon me, sir, I couldn't make it to the mourning ceremony . . . I'd gone off to the shrine at Sha'abdolazim."

"May your prayers be answered."

"Very good of you, sir, I'm sure . . . I hadn't actually gone to the shrine like . . . I'd gone to settle up the account I've got with Kol Asghar the sheep-dealer . . . if you'll pardon me saying so, sir, the bastard had palmed off a rotten sheep on me . . ."

Dear Uncle said in a loud voice, "God willing, the account was cancelled and you got your money back?"

"You bet your life, sir . . . no one's gonna walk off with my money . . . of course, at first he was a bit unwilling but when I'd slapped him about a bit with the carcass of the sheep he'd sold me—well, he didn't just give me back the money for the sheep, that was nothing, he gave me the fare to Sha'abdolazim, too."

"And what disease did the sheep have, Shir Ali?"

"I don't know, but it was really rotten . . . I was afraid the people in this area'd be poisoned . . . and, if you'll pardon me, his organ was all swollen. I didn't realize it at first and I sold two or three fillets. To cut a long story short, I came home tonight and my missus told me you'd had a mourning ceremony, I was really sorry I wasn't there. On the way I said if you're still awake I'll go and say I didn't mean no disrespect, just I wasn't here. I'm really sorry and I hope you'll excuse me."

Asadollah Mirza could not resist the opportunity for mischief; he pointed at Dustali Khan, "Mr. Dustali Khan was asking after you . . . he's very partial to you . . . just a minute ago he was remembering you very affectionately."

Dear Uncle wanted to cut him off somehow or other because Dustali Khan was in a bad way and it was possible that Asadollah Mirza's joking might end up by having a serious effect on his health. Everyone was aware of this but they couldn't openly interrupt and Asadollah Mirza wouldn't let the subject go, "By the way, Shir Ali, you said the sheep's organ was swollen; did you cut it with a knife or with a cleaver?"

Fortunately Shir Ali didn't hear this question properly but Dustali Khan pushed his hands into his groin, his pallid lips started trembling, and a moaning sound came out of his throat.

Dear Uncle gave Asadollah Mirza an angry look and said, "Asadollah, you should be ashamed of yourself."

And then in a loud voice he said to Shir Ali, "In any case, I'm very grateful to you . . . God willing, you'll come next time."

"At your service, sir. God willing, the prayers of your ceremony will be answered."

Luckily Shir Ali didn't stay any longer; after he had said goodbye to each person in turn, he was on his way.

When Mash Qasem had closed the door behind him and returned to the group, he heaved a sigh of relief, "Thank God he didn't get wind of it that Dustali Khan . . . I mean I was really afraid that . . ."

Shir Ali's arrival and departure had thoroughly discomposed Dear Uncle and he cut Mash Qasem off, "Now don't you start speechifying . . . as far as I can see it's better that we leave the rest of this discussion until tomorrow . . . of course, until I've got to the bottom of this business I'm not going to leave it alone."

Then he turned to Aziz al-Saltaneh, "Madam, please return to your house and rest there until tomorrow."

Aziz al-Saltaneh turned to her husband, "Get up, let's go home."

Dustali Khan who was just beginning to recover his breath looked at her with round, terrified eyes and said, "What . . . we're going home? I go into that house with you?"

"I didn't say a word in front of Shir Ali because I'm going to settle up with you myself . . . but tonight I'll leave you alone. Get up, you deadbeat, and come and sleep."

"I'd a thousand times rather go under Shir Ali's cleaver than go back with you to that . . ."

Dear Uncle Napoleon cut him off, "Madam, tonight let Dustali sleep at my house and then we can talk tomorrow."

Aziz al-Saltaneh wanted to object but once again there was a knocking at the outer door. When it was opened, the voice of Qamar—Aziz al-Saltaneh's fat, simple daughter—could be heard, "Is my mummy here?"

And she came toward the group. As soon as she saw her mother and Dustali Khan she started to laugh idiotically, "Did mummy finally cut off Dustali daddy's willy, then?"

Aziz al-Saltaneh said in an irritated voice, "Qamar! What kind of language is that!"

Seeing his stepdaughter there, Dustali Khan became angry and shouted, "When that woman started after me with a knife, this girl was shouting 'Mummy, cut it off! Mummy, cut it off!' She should be put in prison, too!"

Then everyone started talking and interfering in the business. Once again Qamar let out a loud laugh and said, "Did you really cut it off?"

Asadollah Mirza, who was laughing helplessly, said in the kind of voice people use to talk to little children, "Well done, little girl . . . if your husband does nasty things, will you cut it off or not?"

"Sure I will."

"Right from the bottom?"

"Right from the bottom!"

"You won't leave one tiny little bit of it?"

"I won't leave one tiny little bit of it!"

Suddenly a tempestuous yell broke from Aziz al-Saltaneh, "Have you no shame! Or modesty either! You're putting words in the child's mouth that tomorrow a suitor's going to hear about . . . O God , O God, I wish I could never see one of my relatives again as long as I live. Are you a relative or a thorn in my side?"

But Asadollah Mirza was not the kind of person to back down so easily. He yelled back, "Moment . . . moment . . . just a minute, my good woman . . . if cutting it off is so bad, why were you cutting it off from this poor motherless child? If this poor motherless child hadn't jumped out of the way, he'd now be Lord High Chief Eunuch!"

"Talking about your exalted ancestors, are you, you rotten brat . . . what I want to know is, don't I have the right to do what I want with my husband? What the hell's it got to do with you? Are you the boss of this town?"

Asadollah Mirza was furious. Dear Uncle and the rest of the group were trying to calm the argument down but he shouted out, interrupting them, "Moment . . . moment . . . What's it to me? To hell with him and his noble member . . ."

People were not used to hearing Asadollah Mirza shout and almost everyone fell silent. But Asadollah Mirza still couldn't regain his normal self control. He took advantage of everyone else's silence and continued in a quieter tone, "No matter how noble the member that does your business is, it's better it be got rid of, condemned . . ."

As he was saying this he took a delicate little penknife from his pocket. He opened it and continued, "But please, next time, use this penknife . . . because it's a pity to use a kitchen knife."

Qamar started to laugh foolishly. Aziz al-Saltaneh, trembling with fury, screamed, "It's a pity for me I'm talking to such trash, such filth . . . come on, let's go, child!"

Immediately she grabbed her daughter's arm and set off for the door to the garden. As she was following her mother Qamar said with a laugh, "It's a pity you didn't cut it off, though, mummy, we'd have had a good laugh!"

Mash Qasem shook his head and said, "Why should I lie? I wouldn't take this Miss Qamar if they gave me all the tea in China . . . God help her husband!"

Dear Uncle's lack of success in his plan to use this event to disgrace my father had left him very gloomy and introspective, and everyone present was waiting to see what he would decide. Shamsali Mirza, who had been silent throughout all this, stood up and said, "Well, in any event, our time has been wasted and we have come to no conclusion. Cross-examination and judicial investigation cannot come to any conclusion in such an atmosphere; with your permission, your humble servant will take his leave. Asadollah, off we go!"

It was clear that Asadollah was sorry to leave the gathering; he stood up and said, "We're off . . . God willing, the prayers of your mourning ceremony will be granted . . . God willing, Dustali Khan will sleep well and won't have dreams of lions and wild animals, and God willing, all five members of his body will stay healthy and in place. Amen!"

Shamsali Mirza and Asadollah Mirza set off and Dear Uncle also turned toward his house. "Get up, Dustali! Get up, stay here tonight and tomorrow, we'll think of something."

Dustali Khan shouted, "There's no way I'm staying . . . I'm going . . ."

"Where are you going? Be sensible! Get up and don't talk rubbish!"

"I'm not staying . . . I'm not staying . . . I don't want to see anyone at all . . . I don't want to see anyone in this family . . . you're all out for my blood . . . Asghar the murderer was an angel compared to the lot of you!"

Dear Uncle Napoleon exploded, "Shut up, Dustali! Get up and get going and if you don't I'll tell Mash Qasem to take you by the scruff of the neck and drag you into the house!"

Dustali Khan quieted down and set off for Dear Uncle's house in front of Dear Uncle and Mash Qasem.

My mother had gone home before the others and it seemed that she had immediately gone under the mosquito net to sleep. I went back to the house on tiptoe. My father, who was quite sure that everyone in the house was under the mosquito nets sleeping, was in a corner talking quietly with our servant. I quietly slid under the net and listened carefully. Just as I'd guessed, our servant had been spying for my father and was telling him what had happened. Every now and then my father would interrupt him and say "I heard that myself." From this I realized that, besides sending our servant to spy for him, he himself had been listening in some corner to the conversation of the people at Dear Uncle's gathering, since he'd even heard the quarrel between Aziz al-Saltaneh and Asadollah Mirza.

When my father went under the mosquito net to sleep, the sound of him and my mother quietly talking caught my attention. Anger and a terrible desire for revenge were apparent in my father's voice, and in my mother's I could sense her worry and sadness.

"Dear, I'd die for you, but, for my sake, let bygones be bygones! Don't keep on with it! Just have pity on me . . . for my sake . . . things have got so bad that my brother's going to have nothing to do with me . . ."

"Well, well! What a noble person, what a great gentleman your brother is, to be sure . . . by the way, which brother are you talking about . . . the hero of the Battle of Kazerun? The Napoleon of our time? The Iron Man? The Holy Man? Because yes, of course, he is a Holy Man too, this evening he put on a mourning ceremony for Moslem ibn Aghil! Wonderful! That's the kind of person people call holy! That's the kind of person they call fearless and brave! He cuts the water off from his sister's family . . . just what Shemr did in the desert at Karbela, and then he has a mourning ceremony for Moslem ibn Aghil. Now just you wait, tomorrow new things are going to happen . . . by the way, tomorrow evening make rice with herbs and fish . . . it's a while now since I promised that poor Shir Ali the butcher that we'd give him rice with herbs and fish."

My mother's pleas for him to calm down had no effect and the conversation ended with her in tears.

FIVE

I WAS LEFT CONFUSED and bewildered and at a loss as to what to do. I'd given up hope that somehow or other the quarrel between Dear Uncle Napoleon and my father would come to an end. O Lord, why hadn't I appreciated how precious those cloudless days had been? What happy days they were, when Dear Uncle and my father would sit on cushions under the sweetbrier arbor, playing at backgammon and smoking the waterpipe, and we would be playing in a corner or in the garden somewhere. Both Layli and I liked to sit next to them and watch. Perhaps it wasn't their game that was interesting to us so much as their habit of reciting poems and bits of epics. When Dear Uncle was winning he would look at the dice in his hand for a moment and then he would stretch out his head toward my father and, in the rhythm of someone reciting an epic, he'd chant:

> *"Backgammon is for heroes, not for you—*
> *A peasant's spade's more suitable for you!"*

And my father would impatiently shout, "Throw the dice, man! And don't count your chickens before they're hatched!" When my father was winning he would say in a perfectly serious voice, "Layli dear, can you do something for me?" Layli would very innocently say "Yes" and then my father would say in that same serious voice, "Can you ask your mother to bring over a few walnuts so that your dad can play marbles with them?" and Layli and I would burst out laughing.

I remember the days they would take us out to a restaurant. It was quite a journey from our house to the restaurant—a distance that nowadays would take a quarter of an hour or twenty minutes by car lasted almost an hour then in a horse-drawn carriage. Usually Mash Qasem would sit next to the carriage driver, since on the return journey he had to hold a lantern up in front of Dear Uncle. The street lamps gave so little light that it was difficult to see and the streets were full of ruts and potholes. Eating ice cream in the restaurant, and sometimes going for a boat ride on the restaurant lake, left me with sweet, heart-wrenching memories. Then I hadn't appreciated the pleasure of being with Layli, but that night memories came before my eyes, moment by moment, of the times I'd spent beside her in the restaurant.

Going to Sha'abdolazim, going for train rides, going to the Davud shrine . . . I had so many memories of being with Layli that I could have filled the rest of my life with them, but these were all memories of Layli my cousin and I didn't have even one hour of memories of the Layli I was in love with. It was just about the time I fell in love with her that the family difficulties started. That damned dubious noise in the middle of Dear Uncle's war story . . . that damned thief who'd come to Dear Uncle's house . . . Dear Uncle's damned support for the Constitutional Revolution . . . my father's damned mention of Colonel Liakhoff . . . and, to cap it all, Aziz al-Saltaneh's damned behavior. Things had turned out in such a way that all these events and people had got mixed up with our blameless love, even Shir Ali the butcher, so that when I thought about Layli, my thoughts inevitably led me to Dustali Khan and Aziz al-Saltaneh's plot to cut off his noble member and finally to Shir Ali the butcher. My biggest bad luck was that I couldn't see Layli any more and had to content myself with thinking about her, and recently thoughts of Layli ended up with Shir Ali the butcher.

⚜ ⚜ ⚜

I jumped up from sleep, wakened by the sound of knocking at our front door. Someone was asking for my father. I listened carefully.

"Very sorry to trouble you at this time, sir. I wanted to know if the water distributor you'd asked for has done his job or not?"

"I can't thank you enough, Mr. Razavi. While you're here we've nothing to worry about. We've filled the drinking-water cistern, and the cistern for the garden, and the pool."

"It was a difficult job because getting water for a distributor one night earlier than the district's turn is quite tricky. He had to bring it from another district to give to you . . . but we couldn't refuse a commission from you, sir."

"I can't tell you how grateful I am, Mr. Razavi. Rest assured that the business of your transfer will be over by the end of the week; I'll go this very night to the engineer."

As soon as Mr. Razavi had gone, everyone was out of the mosquito nets. The big pool in the middle of the yard was full to the brim and my father was walking up and down, looking at the water with pleasure. Our eyes were fixed on my father's lips; finally he said with a satisfied smile, "The evil warrior Shemr has been confounded and water flows abundantly in the desert of Karbela . . . just that behind the desert there's still no water . . . now the colonel will have to get water from us in water-skins."

I stood there petrified; the problem of our being without water was solved but I knew that Dear Uncle Napoleon would not take this defeat lying down. I looked worriedly toward his side of the garden but as yet there was no sound from there.

After breakfast, which passed in silence, I made my way, step by step, toward Dear Uncle's house and, by going from tree to tree, I got myself to Dear Uncle's door. Suddenly I heard a voice from the balcony overlooking the garden, which was where Dear Uncle slept during the summer. I hid behind a tree.

It was Dear Uncle's voice, trembling with rage and hardly able to emerge from his throat. I climbed onto a branch and looked over toward the balcony. Dear Uncle had slipped the cord of his field glasses around his neck, over his nightshirt; he was looking attentively through the field glasses at our pool and insulting Mash Qasem. "Idiot, traitor . . . you fall asleep and they come and bring water . . . Marshall Grouchy betrayed Napoleon at the Battle of Waterloo . . . and you've betrayed me in the battle with this devil!"

Mash Qasem, who was hanging his head and standing behind Dear Uncle, began whining and pleading, "Sir, as God's my witness, it's not my fault. Why should I lie . . . to the grave it's . . ."

"That day I risked my life to save you from certain death in the Battle of Kazerun, you traitor, if I'd known that you'd betray me like Grouchy one day, I'd have cut my hand off and not bothered to carry your filthy body on my shoulders . . ."

"God, sir, if it was my fault, I hope I never eat in your house again, sir. Why should I lie, sir? To the grave it's ah . . . ah . . . This man you're talkin' about, sir . . . this Guchi guy, I dunno what kind of a man he was, but I've eaten your bread and salt, sir . . . if there's another hundred wars, while there's a drop of blood still in my body I'll be there for you, sir. But this time they caught us nappin', sir . . . last night it wasn't the turn of round here for water . . . they must've slipped the water guy a sweetener to bring 'em water . . . the water's supposed to come here tonight . . . I was asleep and they came and opened the channel . . ."

As he was insulting Mash Qasem in the most violent language, calling him traitor, spy, filthy dog, lackey of the British, and so forth, Dear Uncle went back into his room with the whining Mash Qasem following him and begging for forgiveness. Although I knew that Dear Uncle had gone to plan some terrible revenge on my father, I mostly felt sorry for Mash Qasem. When I got back to our house, I saw our maidservant engaged in cleaning smoked fish. I thought perhaps the notion of Shir Ali the butcher coming for supper was actually going to happen.

My mother was busy talking to my father in the cellar. "All right, you want to give that fat pig Shir Ali rice and herbs, give it to him, but for God's sake don't talk about this particular business. The man's always looking for a knife fight, he's crazy . . . if he kills someone you'll be to blame . . . you told Aziz al-Saltaneh, that's enough . . . that woman's enough for seven poor wretches like Dustali Khan . . ."

"I didn't say a word to Aziz al-Saltaneh, but if I'd known, I'd certainly have told her. It's a pity for the great deeds of this family to stay hidden, such select nobility as they all are. The aristocracy of Iran's ashamed to lift its head up. One of its exalted members has been messing about with a woman from the lower classes and must be destroyed for the crime of ruining the aristocracy's reputation."

"Dearest, darling, have some pity on yourself . . . if you say anything to that crazy fool Shir Ali, you'll be the first person he'll chop to pieces with his cleaver."

"It's not at all clear what I'm going to say to Shir Ali. First of all, if I want to tell him, I've other methods. Second, I'm not an underage child who doesn't know what he's doing. Third, I've no patience for more explanations. Fourth . . ."

My father cut the conversation short and went about his business, and I went off to a quiet room to write a love letter which I'd already spent about twenty hours on and which still wasn't ready to be sent.

Toward noon the coming and going and various other noises emanating from the direction of Dear Uncle Napoleon's house caught my attention.

When I reached the garden I realized that something new and unexpected had happened. During the night Dustali Khan had disappeared. The previous night they'd prepared a room in Dear Uncle's house for him to sleep in, and he had slept there, but when they went to call him to come and eat breakfast in the morning, he couldn't be found.

On Dear Uncle's orders people had either phoned or been to the house of everyone in the family, but not the slightest trace of Dustali Khan had been discovered.

The search went on until the evening, but without result. Around sunset I heard Aziz al-Saltaneh screaming and went over toward Dear Uncle's house. Dear Uncle had hidden himself, apparently because he was afraid of her, and since Aziz al-Saltaneh could find only Mash Qasem, she had made him the target of a furious attack. "You've destroyed my husband . . . you've wiped him off the face of the earth . . . I'll have my revenge on the lot of you . . . my poor husband . . . maybe you've killed him . . . maybe you've thrown him down a well . . . Dustali wasn't the kind of man to go off somewhere. O God, where is he?"

"Well now, why should I lie? To the grave it's ah . . . ah . . . What I've seen with my own eyes is this, that your husband went in this room to sleep. Maybe he went to get a bit of air. I swear to God the Master's even more upset than you!"

"Talk sense, man, in a long nightshirt where's he going to go to get some air?"

And finally shaking her finger at him in a threatening manner, she said, "Tell your master, last night you kept my husband here by force; wherever you've hidden him you have to produce him safe and sound and hand him over to me and if you don't, tomorrow I'll go to the magistrate, I'll go and lodge a complaint, I'll go and stand in front of the minister of justice's car."

Then she slammed the door leading into the inner apartments and set off for the garden door. When she was nearly at the garden door my father appeared—I've no idea from where—in front of her. "My dear lady, please calm yourself a little . . . Dustali Khan is not the kind of person to go very far . . . do come and have some tea . . . no, no, I won't take no for an answer, you've got to come and have some tea."

Aziz al-Saltaneh suddenly burst into tears and, as she was walking with my father toward our house, sobbed out, "I know they've hidden him somewhere. From the beginning they couldn't bear to see my husband's and my life together . . ."

As he was leading her into our reception room my father said, with every appearance of sympathy, "You poor thing! And poor Dustali Khan . . . but don't be upset, he's sure to turn up!"

My father and Aziz al-Saltaneh went into the reception room and the door closed behind them. I waited for a while for them to come out. Since it was a long wait I went over to the door of the room and listened carefully. Aziz al-Saltaneh was saying, "You're quite right . . . I have to say they've killed Dustali . . . they had real differences over property . . . until they're forced to, they're never going to confess where they've hidden Dustali . . . first thing tomorrow morning I'll get started . . . you said Mr. Who?"

My father quietly said a name to Aziz al-Saltaneh, and then a little louder he added, "In that same building where the mayor's office is . . . when you go in you ask on the right for the office of criminal affairs."

After Aziz al-Saltaneh had gone, my father told our servant to go and invite Shir Ali for supper, but my mother started pleading and begged and beseeched so much that finally my father agreed to send the saucepan of rice and herbs and fish over to Shir Ali's house.

Not long passed before uncle colonel turned up. In all this business uncle colonel was the most innocent and put upon, since the trees and flowers belonging to his house were drying up completely. Up till that moment he'd been hopeful that my father's lack of water would persuade him to be less aggressive, but my father had filled his pool and cistern and my uncle was going to have to put up with having no water for at least another week. A little window of hope opened in my heart when I saw uncle colonel. Finishing this quarrel would be to the advantage of both of us—he for his many flowers and I for my one flower, Layli.

Uncle colonel's requests and pleading got nowhere, and my father repeatedly said, "Until he apologizes to me, in front of the whole family, I am not ready to yield one inch."

And uncle colonel knew very well that his brother was not some-one who was going to apologize, not at any price. Only in answer to his request that, since my father had filled his own pool and cistern, he'd let the water flow through to their house, did my uncle hear a more or less favorable answer. "If they send the water over to our house, maybe we'll send it over to you as well."

And all the worries of uncle colonel—who'd repeatedly said "What are my flowers compared to your peace of mind? It's our family unity I'm really upset about"—were laid to rest by this favor-able promise, so that he went back to his house happy and smiling.

However, before going back to his house he did extract an assur-ance from my father that he would, for the time being, forget about the matter of Dear Uncle Napoleon's being terrified at the sight of a thief, until he had tried to get Dear Uncle to agree to an apology.

When my father gave him this promise, I felt strongly that, in the midst of all this enmity and hostility, he missed playing back-gammon with Dear Uncle Napoleon. Everyone in the family knew how to play this game, but my father and Dear Uncle would only play with one another, and from the moment the battle between them started, no one had heard the sound of backgammon being played, neither from Dear Uncle's house nor from ours. The thread of my thoughts even led me to believe that, at the bottom of their hearts, they liked each other without their realizing it, but I laughed at this idiotic notion of mine.

At the beginning of the evening my father went to see Dr. Naser al-Hokama. My mother seemed very preoccupied and upset. I went over to her. As soon as I broached the subject of these recent events the poor woman burst out sobbing and, with tears running down her face, said, "I swear to God I wish I were dead and free of this life."

I was deeply moved by my mother's crying. When I saw that her grief and sorrow were so great I almost forgot my own sorrow.

Still crying my mother said, "I'd wanted that when you were old enough . . . when you were twenty, that I'd arrange for you and Layli to be married." I blushed with embarrassment. With difficulty I managed to restrain the tears that welled up in me.

I went back to my room, deep in thought. I loved Layli. A seri-ous difference had arisen between her father and mine and I had done nothing to resolve it. It's true that a child of thirteen has no strength to do anything, but when he falls in love like an adult, then like an adult he's got to do something to fight for his love. I thought for a long time. What could I do? I couldn't order either my father or Dear Uncle to lay aside their differences. O God, I wished I were as old as Puri, uncle colonel's son, then I'd have married Layli and we'd have gone away together, far from the atmosphere they'd created. But I was still just a child in years. But . . . but if I really concentrated, perhaps I could find a way to resolve the differences between my father and Dear Uncle . . . suddenly, I'd got it, I needed a helper, an ally!

Whichever way I looked at it, I couldn't think of anything or anyone except Mash Qasem. What was to prevent me from telling Mash Qasem—who was really a good man—and asking for his help? But would he be ready to help me?

I stole a small coin from my mother's bag and, with the excuse that I was going to buy a notebook, went off to the covered bazaar. I bought a candle and lit it at the drinking fountain in the bazaar. "O God, first forgive me for lighting a candle with stolen money; second, either help me solve the argument between my father and Dear Uncle, or you solve it."

But I was certain that if God wanted to help He would chose the second of these two ways of solving the problem. I knew this, and only said the first way out of politeness. And anyway, as a priority I asked God to find the lost Dustali.

There was a knock at our door early in the morning. I jumped up from sleep at the sound. I listened carefully. I heard the pharmacist's voice greeting my father and asking how he was.

My father had a pharmacy in the covered bazaar and the pharmacist was in charge there. This meant he received a small monthly salary from my father and a share of the pharmacy's profits. As a result, my father had nothing to do with the running of the pharmacy; he just collected the income at the end of the month. Worry and extreme agitation were apparent in the pharmacist's voice, "Last night Seyed Abolqasem, the preacher, said from the pulpit in the mosque that the medicines and drugs in our pharmacy are all made with alcohol and that it's religiously forbidden to use them . . . I don't know what filthy bastard has stirred this up . . . I beg you to think of something today. This Seyed Abolqasem is a tenant of your wife's brother, please have him do something about it because I'm sure that no one's going to set foot in our pharmacy any more."

My father was silent and the pharmacist added, "It's not just that now they won't buy medicine from us; it's quite possible the people in the area will set fire to the pharmacy and tear me to pieces!"

When my father replied, I was terrified by the fury and malice that could be heard in his voice, "I know who has stirred this up, the shameless wretch! I'll have my revenge on him in such a way that they won't forget it for five generations. You carry on as normal until I've fixed him once and for all."

"But sir, I daren't open the pharmacy today."

My father's speech on the advantages of bravery and standing firm had no effect on the pharmacist and he wouldn't budge from his position. Finally my father gave in and said, "All right, don't open the pharmacy today and I'll see what's happening tomorrow . . . but stick a note on the door . . ."

"What should I write on it?"

"I don't know but it should certainly have something religious about it. For example, write 'Due to a pilgrimage to the sacred shrine in Qom . . . ,' because if you don't, they'll think up some other trick."

"As you say, sir, but don't forget to tell your wife's brother to say something to this preacher."

Between clenched teeth my father said, "Yes, yes, I'll certainly say something to my wife's brother . . . in fact, I'll fix my wife's brother so that he won't know what's hit him or whether he's coming or going."

The pharmacist, who apparently understood nothing of what my father was talking about, left, and my father busied himself in pacing up and down the yard.

A deathly quiet reigned on the opposite front. It was as if, after their successful attack through Seyed Abolqasem the previous night, they were resting. There was no sign even of Mash Qasem. It looked as though he had watered the flowers early in the morning and then gone back to the house. This calm worried me. I went over to the door to the inner apartments of Dear Uncle's house a few times but heard nothing. Finally I saw Mash Qasem in the alleyway; he'd bought some meat and was on his way home.

"Mash Qasem, isn't there any news about Dustali Khan?"

"Well m'dear, why should I lie? It's like the little fellow'd turned to smoke and disappeared into thin air . . . we've been every place we could go and no one's seen hide nor hair of him."

"Mash Qasem, we've got to think of something. Today Mrs. al-Saltaneh's gone to lodge a complaint . . . they'll think Dustali Khan's been killed in your house."

"You don't say so! Now it's sure to be detectives and I don't know what . . ." And he hurried on home and wouldn't let me finish what I was saying.

An hour later I saw Mash Qasem once again returning to the house. As soon as he saw me, he said, "M'dear, now I know that you want this row to be over and done with, too . . . well, the Master's told everyone that if a detective comes they're not to say a word about Dustali Khan's knowin' Shir Ali the butcher's wife, nor that his wife wanted—God forbid—to cut off his privates. So don't you be sayin' nothin' neither!"

"Mash Qasem, you can be sure I won't say anything, but . . ." Again Mash Qasem hurried home and wouldn't let me say what I wanted to tell him.

Around noon I heard Aziz al-Saltaneh making a racket in our yard and ran out. "Now they'll realize just who it is they're dealing with. And it so happens that the head of the criminal division turned out to be a friend of the late lamented . . . he said he'll send Deputy Taymur here before noon . . . that's the man who found Asghar the murderer and arrested him . . . and he was so polite to me, a real gentleman. He said, 'Rest assured Deputy Taymur will find your husband dead or alive in one day.' He said Deputy Taymur's method of surprise attack is famous even in Europe!"

My father took Aziz al-Saltaneh into the sitting room and shut the door. My curiosity wouldn't let me just sit there and I got behind the door where I could eavesdrop.

"My dear lady Aziz, my dear lady, take my word for it you have to insist that they've killed Dustali Khan . . . even say they've buried him under the big sweetbrier bush; if the officials make so much as a move toward that sweetbrier bush, they'll confess where Dustali is because this man would die for that sweetbrier bush . . . he loves it more than his own children."

"But to bury someone the size of Dustali they'd have to dig a big pit at the foot of the sweetbrier. No one's going to believe it when they see the ground under the bush hasn't been disturbed."

"Don't worry about that; I'm working on this because of my devotion to you and because of the concern I have that Dustali Khan be found soon. He really must be found soon because, as you know better than I do, they want you and Dustali Khan to separate; that old maid of a sister of theirs, who for years was supposed to marry Dustali Khan—they're trying to fix him up with her again."

"Oh yes! In their dreams! The angel of death wouldn't take that old maid of a sister of theirs. I'll fix them good and proper so it'll be a legend in their lifetime! First I'm going to settle accounts with the Master and then with the rest of them . . . especially that rotten 'moment, moment' brat."

A few minutes later Qamar, Aziz al-Saltaneh's daughter, led Deputy Taymur into the garden.

My father ran out to greet him, "Good day, sir . . . this way, please . . . heh boy, bring some tea."

"Very grateful, I'm sure, but no tea while I'm working!"

Deputy Taymur refused my father's offer of tea in a dry tone of voice. The deputy had a strange face. The features of his face and his hands were heavy and shapeless like those of a person suffering from elephantiasis; his pince-nez, perched on his huge face, seemed very tiny, and he spoke Persian with the accent of someone from the Indian subcontinent. Leaning on his cane and gazing steadily round the yard, he said, "If you'll permit me to suggest . . . we'd better get down to work. Madam, I must request you to lead me to the scene of the crime."

"As you wish, please come this way."

My father didn't want to let the detective get away from him so easily. "Sir, if you will allow me, I can clarify the details of this case to you . . ."

Deputy Taymur dryly cut him off, "If you'll permit me to suggest . . . no clarification is necessary. If it becomes necessary, I shall question you later."

And he set off after Aziz al-Saltaneh in the direction of Dear Uncle's house. Qamar and I set off after them. I threw caution to the winds. I had to know what was going on even at the risk of enraging Dear Uncle. Besides, I was hopeful that in this way I might see Layli for a moment.

Mash Qasem opened the door of the inner apartments a crack. Aziz al-Saltaneh pushed him in the chest, "Out of the way. It's the detective from the police."

Mash Qasem didn't resist for a moment and stood aside. At that time not only people like Mash Qasem but also people who were considerably his social superiors respected police detectives.

Deputy Taymur and Aziz al-Saltaneh and Qamar and I entered Dear Uncle's inner apartments. Dear Uncle seemed to have been waiting for the detective to appear. He was wearing his military jacket over his Napoleonic winter longjohns, and they were covered by his cloak which he'd slung over his shoulders. Shamsali Mirza was also there. I guessed that, as soon as news of the arrival of the detective had come, he'd sent for Shamsali Mirza, the cross-examining magistrate, to be present so that he wouldn't be alone, because the moment the detective entered, before anything else, he introduced Shamsali Mirza to Deputy Taymur as the cross-examining magistrate of Hamadan. The detective greeted him but didn't treat him with any special respect.

As soon as Dear Uncle saw me he pointed at the outer door and said, "You, out!"

But before I could make a move the police detective shouted, "No, no . . . let him stay, let him stay!"

And he immediately began his investigation, "If you'll permit me to suggest . . . now, let me see, on the last night of his life, the murder victim slept in which room?"

Dear Uncle and Shamsali Mirza, virtually in chorus, objected, "Murder victim?! . . . Dustali Khan?"

In the voice of someone who catches a man red-handed, the detective shouted, "When I said 'murder victim,' how did you know I meant Dustali Khan? Let us continue . . ." and he immediately turned to Aziz al-Saltaneh, "Show me the murder victim's room."

Dear Uncle wanted to object again, "Sir . . ."

But the detective didn't let him interrupt. "Silence! Every form of interruption of the investigation is forbidden!"

With a show of grief Aziz al-Saltaneh said, "God bless you, sir, how should a poor woman like me know which room they put my late husband to sleep in . . . if I'd known I wouldn't be in this mess now. Perhaps Mash Qasem . . ."

The detective asked, "Who is Mash Qasem?"

Mash Qasem, with his head bowed, said, "Well now, why should I lie? To the grave it's ah . . . ah . . . I'm Mash Qasem, your humble servant."

The detective scrutinized him suspiciously.

"If you'll permit me to suggest . . . who told you to tell lies . . . so you really want to tell lies, do you? Answer! Answer! Speak, speak! They've taught you to tell lies, have they? Now, quick, immediately!"

"Well now, why should I lie? You haven't asked me anythin' yet!"

"Then why did you say 'lie'?"

"Why should I lie? To the grave it's ah . . . ah . . . it's just four fingers to the grave . . . when did I say a lie?"

"I'm not saying why did you say a lie. I'm saying why did you say 'lie'?"

Aziz al-Saltaneh interrupted, "Mr. Deputy, sir, forgive him . . . it's his habit, whatever anyone asks, he says 'why should I lie'."

"Well, Mr. Mash Qasem, where did the murder victim sleep on his last night?"

"Well now, why should I lie? In this room the murder victim . . ."

The detective stared at Mash Qasem over the top of his pince-nez and shouted, "Then you admit there is a murder victim? That a murder occurred?"

Dear Uncle Napoleon angrily shouted, "Sir, are you putting words in my servant's mouth?"

"You, be silent! Even if this man is under normal circumstances your servant, he is now a witness!"

"But you are making this poor devil . . ."

"Silence! Mash Qasem, take me to the murder victim's room!"

Mash Qasem gave Dear Uncle a helpless look and set off toward one of the rooms. The detective and Aziz al-Saltaneh, Dear Uncle and Shamsali Mirza, who was on tenterhooks, and Qamar and I set off after them. As soon as we entered the room Deputy Taymur raised his arms, signalling everyone to stop and be silent. "If you'll permit me to suggest . . . let me see! Where are the murder victim's bedclothes?"

Mash Qasem answered, "Well now, why should I lie? That mornin', when I saw that Dustali Khan wasn't there, I collected 'em up."

The detective was silent for a few moments. Suddenly he grabbed Mash Qasem's chin with two fingers and shouted, "Who ordered you to collect the murder victim's bedclothes? Eh? Eh? Who? Who? Answer quickly! Quickly!"

Mash Qasem, who was utterly confused, said, "Well now, why should I lie? To the grave . . ."

"Lies again, eh? Who told you to tell lies? Eh? Eh? Answer, answer, quick, quick, immediately, now!"

Red in the face, Shamsali Mirza said, "Officer, this is a completely new method of investigation. By confusing people you're trying to put words in their mouths."

"If you'll permit me to suggest . . . please do not interfere . . . tomorrow simply ask here and there what kind of a man Deputy Taymur is! No murderer has been able to withstand my international system of surprise attack. Now you, Mr. Mash Qasem, you haven't answered my question! Who ordered you to collect the murder victim's bedclothes?"

"Well now, why should I lie? To the grave it's ah . . . ah . . . in the mornin's me and old Naneh Bilqis collects up all the bedclothes. Yesterday we collected up Mr. Dustali Khan's, too."

"The murder victim's bedclothes?"

"Yes, that's right . . ."

"Aha! If you'll permit me to suggest . . . for the second time you've confessed that Dustali Khan is this murder victim . . . if you'll permit me to suggest . . . we've made a lot of progress, we've made a lot of progress: the fact of a murder has been established, but the murderer . . ."

Dear Uncle objected, "Officer, this is meaningless chatter, you . . ."

"If you'll permit me to suggest . . . you, be silent! Mr. Mash Qasem, you said that in the mornings you collect the bedclothes? Who gave you this order? Your master? His wife? This man? That man? Who? Silence! It's not at all necessary for you to answer! Who was the last person to see the murder victim? You, Mash Qasem? Answer! Quick! Quick! Did you see Dustali Khan before he was murdered? It's not necessary for you to answer. If you'll permit me to suggest . . . why did Dustali Khan sleep here? Didn't he have a house and a life of his own?"

"Well now, why should I lie? To the grave . . ."

Dear Uncle Napoleon jumped into the conversation, "The night before last, Dustali Khan till very late . . ."

"You, be silent! Mash Qasem, answer my question!"

Mash Qasem's mind was in a complete tangle. "What did you ask?"

"I asked why the murder victim slept here instead of going to his own house. Answer! Quick, quick, quick! Eh? Why?"

"Why should I lie? Everyone was here. Mr. Asadollah Mirza was here, Mr. . . ."

"And who might Mr. Asadollah Mirza be? Answer! Quick, quick."

"Asadollah Mirza's one of the Master's relatives . . ."

"Is he related to the murder victim?"

"Yes, he's also a relative of the murder victim."

Dear Uncle Napoleon ground his teeth in fury. "God damn you and your murder victim! Idiot! Blockhead! Have you any idea what you're saying?"

In a miserable voice Mash Qasem said, "Sir, it's not my fault, this detective's got me all confused. I wanted to say that Mr. Asadollah Mirza's . . ."

Staring fixedly at Mash Qasem's eyes, the detective cut him short, "Tell me a little about Asadollah Mirza!"

"Well sir, as God's my witness, poor Asadollah Mirza's not done nothin' wrong!"

"If you'll permit me to suggest . . . when a murder occurs I suspect the whole world . . . anyone could be the murderer . . . the Master . . . this gentleman . . . that gentleman . . . this boy . . . even you! It's possible you killed Dustali Khan! . . . Yes, you, you . . . confess! Come clean! I promise that we'll be lenient in your punishment . . . quick, quick, eh?"

Mash Qasem was terrified and furious at the same time; he shouted, "Me, a murderer! God in heaven, why me and not them?"

Deputy Taymur brought his huge face close to Mash Qasem's and shouted, "Aha! 'Them,' you say . . . and who are this 'them'? Speak! Speak!"

"Well now, sir, why should I lie? To the grave it's ah . . . ah . . . I . . . I mean to say that I . . . I just kind of said it! You was talkin' about Mr. Asadollah Mirza, so how all of a sudden . . ."

The detective once again cut him short, "Yes, yes, Asadollah Mirza . . . what kind of a man is he?"

Shamsali Mirza, who could hardly speak with rage, said in a strangled voice, "I ought to bring it your esteemed attention that Asadollah Mirza is my brother."

"If you'll permit me to suggest . . . so he's your brother, sir! And can't a brother of yours be a murderer? Couldn't this Asadollah Mirza of yours have killed Dustali Khan? And just why are you interfering in my investigations? Eh? Answer, answer! Quick! Quick!"

Shamsali Mirza was so furious he was on the point of fainting. He opened his mouth to say something but the noise of the garden door and the loud sound of Asadollah Mirza's voice gave him no opportunity.

"Moment, moment, what's going on here? Are we talking about Dustali Khan's noble member again?"

Everyone present said under their breath and virtually together, "Asadollah Mirza."

Deputy Taymur gave a little jump. Then he stood still in one place. By raising his arms he signalled everyone to be quiet and muttered, "Well, well! Well, well! Asadollah Mirza; the murderer always returns to the scene of the crime. Silence! Absolute silence! It is forbidden to breathe!"

SIX

SINCE ASADOLLAH MIRZA couldn't hear any sound from within the house, he stood for a few moments waiting on the threshold of the main entrance. Then he called, "Hey! Anybody home? Is my brother Shamsali here?"

Deputy Taymur, keeping his hands up to indicate absolute silence, went quietly toward the door of the room and said in a loud voice, "Yes, he's here . . . everyone's here. Please come this way, sir."

Dear Uncle Napoleon had previously told everyone except Asadollah Mirza about the detective's arrival. Asadollah Mirza had gone to his office and so he knew nothing about the detective's coming. When he saw an unfamiliar face in the doorway he said, while with both hands he adjusted the knot of his bow tie, "Moment, are you the Master's new servant?"

And before hearing an answer he went on, "That poor Mash Qasem, he was a good man. I suppose he's been sacrificed to Dustali's noble member, too!"

Deputy Taymur ground his teeth together in indignation, but said mildly, "Please do come in . . . please come this way."

Somewhat surprised, Asadollah Mirza came over to the room and entered it. "Well, well, hello, hello . . . let me guess, another family council's been called? So why are you all standing here? Let's all go through to the other room and sit down." And then he said to Taymur, "And you run along and tell them to make tea."

Shamsali Mirza said in a strangled voice, "The gentleman isn't a servant . . . he's Deputy Taymur, a detective from the police."

Asadollah Mirza, who had been on his way to the next room, stopped and said, "I do apologize! Perhaps the gentleman's come about the disappearance of Dustali! By the way, Mrs. al-Saltaneh, hasn't Dustali been found? Where can the poor wretch be?"

Before Aziz al-Saltaneh had the opportunity to answer, Deputy Taymur began his attack, "Yes, yes, this is the question: where can he be? You, my dear sir, don't happen to have any news? You don't know where he could be?"

"Moment, moment . . . now I remember . . . yes, yes, I do know one thing."

The detective brought his huge face close to Asadollah Mirza and shouted, "Quick, quick, immediately, now, say where, where?"

Dear Uncle Napoleon and Shamsali Mirza tried, in such a way that the detective wouldn't notice, to signal to him to stay silent, but Asadollah Mirza was in his own world. With a mysterious face he said, "Is there a reward involved?"

"Perhaps, perhaps, quick, now, immediately answer; tell me quickly!"

"If you really promise to give me the reward for finding Dustali Khan, I think I can say that fortunately he's very nearby . . ."

As he was saying these words he started searching through his pockets. "That's strange! Which pocket did I put him in . . . moment, moment, I thought I'd put him in this pocket! Perhaps he's in my inside pocket!"

Deputy Taymur turned red as a tomato with rage. Through gritted teeth he said, "So that's how it is! I see . . . murder . . . concealing the corpse . . . insulting a representative of the state while executing his duty . . . hindering the course of a legal investigation . . . instead of that bow tie, I'm very soon going to see a hangman's rope around the gentleman's neck!"

Asadollah Mirza was somewhat taken aback and stared in astonishment at Deputy Taymur's huge face. During these moments both Dear Uncle Napoleon and Shamsali Mirza were signalling to him from behind the detective's back. By bringing the right hand down like a blade on the left wrist and then by immediately raising both hands they were telling him to say nothing. Even I realized very well that they meant Asadollah Mirza was to say nothing about Aziz al-Saltaneh's attempt on her husband or about the rest of the affair, but Asadollah Mirza didn't pay much attention to their signals and kept on staring in astonishment at the detective. Deputy Taymur, who was well aware of the effect of his threats, added, "The sooner you confess the better it'll be for you! Answer, quick, now, immediately, how did it happen? Quick, immediately, answer!"

"Moment, moment, now really moment! I'm to confess? What have I done that I should confess? Ask his wife, she's the one who was about to cut it off!"

Deputy Taymur suddenly gave a little jump. He raised his hands and shouted, "What? How? Cut it? When was she cutting it? What was being cut? What was his wife cutting? Madam, were you cutting? What were you cutting? Quick, quick, immediately, now, answer!"

Everyone was struck dumb and stared at everyone else. At this moment Qamar, Aziz al-Saltaneh's simple daughter, who was staring at her doll, gave an idiotic giggle and said, "Dustali daddy's little flower."

Deputy Taymur jumped over to Qamar and took her by the chin and shook it, "Speak! Quick, now, immediately, answer!"

Shamsali Mirza interrupted him, "Be careful, this girl's a bit simple."

His sentence wasn't finished before Aziz al-Saltaneh screamed out, "A bit simple yourself! And your brother! And your father! So you'll finally get round to ruining this poor orphan's chances of getting married with your language, will you?"

But the detective paid no attention to this argument. Holding Qamar's chin in his hand, he shouted, "Answer, what's the flower? Where's the flower? Did someone pick the flower? Quick, now, immediately, at the double. If you answer immediately, your sentence . . ."

But he couldn't finish his own sentence; from the depths of his being he gave an anguished scream. Qamar had bitten his finger with all her strength; she was gripping it between her teeth. With difficulty they managed to pry Qamar's jaws apart, and when the detective's finger was freed, blood flowed from the wound like a fountain.

Aziz al-Saltaneh began beating herself on the head. "God help me now!"

"Rabid bitch! Murderer! Killer! Quick, now, immediately, bring a piece of cloth, bring tincture of iodine, quick, now! A plot . . . hindering the course of a legal investigation! Wounding a representative of the state during the execution of his duty! Three years correctional imprisonment!"

During all the confusion and shouting and profound grovelling apologies, the detective's hand was bandaged up and relative peace was restored. Everyone's eyes were fixed on Deputy Taymur, who was pacing up and down the room. Finally the police detective opened his mouth; an extraordinary rage was apparent in his voice. "Complicity in the crime of murder . . . concealing the corpse . . . insulting a representative of the state during the execution of his duties . . . hindering a legal investigation . . . wounding a representative of the law . . . I'll see your daughter, too, in the same state with a rope round her neck. From now on you are under arrest for complicity in the commission of a crime . . . but let us return to the principal criminal!"

And he suddenly stopped in front of Asadollah Mirza. "If you'll permit me to suggest . . . you were saying, sir . . . who was doing the cutting? What was being cut? At what time was this cutting going on?"

Dear Uncle Napoleon interrupted, "Officer . . . with your permission, the children should go out . . . I mean this child . . ." and he pointed at me.

The detective cut him off, "Why should the child go? And anyway this person is not a child, he's taller than I am. Why should he go? Eh? Well? Answer, quick, immediately, now! Perhaps his presence disturbs you! Perhaps you're afraid he'll speak? Eh? Well? Answer, quick, immediately . . . it's not necessary for you to answer! If there's another child let him come, too! We must always listen to the truth, out of the mouths of babes and sucklings! Do you have another child in the house? Well? Quick, now, immediately, answer!"

Dear Uncle was boiling with rage inside but he tried to appear unconcerned; he shrugged his shoulders and said, "No, officer . . . there are no other children here!"

Without thinking I said, "Yes, there are! There's Layli!"

The detective turned toward me and attacked, "Where is she? Who is Layli? Where is Layli? Answer, quick, immediately, now!"

In my confusion I answered, "Layli is uncle's daughter."

And I immediately glanced at Dear Uncle. I was appalled at the glint of rage I saw in his eyes. Dear Uncle had wanted to be free of this spy from hostile territory and now he was getting even more tangled up with him.

In a calm voice the detective said, "Call Layli!"

"It's in conformity with no ethical or legal principles that a child of ten years old . . ."

Without knowing what I was saying, or realizing how I was digging the ditch between myself and Dear Uncle ever deeper, but just out of a desire to see Layli, I shouted out, "Layli's fourteen years old!"

And I didn't dare look at Dear Uncle. I just heard his voice, "He's talking rubbish, officer! My daughter is twelve, thirteen years old and I'm not giving permission for . . ."

The detective cut him off, "Murder . . . concealing the corpse . . . insulting a representative of the state during the execution of his duties . . . hindering a legal investigation . . . wounding a representative of the state . . . refusing to carrying out an order given by a representative of the state . . . your situation doesn't look too good to me either, sir!"

Dear Uncle, his face knotted with rage, shouted, "Layli, Layli, come here!"

Layli's appearance, like the warm sun on a chilly autumn day, warmed my whole being. It seemed as though a whole lifetime had passed since I'd last seen her. Finally her black eyes returned my eager gaze. But I didn't have much chance to savor and enjoy her presence. The detective's shouting interrupted my rapt feelings of love. "Mr. Asadollah Mirza, don't be too pleased with yourself, I haven't forgotten my question! Who cut, and what was cut?"

"Moment, officer! Am I the keeper of Dustali Khan's members? Why are you asking me? Ask his wife!"

"It happens I wish to ask you! Answer. Quick, now, immediately!"

I think that under cover of the confusion that reigned after Qamar had bitten the detective's finger, either Dear Uncle or Shamsali Mirza had got it through to Asadollah Mirza that he was to say nothing about Aziz al-Saltaneh's attempt on Dustali Khan, because he nonchalantly answered, "Well, I don't actually know anything!"

"Strange! You don't know? First you knew that you didn't know that you'd said you know, or you didn't know that you know? Well? Answer! Quick, now, immediately! You don't know anything! Murder, concealing the corpse, insulting a representative of the state while . . ."

Asadollah Mirza took up the list, ". . . executing his duty . . . hindering a legal investigation . . ."

The detective cut him off in a threatening tone, "Mocking and deriding a representative of the state while executing his duty . . ."

"Moment, moment, now don't you one-two-three with a list with me! The truth is that . . ."

"The truth is . . . ? Well? Eh? Answer, quick, now immediately!"

"Well, quick, now, immediately, the truth is that since Dustali Khan had not been circumcised, his wife decided to circumcise him!"

"Strange, very strange! And how old was the late Dustali Khan?"

"The late Dustali Khan was about . . ."

"Aha! So you confess that he is now the late Dustali Khan . . . another confession! Speak! Answer, quick, now, immediately, how old was he?"

"Moment, officer, I wasn't keeping a record . . . from his face he was about sixty."

Aziz al-Saltaneh lost all self-control. "Sixty yourself . . . shame on you. Sir, Dustali Khan, the poor thing, was fifty."

Taking no notice of what Aziz al-Saltaneh was saying, the detective went on with his interrogation of Asadollah Mirza. "Well, you were saying . . . quick, now, immediately, answer! They'd brought a barber to circumcise Dustali Khan . . . what was the barber's name? Quick, now, immediately answer!"

"The barber's name was . . . Aziz al-Saltaneh!"

Aziz al-Saltaneh opened her mouth to scream but the detective didn't give her permission. "You, madam, silence! You said the barber's name was what? Now, immediately, quick! No, don't you answer. You, Mr. Mash Qasem . . . tell me! Quick, now, immediately! Where is the barber Aziz al-Saltaneh?"

Mash Qasem bowed his head and said, "Well now, why should I lie? To the grave it's ah . . . ah . . . Mrs. Aziz al-Saltaneh's this lady who's present here."

"Aha! Very strange! The matter is becoming very *intéresstant.*"

Asadollah Mirza interrupted, "He means *intéressant*, of course!"

"You, silence! It's not necessary for you to give me lessons. I know Russian and Istanbuli Turkish like the back of my hand!"

Then once again he leaned over Asadollah Mirza's chair. "Then, in your opinion, it was the lady herself? Silence! You're making fun of me? They want to circumcise a man of fifty or sixty years old. And his wife with a barber's circumcising knife . . ."

Mash Qasem interrupted, "Sir, it wasn't with a circumcising knife. The lady was . . ."

"Silence! . . . If it wasn't with a knife, what was it with? Answer quick, now, immediately answer!"

"Well now, why should I lie? To the grave it's ah . . . ah . . . It was with a kitchen knife . . . one of them pointed knives they cut meat with."

Deputy Taymur said with a mocking laugh, "The matter's becoming even more *interesstant*. They want to circumcise a man of sixty. His wife circumcises him, and she does it with a kitchen knife . . ."

Asadollah Mirza jumped into the conversation, "You should be aware that they're very thrifty people. So that they wouldn't have to pay the barber, his wife agreed to put herself out and . . . besides, his wife's an expert at this work, she circumcised her late first husband too, and to be fair, she made a very nice neat cut. Once I was in the public baths and I . . ."

Aziz al-Saltaneh attacked Asadollah Mirza with such fury that, if the detective hadn't prevented her, she would have pounded the poor gentleman into pieces with her blows and kicks. Deputy Taymur screamed, "Silence! Go and sit in your chair, madam! Immediately, quick, at the double!"

And he turned to Asadollah Mirza. "Continue, sir! The matter has become extraordinarily *interesstant*."

Asadollah Mirza was a little taken aback. He looked from side to side searching for help but Dear Uncle and Shamsali Mirza, though they were trembling with rage and discomfort, were staring down at the floor. He had no choice but to continue, "But what I mean to say is this . . . that the lady wasn't able to carry out the task. Because before she could cut his little flower the kid had run away . . ."

Deputy Taymur, who was pacing around the room, suddenly— like a teacher who wants to surprise a naughty, daydreaming child— stopped in front of Mash Qasem, who was standing at one side of the room, and shouted, "You, tell me! Why did he run away? Why did the late Dustali Khan run away? Quick, now, immediately! Silence!"

"Well now, why should I lie? To the grave . . ."

"Silence! Speak, quick! Why did he run away?"

Asadollah Mirza answered instead of Mash Qasem, "Moment, moment, if it had been you and a woman like her had wanted to cut your flower with a kitchen knife, wouldn't you have run away?"

Deputy Taymur turned round and gave Asadollah Mirza a furious look. "Who gave you permission to speak? Well, so let's hear you speak . . . you who clearly have a great deal of information about the matter in hand, tell me just why the lady wanted to circumcise the late Dustali Khan at his time of life?"

"Well, for that you'd better ask the lady herself . . ."

"Silence! It has occurred to me to ask the lady . . . I'm asking you. Why did she want to circumcise him? Answer, quick, now, immediately, at the double!"

"You'll have to excuse me on this one . . . I suppose there was some problem with the traffic on the road to San Francisco."

Deputy Taymur suddenly leapt from the middle of the room toward Asadollah Mirza and shouted, "Aha . . . so there's a secret in San Francisco, too! Well . . . well . . . San . . . Fran . . . cisco! Answer, quickly! What happened in San Francisco? Quick, now, immediately, at the double!"

Dear Uncle Napoleon, who was close to exploding with rage, jumped up from his chair and shouted, "That's enough! Officer, let the children go out. It's shameful, I cannot allow that in the presence of children . . ."

Deputy Taymur screamed, "Silence! Silence!"

And he narrowed his eyes, staring at Dear Uncle's sunglasses; weighing each word, he said, "Now that you see that with my scientific system of attack I have got hold of the important thread that will lead me forward, you're being insolent? How is it at all clear that you are not an accomplice to this crime?"

Shamsali Mirza took Dear Uncle by the arm. "Sit down, sir . . . let this charade, this circus, finish by itself, then I know, and this gentleman . . ."

Deputy Taymur, who had been moving toward Asadollah Mirza, suddenly stopped and drew himself up to his full height and, without turning round, once again spelled out the desperate situation of everyone present, "Murder . . . concealing the corpse . . . insulting a representative of the state while executing his duty . . . disturbing the course of a legal investigation . . . wounding a representative of the state . . . and finally threatening a representative of the law!"

Raising his hands, Asadollah Mirza tried to act as go-between, "Moment, moment, you must excuse us, officer, my brother's a little angry . . ."

Deputy Taymur went for him. "Fine, and so you who are not angry, tell me the secret of San Francisco! Quick, now, immediately, at the double! My sixth sense tells me that the key to this complicated criminal enigma lies in this very San Francisco! Answer!"

"It so happens that's exactly right. But would you allow me to whisper in your ear?"

"Silence! In the ear is forbidden!"

Asadollah Mirza was having great difficulty holding back his laughter; scratching the back of his head, he said, "Well now, how can I put it . . . San Francisco's a city . . . a big city that . . ."

"Silence, please do not give me a geography lesson. San Francisco is a big city in Europe. This I know for myself . . . then what? Answer!"

"Moment, whether San Francisco's in Europe or in America, it's a port . . . since Dustali's ship couldn't dock in this port . . . now the ship being wrecked, the port sadly dilapidated . . ."

Suddenly Aziz al-Saltaneh's yells and screams interrupted Asadollah, "Shut up, you rotten brat! I'll smack you in the face so that your teeth rattle down your throat!"

And she pretended to burst into tears.

Deputy Taymur went over to her and said, "Madam, I understand your pain and suffering, but be patient . . . the murderer cannot escape from my clutches!"

"Oh sir, how can I ever thank you enough . . . but I . . . I . . . I've an intuition. I'm certain that the murderer of my poor husband is this brat. It's an old story, ever since he had eyes for me, he could never bear to see my husband."

Asadollah Mirza jumped up from his chair. "Moment, now really moment . . . who are you talking about? I had eyes for you?"

"It's obvious you did . . . with those cheeky come-to-bed eyes of yours staring at me, just say you didn't!"

"My God, may your kitchen knife that you wanted to cut off Dustali Khan's noble member with gouge out both my eyes!"

"I spit on your shameless face . . . when my first late husband was alive you used to flirt with me; that time when he was praying, didn't you kiss me in the hallway?"

"My God, may my lips get stuck to a scalding samovar!"

Aziz al-Saltaneh made a lunge for Asadollah Mirza but Deputy Taymur and Dear Uncle Napoleon rushed between them. In a moment there was a general confused noise of arguing voices, but Aziz al-Saltaneh's voice drowned out everyone else's, "Officer, sir . . . this is the man who killed my husband . . . I'm positive of it . . . I've proof, I've information that this rotten brat, even though he doesn't look the part, is a dangerous murderer. He's a pitiless killer . . . and I've information as to where they've buried my husband's body . . ."

Deputy Taymur's shouting silenced everyone, "Silence!"

Then the deputy brought his huge face close to Aziz al-Saltaneh's face and said in a quiet voice, "Madam, this is a sensitive moment! You said you know where the murderer has hidden the corpse?"

"Yes, I do, I know."

"Then why didn't you say so before?"

"So that you could catch the murderer first . . . so that this killer wouldn't get away from you!"

"Silence! Where is the corpse? Answer! Quick, now, at the double!"

"They've buried it in the garden."

Dear Uncle Napoleon yelled, "Madam, this is shameful, what kind of rubbish are you talking?"

"You, silence! Let us go to the garden!"

Deputy Taymur patted Asadollah Mirza's pockets with his hands to be sure he had no weapons. "You are under arrest! You have no right to make any move without my permission! Silence!"

Aziz al-Saltaneh went ahead, with everyone else following her, to the large, beautiful sweetbrier bush in the garden, which more than anything else, and perhaps more than any member of his family, was Dear Uncle Napoleon's chief pride and joy.

With a little care I could make out my father's profile among the branches of the boxtree; with a wicked smile he was listening avidly to the events he'd been waiting for. But I had got hold of Layli's hand and was standing a little apart from everyone else, and in this state nothing else mattered to me.

Aziz al-Saltaneh stamped on the ground and said, "They've buried Dustali underneath this sweetbrier."

In a calm voice Deputy Taymur said to Mash Qasem, "A spade and a pickax."

Thunderstruck and appalled, Mash Qasem looked at Dear Uncle. Dear Uncle Napoleon, who was foaming at the mouth with rage, grabbed hold of the detective's collar and yelled, "What do you want to do? You want to dig at the foot of my sweetbrier?"

Deputy Taymur calmly removed his collar from Dear Uncle's grasp and shouted, "Silence! It is exactly as I said . . . it's not possible to have a quicker confession . . . a spade and a pickax! Quick, now, immediately, at the double! It's clear that the ground here has recently been dug!"

Trembling with rage, Dear Uncle screamed, "If you touch the roots of this sweetbrier, I'll knock your brains out with the pickax!"

"Well, well! Well, well! Wonders will never cease! Murder . . . concealing the corpse . . . hindering a legal investigation . . . insulting and wounding a representative of the state during the execution of his duties . . . and now starting on the crime of murdering a representative of the law . . . silence! From now on you also are under arrest! Silence!"

Deputy Taymur had struck an extraordinary fear into the hearts of those present. Shamsali Mirza, who had gone pale with anger, took Dear Uncle's arm and sat him down on the stone bench. In the midst of this silence the deputy stood in front of Mash Qasem and shouted, "Silence! What's happened to the pickax?"

"Well now, why should I lie? To the grave it's ah . . . ah . . . My master has to give me orders to bring the pickax . . ."

The deputy's scream went up to the heavens, "What? My orders are not sufficient? Murder . . . concealing the corpse . . . disobeying the orders of a representative . . ."

His words were cut short by the sound of hammering at the garden door. The deputy jumped and placed a finger on his lips, "Silence! Everyone, silence! It is forbidden to breathe! Open the door very gently . . . if you make the smallest sign, God help you!"

And then he went on tiptoe after Mash Qasem up to the main door to the garden. He hid himself to one side of it, and as it opened the deputy was about to fling himself on the newcomer. But as soon as he saw him he stopped in midstride, "You idiot . . . you utter cretin, where have you been till now?"

The newcomer, who was wearing old civilian clothes, clicked his heels together and, instead of saying hello, snapped his hand up to the rim of his hat and said, "At your service, sir!"

Deputy Taymur whispered in the newcomer's ear for a few moments and then walked with him toward the group of people there, and while everyone waited in absolute silence, with their eyes fixed on his lips, he shouted, "Silence! The orders of my assistant, Cadet Officer Ghiasabadi, have the same force as my own orders!"

Mash Qasem went toward the newcomer excitedly, "Are you from Ghiasabad? Which one? The one near Qom?"

"Yes; so what?"

"Well, am I glad to see you . . . I'm glad to see anyone from Qom. I'm from Ghiasabad near Qom, too . . . how are you, then? Good, I hope. You're not sick, are you? You're keepin' well, are you? Where in Ghiasabad?"

His voice shaking with anger, Deputy Taymur interrupted him with a yell, "Silence! Instead of this chatter, bring a pickax for your fellow townsman!"

"Well now, why should I lie? To the grave it's ah . . . ah . . . our pickax is broken, we've given it to be mended."

Deputy Taymur sneered between gritted teeth, "Well, well, so your pickax is broken and you've given it to be mended? I suppose it's blown a fuse, has it? Answer, now, immediately, quick, at the double, answer! Or its pendulum's broken? Eh?"

"Well now, why should I lie . . . I've no learnin' and I don't get these things . . . in the middle . . . I mean at the side . . . imagine this is the pickax . . . the iron part's there and fits in the wood . . . now imagine this is the wood and this is the iron . . ."

"Silence, and I hope the wood of it splits your head open! You're making fun of me? Silence!"

Dear Uncle wanted to interfere but, before the first word had left his mouth, Deputy Taymur screamed, "You, silence! Cadet Officer Ghiasabadi! The pickax is sure to be in the shed; run and fetch it!"

Shamsali Mirza protested in a strangled voice, "Deputy, officer, this is violating the boundaries of a home and personal property! Do you know what you're doing?"

"Silence! When your brother was violating the boundaries of that poor murder victim's soul, why didn't he think of that? Silence!"

Asadollah Mirza cried out, "Moment, moment! Now they really are going to pin the murder of that donkey on me! God damn him and his soul's boundaries!"

Again the deputy's voice rang out, "Silence!"

Cadet Officer Ghiasabadi, who had ignored everyone's protests and gone looking for the pickax, returned and clicked his heels again and said, "Sir, the door to the shed's locked."

The deputy stretched out his hand toward Mash Qasem, "The key!"

"Well now, why should I lie? To the grave it's ah . . . ah . . . the key to this shed . . ."

"I'm sure the key's blown a fuse, too, and you've given it to be mended."

"No sir, why should I lie? This key . . . I mean to say, with all due respect, sir, the key's fallen in the pool . . . however much we tried with the grapplin' hook, we couldn't get it out . . ."

With his knotted, furious face the deputy stared into Mash Qasem's eyes. Mash Qasem went on in exactly the same tone of voice, "I mean, you know it's a tiny little key and the grapplin' hook couldn't hold it . . . you want me to bring a towel and then Mr. Ghiasabadi can go in the pool and get it out . . . I don't think it's very warm, though, maybe he'll catch a cold in his head."

"Silence! Murder . . . concealing the corpse . . . insulting and wounding a representative of the state during . . ."

Deputy Taymur was suddenly quiet for a moment. And then, walking on tiptoe toward the boxtree, he continued, ". . . during the execution of his duties . . . ridiculing and mocking a representative of the law . . . Aha! What are you doing here?"

And in this way the deputy ambushed my father, who was busy eavesdropping behind the boxtree. "Silence! What were you doing here? Answer, quick, now, immediately, at the double!"

Dear Uncle jumped forward and stared at the scene, his eyes round with astonishment and filled with malice and loathing. Involuntarily I left Layli's side and went over to my father.

The deputy walked round the boxtree and stood in front of my father. Bringing his huge face close to my father's face, he said, "Why are you behind the boxtree? Why didn't you come round this side? Eh? Answer! Quick, now, immediately, at the double!"

"Because on this side of the boxtree I'm in my own house and on that side I'm in the house of people who mercilessly and savagely kill a poor innocent young man over some trivial argument about property! And chop his body into pieces! And bury him in the earth!"

Dear Uncle's voice could not escape from his throat, he was so enraged, but from a few feet away I could hear him panting heavily.

Aziz al-Saltaneh suddenly burst out with an artificial-sounding cry, "Oh your poor little chopped-up innocent young body that they've buried under the cold ground!"

Asadollah Mirza imitated her fake sobs. "Oh your poor little chubby potbelly that didn't get to eat its special circumcision supper."

Deputy Taymur's yell drew everyone up short, "Silence! What kind of games do you think you're playing?"

My father took advantage of everyone's silence, "Officer, as I stated, I have detailed information about these events. If you will allow me to talk to you, sir, in private for a minute . . ."

"Silence! Private conversations are forbidden!"

"But sir, you, whose system of surprise attack is famous throughout the whole city, must know that if I discuss the matter in the presence of the murderer and his accomplices, this will hamper the discovery of the truth."

His flattery had its effect. The deputy glanced at the group awaiting his decision beside the sweetbrier bush and said, "No one has the right to leave this place until I return. Silence! Cadet Officer, keep an eye on them until I return."

Dear Uncle, who was trying to keep a hold on his self-control, said, "I hope you will allow my daughter to go and eat her lunch."

"She may go! But she is not to leave the house. It's possible we will have to question her."

At a sign from Dear Uncle, Layli went toward the inner apartments. And I was quite content that Layli go because I didn't want her innocent ears to hear about these upsetting and idiotic events.

Asadollah Mirza ran toward my father and yelled, "Brother, even in a joke, enough's enough! That prize donkey Dustali's gone off on a jaunt somewhere and, as some kind of crazy joke, they're trying to make out I killed him . . . his wife's a lunatic, his stepdaughter's even worse, you say something! If you've your differences with the Master, what's that to me? If you or someone else makes a noise in the middle of one of his stories, what's that to me? If this woman wants to castrate her husband, what's that to me? You know perfectly well that I'm not blame!"

Without looking in his eyes, my father shook his head and said, "I don't know anything. I don't know where Dustali is or when they killed him. I'll offer the information I have to Deputy Taymur. He's an expert in this business and he'll come to whatever conclusion seems best to him. Justice must be done. Isn't that so, Deputy Taymur?" And having said this, he set off with Deputy Taymur.

To stir things up as much as possible, Aziz al-Saltaneh squatted down by the sweetbrier bush where they were supposed to have buried her husband and, putting a finger on the earth, she began to recite the first chapter of the Quran. The deputy called to her, "Madam, you come with us."

I went after them, too, but at the door to the reception room the detective turned me back and wouldn't let me enter. When I started back to the others, I saw that Dear Uncle and Asadollah Mirza were sitting, talking quietly under the sweetbrier; Mash Qasem was in another corner some distance away from them, talking to the detective's assistant; and Shamsali Mirza was angrily pacing up and down the yard in front of the inner apartments.

I was tempted to listen surreptitiously to Dear Uncle's and Asadollah Mirza's conversation, as they seemed to be chatting in a secretive way. Gradually, without making any noise, I positioned myself behind the sweetbrier.

"Have you any idea of what you're saying? How can I . . ."

"You're not listening to me, Asadollah! I'm almost certain I know where Dustali has hidden himself. This evil-minded so-and-so has told Aziz al-Saltaneh to say they should dig up the ground under my sweetbrier. He knows how much I like this bush; if they disturb the sweetbrier's roots during this season, it's sure to wither away, and you can see someone's already turned the ground over a bit with a trowel . . ."

"Moment, because they might disturb your sweetbrier's roots, I'm to confess that I killed Dustali?"

"I just need two or three hours to find Dustali safe and sound. It's enough for you to confess and then, with the excuse that you want to show him where the body is, you take this idiot of a detective away while I find Dustali. It's got so that I have to find Dustali and talk to him first!"

"Suppose he can't be found, or suppose he's found and the detective arrests me for the crime of deceiving a representative of the state? Has it occurred to you how that'll go down in my office?"

"You've been accused in any case already, Asadollah! It's possible you'll be arrested in any case!"

"Moment, moment, they can't arrest someone on the word of that lunatic woman. They'd better not try and do such a thing!"

"But if they do, there's nothing you can do about it! You'll stay under arrest until it comes to court . . . I promise you that I'll find Dustali before tonight, and for the rest, don't worry about it. I've a lot of friends in the police. It's impossible I'd let you stay there for the night."

Asadollah Mirza shouted, "I don't understand how it's possible, with your intelligence and at your age, for you to make such a suggestion! I wish I'd broken my leg and never come here."

"Look, Asadollah, I'm begging you. It's a very simple matter; when the detective gets back you pretend that your conscience has got the better of you, and then straightaway you confess that you killed Dustali and buried him under the floor in your house, and then I'll find Dustali, because I'm just about certain I know where he is. I'll send Mash Qasem to give you the news that Dustali's been found and I promise you there won't be any trouble for you as a result!"

"I'm very sorry, you'll have to excuse me on this one. Even if Deputy Taymur arrests me . . . an innocent man can go to the foot of the gallows but he's not going to climb up and slip the rope round his own neck . . . I can't be a murderer just for the sake of the roots of your sweetbrier bush!"

And he stood up to go. But Dear Uncle angrily said, "Asadollah, sit down! I haven't finished talking yet. Dustali left a message for me."

"A message? Then why didn't you say anything? Why didn't you say so instead of letting me suffer . . ."

"Listen . . . the night he slept here, I went to see him early the next morning. I saw a bit of paper with my name on it in his empty bed. Dustali had written that he'd hide for a while and we, the members of this family, were to smooth over the fuss his wife was making and the fuss about Shir Ali the butcher . . ."

"Moment, moment, this prize donkey goes off on a jaunt somewhere while the helpless members of his family are to smooth over the results of his filthy carryings on?"

"Be patient, Asadollah! The members of his family aren't so helpless after all. If there are difficulties for him, everybody's going to land in it."

"What's that to me! I'm not this family's keeper . . ."

"I think it would be better if I read you his note . . ."

Dear Uncle put his hand under his cloak and drew out of his trouser pocket a folded piece of paper that had obviously been torn from a child's exercise book.

"Marvelous, what fine handwriting Dustali has!"

Dear Uncle drew his hand back and placed the note before his eyes in such a way that Asadollah Mirza couldn't read it. And then he slowly said, "Open your ears and listen carefully. He's written, 'If, in the next two days, this fuss doesn't die down, I will have to publicize the names of the people who've been carrying on with Tahereh . . .'"

Asadollah Mirza jumped. "Tahereh, the butcher's wife?"

Dear Uncle gave him a meaningful look and said, "Yes, Shir Ali the butcher's wife . . . listen . . . and then Dustali's listed the names of a few people that he's heard from the mouth of that woman herself . . ."

With his hand over his mouth, Asadollah burst into peals of laughter, "Moment, this is really delicious!"

"Truly delicious! Especially when you know that your name is there, too."

"What? But how? I don't get it. My name? My name? I swear by our friendship, on my life, on your . . ."

"And on your father's, too, I suppose, you shameless rat! That agate seal of your late father's which you had made into a signet ring and then said you'd lost—Dustali's seen it in this woman's possession. If you aren't blind, take the note and read it for yourself."

Asadollah Mirza didn't know whether he was coming or going. "I . . . I mean . . . as God's my witness . . . I mean, just think of it for yourself . . ."

And then he fell silent with his mouth open. It was clear that his morale was failing before the terrifying vision of Shir Ali the butcher. Dear Uncle kept staring at him. With a pallid face and with his voice trembling, Asadollah Mirza said, "You yourself know that relationships like that are not my kind of thing."

"It so happens that if there's one man whose name's there whose kind of thing they are, then you're that man, you impudent lecher."

For a moment Asadollah Mirza was silent again, then he said excitedly, "Who else is on it?"

Dear Uncle snatched the paper back from his hand and said, "That's nothing to do with you."

"Moment, how come it's nothing to do with me?"

Somehow Asadollah Mirza appeared to feel calm again and in a decisive voice he said, "I have to read that note, and if I don't, I will not cooperate with you under any circumstances."

Dear Uncle hesitated for a moment but then it seemed that he caught sight of his sweetbrier bush again and, with a brusque gesture, he thrust out the note toward him.

Asadollah Mirza started to read carefully. Occasionally he placed his finger on his lips in astonishment, sometimes he slapped his knee, and sometimes he laughed. "What! Wonderful! The colonel . . . God bless you, colonel, who would have guessed it from your face . . . incredible! Well, really incredible! And Madhosayn Khan, too . . ."

Asadollah Mirza suddenly slapped his hand in front of his mouth and smothered a laugh that would have been heard five streets away; with tears of laughter flowing down his cheeks, he said in a broken voice, "This . . . this . . . this is impossible . . . my brother Shamsali . . . moment, moment."

Dear Uncle put one hand over his mouth and with the other snatched the note back. "Quietly! If Shamsali realizes, he'll raise the roof . . . now do you understand why I didn't show the note to the detective? Now do you realize it's not just my sweetbrier bush that's at stake? Just think if this should get into the hands of that filthy fellow . . . do you think he'd have mercy on you or the others or especially on my brother?"

Asadollah Mirza, who was having difficulty controlling his laughter said, "By the way, where is the colonel?"

"Since I told him about it, he's been too ashamed to put in an appearance today."

Asadollah Mirza threw caution to the winds and with a laugh said, "Well, whatever, we're all in the same boat!"

Dear Uncle grabbed him by the arm and said, "Asadollah, think properly! It's possible that Shir Ali the butcher won't believe it of the others, but you're a lady-killer, randy, horny, with a roving eye and handsome to boot . . . it'll be you he'll come after first with the cleaver, so think about it!"

Asadollah Mirza suddenly became very thoughtful and after a few moments he said, "Whatever you say . . . I agree! From this moment on, I'm a murderer. I slit Dustali's neck from ear to ear. And he died just like that! In fact, I wish the prize donkey was here and I'd cut his head off right now. It's a real pity that beautiful Tahereh's paired off with that old jackal . . . with a whole pack of jackals, come to that . . ."

"I promise you there'll be no difficulties for you in all this. But that filthy fellow mustn't be able to use this against us, too. When this business is all over, if my sister doesn't leave the evil bastard, I'll never mention her name again as long as I live. As Napoleon said, sometimes holding back and fleeing from the battlefield is the best strategy. But what's going on? The detective's talk with this fellow's lasted a long time . . . I'm afraid he's cooking up some new scheme . . . anyway, Asadollah, my whole strategy, all my hopes for victory in this conflict rest in you!"

"Rest assured, I'll play my part well because, to be honest, if I weren't so afraid, as well as Dustali I'd have strangled that witch Aziz al-Saltaneh, too, with my own bare hands. But if the detective asks why I killed him, what shall I say?"

"That doesn't matter; first, I'm sure that filthy fellow has been telling the detective about the property in Ali Abad that Dustali Khan bought three parts of and all that fuss there was a few years ago, and that you came under suspicion about, and then you can re-peat what Aziz al-Saltaneh said."

"Moment, you mean I'm to agree that I was interested in that whining witch?"

Dear Uncle had no chance to respond because there was a knock at the door and the preacher Seyed Abolqasem came in. With a wor-ried, confused look on his face, he came panting over to Dear Uncle and started, "Sir, you must help me . . . after I'd spoken about the matter of the drugs in your brother-in-law's pharmacy, his manager closed the shop, but today he came to me and said that if I didn't clear the matter up by tonight, tomorrow he'd tell everyone in the neighborhood that my son has had an unlawful relationship with the wife of Shir Ali the butcher . . ."

Asadollah Mirza jumped up, "Moment, moment, Your Reverence's boy, too . . . yes, indeed . . . God bless . . . I mean, God bless Tahereh, what a woman!"

"But God forbid, it's completely untrue, completely . . . it's slander, it's calumny, it's spreading false reports, it's pure malice . . ."

Asadollah Mirza brought his face close to the preacher's, in the manner of Deputy Taymur, and shouted, "The truth shall set you free! Confess! Make a clean breast of it! The truth, unvarnished, quick, now, immediately, at the double!"

The terrified Seyed Abolqasem drew his head back and said, "It's a lie, it's a falsehood . . . now, perhaps when one is young and ignorant . . ."

Asadollah Mirza once again adopted the detective's system of surprise attack and pressured him, "When one is young and ignorant, what happened? Quick, now, immediately, at the double . . . did San Francisco happen? Quick, now, at the double!"

"Asadollah, will you let me hear what the gentleman has to say?"

But Asadollah Mirza cut Dear Uncle off. "Moment, quick, now, immediately, answer!"

Seyed Abolqasem, who was very taken aback, said, "I've thoroughly questioned this degenerate son of mine, and he says that occasionally he's felt that, if one day Shir Ali were to divorce his wife, he'd like to marry her; but an unlawful relationship, God forbid!"

Asadollah Mirza lifted his head up victoriously and with a laugh said, "The deputy's system of surprise attack's not a bad system after all. My congratulations, sir . . . encourage him as much as you can . . . it's a real pity that a woman with such a reputation, such a fine housewife and so pretty, should be married to that donkey of a butcher, that ogre in human form who's so frightening no one dares pass by their house. This woman needs a kind, meek husband like Your Reverence's son who won't frighten people away like that . . . God willing, it'll all turn out well. Why is Your Reverence's son so rarely seen around and about? Please tell him to drop round to my house sometimes . . . especially after the wedding, have him come over with his wife . . ."

Dear Uncle shouted, "Asadollah, will you shut your mouth or not? Sir, please go home now; tonight I'll come by and we can talk. You can be sure we'll find some way out of this difficulty, but please go immediately . . . we've a difficulty of our own here and we have to solve that first . . . please, this way, please . . ."

Dear Uncle was so afraid that the detective would appear, and that when he saw Seyed Abolqasem he'd start some new incident, that he almost threw the preacher out of the house. But he didn't have the opportunity to express an opinion on the matter. As soon as he'd returned to Asadollah Mirza, Deputy Taymur's yelling became audible, "Hey! Where is that utter cretin . . . Cadet Officer Ghias-abadi! Idiot! Instead of guarding the accused, you're off chewing the cud about Ghiasabad near Qom, are you?"

The cadet officer ran to the deputy as fast as his spindly legs could carry him. He clicked his heels together and, with an informative air, said, "Sir, the accused are all present."

The detective and Aziz al-Saltaneh came over to Dear Uncle and Asadollah Mirza. Aziz al-Saltaneh was making a show of grief and tears. The deputy suddenly thrust his finger under Asadollah Mirza's nose and shouted, "Mr. Asadollah Mirza, there is such an accumulation of evidence against you that if I were in your shoes I would confess immediately. Confess! Quick, now, immediately, at the double!"

Asadollah Mirza bowed his head and in a muffled voice said, "Yes, officer, perhaps you're right . . . I confess that I killed Dustali."

SEVEN

FOR A FEW MOMENTS after Asadollah Mirza's sudden confession Deputy Taymur stood still and speechless. Gradually, with his mouth still closed, he began to laugh. "Silence! Another success for the international system of surprise attack! Another murderer is in the clutches of the law! Cadet Officer Ghiasabadi, the handcuffs!"

Everyone stood rooted to the spot. I quietly went over to the group. As if it were coming from the bottom of a well, Shamsali Mirza's voice broke the silence, "Asadollah . . . Asadollah, what's this I hear?"

Dear Uncle had had no opportunity to pass on to Shamsali Mirza his collusion with Asadollah Mirza, and perhaps he was worried about this. He said, "Sir . . . your honor . . . don't worry, it's sure to be just a misunderstanding."

Suddenly everyone burst out at everyone else. They were having difficulty controlling Aziz al-Saltaneh and she tried to throw herself at Asadollah Mirza. "Then you really truly did kill Dustali? You shameless bastard! You murderer!"

Shamsali Mirza sank down in a faint on the bench. Dear Uncle, for credibility's sake, addressed Asadollah Mirza in the most violent manner. Finally Deputy Taymur's voice rose over everyone else's, "Silence . . . I said silence!"

But Aziz al-Saltaneh didn't pause for a moment in her attempts to attack Asadollah Mirza, who stood there with his head bowed. "I'll scratch your eyes out with my own fingernails. God, I'll see you on a mortuary slab . . . I'm not my father's daughter if I don't kill you with my own hands . . . may you die of bubonic plague! What had that poor innocent child done to you?"

At a sign from the deputy, Cadet Officer Ghiasabadi, with both hands, grabbed Aziz al-Saltaneh from behind. It took a few moments for her to calm down. Deputy Taymur wiped the sweat from his brow and said, "Madam! An individual must not take the law into his own hands! The angel of justice watches over us; this murderer will receive his just desserts for his evil crime. I promise you that within a month I will deliver his body to you on the gallows."

And then he said to his assistant, "Cadet Officer, what's happened to the handcuffs?"

"Sir, I went to the office and they said you'd given an order that I was to come to this address . . . I wanted to pick them up on the way but I didn't get a chance . . . if you remember the lock was broken and we'd given them to be mended."

"Idiot! . . . you utter cretin . . ."

Mash Qasem pushed into the conversation, "Do you want me to bring a clothesline and tie up his arms?"

Dear Uncle interrupted, "Officer . . . I still can't believe . . . but I beg you, sir, to forget about handcuffs and ropes. I guarantee that Asadollah will not run away. Just consider, would a man who's so conscience-stricken and who confesses so candidly run away? You only have to look at his face!"

Asadollah Mirza had such an ashamed, penitent look on his face that if I hadn't known the truth of the matter, I'd certainly have believed that he had killed Dustali.

The detective pretended he was satisfied, but in any case he had no choice since Cadet Officer Ghiasabadi hadn't brought the handcuffs with him. "If I don't handcuff you, do you promise that you'll accept your fate like a man and not think of running away?"

"I promise."

Mash Qasem suggested that he go and fetch some water to splash on Shamsali Mirza's face, but the detective stopped him. "Silence! The gentleman is very excitable . . . it's better that he remain in this state until we've finished our investigation."

Then he stood in front of Asadollah Mirza. Cleaning his pince-nez with a folded handkerchief, he said in a triumphant voice, "It's impossible, with this system of surprise attack, for a criminal not to confess . . . but, all the same, since you quickly realized that logically you had to confess, it's clear that you are not a very foolish person. Now I want you to answer my questions very carefully, and, obviously, sincerity and truthfulness will not be without influence on your ultimate fate."

Once again Aziz al-Saltaneh went for Asadollah Mirza but Cadet Officer Ghiasabadi stopped her in time and, on the deputy's orders, sat her down on the stone bench, and then threw his whole body's weight down on the lady's ample form to keep her from moving. The deputy continued his cross-examination, "Silence! I asked when you killed the poor wretch?"

Without raising his head, Asadollah Mirza said, "That same night he'd run away from his house . . ."

"Just a minute! Why had the murder victim run away from his house? Answer, quick, now, immediately, at the double!"

"Moment! First, now I've confessed, why do we need all this quick and at the double and immediately? Second, how many times do I have to tell you? I told you his wife wanted to circumcise . . . thingy . . ."

"Thingy? What thingy? Answer, quick, immediately, at the double!"

"I mean the murder victim. I'm so conscience-stricken I can't bring myself to pronounce his name."

"Well, and then?"

"When he came here, he was afraid to go back to his house, God forbid his wife would want to circumcise him again . . ."

"But hadn't she circumcised him once? How could she do it again?"

"No sir, I meant he was afraid she'd circumcise him. He said, 'I'm not going home.' The Master insisted that he sleep here that night. When I saw that he was uncomfortable about staying here, too, I secretly suggested to him that when everyone was asleep he come over to my house."

"Well, did he come or not?"

"Moment, officer! What kind of a question is this? If he hadn't come, it wouldn't have happened."

"Well, and then? He came, and what happened next?"

"Nothing . . . it was three in the morning when he came. My brother was asleep. I saw it was the best time for it, I cut his head off . . ."

With a sudden heave Aziz al-Saltaneh threw Cadet Officer Ghiasabadi's body to the floor and went for Asadollah Mirza. "I'll gouge your eyes out . . . may you rot in hell!"

Once again, and with some difficulty, they immobilized her.

"So you cut his head off?"

"Yes, I cut it off."

"Then what did you do? Quick, now, immediately, at the double!"

"Quick, now, immediately, I threw his head away!"

Mash Qasem slapped himself on the thigh. "Eh, God in heaven! Well, 's obvious a guy what drinks wine and whisky's gonna finish up like this."

Dear Uncle impatiently said, "You just shut up, Qasem!"

"Silence! Everyone here makes fun of me! You threw his head away? Was it the head of a cucumber, that you threw it away?"

"I meant that I separated his head from his body."

"What with? With a knife? A cleaver? A stiletto? A dagger? Silence! What was the reason? Why did you kill the victim?"

"Well, I . . ."

"Quick, now, at the double, answer!"

Once again Asadollah Mirza bowed his head, "I've said everything; this is one thing I can't say."

The detective narrowed his eyes and brought his huge face close to Asadollah Mirza's face. "Aha . . . so you can't say! Well, well! The gentleman can't say this one thing . . ."

When they'd once again seated Aziz al-Saltaneh, whose eyes were like two saucers of fire from the intensity of her rage and fury, the detective continued, "So you cannot say the reason? Let me see! Perhaps there are other crimes still hidden here, eh? Yes? Quick, now, immediately, at the double, answer!"

"Moment! So you're making me out to be Asghar the murderer, are you?"

"Silence! You are even more dangerous than Asghar the murderer! Asghar the murderer didn't cut off some huge fellow's head! Why did you kill him? Answer! Quick, immediately, at the double!"

"I'm very sorry, officer, I can't answer this question."

"Silence! Well, well! You can't answer? We shall see . . . Cadet Officer Ghiasabadi . . . !"

"Moment, moment! I agree . . . now you're putting pressure on me, I'll talk . . . I killed . . . I killed . . . I killed Dustali . . . because . . ."

"Because what? Immediately, now, at the double!"

Asadollah bowed his head even further than before and like a shy little boy said, "Because I was in love with his wife . . . because Dustali had stolen my love . . . because he had inflicted the most terrible wound on my heart."

Everyone was silent. The detective's mouth hung open in amazement. I involuntarily looked at Aziz al-Saltaneh. She was standing stock-still, with round astonished eyes and her mouth wide open. In a quiet voice the detective asked, "This lady here? You loved this lady here?"

Asadollah Mirza sighed and said, "Yes, officer! Now that my life has come to an end everyone may as well know."

Aziz al-Saltaneh was staring at Asadollah Mirza, still with her mouth wide open. Finally and with difficulty she closed it, swallowed, then moaned plaintively, "Asadollah! Asadollah!"

Asadollah Mirza, who was perhaps allowing his role to influence him more than was strictly necessary, said in a voice filled with sorrow and longing, "How many times have great poets let concealment like a worm in the bud . . . this time the veil has been torn aside from the secret."

Everyone present was deeply touched and remained silent. Aziz al-Saltaneh said in a way that was sorrowful and at the same time flirtatious, "Well, God strike me dead! Asadollah! O Asadollah! What have you done? Why didn't you tell me?"

Asadollah said in a lovesick tone, "Madam, don't heat the brand again! Don't turn the knife in my heart's wound!"

"O Asadollah, I wish I were dead rather than see you in this state! Why didn't you say? Oh, why did you cut his head off?"

"Dearest, enough! Don't break my heart!"

"O God strike me dead, Asadollah . . . don't worry, I've got to let bygones be bygones, and I shall, too . . . these things happen!"

Deputy Taymur could not stand any more of this. He yelled, "Silence! Madam, the murderer must proceed to punishment. Your forgiveness of bygones doesn't have very much to do with it!"

Aziz al-Saltaneh suddenly exploded in fury against the deputy, "Silence yourself and to hell with you! What are you talking about! Is it my husband he's killed or your husband? He was my husband and if I don't want to take it any further . . ."

"Silence! How can you not take it any further?"

"Any way I want . . . he'd had his life, God rest his soul. He used to say he was fifty but he was sixty if he was a day . . ."

Deputy Taymur brought his huge face close to hers and shouted, "Silence! Then in that case it's not at all unlikely that you two colluded in a plan to do away with this innocent child! Silence! How long ago was it that you . . . Ough!"

The deputy could not finish what he was saying because Aziz al-Saltaneh had sunk her nails into his thick neck. "I'll do away with you, too, so think on!"

"Murderer! Killer! Silence! Do you take me for another innocent helpless victim?"

Aziz al-Saltaneh shouted, "Murderer yourself! God rest his soul, he was innocent the same way you are. With the wife of Shir Ali the butcher . . ."

Dear Uncle and Asadollah Mirza together started making a racket so that the detective wouldn't hear anything about Shir Ali. Deputy Taymur seemed not to hear anything and was silent, but, when the noise had died down, he suddenly jumped toward Asadollah Mirza and said, "And who was Shir Ali the butcher? Answer! Quick, now, immediately, at the double!"

Virtually together, Dear Uncle and Asadollah Mirza noisily started to respond. Finally Dear Uncle said, "Sir, that's a subject of no importance. Shir Ali was the butcher in this neighborhood. A few years ago he passed away."

With a sad face Asadollah Mirza added, "God rest his soul, he was a good man. Shir Ali . . . he caught typhoid two years ago and died."

"Silence! And how is it clear that you didn't kill this poor wretch, too?"

"Moment, moment, why don't you just announce once and for all that I've no other profession or occupation than killing people? When I killed Dustali, that was enough for the rest of my life and more!"

"Is that so! Is that so! Well, you haven't said where you've hidden the body."

"I took him in the yard of my house and buried him."

The deputy once again jumped at him. "Who helped you? Quick, at the double, immediately, answer!"

"No one, officer. I took him myself to the entrance to the yard . . ."

Asadollah Mirza put his hand on his back and wrinkled his eyebrows, "Ouch, my back . . . my back still hurts. You've no idea how heavy his body was!"

Aziz al-Saltaneh raised her eyebrows and said, "Well, he ate so much!"

Dear Uncle shouted, "Madam, this is shameful. That's enough!"

The detective shouted, "Silence! You, too, silence! Everyone, silence! I shall proceed to the site of the concealment of the corpse! No one has the right to leave this garden until we return! Silence! Madam, you stay here, too, until we return!"

"Forget it! I'm coming with you."

"Madam, seeing a headless corpse will not be a very pretty sight for you. It's better that you . . ."

Aziz al-Saltaneh decisively cut him off and, pointing at Asadollah Mirza, said, "I let you lead a young man off like a sheep to the slaughter while I stay here? No way, I'm coming, too . . . let's go. Besides, is it my husband's head or your husband's head?"

When Asadollah Mirza set off to go with them I heard him say under his breath, "God and all the saints help me now . . . I wasn't prepared for this!"

✤ ✤ ✤

As soon as the detective and his assistant had left, together with Asadollah Mirza and Aziz al-Saltaneh, first Dear Uncle told Shamsali Mirza about the plan, and then a feverish search for Dustali Khan began. Dear Uncle sent people off to two or three places where he guessed Dustali Khan might be hiding. At the same time, uncle colonel, who had not shown his face during the whole affair, came out of his house and, after he had gathered what was going on, began to bend all his efforts toward settling the differences between Dear Uncle Napoleon and my father. His first step was to prepare the ground for a solution. In a decisive voice he told Dear Uncle Napoleon that if peace had not been achieved by the end of the night, he would without hesitation leave the paternal home and he would let it to some disreputable lout living in the neighborhood. At his instigation my mother threatened my father that if the differences were not solved, she would kill herself by eating opium.

While Dear Uncle Napoleon and his emissaries were busy running everywhere looking for Dustali Khan, and Asadollah Mirza and Aziz al-Saltaneh were off with the detective and his assistant to Asadollah Mirza's house to find Dustali Khan's corpse, uncle colonel arranged for an extraordinary meeting of the family council.

Negotiations for ending the differences between the two sides began. Uncle colonel and Shamsali Mirza frequently went off to see Dear Uncle Napoleon and my father and then returned.

Many of the differences between them could be solved and the two parties didn't make many difficulties about them. Dear Uncle Napoleon agreed that henceforth he would not hinder the free flow of water. My father was prepared to forget about both Aziz al-Saltaneh's attempt on her husband and the relationship between Dustali Khan and Shir Ali the butcher's wife. Dear Uncle was prepared to ask the preacher Seyed Abolqasem to put right the matter of the presence of alcohol in the drugs manufactured in my father's pharmacy, and, in order to facilitate the preacher's task, my father was ready to dismiss his pharmacist and engage another manager. My father was ready to stop making contemptuous remarks in public about Napoleon, but he drew the line at praising him and paying tribute to him. After renewed comings and goings by uncle colonel and Shamsali Mirza, he finally agreed to say publicly at a family gathering that, although Napoleon's activities had ended by harming France, he had, when all was said and done, loved France.

But despite persistent pressure from his relatives my father refused to admit to Dear Uncle's support for the Constitutional Revolution. The only concession he made was that he agreed not to deny Dear Uncle's bravery in putting down the insurgents in the south of the country, especially at the battles of Kazerun and Mamasani and so forth.

The only remaining bone of contention was the matter of the dubious sound. Dear Uncle expected my father to say in front of everyone that, although the dubious sound had in fact come from his direction, it wasn't done on purpose. My father was not going to agree that the dubious sound had come from him and he wanted Dear Uncle to apologize for publicly reciting the verses beginning "To raise up someone vile . . ." with him in mind. Finally the notion was put forward, and gathered strength, that the dubious sound be attributed to someone else and that this person should provide proof positive that the sound had come from him.

This notion received virtually unanimous support, but three difficulties still remained. The first was that neither uncle colonel nor Asadollah Mirza nor any of the others who were ready to take this upon themselves were anywhere near Dear Uncle on the night of the party. And Qamar's mother was under no circumstances going to allow her daughter to be sacrificed for the sake of making peace. In sum, the first difficulty was in attributing the sound to someone who was near Dear Uncle Napoleon at the time that it became audible. The second difficulty was in persuading that person to acknowledge that the sound came from him. The third difficulty lay in how those who were interested in resolving the quarrel could convince Dear Uncle Napoleon that this person was telling the truth and that the dubious sound had in fact come from him.

In the midst of this discussion Shamsali Mirza suddenly shouted, "Wait! If you remember, besides those two, Mash Qasem was standing near the Master on that night."

Two or three relatives objected, "But Mash Qasem wasn't standing next to the Master, he was standing behind him."

Angrily and impatiently Shamsali Mirza shouted, "Look, the Master didn't have a compass with him to tell him which direction the noise was coming from!"

One after another, everyone present recalled that on that night when Dear Uncle Napoleon was describing the Battle of Kazerun and how he had taken aim at the leader of the insurgents' forehead—and especially when the dubious sound became audible—Mash Qasem was standing behind Dear Uncle.

But with a gloomy face uncle colonel said, "But don't be too optimistic. I know this Mash Qasem very well. He's not the kind of person to be put upon. He'll consider this kind of noise to be a shameful matter."

Shamsali Mirza also became very thoughtful and after a moment said, "That's true. If you remember he's told that story a few times about his niece who killed herself because her body let one fly during a wedding party."

"If we give him a nice sum of money, maybe . . . not that he's very mercenary."

I didn't want the vista of peace that had appeared on the horizon to be obliterated; excitedly I said, "You know, uncle, a while ago Mash Qasem was saying that he has only one wish in all the world, and that's to build a water cistern in Ghiasabad and donate it to the people there."

Everyone noisily confirmed this; Mash Qasem might be ready to help, in order to make the gift to his village possible.

Before having Mash Qasem come in to discuss the matter, the subject of how to convince Dear Uncle Napoleon was brought up. After a good deal of discussion and argument one of those present said, "Please excuse me . . . I hope that you won't be very upset by this suggestion that I want to make, but this is the only way to do it . . . I really apologize but we, and everyone who was present on the night of the party, or at least some of us, must swear by the soul of the Late Grandfather that the dubious sound came from Mash Qasem."

"By the soul of the Late Grandfather?!"

"By the soul of the Late Grandfather?!"

"By the soul of the Late Grandfather?!"

Two people more or less fainted and an indescribable commotion ensued. After a few moments profound silence reigned. Everyone stared with eyes bursting from their sockets at the person who had made the suggestion. The Late Grandfather was Dear Uncle Napoleon's grandfather, and within the family no one, not even to claim it was hot in the hottest days of summer, dared swear by his name.

At a time when Dear Uncle Napoleon, in his own house and with all his strength, was striving to save his family from being dispersed and to preserve its identity and sacred unity, and Asadollah Mirza was inextricably caught in the clutches of the law and of Aziz al-Saltaneh—and in truth was in his own way sacrificing himself for this very cause—at such a time someone dared in this appalling way to take in vain the name of the Late Grandfather, who was the symbol of precisely that identity and sacred unity. It seemed as though the sad moans of the soul of the Late Grandfather were echoing in the ears of everyone present.

The relative who had made the suggestion that they swear by the soul of the Late Grandfather was so confused and upset that he didn't know what to say. Finally, with the help of one or two who felt sorry for his condition, he swore by all that was noble and all that was holy that the word "grand" had never crossed his lips and that he had meant "by the soul of the Late Father," meaning Dear Uncle's father, not "by the soul of the Late Grandfather."

After scorn was heaped on the unfortunate proposer of this idea, and he'd been well and truly lectured on the error of his ways, another suggestion, to add one or two meters to the length and breadth of Mash Qasem's donated water-cistern, which of course would increase the expense, was discussed. Finally, they decided to have Mash Qasem in and to put the matter to him.

In moving, poignant language Shamsali Mirza told Mash Qasem that his decision would have a vital effect on whether or not a great and noble family was to be saved from discord and destruction, and then, looking him straight in the eye, he said, "We are asking you for a favor, a sacrifice, Mr. Mash Qasem! Are you prepared to help us for the sake of this sacred goal?"

"Well sir, why should I lie? To the grave it's ah . . . ah . . . just four fingers. First, that I've ate the bread and salt of this family; second, that the Master—and God keep him the noble gentleman he is—has saved me from the hand of death not once, not twice but an hundred times; third, that I know all about these jobs . . . I remember in the thick of the Battle of Kazerun, a bullet went right between the eyes of one of our men and come out the back of his head, poor devil, he was from Malayer . . . however much I tried to get him down off his horse and off of the battlefield he wouldn't have it. 'Mash Qasem, you go,' he says, 'I haven't got long to live,' but d'you think I'd leave him there, no way . . ."

Shamsali Mirza impatiently said, "Mr. Mash Qasem, please leave this story for later . . . give us an answer! Are you prepared to help us at this crucial moment?"

Mash Qasem, who had imagined that at least at this moment they would listen to his story, went very quiet and said, "Of course, I'm your humble servant."

Weighing his words, Shamsali Mirza said, "Mr. Mash Qasem, we have more or less prepared the ground for solving the differences between the gentlemen. There's just one problem left, and that's the matter of the dubious sound on the night of the party."

Mash Qasem suddenly burst out laughing, "The tale of that dubious sound's not over yet? Please God, what a tale with a tail that's turned out to be, eh?" And then, seeing the serious, glum faces of everyone there, he controlled his laughter and said, "Damn the fellow what did it! If that fellow what did it had had the guts to hold himself in a bit and not let fly in that shameful way, all this row and carryin' on would never have started."

"Mash Qasem, I've heard that you wish to build a water cistern in the village of Ghiasabad near Qom and donate it to the people there. Is this so?"

"Why should I lie? Ever since I've been a nipper knee high to a grasshopper I've wanted to, but God hasn't seen to send the money for the expense of it. The poor folks in Ghiasabad still get water from the creek and it's all dirty. Just today I asked that detective's helper if anyone's built a cistern in Ghiasabad or not. 'No,' he says . . ."

Uncle colonel cut him off, "Now, Mash Qasem, if we were to cover the expenses of this water cistern of yours, would you be ready to help us?"

"Why should I lie? If you was to say, savin' your reverence, go climb the Caucasus, I'd go, to get this job done . . ."

Shamsali Mirza jumped up and said, "Mash Qasem! The help we need from you is that you accept that the dubious sound on the night of the party came from your direction."

"You mean from around where I was standin'?"

"No, you haven't understood, no, that the sound came from you . . . of course by accident . . ."

Mash Qasem suddenly turned crimson and in an extremely agitated voice said, "I swear by all the saints in heaven it weren't me, I love the Master like he's the apple of my eye, may I drop down dead if it were me . . . you mean you think I've no shame . . . you mean you think I'm that shameless . . ."

Shamsali Mirza shouted, "That's enough, Mash Qasem! Why don't you understand? We all know that you didn't do it, but we want you to grant us a big favor and say that you did, so that maybe this quarrel will be over and done with."

"Me come and tell a lie? Tell a lie, and to the Master as well? God forbid! Just how far from the grave are we?"

"Think about it for a moment! A water cistern donated by you . . . Mash Qasem's water cistern, the answer to the prayers of the people of Ghiasabad, an eternal reward . . . how can you not be ready to . . ."

Mash Qasem jumped into the middle of his sentence, "I'm to make myself out to be that shameless so the folks in Ghiasabad can drink water? I don't care if they don't drink water for another seventy years! And if them in Ghiasabad was to know I'd built the water cistern with money got from shamelessness, they wouldn't let that water touch their lips for a hundred years, not even if their dirty creek was to dry up . . . but it so happens I've thought of somethin' that could fix it for you."

Everyone stared at Mash Qasem's mouth. "If you remember, that night at the party, that cute little cat of Miss Layli's was hangin' around under everyone's feet the whole time . . . how come the dubious sound couldn't be from that cat?"

Shamsali's yell went up to the heavens, "There's a limit to talking rubbish, too, you know, Mash Qasem . . . you expect reasonable adult people like us to go and say to the Master that right in the middle of his story about the Battle of Kazerun, just when he had taken aim at a spot between the eyes of the leader of the bandits, Layli's cat produced such a noise?"

The meeting rang with the confused noise of some people's objections and others' laughter. Mash Qasem was trying to speak but no one was listening to him. In the midst of all this I was angry; I wanted to hit Mash Qasem on the back of the neck for daring to talk badly about Layli's cat. It had made me feel similar to how the relatives had felt when they heard "the soul of the Late Grandfather."

Finally Mash Qasem was able to get everyone to listen to him. "Let me speak . . . let me speak . . . I've somethin' to say. How come sayin' I did it's not bad but sayin' the cat did it is bad . . . you mean the cat's reputation's more important than my reputation?"

"Think straight, man, it's got nothing to do with reputation. Look, how could a little cat like that . . ."

Mash Qasem cut uncle colonel off, "Not at all, not at all, it's got nothin' to do with how big or how little. First of all animals do these shameless things; second, why should I lie, I myself I've heard these dubious sounds from swallows up to buffaloes. Third, it's got nothin' to do with size. That time right in the thick of the Battle of Kazerun I saw a little bastard of a shameless snake. He made such a dubious noise that all of a sudden Deputy Gholamali Khan, who was a bit deaf, too, jumped up from his sleep. One time I saw two green-finches that it was like they'd got together to . . ."

Uncle colonel's shouted, "Will you stop or not? How much rubbish are you going to talk? How much nonsense? I don't want to hear a word from you ever again! Just get out of here!"

Sulky and gloomy, Mash Qasem left.

After Mash Qasem's departure the meeting more or less fell apart, and with one excuse or another the participants in the family council took their leave.

No one was left in uncle colonel's sitting room except the colonel himself, his son, and Shamsali Mirza. Hopeless and upset, I walked up and down in the hallway; without realizing it, I was waiting for a flash of inspiration to strike in either uncle colonel's or the cross-examiner's brain, but it was clear from what they were saying that they were completely stuck.

EIGHT

WHEN I RETURNED to the garden, Dear Uncle Napoleon was walking up and down with an extremely troubled face, sunk in thought, and Mash Qasem was busying himself by calmly tending to the flowers.

Dear Uncle Napoleon caught sight of me. His glance frightened me. It seemed that he considered me an accomplice in my father's crimes. I took myself off to a corner so that I was safely out of the range of his furious looks. For a moment I once again went over ways to escape from love, but nothing occurred to me. For the first time in all this I talked to God from the bottom of my heart. This was the second time I had thought of God in such an intimate way. The first was on the night of the earthquake when I had asked God that the ceiling of our room not fall on us before morning. But this time I didn't really know what I should do. I didn't really know what I should ask God for. I asked him to free me from being involved with Layli. Then I immediately bit between my five fingers and blew on them. I don't know where we children got this way of showing that we were asking for forgiveness. But this was the simplest way, because otherwise I would have had to ask for lots of things. O God, make Dear Uncle open the water channel to our house and my father open the channel to uncle colonel's house . . . O God, make my father believe in Napoleon's bravery and genius . . . O God, make Dear Uncle force Seyed Abolqasem to lift the ban on the drugs made in my father's pharmacy . . . O God, make my father believe that Dear Uncle had done sterling service during the Constitutional Crisis and that the safety and security in the southern regions were due to his bravery . . . O God, make Aziz al-Saltaneh not have designs on her husband's member . . . O God, make Dustali Khan appear . . . O God, after he appears make him an honorable man who'll leave Shir Ali the butcher's wife alone . . .

I was struggling with these thoughts when the garden door, which had been left unbolted, opened and Mrs. Aziz al-Saltaneh entered. When she was face to face with Dear Uncle Napoleon she frowned like a fighting cock and stared at him without saying a word. Finally Dear Uncle anxiously asked her, "Madam, what's happened?"

Without answering his question, Aziz al-Saltaneh said, "Can I telephone from here?"

"Who do you want to telephone?"

"The head of the police."

And then after a moment's silence she screamed, "Those detectives are torturing my young man! However much I tell that stupid deputy that the poor child is innocent, he won't listen. Now I want to phone his boss and tell him that this poor helpless little waif Asadollah is innocent. I want to tell him that one of you has done away with Dustali. I want to tell him that poor Asadollah is sacrificing himself to save the lot of you . . . God, I wish there was just one scrap, one hair, of the goodness of Asadollah in you. Good God! Such a gentleman, so noble . . . how could such a sensitive person possibly kill someone?"

"My dear madam, please don't shout so loud . . ."

"Oh, I'll shout, I'll scream . . . do you imagine I don't know what's going on . . . either you have done away with Dustali and framed that poor innocent child . . . or you've hidden him somewhere so that you can get him for that dried-up sister of yours . . ."

With a great deal of effort Dear Uncle calmed Aziz al-Saltaneh down somewhat and said, "Madam, I've no idea what base wretch has put these ideas in your head . . . no one has killed Dustali . . . Dustali's more healthy than either you or me . . . he's gone off and hidden because he's afraid of you . . ."

Aziz al-Saltaneh sprang at Dear Uncle and screamed, "So now I'm frightening, am I, and Dustali's hidden because he's afraid of me? Do you have any idea what you're talking about, old man? It's a pity poor Asadollah belongs to the same family as you! Are you going to let me phone or shall I go down the bazaar?"

Once again Dear Uncle exerted himself for a while until Aziz al-Saltaneh calmed down. Then he said in an extremely mild voice, "Madam, I don't know where Dustali is but I promise you upon my honor that he hasn't gone far and that by tomorrow I shall deliver him to you safe and sound. With your permission I'll send someone for the deputy. When he comes, you tell him that you've found Dustali, meaning you know where he's gone . . . if you waste any more time they'll take poor Asadollah off to prison!"

"May God strike me dead if they put such a sweet young man as that in prison. I'll tell the detective I've completely withdrawn my complaint . . ."

"Madam, that won't do any good. You have to say that Dustali's alive and that he's talked to you, meaning he's phoned you and talked . . . I promise you that by tomorrow Dustali . . ."

Aziz al-Saltaneh angrily interrupted him, "I don't care if I never see him alive for another seventy years. If I don't want to live with that Dustali of yours, what on earth am I supposed to do, eh?"

Aziz al-Saltaneh was silent for a moment, then she said, "Heh, Mash Qasem! Come here and God bless you and run along to Asadollah's house and say that madam says come quick because Dustali's been found."

Mash Qasem put his watering can down and said, "Well, that's good news and no mistake, ma'am, and don't you be forgetting my tip . . ."

"Just you wait, my lad, just wait till Dustali really comes back and then your tip'll be a cleaver and I'll smash his head and yours in with it."

It was almost dark when Deputy Taymur Khan, followed by Asadollah Mirza with Cadet Officer Ghiasabadi and Mash Qasem, entered the garden. As soon as the detective arrived he shouted, "Silence! Where is the murder victim? Quick, now, immediately, at the double! Silence!"

Dear Uncle went forward to welcome him and said, "Officer, I'm very pleased to inform you that the misunderstanding has been cleared up. The lady's husband is in the best of health and is staying comfortably in the house of one of his relatives . . ."

"You, silence! Where is the murder victim? Quick, now, immediately."

Then he brought his huge face close to Dear Uncle's face and said in a very suspicious tone, "Are you quite sure the murder victim is alive?"

Aziz al-Saltaneh interrupted, "Officer, fortunately it's become clear that Dustali is alive . . . the cat's got nine lives, he has that. You won't find that donkey dying till he's killed me first!"

It was clear that Asadollah Mirza, who had been busy flicking the dust off his clothes since he'd come in, could no longer be bothered to carry on a conversation; he heaved a sigh of relief and said, "Thank God a hundred thousand times over, husband and wife are together again."

The deputy quickly turned in his direction. "Don't be too quick about giving thanks. Now let me see! If the murder victim is alive, why did you confess to killing him? What was the reason for your confession? Well? Quick, now, answer!"

"I think I must have had a dream . . ."

"Silence! Have you been making fun of me? They kill someone, and then the murderer charms the murder victim's wife with his sweet talk, the murder victim's wife claims that her husband's alive, the detective in charge of the investigation says 'Good night' to them like a good little boy and goes off home! Silence! I hope I place the hangman's rope round your neck myself."

Aziz al-Saltaneh sprang at the deputy like a panther. "What? A hangman's rope? Put a hangman's rope round your own dad's neck first! I'll claw your eyeballs out of their sockets . . ."

Dear Uncle anxiously interposed himself. "My dear madam, madam, please, I beg you, the deputy is only fulfilling his duty according to the law. You have to explain to him, not . . ."

"Why are you interfering? Who the hell do you think you are? My idiot of a husband goes off on one of his jaunts . . . we get a detective in who's a half-wit and he accuses an innocent young man, I tell him where to get off, and what's it all got to do with you, eh?"

"Silence! Everyone, silence! I said silence!"

"Oh, shut up, you and your damn silence! I've a mind to hit you on the head with this rake so your glasses'll smash into your blind eyes!"

Aziz al-Saltaneh joined the action to her words, threatening the deputy's head with the rake. Asadollah Mirza grabbed her arm. "My dear madam, please calm yourself."

Aziz al-Saltaneh calmed down. With unexpected mildness she said, "Whatever you say, Asadollah . . ."

The deputy, who had been taken aback by Aziz al-Saltaneh's assault, took courage. "Silence, madam! Until I see the murder victim with my own eyes, I cannot let the accused go free. Cadet Officer Ghiasabadi! Take charge of the accused!"

Cadet Officer Ghiasabadi clicked his heels together and took hold of Asadollah Mirza's arms. "At your service, sir!"

But before anyone realized what was happening, the cadet officer began screaming and yelling. Aziz al-Saltaneh had jabbed the detective's assistant violently in his hindquarters with the rake.

The deputy screamed in a voice shaking with anger, "Silence! Inflicting an injury on a representative of the state while performing his duty! Madam, you, too, are under arrest! Cadet Officer Ghiasabadi, arrest this woman, too!"

Clutching his behind, with all the muscles of his face twisted in pain, the cadet officer said, "Sir, please, you arrest the lady yourself, I'll bring the murderer!"

At this moment uncle colonel and Shamsali Mirza also arrived, but confronted by the determined face of Aziz al-Saltaneh, who was holding the rake aloft in a threatening way, they stood rooted to the spot. Quietly, Dear Uncle Napoleon said, "Asadollah, you do something!"

Very quietly Asadollah Mirza answered, "Moment, moment . . . so now I've become a wild animal tamer have I!" But he went over to Aziz al-Saltaneh and said out loud, "Aziz, my dear, put that rake down . . . give us a chance to explain the matter to his excellency Deputy Taymur Khan. We're not going to get anywhere by quarreling."

"I'm only letting them off for your sake, you handsome devil!"

As Aziz al-Saltaneh was putting the rake down, Cadet Officer Ghiasabadi, who had no thought in his head except to carry out his orders, quietly made his way over to Asadollah Mirza and said in a mild voice, "We'd better be on our way. You're a sensible fellow . . ."

Asadollah Mirza jerked his arm free of the officer's hand and said, "Get back, or the lady'll get angry again."

Dear Uncle Napoleon interrupted, "Deputy, sir, taking into account that Dustali Khan has been found and has given news of his health over the phone to his wife, all this business of the investigation and complaints and so forth has become pointless."

"You seem to be the most senior of this group, get it into their heads that a prosecution that begins as a result of a private complaint does not end with that private complaint when murder is involved. I am arresting the murderer; you come tomorrow to my office with the murder victim and arrange for his release!"

Asadollah Mirza could not contain himself, "Moment, moment, deputy sir, but what if the murder victim doesn't want to come along, too?"

The deputy screamed, "Silence! Off to prison with you! Cadet Officer Ghiasabadi!"

Mrs. Aziz al-Saltaneh shouted in a louder voice, "And both of you two off to the graveyard with you!"

Once again she made a quick lunge and grabbed the rake from Mash Qasem, who had picked it up, and said, "Come on, I'm going to phone their boss and see what's what. Asadollah, come with me!"

And she took hold of Asadollah Mirza's hand and set off toward the inner apartments of Dear Uncle's house. The deputy and Cadet Officer Ghiasabadi followed her at a distance, along with everyone else.

While Aziz al-Saltaneh, with the rake in her hand, stood in the hall of Dear Uncle's house trying to get in touch with the deputy's superior on the phone, everyone gathered in a circle around her, at a sufficient distance, and no one dared go any closer. Only Asadollah Mirza was next to her. Finally she got through.

"Hello . . . good afternoon, sir . . . that's very kind of you, sir . . . yes, he's been found, he'd been sulking and had gone off to stay with one of his relatives. Thank you. Thank you very much . . . but you see this deputy of yours, Taymur Khan, he won't give up . . . just imagine . . . he insists they must have killed Dustali and he wants to arrest Asadollah Mirza . . . Yes? Yes, yes, that's right . . . the grandson of Uncle Rokn al-Din Mirza . . . You can't remember him? That year you came to Damavand he was with us . . . yes, yes, that's exactly right . . . you don't know what an angel he is, such a good man, such a gentleman he is . . . certainly, I'll hand the receiver over to the deputy . . ."

Aziz al-Saltaneh held out the receiver to the deputy and said, "All yours!"

And when she saw that the deputy wouldn't come any closer out of fear of the rake, she shouted, "Come here, I won't bite you!"

The deputy took the receiver, clicked his heels together, and said, "Good afternoon, sir . . . yes, sir . . . of course, whatever you say, sir . . . but you must realize, sir, that in the statement I prepared I wrote down the lady's complaint concerning the murder of her late husband, and now unless I see the murder victim and establish his identity . . . Yes, sir . . . the lady herself? How can the lady herself be a guarantor for the accused? Yes?"

With a sharp shove from behind, Aziz al-Saltaneh pushed him aside and snatched the receiver from his hand, "Hello . . . yes, I myself will be guarantor for Asadollah Mirza . . . there's no question . . . tonight I'll keep Asadollah Mirza at my house, and your deputy can sleep at my house, too . . ."

With round astonished eyes, Asadollah Mirza said, "Moment, moment, madam, what are you saying? What do you mean, you'll keep Asadollah Mirza at your house?"

Aziz al-Saltaneh put her hand over the receiver and in a somewhat reproachful voice said, "Don't talk so much, Asadollah; let me hear what the chief has to say. The room upstairs is empty, you can go up there and sleep. Deputy, sir, come here, the chief wants to talk to you again . . ."

"Hello . . . Yes, sir . . . certainly, sir, it shall be done, sir, that's right . . . so that nothing will be against the regulations . . . as you say, sir . . . certainly . . . very good, your excellency."

Deputy Taymur replaced the receiver. He brought his huge face close to Asadollah Mirza's anxious, dumbfounded face and said, "Silence! Tonight I am letting you go free with this lady as your guarantor; you must not leave the lady's house! Cadet Officer Ghiasabadi will also stay in the same house to see that you don't leave . . . Silence! Cadet Officer Ghiasabadi, open your ears and pay attention: tonight you will sleep in this lady's house! The accused has no right to set foot outside of her house, and if he does, you will be held responsible!"

In a voice of mingled triumph and sympathy Aziz al-Saltaneh said, "Asadollah, I'd rather die than let them drag you off to jail!"

As he was wiping the sweat off his forehead Asadollah more or less collapsed onto a bench in the hallway and in an appalled voice said, "Moment, moment, now really moment! If it so happens that that prize donkey Dustali comes back to his house, then what? And what will people say? Give me permission to sleep right here; the cadet officer can keep me under observation here, too . . ."

"Silence! I said Silence! It is only on this lady's guarantee that the murderer is not going to prison; he must remain under her observation! This lady is your legal guarantor! Cadet Officer Ghiasabadi, quick march with the accused! Silence!"

With his cheeks glowing, retired prosecutor Shamsali Mirza bawled, "Gentlemen, this is shameful! How can a healthy, full-grown man spend the night in the house of a respectable woman when her husband's not there? You're flinging the family's honor and reputation to the winds!"

Dear Uncle Napoleon interrupted him, "Stop shouting, Shamsali! Let this damned row die down . . . Asadollah's not a mouse to be afraid that some cat's going to eat him!"

"What are you talking about, sir! What regulation is it contrary to that Asadollah can't stay the night at his own house, or at least stay here?"

Deputy Taymur Khan roared out, "Silence! Who gave you permission to interfere in the business of a representative of the law? Well? Answer! Quick, now, immediately, at the double! Silence!"

Shamsali Mirza summoned up all his reserves of strength in order to answer calmly, "Officer, I also have some experience of the law. And I ask you, as a reasonable man, what is there to prevent my brother, on my guarantee, and that of this gentleman here, and even of the lady in question, from staying in his own house tonight?"

"Silence! The guarantees of you and this gentleman and so on and so forth are of no interest to me. Mrs. Aziz al-Saltaneh is the gentleman's legal guarantor. If she agrees, I have no objection. Madam, do you agree?"

Aziz al-Saltaneh had seen no reason up to that moment to interfere; now she suddenly burst out, "And how am I to know they won't make this young fellow run away the same as they made that poor devil Dustali run away? I can only answer for him if I can see him with my own eyes."

Shamsali Mirza was so angry the veins on his neck were swollen; he turned to Asadollah Mirza. "Asadollah, why have you been struck dumb? Say something!"

With an innocent face Asadollah Mirza bowed his head and said, "Brother, what can I say against the power of the law?"

Everyone present looked at him in astonishment, since they thought they'd been working to save him from the clutches of Aziz al-Saltaneh, but now they saw that Asadollah Mirza had submitted to his fate and perhaps he didn't even feel too bad about it.

Asadollah Mirza was famous in the family for his flirtatiousness and lascivious behavior, and there was no one the women of the family gossiped about so much, but even while they were damning him and calling him "shameless," there would be a kind of knowing coquettishness in their voices which showed that the soft soap of his flirting had rendered all of them more or less compliant. In general, everyone knew about his lecherous behavior, but they never imagined that he wouldn't pass up even a woman who was perhaps twenty years older than himself.

Deputy Taymur Khan's voice roused everyone from their incredulous astonishment, "Silence! Madam, take this pen and paper and write down whatever I say."

Aziz al-Saltaneh put the rake down and took the pen and paper.

"Write, please: I the undersigned . . . write your name and first name . . . hereby undertake that I shall deliver Mr. Asadollah . . . write his family name and his father's name . . . first thing tomorrow . . . to the criminal desk at the police station . . . Have you written that? . . . And will hand him over to the proper authorities . . ."

"Moment, moment . . . she should write that she's received him whole and in good health and that she'll hand him over in the same condition . . ."

"Silence! Who gave you permission to interfere? Well? Who? Quick, immediately! Silence!"

"What do you mean, silence? The five limbs of my body are healthy. All its members, noble and not so noble, are healthy. God forbid that tomorrow they should say something was missing."

Coyly and flirtatiously, Aziz al-Saltaneh put the pen between her teeth and said, "Well now, God strike me dead, what things you do say, Asadollah!"

"Officer, if this is to be completely according to law, there should be an official record of the extant members of the body . . ."

Aziz al-Saltaneh burst out in a coy laugh and said, "O Asadollah, you're such a rascal, you are!"

"Silence! I personally shall accompany you to the lady's house. Cadet Officer Ghiasabadi, quick march!"

Asadollah Mirza sat on a chair. He gripped the chair's arms firmly and, with a mischievous glint in his eye, said, "I'm not coming unless they drag me there by force!"

"Silence! Cadet Officer Ghiasabadi!"

Deputy Taymur Khan and his assistant took Asadollah Mirza by the arms and, while he was pretending to resist, lifted him up and set him on his way.

As Asadollah Mirza was leaving between the two officers, he turned his face toward Dear Uncle Napoleon and said, "Moment, if—God forbid—something happens, you're responsible because it was you who made me a murderer. Cadet Officer Ghiasabadi, we're off to San Francisco!"

Shamsali Mirza was on the point of fainting from rage; with a voice he could hardly drag from his throat he shouted, "Asadollah, God damn your impudence!"

"Moment, moment, this is a fine to-do! I came here today just to make a friendly call and leave. I became a murderer, I was sworn at, I've had a square yard in the garden of my house dug up, and now, just as I'm off on a little trip, I have to hear an argument?"

Mash Qasem, who was standing motionless in a corner, said with a grin, "Good luck to you, sir, so you're going on a trip, are you? Where are you going?"

"Somewhere close to San Francisco."

"God be with you then . . . don't forget to bring back a present."

"God willing, the present should turn up in nine months' time."

"Silence! I said silence! Good day to you, gentlemen!"

As Deputy Taymur Khan and Cadet Officer Ghiasabadi were leading the accused out behind Aziz al-Saltaneh, uncle colonel weighed in for the attack against Dear Uncle Napoleon. "And you're just standing there silent, as if it had never entered your mind that you were the head of this family . . . how much shameful behavior are we going to have to put up with? How much stubbornness? Just think about it! Now that he's climbed down, you leave off, too! He says he's ready to open the water so it can come through to us . . . forget this whole business . . ."

Dear Uncle Napoleon's patience and strength were stretched to the point of exhaustion; in the detective's tone of voice he yelled, "Silence! You're here plunging a dagger in my back, too! I've had just about all I can stand! On the one side that . . . that filthy fellow, and on the other side all of you! God help me, what have I done to deserve this?"

In a gentler tone of voice uncle colonel said, "Brother, now that this filthy fellow is ready to let bygones be bygones, why don't you . . ."

Dear Uncle Napoleon interrupted him, "Why have you become so stupid? Don't you know this filthy fellow? Don't you know how dangerous this snake is? As Napoleon said, the time the battlefield falls silent is the most dangerous moment. I promise you that right now that man is hatching some new evil plot."

At this moment, the group was in front of the private apartments of Dear Uncle's house. Involuntarily I looked toward our own house. It occurred to me that Dear Uncle had guessed correctly, but I saw no sign of my father or of our servant who usually did his spying for him. Although for the whole time this was going on I'd tried to stay hidden in a corner out of Dear Uncle's sight, it was still possible he would see me. I tiptoed away, back to our own house, to see where my father was and what he was up to.

I saw no sign of him in the yard or in any of the rooms. The front door stood open and I peeped out. Looking carefully and searching around a little in the darkness of the street, I made out my father standing behind a thick tree trunk, and it was clear that he had hidden there and was waiting for something or someone.

After a few moments I saw that my father had suddenly become rather agitated. I looked in the direction he was looking. Deputy Taymur Khan had come out of Aziz al-Saltaneh's house and was walking so that he would pass by our house and then be on his way. When he had come a little closer my father came out from behind the tree and pretended that he was returning home.

"Hello, detective inspector. I hope that you've been successful in your investigations!"

"Silence! Oh, excuse me, you are . . . ? How are you, sir?"

"Thank you very much, officer. You didn't say how your investigations had turned out . . . although with someone like yourself whose fame has spread everywhere, I don't think there would be any problems left to clear up . It so happens that only an hour ago I met one of my friends and, as soon as he heard your name, he said there's no one to touch Deputy Taymur Khan in the whole country! Well, and how did your investigations turn out?"

"Well, the complainant claimed that the murder victim is alive and I . . ."

"Extraordinary! But how could you believe it? Did you see Dustali Khan?"

"No . . . but . . . of course, I should point out that on principle I regard every statement and action with suspicion . . . I have not personally seen the murder victim but he has telephoned the complainant, and I've temporarily released the accused."

"You've let the accused go? It's extraordinary that a person like yourself should . . ."

"Of course, I haven't completely let him go. With the complainant's written guarantee I've left him to stay for the moment under the complainant's and my assistant's observation in the complainant's house, until tomorrow morning . . . I mean, this was at the insistence of my supervisor, and if it hadn't been for that, I'd certainly have arrested the accused."

In this way my father became informed of what was going on and that Asadollah Mirza had been placed under observation in Aziz al-Saltaneh's house. After the detective had gone my father returned home and, with a thoughtful frown, he paced up and down for a few minutes in the yard. From his footsteps, which became louder from moment to moment, I knew that he was very annoyed and was probably waiting for something.

From my hiding place I heard the outer door open and shut. It was our servant, who came in and immediately went over to my father. As soon as he saw him my father said in an angry voice, which he tried to keep from being too loud, "Idiot! Where have you been from noon till now? I've a good mind to brain you . . ."

"That tip you said you'd be kind enough to give me if I found out where Mr. Dustali is . . ."

"What? Really? Quick, tell me. Where is he?"

"I swore I wouldn't let on to a soul."

My father flung his hand out, grabbing one of our servant's big ears, and in a smothered voice said, "Are you going to talk or am I going to twist off this ass's ear of yours?"

"All right, all right . . . he's hidden in the doctor's house."

"What? Dr. Naser al-Hokama's house?"

"Yes, sir . . . but Sadiqeh got me to swear I wouldn't let on to anyone."

Without paying attention to what the servant was saying, my father said under his breath, "Just look where that bastard's been found . . . right under everyone's nose . . . who'd have thought it. Listen, you go immediately to Dr. Naser al-Hokama's house . . . tell him I've got some business with him, say it's a very urgent matter; got it?"

A few moments later Dr. Naser al-Hokama, wearing his wide striped pajamas, came into our house. My father took him by the arm and together they went into the room with French windows, by the door to the yard. When our servant had gone about his business, I got behind the door to listen; they were in the middle of a conversation.

". . . agreed, but now how can I get him to leave my house? I can't say to him . . ."

"Listen, doctor, as far as I can see, the best way to get Dustali Khan to leave your house, so you'll be free of these headaches I mentioned, is like this. Tell him that everyone thinks he's been killed, and that the detective from the police suspects Shir Ali the butcher, and that he's sent someone to arrest Shir Ali. Say that if they arrest Shir Ali they'll have to tell him that they suspect him because Dustali has had an affair with his wife. As soon as you mention the name of Shir Ali the butcher, you can be sure that Dustali will appear of his own free will . . ."

Poor Dr. Naser al-Hokama was extremely upset. From his worried tone of voice it was clear that my father had painted him a very gloomy picture of the results of keeping Dustali in his house. He left with a worried thoughtful face and my father lay in wait, behind the half-open door to the street, for Dustali Khan to come.

He waited for perhaps half an hour. Suddenly he jumped, shoved his head out of the door, and immediately ran into the street. I was thinking I would go after him, but I had no chance to because Dustali came into the yard with my father following him.

My father got rid of Dr. Naser al-Hokama, who seemed to want to come in after them. "Dr. Naser al-Hokama, sir, you go and have a

rest. Thank goodness everything has turned out just fine, doctor."
Then he took Dustali Khan into that same room where he'd previously gone with the doctor.

It was important for me to hear their whole conversation. Although I didn't know what my father's plan was, I guessed that things hadn't turned out as well as my father was claiming.

After spending a few moments scolding Dustali Khan for running away, my father said in a sympathetic voice, "But really, you know, you're very childish; don't you realize that a man mustn't leave his wife and run off just because of one of these little arguments that happens between every husband and wife?"

"I hope I never have a wife again as long as I live; you call that witch a wife?"

In a fatherly tone my father said, "Oh, come on now, how many years have you lived together, sharing in your sorrows and joys, and now you've to go on living together . . ."

My father's tone was so kind that I was ashamed I'd ever doubted his good intentions. He continued in the same tone, "When you're alone, without anyone, you've no one to back you up except her and she has no one except you . . . when all's said and done she's your wife . . . your better half . . . your honor . . . you don't seem to care that when you carry on like this and disappear, there are all sorts of wolves around these days ready to take advantage of your house and home . . ."

Dustali Khan impatiently said, "I wish these wolves would tear her to bits!"

"Well, you say these things, Dustali, but just think for a moment . . . people are really evil . . . people have no humanity or compassion . . . I'm like an older brother to you . . . I want you to understand clearly. If it should turn out, and God forbid it should, that something had happened while you were away . . . that something had occurred . . . you ought to realize that it's not your poor wife's fault."

Dustali Khan pricked up his ears, "I don't get what you're talking about . . . what is it that might happen?"

"I don't want to worry you but these relatives of yours are not the purest of people . . . this man who as they say is the head of the family . . ."

Agitatedly Dustali Khan said, "It's as if you want to tell me something! What's happened?"

"You have to swear you didn't hear it from me!"

"Please, tell me what's going on, what's happened?"

"I swear on your life, and by the death of my children, that I'm only telling you this because I want everything to be for the best . . ."

"What's going on? What's happened? What are you talking about?"

"When you were hiding . . . they put it about that—God strike me dumb if I tell a lie—something awful had happened to you . . . and then the head of the family told that Asadollah Mirza fellow, the one who's always flirting and is such a notorious lady-killer, to go and sleep tonight at Mrs. Aziz al-Saltaneh's so that she shouldn't be afraid. Of course, Mrs. Aziz al-Saltaneh's not the kind of person who would enjoy a relationship like that, God forbid, all right, but neighbors' tongues . . ."

Dustali Khan was silent for a moment, and then in a voice trembling with rage, he said, "That fellow has gone in my house tonight, with my wife?"

"Don't upset yourself . . . he's not the kind of person to . . ."

"He's not the kind of person to what? I'm afraid to be in the same room as that thief of everyone's honor myself. I'll kill that fellow . . . I'll . . . I'll . . ."

My father sat Dustali Khan down on a chair, so that he could finish talking to him.

For a moment I stood frozen to the spot, dumbfounded. This was really terrible. In his enmity toward Dear Uncle and his family my father would stop at nothing. In a flash I decided to run as fast as I could to Dustali Khan's house.

I pounded on the door with all my strength. After a few moments Aziz al-Saltaneh herself opened the door. I threw myself into the yard and shut the door behind me. Aziz al-Saltaneh was wearing a lace nightdress and Asadollah Mirza had stuck his head out of an upstairs window to see who had come.

I quickly ran upstairs and Aziz al-Saltaneh ran after me shouting, "What do you want? What's happened? What's going on?"

When I got to Asadollah Mirza I panted out, "Uncle Asadollah, get out of here quickly, my father's found Dustali Khan and has told him you're sleeping here with his wife."

Asadollah Mirza looked at me thunderstruck for a moment, and then ran toward the chair where he'd put his jacket and bow tie.

While he was putting his jacket on, he said, "Moment, really moment . . . now I have to answer to that idiot!"

Aziz al-Saltaneh took him by the arm, "I'll answer to him. Don't be afraid!"

Agitatedly I said, "Please, let him run away. Dustali Khan's eyes were like two bowls of blood . . . where's the detective's assistant? If he comes, tell him to stop him."

"I sent him to buy some things at the end of the road."

Asadollah Mirza was hurriedly knotting his bow tie. "God bless you and keep you, my dear . . . God willing, I'll come and see you another time." At this moment there was suddenly the noise of banging on the door.

"God strike me dead, he's come!"

Aziz al-Saltaneh said this and looked wildly round. Asadollah Mirza was also distractedly looking for somewhere to hide. A thought occurred to me. I said, "How about if you ran away over the roof?"

"Yes, Asadollah, run."

Asadollah Mirza ran toward the stairs to the roof, holding in his hand one of his shoes that had a knot in its lace, and I went with him. Aziz al-Saltaneh locked the door to the roof behind us and then went toward the outer door, where the noise of the banging hadn't stopped for a moment.

A little later we heard the sound of Dustali Khan shouting furiously in the yard, "Where is the shameless bastard . . . where is he, that thief of everyone's honor?"

Very quietly Asadollah Mirza said, "What a hoarse voice he's got. But I owe you one for having saved me from this wild bear. May you live to a ripe old age, lad!"

The sounds of Dustali's and Aziz al-Saltaneh's shouts and screams could be heard mingling and clashing with one another. Aziz al-Saltaneh swore on the soul of her dead grandfather that such a thing was a complete lie and Dustali Khan searched one room after another, roaring as he went. At this moment the sound of someone banging on the outer door started up. Aziz al-Saltaneh insisted they shouldn't open the door and said it was certainly some guest who'd turned up at the wrong time and would stop them from sleeping, but Dustali Khan, still in a fury, opened the door and came face to face with Cadet Officer Ghiasabadi.

"Ma'am, they didn't have any of the wine you wanted . . . I bought this . . . so, let's see, where's Asadollah Khan? Well? Where is he? Where's he gone? Quick, now, answer!"

Asadollah Mirza, who had been stretched out at the edge of the roof listening, said under his breath, "Saints alive . . . let's get out of here, the cat's out of the bag."

While the voices of Dustali Khan and Aziz al-Saltaneh and Cadet Officer Ghiasabadi mingled and clashed, we doubled over and took to our heels across the rooftops. We'd got clear across the roof of one house when we heard a racket on the stairs leading to the roof in Dustali Khan's house. Dustali Khan was yelling, "The key . . . what have you done with the key?"

We quickly got across one or two more roofs. But we'd reached a dead end, because to get to the next house we'd have had to cross over a narrow wall. We were scrambling about in the dark looking for a way to escape when suddenly a gruff voice stopped us in our tracks, "You bastard, come here thievin', have you?"

I turned round; a monstrous silhouette had grabbed Asadollah Mirza from behind and lifted him off the ground and, before he could protest, had dragged him over to the stairs up to the roof we were on.

I ran after the silhouette that had lifted Asadollah Mirza up and dragged him off. When everyone's face was lit up by the lamps in the yard I recognized Shir Ali the butcher, and Shir Ali recognized Asadollah Mirza.

He gently put him down and said, "I'm really sorry, Mr. Asadollah Mirza, sir . . . I didn't recognize you . . . but what was you doin' on the roof?"

Asadollah Mirza still hadn't shaken off his terror at being suddenly attacked in this way; he said, "You frightened me, Mr. Shir Ali Khan . . ."

"Shame on me, sir . . . I'm at your service, sir . . . I never forget your kindness to me, sir . . . but what was you doin' up there?"

"Don't ask, Shir Ali, don't ask . . . people are so bad, so evil. That Dustali had invited me to his house to get revenge for that argument about property we'd had. I went to his house, the shameless so-and-so wasn't there himself, I sat down to chat with Mrs. Aziz al-Saltaneh and all of a sudden he bursts in to accuse me of acting in a dishonorable fashion . . ."

"You don't say so, sir? Spit on him for a shameless bastard."

"Think of it, a man who's ready to impugn his own honor just so he can annoy people."

Shir Ali picked up a long knife that was lying next to the garden pool and in a terrifying voice said, "You give the word and I'll spill his guts!"

"Moment, moment, I beg you not to do anything you might regret later. I'll hide somewhere tonight, till tomorrow, and by then this shameless fellow will have calmed down."

"You'll do me the honor of stoppin' here tonight . . . your humble servant, sir, I'll fix you up a place in the cellar . . . don't give it a second thought. An accusation like that, and against someone like you! I'd put the honor of my sister, my mother and the whole house in your hands . . ."

"My dear Shir Ali . . . you're a real brother to me . . ."

And then he turned to me, "Now lad, you be off home . . . you have no idea where I am."

And immediately he said to Shir Ali, "If it weren't for this young fellow, that shameless wretch would have really done for me tonight. Just think of it, is it conceivable a man like me would be involved in a relationship like that? And then with that witch of a wife he's got?"

"God forbid, Mr. Asadollah Mirza . . ."

And he laughed and added, "It's not like you and it's not like that Mrs. Aziz lady neither, who's old enough to be your mother, God save her. A woman's got to look out for her own reputation. You're just like my own brother. My missus is young enough to be Mrs. Aziz's granddaughter . . . the nail of her little finger's worth a hundred Mrs. Azizes. Have you caught sight of her in the street or down at the bazaar?"

"Good heavens, no, God save the mark, why are you comparing your wife with that witch? God forbid! God forbid!"

"A young woman, sir, well . . . whatever happens, the young men are bound to be flockin' around her, but first, my missus never goes out the house, and second, every mornin' when I leaves the house, I leaves her in God's hands, then I goes off to work with an easy mind. I don't make eyes at nobody else's better half and God keeps my better half safe."

"Wonderful, wonderful . . . this is *la mieux garantie*. Well done! Leave her in God's hands and then rest assured all is well!"

Shir Ali went to fetch some bedclothes from upstairs, to make up a bed for his unexpected guest. I was about to leave, when just at that moment I became aware of a twinkle in Asadollah Mirza's eye. When I looked in the direction he was looking I saw in the dimly lit porchway the beautiful glittering eyes of Tahereh, Shir Ali's wife; she was watching the scene with a winsome smile, peeping out from behind the veil she wore for prayers.

I said, "Goodbye. You don't want me to bring you anything, Uncle Asadollah?"

Without taking his eyes off Tahereh's beautiful face, Asadollah said, "No lad, there's everything here, you go and sleep, but don't forget, you don't know where I am. Especially don't tell that witch that I'm here . . ."

And as his greedy eyes were wandering over the body of Shir Ali's wife, he added, "God works in mysterious ways, His wonders to perform . . . Don't you forget, if any time you need something done or you're in some difficulty, you tell your uncle. You've really done me a very good turn tonight. I hope you live to a ripe old age!"

At this moment Shir Ali, with a huge bundle of bedclothes and rugs under his arm, came down from upstairs and stepped into the yard. I went toward the outer door. Before I left I glanced at Asadollah Mirza. With smiling eyes he was staring at Tahereh's breasts and saying, "They'll kill me in the end . . . oh, I wish they they'd kill me soon and get it over with! Oh, let them kill me soon!"

Shir Ali's gruff voice could be heard, "Over my dead body they'll be killin' you . . . anyone looks at the door to this house, your humble servant here'll cleave him down the middle. I'm not called Shir Ali for nothin'; up till now I've cleaved two of 'em in two, and this'll be one more!"

NINE

I COVERED THE DISTANCE between Shir Ali's house and our garden quietly and with no problem. The door to the house was ajar; softly I went in. Suddenly I found myself face to face with my father, who had apparently been lying in wait behind the door.

"And where have you been?"

"I've been to aunty's house."

"Well, you shouldn't have stayed so long . . . go quickly and eat your supper and get to bed."

"Aren't you coming to eat supper?"

"No, I've got something to do; off you go."

I realized he was desperately waiting to find out the results of the plot he'd hatched. I ate supper with my mother and sister and went to my room, but I had no hopes that the business of that eventful day was over yet.

Although I was sure of how Asadollah Mirza's circumstances stood in Shir Ali's house, there were still many things I didn't know. I didn't know what had happened in Dustali Khan's house, I didn't know what was going on in Dear Uncle Napoleon's house, and, more important than everything else, I didn't know what new plot my father was brooding about. I was really tired. I went over to the mosquito net to sleep, but with the anxiety and curiosity I felt, I wasn't very hopeful I'd be able to sleep, especially since my father was standing guard at the door to the yard. But as soon as I set foot inside the net I had no opportunity to think further since I was so exhausted I immediately fell into a deep sleep.

When I awoke in the morning, silence and profound peace reigned over the house. I was really eager to know what had happened while I slept. I went into the garden to see Mash Qasem but there was no sign of him. I opened the garden door to see if I might catch sight of him in the alleyway. I suddenly became aware of Aziz al-Saltaneh who was hurrying toward the garden. I went to welcome her. As soon as she saw me she said, "What luck to see you, my dear. I was coming to find you, to ask where Asadollah's gone."

"Well, Mrs. Aziz, we went over the rooftops until we got close to the canal, and there I jumped down from a little wall into the street and then Asadollah Mirza went on his way."

"He jumped down from a wall? Good heavens, what things that Asadollah gets up to! Didn't you see where he went?"

"I don't know. Maybe he went to his house."

"No, he didn't go home last night. I'm really worried. That fool Dustali's been imagining such stuff, he's sworn he'll kill poor Asadollah. Not that he's got it in him to manage it, but you never know . . . I wanted to say to you if Dustali asks you anything, don't breathe a word."

"No, Mrs. Aziz, you needn't worry about that. I haven't seen a thing . . . by the way, what did you do with the detective's assistant?"

"Nothing, I threw him out in the street and shut the door on him. After Dustali'd been found, he'd no business staying in our house. Now I'll go and drop by Asadollah's house again and, if he's there, I'll tell him to steer clear of this area for today. He shouldn't go to his office either because that idiot Dustali might do something crazy. Anyway, remember, if Dustali asks anything, don't breathe a word!"

"Don't worry."

Aziz al-Saltaneh hurriedly went on her way and I returned to the garden. Mash Qasem was busying himself seeing to the flowers.

It was from him I heard what had happened after I'd fallen asleep. Dustali Khan had gone to Dear Uncle's house with a shotgun and searched through all the rooms looking for Asadollah Mirza. Dear Uncle had become so angry that he had slapped him but Dustali had sworn that he wouldn't be content until he had emptied the shot in his gun into Asadollah Mirza's belly.

To make sure that Mash Qasem knew nothing of where Asadollah Mirza was hiding, I asked him, "Mash Qasem, where's Asadollah Mirza now?"

"Well, m'dear, why should I lie? To the grave it's ah . . . ah . . . four fingers. This mornin' at the crack of dawn the Master sent me to his house, but he hadn't been there all night; Shamsali Mirza's really worried, he should turn up here any minute . . ."

"So what's happened to Asadollah Mirza?"

"Well, m'dear, it's like he's turned to smoke and gone up to heaven . . . or he's so afraid of that Mr. Dustali he's hidden himself someplace . . ."

"So now we've another to-do to find Asadollah Mirza."

"Too right, m'dear. Your dad's good at stirrin' things up and no mistake. Last night, middle of the night, he dragged that Ghiasabadi guy into his house, I heard him, he was tellin' him Dustali had killed Asadollah Mirza. It was lucky I heard and I told that feller—he's from my town, you know—that they're all against one another and they want to stir things up. If it hadn't been for me that deputy'd 've been here again today shovin' his nose in."

"Well, God bless you, Mash Qasem."

After hesitating a few moments and turning one color after another, I managed to ask Mash Qasem if he would tell Layli to come into the garden for a minute. I didn't know what I wanted to say to her but I was extremely anxious to see her. I really missed her. Things had been happening so fast, one after another, that I hadn't even had time to think of Layli, but for all that I was desperately in love and had to see my beloved.

Mash Qasem nodded his head and said with a smile, "Eh m'dear, if I'm not mistaken, you've fallen for Miss Layli?"

However violently and insistently I protested, Mash Qasem had seen from the color of my face what was there to be seen. In a kind voice he said, "All right, m'dear, I was just talkin', there's nothin' wrong with it . . ."

When Layli came into the garden Mash Qasem said close to my ear, "I'll be by the door to the inner apartments. If the Master turns up, I'll cough and you take to your heels, m'dear."

It looked as though Mash Qasem was fully aware of my secret, but the warm look in Layli's eyes swept from my heart any horror of its becoming public. And then hadn't I myself thought of telling my secret to Mash Qasem?

"Hello, Layli."

"Hello. You wanted to talk to me?"

"Yes . . . I mean no . . . I missed you."

"Why?"

Layli's caressing look seemed to want to plunge into my throat, and to drag up from the depths of my larynx the things I didn't dare say to her. And for my part I was really determined to tell her of my love but I couldn't find the words. The lovers' sentences I'd read in books flashed through my brain: "I'm in love with you," "I've fallen in love with you," "I love you." Finally, as I felt my face burning bright red, I blurted out, "Layli, I'm in love with you."

And then, like lightning, like the wind, I fled so fast toward our house that in one short moment I found myself in my room.

O God, why had I run away? Why hadn't I waited to see her reaction? I didn't understand it myself. I went over what I could remember; I hadn't read or heard anywhere of a lover running away as soon as he had declared his love.

After severely reproaching myself and with considerable hesitation and internal debate I once again decided that the best thing for me to do was to finish my love letter and hand it to Layli.

Again I wrote it out several times and tore it up. I don't know how many hours had gone by when I heard a racket coming from the garden. Almost all my aunts and uncles were gathered in the area near the sweetbrier arbor. Shamsali Mirza was there, too. When I saw my mother in the midst of the group I hurriedly made my way there. From odd scraps of conversation I learned that uncle colonel had taken upon himself the responsibility of leading a concerted action by the family, and under his leadership the family members had decided to go in a body to Dear Uncle Napoleon and to stay there until the family quarrels were all settled. But their resolve had been somewhat distracted by the subject of Asadollah Mirza's disappearance. I went after them to Dear Uncle Napoleon's house.

Uncle colonel was in the middle of a rousing speech when he was interrupted by Dear Uncle Napoleon shouting, "Couldn't you find someone smaller than me to pick on? Why don't you go to that filthy fellow's house and make a fuss there? Don't you ever consider what new evil plots he's thinking up now? Haven't you realized that this swine found Dustali and sent him home just to create trouble? Aren't you aware that poor Asadollah has hidden himself away from last night until now, out of fear of Dustali?"

Dear Uncle Napoleon had such a blazing red face and shouted in such tremulous tones that no one dared open their mouths.

Only when Shamsali Mirza began to put forward his notions about Asadollah Mirza's disappearance did a general commotion start among those present. Everyone realized that Asadollah Mirza had run away from Dustali Khan's house because of Dustali's arrival there, but, with an eye to her husband, Aziz al-Saltaneh said that Asadollah Mirza had left the house before Dustali's arrival there, and she mentioned nothing about his escaping by way of the roof.

In a calmer voice Dear Uncle Napoleon said, "Last night that filthy fellow wanted to phone the detective's assistant and say Dustali had killed Asadollah Mirza; instead of all coming and giving me an ultimatum and protesting here, go and get hold of Asadollah."

Dear Uncle was silent for a few moments, then with a gloomy face he said to Mash Qasem, "Say whatever you know . . . ladies and gentleman, pay attention and then you'll see what difficulties I have to put up with . . . Qasem, tell them about this Asadollah business!"

Mash Qasem scratched his head and said, "Well now, why should I lie? To the grave it's ah . . . ah . . . I was in the covered bazaar, that baker's boy was sayin' that in the mornin' when he took bread to Shir Ali the butcher's house, he saw through the crack in the door that Asadollah Mirza was there . . ."

"What?"

"How?"

"Really?" Each person's mouth dropped open in astonishment. Then a general hullabaloo ensued. Everyone started denouncing Asadollah Mirza and the air was full of words like "idiot," "shameless," "brazen," "outrageous," and so forth.

Finally uncle colonel shouted, "Silence, everyone! Let me understand what you're saying. This baker's boy's sure he hasn't made a mistake? Didn't you go and see if he was telling the truth or not?"

Mash Qasem nodded his head and said, "God help me, sir, I went to the door of Shir Ali's shop to ask if it was true or not. As soon as the bastard heard the name Asadollah Mirza he gave such a roar as you'd think it was a buffalo roarin' . . . 'who told you,' he says . . . then he comes after me with his cleaver and I was that scared I said 'the baker's boy' and I got out of there as fast my legs'd carry me, like I'd borrowed an extra pair . . ."

"And now he's certainly gone after the baker's boy, the poor devil!"

"No, after that I saw the baker's boy in a street around here and I says to him not to show himself near Shir Ali's shop."

With a frown on his face uncle colonel said, "Sir, think of something! I'll have to send someone to this idiot to tell him to get out of Shir Ali's house. This imbecile Asadollah is destroying the centuries-old reputation of our family! Have you considered that? For a respectable person from a good family to go to this butcher's house . . ."

At this moment Dustali Khan arrived as well. Outwardly he seemed to have calmed down somewhat and it was clear he'd come there at uncle colonel's invitation to be part of the deputation and that he was no longer burning for revenge, but as soon as he heard about Asadollah Mirza hiding in Shir Ali's house, he became violently upset and started cursing not only him but every wellborn loafer. Finally, his voice barely emerging from his throat with rage, he said, "I . . . I'm not a man if I don't kill that man . . . that shameless . . . that destroyer of people's honor . . ."

Dear Uncle Napoleon interrupted, "Enough, sir! Nothing's happened to your honor, has it, for you to get so upset about Shir Ali's?"

"For the reputation of our family . . . for the reputation of the place where we live . . . think of it: a man from our family in Shir Ali's house, someone from the flower of this country's aristocracy in Shir Ali's house . . . with a young woman. If I'd found him last night he wouldn't have been able to perpetrate this new outrage . . . the snake must be killed, otherwise it'll bite! The shameless degenerate!"

The only person who had more or less retained his self control was Dear Uncle Napoleon; the rest of them, the women as well as the men, were furious and screaming and shouting that Asadollah must at all costs be persuaded to leave Shir Ali's house.

Finally, after explaining Napoleon's tactics under similar circumstances, Dear Uncle Napoleon suggested that a party go and talk to Asadollah Mirza and allay his fears and convince him by all means possible to leave his sanctuary. Uncle colonel and Shamsali Mirza volunteered to be members of the party. But Dear Uncle Napoleon said in an imperious voice, "No, you can stand aside, I shall go myself."

Voices were raised in protest, "It's not right for you to go, sir . . . it's beneath your dignity to go to Shir Ali's house."

Dear Uncle cut them off, "It so happens that it's exactly right. Because someone who is impartial and unbiased should go."

Uncle colonel wanted to protest but Dear Uncle Napoleon said in a curt voice, "I said someone who is impartial and unbiased should go."

And he particularly emphasized "impartial and unbiased." Then he adjusted his cloak over his shoulders, "Come on, Qasem, come and show me where Shir Ali's house is . . . hurry up, I have to talk to that silly fool before Shir Ali returns home."

I set off like a shadow after Dear Uncle and Mash Qasem. Dear Uncle strode toward Shir Ali's house. It was obvious he didn't want to attract the neighbors' attention.

They knocked at the door once or twice and then the delicate voice of Tahereh, Shir Ali's wife, could be heard from behind the thick door, "Who is it?"

"Is this Mr. Shir Ali's house?"

"He's not in. He's gone to the shop."

Dear Uncle brought his head close to the door; while trying not to raise his voice too much he said, "Ma'am, would you please tell Asadollah Mirza to come to the door."

"Who? We haven't anyone like that here."

"Ma'am, please listen to me. We know Asadollah is there. It's a matter of vital importance . . . if he doesn't come he'll be sorry . . . it's a matter of life and death . . ."

After a moment's silence Asadollah Mirza's voice came from behind the door, "You wanted me, sir?"

"Asadollah, come outside, I want to talk to you."

"Moment, is that you? How are you keeping?"

"Asadollah, open the door!"

Asadollah answered from behind the door in a terrified voice, "I daren't, sir. It's not safe for me. My life's in danger . . ."

"Listen Asadollah, open the door! I give you my word the matter's been solved . . . it was a misunderstanding. Dustali has given me his word that he'll forget the matter."

"Moment, moment, even if you accept the word of that wild raving idiot, I don't."

Dear Uncle said, in a voice trembling with rage but which he tried not to raise too much, "Asadollah, I'm telling you, I order you, to open the door!"

The tone of terror and anxiety in Asadollah's voice increased. Emotionally he said, "Sir, I don't want to disobey your order, but my life's in danger. I know I've no way to escape from this savage executioner . . . I'm an inch away from death, but I want to live a few hours longer."

"Asadollah, shut up! Open the door!"

In a grief-stricken voice Asadollah said, "Why, have you no mercy . . . if you saw my face you wouldn't recognize me . . . in one night worry and the fear of death have aged me twenty years . . . tell my brother to forgive me . . . I've given the matter some thought, and Dustali won't have to go to any more trouble."

"Damn you and your face! Damn you and your brother!"

Dear Uncle said this, and then, with the veins on his neck standing out in rage and with his complexion deep crimson verging on black, he turned his back on Shir Ali's house and set off toward his garden. I put my eye against a crack in the door of Shir Ali's house and peered into the yard. I was curious to see Asadollah Mirza's aged face. I wanted to tell him that I hadn't let on about his hiding place and that I wasn't responsible for his pain and suffering and getting old. He was wearing a shirt and trousers. The buttons on his shirt were completely open, his face was fresher and more cheerful than usual. He had a bowl of sherbet in his hand and he was stirring the ice in it with one finger. Shir Ali's wife, Tahereh, stood a little further off with her fingers pressed against her white flashing teeth to stop herself laughing out loud. I stopped worrying.

When I returned to Dear Uncle's house, Dear Uncle was telling the family members, in a choked voice, about his unsuccessful expedition.

After a few moments of everyone shouting at everyone else, Mash Qasem's voice was heard saying, "We have to think of somethin' quick . . . that poor innocent gentleman, he's in a really bad way . . . and he might do somethin' terrible to himself."

Uncle colonel exclaimed, "He's doing something terrible to us . . . he's destroying our reputation. What the hell's the matter with him? And what better place . . . ?"

"Well now, why should I lie? To the grave it's ah . . . ah . . . When I heard his voice from behind the door it was really upset . . . you'd think his voice was thirty years older . . . like his head was trapped in a leopard's jaws . . ."

Impatiently Dear Uncle Napoleon said, "Don't talk such rubbish, Mash Qasem . . . now that this man shows no concern for the reputation of his family, it seems to me we should think of something else."

Once again there was excited talk back and forth. The meeting became heated, with various discussions and arguments going on. Virtually everyone agreed that they should send someone to Shir Ali the butcher, to say to him that it was not right for Asadollah Mirza to be staying in his house, and that it might become a subject of gossip. However, no one who was there wanted to take on this difficult task, and they said that the only man for the job was Dear Uncle Napoleon.

But as Dear Uncle Napoleon wasn't having it, Dustali Khan suddenly burst out in an excess of bravery, "Tell him to come here. I'll tell him." He was so eager to be revenged on Asadollah that he had turned into a brave and fearless man.

They sent Mash Qasem to fetch Shir Ali. While they were waiting for the butcher to appear, a regular storm of reproaches rained down against Asadollah, with the men blaming him and the women objecting to his unsavory character. Finally the door opened and Mash Qasem entered alone.

"Praise the Lord . . . nothin' happens in this world without its punishment comin' after."

"What's happened, Mash Qasem? Where's Shir Ali?"

"Well now, why should I lie? His shop was closed. He'd been fightin' and they'd taken him to the lockup. It was like this, see, the baker's boy had said to the kneader who kneads the bread dough that Mr. Asadollah Mirza was in Shir Ali's house . . . the kneader had pulled Shir Ali's leg about it, and then Shir Ali had hit the kneader around the head with a leg of mutton . . . and the kneader had passed out and they'd taken him to the hospital. The cops took Shir Ali to the lockup . . ."

Virtually simultaneously various voices said, "The lockup?"

"They took Shir Ali?"

"How long are they keeping him?"

When the racket had quieted down somewhat, Dustali Khan, who it seemed had only just realized the important factor in all this, said with a flabbergasted expression on his face, "Then . . . then . . . if they've taken Shir Ali off to prison . . . it means . . . that man . . . perhaps ten days . . . twenty days . . . he might be in prison for six months."

Then he turned to Dear Uncle and screamed, "Sir, think of something! What the hell are we to do?"

Dear Uncle Napoleon screamed right back, "What's going on? Why are you yelling? Why's Shir Ali so special all of a sudden?"

This argument was cut short when the door opened and Mrs. Aziz al-Saltaneh entered; it was clear that she had gone to the police station to withdraw the complaint she had made the previous day. As soon as he saw his wife, Dustali went over to her and said in a voice filled with emotion, "Did you know they've arrested Shir Ali?"

"Wonderful . . . God damn him and his rotten meat, too."

Dustali Khan took her arm and said even more wildly, "But that thief of everyone's reputation is in Shir Ali's house. That shameless loafer . . ."

Aziz al-Saltaneh said with a very knowing, coquettish smile, "Oh, that Asadollah and the things he gets up to, he's a real rascal."

But then suddenly, as if a light had flashed on in her brain, the smile died on her lips. Wide-eyed, she stared at the door to the room and roared between clenched teeth, "What . . . Asadollah . . . that . . . that . . . that slut of a little bitch, is she there, too?" Everyone stared, silent and astonished, at Aziz al-Saltaneh's contorted face.

Dustali was silent, too, but his upper lip and its mustache trembled with the effort of holding back his fury. Finally he said from between clenched teeth, "God rest that Rokn al-Din's soul, by spawning this child in his old age he's ruined the whole family's reputation . . . and spawning it with his gardener's daughter at that!"

Shamsali Mirza frowned and angrily said, "Mr. Dustali Khan, I'll ask you to leave the dead in peace."

And even more angrily, Dustali Khan answered, "The dead are at peace, with God. It's just that they land the living in such a mess . . . God rest his soul, if your late father hadn't been so free and easy about undoing the belt on his pants and hadn't spawned this Asadollah, would it have been any great loss? Would it have been the end of the world if he hadn't set this wolf among people's women and children?"

"Mr. Dustali Khan, I'll ask you not to talk about being free and easy undoing the belt on someone's pants! Was it for my sake Mrs. Aziz al-Saltaneh brought a carving knife into bed with her?"

It seemed that Dustali Khan was so livid that he had forgotten all about the presence of his wife and the events of the night of the mourning ceremony, and, paying no attention to Shamsali Mirza's remark, he shouted, "Stop defending that shameless thief! All right, so he's your brother. He's a thief . . . a thief of reputations. Yes sir, the high and mighty Asadollah Mirza is a thief of people's reputations!"

Aziz al-Saltaneh was completely lost in thought and seemed not to hear the noise going on around her, but when she heard the name Asadollah she came back to herself and, in a terrifying voice, said, "Dustali, shut up! I wish there was just one hair of his on your body! I wish all thieves were like him!"

Then under her breath she said, "I'm sure that slut of a little bitch has tricked the poor boy!"

Then she suddenly turned on Dear Uncle Napoleon and shouted, "And you're just sitting there! A respectable member of this family is a prisoner in that butcher Shir Ali's house and you're not doing anything? If that slut's slipped him a love potion, what are you going to do?"

Calmly Dear Uncle said, "Don't get angry, ma'am . . . I've just come from Shir Ali's house. I talked to Asadollah from behind the door and he wasn't coming out and that's that. However much I begged, however much I shouted, he wouldn't budge."

"Why? What did he say?"

"How should I know, ma'am, a thousand ridiculous things, a thousand bits of nonsense, he says he daren't come out from fear of Dustali but . . ."

"Out of fear of Dustali? And whose dog is Dustali to raise a hand against my uncle's son? I'll have to go and get him myself . . . I'll have to go, because that slut with that disgusting figure of hers, she's got a thousand ways to put spells on people . . . and she must have put a spell on him now, otherwise Asadollah's not the man to stay there . . ."

Dear Uncle Napoleon said, "Ma'am, consider that he himself may be quite happy for this spell . . ."

But Aziz al-Saltaneh interrupted him, "Why are you talking so much? A terrible catastrophe might happen to the young man."

Mash Qasem found an opportunity to speak, "The lady's right . . . when I heard Mr. Asadollah Mirza's voice from behind the door it was shakin' like a little kid's. He was in a really bad way. It was like he'd got typhoid fever. His voice could hardly come out of his throat . . . like his head was trapped in a leopard's jaws . . ."

Aziz al-Saltaneh slapped herself on the cheek, "O God strike me dead . . . the poor young man, what kind of a state's he in? And this crowd are supposed to be his relatives."

Having said this she prepared to set off. "I know as soon as I've said one word to him he'll come out . . . up till now the poor thing hasn't heard a kind word from you, so why should he listen to you!"

Dustali Khan got up, too. "Then I'll come, too, and tell him I've forgiven his sins . . . I'll have to make it clear to him that . . ."

"Sit down where you were . . . if the poor thing hears your ugly voice, his courage'll melt away to water."

When Aziz al-Saltaneh was in the hall, Dear Uncle Napoleon called after her, "Don't tell him they've taken Shir Ali off to prison . . . and I didn't tell him, because once he finds out it'll be impossible to get him to move."

"And if you're so good at lullabies, how come you haven't sung yourself off to sleep?"

Aziz al-Saltaneh set off for Shir Ali's house. And just as I'd done the previous time, I followed her like a shadow.

The alleyway was quiet and I tracked her from a distance. She knocked at the door a few times before the voice of Tahereh, Shir Ali's wife, could be heard from behind the door; for a while Aziz al-Saltaneh bargained with her and threatened her, until the mistress of the house agreed to bring Asadollah to the door so that she could talk to him.

In a voice that she tried to keep calm and enticing, Aziz al-Saltaneh said, "Asadollah, open the door so I can have a word with you."

"My dear lady, ask me anything you want except that I leave this house. I fear for my life."

"I'm telling you to open the door! Dustali wouldn't dare raise his hand against you; I've completely forgiven Dustali and he's forgiven us . . ."

His voice trembling, Asadollah said, "My dear, I'm afraid . . . I know that Dustali's there with you now . . . I know that now he's got his knife hidden behind his back ready to sink it into my heart . . ."

"Asadollah, open the door a crack and see for yourself that Dustali's not here . . . just think what people are saying, you're alone in the house with a woman . . ."

"Moment, moment, praise the Lord such relationships aren't at all my kind of thing. Shir Ali's like my brother, his wife and children are like my own wife and children . . . just wait till Shir Ali comes home and I'll hand his house over to him, then I'm at your service."

"Asadollah, you know Shir Ali had a fight and they've taken him to the lockup? How can you want . . ."

"What! Good God! Shir Ali's gone to prison . . . well then, it's quite impossible for me to set foot outside this house . . . duty, ethics and conscience all command me to stay. Dear God, what a heavy duty it is, too!"

From his voice it was clear that he'd already heard about Shir Ali's going to prison and that he was play acting.

Aziz al-Saltaneh brought her head closer to the door and softly said, "Asadollah, please, for me, come out of there. Don't show me up in front of them."

Asadollah Mirza said, "Ma'am, I'm ready to give my life for you, but I've a duty my conscience won't release me from. You couldn't accept it if I left Shir Ali's wife and children alone and without a protector when they've been given into my hands and he's been taken off to prison."

"Shir Ali doesn't have any children, Asadollah!"

"Well, there's his wife, my dear lady . . . and she's just like a child . . . poor thing, now she's crying like a cloud in springtime . . . I can't see her face from under her veil but I can hear her sobbing. The poor innocent child!"

For a while Aziz al-Saltaneh kept trying, but without success. Finally, while showering the most indecent curses on Shir Ali and his wife, she set off for the garden like a walking volcano.

I set off after her, dogging her like a shadow, but I suddenly became aware that the pharmacist who managed my father's pharmacy had entered our house. This was an important matter to me. I quietly went over to our house. My father and his pharmacist had gone to the room with French windows near the door to the yard. During all the recent goings on I had got used to eavesdropping, and I put my ear against the window.

As he wiped the sweat from his forehead with a handkerchief the pharmacist said, "Sir, you can be saying the burial service for the pharmacy; it's all over. Despite the fact that we closed for a day and put a notice up that the pharmacy's closed for a pilgrimage, it hasn't done any good."

"But didn't the Seyed say what we told him?"

"He did, sir. That poor Seyed Abolqasem has gone up in the pulpit twice to put things right, but it looks as though no one's paid any attention to him. Once something gets into folks' heads it's hard to get it out again."

"But what are people saying? What's the matter with them?"

"Nothing, sir, they aren't saying anything. But not even one person has come to buy so much as a couple of grams of Glauber's salts. Today someone who was just passing by was about to step into the pharmacy but the tradespeople roundabout cursed him out so much he changed his mind and went . . ."

I saw my father's face through the crack between the windows. He had turned white and was grinding his teeth. Finally, in a strangled voice, he said, "A way has to be found . . . we have to think of something."

"There's nothing to think of, sir, I know the people of this area very well; if they're at the point of death they won't buy drugs from us because it's got into their heads that we make our drugs with alcohol . . . and I can't stay in this area any more . . . because everywhere they're saying that I'm a heathen with no religion . . . for now I've closed up shop until we think of something . . ."

Frowning, my father paced in the room for a few moments; then he stopped and, in a voice that was unrecognizable from the violence of his fury, he said, "This filthy shameless bastard has taken my livelihood away from me . . . I'm not a man if I don't get my revenge, if I rest before I put his body in the grave . . . shameless! Obscene! I'll give him Napoleon, I'll Napoleon him till he doesn't know whether he's coming or going!"

"What should I do for now, sir?"

"Nothing, you can . . . you can . . . until we see what's going to happen . . . for now turn the electricity off and the pharmacy can stay closed until later . . ."

With a worried face, the pharmacist said goodbye and left and my father started pacing back and forth in the room. He was in such a bad way that I stayed there fearing that he might collapse. When I could tell from his movements that he was a little calmer, I went to

Dear Uncle's house to see what was happening there. Everyone was still there. Aziz al-Saltaneh's simpleminded daughter, Qamar, who had been sent to a relative's house the day before, had arrived.

Discussion and argument were still raging. In particular, Aziz al-Saltaneh and Dustali Khan were extremely angry and agitated. During my absence Dustali Khan had phoned the police station to see if he could arrange the temporary release of Shir Ali, but they had answered that until the condition of the victim—meaning the baker's dough-kneader—was known, they could not release Shir Ali.

As I arrived Aziz al-Saltaneh was saying, "I know that slut has put a spell on poor Asadollah; if she hadn't, he's not the kind of man to ignore what I say. Why don't we send for Mr. Khorasani, to splash a vinegar mixture against spells on the door to Shir Ali's house?"

Dustali Khan impatiently yelled, "What do you mean, spells, what kind of balderdash are you talking . . . that lout has stayed there so that he can play around with Shir Ali's wife."

"What! Damn your cheek! A man is going to leave real respectable women so that he can go and play around with that ugly fright! And a man like Asadollah into the bargain!"

Dustali couldn't very well defend Shir Ali's wife's appearance but he let loose a flood of bad language and curses against Asadollah, and Aziz al-Saltaneh exploded in fury, "Dustali, I'm ready to slap you round that snout of yours so that all your false teeth shake out of your mouth! If you curse my uncle's grandson it's like you're cursing me!"

Dear Uncle had no choice but to intervene; he shouted, "Silence! Why don't you go and have this quarrel in your own house? What sin have I committed that I have to listen to your rubbish? Asadollah can stay in Shir Ali's house till the grass grows green under his feet! What's it to you? Are you Asadollah's or Shir Ali's guardian or lawyer?"

Uncle colonel said, "Brother, I beg you not to get angry again . . . you at least should stay calm. We came to . . . ."

"You came to what? What do you want from me?"

"Don't get so angry! We came to solve our existing differences . . . but, as you can see, a more important matter has come up . . . the honor and reputation of the family are in danger. We have to get Asadollah out of Shir Ali's house in any way possible . . . I suggest we go and visit the dough-kneader who's been wounded on the head, perhaps the wound isn't a serious one, perhaps he's only faking to get revenge on Shir Ali . . . in this case, with a bit of pecuniary encouragement, we might be able to persuade him to drop his complaint, and they'll release Shir Ali today."

Dear Uncle Napoleon yelled, "And now I, in my situation, in my condition, am to go and visit a dough-kneader to persuade him to drop his complaint against a butcher?"

"I didn't mean you . . . one of us . . . or, for example, we could send Mash Qasem . . ."

Dustali Khan interrupted, "It's a good idea. It's very logical. Of course it's beneath the dignity of the family to go and visit a dough-kneader. But we could send Mash Qasem."

Dear Uncle Napoleon angrily yelled, "Why ever is it necessary that Shir Ali be released? It serves him right if he wants to hit people on the head with sheep's carcasses. This man has harassed the whole neighborhood, and now that for once the state wants to punish him, why are you interfering?"

"We're not interested in Shir Ali . . . it serves him right, he got what was coming to him. May he rot in jail . . . but we're concerned about the family honor, we're concerned about Asadollah. Just think of it, our Asadollah is in Shir Ali the butcher's house! Tomorrow how are we going to be able to look the people of this neighborhood in the eye?"

Trying not to show his anger, Dear Uncle Napoleon said, "Gentlemen, is this the first time that Asadollah Mirza has gone into people's houses . . . is it even the first time he's been to Shir Ali's house? Really, gentlemen, do anything you want to do . . . as for Mash Qasem, send him to visit the dough-kneader, the baker, the draper, the grocer . . ."

Aziz al-Saltaneh's daughter, Qamar, who had been busy licking a barley-sugarcane up to that moment, asked, "Mummy dear? Have they taken Asadollah off to prison then?"

"No, my darling, they haven't taken Asadollah to prison, a nasty person is keeping the poor thing prisoner . . ."

"O God strike me dead, poor Asadollah Mirza . . . I hope they let him go soon, because he's going to take me on a trip."

"What? A trip? Where's he taking you?"

Still licking her barley-sugarcane Qamar said, "That night at the party he said to me, 'If you're a good girl and don't tell anyone, I'll take you on a trip to San Francisco' . . . by the way, mummy dear, is San Francisco nice?"

Aziz al-Saltaneh gave her an angry look to silence her, but Qamar wasn't going to give up so easily. "Really, mummy dear, is it nice?"

"No, it's not for children . . ."

Then without getting angry she shook her head and said under her breath, "God cripple him, the things that Asadollah says!"

In a voice shaking with anger Dustali Khan said, "You see? Are you still going to defend this thief of people's honor?"

Aziz al-Saltaneh gave him a threatening look and said, "You just shut up! The poor thing was making a joke."

Uncle colonel jumped into their conversation, "Now that the Master has given permission, it's better that we don't delay any more. Run, Mash Qasem, run, my man! Go and find that dough-kneader . . . here's some cash . . . persuade him any way you can to drop his complaint."

Without raising his head, Mash Qasem said, "There's a problem with this job."

"What problem?"

"Well now, why should I lie? To the grave it's ah . . . ah . . . I saw them takin' the dough-kneader to his house an hour ago, with his head bandaged, and now Dr. Naser al-Hokama must be at his bedside . . ."

"Then he's not badly hurt."

"No, not too bad . . . but the thing is that for ten or twelve days now I'm not talkin' to this dough-kneader. You remember that time there was a bit of sackin' in the bread? Me and the dough-kneader had a bit of an argy-bargy about it, and he hit me right here, the cheeky beggar, with one of the weights off his scales . . . it really winded me, so I banged him round the head with my basket, then they came to separate us . . . but from that day till now I'm not talkin' to him, not a word."

"What do you mean, not talking? A grown-up man doesn't go around not talking like a child."

"Not talkin's nothin' to do with how big you are . . . right now isn't the Master not talkin' to his own sister's husband?"

"Don't talk rubbish, be off with you!"

"Well sir, why should I lie? You could cut my jugular and I wouldn't spit in that dough-kneader's face, so how can I be goin' and makin' up to him nice like?"

For a while uncle colonel and Dustali Khan and Aziz al-Saltaneh and even Shamsali Mirza begged and insisted, but Mash Qasem wasn't having it. "We Ghiasabadi folks won't be doin' these shameful things. There was a man from our town once who . . . and he wasn't exactly from Ghiasabad neither. He was from the other side of Qom, over toward the place where they have prayers at Musa Mobaraghe . . ."

Uncle colonel yelled, "All right, so you're not going, don't make a song and dance about it, God damn you and the man from your town . . . I'll go myself!"

At this juncture Dear Uncle Napoleon interrupted. In a severe voice he forbade his brother to go on this lowly mission, but since he saw that everyone was determined that, at whatever cost, the dough-kneader had to be brought round so that Shir Ali would be released, he turned to Mash Qasem, "Mash Qasem, I command you to carry out this undertaking. Just as on the battlefield I gave you my orders and you carried them out, so today I order you to go . . . imagine we are at the Battle of Kazerun."

Mash Qasem drew himself up to his full height, "Very good, sir, but just look at the power of God, will you . . . at how times change . . . those days you was orderin' me to fight against the English. Now I have to go after this here dough-kneader. I remember once in the thick of it at the Battle of Kazerun, I'd got my rifle in my hand . . ."

"That's enough, don't talk, Qasem! Go! Your commanding officer is giving you an order, execute it immediately!"

By the time Mash Qasem returned all present were regularly pacing up and down the room and were at the extreme limit of their patience; they crowded round him.

"What happened, Mash Qasem?"

"Well now, why should I lie? To the grave it's ah . . . ah . . . I didn't speak to him himself, I called his brother to the door so he would give him the message . . . he kept comin' and goin' but in the end nothin' came of it . . ."

"How did nothing come of it?"

"Well, he says that Shir Ali's to come and kiss his hand in front of all the shopkeepers in the neighborhood before he'll forgive him."

Helpless and exhausted, Dustali Khan fell back on a sofa. "No, that shameless bastard's going to be staying in Shir Ali's house!"

Mash Qasem continued, "And then I've just seen Esmail the master cobbler, and he was sayin' how he'd seen Shir Ali in the lockup, and Shir Ali'd said to him, 'Go to my door and tell the wife she's not to worry and she's to do everythin' in her power to be hospitable to our guest till I come back!'"

Uncle colonel shook his head and said, "Well well, well well, he must be a very gracious host to be offering him that kind of welcome . . . really, as the man himself would say, really moment . . ."

TEN

IN THE MIDST of the back and forth of the arguments over Shir Ali the butcher's fight with the dough-kneader, an unexpected event suddenly occurred which left each person rooted to the spot in astonishment. Everyone held their breath. Perhaps no one could believe what they were seeing: my father had appeared in the doorway of Dear Uncle Napoleon's sitting room. I glanced over toward Dear Uncle Napoleon. His tall stature seemed to grow even taller. Wide-eyed, stock-still, and with his mouth open, he stared at the new arrival. My father stretched out his hands toward Dear Uncle and said in a voice filled with emotion, "I have come to kiss your hands and beg your pardon . . . please forgive me, sir."

And he went toward Dear Uncle; he stopped two paces from him but Dear Uncle made no movement. My heart was beating violently. I wanted to shout out and ask Dear Uncle not to leave my father's gesture unanswered; perhaps everyone there wanted this. What to me seemed an extremely long moment passed. Suddenly Dear Uncle opened his arms. The two strenuously embraced.

Happy voices suddenly rose on every side. My mother threw herself on the two and kissed their faces.

I ran toward Layli's room, where I knew she had been confined without permission to leave, and shouted, "Layli, Layli, come and see . . . come and see . . . my dad and Dear Uncle have made up." Layli put a hesitant foot out of her door. When in the distance she saw my father beside Dear Uncle, she took my hand and squeezed it tightly. Quietly I said in her ear, "Layli, I'm very happy."

"So am I."

"Layli, I love you."

Layli blushed and, in a voice I could hardly hear, said, "I love you, too."

My whole body shook, a burning wave enveloped me, scalding me from the tips of my toes to the top of my head. Without thinking I opened my arms to crush her against my chest, but then I came to my senses and led her toward the sitting room. My father had taken Dear Uncle's hand in both his own and was in the midst of apologizing for what he had said and done, and Dear Uncle was very calmly shaking his head and saying it was nothing important and that he had forgotten everything. I went over to my father, but I had released Layli's hand because those present might have noticed.

When everyone had sat down, my father stared at the flowers on the carpet and said in a strange voice, "Today something happened which completely turned my life upside down. I met a well-known person, and when the talk turned toward you he said something which shook me. He said, 'You should take pride in the fact that you have such an individual in your family.' I wish you could have heard the passion with which he talked about you. He said he'd heard from Major Saxon, who was stationed here for years during the First World War, that if it hadn't been for you there were many things in this country that would be quite different. If it weren't for your struggles and your patriotism the English could have done many things. He said that when the war in the south was going on, the English were ready to give a thousand pounds to anyone who would get rid of you."

Dear Uncle's face palpably opened and blossomed, gradually a seraphic smile spread about his lips; he didn't take his eyes from my father's mouth. My father went on in the same tone of voice, "This same person talked about your struggles against despotism. He said that if it weren't for your sacrifices perhaps we wouldn't now have a constitution . . ."

With childish excitement Dear Uncle asked, "Who is this person?"

"I'm sorry but I can't say his name . . . since he repeated to me what Major Saxon had said it would be dangerous for him. You yourself know that the English have no mercy, especially now when they've started such a huge war and Hitler is raining bombs down on them every night . . ."

Dear Uncle was so transformed that he was on the brink of throwing his arms around my father's neck and kissing him on the lips.

Mash Qasem, who had been listening carefully to this conversation, said, "Like they say, the moon doesn't stay behind a cloud all the time . . . I myself know how the Master thrashed them English . . . and right now if they'd let him the Master could whip them English better than three Hitlers . . ."

My father continued, "I really felt proud and privileged . . . and ashamed there'd been such a misunderstanding. This chance event really taught me something new."

Perhaps everyone there had guessed that my father was lying. All of them knew that Dear Uncle's struggles against the rebels in the south, his struggles against foreigners, and his struggles on behalf of the Constitution were his own invention, and they knew that my father believed these fantasies less than anyone else.

But these empty words of praise made everyone extremely happy, because they believed that my father was doing all this in order to put an end to their differences and quarrels. But my morale sank further and further from one moment to the next. The vague feeling I had as soon as my father started on his flattering speech became horrifyingly clear as I remembered my father's conversation with the pharmacist, and my confidence in my father's good faith disappeared.

O God, let me be wrong! Let it be that my father is really sorry about all the fighting and arguing! O God, I beg you with all my heart that there be no wheels within wheels involved in what my father is saying. The flood of praise was still flowing from my father's lips, "This same person was saying that if it weren't for the fact that the English were busy fighting against Hitler they would never leave the Master alone. He said that in the whole of the East there wasn't a single person who'd done such harm to the plans of the English as you had . . . he said he's heard from Major Saxon's own mouth that there were two people who'd really given the English a hard time, one the Master in World War I, and the other Hitler in this war . . ."

If someone had seen the gathering in Dear Uncle's house an hour before and then seen it again now, it would be impossible for him to recognize it. The sad, frowning faces had completely opened up. Everyone was happy and cheerful. The only sad face was Dustali Khan's; every now and then he would regret Asadollah Mirza's absence, but I easily guessed that the thought of Asadollah Mirza being in Shir Ali the butcher's house tormented him. Basically Dustali Khan didn't like Asadollah Mirza. Perhaps the reason was that at gatherings and parties Asadollah Mirza used to tease him too much, and in his absence, sometimes referred to him as "that ass Dustali." There was also the fact that Dustali Khan was lecherous and couldn't bear Asadollah Mirza because all the women of the family and their friends liked Asadollah Mirza's company. Every time poor Dustali Khan related a bit of juicy gossip he would be faced with the women's reproaches, "Please don't make fun of Asadollah!"

"What a sweet turn of phrase Asadollah has."

"If a woman's going to have a fling, it should be with Asadollah. You want someone who's going to be witty and charming about it!"

Sometimes Dustali Khan lost all patience and let loose a flood of curses against Asadollah Mirza. Another reason for Dustali's malicious feelings toward Asadollah Mirza was that whenever he became interested in a woman, there were signs of Asadollah Mirza's already having passed that way before him. Especially in the case of Shir Ali's wife, with whom he apparently hadn't been successful.

While my father was having his say about Dear Uncle's bravery, Dustali once again jumped into the conversation, unable to contain himself, "But give a thought to Asadollah! How long do you want him to stay in that wretched butcher's house?"

Dear Uncle Napoleon angrily cut him off, "Dustali, where are your manners! Can't you see the gentleman's talking? Now, you were saying . . ."

My father continued, "Yes, it was in the middle of the First World War that they sent Major Saxon here . . ."

Mash Qasem, who had been listening carefully, asked Dear Uncle, "Sir, wasn't he that tall feller who you went for with a sword? Who was squint-eyed?"

Dear Uncle quieted him with a wave of his hand, "Just a moment, let me understand . . . so this person you're talking about, had he seen Major Saxon recently?"

"Yes, oh yes, just two or three months ago in Istanbul . . . I didn't really follow, it seems he'd come from Cairo and was on his way somewhere . . . God willing, when these problems are out of the way I'll have to invite him to my house and then you can hear from his own mouth the things Major Saxon has said about you. I'm sorry to say he did a lot of cursing . . . he even said you had connections with other political developments."

Dear Uncle was in seventh heaven; with a seraphic smile he said, "That's very natural . . . it would have been surprising if he had said anything else . . . of course, I don't personally recall this Major Saxon. But then the English don't push their people forward . . ."

Mash Qasem interrupted, "Sir, how can you not remember? He's that tall feller who we saw once two or three years ago in Cheragh Bargh Street. Don't you remember I said to you 'Why's that foreigner lookin' daggers at you?' Right then I said you'd think . . ."

Dear Uncle impatiently cut him off, "No, Mash Qasem, don't talk rubbish . . . though perhaps he was one of their pawns . . . anyway, I can't remember the face of this foreigner you're talking about."

"How's it possible you don't remember him? But why should I lie? To the grave it's ah . . . ah . . . it's like he's standin' before my eyes right now . . . he'd eyes like bowls of blood . . . he gave you such a look my stomach turned over. Right there I said 'Blessed Morteza Ali, save the Master from these evil English!'"

Dear Uncle didn't pay much attention to what Mash Qasem was saying. He stared into space with the same seraphic smile on his face. "Yes, I've done my human and patriotic duty, and I was aware of the consequences. You think I didn't know what it means to fight with the English? You think I didn't know they'd block my career? You think I didn't know they'd never forget their hatred and enmity for me! On the contrary, I knew all this but I anointed my body with the fat of every hardship and humility and I fought . . . now how many go-betweens they've set up, how many people they've sent, well, never mind . . . I remember my last commission in Mashhad . . . one day toward sunset I was walking home, perhaps it was Mash Qasem here following on behind me."

"Of course it was me, sir."

"Yes, just as I was going along I saw someone like an Indian trailing me. Well, I paid no attention; then in the evening I was at home and there was a knock at the door. A private went to the door . . . I think it was Qasem here . . ."

"Yes, it was me, sir."

"He went to the door and came back and said, 'There's an Indian come who says he's on the pilgrimage, but a problem's turned up and he wants to talk to the Master for a moment' . . . I immediately suspected he was one of their pawns . . . I swear by the soul of Layli I didn't even go to the door . . . I shouted 'Tell the gentleman he can only see my corpse' . . . I wasn't even prepared to say one word to him."

Mash Qasem interrupted, "I remember very well . . . when the Master said that, I went and slammed the door in his face and his turban fell off on the ground."

Dear Uncle continued excitedly, "I sent him off with a flea in his ear, and I shouted after him, 'Go and tell your masters that this one's not for sale.'"

Mash Qasem nodded his head and said, "That Indian gave such a look as he was goin' that a shiver went down my spine . . . right there I said 'Blessed Morteza Ali, I'm lookin' to you to save the Master from this crowd.'"

My father said, "And instead today you walk with your head held high. Your family respects you."

Dustali Khan, who was in a constant state of excitement, said, "But once respect and reputation have been acquired, you can't allow a shameful blot to stain it. At the moment an individual from this family is in the house of a lout of a butcher and no one is even . . ."

Shamsali Mirza said in a forceful voice, "Mr. Dustali Khan, stop making such offensive references to my brother. The poor wretch has taken refuge with the butcher because he's afraid of your violence and your foul mouth. If you're worried about the butcher's wife, that's another matter."

Aziz al-Saltaneh suddenly jumped up, "God damn him and his worries . . . if he talks rubbish behind my cousin's back once more I'll knock his false teeth down his throat . . ." Then she sat down again and said, "I talked to Asadollah; poor thing, he doesn't want to leave Shir Ali's wife and children alone without anyone to look after them."

Dustali Khan yelled, "My dear woman, Shir Ali doesn't have any children."

"That wife of his is just a child . . . Asadollah's a sensitive person . . ."

His face contorted, Dustali Khan said through clenched teeth, "I'll give him sensitive . . ."

And with quick angry steps he strode from the room. With her eyes full of malice, Aziz al-Saltaneh watched him leave and said, "I'm going to do something now that'll put Asadollah's mind at rest so he'll come out. Shir Ali's mother-in-law's house is close by. I'll go and send her to stay with her daughter so she won't be alone till that bear Shir Ali gets out of jail."

Uncle colonel's face brightened. He also was uncomfortable with the notion of Asadollah being in Shir Ali's house but he wasn't showing it. Excitedly he said, "That's a very good idea . . . because it would be a pity if Asadollah couldn't share in our happiness and pleasure . . ." And then he addressed everyone present in a loud voice, "I would like to invite everyone here to come for supper tonight at my house. To celebrate our good fortune in clearing up this misunderstanding, I'm going to serve you a very fine vintage wine, twenty years old . . ."

"No, this is far too much trouble, Colonel. God willing, we'll do it another night . . ."

"It's no trouble at all . . . everything is ready. My wife's made a beautiful dish of rice and herbs; those of you who've cooked supper, you can bring it over and we'll eat together."

This suggestion of uncle colonel's met with a warm welcome. My father's conversation with Dear Uncle continued, and after a few minutes the sounds of backgammon, which hadn't been audible for many a long day, could be heard once again.

Despite the fact that I was suspicious of my father's hidden intentions and was extremely worried about this, I was still ready to burst with happiness at seeing myself once again with Layli next to my father's and Dear Uncle's backgammon board. Layli's surreptitious glances sent a wave of pleasure over me from head to toe. My father threw out challenges apparently with the same old cheerfulness, "You fought against the English but admit it, you don't know how to play backgammon . . . if I were in your shoes I'd give up backgammon . . . Layli dear, go and get some walnuts for your dad to play with . . . let's have two sixes now!"

And Dear Uncle was ready with his answer, "Throw the dice . . .

Backgammon is for heroes, not for you—
A peasant's spade's more suitable for you!"

Layli's mother called her and gave her some work to do. I took a turn around the garden. It was as though peace and reconciliation between the hostile factions had had an effect on the garden, too. The flowers and trees looked more flourishing to me. But through the trees I could see Dustali Khan talking earnestly in Mash Qasem's ear and from their gestures I could guess at his insistence and Mash Qasem's refusal. Finally it seemed as though either his logic or his threats and promises convinced Mash Qasem because he rolled down his trousers, which he had hitched up in order to water the flowers, and left the garden. I guessed that Dustali had sent him to satisfy the dough-kneader and procure Shir Ali's release from prison, and later I found out that my guess was correct. If Shir Ali hadn't returned home, and Asadollah had stayed the night alone in the house with Tahereh, Dustali would have died of chagrin. From his condition and his actions it was clear that he was prepared to do anything at all to get the philanderer out of the butcher's house.

It was nearly sunset when Mash Qasem returned and took Dustali Khan aside. I was very curious to know how his mission had turned out. I quietly went over to them and stood eavesdropping behind a clump of trees.

"Sir, you really put me in some shameful fixes . . . although I wasn't talkin' to that dough-kneader feller, I went to see him. And after he'd taken the money he was messin' me about and playin' hard to get for an hour till we went together to the lockup so as he could say how Shir Ali could . . ."

Dustali Khan impatiently said, "What happened? Did they let Shir Ali out?"

"Well sir, why should I lie? To the grave it's ah . . . ah . . . this dough-kneader feller wrote down he'd withdrawn his complaint and handed it over but the boss wasn't there and they said if the boss weren't there they couldn't let Shir Ali go."

"When will the boss get back?"

"Well, he's gone till tomorrow . . . though they said how it was possible he might pop in tonight."

In a voice trembling with anger, Dustali Khan said under his breath, "I spent all this money so they could release him tomorrow? And so tonight this shameless, unprincipled . . ."

"All the better, sir, serve him right so he won't be wavin' his cleaver at folks!"

Dustali Khan yelled, "I'm not talking about him, where's your common sense?" Then he took Mash Qasem's arm and guided him out of the garden.

Half an hour later when there was still no sign of them, I too went out. The alleyway was dark and completely quiet as I walked toward Shir Ali's house. In the darkness of the night I saw Dustali Khan hidden behind a tree near the butcher's house. For a while I watched him from a distance, but when he didn't move, I had no choice but to go back to the garden.

The party at uncle colonel's house was well under way. Virtually everyone from our close family was there. Dear Uncle Napoleon and my father were sitting next to one another at the end of the room, chatting away like a bride and groom, and loud music was coming from uncle colonel's ancient horn gramophone. Some people were clapping in time to the records and uncle colonel was insisting that everyone drink some of his vintage wine. Aziz al-Saltaneh looked very merry, except that occasionally she seemed worried that Dustali Khan hadn't turned up. It seemed as though Asadollah Mirza's absence had been completely forgotten; even his brother Shamsali Mirza made no mention of him. The retired examining magistrate's frowning face had, for the first time, completely opened up, and he was even encouraging fat, simpleminded Qamar to dance.

I was wallowing in a sea of happiness, whispering in Layli's ear, despite the furious glances of Puri. We laughed out loud. Uncle colonel gave orders for a fire to be lit to barbecue kebabs. At this moment Dr. Naser al-Hokama entered, saying "Your good health," and, before he had time to turn round, uncle colonel poured a glass of wine down his throat. As soon as he sat down, the doctor looked about him and said, "Your good health . . . your good health . . . but where's Mr. Asadollah Mirza?"

Aziz al-Saltaneh answered with a laugh, "The little devil's attending to wives and widows as usual."

Uncle colonel gave a forced laugh and said, "But weren't you supposed to tell Shir Ali's mother-in-law so that she could go and stay with her daughter and let Asadollah go free?"

"God damn her if she hasn't gone off to Qom."

When I heard the name Qom I glanced around; there was no sign of Mash Qasem either. And this was strange because there never was a party when Mash Qasem wasn't in the main room, or busy going back and forth nearby and adding his opinions to the guests' conversation.

Dinner wasn't yet ready when two or three women who were out in the yard could be heard joyfully shouting, "Well, I never, Asadollah!"

And a moment later Asadollah rushed into the party, shouting, "My dear brother, what's happened?" But when he saw Shamsali Mirza's shining, cheerful face he stood there rooted to the spot.

When the sounds of happiness and welcome from those present had died down, Asadollah Mirza said, "So what were they talking about when they said you'd collapsed?"

With a loud laugh that was not at all part of his usual behavior Shamsali Mirza said, "I've never felt better in my life."

Asadollah Mirza frowned for a moment, but his face soon resumed its usual cheerful expression and he said, "Moment, so that little bastard Mash Qasem wanted to drag me here?"

And he immediately began singing:

"Oh, we've come, we've come,
With guitars and a drum we've come . . ."

Aziz al-Saltaneh pinched his cheek and said, "God bless you and keep you for all your fooling . . . however did you drag yourself away?"

"Moment, moment . . . I'll just say hello and be back there again."

Aziz al-Saltaneh drew her eyebrows together, "You want to go back to that butcher's house again?"

With an innocent face Asadollah said, "Just think, Aziz . . . they've taken this poor helpless woman's husband off to prison and she's all by herself. She's got no friend or protector there . . . and if I want to leave her all alone, too, your conscience shouldn't stand for it."

What with all the confusion and getting up and sitting down by the guests Asadollah hadn't seen my father and Dear Uncle sitting next to each other, and suddenly he stopped dead in his tracks. Staring straight at them he shouted out, "Well well, God willing, it's all for the best . . ."

And he immediately started snapping his fingers, "Here's to friendship and all for the best, all for the best . . . a splendid wedding and all for the best, all for the best . . . a fancy party and all for the best . . ."

All the guests started singing along with him. Asadollah Mirza drained a glass of wine and went on, snapping his fingers, "From garden to garden . . . they're bringing the sweets, and San Francisco's coming!"

And Aziz al-Saltaneh, her gaze lovingly fixed on his face, said with an extremely coy giggle, "My God, it kills me, the things he gets up to!"

The party had reached a peak of happiness and enjoyment and everyone was capering around in the middle of the room dancing to Asadollah's racket.

At this moment an unexpected event occurred. Mash Qasem threw himself, panting for breath, into the hallway and screamed out, "Help . . . he's killed him . . . he's cut off his head . . . Blessed Morteza Ali help us now . . ."

Everyone stood as if transfixed and held their breath.

Pallid and gasping, Mash Qasem said, "Run . . . help him . . . Shir Ali's killed Dustali Khan."

"What? Why? How'd it happen? Speak man!"

In broken sentences Mash Qasem explained what had occurred. "It seems like Dustali'd gone in Shir Ali's house . . . and all cheeky-like he was wantin' to give Shir Ali's wife a kiss when Shir Ali comes back; he really swiped him one . . ."

"Shir Ali was in prison!"

"They let him out . . . the dough-kneader feller said it was all right for them to let him out."

"Where's Dustali now?"

"He ran away, he threw himself into the garden here. I shut the door after him . . . but Shir Ali's behind the door with a cleaver . . . he's tearin' the door off of its hinges . . . can't you hear?"

We listened for a moment. Such heavy blows were being struck against the door that the noise was audible where we were. The men ran toward the door with the women following. Mash Qasem yelled out, "Run . . . that poor Dustali Khan's fainted . . ."

When we arrived at the garden door, which was shaking under the kicks and blows being showered on it, we saw Dustali Khan lying limply by the wall with his clothes all torn and a bloody nose. In a weak voice he whined, "Phone the lockup . . . get the police . . . he was going to kill me. He's after me now with a cleaver . . . help me . . . call for a cop."

Dear Uncle shook him by the shoulders and said, "What's going on? What's happened? Why did you go to Shir Ali's house?"

"This is not the time to discuss that . . . phone the lockup . . . that bear's going to break the door down any minute, he'll kill me . . . tell the police to come."

"Why are you talking such rubbish? You want the police to come and I tell them you went after someone's wife in someone's house?"

The thumping and kicking against the door went on uninterruptedly, and Shir Ali's hoarse voice could be heard, "Open up, and if you don't, I'll tear the door down . . ."

In the midst of the general tumult Asadollah Mirza said, "Well really, what people there are to be found in the world . . . have you no sense of honor, Dustali, that you go and insult other people's honor in this way?"

Dustali Khan threw a furious look at him and yelled, "You just shut up!"

"Moment, moment, then if you'll allow me to open this door and see who it is that Mr. Shir Ali is looking for."

Dustali Khan let out a loud wail, "I beg you all, don't let him open the door . . . that bear'll kill me."

At this instant Aziz al-Saltaneh hit Dustali Khan such a blow on the head with her shoe, which she had taken off, that a sob escaped from the helpless wretch's throat. "God damn you and your dirty-minded manners . . . so now you're carrying on in front of everyone's eyes are you?"

Asadollah Mirza grasped her hand, which she had raised to deliver a second blow, "My dear lady, forgive him, he's at fault . . . he's an ass, he's a fool, he has no common sense, he's an idiot, out of the greatness of your heart forgive him!"

Aziz al-Saltaneh lowered her hand and said, "Well, and why should I be bothered . . . I'll let that fellow with the cleaver behind the door take my revenge for me." Having said this, before anyone could move, she made a lunge for the door and lifted the latch.

The mountainous body of Shir Ali the butcher burst into the garden, dragging after him his dainty wife, Tahereh, who with one hand was clinging onto her veil and with the other was clutching his massive arm. Anyone colliding with this 250-pound body would have been reduced to a fistful of mincemeat and bone on the spot.

Luckily he crashed into the trunk of a walnut tree and a few walnuts pattered down to the ground. His roar, which was a match for any lion's, resounded throughout the garden, "Where is the bastard?"

Dear Uncle, my father, and Shamsali Mirza shouted at the tops of their voices, "Shir Ali . . . Shir Ali . . ."

Tahereh's voice could be heard, too, "Shir Ali, I beg you, on my life, let him go."

Asadollah Mirza was standing to one side, staring at Tahereh's body; under his breath he said, "My God, I'd die for you . . ."

For a moment all was confusion and voices on all sides, but with a quick movement Shir Ali scooped up Dustali Khan, who had been hiding behind Dear Uncle, as if he were a babe in arms. Tahereh's pleading cries and Dear Uncle's and everyone else's angry reproaches fell on deaf ears; still roaring, Shir Ali carried off Dustali Khan, who was waving his arms and legs about, toward the garden door. Suddenly Aziz al-Saltaneh blocked his way, "Put him down!"

"Ma'am, get out of me way or I'll . . ."

"Damn your impudence! Are you threatening me now as well? Put him down, and if you don't, I'll smash your false teeth down your throat!" And she set about kicking and punching Shir Ali. But neither her kicks nor her blows had any effect on Shir Ali and many of them landed on the head and face of Dustali Khan, whose teeth were clenched in terror.

Aziz al-Saltaneh shouted, "Asadollah, you say something!"

Asadollah came forward, without taking his eyes of Tahereh, "Shir Ali Khan, I beg you to forgive him . . . he's an ass, he's a fool, he's no common sense, he's a donkey . . ."

Without releasing Dustali Khan, Shir Ali said, "Mr. Asadollah Khan, sir, ask me anythin' you want but don't ask me that . . . I've got a bone to pick with this here shameless person."

"Shir Ali, I know this man better than you do, he didn't mean anything by it, it's just he's an ass, he's no common sense, he's a donkey . . . it's because he's such an ass he did something wrong . . ."

Then he lectured Dustali, "Dustali, say you're an ass, say you've no basic common sense . . . well, say it, man!"

With difficulty, through gritted teeth and in a whining voice, Dustali Khan said, "I'm an ass . . . I've no common sense."

"Say, 'I did it because I'm such an ass'."

"I did it . . . I did it because . . . because I'm such an ass."

Asadollah Mirza laid his hand on Shir Ali's arm. "You see, Shir Ali . . . now I beg you to forgive him . . . for the sake of your Tahereh, poor thing, whose body's trembling like a sparrow's, forgive him . . ."

Shir Ali had softened. "But just think of it . . . Tahereh's like your sister . . . if I forgive this shameless thing, you can't forgive him!"

"Obviously I won't forgive him . . . I'll give him a very hard time indeed . . . but you leave him be for tonight, until I teach him some manners . . . God damn his senseless head!" And saying this Asadollah Mirza hit Dustali, caught as he was in Shir Ali's embrace, smartly over the head.

Shir Ali brought his arms down and set Dustali on his feet so forcefully that a sobbing sound came up from his throat. "I'm doin' this only for you, because you're a real gent, a gentleman among gentlemen . . . you get someone like yourself what goes and gives money to this lousy dog of a dough-kneader so as he'll come and withdraw his complaint and I won't have to go to jail . . . and then you gets one like this shameless gentleman here who, as soon as my house is empty, comes after my missus . . ."

"Oh, don't mention it, Mr. Shir Ali . . . you're like a brother to me, your wife is like my sister, she's the light of my eyes . . . and you'll see that I'll be teaching this Dustali a lesson he won't forget in a hurry . . ."

"You're such a gent. I don't know how to thank you . . ."

Everyone breathed a sigh of relief. Surreptitiously staring at Tahereh, Asadollah Mirza said, "Now, Mr. Shir Ali, if you really want to make us all happy, do us the honor of coming to the colonel's house tonight and having supper with us . . . tonight we're having a celebration, a party."

Shir Ali bowed his head, " 'S very kind of you I'm sure, sir, but I wouldn't want to put you to the trouble."

Dear Uncle Napoleon threw an angry look at Asadollah Mirza and quietly whispered in his ear, "Asadollah, what kind of rubbish are you talking . . . this lout of a butcher's to come to my brother's house?"

Asadollah Mirza answered as quietly, "With your permission, I'll explain why later."

Quietly but in a furious tone Dear Uncle said, "I don't care if I never hear one of your damned explanations again . . . how can a butcher come and eat with us?"

Asadollah shook his head and said, "Fine, fine . . . then we can let him take Dustali . . . Mr. Shir Ali Khan . . ."

Dear Uncle put his hand over Asadollah's mouth and hissed, "All right, let him come, let him come."

Asadollah Mirza went on, "Mr. Shir Ali Khan, if you don't accept I'll be really upset . . . and your wife Tahereh is just like my sister to me . . . don't worry about Dustali, I'll send him off to bed."

A few minutes later uncle colonel's party had livened up again. Asadollah Mirza made Shir Ali—who was kneeling on the floor at the end of the room—drink two or three of glasses of uncle colonel's vintage wine.

After drinking a glass of wine at Asadollah Mirza's insistence, Dear Uncle Napoleon, who was extremely put out by the presence of a butcher at a gathering of his family, forgot about the family's high and mighty position, and his expression relaxed.

After Aziz al-Saltaneh had interceded for him, Dustali Khan was also given permission to be in the room, but he sat sulking and silent in a corner.

Asadollah kept plying Shir Ali with wine. When the butcher's thunderous laugh began to resound through the room, Asadollah knew that the wine was taking effect, and suggested that his wife Tahereh should dance; to everyone's astonishment Shir Ali agreed that his wife should dance.

They put a record on and Tahereh's beautiful, elegant body began to sway. Asadollah Mirza was clapping and repeating, "My God, I'd . . . My God, I'd . . ." And those who weren't too affected by the wine realized what he meant. Even the women in the family were cheered by Asadollah's cheerfulness and perhaps this was the only time in which malice and spite against Tahereh were not apparent in their glances.

After supper my father seemed extremely merry and jovial; once again he sat down next to Dear Uncle Napoleon and after a while suggested to him that he tell the rest of the story of the Battle of Kazerun, which, because of the dubious sound, had remained unfinished on the famous night of the party in uncle colonel's house. Dear Uncle mildly protested that it was a trivial subject, but as my father insisted, he agreed to talk about it. As soon as Mash Qasem heard mention of the Battle of Kazerun he stationed himself near them.

Dear Uncle adjusted his cloak over his shoulders, "Yes, it was a battle such as used to be fought in those days . . . now with these new inventions like machine guns and tanks and planes, bravery and a man's initiative take second place. There were us and four decrepit rifles . . . none of my men had the right equipment. Their stomachs were empty, their rations and pay weren't getting through . . . the one and only secret of our success was our faith in our cause, but the other side was well equipped, you understand. Khodadad Yaghi wasn't alone, he had the whole British Empire behind him, and if we had two or three good rifles, they were booty we'd taken from them . . . I had one good rifle and I'd given a couple out to my men . . ."

Mash Qasem interrupted, "You was kind enough to give one of 'em to me."

"Yes, I'd given one to Qasem . . . not, of course, that he was a good shot but because he was my orderly, and it was his duty to protect me . . . would you believe that during that time the English frequently plotted against my life . . . especially after Khodadad Khan was killed by me."

Mash Qasem said, "That was a good job you did, sir; if you hadn't killed that bastard, I don't know what kind of troubles there wouldn't have been in them parts."

My father said, "But you haven't told us how you were finally successful in killing Khodadad Khan."

"That was really God's work . . . because there were perhaps a hundred paces between us . . . I took aim right at his neck."

Mash Qasem objected, "Between his eyebrows."

"That's just what I meant . . . you see my rifle used to fire upward a little, I aimed at his neck so that I'd hit him in the middle of the forehead . . . I entrusted my soul to the Lord and pulled the trigger."

Mash Qasem slapped himself on the knee, "Bang bang . . . as God's my refuge . . . when the bullet hit his forehead he let out such a howl as all the mountains and desert shook."

"I realized from the yelling and the commotion the bandits made that the bullet had hit its target . . . all hell broke loose and they were running off in all directions . . . but we stuck with them. We took around thirty or forty of them prisoner . . ."

With a derisive smile Mash Qasem said, "Sir, what are you sayin'! Forty of 'em? God keep you, sir, you've fought so many battles you can't remember right . . . I counted 'em myself and they was just ten shy of three hundred . . . Khodadad's brother was one of 'em, too."

Asadollah Mirza, who was surreptitiously exchanging glances with Tahereh, said, "My God, what I wouldn't . . . Khodadad's brother, eh?"

Layli and I were near him and, realizing what his words meant, burst out laughing. Asadollah Mirza turned round and gave me a very reproachful look, "My dear boy, you don't laugh when your elders are talking." And he went back to ogling Tahereh.

Dear Uncle, who was vaguely staring into space, said, "Now, do you think after the English had taken all that trouble for all those years setting up Khodadad Khan, they would forget this? A year later, they'd lost one of their pawns, so they opened a dossier on me and it was touch and go they didn't wipe out my whole family."

With a philosophical expression on his face my father said, "When the going gets tough, the tough get going; to a wolf, the dust sent up by a flock of sheep's a sight for sore eyes."

Asadollah, still staring into Tahereh's eyes, said, "Oh, I'd do anything . . . to a wolf, eh?"

Dear Uncle asked, "What are you saying, Asadollah?"

"Nothing, I said that that's really true . . . that bit about the wolf's eyes is completely true."

My father said, "But then, your troubles weren't confined to the battles in the south . . . you gave the English a hard time in many places . . . and a wounded leopard is much more dangerous than a healthy one."

With a knowing smile Dear Uncle said, "But I'm no weeping willow to tremble in that kind of a wind . . . I didn't leave a single place for them where they were safe . . . during the Constitutional troubles I'd made so many sacrifices for the cause they wanted to blacken my reputation . . . to drag my name in the mud. They said it everywhere, I even heard they'd written it in the newspapers, that I'd had a hand in Colonel Liakhoff's bombardment of the parliament building . . . whereas in fact, well, it's true that I was part of the Cossack regiment but I swear by the sacred soul of my father that not a single bullet was fired from my rifle in all that. Well, why beat about the bush, Mash Qasem here was with me every step of the way, ask him what I said to Shapshal Khan."

Without waiting to be asked, Mash Qasem said, "Why should I lie? To the grave it's ah . . . ah . . . The Master here, God bless him, said such a thing to that Shapshal Khan, he was ready to melt away like water and hide himself seven yards underground, he was that put out."

Asadollah Mirza's eyes were wandering over Tahereh's elegant body; quietly he said, "Who was this Shapshal Khan person? . . . my God . . . my God, you'll come to no good, my little Shapshal Khan!"

Dear Uncle had heard what he said and explained, "How can you not know who Shapshal Khan was? Shapshal Khan was a Russian, and the tutor of Mohammad Ali Shah. In the whole of Iran there was no one as opposed to the Constitution as he was."

In a loud voice Asadollah Mirza said, "God damn him and may he come to no good!"

And still staring at Tahereh he said, "God willing, I've got big constitutional troubles of my own here . . ."

Uncle colonel realized what was going on and said in an angry voice, "Asadollah, shame on you!"

"Moment, moment, and so I've no right to be concerned about the constitution . . . and so you're all for tyranny, are you?"

For the first time Dustali Khan opened his mouth, "But you mean something else."

"Moment, I'm not following. This thief of everyone's honor is opening his mouth again . . . well, let me see, where is Mr. Shir Ali Khan?"

Shir Ali was busy chatting to uncle colonel's servant in the hall; he appeared in the doorway, "You wanted me, Mr. Asadollah Mirza, sir?"

"No, no, we were just saying what a splendid fellow you are . . . you carry on with your conversation."

Dear Uncle Napoleon continued with his story. "On the evening of that day, when they'd taken Malek al-Motakalemin and Mirza Jahangir Khan and the rest of those who were fighting for the constitution off to the Bagh-e Shah, Mohammad Ali Shah received Colonel Liakhoff and the officers of the Cossack regiment to thank them for their trouble, as you might say, and just as he was passing me I shouted out, 'Your majesty, you're making a mistake, these are good people, don't spill their blood.' Mohammad Ali Shah stopped short and frowned and in an undertone asked Mohammad Khan Amir al-Amara, his court minister, 'Who is this?' . . . and when they'd told him 'This is so-and-so, the son of so-and-so, and the present peaceful situation in the south of the country is due to his self-sacrificing efforts,' as God's my witness and on the sacred soul of my father, he went as red as a red mulberry. He didn't say anything, he just left, but the next day I was posted to Khorasan . . . and you can make enquiries about this. I wasn't alone, lots of people were present and witnessed it . . . God rest his soul, Madvali Khan was there . . . God rest his soul, Alireza Khan Azod al-Molk was there . . . and God rest his soul, Aliqoli Khan Sardar Asad was there . . . there were lots of people . . ."

Mash Qasem said, "I was there too. Why should I lie? To the grave it's ah . . . ah . . . it's like it was yesterday . . . when the Master said them words I swear by God in heaven that Shapshal Khan, it was like the ground was shakin' under his feet, every bit of his body was tremblin' like a willow . . . he didn't dare say a word to the Master here so he started on sayin' bad cuss words to me . . . I couldn't say a thing and I leaves it up to Him who's up there watchin' over us all."

Without paying any attention to Mash Qasem's interruption, Dear Uncle continued, "Now given all this, with such a past as I had, one that was so full of self-sacrifice, when they put it about that such and such a person under the command of Colonel Liakhoff had bombarded the parliament building—well, whose work do you think that was? Could it be anybody's but the English? Was there anybody except the English wanting to get revenge for the defeats they'd suffered?"

Nodding his head my father said, "Yes, that's absolutely right . . . and haven't they acted in exactly the same way toward Napoleon and a thousand other men? That hypocritical old wolf doesn't easily forget the blows it's received."

Dear Uncle's face clouded over. "Their hatred of Napoleon reached such a pitch that before he set off for St. Helena, they wouldn't even let him see his son . . . the day I started to fight against the English the history of Napoleon's life was there before my eyes, but it didn't change my decision."

Although I was almost drunk with pleasure at being with Layli, I couldn't ignore the conversation between my father and Dear Uncle. From one moment to the next, I doubted my father's sincerity more and more. My father was not the kind of person to swallow Dear Uncle's imaginary exploits, or to encourage him to talk about them. I wished I could plumb the depths of his mind and understand what he was planning.

Asadollah Mirza's voice rang out, "Moment, the English haven't turned up yet tonight . . . leave Hitler to deal with them . . . I want you to put that dance music on again so that Tahereh can dance."

The women, who were bored by the monotonous tale of Dear Uncle's self-sacrificing exploits, added their voices to his, "Run, boy, run, Layli dear, put the dance music record on."

A moment later Tahereh started dancing again. Shir Ali was sitting in the hallway more or less drunk, telling Dear Uncle's servant and one or two of the other domestics the story of his quarrels and brawls.

Asadollah made good use of Shir Ali's absence. Snapping his fingers, he circled Tahereh, at the same time letting his gaze travel over every curve and crevice of her elegant and beautiful body, and singing, "Sweet thing, I'm circling you . . . sweet thing, so tall and fine you are . . . sweet thing, such lips you have, sweet thing, such eyes . . ."

And as he circled her he bent at the knees and swayed his hips. Meanwhile Dustali Khan sulkily, and with poison in his gaze, stared at him, and Layli and I clapped and laughed with all the warmth and enthusiasm of young people in love.

PART TWO

PART TWO CONTENTS

ELEVEN

THE SAMOVAR WAS BUBBLING away on a wooden table beneath the vine pergola in the garden to our house. My mother had just made the tea for breakfast and my father was passing a saucerful of jasmine flowers back and forth under his nose and sniffing them as he waited his turn to be served. It was a Friday toward the end of the summer of 1941, and we were sitting there for breakfast, in our flannel pajamas as the weather was no longer too hot.

Suddenly the sound of footsteps coming from the yard attracted our attention. For Dear Uncle Napoleon to show up at such a time was unusual, especially as he had a severe frown on his face. His right hand was thrust out from his cloak and rested against his stomach, while with his left hand he angrily shifted the beads of his Moslem rosary back and forth. I had never seen Dear Uncle looking so preoccupied and upset. It was as if the sky had fallen in on his head. In a strangled voice he asked my father for a few minutes' private conversation, and in answer to my mother's invitation to sit and drink a glass of tea he shook his head and said, "Sister, it's far too late for your brother to drink any tea."

With a worried face my father accompanied him into the room with the French windows.

What in heaven's name could have happened? I couldn't remember even once in my whole life having seen Dear Uncle looking so melancholy and hopeless! Why was it far too late for him to drink any tea? He was just like someone who was going to have to mount the scaffold in a few minutes' time. I'd no idea what was going on and couldn't understand it at all. More than a year had passed since that thirteenth of August when I had suddenly fallen in love with Dear Uncle's daughter Layli.

In this period nothing extraordinary had happened, except that I had grown more in love with Layli with every day that passed, and had occasionally written her love letters, to which she had sent me loving answers. But we conveyed these letters to each other with a great deal of care. Once every few days Layli would borrow a novel from me, within the pages of which I had placed my love letter, and when she returned the book I would see her answer tucked between its pages. Like all the love letters of that period, ours were very romantic, to the point of morbidity, and talked about death and disaster and "that moment when my helpless body will be laid in the earth's dark heart." Apparently no one had stumbled on our secret. The main difficulty along the road of our love was the existence of Shapur, a.k.a. Puri, uncle colonel's son, who also wanted Layli, but fortunately his military service had intervened and the formal proposal and engagement party had been put off until after his discharge. In her letters to me Layli had written that if one day she were forced to become Puri's fiancée she would kill herself, and in my letters I had sincerely promised her that I would not allow her to go on such a journey alone. Nothing important had changed in the situation of the other members of the family, except that the examining magistrate Shamsali Mirza, who had been temporarily relieved of his duties with the ministry of justice, had been in this indeterminate state for such a long time that he had resigned from the ministry altogether and set up as an attorney.

Relations between Dustali Khan and Aziz al-Saltaneh had returned to normal, but the suitor of Aziz al-Saltaneh's daughter Qamar had, by some divine providence, decided to back out of his chivalrous proposal and had taken to his heels.

Relations between Dear Uncle Napoleon and my father were in a peculiar state. Apparently all was sweetness and light, and Dear Uncle was even closer to my father than before and admitted no one into his confidence as much as him, but my doubts and suspicions concerning my father's good intentions and sincerity increased daily, to such an extent that I was positive that in reality, in the depths of his heart, my father intended to destroy Dear Uncle. And the reason, as far as it could be fathomed by a fourteen or fifteen year old boy, was the setbacks my father had suffered as a result of the events of the previous year. My father's pharmacy—which before all this happened was one of the most important and respected not only in our neighborhood but throughout a whole area of the town, and which was always filled to overflowing with customers—had completely lost all its business after Seyed Abolqasem's accusations (which had been made at the instigation of Dear Uncle) against the pharmacist who managed the shop, and even after my father had replaced the pharmacist, no one would go there for medicine. Things had reached such a state that my father had taken on the son of the preacher Seyed Abolqasem as an apprentice in the shop, in order to restore its prosperity, but the things which Seyed Abolqasem had said about the medicines of the pharmacy being made with alcohol had become so firmly implanted in the minds of the people of the neighborhood that even the presence of the preacher's son among the employees had no effect.

When after two or three months of pointless struggling the pharmacy had gone bankrupt, and the empty shelves and bottles of sodium sulphate and boric acid had been brought and dumped outside our house, my father was in a strange state; sometimes I heard the curses and profanities he muttered under his breath and I saw other signs of the revenge he was plotting against those who had brought this on him. I was quite sure that Dear Uncle Napoleon was going to be the target of some terrible disaster. But my father was not a person to make a show of his malice and hatred. He was extremely friendly to Dear Uncle. The one thing I knew was that for a year now he had been flattering Dear Uncle more and more from one day to the next and beating the drum about his bravery and glory and might. I couldn't guess at what all this was leading toward, but someone who up to a year ago had even treated Dear Uncle's skirmishes with the insurgents when he had been in charge of a gendarmerie post as a ridiculous joke, was now elevating him to the status of a military leader on a par with Genghis Khan and Hitler.

With such helpful backing Dear Uncle ascended every day further up the ladder which my father had placed beneath his feet. The clashes with the insurgents in the south of the country (which before the events of a year ago had reached the stage that the "Battle of Kazerun" and the "Battle of Mamasani" possessed all the features of Austerlitz and Marengo) had gradually, under the influence of my father's promptings, changed to larger and more terrible battles in which Dear Uncle and his men had been face to face with the military might of the British Empire.

Of course in their hearts members of the family laughed at these fantasies, but no one dared express doubts about them, and if someone did dare to say to Dear Uncle that previously the battle of Kazerun had been a skirmish with Khodadad Khan Yaghi, Dear Uncle's furious protests would be heard and a fierce malice against the speaker would take hold of him.

Once when Dr. Naser al-Hokama had finished building a new addition to his house and had thrown a party to celebrate this, an interruption by Shamsali Mirza almost produced a major disaster.

In the midst of talking about the Battle of Kazerun Dear Uncle said, "I was there with about three thousand exhausted, hungry, poorly armed men, and against us there were four British regiments fully armed, with infantry, cavalry and all their artillery . . . the only thing that saved us was that famous tactic of Napoleon's at the battle of Marengo . . . I entrusted the right flank to Soltanali Khan, God rest his soul . . . and the left flank to Aliqoli Khan, God rest his soul . . . and I took responsibility for commanding the cavalry . . . mind you, what kind of cavalry . . . in Mohammad Ali Shah's time they called it the 'cavalry' but it was just a name . . . four lame hungry old nags . . ."

Mash Qasem interrupted, "But sir, God rest its soul, that bay horse of yours was worth forty ordinary horses, you'd have thought it was the great hero Rostam's horse Rakhsh. One tug on the reins and it was like an eagle flying down from the mountain to the valley . . ."

"All right, there was that one that was a real horse . . . can you remember what his name was, Mash Qasem?"

"Well now, why should I lie? To the grave it's ah . . . ah . . . 'sfar as I can remember you'd called him Sohrab."

"Well done . . . yes . . . your memory's stayed better than mine. His name was Sohrab." During these days Dear Uncle's behavior toward Mash Qasem had greatly improved. Because apart from my father who listened to these stories carefully and with apparent interest and pretended to believe every word of them, none of the rest of his audience showed any signs of believing him, and Dear Uncle felt the need—even more strongly than before—for a witness who could confirm his claims. This witness couldn't be anyone else but Mash Qasem, and this new role of his had transported Mash Qasem into a seventh heaven of happiness.

Dear Uncle went on as before. "It was sunset when we saw a rifle barrel with a white flag on it stuck up from behind a hill. I ordered them to stop firing. An English sergeant came toward us on horseback wanting to discuss a truce. The first thing I asked him was his rank; when he said he was a sergeant I said he couldn't discuss matters with me and that he should discuss things with one of my men who was of his own rank, I can't remember which of our fellows I delegated to talk to him."

"How can't you remember, sir? It's very strange how, God save the mark, you're forgettin' everythin' . . . it was me you gave the order to."

"No, now . . . why are you talking nonsense, Qasem? I think it was . . ."

"Why should I lie? To the grave it's ah . . . ah . . . it's like it was yesterday. You were walkin' up and down in front of the tent . . . field-glasses round your neck too. You said, 'Mash Qasem, I won't talk to this sergeant. See what he wants.' Then they brings the sergeant in front of me and he falls to the ground, all beggin' and pleadin' he was, and I couldn't understand his lingo, there was that Indian boy with him that was his interpreter . . . and he said how the sergeant says to tell the Master that their army's been destroyed . . . that we was to be generous and give 'em safe conduct . . . so I says tell him 'why hasn't his commandin' officer come? It's beneath the dignity of my master to be talkin' to a sergeant.' He says somethin' in his foreign lingo to the Indian. The Indian says he says how he swears by Morteza Ali he's wounded and can't move . . ."

Dear Uncle cut him off. "I didn't follow all these details . . . the conversation went on for a long time. When it was over and I'd given their men promise of safe conduct, I myself went and saw the colonel in charge, who'd been wounded. I stood to attention in front of that shattered enemy commander and greeted him . . . poor devil, a bullet had gone right through his larynx, but he couldn't stop himself, weak as he was he said, 'Monsieur, you from noble family, you aristocrat . . . you great commander . . . we English giving great importance to these matters . . .'"

It was at this moment that Shamsali Mirza, who had perhaps had a couple more glasses of wine than usual, interrupted and said, "God bless the man, what a pair of lungs he had! For someone whose larynx had been split from end to end, what a lot of talking he did!"

Dear Uncle burst out in such a way that everyone held their breath, "Politeness and intelligence and human decency are gradually deserting this family, and their place is being taken by vulgarity and shamelessness and disrespect toward one's elders and betters."

Having said this Dear Uncle stood up to leave, but the whole family flocked around him, and my father in his capacity as a pharmacist gave an eloquent speech on the scientific possibility of a man talking with his larynx split open and so was able to persuade Dear Uncle to come down off his high horse.

Without the slightest demur my father confirmed all of Dear Uncle's fantasies, and in particular he never forgot to add the sentence "It's impossible the English will forget this" at the end of Dear Uncle's adventures.

My father egged Dear Uncle on so much and made such dire predictions of the English seeking revenge that Dear Uncle gradually became suspicious of everyone and everything. He saw the English after him everywhere, to the extent that Mash Qasem said that for the past two or three months Dear Uncle had placed his revolver under his pillow every night, and we ourselves had heard him repeatedly say in a resigned, submissive voice, "I know they'll get me in the end. I'm not someone who's going to die a natural death."

After a while this manner of thinking affected Mash Qasem too, and I had personally many times heard him state his worries about the revenge of the English. "Well m'dear, why should I lie? To the grave it's ah . . . ah . . . of course it's not as much as the Master's done, but in my own way I've really given them English a run for their money. And they won't be forgettin' it, not for another hundred years!"

The only thing which throughout this year somewhat disturbed the outward amity and harmony between my father and Dear Uncle was the matter of Brigadier Maharat Khan.

I think his real name was Baharat or Baharot but in our area they always called him Brigadier Maharat Khan. Three or four months previously this Indian businessman had rented a little house which belonged to my father and was situated opposite our garden.

The day that Dear Uncle found out that my father had rented his house to an Indian he was even more disturbed than usual, but my father swore by all the saints in heaven that he hadn't known that the tenant who had rented his house was Indian. And this was despite the fact that I was present right from the beginning of my father's discussions with this Indian gentleman about renting the house, and that I well knew that my father had rented the house to him with full knowledge of his background and nationality.

On that day, faced by Dear Uncle's furious objections, my father—who had always tried to insinuate to him that the English were after him, either personally or through their Indian agents—brought a thousand reasons forward to prove that Brigadier Maharat Khan was entirely innocent and was not to be suspected under any circumstances. Dear Uncle apparently acquiesced, but it was clear that he believed the English had deliberately sent this Indian to rent somewhere near his house in order to keep an eye on what he was doing.

Later, of course, I realized that my father had done this deliberately, and he had even given the Indian a considerable discount on his rent. For a while Dear Uncle insisted that my father must get rid of the brigadier by any means possible, but another factor came to my father's help and this resulted in the brigadier's staying in the house. This factor was Asadollah Mirza. The reason that Asadollah Mirza intervened on the Indian's behalf was that Brigadier Maharat Khan had an English wife who was quite attractive and Asadollah had determinedly set his sights on her.

Asadollah Mirza had even made overtures of friendship to the Indian and two or three times invited him and his wife, to whom he referred as *"Lady Maharat Khan,"* round to his house. Dear Uncle was extremely annoyed with Asadollah over this. Once he had even threatened him, in front of the rest of the family, saying that if he had anything further to do with this Indian, he had no right to set foot in his—Dear Uncle's—house, but with a face that was all innocence Asadollah Mirza sprang to the Indian's defense. "Moment, and aren't we supposed to be Iranians . . . and aren't Iranians supposed to be famous for their hospitality? This poor man's our guest, he's alone, a stranger . . . once I translated for him that poem of Hafez's about the stranger's evening prayer and, would you believe it, he burst into tears like a cloud in the springtime . . . you can kill me, you can throw me out of your house, but I can't not comfort a man who's a stranger and a guest . . . especially now there's a war on . . . it's an age since the poor thing's had news of his family, of his mother, of his father . . ."

The upshot of it was that, although Dear Uncle, with some difficulty, put up with the presence of Brigadier Maharat Khan near his house, he did not relax his suspicions about him for an instant, and from time to time when he was talking about the vindictiveness of the English, he would refer to the Indian gentleman.

That morning when Dear Uncle and my father went into the room with the French windows and closed the door behind them, I was seized with curiosity, and I somehow felt that what was about to happen was something that would profoundly affect me.

I ate my breakfast and walked from the garden over to the storeroom behind the room with the French windows; its window opened onto the garden. I was dying to hear their conversation.

I climbed through the little window into the storeroom and peered through the crack in the door into the sitting room. Dear Uncle was standing tall and erect, his cloak over his shoulders, in front of my father. Under the cloak, there was a long-barreled revolver at his belt.

"I don't even trust my own brothers and sisters. I've decided to confide only in you, and I hope that in that same way that you've always been like a brother to me, you won't deny me your kindness and help at such a critical moment."

With a thoughtful expression on his face my father answered, "Well, whatever I do, I can see that on the one hand you're right. But on the other hand . . . it's a tricky business. And then what are you going to do with your wife and children?"

"I'll set off this very night, and you arrange for them to come along in a few days, in a way that won't attract attention."

"But you should consider that the driver who takes you is going to come back eventually, and how can you be sure he won't reveal your hiding place?"

"On that point you can set your mind at rest. I'll go with Dabir Khaqan's car . . . for years during the war his driver was under my command, he'd sacrifice his life for me. I mean he's like Mash Qasem in his feelings for me . . ."

"But I'm of the opinion that you should wait one or two days while I study all sides of the question."

In a voice that he tried to keep from being too loud Dear Uncle screamed, "But they won't wait. The British army is marching on Tehran . . . it's not at all unlikely that today or tomorrow they'll enter Tehran . . . believe me I'm not thinking of myself. I've lived with danger and I'm used to danger, as Napoleon says 'great men are the children of danger,' but I'm thinking of my little children. You can be sure that as soon as the English have entered Tehran the first thing they'll do is settle their old accounts with me."

My father once again shook his head and said, "Of course I know the English don't forget these old accounts but . . . how can we trick them? Do you imagine that in Nayshapur you'll be safe?"

At that moment it occurred to me that my father was reluctant to lose his backgammon partner.

Dear Uncle thrust his cloak aside, laid his hand on the holster of his revolver, and said, "First, six bullets in this are for them and the last is for me. It's impossible they take me alive. Second, when I leave here it'll look as though I'm going to Qom. No one—you hear, no one, not even my faithful driver—knows where I'm going. I'll even tell him I'm going to Qom. And then when we get out of the city gates I'll turn off toward Nayshapur."

"But when you've got there, then what will you do? You think they don't have one of their men in Nayshapur?"

"Dabir Khaqan's village isn't in Nayshapur itself. And I've thought that for now I'll arrive under an assumed name."

I didn't hear any more of their conversation. The horrifying prospect of being separated from Layli took shape before my eyes. The English were approaching Tehran and Dear Uncle wanted to get away from Tehran. O God, how could I live separated from Layli? Who knows how long this trip would last. This was the first time that I really felt the ugliness of war and the foreign occupation of our country. For twenty days now the allies had been overrunning the country, but this had had little effect on the lives of young people, apart from the fact that it had been announced the schools would open a few days later and that we had heard that food supplies had become scarce and expensive. But we ate as well as before and laughed as loudly as we used to.

On August 26, 1941, Dear Uncle, with his cloak over his shoulders and his revolver on his hip, together with Mash Qasem who had slung the strap of Dear Uncle's double-barreled shotgun over his shoulder, had assumed command of the garden and for a few days they did not allow us to come out of our rooms. Even during those days we hadn't taken the war very seriously, but now it became the most important thing of all for me. I wished I could have jumped into the midst of their discussions and shouted that the whole family was making fun of Dear Uncle's terror of the English; I wished I could have told him that, if my father had put this notion into his head, it was only to make him appear ridiculous in their eyes and that the English were not going to waste their time bothering to take revenge on some simple Cossack who had shot off a few bullets at a couple of footloose bandits during Mohammad Ali Shah's reign. But I knew that not only would my words have no effect but that I'd probably be scolded by my father and get a slap into the bargain.

I didn't stay there any longer. I went off to a quiet room and tried to think of a solution to this whole complicated dangerous business. In some way or another I had to stop Dear Uncle from going on this trip, but how? I don't know how long I thought about it without getting anywhere.

It was almost noon when I went despondently and wretchedly back to the garden. I caught sight of Mash Qasem. We greeted one another warmly and then I asked him what information he had.

"Well m'dear, the Master's thinkin' of goin' this evenin' to Qom for two or three days . . . the lucky devil, and no matter how much I asked him if he'd take me along so as I could make a little stop at Ghiasabad, he wasn't havin' it. Well, what can I do, the blessed Masumeh didn't want me, it was the Master she wanted . . ."

"Mash Qasem, how's he going? By train or car?"

"Well now, why should I lie? It's like he's goin' by car . . . because I heard him telephonin' Mr. Dabir Khaqan and sayin' how he should send his car and his driver Mamad over here . . ."

There could be no further doubt that Dear Uncle's decision to take this trip was completely serious.

O God, show me what to do! If I couldn't stop this trip of Dear Uncle's, Layli would go, too. How could I live without Layli? O God, wasn't there anyone who could help me? Just a minute . . . maybe . . .

perhaps . . . a light flashed through my mind: Asadollah Mirza. He was the one person I could at least explain my troubles to. His warm, kind glances were so reassuring. Running as fast as I could, I set off for Asadollah Mirza's house. I still didn't know what I wanted to say to him, but it seemed to me that a hopeful path was opening up.

His excellency lived near us, in an old-fashioned house, with an ancient maidservant. When I asked her for him she said he was still asleep. But I saw his head poking out of a window, and it was clear he had just got up. As soon as he caught sight of me in the yard he said, "Moment, moment, what are you doing here, lad?"

"Good morning, Uncle Asadollah. There's something very important I want to talk to you about, I'm sorry."

"You needn't be sorry, come on up."

He was sitting on the edge of his bed, wrapped in a flowered silk dressing-gown.

"What's the matter? You look upset!"

It took a while before I was able to tell him I was in love with Layli.

He gave a great guffaw of laughter. "Is that what you've come about? Well congratulations, lad! Now let's see, have we got to San Francisco yet or not?"

From the warmth I felt in my face I realized that I had turned crimson to the tips of my ears. For all the affection I felt for Asadollah, for a moment I hated him that he could talk in this disrespectful way, soiling our celestial love like this. He interpreted my silence badly. "So now I suppose you're looking for one of those doctors who do abortions? Don't you worry about it, I know a good dozen of them."

I shouted, "No, Uncle Asadollah, it's nothing like that."

"So there hasn't been any San Francisco? Answer . . . quick, now immediately, at the double; there hasn't been any?"

"No, no, no."

"So you've fallen in love so you can sit and play marbles with each other? It doesn't do for a grown up man to be shy."

With my head bowed I said, "Later, when we're older, we want to get married."

He laughed again and said, "If it was me, I wouldn't be able to wait . . . and by the time you've got round to it that girl'll have had three kids . . . if you want her to wait for you, you've got to take another line."

"What line should I take?"

"Off to San Francisco for a moment and back again!"

In the course of his joking and fooling I managed, with a lot of difficulty, to tell him about Dear Uncle's flight in Dabir Khaqan's car, and to ask him to do something so that Dear Uncle would change his mind about the trip.

Asadollah Mirza thought for a moment and said, "But if Churchill himself came and swore by a hundred and twenty-four thousand prophets that he wasn't interested in a warrant officer in charge of a motley crew of Cossacks, this Dear Uncle of yours wouldn't believe him. He's convinced that the English will forgive Hitler's sins but they won't forgive his. Let's see, you said he wants to set off as if for Qom and then go to Nayshapur?"

"Yes, but only I and my father know this."

Once again Asadollah Mirza thought for a moment. Suddenly his face lit up and he murmured, "Moment, moment, if the English also realize that he wants to go to Nayshapur, he'll certainly change his mind about going! We must do something so that the English realize he wants to run off to Nayshapur and that he realizes that the English have realized this."

And then in a teasing voice he said, "We'll save those poor English devils too, because otherwise they'll have to send a special bomber from London so that it can bomb Dabir Khaqan's car somewhere in all the twists and turns of that road of a thousand valleys and then there's a major danger threatening the plane and its pilot. Suddenly the Master, who's a champion shot, lets off his double-barreled shotgun and there goes the pilot's noble member."

While he was hurriedly getting dressed he was shouting at my stupefied and anxious face, "Forward to the English to save a great hero! . . . Stop press . . . collaboration of the secret service with a secret opponent and all for love! On the command, about turn! Quick march!"

I had no idea what kind of a plan he had in mind but his contented, happy face restored my confidence.

In the street, as he was slipping his arm into mine, he said, "Well now, let's see, tell me, lad, does Layli like you too, or not?"

In a modest tone I answered, "Yes, Uncle Asadollah, Layli likes me, too. But you must promise me you won't talk about this to anyone."

"You needn't worry about that, but tell me how long is it since you fell in love?"

Without any hesitation I answered, "From the thirteenth of August last year."

Laughing, he said, "I bet you know the hour and the minute too!"

"Yes, at a quarter to three . . ."

His shrieks of laughter rose into the sky so loudly that I burst out laughing too. When his laughter quieted down he placed his hand on my shoulder and said, "But I have to give you a few bits of advice, lad. First, don't show her too much that you like her . . . second, if you see that she's getting away from you, don't forget San Francisco."

Once again I blushed with embarrassment and didn't answer. Suddenly Asadollah Mirza stopped in his tracks and said, "Now I'm going to manage things so that they won't separate this child from you, but what are you going to do about that blabbermouth? As soon as Puri's military service is over, he and Layli are supposed to get engaged."

At the thought of this my whole body began trembling violently. He was right, if something like that happened there was nothing I could do. When Asadollah Mirza saw my anguished, unhappy face he laughed again and said, "Moment, don't be too worried. God's on the side of lovers."

We had almost reached the garden. He looked this way and that and when he saw there was no one in the alleyway he knocked at the door of the Indian's house. I didn't have a chance to ask him what he meant by this because a moment later the English wife of the brigadier opened the door. Asadollah Mirza's eyes glittered. In English he said, *"Good morning, my lady."*

With my two or three years of high school English I could see that Asadollah Mirza didn't know English well, but he spilled the words out one after another in such a way that it made you not so sure. With glances and gestures he engaged the English woman in conversation, and he managed things so that even though she didn't want to invite him into the house she was left with no alternative. She said that her husband had gone out but that he would be back soon. Faced with his lordship's warm ingratiating words she had to invite us to sit and wait for her husband's return. A moment later Asadollah Mirza and I were ensconced in Brigadier Maharat Khan's sitting room. The English woman offered him a glass of wine.

When, in response to our host's offer of a glass of wine, I said that I didn't drink wine, Asadollah Mirza frowned and said, "Moment, moment, you fall in love but you don't drink wine? If you're a child you've no right to fall in love, and if you're an adult you've no right not to drink wine . . . take a glass."

And when I had no choice but to take a glass, he said quietly, "You should remember this, too, that from the hand of a pretty woman you shouldn't refuse even deadly poison."

And immediately he busied himself in conversation with the brigadier's wife, or the *"lady,"* as he called her; my presence there was no hindrance to him and he frequently interrupted his broken English phrases with expressions (in Persian) of undying devotion, "*Good wine . . . my God, what I wouldn't do for you . . . very good wine . . .*"

The English woman started to laugh at his gestures and glances and sometimes she would ask the meaning of the Persian phrases that flowed from his lips.

A few minutes hadn't gone by before the Indian gentleman returned. At first he was surprised, and perhaps somewhat upset, to see Asadollah Mirza in his house, but his lordship very quickly cheered him up. The brigadier knew Persian but he spoke it in an idiosyncratic way and with an accent. After a few minutes in which the conversation drifted this way and that, and touched especially on news of the war, Asadollah Mirza brought the conversation round to the point of his visit and said that Dear Uncle Napoleon was thinking of going on a trip to Qom and that he—meaning Asadollah Mirza—as a friendly gesture, wanted the Indian gentleman to be there when Dear Uncle was getting into the car, in order to bid him goodbye, and for him during the course of the conversation to mention, casually and naturally as it were, the name of the town Nayshapur.

With some surprise the brigadier asked why. Asadollah Mirza said that there was a joke involved and then he so livened up the chat with laughter and fooling that the Indian made no further objections. He only asked how he was to know when Dear Uncle was setting off so that he could come out of his house to say goodbye.

"Well now, what do you mean, brigadier! It's not as if our alleyway were the main square of the city with a thousand cars going through it every day. When you see a car has come and parked outside the garden you'll realize that's the moment the master's setting off."

"Sahib, it so happens that I am thinking of something that is extremely natural for saying Nayshapur . . ."

"I'm eternally grateful . . . you are really being too kind, oh yes indeed."

"Sahib, how many days is the Master being in Qom?"

"Well, I don't rightly know, I think he'll stay seven, eight, perhaps ten days."

"Sahib, how can the Master put up with the being away from his family?"

Asadollah guffawed with laughter and said, "Well, these days the master's natural vitality's *bahot* wilted."

This was an expression which Asadollah Mirza seemed to have learned from the Indian, and from the situations he used it in, and the people to whom he applied it, it was clear that the phrase was used to indicate the condition of someone who could not perform his conjugal duties.

Laughing as he did so, Asadollah Mirza repeated the phrase, "When women are sure that the natural vitality's *bahot* wilted, they don't raise any objection to their husbands' going on trips, oh no, indeed not."

Asadollah Mirza's laughter set the Indian laughing, too, and the meeting came to an end in an atmosphere of happiness and pleasantries. We left the Indian's house with Asadollah Mirza's eyes still glued to the tall form of Lady Maharat Khan. Naturally, before we left, Asadollah Mirza put his head out to be sure there was no one in the alleyway.

I accompanied him a few steps of the way toward his house. With a cheerful look on his face he said, "Rest assured, as things are now, Dear Uncle won't be going anywhere, at least he won't be going to Nayshapur, and your little Layli will stay with you, and you for your part should give some thought to San Francisco."

"Uncle Asadollah, please don't say those things!"

Asadollah Mirza raised his eyebrows and said, "Then it's possible that your vitality's *bahot* wilted too, and in the flower of your youth at that."

I returned home with a heart filled with hope. Whichever way I looked I saw no sign of my father; I asked our servant where he was and he said that he had gone with the Master into the room with

French windows. I had to know everything that Dear Uncle was doing and saying. Layli's departure, and a dangerous separation for both of us, all hung on a hair and I couldn't leave anything to chance. Once again I got myself into the storehouse behind the sitting room. Dear Uncle was standing sad-faced in front of my father and quietly spelling out his final instructions, "I'll send a telegram in the name of Mr. Mortazavi . . . of course I won't mention the children. When I say send on the baggage you're to take it as meaning my wife and children. I especially need your help even more now, because I've decided to take Mash Qasem along with me, too."

"Why have you suddenly changed your mind?"

"I thought that my going without Mash Qasem, as he's from Qom, might arouse suspicion. Outwardly we have to do things in such a way that their agents don't get suspicious. In particular I'm asking you to say to the driver, when the car's about to set off, that as the road to Qom's very busy these days he's to drive carefully."

"Have no worries on that score."

Like a Roman general going off to war, Dear Uncle gathered the skirts of his cloak and draped them over his left shoulder as if he were wearing a toga; placing his right hand on my father's shoulder, he said, "I hand over command of the rear guard to you; in my absence you are my representative."

Then he drew himself up to his full height and left the room.

An hour later Dabir Khaqan's car was waiting outside the garden door. The members of the family had all gathered in the garden to say goodbye to Dear Uncle. Naneh Bilqis had a tray with a mirror and a copy of the Quran on it, for the goodbye ceremony.

Poor little Layli had no idea of her father's real destination, but although I tried to be calm, my heart was filled with confused emotions and an untoward anxiety. Even though Asadollah Mirza had convinced me that, given how he had arranged things, it was impossible that Dear Uncle would be going to Nayshapur, or if he did go that he would stay there, I was still extremely worried. Every now and then I glanced over to where Asadollah was busy laughing and joking in the midst of the family group, and he would answer me with a meaningful, reassuring look.

Dear Uncle came into the garden dressed in his travelling clothes, but before kissing everyone goodbye he began looking for

Mash Qasem, and became annoyed that he wasn't there. In an angry tone he said to Naneh Bilqis, "Put that tray down and go and see where that idiot Mash Qasem has got to at a time like this."

But Naneh Bilqis hadn't even left the garden before Mash Qasem entered it and made straight for Dear Uncle. Before Dear Uncle had a chance to say anything to him he said, "Sir, you know best but please forget about this here trip. Just now in the bazaar they were sayin' as how the English are six miles outside Qom . . . they're sayin' how they've got rifles and field-guns that can shoot nine miles . . ."

Dear Uncle threw him a contemptuous look and said, "So now they're trying to frighten me with the English!" And with his eyes fixed on the highest branches of the walnut tree he recited:

"We've no complaint against the will of God—
The lion does not disdain the raging flood."

But Mash Qasem went on trying, "You know me, sir, I'm not afraid of these things, but why should a man make trouble for himself when there's no need? . . . the blessed Masumeh herself, who's shrine's there in Qom, doesn't want us to fall into the hands of them there English . . ."

"If you're so afraid, stay here and hide in the cellar like an old woman!"

It seemed as if he were really annoyed with Mash Qasem since he tucked his bundle of bedding under his arm and said, "I'm not afraid of the English nor of all their ancestors either!" And he set off for the garden door.

At this moment the preacher Seyed Abolqasem entered, panting for breath. "I've heard you're going on a pilgrimage to the shrine. God willing it'll go well and bring you good fortune."

Whenever my father happened to bump into this preacher he tried to stay calm, but I always saw hatred and a longing for revenge flash in his eyes. It was clear that the pain of his pharmacy's failure was still fresh in his heart.

That day when he saw the preacher he said with an artificial laugh, "Your excellency, sir, how is your son doing?"

"You are always in his thoughts."

"Does he still have those same feelings for Shir Ali the butcher's wife or has he forgotten about her?'

The preacher glanced uneasily around and said, "I must ask you not to make such jokes . . . we're hoping to get him engaged to a very nice girl in a day or two . . . the daughter of Haji Alikhan Ma'mar Bashi . . ."

Asadollah Mirza jumped into the conversation. "Wonderful, wonderful, congratulations! She's a really, really nice girl! And what a fine family! What a beautiful and sensible girl! Apart from the fact that she had a husband, Shir Ali's wife wasn't at all fit to join your family. But Ma'mar Bashi's daughter's a very nice girl, I've seen her a couple of times at my sister's house . . ."

Dear Uncle was ready to leave. "Well, farewell to you all, I'm on my way."

And he started kissing everyone present. At this moment Mash Qasem ran back into the garden from the street. He took Dear Uncle aside and whispered something to him in his ear. The color drained perceptibly from Dear Uncle's face, but a moment later he puffed out his chest and in a rather loud voice said, "So what if he's there?"

I guessed that Mash Qasem had told Dear Uncle that the Indian gentleman was out by the car. As he was going toward the garden door Dear Uncle told the children in a loud voice that he would bring them back a present of *sohan*, the local candy made in Qom, and to the adults he said that he would pray for them at the shrine.

Dabir Khaqan's car was waiting at the door, with Dear Uncle's luggage tied down on its roof. The Indian was walking up and down beside the car. As soon as he saw him Dear Uncle said, "How lucky to see you, brigadier, and to be able to say goodbye to you."

"Have a good trip, sahib."

Dear Uncle sat in the back of the car and Mash Qasem took his place beside the driver. At the same time Dear Uncle kept up his conversation with the Indian, "Yes, it's quite a while since I've been on a pilgrimage to Masumeh's shrine . . ."

The Indian cut him off, "But aren't you afraid, sahib, that the road might be unsafe with all these goings on?"

"No, my dear sir, that's just talk, rumors, the fighting's over . . . and then I've faith that the blessed Masumeh will protect her own pilgrims."

All the relatives were crowded around the car, but the Indian wasn't going to give up.

Asadollah Mirza, who I'd expected to pay more attention to this conversation than anyone else, was busy exchanging glances with

Lady Maharat Khan, who was peering into the street from behind her lace curtains. I had my eyes fixed anxiously on the Indian's mouth.

"Sahib, you aren't taking your lady wife with you?"

I could guess that Dear Uncle was raging inwardly, but he answered in an apparently calm voice, "No, I won't be staying more than a few days."

"But sahib, however short separation might be it is being very hard on the heart, as the poet says, 'My love's in Lahavard, while I am here in Nayshapur. . . .'"

I stared at Dear Uncle's face. When he heard the name "Nayshapur" come from the Indian's mouth he suddenly gave such a start that it was as if someone had passed an electric current through his body. For a moment he stared at the Indian with his mouth wide open, and then in a voice that could hardly struggle out of his throat he said to the driver, "Mamad, drive on!"

The engine started, the driver revved it and everyone took a step backwards. The car set off and dust filled the alleyway.

I made my way over to Asadollah Mirza and looked at him. He put his hand on my shoulder and said quietly, "Dear Uncle's goose is well and truly cooked. You can go and sleep easy . . ."

At this moment Dear Uncle's wife's voice rose above the hubbub, "Don't forget tonight . . . we're having *ash-reshteh* soup, to remember the Master and give him a good send off."

Asadollah Mirza quickly went over to the Indian, who was about to return to his house and quietly said to him, "Brigadier, you said it beautifully . . . well done!"

And then he went on in a louder voice, "But the Master's wife's cooked *ash-reshteh* tonight, and they're asking you and your wife to do us the honor of joining us."

Everyone looked at Asadollah in astonishment, because relations with the Indian were not of the kind that involved their being invited to the house, but Dear Uncle's wife could not refuse an invitation now and she said, "Of course, they'll be more than welcome."

The Indian stood on ceremony, too. "No, sahib, we won't trouble you . . . there'll be many opportunities, another day . . ."

But Asadollah Mirza wasn't giving up so easily. "Moment, brigadier, you're like a brother to us. What do you mean, 'trouble'? I promise you the Master's wife will be very upset if you refuse her invitation!"

And he turned his face toward Dear Uncle's wife. "Isn't that so, ma'am? I know the kind of person you are . . . of course you'll be upset . . ."

"Sahib, perhaps my wife will be being busy . . . perhaps I might be able to be coming by myself . . ."

"Well, if your wife is busy you can't leave her alone, and we'll have to leave it for another time. But please, ask her . . ."

And he glanced over at the window of the Indian's house. When he saw the English woman behind the window he shouted across, *"My Lady! Lady Maharat Khan!"*

And when the English woman stuck her head out of the window he invited her to supper in his broken English. Lady Maharat Khan said simply that if her husband had no other plans, she had no objection.

"You see, brigadier . . . and so we'll certainly expect you. You are doing us a great honor, oh yes indeed."

The Indian promised he would be there and we went back to the garden. I went over to Asadollah Mirza again and said, "Uncle Asadollah . . ."

But he cut me off, "Let me see now . . . Dustali, tonight you'd better keep your eyes to yourself! Because this Brigadier Maharat Khan has two cobras that he keeps in a cage in his house, and if anyone starts ogling his wife he takes one of these snakes and throws it in the fellow's bed . . . not at all funny! Don't think I'm joking! Do you want me to take you now to see the snakes?"

Asadollah Mirza spoke in such a serious way that Dustali Khan turned pale. "Good God, are you telling the truth, Asadollah?"

"You bet your life I am! . . . of course he doesn't tell people why he keeps them, he doesn't even let on that he has any snakes . . . but Lady Maharat Khan told me one day."

Dustali Khan looked over his shoulder and said, "Now please don't mention the name of Lady Maharat Khan in front of Aziz al-Saltaneh, because tomorrow she'll be imagining that I'm in love with this English woman. It was your jokes that started all that ruckus last year."

TWELVE

AT THE BEGINNING of the evening all our close relatives were gathered in Dear Uncle's house. Although I was very happy to be together with Layli and away from Dear Uncle's watchful eyes, occasionally I'd fall to thinking of Dear Uncle's trip and then a kind of horror would take hold of me from head to toe. A few hours had gone by since Dear Uncle's departure and I had no idea where he was. Asadollah Mirza had assured me that Dear Uncle hadn't gone to Nayshapur, but I knew very well that he wasn't the kind of person who would go toward Qom when according to Mash Qasem the English were within six miles of it. And so where was he?

At every moment I wanted to ask Asadollah Mirza's opinion, but he was so deeply engaged in conversation with Lady Maharat Khan that it was impossible to get near him.

In the midst of the party's cheerful laughter and chatter my father was called to the front door. Hoping that there was some news of Dear Uncle I went to the door after him.

It was Seyed Abolqasem's son. He said that his father was asking that my father come by to see him for a moment. At first my father was livid and said that he would never set foot in the house of that worthless fake Seyed, but the messenger's insistent pleading—he said it was an important matter, a matter of life and death—finally convinced him to go. When he was ready to set off I managed, by pleading and begging, to get him to let me come along too.

"All right, all right, you come, too . . . but I can't understand why you'd want to leave a party to come to a preacher's house!" When we reached Seyed Abolqasem's house the preacher's son acted like someone who wanted to enter a place surreptitiously. First he glanced all round, and when he saw that the street was empty he knocked at the door in a special way. The Seyed himself opened the door, quickly ushered us into the yard, and closed the door again.

"This way please, this way, if you'd go into the sitting room . . ."

My father went ahead and I followed him into the sitting room. We both stopped dead in our tracks with astonishment. Dear Uncle Napoleon was sitting on a mattress, still in the same travelling clothes, slumped back against some cushions. And Mash Qasem was there too, kneeling on the floor at the end of the room.

"You? What are you doing here, sir? But didn't you go to Qom?"

Dear Uncle's face was even paler and more contorted than usual. In a strangled voice he said, "Please, sit down and I'll explain . . . but I asked that you come alone, and now this boy . . ."

My father interrupted him, "The Seyed's son didn't say anything about that. He just said that the Seyed had something he needed to talk to me about."

Dear Uncle turned to me, "There's a good lad, go in the yard for a moment, I've something private I have to discuss with your father."

I immediately left the room. Seyed Abolqasem was just getting on his donkey to go out; when he saw me he said, "Hey boy, do me a favor, I've sent my son on an errand . . . there's no one in the house, bolt the door behind me as I go out, and tell the Master I'll be back in half an hour."

I closed the door behind the preacher. The preacher's wife wasn't there, his son had gone out, the situation couldn't have been better for me. I stood behind the door to listen to their conversation. Dear Uncle was saying, "When I say the English don't take their eyes off me for a minute, my brothers and the rest of the family say I'm exaggerating . . . but did you see how they'd discovered my plan to go to Nayshapur! Did you see how he talked about Nayshapur?"

My father said, "But don't you think this Indian just happened to say the poem by coincidence?"

"My dear sir! I'm supposed to be going to Qom; no one besides you and me knows that in fact I'm going to Nayshapur. And then this Indian just accidentally at the last moment recites that 'My love's in Lahavard, while I am here in Nayshapur' verse?"

Mash Qasem jumped into the conversation too. "Why should I lie? To the grave it's ah . . . ah . . . even I didn't know the Master wanted to go to Nayshapur. What buggers them English are! . . . O God, just let me go on a pilgrimage to the saintly Hasan's tomb so's I can light a candle to him and he'll destroy them English. You don't know what miracles the saintly Hasan's performin', I'd die for him, I would . . . there was a man in our town once who . . ."

Dear Uncle cut him off, "That's enough, Qasem! Let us talk, will you! Now what do you suggest I do? When I left the town today, however much I thought about it I couldn't see my way clear, and so through back streets and I don't know what we came here to Seyed Abolqasem's house . . . and now I'm to go back home so that this Indian will immediately inform London . . . I'll bet you anything you like that now that Indian is lying in wait with a telescope behind a window in his house spying on what's going on in our home . . ."

My father interrupted him, "Then I've some good news to give you. At this very moment the Indian brigadier is in the sitting room of your house eating *ash-reshteh* at the gathering for your send-off!"

Dear Uncle suddenly froze to the spot as if electrocuted, and in a voice that sounded as though it were coming from the bottom of a well he said in broken phrases, "What? What? . . . the brigadier . . . the Indian brigadier . . . in my house . . . mine? Then they've stuck the dagger into my back?"

When he heard this news Dear Uncle's condition worsened. His face turned a whitish yellow, his upper lip and his whole mustache trembled. He spoke in broken, incomprehensible phrases.

My father seemed to be enjoying torturing Dear Uncle in this way. But of course he outwardly showed himself to be sympathetic and concerned. Once more he turned the knife in Dear Uncle's wound. "As you yourself say, they stuck the dagger into your back . . . though it seems to me that the instigator isn't the Indian fellow . . . they've a thousand ways to close their files . . ."

He was silent for a moment and then went on, "I've never had the slightest suspicion of Brigadier Maharat Khan, but tonight in your house I was a bit worried about his wife. That English woman . . ."

In a strangled tone, his eyes popping out of their sockets with rage and astonishment, Dear Uncle cut him off. "Then the brigadier's wife came to my house, too? All of a sudden people have taken it into their heads to make my house a meeting place for the British Army's General Staff, have they? What I have to know is, who brought them to my house?"

My father wasn't going to give up; with a thoughtful, mysterious air he said, "The thing which made me suspicious of her was that when she was looking through your photo album she stared a great deal at a big old photo of you in your Cossack uniform . . . and when someone there said it was a photograph of you she showed it to her husband and said something in English that I didn't understand and then they whispered to each other for a moment."

Dear Uncle, who had been staring at my father's mouth wide-eyed and with his own mouth wide open, suddenly clasped his hand against his heart, moaned, and slumped to one side.

My father ran over to him and said, "The Master's fainted . . . Mash Qasem, run and get Dr. Naser al-Hokama."

Dear Uncle suddenly raised his head and screamed out with all the strength left in his body, "No . . . no . . . sit down . . . I'm perfectly all right . . . Dr. Naser al-Hokama's a lackey of the English . . . his cousin works for the Anglo-Iranian Oil Company."

While he was massaging Dear Uncle's hands my father said to Mash Qasem, "Run and get a bowl of water."

Mash Qasem ran quickly into the yard. I hid myself in a corner until he took the bowl of water back into the sitting room. A swallow of water was enough to bring Dear Uncle back to himself. Leaning back against the cushions and with his eyes closed he whispered to himself:

"When once a savage lion's cornered you
Accept your fate—what else is there to do?"

In a reproachful voice my father said, "This accepting your fate talk isn't like you. You've spent your life in the struggle, you can't give up like this and let yourself be borne along by whatever happens. Great men are recognized as such at times of crisis . . . they appear in the midst of catastrophe . . . excellence and magnanimity and leadership . . ."

Dear Uncle raised his head and with a thoughtful face said, "You are right. This is no time to take a back seat, in fact it's impossible to take a back seat. We must continue the struggle. But the first factor for carrying on the struggle is that I have to stay alive, and with the malice they have against me it's impossible the English will leave me alone. Today I stopped outside the city gate and stood at a café there to drink a glass of tea. You should have heard the stories about their atrocities that the people coming up from the south were telling."

It was a long time since Mash Qasem had said anything. He nodded his head and said, "God help us all, so far they've slaughtered two and a half million folks. God help Ghiasabad near Qom. Because the folks in Ghiasabad have really hammered them English . . . Ghiasabad's done more 'n all the other places in the country put together . . . why there was a man in our town who . . ."

Dear Uncle impatiently said, "Qasem! Enough! Let us think about the difficulties of our own situation."

Then he turned to my father, "What in your opinion should I do now?"

My father stroked his chin and said, "In my opinion your continued existence is necessary for the country. You have to keep yourself alive for the sake of the people, and in a blind alley like this the best way is to hit the enemy by means of an enemy of his own. In my opinion your only means of salvation is the Germans. You have to place yourself under the protection of the Germans."

"The Germans! But there's neither hide nor hair of them left here."

"Don't you be so sure, sir! As far as appearances are concerned they've gone, but they have an immense underground organization in this very city. In my opinion you should write a letter to the Germans asking them to place you under their protection."

Dear Uncle was leaning forward with his neck stretched out, listening intently. My father went on, "It just so happens I know a means of sending such a letter . . ."

"Who should I write the letter to?"

"To Hitler in person."

Mash Qasem burst out joyfully, "Brilliant! I was wantin' to say exactly that same thing. If there's one man in the world, that man is Hitler."

"So you pen a letter to Hitler asking that they look after you for a few months, until their army gets here, because there can be no doubt that in a few months' time the German army will be here."

For a few minutes Dear Uncle, my father and Mash Qasem talked amongst themselves in such a way that it was difficult to make out the subject of their conversation. But it became clear when Mash Qasem got up and started looking for a pen and paper. The preacher's inkstand was on a shelf in that same sitting room. Dear Uncle started writing with my father dictating the contents of the letter to him.

"If you would write as follows: 'To his esteemed excellency Adolf Hitler, great and glorious leader of Germany; in token of profound devotion and respect to your exalted glory. Your humble servant is sure that your exalted self is sufficiently aware of your humble servant's and his late father's long and arduous struggles against English colonial adventurism, nevertheless I shall take the liberty of setting out my struggles below . . .' have you written that?"

Dear Uncle was busy carefully writing.

My father said, "Now write down a description of the Battle of Mamasani and the Battle of Kazerun and the other clashes with the English you were involved in, and then make some reference to Brigadier Maharat Khan and his English wife, and the fact that they've been detailed to keep you under observation . . . of course we're not absolutely certain that this Indian is an English spy, but you write down with no ifs, ands or buts that you're sure he's one of their agents and . . ."

Dear Uncle interrupted him, "What do you mean, we're not absolutely certain? I'm as certain as the fact that I'm here in this room that this Indian is one of their agents and that he's been detailed to keep me under observation."

"In any case write about him to the German leader . . . and at the end of the letter write down the phrase 'Heil Hitler.'"

"And what does that mean?"

"It's a modern German custom. It means 'Long live Hitler' . . . especially don't forget to write that you're ready to undertake any service on their behalf, and ask him to arrange for your immediate protection."

With an innocent look on his face Dear Uncle asked, "And then where will they take me?"

"They'll take you to Berlin. . . . and then a few months later they'll bring you back here with the German army . . . in any case you'll have to put up with being separated from your wife and children for a few months."

"I couldn't ask them to take Mash Qasem with me, too?"

"No reason why not; add a couple of lines at the end about Mash Qasem saying he's in mortal danger, too."

Mash Qasem nodded and said, "Well now, why should I lie? To the grave it's ah . . . ah . . . them English have really had enough of me, too . . . I killed that many of 'em at the Battle of Kazerun! It's like it was yesterday . . . with one swipe of my sword I slashed off the head of one of their colonels and it fell at his feet . . . and I hit him so fine he never realized . . . his body fell down, too, with no head on it, and for a good half hour it was swearin' and cussin' at me . . . finally I stuffed a handkerchief down his throat . . ."

Dear Uncle angrily interrupted him, "That's enough, Mash Qasem! And so how did you say you would get this letter to Hitler in a hurry?"

"Don't worry about that, I know one of their men here who can radio your message, just as you've written it, to Berlin. You can be quite sure that they'll be in touch with you within a couple of days . . ."

"And what am I to do till I get news from them?"

"In my opinion it's best that you go home, don't show them that you're at all concerned about anything, be really friendly with the Indian . . . say the car broke down on the way and you had to come back."

"You don't think that . . ."

"Obviously the English won't reach Tehran before five or six more days are up, and you should act as if you couldn't care less about them . . . in principle it's better if this Indian—if in fact he really is one of their agents—should report that you're in your house, so that they don't take any further steps before their army gets here. I'll go back now, and you come in a quarter of an hour or so, looking like someone who's just got back from a journey. In the meantime make a fair copy of the letter, slip it to me when no one's looking, and you're all set."

My father made a few more recommendations concerning the humble, imploring tone of the letter to Hitler, Dear Uncle's announcement that he was ready to be of service to the Germans, and the necessity for revealing the connections between Brigadier Maharat Khan and the English, and was then ready to leave.

I immediately got myself to the other side of the yard where I sat down on the step with my back against the door to the street; with an innocent look on my face I pretended to have dozed off.

"Get up, let's go . . . don't go to sleep in other people's houses."

While we were on the way back home I asked my father, "By the way, Dad, why didn't Dear Uncle go to Qom?"

It seemed that my father was deeply involved in thinking about his plot, because I repeated the question two or three times before he heard. In an impatient voice he said, "The car broke down along the way and they came back."

While we were on the way home I watched him out of the corner of my eye. He was talking to himself, though no words were audible. I involuntarily raised my head to the heavens and said under my breath, "O God, put it into my father's heart not to start any more arguments."

I had no idea what my father wanted to do with Dear Uncle's letter to Hitler, but I decided that in any case I was not going to sit idly by; I was going to try to neutralize whatever steps he was taking that might once again lead to battles and rows likely to bring sorrows and suffering down on my head.

The main living room of Dear Uncle's house was still full of bustle and noise, and the guffawing laugh of Asadollah Mirza could be heard from the middle of the yard.

I saw Layli before anyone else; she was laughing loudly and for a moment I forgot all my worries. When I asked her why she was laughing, she said quietly, "You should have seen how Asadollah has been teasing Dustali Khan."

Dustali Khan had a grim frown on his face; every now and then he tried to manage a laugh but he wasn't being very successful. As usual Asadollah Mirza had had a drink or two; he was describing to the Indian his memories of a night on the prowl he had spent with Dustali Khan. "And then after all this arguing Mr. Dustali Khan was left alone with the girl but—God forbid such a thing should ever happen to you, brigadier—it seems his natural vitality was quite *bahot* wilted . . ."

His lordship gave another great guffaw and, with his shoulders shaking with laughter, went on, "And he was young then too, when his vitality was *bahot* wilted . . . so now his vitality's more *bahot* wilted than ever."

Asadollah Mirza's laughter had set the English woman laughing; she constantly praised him with the English word *"lovely"* and such like expressions and begged him to explain everything to her in English.

Although Asadollah didn't really know English, he wasn't a man to let that stop him, and he began, *"You know, my dear Lady Maharat Khan . . ."*

In a quiet smothered voice Dustali Khan said, "I know a good story about Emamzadeh Qasem."

Asadollah Mirza assumed a serious face and said, "Ladies, gentlemen . . . *ladies and gentlemen* . . . silence, please! Our noble friend, that brilliant orator Mr. Dustali Khan, will relate for our esteemed listeners the story of Emamzadeh Qasem . . . and now I hand the floor over to him."

Dustali Khan knew that his words would never shine anywhere Asadollah Mirza was and, despite the urging of everyone present, he remained silent.

In a reproachful tone Asadollah Mirza said to him, "Dustali you're making me look silly in front of the brigadier and his wife . . . the brigadier and his wife are my guests tonight, and you mustn't deprive them of your charming conversation."

Dustali Khan angrily said, "The brigadier and his wife are friends of all of us . . . and in fact it was because I asked that they came tonight."

"What a nerve you've got, Dustali!"

"Oh yes? Well, you invited the brigadier and he didn't accept, but when I insisted they come, he accepted."

Asadollah Mirza said with a laugh, "All right, let's pretend that Mrs. Brigadier Maharat Khan is my guest, and the brigadier is your guest!"

But Dustali Khan was angry, and like a child who stubbornly argues and contradicts himself he shouted out, "You've no right to say that! I invited Brigadier Maharat Khan and his wife here tonight and they are my guests!"

At this point I became aware of amazed looks on the faces of everyone present; they were staring at the entrance, and I turned to see what was there. The tall figure of Dear Uncle, who was still wearing his leather travelling goggles, was standing in the frame of the living room doorway; there could be no doubt that he had heard Dustali Khan's last sentence, because he glared at his face in astonished fury.

There was a short moment of silence, and then the noise of everyone's questions as to why Dear Uncle had returned set the party in an uproar. With a smile on his lips Asadollah Mirza glanced over at me and winked; I thanked him with a slight nod of the head. Dear Uncle started playing the role he had taken on; after greeting everyone and giving the Indian and his wife a pretended welcome to his house, he told the story of the car breakdown.

My father said, "It's all for the best, there's lots of opportunities to go on pilgrimages. God willing, next month we'll go together."

And in order to say something the Indian said, "The gentleman could not be putting up with being away from his lady, so he commanded a return . . ."

And then the joke about Nayshapur, that Asadollah had suggested to him at noon that day, suddenly seemed to occur to him, and he added, "The beloved commanded a return from Nayshapur to Lahavard."

When he heard the name Nayshapur Dear Uncle gave a start, but he tried to act as if nothing had happened; he gave a forced laugh and then took an envelope out of his pocket and stretched out his arm toward my father. "By the way, the address of that hotel you gave us was no use. You might as well keep it!"

Although I was trying to stay calm I couldn't tear my eyes from the envelope. My gaze followed its movement from Dear Uncle's hand to my father's, and then into my father's pocket. O God, what had my father trapped our naive Dear Uncle into this time?

Dear Uncle struggled to hide his anger and anxiety at the Indian's presence, and at his own dark prospects. He spoke even more than usual, and contrary to his usual practice—since he found Asadollah's jokes difficult to put up with—he tried to get Asadollah Mirza to talk. "By the way, Asadollah, where has Dustali Khan hidden his wife Aziz al-Saltaneh away tonight?"

"I imagine Mrs. Aziz al-Saltaneh has gone to the shrine of Davud to pray for intercession."

"Intercession for what?"

"To get rid of Dustali Khan's infirmity . . . as Brigadier Maharat Khan puts it, unfortunately Dustali Khan's natural vitality is *bahot* wilted . . ."

The brigadier protested, "I am never saying such a thing."

Asadollah Mirza said, "Brigadier, sir, I said as you put it, meaning in your language . . . I didn't say you had said it. Everyone says it. It's obvious from his face that his natural vitality's *bahot* wilted."

In a quiet but furious voice Dustali Khan said, "Asadollah, I'll make you eat your words . . ."

Asadollah Mirza shouted out, "What's this I hear? All right, all right then. Your natural vitality is not being *bahot* wilted . . . it is being in complete working order . . . it's the vitality of the great hero Rostam, the vitality of Hercules, oh yes indeed."

At the end of the party when everyone stood to say goodbye and leave, Dear Uncle indicated to Dustali Khan that he should stay; my father seemed to guess that he wanted to ask him why he had invited the Indian and signalled to him to change his mind. Dear Uncle let Dustali leave with the others. Only Dear Uncle and my father remained in the living room. I couldn't go, I wanted to hear what they would say to one another. I pretended to be busy behind the door.

My father quietly asked, "You wrote the letter just as we said?"

"Yes, exactly as you said, but please act quickly. My situation is very dangerous."

"Rest assured that first thing tomorrow this message will be sent to the city we mentioned."

At that moment Mash Qasem entered the room, grumbling and muttering under his breath; he went over to Dear Uncle. "Sir, you know what that bastard's done?"

"Who, Qasem?"

"That Indian brigadier."

With extreme agitation Dear Uncle said, "What's he done?"

"Just half an hour ago he came out of the room, looked all round and then goes in the yard . . . I went after him all quiet . . ."

"Get on with it, don't be so irritating. Then what happened?"

"Well now, why should I lie? To the grave it's ah . . . ah . . . he went straight to the roots of the big sweetbrier bush . . . then cheeky beggar if he didn't stand there and do his stuff like."

"On the roots of the big sweetbrier?"

"Yes, sir . . . on the roots of the big sweetbrier."

His face contorted, Dear Uncle gripped my father's arm. "You see that? . . . these English . . . they want to get at me from every side! This is part of their plan, they want to destroy my soul so I'll submit to them, bound hand and foot. This is the beginning of their war of nerves against me!"

Then he suddenly thrust aside his jacket, put his hand on the leather holster of the revolver at his belt, and shouted, "I'll kill that Indian with my own hands . . . on the roots of my big sweetbrier! This is really hitting below the belt! Even if I die under the tortures of the English, I have to pay this Indian back for what he's done."

My father put his hand on Dear Uncle's shoulder and said, "Calm down.

> 'An ant that's slithering in a slippery bowl
> Needs skill not strength to save his soul.'

Be patient, when your friends arrive, they'll sort this Indian fellow out."

Dear Uncle muttered under his breath, "With my own hands I'll string them all up on the vine trellis."

Mash Qasem raised his eyes to the heavens and said, "God help us all . . . I didn't want to say everythin' . . . the bastard did somethin' even worse."

With his eyes bulging from their sockets Dear Uncle said, "What else did he do? Why didn't you say everything?"

"Well now, why should I lie? To the grave . . . Never mind he did that, that was nothin', savin' your grace and rose water on your face, but he let fly one of them shameless noises like that I heard a good four yards off."

Dear Uncle clutched his head in his hands and said, "My God, just give me the chance to be revenged on these English wolves for this insolence!"

A few minutes later, when we'd gone back to our own house, Dear Uncle turned up again. He signaled my father to go into the room with the French windows.

I had already made up my mind that I would not miss what they were up to at any price. I quickly made my way to my hiding place.

"There's always something wrong when things are done in a hurry. I've just realized that I didn't put anything in my letter about how I was to recognize their representative. Just imagine their representative wants to get in touch with me, how's he to introduce himself and how am I to understand that he's come from them?"

My father wanted to dismiss the matter as trivial, but it seemed that he straightaway realized that Dear Uncle's question was a logical one, and after a moment apparently spent sunk in thought he said, "You're quite right. In such a situation one has to think of everything. You must establish some kind of secret sign. How about if . . . ?"

"I thought I'd specify a sign that would be a special password for when we got in touch."

My father stroked his chin and said, "That's not a bad idea, but you'd have to write the password down and this is not a good time to be writing things down; you have to think of the enemy's agents. If you ask me, I think . . ."

He remained deep in thought for a few moments. Dear Uncle said, "How about if we used the name of one of my family?"

My father's eyes lit up, "Not bad. For example we could use your late grandfather's name, but it would have to be in such a way that it couldn't be copied. How about, 'My late grandfather is eating *ab-gusht* with Jeanette McDonald'?"

In a choked voice Dear Uncle said, "I don't think this is the right time to be making jokes."

"I'm not making a joke; just as I suggested, it has to be a sentence that it would be impossible for the enemy's spies to guess at."

His voice trembling with anger, Dear Uncle said, "I'd rather mount an English scaffold than put my late grandfather's name next to that of some loose woman."

My father shrugged his shoulders and said, "Well, you can't have your cake and eat it, too . . . if you really don't want to . . . then we can just leave everything in the hands of fate . . . after all, it's not certain that the English want to take revenge on you. Perhaps after all this time they've forgiven your sins."

"It looks as though you're trying to torture me. You know better than anyone else what horrible plans the English have for me. The roots of my sweetbrier bush aren't dry yet from that filthy Indian's evil plot against me . . ."

"Then why are you being so difficult? Do you think if Napoleon could have escaped from all his troubles on St. Helena under such conditions he would have hesitated? You're not alone in this. A great family, a city, a nation are all waiting for your self-sacrifice."

Dear Uncle closed his eyes for a moment; clutching his temples in his hands he said, "I accept, for the people's sake! Give me the letter and I'll add the secret password."

My father handed him the letter and placed pen and ink before him. "Write as follows: 'Finally it is requested that in order to establish contact with me it be established that the following secret password is to be used . . .' Have you written that? Now write between quotation marks, 'My late grandfather is eating *ab-gusht* with Jeanette McDonald.'"

When Dear Uncle raised his head from the paper his brow was covered in sweat. He said under his breath, "God forgive me that in order to save my own soul I've made my late grandfather turn in his grave like this."

"Rest assured that if your late grandfather were alive he would be completely behind you."

After delivering himself of a short speech about his own innate bravery, together with a few anecdotes drawn from the life of Napoleon, Dear Uncle returned to his own house.

I was really confused and at a loss. However hard I tried to guess what my father's plan was, my brain couldn't come up with anything. I spent a restless night. It occurred to me to turn to Asadollah Mirza again. But although I went to find him early next morning, he had already left the house and still hadn't come back late that night, so I had to spend the whole day—which seemed endless to me—alone with my own thoughts and wild imaginings. The thing which particularly caught my attention that day was my father's expression and general manner. I thought I saw in his glance a certain mental self-satisfaction, as if he'd triumphed over an enemy.

I didn't see Dear Uncle for the whole day. Toward dusk, when Mash Qasem was busy watering the flowers, I was able to have a few words with him. He too seemed filled with anxiety and alarm, under the influence of Dear Uncle's hints.

"It's no joke m'dear, the master's right not to sleep at night. Them godless English are gettin' closer. And God strike me dumb, who knows if their agents aren't on their way to do the Master some terrible injury . . . me and the Master won't be livin' for much longer . . . though I was sleepin' with my rifle outside the Master's bedroom last night he woke up ten times before mornin'. And when he was asleep he was screamin' out, 'They're comin', they're here.' You'd think he felt the blade of a British sword against his throat . . . and my situation's none too good neither, but I put my trust in the Lord . . . I mean them English have a right to . . . if we was in their place we'd've given us such a hidin' as we wouldn't've got out of it alive."

"Mash Qasem, I don't think that you're in such . . ."

Mash Qasem put his watering can down and said, "What are you thinkin' of, m'dear, us and them English are like a devil and an angel . . . and just say they've forgotten about the Battle of Mamasani, what are they goin' to do about the Battle of Kazerun, eh? And if they've forgotten about the Battle of Kazerun what about the Battle of Ghiasabad? But m'dear, why should I lie? To the grave it's ah . . . ah . . . as God's my witness, I'm ready for them English to lash me to a cannon's mouth so as they don't bother the Master."

Mash Qasem spent a long time describing his bravery and the crushing blows he had struck against the British army, and threw out hints about the possibility of the means of their salvation being at hand.

Fortunately the following day was a national holiday. I went a few times to Asadollah Mirza's house, and the old servant woman there said that the master had given orders that he wasn't to be woken till an hour before noon, not even if the world were to come to a end. It was gone eleven by the time his lordship woke up. When I went to his room he was eating his breakfast. It was clear that he'd slept well; he was very cheerful and good-humored and was busy wolfing down fried eggs and tomatoes; the sound of the singer Qamar al-Moluk's voice was coming from the gramophone. He welcomed me with open arms and offered to share his breakfast with me, but I'd no appetite.

"Why won't you have some? Has being in love blunted your appetite?"

"No, Uncle Asadollah, things are really in a terrible mess."

When I told him about what had happened at the preacher's house, and about Dear Uncle's letter to Hitler, he burst out with a great guffaw of laughter and said, "I don't know what your father's planned for this old man. And to some extent he's got right on his side because when he had the pharmacy he was a wealthy man, and now he's about at the level we civil servants are. Dear Uncle rubbed his nose in it and he's rubbing Dear Uncle's nose in it. If you weren't in love and stuck in the middle, I'd have just laughed and let them fight it out."

"But Uncle Asadollah, you have to think of something. I really don't understand what my father's up to."

"Moment, don't get too upset, your father's not such a simpleton as to send the letter to Hitler, or to show it to anyone, because he'll be the first person people will collar demanding to know what all this is about."

"Then why do you suppose he dictated this letter to Dear Uncle?"

"I suppose he wants to have something in his hands to bring pressure on Dear Uncle, so that he'll have to dance to his tune, or he just wanted to have something which he could use to make fun of the old man. You said they fixed on a secret password?"

"Yes, the secret password to be used for contacting him later was this: 'My late grandfather is eating *ab-gusht* with Jeanette McDonald.'"

Asadollah Mirza laughed so violently that he fell on the floor, and I burst out laughing too. I said, "When Dear Uncle heard the name of his late grandfather he nearly had a heart attack, but my father forced him to accept it."

"Your father's no fool . . . they've pushed the name of the Master and this late grandfather down his throat so often that this is apt revenge . . . but it's incredible the Master should've gone along with it."

"He didn't accept it so easily as all that. At first he said he'd rather mount an English scaffold than have his late grandfather's name associated with that of a loose woman."

Asadollah Mirza's eyes grew round with astonishment, and with a loud laugh he said, "He's got a nerve . . . Jeanette McDonald's a great artist, and the whole world would love to kiss her hand . . . he can't hold a candle to one of her (—)s."

(The word Asadollah used in this expression, and which is here indicated by parentheses, is too vulgar for me to record. It indicates a gas silently produced by human agency, and with an unpleasant smell.)

"My father said that if Napoleon had found himself in such a situation he would have been ready for such a sacrifice. To cut a long story short, he frightened Dear Uncle so much he agreed that his late grandfather and Jeanette McDonald could eat out of the same dish."

Wiping his lips and mouth with his napkin, Asadollah Mirza said, "Moment, they talk about this late grandfather as if he were Victor Hugo or Garibaldi; do you have any idea who this late grandfather was?"

"No, Uncle Asadollah."

"The father of this grandfather was architect to the court, in the time of Mohammad Shah and Naser al-Din Shah; he was someone who'd done quite nicely for himself out of the bricks and mortar he'd knocked up for people. Well, one day he sent a present of five-hundred *tomans* to Naser al-Din Shah, and Naser al-Din Shah gave him some sonorous seven-syllable title—something like 'His Dropsical Excellency' or some such—and he became architect to the court, and his son, this late grandfather who'd taken the money to Naser al-Din Shah on a silver salver, received some six-syllable title like 'The Royal Disquisition' . . . and then all of a sudden, from one day to the next, they became members of the country's aristocracy . . . and it's natural that the son of the royal leopard should be his excellency the tiger, and his excellency the tiger's son should be the lion of the state . . . and to cut a long story short, there isn't now a person in the world they'll give the time of day to. But, moment, don't you repeat what I've just told you!"

"No, you can be sure of that, Uncle Asadollah."

"Right, now we must think of something so that, God forbid, Hitler doesn't send Marshall Goering to the house of this pensioned-off Cossack lieutenant . . . by the way, do you know what this Dear Uncle of yours—who's now posing as Marshall Hindenburg—actually did? When he was pensioned off he'd just got to the rank of third lieutenant. And he applied to be pensioned off earlier than he was due for it, do you know why?"

"No, I don't know."

"You were just a little boy, there's no reason you should remember. He was so high and mighty around the house, and put on such airs in front of your father, that your father rented that house out—the one he's now rented out to Brigadier Maharat Khan—to a young second lieutenant. And every time Dear Uncle, who acted in the house as though he were some great historical military commander, was in the street and met this second lieutenant—who was young enough to be his grandson—he had to click his heels together and salute him. At that time military discipline was no joke. And people laughed so much at this that Dear Uncle applied for his pension early. That's when he first fell out with your father. Right, now get up and let's think of something."

Asadollah Mirza continued talking while he was getting dressed. "As we know the secret of how Hitler's agent is to get in touch with Dear Uncle, we must get in touch with him and neutralize whatever plans your father has . . . but where can we phone from? We can't do it from your house, and we can't do it from Dear Uncle's house either . . . how about we pay a visit to that ass Dustali Khan's house, I don't think they'll be in at the moment."

We went out hoping that we'd be able to phone from Dustali Khan's house. As we were on our way Asadollah gave me some bad news that made me even more upset than before; everyone who was doing his military service had been demobilized, and this being the case it wasn't going to be long before Shapur, aka Puri, uncle colonel's son, turned up again.

When Asadollah Mirza saw my sorrowful face he put his hand on my shoulder and said, "Now don't be so mournful! Trust in the Lord! When I said 'Don't forget San Francisco,' it was for a situation like this . . . don't worry about it so much. In the end it'll turn out either that you're free of it all, or you'll get to San Francisco, or that blabbermouth will think of some other woman."

But his words were small consolation to me. We paused for a moment and listened outside the door to Dustali Khan's house. We could hear nothing of Aziz al-Saltaneh's racket, which was normally audible from two houses away.

Asadollah Mirza said, "It seems that the old witch isn't in. If only her maid's here this is the best place to phone from. We'll send her packing somehow or other, so that we can get down to business."

When the door opened Asadollah Mirza's eyes glittered and a smile transformed his mouth. A pretty young woman of about twenty had opened the door for us. She politely and warmly greeted us and invited us in. At her first "Won't you come in?" his lordship entered the house and started looking for Aziz al-Saltaneh and Dustali Khan. It was clear that everyone had gone out and that the young woman was alone.

She was wearing a prayer veil over her hair; with a charming smile she said, "Mr. Asadollah, sir, it seems you don't recognize me."

As if he had forgotten all about our business and our plans, Asadollah Mirza was eating the girl alive with his eyes; smiling, he said, "Moment, how could I not know you . . . you're Miss Zahra, aren't you? . . . How are you keeping? And is your dad well? . . . Where have you been, we never see you?"

The girl laughed again and said, "I'm Fati, Mrs. Khanomha's daughter . . . Mrs. Khanomha is Miss Qamar's aunt . . . can't you remember that when I was little you used to say my lips were like apples from Khorasan?"

"Aha! My dear Fati . . . well well, God be praised, what a fine young woman you've grown up to be . . . and where are those red lips? You'd never let me take a bite out of them and now their red's turned all pale! And now won't you give your uncle a kiss?"

The girl blushed and hung her head. Asadollah Mirza took her by the arm. Looking her up and down as he spoke he said, "I've asked Mrs. Khanomha about you constantly. I think she said you'd got married!"

"Yes, I got married and went to Esfahan . . . but after four years I got divorced . . . he was a bad man . . . he was really nasty to me."

"May he rot in hell, how could anyone be nasty to such a pretty girl? Any kiddies?"

"No . . . no children came . . ."

"Well well . . . well well . . . splendid . . . and so what are you doing now?"

Asadollah Mirza was so busy with this girl that it seemed that he'd forgotten all about why we had gone there. I signalled to him to draw his attention. Without taking his eyes off Fati's body he said, "So we'll just sit here a while until Dustali . . ."

The girl interrupted him and said warmly, "Oh please, treat it as your own house. Come into the sitting room."

"Fati dear, is there anything cold to drink in your house?"

"Certainly, there's some cherry cordial, and there's quince cordial. Which would you like?"

"No my dear, I'd really like some lemonade. If you could just step out and go down to the arcade and fetch us two lemonades, that would be really nice of you! . . . Here's the money for it!"

"Please, what are you saying? I've some money."

Asadollah forced a bank note that was twenty times the cost of the lemonades into Fati's hand. As soon as she had gone he went to the telephone and dialled Dear Uncle's number. He placed his handkerchief over the mouthpiece and waited. When he heard Dear Uncle's voice on the phone he spoke in a disguised voice, with an accent like that of a White Russian, "Sir, is you alone? . . . Then pays attention . . . My late grandfather is eating *ab-gusht* with Jeanette McDonald . . . you understand? You not worried. The necessary orders gav comes. The day after tomorrow we was in touch with you . . . whatever anyone says do, you not done; you waited our orders . . . even if the gusband of you sister was saying you not listening . . . completely in the confidence. You not doing anything. You waiting . . . excellent. This is correct. You not speaking with anybody until we gives order . . . you understand? . . . You make promise? Excellent . . . Heil Hitler."

Struggling hard to control his laughter, Asadollah Mirza put the phone down and said to me, "The poor thing was trembling. But the way things are now if your father wants to prod him any further Dear Uncle won't fall for it until we can work out what we have to do."

A moment later Fati came in with the lemonade; she was panting and it was clear she had run all the way.

Sipping at his lemonade and never taking his eyes off her, Asadollah said, "Well, Fati dear, and when are you going to come and visit your uncle? You know where my house is, don't you?"

"You're still in the old house?"

"Yes, the same place . . . now you're here you must come and see your uncle regularly."

"God willing, I'll come one day with my mom."

"Moment, moment . . . no need to trouble Mrs. Khanomha with that bad back of hers . . . I couldn't agree under any circumstances for you to drag that lovely woman all that way . . . she has to rest."

"Her bad back's better now, Mr. Asadollah, sir."

"Moment, moment, she absolutely must not walk anywhere. A person thinks she's all better, off she goes walking, and then she's worse off than before . . . Well, it seems as though Dustali Khan and his wife are not coming back any time soon, so we'll be on our way!"

"Please stay, they'll be here directly."

"By the way, you don't know where they went do you?"

"Well, you know . . ."

Fati hesitated for a moment. Asadollah Mirza pricked up his ears. He sensed that Fati knew something she didn't want to say. With apparent negligence he stretched out his hand to her.

"Aha, I get it. They've gone about that matter . . . that business there was talk of yesterday. But really, the poor devil, what troubles do turn up for him!"

Fati naively said, "Eh! So you know about it too?"

"Don't be such a child! I was the first person they mentioned it to . . . the whole family more or less knows about it."

The flood gates opened, "They had guests here last night. The Indian neighbor and his foreign wife had supper here. An hour after they'd gone there was suddenly a lot of noise and I went behind the door to listen and saw that Mrs. Aziz al-Saltaneh was interrogating Miss Qamar and saying 'Whose baby is it?' And Miss Qamar was completely off her head giggling about it. She said the names of the strangest weirdest people you could imagine."

Asadollah Mirza tried to hide his astonishment. He glanced across at me and then, to get the girl to talk further, said, "Moment, really moment. What dishonorable people there are in this world. To come and do such a thing to a half-witted girl like that!"

Fati looked down and said, "Today they've taken her to a doctor to see if he can get rid of the baby . . . Mrs. al-Saltaneh was crying and beating herself on the head all night till morning, but Miss Qamar herself was happy as a lark and laughing and saying she wanted to knit the baby a matinee jacket."

Asadollah Mirza was clearly affected by the news; he said, "The man who did this to that girl must be found and his head cut off."

Fati made a moue and said, "But sir, if I say something will you swear you won't say I said it?"

"On your life, I won't say a word . . . on your life, which is dearer to me than my own." Fati glanced at me. Asadollah realized what she was thinking. He said, "This boy's just like me. You can be sure that his lips are more sealed than anyone's."

Once again Fati hesitated for a moment; finally she said, "This morning Mr. Dustali Khan was saying to his wife that this was your doing. Meaning it was your baby."

Asadollah Mirza started up and shouted, "What? . . . the creep, the impudent bastard . . . I'd come and do such a thing with a girl who's a half-wit?"

A stream of curses on Dustali flowed from Asadollah Mirza's mouth. "I'll destroy that ass Dustali, he won't know what's hit him . . . that wretch invites the Indian and his wife here and spreads stories about me behind my back."

For a moment he was sunk in thought. Then he raised his head and said, "Get up, let's go now, we'll deal with Dustali later."

Fati was very insistent that we stay until her master returned but Asadollah Mirza promised he would look in again later.

When we were outside I said, "Uncle Asadollah, do you think this girl . . ."

He interrupted me, "With Fati it's all over bar the shouting. With women if you get them in the first few minutes you've got them, and if not then leave them be! She's one of those who'll come of her own accord. I'm going to have to give you a few lessons. For now let this be your first lesson: when you approach women show them you're interested, that you're looking for custom, that you're ready to buy, and then clear off and don't give them another thought and they'll come after you on their own, and then San Francisco!"

"Uncle Asadollah . . . I thought what this girl said . . ."

"Damn you and your Uncle Asadollahs . . . do you want to tell me yet again that your heart's thumping in your chest for the sake of some heavenly, innocent love? . . . keep telling me rubbish like that till someone else takes the girl off and you sit sighing for her memory!"

I closed my eyes for a moment and saw the terrible scene in my mind—someone else taking Layli away from me. But I didn't have much opportunity to think about this appalling notion. Fati caught up with us, panting and out of breath, "Mr. Asadollah Mirza, I still had your change."

Asadollah Mirza pretended to be upset, "For goodness sake, a girl doesn't give money back to her uncle!"

And after a moment's pause he took another bank note out of his pocket, "To tell you the truth, Fati dear . . . the woman who looks after me's got no taste at all. You take this money, and whenever you've time buy me a few glasses of that lemonade that you bought today. According to your own taste."

Fati said warmly, "Do you want me to go and buy it now?"

"No, my dear. Tomorrow or the day after tomorrow, whenever you've time. If I'm not at home, just leave it with the maid. Bye-bye dear."

When Fati had gone I said, "Uncle Asadollah, do you have to have taste to buy lemonade?"

"Moment, really moment; you're such a big lad and you've no idea what's going on yet. Well, I'll have to give you your second lesson. The second lesson: always provide her with an excuse which she can make use of in order to deliver the goods."

"But what if she brings the lemonade when you're not there and leaves it with the maid, then what?"

"Moment, then I have to accept that I didn't get it across to her properly that I was in the market . . . Shall I give you your third lesson or will it be too much for you? The third lesson is never put on a grave serious face. As soon as women see you've a grave face and you hang your head, even if you were Cicero they'd say, 'Ugh, he can't talk to save his life!' If you were Clark Gable they'd say, 'Ugh, handsome maybe but pathetic.' If you were Avicenna they'd say, 'What does he know about anything?' You don't seem to be following. I'll leave the lesson for another time."

"You're right. I'm very worried. I'm afraid that all this is going to land me in the soup again."

"And you'll lose your dear Layli! . . . Learn this one thing from me, that with your big innocent eyes they'll take Miss Layli away from you and you'll have to spend the rest of your life sighing."

"So what should I do, Uncle Asadollah?"

"San Francisco!"

"Please don't say those things."

"If you're not going to San Francisco itself, at least tour the suburbs a bit, show that you basically know your way around the city."

Asadollah's cheekiness made my blood boil. If I hadn't needed him so much I'd have said whatever came into my head and gone on my way. But I didn't want to do this, and I couldn't afford to lose him as he was perhaps my only friend and support. I changed the subject. "Uncle Asadollah, are you sure that my father won't do anything with Dear Uncle's letter?"

"Yes, unless he's really soft in the head. Say he sends this letter to Hitler or to Churchill. At least they'll know that there never was a Battle of Kazerun so they'll say, 'One more nut, one more fruitcake.' If they're in a good mood they might get a bit of a laugh out of it; in any case if you can lay your hands on that letter, grab it and run. Before you tear it up bring it here and we'll read it together and we can have the laugh instead of Hitler and Churchill . . . but you know where the real danger lies? The real danger is that this poor old man . . ."

Asadollah laughed and said, ". . . will go crazy from fear of the English."

"By the way, Uncle Asadollah, who do you think is responsible for Qamar's baby?"

"How should I know? It must be some water carrier, some porter . . ."

"What will they do now? I suppose they'll have to force this man to marry Qamar?"

"Moment, moment, it's clear you don't know this crowd. They'd rather cut the poor crazy girl's head off than hear that a great-grandchild of his Royal Leopardship has become the wife of some commoner . . . tonight when I'm having supper at the colonel's house I must keep my eyes and ears open to see what's going on . . . I'm afraid they'll do something awful to this poor child."

When I separated from Asadollah Mirza I went home and saw that everything was peaceful and quiet in the big garden. At lunch I tried to read what was in my father's face, but he was silent and uncommunicative.

THIRTEEN

THAT AFTERNOON we found Layli and her brother in the garden. My sister and Layli's brother suggested various games, but since Layli and I had fallen in love we had felt no real interest in children's games. It was as if love had suddenly aged us a few years, but so that no one would realize our feelings we took part in their games, meaning that in reality we let Layli's brother and my sister play while we chatted together in the sweetbrier arbor.

It wasn't long before we heard the cry of an itinerant photographer coming from the alleyway. My sister ran over to us shouting, "Come on, it's Mirza Habib the photographer . . . let's have a photo done."

We had often brought this itinerant photographer into the garden before. With his old box camera, complete with its black hood, he had frequently taken photographs of us children, charging only a tiny fee.

When we called out to the photographer we were surprised to see that it wasn't Mirza Habib. We recognized the camera, that was just the same, with the same photographs stuck on its casing. But its owner had changed.

When the photographer saw our surprise he seemed to realize what had caused it, because before we could ask him anything he said in an Armenian accent, "Mirza Habib sold me his camera. If you like I'll take your picture. You know that in fact Mirza Habib was my apprentice. I take much nicer photos than him."

We all looked at one another, and since the price was unchanged we asked him to come and take a picture of us.

I still have the photograph we had done that day. I'm wearing my striped pajamas, standing next to Layli; my sister and her brother are sitting on a chair in front of us. When the photographer had colored the cardboard negative red and placed it upside down in front of the camera's lens in order to produce the final print, I suddenly realized that Dear Uncle Napoleon had come out of the door to the inner apartments of his house. Then he whispered something to Mash Qasem, who had followed him out. As he was speaking he didn't take his eyes off the photographer. He stared at him as if he were a police officer staring at someone suspected of theft or murder.

Dear Uncle Napoleon started walking up and down with a preoccupied look on his face, and Mash Qasem, who it was clear had been entrusted with some task or other, walked over toward us.

He beckoned me aside and quietly said, "That's not the usual photographer, m'dear. Where did he turn up from?"

"Mirza Habib has sold his camera to this photographer."

Mash Qasem walked back to Dear Uncle and whispered something in his ear. Dear Uncle stared at the photographer, his face preoccupied and filled with suspicion; then he seemed to give Mash Qasem another order.

This time Mash Qasem walked over, with apparent unconcern, toward the photographer.

"Well hello, sir, how are you keepin', you're well, God willin'?"

And after a few greetings and pleasantries he asked him his name.

"Bughus, at your service."

With his head twisted round so that he could look at the upside down negative Mash Qasem said, "But why should I lie? To the grave it's ah . . . ah! It looks like you really know what you're doin'. You've taken a grand photograph! The photographer before you didn't take 'em this good."

The photographer visibly swelled with pride and said, "Mirza Habib learned photography from me. I've been a photographer twenty years. I had a photographer's studio. First here, then in Ahvaz . . . but I had bad luck, I was forced to sell up . . ."

"Then you've been to them places down south then?"

"You bet your life I've been there. Why, all the important folks came to me to have their photos done. All the oil company people came and had their photos done with me."

Mash Qasem's eyes momentarily widened, but he tried to hide his astonishment and terror. He said in a calm voice, "And them English must've had their photos took with you, too?"

"In fact most of my customers were English."

The photographer took the photograph out of his camera and showed it to Mash Qasem, "Take a look! That's what they call a real photograph."

We didn't give Mash Qasem the chance to look, but snatched the photograph from his hand. Layli took the photograph and ran toward her father, "Daddy, look, isn't it a beautiful photo?"

Dear Uncle was looking at the photographer in an openly suspicious way. At this moment Mash Qasem whispered something in his ear. The photographer came over toward us too. He greeted Dear Uncle and said, "If you'll allow me, I'll take a photograph of you too."

In a smothered voice Dear Uncle said, "No, thanks all the same, that won't be necessary."

"Just say the word. I'd like to take a photograph of you, sir, as a souvenir. If you like it give me whatever you want, and if you don't then it's on me."

Dear Uncle was silent for a moment but he couldn't hide his discomfort and he burst out angrily, "Why do you want to take a photograph of me? Who told you to take a photograph of me?" The photographer looked at him in amazement and said, "What are you upset about? I only wanted to be of service."

Dear Uncle lost all control of himself and screamed out, "They've a thousand photographs of me in their dossier. Go to hell, and tell your masters that even if they take a hundred more photographs of me they won't be able to take me alive."

Then he suddenly thrust aside the front of his cloak, pulled his revolver from its holster and went on in the same trembling voice, "Six of these bullets are for you and their lackeys and the last is for myself."

The hapless photographer, his eyes bursting from their sockets, stared wildly at the gun for a moment and then suddenly took to his heels. In full flight he whisked the camera tripod under his arm and left the garden in such a hurry that our mouths hung open in surprise.

We stared at Dear Uncle in astonishment. He put the revolver back in its holster. There were large beads of sweat on his forehead. He struggled over to the stone bench and sank down on it. Unlike me, Layli and the other children had understood nothing of what Dear Uncle had said or the reason for his sudden wild behavior.

Massaging Dear Uncle's hands, Mash Qasem said, "Well done, sir! For the sake of all the saints may God keep you so the people of this here country can live protected by you. You gave him just what he deserved. A man can only die once. Let him go and tell that to his bastard masters!"

I ran quickly home and told my father that Dear Uncle had collapsed.

My father hurriedly made his way over to Dear Uncle.

"What's happened, sir? What's going on?"

Mash Qasem answered for Dear Uncle, "Them bastards had sent a spy here to take a photo of the Master . . . the Master sprang at him like a lion . . . he near as anythin' emptied a bullet into his belly, and I wish he had."

In a voice quite devoid of sincerity my father sympathized with Dear Uncle for a while and then quietly said to him, "You can be sure that news of the arrival of the letter has reached them."

Mash Qasem helped Dear Uncle return to the inner apartments and, more worried than ever, I followed my father back to our house.

Supper at uncle colonel's house was not a very elaborate affair. In addition to my father and mother and Dear Uncle Napoleon and the children, Asadollah Mirza and Shamsali Mirza were there.

A little later Dustali Khan came and said that Aziz al-Saltaneh wouldn't be coming because Qamar felt unwell. At first the conversation revolved around Shapur, aka Puri, uncle colonel's son. Shamsali Mirza said, "Now that Mr. Puri's coming home safe and sound, the colonel should roll his sleeves up as soon as possible and get preparations for the wedding underway."

Uncle colonel said, "Thank God a thousand times over, you don't know what a state I've been in these days what with all this trouble and confusion, what I've been through till the right papers came. If the Master agrees, God willing we can fix the engagement date for the Qorban holiday."

Dear Uncle Napoleon was silent and withdrawn. I peeked at Layli who was looking down, and then gave Asadollah Mirza a helpless, imploring glance.

Asadollah pretended he'd no idea what was going on.

"Very nice, too, have you got someone in mind for him?"

Uncle colonel said, "You mean you don't know, Asadollah?"

"Moment, how am I supposed to know? And then I wouldn't have thought you could find a girl willing to take on someone who's just got through with his military service and hasn't a proper job to his name."

"What nonsense you're talking! With the education Puri's had, any office would take him sight unseen. It's no joke, the boy's had fifteen years of education and got his degree, all my friends in government offices are begging to have Puri work with them . . . the boy's a real genius."

Asadollah laughed and said, "That's clear from his face. But who have you got in mind for him?"

Uncle colonel gave Layli a fatherly look and said, "The marriages of first cousins are made in heaven."

Asadollah Mirza wrinkled his brow and said, "Moment, moment, I'm very against this. Little Layli isn't any more than fourteen or fifteen and she has to finish her schooling."

Before uncle colonel had the opportunity to answer, Dustali Khan said, "I'd like to know if when his lordship got married his bride had finished her schooling. And anyway this kind of talk doesn't mean anything when it comes to girls."

Asadollah Mirza immediately bristled and said, "Now, Dustali . . ."

But it seemed that a thought suddenly occurred to him and he stopped talking. After a moment he said, "By the way, did you read in the paper how the Germans have sunk some more Allied ships?"

Dustali Khan never had the least idea of what was going on in the world, but in order to annoy Asadollah Mirza he started to make provocative remarks, "Even if they sink a thousand of their ships, in the end the English will smash them to bits. In the first World War didn't the Germans almost get to Paris, and then they were made mincemeat of?"

In a loud voice Asadollah Mirza said, "I don't know why you back the English up so much. It looks like there's some kind of pay-off involved."

Involuntarily I glanced across at Dear Uncle Napoleon; from the tensed swollen muscles on his face I realized he was thinking about the English.

After bursting out in a loud artificial laugh Dustali Khan said, "You take money from the Germans, why shouldn't I take it from the English?"

His eyes glittering, Asadollah glanced at me. He drained his glass of wine and said, "And much good I hope it does you. You get a consultancy fee then. If it wasn't for your great brilliant brain, who would Churchill have to advise him?"

Dustali Khan had no chance to answer him, because at this moment the sounds of a commotion in the hall became audible. A moment later Qamar threw herself into the room, panting and out of breath, and said, "Daddy Dustali, help me, mummy wants to kill me."

Everyone jumped up. Dustali went over to Qamar and said, "Why are you talking nonsense, child? Where's mummy?"

"She's coming, she's after me . . ."

And at that instant Aziz al-Saltaneh burst in on the company like a smouldering volcano. She screamed out, "As God's my witness, child, I hope I see you in the grave, you're making me old before my time."

Dear Uncle Napoleon had stood up and said to her, "Madam, stop yelling, what kind of a racket is this you're making?"

Without paying any attention to his objections Aziz al-Saltaneh addressed her daughter, "Get out and back to the house with you before I break something over your head."

Qamar, who was hiding behind Dustali Khan, screamed out, "I'm not going home. I'm afraid of you."

"You're not coming home? Then just you wait."

She looked around, snatched up a cane that was lying on the arm of a chair, and raised it over her head, "Get going!"

With an angry expression on his face Dear Uncle Napoleon drew himself up to his full height in front of her.

"Madam, put that cane down."

Asadollah Mirza interrupted, "Moment, madam, this innocent child . . ."

Dear Uncle cut him off, "You be quiet!"

In a mournful voice Aziz al-Saltaneh said, "But sir, you don't know what I have to put up with. Let me take her."

"I said put that cane down!"

Faced by the firmness of Dear Uncle's tone, Aziz al-Saltaneh lowered the cane. When he saw that Aziz al-Saltaneh had calmed down Dear Uncle turned to Qamar and said, "Now, my dear child, off you go to your house with your mother."

The fat simple girl said in a trembling voice, "No, no, I'm not going, I'm not going."

"I said be off with you now and go back home with your mother. In our family disobeying one's elders is a big sin."

"I'm not going. I'm not going."

Suddenly in a voice shaking with anger Dear Uncle yelled, "I said go home . . . home!"

A deathly silence succeeded Dear Uncle's terrifying outburst. For a moment Qamar stared at him dumbfounded; suddenly she burst into tears and sobbed out, "I'm not going, I'm not going; mummy wants to kill my baby."

Then she placed her hand on her belly and said, "They want to kill this baby I've got. I love my baby, I want to knit him a matinee jacket."

"What? A baby? . . . a baby? . . . a matinee jacket?"

After this unexpected confession and Dear Uncle Napoleon's noisy reaction, everyone was frozen to the spot for a moment. Only the sound of Qamar's snuffling sobs broke the silence. Suddenly Aziz al-Saltaneh hit herself on the head and said in a strangled voice, "God strike me dead so I don't have to put up with the shame of all this."

Dear Uncle turned to her and said, "And so . . . you . . . you . . . the English . . ."

But he couldn't finish his own sentence. He pressed his hand against his chest, in the region of his heart, and struggled to take the two steps to his chair. Pale, and with his eyes closed, he sank down into the chair. Everyone ran toward him and began talking at once, "Sir . . . sir . . ."

"Sir, how are you? Drink a little water."

"Mash Qasem, a glass of water!"

Mash Qasem brought the water. But Dear Uncle's mouth wouldn't open. They splashed a little water on his face, but he made no move.

My father said, "It's his heart, water's no use. Mash Qasem, run and fetch Dr. Naser al-Hokama."

As Mash Qasem was running out he said, "Eh, m'dears, they'll be the death of the Master in the end."

I went over to Asadollah Mirza and told him about the arrival of the photographer, and Dear Uncle's getting angry. Meanwhile everyone was talking at the same time and running distractedly back and forth. But Qamar was now utterly calm and was busy enthusiastically eating cookies. With her deficient intelligence the poor thing had no notion that she was the cause of all this confusion.

Uncle colonel, who had somewhat recovered his composure, abruptly realized there were children present and said, "Children, please, go and play in the next room."

Asadollah Mirza interrupted him, "Moment, colonel, we don't have any small children here. They're all big enough. Besides they've heard the whole affair. If it's so that no one should hear of the matter you'd better let them stay, but ask them not to mention it anywhere."

Uncle colonel had nothing to say to this logical remark. With a smile on his face Asadollah addressed the children, "The colonel is asking you, for the sake of our family honor, to promise not to say anything about what has happened to our dear Qamar."

With a noisy laugh Qamar said, "I promise I won't tell anyone."

This interruption of Qamar's started many of those present laughing, and she herself let out another laugh.

Dr. Naser al-Hokama gave Dear Uncle an injection; a moment later Dear Uncle opened his eyes. When he had quite come to himself the first thing he said was that he had no need of a doctor and that they shouldn't have given him an injection.

It was clear that Dr. Naser al-Hokama was upset by this remark and he closed his bag and stood up. "Your good health, your good health . . . but see to it that the Master doesn't collapse again; because I'm invited out and I'm on my way now. You've all been very kind, your good health." And he left the room with a frown on his face.

My father said, "These unfortunate things can happen to anyone. You shouldn't upset yourself so much. At this age any untoward excitement can cost a man his life."

Dear Uncle took a sip of water and said, "You're quite right. We mustn't lose control of ourselves . . . and Mrs. Aziz al-Saltaneh, stop all that pointless crying."

At this moment my mother took my sister and Layli's brother out, on the pretext of giving them supper.

Dear Uncle turned toward Qamar and said gently, "Come here, my dear, and sit by me so we can talk a little . . . and Mrs. Aziz al-Saltaneh, please leave her alone."

Still busy eating cookies, Qamar got up without any hesitation and sat next to Dear Uncle.

"Now my dear, you tell your uncle how you realized you were going to have a baby."

Qamar laughed and said, "Because he moves about in my tummy."

"When did you realize?"

"A few days ago . . . I went and got the money out of my money-box and bought some red wool and knitted my baby a jacket . . . I want to knit another one, too."

"But my dear, until a girl has a husband she can't have a baby. When did you get married without our realizing?"

"It was around the beginning of summer."

In spite of all his attempts to remain calm, it was clear that Dear Uncle was seething inside. He gritted his teeth. And in the same gentle voice he went on, "Who was your husband? Where is he now?"

Qamar thought for a moment, then answered, "I don't want to say."

"Just whisper it to your uncle."

Dustali Khan said, "We killed ourselves but couldn't get her to say the fellow's name, don't wear yourself out for nothing. We must think of something else."

Dear Uncle said, "But you'll tell me. Won't you, my dear?"

Everyone stared at Qamar's mouth and pricked up their ears. In the same artless fashion Qamar answered, "I don't want to say."

And she stood up to get another cookie. Dear Uncle, too, suddenly stood up. He grabbed her by the wrist and yelled, "You have to say! Understand? You have to say!"

With her free hand Qamar took a cookie from the cookie plate and as she was stuffing it into her mouth said, "I don't want to say."

Dear Uncle's eyes were popping from their sockets; his lips were trembling. He twisted the girl's wrist, pulled her toward himself, slapped her hard across the face and yelled, "You have to say!"

Qamar froze with her mouth open. She sobbed like a little child. A drop of blood, together with a half-chewed morsel of cookie, came out of the corner of her mouth. With her mouth full she said,

"I don't want to say . . . if I say they'll kill my baby. I want to knit him a jacket."

I don't know what the others felt, but I was close to exploding when I saw this upsetting scene. My heart seemed to be about to burst from my chest. Why didn't anyone interfere? Why did they allow this innocent girl to be tortured like this?

My father ran over to Dear Uncle and said, "Sir, it's not right. Leave her alone. The girl isn't right in the head."

Dear Uncle said angrily, "You keep out of it!"

And Aziz al-Saltaneh, who had been quietly crying, suddenly stood up and shouted, "Just realize what you're saying, you; it's you that's not right in the head. You're trying to say my girl's crazy? God blast and damn you, girl, for putting me at the mercy of this family's gossip!"

Asadollah Mirza found a suitable opportunity to interrupt and came forward. "Moment, my good woman, don't shout, calm yourself. Nothing is put right by shouting." Then he turned toward Qamar. With a handkerchief he cleaned the blood away from the corner of her mouth. He took her in his arms and in a voice filled with kindness said, "Don't be upset, my dear! No one can kill your baby. They won't kill a baby that has a daddy. If the gentleman asks who the baby's daddy is it's so they can find him and tell him to come and live with his wife and baby—meaning with you and your baby."

Qamar laid her head on Asadollah Mirza's shoulder and said quietly, "But he isn't here."

"Where is he, my dear?"

In an angry voice Dustali Khan said, "Leave her alone, it's impossible this girl'll say anything. We interrogated her all one night until morning."

Asadollah Mirza shouted, "Churchill's special advisor, shut up!"

Dustali Khan started up and lunged toward him. With his arm still around Qamar, Asadollah Mirza gave him a push with his free hand and said, "Hey, someone come and sit this donkey Dustali down in his chair."

Shamsali Mirza and my father sat Dustali Khan down. Dustali Khan muttered under his breath, "If it wasn't out of respect for the Master I'd have given him such a swipe in the mouth I'd have knocked his teeth down his throat!"

Without paying him any attention Asadollah Mirza went on talking to Qamar in the same kind tone, "My dear, if you say where he is, perhaps we'll be able to find him."

"If I say will you promise not to kill my baby? I've knitted him a jacket, there's just the sleeves still to do!"

"I promise, my dear."

Dear Uncle Napoleon's complexion had turned deathly pale. He was quiet, but from his gestures and appearance his internal turmoil could be guessed at.

Qamar's lips widened in an innocent smile and quietly she said, "His name was Allahverdi."

Everyone stared at Qamar's mouth. But she bent her body forward slightly so that she could reach the cookie plate. She took a cookie and stuffed it into her mouth.

At this moment Mash Qasem stepped forward and said, "You don't mean Allahverdi, the servant of that Indian brigadier, do you?"

With her mouth full Qamar repeated, "Allahverdi."

"Eh, can you beat that! You mean that Indian servant that swiped his master's money out of his pocket and they fired him?"

"Yep, Allahverdi."

Everyone spoke at once. Dear Uncle had reached the point that he was ready to explode, but at a sign from Asadollah Mirza he controlled himself. After a moment of dumbfounded consternation Aziz al-Saltaneh suddenly burst out, "As God's my witness, child, I hope I see you in the grave . . . that they bring me the news you're dead and gone . . . with an Indian servant, God strike me dead!"

Finally Dear Uncle could control himself no longer; in a voice that sounded as if it were coming from the depths of a well he said, "The servant of that Indian brigadier! It's obvious . . . it's obvious . . . I'm the target of all this! So that I and my family will be destroyed!"

Dustali Khan said, "The English did this too? God help the English then!"

His face contorted with rage, Dear Uncle turned toward Dustali Khan and through clenched teeth said, "You too? You're backing them up, too, are you? . . . You, my own cousin?"

Dustali Khan started to stammer, "I . . . I . . . I . . . ha . . . ha . . . haven't done anything."

Asadollah Mirza placed his hand on Dear Uncle's shoulder, "Forgive him, sir, the man lacks all basic common sense . . . it's no time to be talking about such things . . . before everything else we have to find this Allahverdi."

Shamsali Mirza jumped into their conversation, "Asadollah's right, before everything else we have to think about finding Allahverdi."

Dear Uncle suddenly shouted, "And when you've found Allahverdi, what are you going to do? Marry the daughter of my cousin off to Allahverdi, this lackey of the English?"

My father said, "If you can see any other way out, then please tell us."

"I'll ask you not to interfere. The lineage and honor of a noble family is not something that . . ."

Fortunately Dear Uncle did not finish his sentence.

My heart was in my mouth. I looked at my father with extreme apprehension.

Asadollah Mirza quickly started talking. It seemed that by making a noise he wanted to head off any confrontation between my father and Dear Uncle.

He took Qamar's hand again and said, "So you and Allahverdi got married . . . it must have been one day when you were alone and he came to your house and said 'Let's get married.' Was that it?"

With a laugh on her face Qamar said, "No!"

"Then one day when his master wasn't home he said to you 'Come to our house and let's get married.' Was that it?"

"No."

"You got married in the bazaar in front of the baker's, the grocer's and the butcher's?"

"No."

Mash Qasem couldn't control his tongue; he shook his head and said, "God help us all, what shameless folks there are about!"

"Then you describe what happened."

With an unconcerned look on her face Qamar went on eating cookies and said nothing. Asadollah Mirza had no choice but to start his questioning over again, but first he told everyone that they had to wait and be patient.

"Well my dear, so Allahverdi came on the roof of your house?"

With a laugh Qamar answered, "No. He didn't come."

Dustali Khan objected once again, "Sir, I've pointed out to you that you're not going to hear any reasonable words from this girl. Leave her alone; we have to think of something else."

Weeping, Aziz al-Saltaneh said, "Let them ask her. I'm done for. And tonight just like last night I'll have to lie awake till morning."

Asadollah Mirza wiped the sweat from his forehead and said, "Moment, I think the Holy Spirit came again and did a San Francisco!"

Qamar said excitedly, "Uncle Asadollah, you remember you told me if I was a good girl you'd take me to San Francisco, so why didn't you take me?"

In a sarcastic tone Dustali Khan said, "Perhaps this is the present uncle brought you back from San Francisco."

Asadollah Mirza, and everyone else, gave Dustali Khan such a look that he directed his gaze at the floor.

Asadollah Mirza turned to Qamar again, "Moment, Allahverdi didn't come to your house, he didn't take you to his house, it wasn't in the bazaar, it wasn't on the roof . . . so where was it, when was it?"

Qamar said simply, "No."

"Aha, maybe it was in a car?"

"No."

Mash Qasem interrupted again, "That Allahverdi was no more'n a beggar, what'd he be doin' with a car? And why should I lie? to the grave it's ah . . . ah . . . The shameless bastard swiped twenty *tomans* from me and took off."

Asadollah Mirza's patience was at an end; irritatedly he said, "Then my dear girl how was it . . . ? You can't do San Francisco by registered mail. Where did you see Allahverdi, my dear?"

"I didn't see him."

"How can you have not seen him? We've telephones and telegrams but unfortunately tele-San Francisco's not been invented yet; do you know Allahverdi at all?"

"No."

"Moment, now really moment, so how can your baby's daddy be Allahverdi?"

Qamar answered as she was eating a cookie, "Daddy Dustali said my baby's daddy is Allahverdi."

Everyone, all at once, froze as though electrocuted. For a moment mouths hung open in complete silence.

Aziz al-Saltaneh, her mouth wide open and her eyes round with astonishment, slowly turned her head toward Dustali Khan who was agitatedly looking from one side to another; in strangled tones she said, "Dustali . . ."

Dustali started stammering, "I . . . I . . . I . . . as God's . . . as God's my witness . . . the girl's crazy . . . she's a half-wit . . . her mind's completely defective . . . I . . . I . . . never ever . . ."

Asadollah Mirza couldn't stop himself from laughing. He gave a great guffaw and said, "Moment, moment, as the Arabs say, *al-moment* . . . so this then is the work of We-All-Know-Who?"

In the middle of the astonished, unmoving group of onlookers Dustali Khan once again tried to exculpate himself, "On the soul of my father . . . on the soul of our late grandfather . . . on the soul . . ."

With an agility that would have been remarkable even in a sixteen-year-old girl, Aziz al-Saltaneh suddenly leaped toward the glass cabinet at the end of uncle colonel's sitting room. With a violent gesture she turned the key in the door of the cabinet and snatched up one of uncle's two double-barreled shotguns that were always in the cabinet. Before anyone could move she pointed the barrel at her husband's belly and screamed, "Tell the truth, and if you don't I'll drill you full of holes."

Uncle colonel had jumped up after her, but he froze in his tracks and shouted, "Be careful, woman, that gun's loaded."

Aziz al-Saltaneh said, "And you sit down as well, because if you don't I'll fill your belly full of holes, too."

"I swear on Puri's soul that gun is loaded. In the evening I loaded it, just to test the mechanism, then our guests came and I forgot to take the cartridges out."

Neither the noise everyone else made nor Dear Uncle Napoleon's peremptory commands had any effect on her. Her lips trembling and her face pale, the furious woman screamed out, "All of you shut up! . . . this orangutan has to speak."

Such fury was apparent in her voice that no one dared move; Qamar wanted to stand up but Shamsali Mirza held her firmly in her place. Dustali was standing up; his legs began to tremble. Stumblingly, with a voice coming as if from beyond the tomb, he said, "On the holy Quran . . . on my father's soul . . . just allow me . . . allow me to speak."

Aziz al-Saltaneh screamed, "Spit it out . . . speak! Why did you tell Qamar to say it was Allahverdi's doing?"

"I . . . I . . . I . . . I . . . because I saw that she didn't know . . . the man's name . . . she'd forgotten . . . I said at least . . . at least . . . it'll save face a bit . . . I mean she herself . . . she said that Allahverdi . . ."

At this moment Qamar laughed and said, "What a whopping big liar this daddy Dustali is! . . . Didn't you say to me that if I didn't say Allahverdi was my baby's daddy, you'd kill my baby?"

Dustali Khan shouted, "Shut up! . . . Believe me . . . sir, you say something . . . After all, would I, with my own stepdaughter . . .? I mean, is such a thing possible?"

No one had any opportunity to intervene because Dustali suddenly and with the alacrity of a young gazelle made a dash for the door and took to his heels. At the same speed Aziz al-Saltaneh went out after him. After a moment's astonished silence everyone started shouting and running after them.

"Mrs. Aziz . . . Aziz . . . just think . . . the gun'll go off . . . put the gun . . ."

The husband and wife were considerably ahead of us and had reached the garden. We were running after them with all our strength when suddenly the sound of a shot rang through the garden and immediately after that we heard the noise of Dustali's heart-rending scream, "Aaaggghhh! She's killed me . . ."

We had reached the walnut tree. We still hadn't properly sorted out what had happened. At this moment Mash Qasem caught up with us, carrying a lantern. The lantern's weak light brought us face to face with a strange scene.

Dustali Khan had fallen prone on the ground, and on the back of his trousers, especially in the area of his buttocks, bloodstains were visible. Aziz al-Saltaneh, gun in hand, was standing by his head, motionless and dumbfounded, like someone who had just woken from a dream.

Everyone was in a state of panic and confusion. My father was the first person to bend down and lift Dustali Khan's head. The head fell back motionless to the ground.

"We must do something. Mash Qasem, run and fetch Dr. Naser al-Hokama."

Over all the voices speaking to each other and past each other Qamar gave a loud laugh and said, "Mummy, did you kill daddy

Dustali? . . . That's good! Do you remember he kept saying let's go to the doctor so he can get rid of the baby?"

Uncle colonel took the gun from Aziz al-Saltaneh's hand and said, "We have to get him to a hospital immediately."

Asadollah Mirza said with a smile, "The wretched fool goes off and does a San Francisco, and now he'll have to sleep on his belly till the end of his life. Because this . . . because not to be impolite about it . . . this sit-upon of his won't be a place for sitting upon any more."

Shamsali Mirza said with a frown, "Asadollah, please! This is no time for joking."

"Moment, moment, do you imagine it's anything serious? What could four bits of buckshot, that can hardly kill a partridge, do in all the fat flesh of this donkey Dustali's buttocks? He's playing dead out of fear of Mrs. Aziz al-Saltaneh."

Uncle colonel said harshly, "Instead of chattering, give some thought to this poor devil. In my opinion Dr. Naser al-Hokama will be of no use. We have to take him to the hospital."

At this moment Mash Qasem came back. "The doctor says we're to take the patient there."

My father also thought that we should take the wounded man to a hospital, but in an imperious voice Dear Uncle Napoleon said, "In my opinion, if it's at all possible, it's better we forget about the hospital."

Naturally Dear Uncle's opinion was the one that was acted upon and the motionless body of Dustali Khan was transferred, on Mash Qasem's back, to Dr. Naser al-Hokama's surgery.

FOURTEEN

A FEW OF THE NEIGHBORS had gathered at the entrance. Shamsali Mirza went to the door and sent them off to their own houses, but before the door to Dr. Naser al-Hokama's house could be closed the Indian brigadier, Maharat Khan, insinuated himself in.

I glanced at Dear Uncle. He was staring at the Indian, pale and wide-eyed, and I could guess what was going on inside him.

Dr. Naser al-Hokama loudly exclaimed, "Your good health, gentlemen, your good health, but I'm not a surgeon, you'll have to take him to the hospital . . . Mash Qasem said he'd been hurt in the leg, but now from what you're saying it seems he's been shot."

Dear Uncle said to him quietly, "Doctor, for the sake of all our former friendship and neighborliness and closeness, I'm asking you to examine Dustali Khan . . . it's out of the question that we take him to the hospital. I'll explain everything to you later."

There was such supplication, and at the same time such firmness, in Dear Uncle's voice that the doctor made no further objections. He simply said, "Then on your head be it. If, God forbid, an infaction develops then I'm not responsible." The doctor always had a strange horror of infection, which he pronounced "infaction," and he even terrified patients who had sprained their wrists with his talk of the consequences of "infaction."

Nevertheless he went over to Dustali Khan, who was lying on his stomach on the consulting room's examination table, and said, "But all you ladies and gentlemen must leave the room. I can't carry out an examination with all these people here."

Everyone made for the door, but Aziz al-Saltaneh, who kept hitting herself on the face and head, said, "But I have to stay . . . I wish my hand had been broken, that I'd been paralyzed so I couldn't have done it . . . I have to stay to see this calamity of mine through."

"Your good health, but you too will have to be so kind as to leave, and if you don't then I shall have nothing to do with the patient."

At this moment the Indian jumped into the conversation. "I have a very efficacious Indian ointment for the treatment of wounds of this nature which is certainly producing the most excellent healing effects in the wink of an eye. Right this minute I will go and fetch it."

And having said this he left in a great hurry.

His face contorted, Dear Uncle said through gritted teeth, "Qasem! Don't open the door to that shameless countryless wretch! Now he's seen his plan didn't work out as expected, he wants to kill Dustali Khan with his Indian ointment. No doubt Dustali Khan wanted to tell me the secret plans of the English."

Mash Qasem nodded his head and said, "If the bastard waits outside the door till mornin', I won't open it. I know what that ointment is . . . it's a black oil that they get from the liver of black vipers. Put a little tin of it in front of an elephant's nose and he'll turn to ashes on the spot . . . there was a man in our town who . . ."

I went over to the patient and the doctor to see what was going on there. Dr. Naser al-Hokama was standing to one side and waiting for everyone to leave his consulting room, and Aziz al-Saltaneh was refusing to move. Finally she too left, at Dear Uncle's insistence. The doctor said, "My assistant isn't here. Just Mash Qasem must stay, to help me."

Mash Qasem dashed forward, "At your service . . . I've a lot of experience at this kind of work. Why should I lie? To the grave it's ah . . . ah . . . One time there was a man from our town who'd been stabbed in the spleen, and by myself, I . . ."

The doctor frowned and said, "Your good health, Mr. Mash Qasem, there's no need for you to stay either, you chatter too much, out you go . . . that gentleman can come and help me."

The doctor pointed at me. He cleared everyone from the room and said, "Either go to your own homes or sit in the waiting room. I don't want to see anyone in the hallway or in the yard outside." The waiting room and consulting room were on each side of the entrance to the building, and the doctor's house was on the further side of the yard.

When everyone had gone into the waiting room and the surgery was empty, the doctor said to me, "Your good health, my dear boy, help me get the clothes off the patient. Now you're not afraid of blood, are you?"

"No, doctor sir, certainly not."

"Then let's get Dustali Khan's jacket and trousers off."

I didn't find this too difficult, because it was as if the motionless patient, even though he was unconscious, actually helped us remove his clothes, and he didn't have the dead weight unconscious people normally have.

The doctor cleaned the places that had been bleeding with swabs and alcohol. The wounds consisted of three small holes. The doctor touched the wounds and said under his breath, "It looks as though the pellets entered his body after they'd been fired from some distance away . . . they haven't gone in very far, they're just under the skin."

I realized that Dustali Khan's forehead was covered in sweat and that he was moving. I drew the doctor's attention to this. He brought his head down close to the patient's ear and said, "Dustali Khan, can you hear me?"

A smothered moan emerged from Dustali Khan's throat, "Yes, I can hear you."

Then he raised his eyelids, looked carefully round the room and in a quieter voice asked, "My wife's not here?"

"Your good health, there's no one here except myself and this young man."

It was as if Dustali Khan had been holding back his cries until this moment; he gave vent to a great moan and said, "What I've been through . . . Doctor . . . what's happened? Where did it hit?"

"Your good health, there's nothing serious. Three little pellets fired from quite a distance away have struck you in the buttocks . . . but they haven't gone in far . . . if you can stand it, I'll be able to get them out . . . or would you rather I sent you to the hospital?"

With a moan Dustali Khan said, "I'm dying of the pain . . . I've been in pain for an hour and haven't dared to utter a sound."

"Why didn't you utter a sound?"

"Out of fear of that running sore . . . that murderer . . . my wife . . . I'll tell you about it later, but I beg you on the soul of your own children not to send me to the hospital, and I'd like to ask you to tell my wife that my life's in danger but that the hospital's not . . ."

The doctor cut him off, "But I haven't got anything to anaesthetize you with here, you'll have to grit your teeth while I get the pellets out with tweezers . . . you'll have to put up with it!"

"Yes, doctor, I'll put up with it . . . but promise you'll tell my wife my life's in danger and that there's not much hope I'll pull through . . . if she realizes I'm not in too bad a shape she'll throttle me before morning's here, she'll kill me."

And then he addressed me, "And you, on your own mother's soul, don't you be saying anything . . . you know Aziz, you know she'll . . ."

"Don't worry about that, Mr. Dustali Khan, I promise I won't say a word to Mrs. al-Saltaneh."

Dustali Khan breathed a sigh of relief and asked for a glass of water. The doctor went out to talk to the people in the waiting room. After I'd given Dustali Khan a drink of water from the doctor's metal washstand, I followed him. The doctor was insisting to Aziz al-Saltaneh that she return home.

"You go back to your house now, Mrs. al-Saltaneh, your husband is not at all well, but I am doing my very best . . ."

As he was saying this the doctor winked at Dear Uncle and the others who were there, and in this way let them know he wasn't telling the truth.

Asadollah Mirza came over to me and quietly asked, "How is he?"

I answered as quietly, "It's nothing serious, he pretended to be unconscious out of fear of Mrs. al-Saltaneh."

Despite the doctor's insistence, no one was ready to leave the premises. The doctor had no choice but to go back to his consulting room. I followed him. With Dustali biting into the pillow while great drops of sweat formed on his forehead, the doctor extracted the three tiny pellets with tweezers, and then dressed the wounds.

In a voice choking from the intensity of the pain, Dustali Khan managed to beg the doctor that he bandage his whole body, and asked him to say that he couldn't be taken home and that he was to sleep in Dear Uncle's house that night.

When the doctor emerged from his consulting room everyone clustered around him. Aziz al-Saltaneh shouted, "Doctor, doctor, tell me the worst, tell me how he is."

"Your good health, ma'am, your good health, at the moment we can't say anything. It depends on how tough his body is. If he makes it through the night, perhaps he'll live . . ."

Once again while he was saying this he indicated, by winking and moving his eyebrows, to Dear Uncle and the rest that what he was saying was just a convenient ruse.

Then he went on, "But let him sleep at the Master's house tonight, so that he'll be closer to me and if he collapses I'll be able to get to him more quickly. I've given him some morphine for now so that if he comes round he won't suffer too much."

We placed the motionless bandaged body of Dustali Khan on a portable cot and transferred him to Dear Uncle's house.

Azizullah Khan, the local constable, who had been pacing up and down at the doorway, accompanied us to Dear Uncle's house. Dear Uncle said to him, "Mr. Azizullah Khan, Dustali is better. You can be on your way."

"But sir, it's my duty to make out a report. Someone's been shot."

"It was an accident, my good man, he was cleaning a gun when it went off. He's in good shape and no one's lodging a complaint."

"But saving your grace, sir, how was he cleaning his gun if the bullet went into that part of his body? Do you take me for a child?"

Mash Qasem became angry, "Why are you makin' things so difficult, Azizullah Khan? All you folks from Malayer know how to do is make things difficult. The poor feller was playin' with his gun and it went off . . ."

Constable Azizullah Khan interrupted him, "Then are you telling me he was playing with the gun with his backside?"

"Well, a gun's a gun . . . sometimes it hits a man in the eye, sometimes in his liver, sometimes in that part. There was a man in our town who . . ."

Dear Uncle angrily interrupted him, "Mash Qasem, can I possibly ask you not to interfere?"

Dear Uncle took Azizullah Khan into a room and there convinced him by logic and irrefutable proofs that it was possible, while a man was playing with a gun, for a stray bullet to strike that part of his anatomy, because when Azizullah Khan emerged from the room he said, "You've really put me to shame, sir, you've been that good to me, sir . . . I'll be off now, and I never heard nothing about all this fuss . . . but if, God forbid, anything should happen to Dustali Khan, you'll have to tell the police station yourself by morning."

When I went into the room where they had lain Dustali Khan down on his stomach, I caught sight of Layli, who was sitting with tearful eyes next to the patient's bed. I couldn't bear to see her upset and unhappy. I signalled her to come over to me and told her that the wounded man was not in a serious condition and was playing the role of a patient at death's door out of fear of his wife.

Aziz al-Saltaneh could not keep still. She constantly slapped herself about the face and head, moaning and sobbing, "God cripple me . . . God strike me dead, I never wanted to see Dustali like this . . . for goodness sake, think of something, bring another doctor . . . let's take him to the hospital."

And Dear Uncle was trying to calm her down. "Mrs. al-Saltaneh, another doctor will be of no use . . . what doctor are we going to get at this time of night? And it's not at all advisable to move him now. He's only just stopped bleeding . . . and then the hospital is going to ask questions about what happened . . . do you want to go to prison?"

There was a moment of silence. Then a moaning sound came from the wounded man, and his lips moved. He seemed to be saying something but no words came from his mouth.

Asadollah Mirza, who had remained quiet during this whole period, said, "Moment, it looks as though he wants to say something."

Then he sat down by the bed and brought his head down to the patient's mouth, "Speak, Dustali . . . if you're still alive say something. If you're already on your way give our regards to those who've gone before."

Dustali's lips continued to tremble. Finally his voice could be heard, "Where's Aziz?"

Striking herself on the head and chest, Aziz al-Saltaneh sat down next to him and said, "I'm here, Dustali, may God let me suffer in your place. I'm here."

With his eyes closed, in a weak voice, Dustali Khan said, "No, no, you're not Aziz . . . I . . . I . . . I want . . . Aziz."

"It's me, it's really me, I'm Aziz, O God, what I wouldn't do to hear that voice of yours . . ."

"You're . . . you're . . . not Aziz . . . I . . . want Aziz."

"God strike me dead . . . he doesn't know me any more . . . Dustali . . . Dustali, open your eyes, I'm Aziz."

A moment later Dustali Khan opened his eyes and stared at his wife's face. "Agh . . . agh . . . thank God . . . I've seen you once more . . . Aziz . . . let bygones be bygones . . . let me depart with an easy mind . . . water . . . water . . ."

We managed to give him a drop of water. He opened his eyes completely and went on in the same weak voice, "Aziz . . . forgive me . . . maybe I've committed many sins but . . . in the matter of Qamar I wasn't . . . I wasn't the guilty one. I was innocent . . ."

Dustali Khan's gaze wandered round the room and he asked, "Where's Qamar?"

"In the other room with the children . . . God, I'd be glad to hear she'd died after she's caused all this . . ."

"Watch over her . . . that girl is crazy . . . to save the family honor I said to her that . . . but . . . but . . . I wasn't the guilty one . . . where's Shamsali Mirza?"

Shamsali Mirza came quickly forward, "I'm here Dustali . . ."

"Please, get hold of a pen and paper and write my will down, so that I can sign it before my strength finally gives out . . . everything I own belongs to Aziz . . ."

Aziz al-Saltaneh struck herself on the face, "What are you saying? May God strike Aziz dead . . . Aziz isn't going to outlive you for you to leave her anything."

Dustali Khan screamed, "Shamsali! Do not refuse me my last request!"

Mash Qasem interrupted, "Eh, don't upset him . . . God rest his soul, he was a good feller." Everybody looked angrily at Mash Qasem and he hung his head.

Shamsali Mirza produced a pen and paper and Dustali Khan began to dictate his will. He left his house, shop and worldly goods to his wife. At the end he said with a moan, "Just a moment, I forgot the property at Mahmudabad. Write that, in the same way, I leave to my wife the entire estate in Mahmudabad near Qazvin, together with its water canals . . ."

Once again Aziz al-Saltaneh struck herself in the face. "May God strike Aziz dead and may she never see the property in Mahmudabad again . . . by the way, was that caravanserai in Mahmudabad yours too?"

"Yes . . . write the caravanserai down too . . ."

Asadollah Mirza couldn't control himself. With a moved expression on his face he said, "Don't forget the sheep."

Aziz al-Saltaneh whined, "To hell with the bloody sheep . . . he sold the sheep last year."

Dustali Khan swallowed and said, "Now . . . now give it to me to sign . . . and all of you must sign it too at the bottom . . . all . . . all of you."

Shamsali Mirza brought the pen and paper over but Dustali Khan's hand didn't move. With a groan he said, "O God . . . O God give me the strength to sign this . . . lift me up . . . lift my hand out from under the blanket!"

Shamsali Mirza raised his upper body a little and took his hand out from under the blanket, but the hand fell back lifelessly.

Dustali Khan seemed to gather all his strength together to scream, "O God . . . O God, my hand . . . my hand."

Aziz al-Saltaneh tried to help him, "Do you want me to help you, dear?"

Once again Asadollah Mirza couldn't control himself and said, "Moment, even if his whole body gets better this right hand will never move again. Poor devil! Well, it's obvious if a bullet strikes in the behind the right hand's going to be paralyzed. The relationship between the right hand and the behind has been scientifically established."

Dustali Khan wanted to say something to him, but he seemed to change his mind. He tried, by himself, to raise himself up, but then gave a cry, fell back unmoving and his eyes closed.

My father, who had remained silent up to this moment, said angrily, "You're killing him bit by bit. Let him rest!"

Dear Uncle gave him a furious look and angrily answered him, "Please do not interfere."

I didn't understand why he was angry. Perhaps his nerves were frayed, but my father was very taken aback by this inappropriate outburst and said, "In any case, there's no point in our staying here. I'm going."

And with an extremely preoccupied look on his face he left the room.

After a few moments' silence Dear Uncle said, "We'd better leave the patient alone for now. Just his wife should stay with him, and we can have Qamar sleep at our house, too."

As we left the room Asadollah Mirza beckoned me over. We walked out of the inner apartments into the garden. I told him what had passed in the conversation between Dustali Khan and the doctor. Asadollah Mirza shook his head and said, "This family is cursed. Some new quarrel's going to start up tomorrow. Did you notice how today Dear Uncle went for your father a couple of times? And each time I saw such fury glittering in your father's eyes I'm certain that any time soon he's going to arrange for some sort of catastrophe to strike this old man. Did you notice?"

"Yes, that time he said something to my father about lineage and honor."

"Then, and he's just gone for him again now."

"I'm really worried about all this, too, Uncle Asadollah. I'm afraid some new quarrel's going to blow up."

"It's obvious it began with that, but in a covert kind of way . . . if this matter of Qamar's pregnancy hadn't come up, your father would have started in at the beginning of the evening . . . it's really ridiculous, they talk about lineage and honor as if they were descended from the Hapsburgs . . . now, if you can, be sure to get hold of that letter of Dear Uncle's to Hitler."

"I haven't been able to yet. I think he's put it in the drawer of his desk, and he's locked it."

Asadollah Mirza remained sunk in thought for a moment. Then his eyes lit up and he said, "I've thought of a way. I think I'm going to have to give the office a miss tomorrow. Drop by at my house tomorrow morning."

The next morning I called on Asadollah Mirza. We left his house together, setting off in the direction away from our house. After going through a couple of alleyways he suddenly stopped in front of a shoeshine man whose little stall had been set up in the street. He put one foot on the man's box and asked the man to shine his shoes. I stood silently to one side, waiting for him.

Asadollah Mirza struck up a conversation with the shoeshine man, who was young and well built, asking after his health and how he was getting on, and I was surprised that he could think of having his shoes shined at such a critical time.

"But I don't think you can do much business around here . . . why don't you go over to the road with the trees, over there? We have to come all this way round to get here, or we have to go round the other way to the main road."

"Well sir, it's all God's will if a man gets by or not; and without that, being in this place or that place's got nothing to do with it."

"Moment, what do you mean this place or that place has got nothing to do with it? If you were nearer I'd come myself twice a day to get my shoes shined. Everyone in my area's looking for a cobbler and shoeshine man."

Asadollah Mirza gave him a thousand reasons why, if he set up his stall opposite our house and garden, his income would double.

The shoeshine man cheerfully welcomed this suggestion and promised that, from that afternoon on, he would set up his stall in our alleyway, which had large shady trees in it, opposite the entrance way to our garden.

Asadollah Mirza gave him a tip, besides the fee for shining his shoes, and we set off back toward our house.

Guessing at what I wanted to ask him, he said, "This shoeshine fellow is going to be very useful to us, you'll realize why later. For now the main thing is to find somewhere from where we can send a phone call from Hitler to Dear Uncle . . . aha, I remember . . . come on, one of my friends who has a telephone lives around here."

An ancient servant opened the door to us. When Asadollah Mirza said we wanted to make a phone call, he immediately led us upstairs to where the phone was. He then went off to the kitchen to make tea.

Asadollah Mirza promptly dialled Dear Uncle's number. When Dear Uncle came to the phone, his lordship put on his representative-of-Hitler accent and said, "My late grandfather eating *ab-gusht* with Jeanette McDonald . . . sir, you listen good . . . it is very important important important what I say . . . first, that our code is changed . . . because it is possible the English spy understood. When our representative say 'My late grandfather eating Irish stew with Jeanette

McDonald,' you asked 'What with?,' and he say 'With pickled marjoram.' If you not know him say this then it is clear he is English spy and you kicked him out . . . Second, that we gav placed an agent looking like tradesman in front of your door that he be looking after you . . .while this tradesman was here you not being at all at all afraid . . . you was completely confident he was looking after you . . . but you must not at all talking to the tradesman about this . . . we was being in touch again, before the time for your departing . . ."

It seemed that Dear Uncle was insisting on some way he could recognize the aforementioned agent. Asadollah Mirza said, "I very very confidential saying to you, is a shoeshine man . . . but you not at all, at all, at all talked to no one . . . gav you understand? God keep you . . . Heil Hitler!"

When he put the receiver down a satisfied smile played across his lips and he said to me, "Poor thing, he's a simple-minded fellow, but now his mind'll be quite made up and your father won't be able to play any more tricks on him . . . so much for Dear Uncle. Now we must think of something for that poor wretch of a girl . . . Dustali Khan or some other idiot has done a San Francisco and now they want to abort the three- or four-month-old fetus, even if it's at the cost of that poor girl's life."

"How about if we told Dear Uncle that Hitler would be upset? . . . but he wouldn't believe that."

As we left his friend's house, Asadollah Mirza said, "Now we must look in on that donkey Dustali Khan and see how he's getting on."

"Are you very worried about him?"

"Moment, not in the slightest, I know that a shrapnel bomb wouldn't harm that tub of lard, never mind three shotgun pellets. No, it's that crazy half-witted girl I feel sorry for."

Mash Qasem opened the door to us and, in answer to Asadollah Mirza's questions concerning Dustali Khan's health, said, "Why should I lie? To the grave it's ah . . . ah . . . 'slike he's not doin' too bad . . . Mrs. Aziz was here till mornin', now she's gone over to her own house and then she'll be back."

When we entered the room Dustali Khan, who was lying on his stomach, had raised his upper body and was eating his breakfast with great relish from a tray on the bed in front of him. As soon as he heard the door he pulled the blanket over both himself and the breakfast tray and lay motionless. Asadollah Mirza laughed and said, "Don't worry, Dustali, it's only us, Aziz isn't here. Fill that gross belly of yours."

"As God's my witness, I'm in a bad way . . . but the doctor said I should eat something to make up for the blood I've lost . . . but on the soul of your mother, don't breath a word to Aziz! On your own death, I swear I'm dying with the pain!"

"Eh, swear on your own dad's death, what's my death got to do with it . . . but you made your bed and now you have to lie on it. You did a San Francisco and now you have to put up with the consequences."

"By your death, Asadollah, by my own death, I never did a thing . . . I just feel sorry for the girl. If we could find someone who wouldn't mind that she's having the baby, then we could get Qamar married off for a few days and I'd give him whatever he wanted . . . and I'd give a notarized undertaking that we'd bring up the child."

"Moment, what simpleton can you find who'd be ready to tie that clog to himself for an hour, never mind a week?"

Dustali Khan answered in a quiet friendly tone, "Asadollah . . . I've been thinking . . . I mean I said to myself that . . . I was thinking that if you . . . if you could . . . ."

Laughing, Asadollah said, "Moment! This would be an expensive business. Dustali, you'd really have to loosen the purse strings."

Dustali Khan had not been prepared for such a mild reaction on Asadollah Mirza's part, and he said excitedly, "I'll give you whatever you want . . . ."

But suddenly he seemed to realize that his excitement and loud tone of voice were not suitable for a wounded man at the point of death; he went on in a quieter voice, "Asadollah, you and I grew up together. If we leave aside a few small childish differences, you and I have always liked each other. I haven't long to live now . . . accept this last request of mine."

Asadollah Mirza well knew that Dustali Khan was playing the part of a man at death's door, and with fake emotion he said, "Don't say that, Dustali, don't say that, you're breaking my heart! You're so young! You had so many high hopes! I promise you that every Friday I'll put a bunch of hollyhocks on your grave stone. Forgive me that my circumstances don't allow me to run to camellias . . . never mind, instead of La Dame aux Camélias, you'll be Le Monsieur aux Hollyhocks . . ."

"Asadollah, please don't joke. This is no time for joking. Tell me how much you want!"

"You'll give me whatever I want?"

"Rest assured, Asadollah. To save this poor girl . . ."

"The property at Mahmudabad, my dear Dustali."

"What? The property at Mahmudabad? Have you gone crazy? I have to give you the whole property just so you'll marry this girl for a couple of days?"

Asadollah Mirza suddenly realized what Dustali Khan was driving at. With fury in his face he stood up. He picked up a small cushion and said, "Moment, Dustali, I really liked you, you were a very fine fellow, but so that you won't talk any more of this nonsense I'm going to have bring the angel of death's job forward a bit."

Then he raised his head to the skies and went on, "God forgive me! In all my life I've never harmed so much as an ant, but the quicker this man reaches you up there, the better it'll be for humanity. Please take him back! Damaged goods returned to sender!"

In the midst of this rhetorical display he placed the cushion over Dustali's mouth and added, "Farewell, Dustali! I am doing you my last favor in the world of friendship. Because every extra minute you stay here you commit another sin. Ready for departure, Monsieur aux Hollyhocks! To the rendezvous in hell . . . at the Boulevard of the Lord of the Inferno, in the alley named after Ali Asghar the mass-murderer, next to the coal shop belonging to Yazid, slayer of the martyrs . . ."

With terror in his face Dustali looked at Asadollah. Asadollah played the role of a man beside himself with rage so well that Dustali was really afraid, and he stammered out, "Asadollah . . . Asadollah . . . I was joking . . . on your own soul . . . on your death I was joking . . ."

Dustali was lying prone and Asadollah brought the cushion down violently on his buttocks. Dustali's scream went up to the heavens, "Agh, I'm dead! . . . That wasn't fair, to hit me on the scars!"

"While you remain alive don't speak another word of that rubbish!"

Dustali Khan whimpered, "What was rubbish that I said? You said if I loosened the purse strings you'd agree to . . ."

Asadollah Mirza cut him off, "You ignorant animal! I thought you expected me to find someone to marry your stepdaughter. Are you telling me that even at death's door you can't give up your wicked ways . . . if Monsieur aux Hollyhocks goes on with his filth and philandering I'm going to have to fix all that . . . you wretch, even in your wretchedness you're lucky your wife shot bullets into your lacerated backside, so that now she has to shut up, otherwise you'd have been in prison for fifteen years."

"Asadollah, believe me, on your death I swear that if it was me . . . on my own death, on your death . . ."

Asadollah was standing at his bedside, and kicked him in the leg with the toe of his shoe, saying, "On your dad's death, on all your ancestors' deaths . . ."

Dustali Khan screamed with pain. Layli's room was across the corridor from the room where we were, and the sound of his voice brought her running into the room; anxiously she asked, "What's happened? What's happened?"

Asadollah Mirza's face widened in a smile. In a voice filled with kindness he said, "Don't worry, my dear, nothing's happened. Dustali has departed . . . God rest his soul, he's now chasing after the gatekeeper of hell's wife."

Dustali moaned, "If I could just get up, I'd give you such a hiding you wouldn't forget it for your whole life."

Layli stared at me with an inquiring look on her face. "Don't worry. Uncle Asadollah and Dustali Khan were joking around."

With the same smile still on his face, Asadollah Mirza placed his hand on my shoulder and said, "Off you go to Layli's room for a moment, lad . . . I want to talk to this aging Don Juan about that poor girl for a moment."

Nothing could have pleased me more and I took Layli's hand. We went to her room together. For a moment Layli's warm intimate glance wiped all memory of the various events of the past day and night from my mind. We were silent for a little while. The sound of Asadollah Mirza and Dustali Khan talking in the next room brought us back to the real world again. Anxiously I said to Layli, "You know, Layli, I'm really worried . . . did you notice how last night they were talking again about Puri coming back?"

Layli's face clouded over. She hung her head. Quietly she said, "Last night I didn't sleep till morning. I'm really afraid . . . last night when I got home daddy talked about the same thing, too."

"What did he say?"

"Just the same as uncle colonel said, about getting engaged. If daddy wants to force me to, I daren't say no. But I've one way left . . ."

"But why? I mean, can they force a girl to . . ."

Layli interrupted me, "It's impossible for me to answer daddy back. But I can do away with myself . . ."

My heart nearly stood still, but I tried to comfort her—and myself at the same time.

"No, Layli, we'll find a way . . . we're sure to find a way . . ." At this moment we heard Dear Uncle's voice calling for Layli from the other side of the yard. Layli said, "Stay here till I get back."

From the window I watched her go over to her father. It seemed that Dear Uncle was entrusting her with delivering some kind of message, because Layli gave a stealthy glance at the window to her room and then after a moment's hesitation went off toward the big garden.

Dear Uncle went toward the room where Dustali was convalescing; as he reached the doorway he was confronted with the glowing face of Asadollah, who was just coming out. I could hear their conversation.

"How is Dustali?"

"He's flirting with the angel of death."

"I don't think this is a suitable time for making jokes, Asadollah."

"I'm not joking at all, but luckily it seems that Aziz al-Saltaneh's bullet has done in his noble member . . . mind you, we're at fault there, if we'd let Madam Aziz cut it off that other time, a bullet wouldn't have gone to waste this time."

Asadollah Mirza left the room and Dear Uncle entered it. I pricked up my ears. The door was ajar. Though I couldn't see them I could hear their conversation well enough. After asking him how he was, Dear Uncle was silent for a few moments; then in a very cold, serious tone he said, "Dustali, I'm going to ask you something and, for the sake of all the kindness I've shown you, I expect you to answer me completely honestly! It's natural for mankind to sin . . ."

"As God's my witness, on your soul, on the soul of Aziz . . . on the spirit of my late father . . ."

"Dustali, talk sense . . . last night I felt you wanted to tell me something but those whose interests were not served by your talking prevented you from speaking . . . now tell me: What did you want to say?"

"I . . . I . . . I mean . . . in fact . . . maybe you're right . . . I wanted to say that, though I'm not at all at fault in this matter, I'm ready to pay any price to . . . in any way . . ."

"Listen, Dustali, as Napoleon said, it's only one step from being a traitor to being a loyal subject, if the step is taken at the right time. If you're looking for some kind of payback, I'll help you so you don't stay stuck in this mess. Recently I've realized that you support certain political interests . . ."

At this point the racket made by Aziz al-Saltaneh in the yard outside cut off the thread of their conversation, "How is my poor little Dustali? After you, doctor."

Aziz al-Saltaneh entered Dustali Khan's room, followed by Dr. Naser al-Hokama. After examining the patient, he pronounced himself satisfied with his condition and left the room, saying "Your good health" as he did so. Layli returned to where I was and the two of us sat in silence listening through the open door to the conversation of Dear Uncle, Aziz al-Saltaneh and Dustali Khan, who spoke in a weak voice interspersed with moans.

Dear Uncle said, "It looks as though the danger's receding, thank goodness."

"I hope the good Lord takes your word for it. I've made a vow, if Dustali gets better I'll go to the Davud shrine and sacrifice a sheep to distribute the meat to the poor."

"But have you thought what to do about Qamar? . . . What did that doctor say to you finally?"

"He said it's way too late for an abortion, it might be dangerous for her."

Dear Uncle said violently, "Doctors always say that kind of rubbish. Why don't you go and find one of those backstreet midwives?"

"Well sir, I'm afraid to. I'm afraid that—God forbid—they might do the poor girl some awful injury."

"You should also be thinking of the family honor. If the girl's poor father had been alive he'd have died of the disgrace. Lucky for him he's dead and never had to witness this shame . . . tomorrow the news'll be all over town."

"I'm afraid of that, too. By now lots of folk must have heard about it . . . the little wretch can't keep her mouth shut . . . I bet you that today that gossip Farrokh Laqa'll turn up."

At this moment uncle colonel's and his wife's voices were suddenly audible from the yard, calling for Dear Uncle with obvious agitation. Everyone, including Layli and I, ran into the yard.

Uncle colonel and his wife were both extremely upset, and both of them tried to tell Dear Uncle why at the same time. Finally uncle colonel quieted his wife down and said, "As the oldest brother, please say something to this woman. She's been crying for an hour . . ."

"What's happened?"

"If you remember, we were so worried about Puri that before his letter arrived I wrote to a friend of mine in Ahvaz asking him to find out how Puri was doing and to let us know. He wrote that Puri was sick. Now no matter how much I tell my wife that Puri wrote to us after that letter, it doesn't do any good."

"But aren't the letters dated?"

"No, they're not, but I'm quite sure that Puri wrote to us after he did . . ."

Weeping, uncle colonel's wife said, "I beg you, I'll do anything for you . . . Sir, please think of something. Send a telegram."

Dear Uncle asked, "How is he sick now? I mean, how was he sick?"

Uncle colonel's wife didn't give her husband a chance to answer. She said, "They wrote that my boy heard a gun go off and went into shock . . . God strike me dead for letting the boy go off to the war, it's so noisy!"

Uncle colonel said with some asperity, "Why are you talking such rubbish, woman? That man writes rubbish and you have to repeat it? He must have eaten some contaminated food and collapsed, and if he didn't, Puri's my son, after all. You won't find one in a thousand young men with the courage and daring and bravery of my Puri."

Layli and I exchanged glances and smothered our laughter. Asadollah Mirza had just come out of Dear Uncle's reception room a moment or so before and had heard the last part of the conversation. As he approached the group he said, "The colonel's right . . . there isn't even one in a million young men as brave as Puri. The boy's appearance reminds me of Julius Caesar."

Uncle colonel turned his head angrily in his direction. But Asadollah Mirza had such an innocent look on his face that uncle's furious glance turned to one filled with gratitude, and he calmly said, "I thank you, Asadollah, with all your faults you've one virtue, that you see people for what they are." Then he turned to Dear Uncle Napoleon and went on, "But in your opinion how would it be if I went to Ahvaz to see for myself . . ."

Dear Uncle Napoleon interrupted him, "What kind of time is this for taking trips, my dear sir? Send a telegram to this friend of yours. This is no time for taking trips. We can't leave the front undefended. For all you know this is some trick of theirs to get you away from me. To clear everyone away from me the better to achieve their goals . . . And now they're approaching Tehran."

Once again Asadollah Mirza couldn't remain silent, "The Master's right . . . it's not at all unlikely that there are wheels within wheels here . . . you'd better send a telegram."

The sound of two people shouting and quarreling in the alleyway became audible. Dear Uncle Napoleon pricked up his ears and after a moment turned to me, "Go and see what's going on, lad. What all the fuss and shouting's about."

I ran into the alleyway.

Mash Qasem was standing with a broom in his hand arguing with the shoeshine man, who apparently intended to set up his little stall opposite the entrance to our garden.

"This here ain't your aunty's house for some feller to come along every day and set up shop."

"Cut the cackle. What are you shouting so much for?"

"Never mind my shoutin'. If you spread out your stuff here, I'll chuck all your tins of polish and rags and leather in the gutter."

For a moment I stood stock-still, but rather than interfere, I preferred to go and tell Dear Uncle what was going on, before the shoeshine man saw me.

I ran quickly back to the house. As soon as Dear Uncle Napoleon saw me he asked, "What's going on?"

"Well, uncle, a shoeshine man has come and wants to set out his stuff in front of the door to our garden, and Mash Qasem is trying to get rid of him."

Dear Uncle was like a man who has been given an electric shock. He stood rooted to the spot; for a moment he froze, his eyes staring and his mouth hanging open. Then he shouted, "What? . . . Mash Qasem? . . . A shoeshine man? . . . What the hell does he think he's doing!"

And he hurried off toward the street. Asadollah Mirza winked at me, but he stayed where he was and didn't move.

I set off after Dear Uncle Napoleon.

When we reached the alleyway Mash Qasem was grappling with the shoeshine man and shouting, "I'll beat the livin' daylights out of you, you callin' me a donkey?"

Dear Uncle came to a standstill and shouted, "Qasem!"

Mash Qasem went on grappling with the shoeshine man and shouted out, "I'm no son of Ghiasabad if I don't teach you a lesson you'll never forget!"

Dear Uncle stepped forward and gave Mash Qasem a blow on the neck. "Qasem! Idiot, I said calm down! What's going on?"

"This feller came and wanted to spread out his cobblin' stuff here. I told him to go, and he started arguin' with me . . ."

I tried to keep myself out of the shoeshine man's line of vision. Panting for breath, the shoeshine man said, "Sir, I came here to work, he came and swore at me . . . look man, can't you keep a civil tongue in your head?"

And as he was gathering up his the materials of his trade he added, "I'm out of here, this alleyway's reserved for the sons of Ghiasabad."

His face flushed, Mash Qasem shouted, "What do I hear you sayin'? If you mention Ghiasabad again I'll give you such a belt on the snout it'll knock your teeth out in your mouth."

Trembling with rage, Dear Uncle said in strangled tones, "Qasem, shut up! And if you don't I'll shut you up with my own hands! What right do you have to prevent people from going about their business? It's not as if he's eating you out of house and home!"

The shoeshine man's face lit up, but Mash Qasem stared at Dear Uncle with round, astonished eyes.

"But sir, didn't you yourself tell me not to let these here gutter-snipes spread their stuff out here? Didn't you say as how they come to case the houses and then come at night, thievin'?"

"Idiot, I said suspicious people, not some poor tradesman who's trying to keep body and soul together!"

"Why should I lie? To the grave it's ah . . . ah . . . Up till now I've not seen a more suspicious feller than this 'un. His eyes are just drippin' with thievin' and oglin' folks and suspiciousness."

The shoeshine man said angrily, "You should understand just what it is you're saying." Then he picked up his box of tools and went on, "I'm out of here, but it's a pity that this gentleman has got such a donkey for a servant."

Mash Qasem made to attack him, but Dear Uncle struck him hard in the chest and pushed him back and said to the shoeshine man, "Sir . . . what's your name?"

"Hushang, at your service."

For a moment Dear Uncle stared at the shoeshine man's face in astonishment and said under his breath, "Strange! Strange! Hushang . . ."

The shoeshine man undid his apron and threw it over one shoulder, "If you ever need a job doing . . . shoeshine, new soles, sandals repaired . . . I'll be two streets further down, by the coal seller's place."

And he prepared to leave.

Anxiously Dear Uncle said, "What's this, sir? Where are you going? This is a very good place right here. From morning till evening we've a thousand jobs of polishing and shoe-repairs. If just my family gives you work you'll have no need of any more."

"No sir, I'm going. It's not worth the bother; a hundred pounds of meat got by hunting's not worth one lousy hunting dog."

And he really started on his way. Dear Uncle threw himself in his path and took his arm, "Sir, please . . . I promise you that Mash Qasem will behave toward you as if he were your brother."

Under his breath, so that Dear Uncle couldn't hear, Mash Qasem said, "Oh yeah, you and your bleedin' ancestors, too . . . I'll show you a lousy huntin' dog, right enough."

Dear Uncle turned to Mash Qasem, "Isn't that so, Mash Qasem? . . . Won't you behave like a brother to Hushang?"

Mash Qasem hung his head and said, "Well now, why should I lie? To the grave it's ah . . . ah . . . whatever you say, sir . . . but if you remember that photographer feller . . ."

Catching sight of Dear Uncle's angry look, he stopped short. "Well, it seems like I mistook this feller for that shoeshine feller in the bazaar."

The shoeshine man put his bundle down. Dear Uncle breathed a sigh of relief and said, "At lunchtime Mash Qasem will bring you out some lunch . . . Qasem! Tell your mistress that if the food's ready she's to send a plate out for Hushang . . . and don't forget to bring salad and bread and yoghurt, too."

With a relaxed, satisfied look on his face the shoeshine man spread his wares out and said, "Very kind of you and God keep you in your generosity, sir . . . but I'll eat my own bread and grapes."

"No, no . . . out of the question . . . today you're our guest. And come in the garden to have lunch."

As we were returning to the inner apartments Mash Qasem, who was extremely put out, tried to give Dear Uncle some guiding advice. But he was confronted by such a furious expression on Dear Uncle's face that he swallowed his words and sealed his lips.

When we reached the inner apartments Asadollah Mirza gave me an enquiring look. With a gesture I reassured him that all had gone as planned.

The subject of Puri's illness was reopened, but it didn't get anywhere because Layli came running out of the living room saying that someone from the office of criminal affairs wanted to talk to Aziz al-Saltaneh.

Aziz al-Saltaneh went to the phone and everyone gathered about her, wondering what could be afoot.

"Hello, yes . . . who? . . . Good day to you, sir, thank you very much, that's very kind of you . . . and how did you get this number? . . . from our house? . . . Yes, yes, no, that's Fati, Qamar's aunt's daughter . . . what? Whatever are you saying? God strike me dead! And did you believe it?"

Dear Uncle kept mouthing that she was to explain what was going on. Aziz al-Saltaneh said to whoever was on the other end, "Hold on, will you please, there's a lot of noise going on in the yard, I'll just shut the door."

Then she put her hand over the mouthpiece and whispered, "It's the head of the criminal office . . . the one I went to see that time, the friend of my late husband . . . he says that today some unknown person phoned him and said I'd shot Dustali and hidden the injured party in the house."

Dear Uncle's eyes widened and his lips began to tremble. After a moment's silence he said in a voice that could hardly drag itself from his throat, "It's their work . . . answer him! . . . tell him he can talk to Dustali himself."

"Hello? . . . Yes, what were we talking about? . . . They must've been joking . . . just hold on, will you, and you can talk to Dustali himself . . . no, no, really, you have to talk to him. Please."

Aziz al-Saltaneh hurriedly took the phone into Dustali Khan's room, explained the situation to her husband in a couple of words, and said, "Take it and talk, but no moaning, eh?"

Dustali Khan had no choice but to obey; he greeted the head of the criminal affairs office in a strong cheerful voice, asked after his health and assured him that all was well. Then he gave the receiver back to Aziz al-Saltaneh. Meanwhile Dear Uncle had been instructing Aziz al-Saltaneh.

"Hello, did you hear, sir? . . . So now you'll realize they were just joking with you. Yesterday Dustali was filling cartridges and some of the gunpowder burnt his leg a bit . . . thank you very much . . . that's very kind of you."

Dear Uncle signalled her to ask the head of the office what he, Dear Uncle, wanted to know. Aziz al-Saltaneh signalled back that she hadn't forgotten. After an exchange of compliments and promises to see one another in the near future she said, "By the way, sir, I had one question . . . can I ask you what kind of person it was who phoned you . . . I mean didn't he have a particular accent? Like for example an Indian accent? . . . No? Then . . . what kind? A Shiraz accent? . . . Are you sure? . . . That's right, you lived in Shiraz for many years! . . . Well, I'm very grateful to you for your kindness . . . obviously . . . and of course if it had been anyone else except you this would certainly have meant problems for us . . . I can't thank you enough."

I didn't dare look at Dear Uncle. Although I was looking down I could guess at the expressions on the faces of those present in the room. Finally I stole a glance at Dear Uncle out of the corner of my eye. I saw from his purple color, and from the muscles starting from his face, that his cataclysmic inward state was even worse than I'd guessed. I was so terrified I almost gave up the ghost. I said to myself, "God help us now!" Because the only person in the whole family, and out of all our acquaintances, who had a Shiraz accent was my father.

FIFTEEN

DEAR UNCLE STOOD stock-still, his face rigid. Finally Asadollah Mirza said, "It must have been some friend or relative who did it as a joke . . . since they've had this automatic telephone system . . ."

Dear Uncle cut him off and said in a choked voice, "Mrs. al-Saltaneh, do you have this gentleman's phone number?"

Aziz al-Saltaneh answered in surprise, "The phone number of the head of the criminal office? Yes, I do, but why?"

"Please call him right now and say that you have to go and see him today about something important."

"What should I go and see him for?"

In a peremptory tone Dear Uncle said, "Please phone him right now. I'll explain later."

Faced with an order from Dear Uncle, Aziz al-Saltaneh had no choice but to obey. She took the relevant number from her handbag and called the head of the office of criminal affairs. An appointment was made for four-thirty that afternoon.

When she had put the receiver down Dear Uncle said, "You and I will go to his office together."

"You want to tell him something about Qamar? . . . look, I beg you . . ."

Dear Uncle cut her off, "No, we'll talk about Qamar later. This is a much more important matter. I have to know who made this phone call to him. Knowing this is a matter of life and death to me."

After pacing up and down in the room for a few moments Dear Uncle said, "Tonight, I'd like you all to come here . . . we have many matters to discuss, including Qamar's difficulties and our dear Puri's illness."

Uncle colonel's wife moaned, "Sir, please do something, I'm afraid it'll be too late . . . I'm afraid something awful's going to happen to my poor little boy."

Dear Uncle said firmly, "No, it won't be too late . . . we'll talk about it tonight. Then whatever has to be done we'll do."

Uncle colonel and his wife went back to their house. I followed Asadollah Mirza out because I wanted to talk to him about this new business of some unknown person phoning the criminal affairs office. Our troubles seemed endless. Every hour of every day some new obstacle came between me and Layli.

When we had left the inner apartments of Dear Uncle's house I said to him anxiously, "Uncle Asadollah, what was all that about a phone call? Do you think that . . ."

"Moment, thinking doesn't come into it, it's clear that this is the work of We-All-Know-Who. Since the moment the Master turned on your father I've been waiting for your father to stir things up somehow."

"Why does Dear Uncle want to go and see the head of the office of criminal affairs? Do you think he'll have recognized my father's voice? Do you think he'll tell Dear Uncle as much?"

"I don't think he knows your father, and even if he did . . ."

For a moment Asadollah was sunk in thought, then he said, "In any case I'm going to have to go and call on this head of the office of criminal affairs before four-thirty and ask him to smooth things over in order to prevent new hostilities breaking out."

At this moment I became aware that Mash Qasem was coming out of the house carrying a tray on which was a plate of rice. After a few steps he looked this way and that, but he didn't see us as we were behind a clump of trees. He put his hand into the plate and took out something which I couldn't see from that far away, but which I guessed was a piece of meat that had been in the rice; then he stretched out his hand and called "Puss, puss." In the blinking of an eye two of the stray cats that were usually hanging about the garden made their way over to him. He threw the piece of meat in front of one of the cats. Both cats went for the meat at the same time and the air was filled with their meows and the sounds of their fighting. Mash Qasem threatened them, trying not to raise his voice, "Drop dead, you little . . . just eat it and shut up!"

And since the cats went on just as noisily he bent down, picked up a stone and shouted, "Eh these damn stupid donkeys, filthy cats . . . get out of it . . ."

It seemed that the door to the inner apartments was ajar and that Dear Uncle was watching Mash Qasem, because at precisely this moment he stepped into the garden. He angrily went toward his servant; the cats fled.

"Qasem, have you given the meat from that rice to the cats?"

Mash Qasem answered fearfully, his voice trembling, "No sir, what a thing to say. D'you think I'm a heathen to be givin' good meat to cats?"

"And so this dish didn't contain any meat?"

"Well now, what can I say? 'Slike it didn't."

"Go back to your mistress and I'll see why she didn't put any meat in it."

Mash Qasem hesitated, hung his head and said, "Well now, sir, why should I lie? To the grave it's ah . . . ah . . . 'slike it did have some but my hand shook and it fell out."

Dear Uncle ground his teeth with rage, "I hope the undertaker soon gets his hands on that miserable lying face of yours."

"But sir, why should I lie? To the grave . . ."

"God willing I'll put you in the grave myself . . . go back and get some meat and take it to him! Why are you so spiteful? . . . What's this poor tradesman done to you?"

Mash Qasem made his way back to the inner apartments, saying under his breath, "I hope he gets knifed in the belly! It'd be a waste of dog-meat to give it to these shameless thievin' rascals!"

Dear Uncle followed him back to the inner apartments. I asked Asadollah Mirza to let me know the result of his interview with the head of the office of criminal affairs. Then I went back home.

A little after Dear Uncle Napoleon and Aziz al-Saltaneh had set off Asadollah Mirza turned up. His face was relaxed and cheerful and when he saw me he said with a smile, "I've fixed it, this head of the office of criminal affairs is a fine fellow. I recognized him when I saw him, I'd seen him a couple of times in Aziz al-Saltaneh's late husband's house . . . when he realized what was going on he promised that he'd do his level best to prevent any kind of quarrel breaking out."

"On the phone he said it was someone he didn't know who had a Shiraz accent, he can't now say it was an Esfahan accent."

"The two of us gave it a lot of thought. Finally he remembered that he'd said it was someone he didn't know and that he hadn't mentioned whether it was a man or a woman . . . we agreed that he'd say to Dear Uncle that it was a woman with a Shiraz accent who had phoned."

"But a woman with a Shiraz accent, who could it be? They won't believe . . ."

Asadollah Mirza laughed and said, "Moment, you've forgotten Farrokh Laqa and how much she dislikes Aziz al-Saltaneh . . . well, a Shiraz accent or just maybe a Hamadan accent."

"Bravo, Asadollah . . . you've managed it brilliantly. If it weren't for you, I'm positive a new quarrel a hundred times worse than the old one would have started. And they'd have separated me and Layli again . . . I don't know how I can thank you."

"Do you want to know how?"

"Yes, Uncle Asadollah."

"Do a San Francisco so that both your mind and mine will be at rest . . . goodbye till tonight."

Asadollah Mirza set off without waiting for my reaction.

Half an hour later a horse-drawn carriage drew up in front of the door to the garden and Dear Uncle Napoleon and Aziz al-Saltaneh got down from it. I was so anxious I didn't dare look at Dear Uncle. He came over toward me. I greeted him and looked down, but as soon as Dear Uncle opened his mouth I breathed a sigh of relief.

"Hello there, lad . . . why are you on your own? Where are the other children? Is your dad at home?"

Nervously I said, "Yes, uncle, do you want him for something?"

"I'll come and see him myself . . . I'll change my clothes and come."

There could be no doubt that Asadollah Mirza's intervention had been successful and that my father had been cleared of all suspicion. The flood of abuse which then followed, directed against that woman who always dressed in black, that bad-mouthed bringer of bad luck Mrs. Farrokh Laqa, confirmed this.

I hung about the garden for a while. Then it occurred to me to take advantage of Dear Uncle's good mood and go and see Layli, but a noise coming from the alleyway drew me toward the garden door.

The noise was the Indian Brigadier Maharat Khan arguing with the shoeshine man. The brigadier was angrily and emphatically telling Hushang the shoeshine man that he should pack up his stall and take it off somewhere else. I decided to tell Dear Uncle about the matter at once. At that moment he himself appeared from the inner apartments, wearing his house clothes with his cloak over them.

"What's going on? What's happened?"

"Uncle, that Indian brigadier wants to send the shoeshine man packing."

Dear Uncle stood rooted to the spot, wide-eyed and with his mouth hanging open. Then, through gritted teeth, he said, "What? The Indian brigadier? . . . the Indian brigadier?"

For a moment he closed his eyes and went on under his breath, "Although it's not surprising! . . . not at all surprising! I should have expected it! . . . he must have got wind of it or suspected something was going on. God damn these English!"

Then he came back to himself. He ran toward the door to the inner apartments, shouting for Mash Qasem, "Qasem, Qasem . . . run . . . run. See what that filthy spy is saying . . . Why does he want to turn that poor tradesman out of the alleyway? Does he think this alley belongs to Chamberlain's father? . . . Run, now . . . Qasem, if you hold back, God help you! But don't mention my name . . . I know nothing about all this."

Biting at the ends of his mustache Mash Qasem set off for the alleyway. "What's goin' on? What's goin' on, Mr. Brigadier, sir?"

"This shoeshine man is setting up his residency in this place and I am saying to him that he should go and he is disobeying my order."

The shoeshine man strenuously objected, "The whole alleyway's next to the Master's garden . . . does this pigheaded brigadier think he's bought the alley with that couple of yards of house he's got?"

"I am someone who is dwelling in this alleyway and I am saying to you frankly that I do not want any shoeshine person."

"Well, that's obvious because you either go barefoot or you wear yokel's sandals, so how would you know what a shoeshine man was for . . ."

Mash Qasem glared at him, "And you watch your mouth when you're interruptin' the Brigadier . . . and you, Mr. Brigadier, sir, as an act of charity like, let him stay here and earn enough to keep body and soul together."

"Let him do his acts of charity for the beggars in his own country. I work for a living, I don't want no acts of charity from no one."

I was standing in the doorway, and I could see both them and Dear Uncle who was in the garden angrily pacing up and down next to the wall, beside himself with anxiety. I heard him say under his breath, "I hope I see you in your grave. He's no idea how to deal with this Indian spy."

I saw that he was pressing his hand against the leather holster of his revolver, under his cloak.

I went forward and said, "Brigadier, sir, we need a shoeshine man or a cobbler all day long, from morning till night. If he's really disturbing you he could stay on this side of the alleyway, next to the door to our garden."

Fortunately at this moment Asadollah Mirza appeared in the distance. I breathed a sigh of relief. As soon as he saw the scene of the argument his lordship shouted, "Moment, moment, brigadier, what's going on? What are you so angry about?"

And he glanced up at the window to the brigadier's house. His eyes glittered and a smile came to his lips. I followed the direction of his gaze. Lady Maharat Khan was standing on the balcony watching what was going on, her long blonde hair spread over her shoulders. The tone of voice in which Asadollah Mirza addressed the brigadier changed, "My dear brigadier, what are you getting so angry for? You, who are an example to us all of good humor and purity of character . . . I couldn't even have imagined your getting angry . . . I know this young fellow, he's not a bad chap, earlier on he was in that alley further down . . ."

"Respected sir, if I have taken up residency in this alleyway it is only for the sake of the peace and quiet and the lack of noise that is prevailing in it. If it is agreed that these louts are to be gathering here . . ."

The word "louts" was too much for the shoeshine man. Despite Asadollah's signal to him to be quiet he shouted out, "Lout yourself . . . and your dad . . . and your granddad . . . and your wife."

His face glowing with rage the brigadier made for the shoeshine man and said, "Say that again!"

"Sure I'll say it again; anyone who calls me a lout is a lout himself and so are all his dad's family for generations back."

Without a moment's hesitation the brigadier gave the shoeshine man a slap on the ear. The shoeshine man, who was young and strong and had an athlete's build, attacked him and a general struggle ensued. Asadollah's shouts to calm them down had no effect, and Mash Qasem, who had supposedly intervened as a conciliator, landed a blow on the shoeshine man at every opportunity that presented itself.

Dear Uncle appeared in the door frame and ordered Mash Qasem to separate the two. Meanwhile Lady Maharat Khan was desperately trying to enlist Asadollah Mirza's assistance.

As luck would have it, at this moment someone with physical authority turned up, and this was Shir Ali the butcher. As soon as he saw him, Dear Uncle screamed out, "Shir Ali, separate them."

Shir Ali ran toward the Indian and the shoeshine man, who were struggling violently with one another. He handed the leg of mutton that he was carrying to Mash Qasem and, grabbing the neck of each of the parties in different hands, pulled them apart. "What's goin' on? Why are you two beatin' each other up?"

The Indian's turban had fallen off, and his long black hair reached down to his waist. Panting, he said, "This unconscionable wretch, this thief . . ."

And he attempted to attack him again, but as his neck was fast in Shir Ali's strong grip he was unable to.

"What's goin' on, brigadier? And do your curls up when you're carryin' on like this."

Apparently the Indian was very sensitive about his hair because he suddenly burst out, "Shut up! What has my hair got to do with you?"

He was so angry that he said the rest of what he had to say in Hindi, and in the midst of his talk there was a phrase that sounded something like "low-life" and which came two or three times. Shir Ali's eyes widened and in a choked voice he said, "Just a minute, are you callin' me low-life?"

And he suddenly released his hold on the shoeshine man's neck. He slipped his arms round the Indian's waist, from behind, and as if he were a sliver of straw lifted him into the air and took a few paces with him toward his house. Then with a violent gesture he flung him into the house, shut the door and grabbed hold of its knocker so that the Indian couldn't open it.

"And now that Indian's sayin' 'low-life' to me . . . I'm tellin' you straight up, it's only because you were sayin' leave him alone that I didn't say anythin' to him, and if it hadn't been for that I'd have taken him by the legs and split him in half."

Dear Uncle was standing between the posts of the garden doorway; a satisfied smile spread over his lips.

Flicking the dust off his jacket, Asadollah Mirza said, "My dear Shir Ali . . . I haven't had the chance to ask how you are . . . how are you getting on? . . . Well, I hope? And your wife is well?"

"I'm your servant till my dyin' day . . . now what's this shoeshine feller got to say for himself?"

Asadollah Mirza quickly said, "He's a very fine fellow. I know him . . . he came here to scrape some kind of a living together . . . and I've a great deal of polishing and repair work . . . leave that door now, Shir Ali, I don't think the brigadier is going to venture out with you here."

Asadollah Mirza's guess was correct, because there was no further sign of the Indian. Shir Ali rolled up the Indian's turban, which had fallen into a puddle, threw it over the wall into his house, and then went on his way.

Asadollah Mirza sympathized with the shoeshine man, "Never mind, my dear fellow . . . wherever a man goes this kind of fuss happens for the first few days . . . the Master's shown you kindness and that's enough."

The shoeshine man had calmed down. In a mild voice he said, "I put my trust in God, and after God in you . . ."

Then he turned to Mash Qasem. "But you, you mean sneak, you got in a good swipe at my head in the middle of the fight."

Out of fear of Dear Uncle, Mash Qasem assumed an innocent face. "Me? Now why should I lie? To the grave it's ah . . . ah . . . I swear by God in heaven that if he hadn't stopped I'd have torn him to bits . . . I don't like raisin' my hand in anger like, and if it weren't for that I could take on a hundred of these here Indians. There was a man in our town who . . ."

Dear Uncle cut him off, "All right so there was a man in your town. Run and fetch a glass of cordial to freshen Hushang's throat."

Then he turned to the shoeshine man. "Don't you worry yourself, from tomorrow on everything will be all right."

"No sir, I'm not a willow to be trembling with every wind . . . the one who's above has told me to stay here and I'm staying here."

His mouth wide open, Dear Uncle stared at him. Then he muttered, "The one who's above told you . . .?"

"Yes sir, the one who's up there keeping an eye on each man's business, and who sees that a man gets his daily allowance."

Dear Uncle gave him a meaning look, gestured stealthily and repeated, "Yes, yes, of course you have to stay where you've been appointed to . . . why don't you come in, my dear sir?"

Before going back to his house Dear Uncle asked the shoeshine man where he slept at night. When he heard that during the night he stayed in a coffeehouse at the end of the alleyway, he felt completely reassured.

We were about to go into the garden when a horse-drawn carriage pulled up, and uncle colonel hurriedly jumped down.

"Brother, good news, good news . . . I've just been at the telegraph office sending a telegram to Khan Babakhan, and he said that dear Puri's health is much better and that together with Khan Babakhan himself he'll be here tomorrow by train . . . I've got to run and tell my wife the good news, poor thing she's been going crazy with worry."

As I was walking in the garden beside Asadollah Mirza he quietly said, "Tomorrow night Julius Caesar will arrive . . . watch out for yourself, Marc Antony! Don't be lolling about so free and easy, they'll take your Cleopatra."

In deep distress I said helplessly, "But what can I do, Uncle Asadollah?"

"What I told you to."

I was so upset I didn't try to remember what he'd said and asked, "What did you say?"

"Open your ears: San . . . Fran . . . cis . . . co!"

"Uncle Asadollah, I'm really in no mood for joking."

"Moment, then just say you're in no mood for anything . . . as the brigadier says, your vitality's *bahot* wilted."

❖ ❖ ❖

A few people gathered in Dear Uncle's house to discuss the family's problems, which now that the news of Puri's recovery had arrived were limited to the subject of Qamar's pregnancy. Asadollah Mirza, Shamsali Mirza, uncle colonel, the injured Dustali Khan and his wife were present. My father arrived a little later.

One thing I realized from the atmosphere in the house, and more particularly from the atmosphere of that meeting, was that they no longer had any strong desire to go into who was responsible for Qamar's baby. The matter had more to do with Aziz al-Saltaneh than anyone else, but either because of the crime she'd committed in going after her husband with a loaded shotgun, a crime that had almost resulted in his losing his life, or because she didn't want to go through any further public humiliation, she accepted the story that the real perpetrator was that wicked Allahverdi, and from time to time in the midst of the conversation she denounced and cursed him. As a result of Aziz al-Saltaneh's turning a blind eye, Dustali Khan also felt easier in his conscience. The person who saw himself as having suffered most in all this was Dear Uncle Napoleon.

It has to be said that as soon as she entered Aziz al-Saltaneh told him he could forget about a midwife/abortionist, and said that even the famous midwife Zayvar had refused to undertake it.

Dustali Khan, who was still lying prone on his belly, said, "As far as I can see there's only one thing to do. We'll have to find someone who'll marry Qamar, even if just for a few days. I don't think that Mamad fellow, the electrician, has a wife and if . . ."

Dear Uncle Napoleon threw him a furious look and said, "Aren't you ashamed of yourself, Dustali? . . . For Mamad to be one of our in-laws? How could we put up with the shame?"

Aziz al-Saltaneh started weeping and wailing, "God strike me dead, what high hopes I had for this poor wretched child!"

Mash Qasem, who was in the room busy serving people, said, "Don't even think of that Mamad feller."

Asadollah Mirza asked, "Why, Mash Qasem?"

"Because he's got a health problem."

"What health problem?"

"Well, not to be rude like, and beggin' your pardon, sir, but he's not a man."

"How do you know?"

Dear Uncle shouted, "The hell with whether he's a man or not, don't even mention him!"

Asadollah Mirza said, "Moment, sir, a little research never did any harm . . . perhaps we'll finally have to . . . so, let's see Mash Qasem, how is it you know that Mamad is not a man?"

"Why should I lie? To the grave it's ah . . . ah . . . I haven't seen anythin' with my own eyes, I heard it from the brother of Ebrahim, the grocer . . . he heard it from the wife of the baker, the baker's wife heard it from Reza who has the cloth shop, Reza heard it from Shir Ali's wife, Shir Ali's wife heard it from Seyed Abolqasem's son, and Seyed Abolqasem's son heard it from someone who's name I can't say . . ."

"What do you mean you can't say it, Mash Qasem?"

"Tear me limb from limb and I won't tell you, because one of your own family's involved."

"Moment, whether he's a man or not's neither here nor there, what he has to do's already been done for him by someone else!"

"But I know someone who'd really fit the bill for this job . . . if he'd accept, he's a very distinguished gentleman with many fine accomplishments . . . I mean to say he's from our own Ghiasabad."

"Who, Mash Qasem?"

"You remember last year that feller from Ghiasabad that came here with Deputy Taymur Khan who, if you'll pardon the expression, was lookin' for Mr. Dustali Khan's corpse?"

"Cadet Officer Ghiasabadi?"

"That's him, I remember when he saw Miss Qamar his mouth was really waterin' . . . he was sayin' he'd really like a wife who looked like that. Well, folks from Ghiasabad like a woman to be a bit chubby and cuddly."

Dear Uncle screamed, "Shut up Qasem! . . . Cadet Officer Ghiasabadi marry into our family? You've forgotten all sense of shame and decency."

Asadollah said with a smile, "And is this Ghiasabadi fellow a man?"

"Why should I lie? To the grave it's ah . . . ah . . . I haven't seen with my own eyes, but there aren't any in Ghiasabad who aren't real men. Women from Qom and Kashan and Esfahan, and sometimes women from Tehran, too, they're dyin' to marry someone from Ghiasabad . . . there was a man in our town who . . ."

Dear Uncle Napoleon's nerves could not stand any more of this talk. He slammed his prayer beads down on the table so hard that its string broke, and the beads went flying off in all directions.

"At least have some shame when you're talking in front of me! There's a limit even to impudence!"

With a very serious face, and in a firm voice, Asadollah Mirza said, "Moment, where's the impudence? An innocent girl who's not quite all there is in difficulties. Either Allahverdi, the Indian brigadier's servant, or some other shameless despicable wretch has done this monstrous thing to her. Her life's in danger if she has an abortion. There's one way left, which is that we find her a husband. And that's only to save your face, because she couldn't care less. She's ready to have her baby without any husband, and to bring her baby up. Do you expect the son of some aristocratic Sir Leopard of the Kingdom or Lord Lion of the State to come and marry the girl?"

"You have to realize that . . ."

"Yes, I know . . . I know what you want to say. A girl descended from this lordship and that ladyship mustn't become the wife of a simple cadet officer. If you're acquainted with Baron de Rothschild, telegraph him and tell him to make sure he sends the fancy marriage mirror for his wedding."

Everyone was appalled and stared at Dear Uncle. But contrary to expectations he didn't become angry, or if he did he suppressed his anger and said in a mild tone, "Perhaps you're right. My interference was entirely unwarranted. Her mother and stepfather are here. They should decide for themselves."

His usual smile returned to Asadollah Mirza's lips. "What a noble sensitive fellow her stepfather is, to be sure! Here he is lying down for all the world as if the matter had nothing at all to do with him!"

Dustali Khan, who had been silent since the beginning of the gathering, raised his face from his pillow and yelled, "Asadollah, I swear on the soul of my father that if you once again . . ."

Asadollah Mirza interrupted him, "Moment, moment, moment, I am really very sorry to have disturbed your innocent, angelic sleep."

Dear Uncle said with some asperity, "Asadollah, please, no more of these jokes! As far as I'm concerned there's no doubt that this incident is another part of their plan to ruin me. A plan hatched by that wretched Indian spy and carried out by his servant and dictated from another place."

Asadollah Mirza laughed and said, "Then according to you, whoever the English are enemies of, they delegate some tough guy to put that person's uncle's grandchild in the family way?"

Dear Uncle was extremely angry and said forcefully, "Don't talk rubbish and don't be so facetious! You've a long way to go before you understand that old wolf's tricks."

"Moment, going by this line of reasoning, the grandchildren of Hitler's and Mussolini's uncles must have had three kids each by now."

"Asadollah!"

"I'm very sorry, I didn't mean anything by it. Just that in my opinion it's not a bad idea. Mind you with this method the English are going to have to turn all their armaments factories into factories for making Dr. Ross's famous virility pills. In any case, I shall be very glad to enroll myself in a special force for paying them back in their own kind."

Everyone was horrified because as Asadollah was saying this my father burst out with a loud roar of laughter. Fortunately an interruption by Mash Qasem cut this line of conversation short, "Now we have to see if this Ghiasabadi feller 'll agree or not . . ."

Dear Uncle's anger turned on Mash Qasem, "What? How? . . . Do I understand correctly what you're saying, Qasem?"

"Well sir, why should I lie? To the grave it's ah . . . ah . . . Last year this feller from our town really took a fancy to Miss Qamar. And just look at it this way, you can put all the country—as far as protectin' the family honor's concerned—on one side, and Ghiasabad on the other outweighin' 'em all . . . There was a man in our town who . . ."

Dear Uncle cut him short, "Yet again there's someone in your town? Qasem, for how long . . . ?"

Uncle colonel interrupted, "Brother, let him talk. We have to find a way out of this fix we're in."

Mash Qasem went on, "Yes sir, there was a man in our town who'd had two sons grown up and married. Then one day he heard that before they'd got married his wife's veil had slipped off in the mosque . . . well, he divorced her. And then all the folks in Ghiasabad blamed him for not killin' the woman . . . he became famous for not carin' about his family honor. And the poor devil was that upset he just wasted away and died . . . I'm tellin' you this so you'll know it won't be that easy, tyin' Miss Qamar round the neck of a man from our town."

For the first time Shamsali Mirza spoke, "Well, it won't be necessary to mention the matter of Qamar's pregnancy to him."

"You mean you're sayin' that folks from Ghiasabad are donkeys? No reflection on you, sir, but there was a man in our town who . . ."

Asadollah Mirza cut him off, "Moment, if we don't say anything, how's he going to know?"

"Well now, why should I lie? To the grave it's ah . . . ah . . . beggin' your pardon like but there's a difference between a girl and a woman."

"Thank you, Mash Qasem, for passing on this completely new piece of information to us. I always thought there was no difference between the two."

Once again Dear Uncle's Napoleon's voice rang out, "Asadollah, do not say such things in front of the children!"

Asadollah Mirza laughed and said, "Moment, this is a scientific discussion, an entirely scientific discussion concerning the difference between women who have been to San Francisco and women who haven't been to San Francisco."

And then he turned to Mash Qasem and said, "After thanking you for the scientific information you passed on to me, I have to say that I also realize that when his excellency Cadet Officer Ghiasabadi has been to San Francisco . . . I mean, after their wedding he'll understand that something's happened, but with this concern for family honor that people in Ghiasabad have, it's obvious he won't be announcing it from the rooftops. The most that'll happen is he'll divorce her. And that's precisely what we want, that someone come along and marry Qamar and then quietly divorce her. And besides, when he's signed the register we'll quietly tip him the wink and grease his palm so that he'll keep his mouth shut."

Dustali Khan raised his head, "This is dishonorable and against all conscience. We have to tell him the situation honestly from the beginning."

Mash Qasem scratched his head and said, "It'll have to be one or the other—conscience or the bridegroom."

Asadollah Mirza threw up his hands and said, "We should vote on it. My vote goes to the bridegroom. Of course, Mr. Dustali Khan, otherwise known as Sir Conscience of the Realm, will vote for conscience. But in defence of my choice I claim that nothing contrary to conscience will happen. Cadet Officer Ghiasabadi arrives with not a stitch to his name, he eats and sleeps here for a while, he becomes Mrs. Aziz al-Saltaneh's son-in-law, it doesn't cost him a thing and he gets a free trip to San Francisco into the bargain. Then if he's ready to die, let him go off to Ghiasabad . . . we should all be so lucky!"

Dustali Khan yelled, "Asadollah, when you were conceived it must have been a union of wine and vodka . . ."

"Moment, moment, first as one whose conception was a union of holy water and rose water, just tell me if it was you, would you be so upset if someone came and took care of all your expenses, asked it of you as a great favor, gave you supper and lunch, and then said off you go to San Francisco four or five times with a nice chubby, cuddly travelling companion? You'd have said 'No thanks,' would you? Even without anybody asking, you're quite ready to look for this kind of . . ."

At this moment Aziz al-Saltaneh burst out with, "God, I hope the gravediggers get their hands on both of you soon! Is my little darling's situation so bad that we have to be asking favors from that Ghiasabadi?"

She was prevented from coming to blows with them by Shamsali Mirza and uncle colonel. Mash Qasem said, "Whatever happens, we have to find out if Ghiasabadi will agree to it or not. Even if the girl was innocent as a newborn just popped out of her mom's belly, maybe he doesn't want to get married!"

"And even if he does, maybe the girl doesn't . . . in my opinion we have to settle this fifty percent of the matter first and then refer to the bridegroom . . . in my opinion Mrs. Aziz al-Saltaneh must have a chat with Qamar. If she agrees, then Mash Qasem can go after the bridegroom."

After a little discussion of the subject Aziz al-Saltaneh went to find Qamar, who was busy chatting and playing with my sister and Layli in the next room. She talked to her for a while, privately in another room. When she came back everyone's eyes were fixed on her mouth.

"What happened, Mrs. al-Saltaneh? What did she say?"

Gloomy faced, Aziz al-Saltaneh said, "That poor little wretch of mine can't think straight. She says things that make no sense at all."

Asadollah Mirza said, "Will you permit me, ma'am, to question her?"

"You won't get anything out of her. God strike her mother dead, I say. From the time this disaster's happened the girl seems to be out of her mind."

"Call her now and I'll question her here."

Aziz al-Saltaneh hesitated for a moment, then went and fetched Qamar. A bland smile played about the child's lips. Asadollah Mirza sat her down next to himself. He talked a little about her doll, which she was clutching against her chest, then he said, "Well, my dear, a nice husband's been found for you . . . would you like to have a husband?"

Although she wasn't all there, the fat child blushed and bowed her head. She mumbled, "No, I wouldn't like to. I like my baby, I want to knit it two red jackets."

"My dear, I'll buy your baby a beautiful jacket, too. But a baby has to have a father. If you don't have a husband your baby will be sad. Because a baby needs a daddy."

For a moment Qamar stared at him silently, and then said, "All right."

"So shall we start getting ready for the wedding? A beautiful white dress with a beautiful veil . . ."

Qamar said cheerfully, "With orange blossom!"

"Of course, my dear, with a crown made of orange blossom."

Qamar thought for a moment then said, "Where's my husband now? . . . You know, Uncle Asadollah, I want him to have really thick, black hair so that my baby will have beautiful black hair like his!"

Asadollah turned round and threw a mournful look at Dear Uncle. "All right, dear, off you go and play now."

After she had gone out Asadollah Mirza said quietly, "Poor thing, what a nice girl she is."

Mash Qasem, who had been standing silently in a corner, said, "This ain't workin' out . . . it's like this business doesn't want to work out."

"Why, Mash Qasem, what's wrong?"

"But didn't you hear her say she wanted her man to have thick black hair?"

"And isn't Cadet Officer Ghiasabadi's hair black?"

"Why should I lie? To the grave it's ah . . . ah . . . Them two or three days I saw this neighbor of mine his hat was pulled right down over his ears but one time when he took his hat off careless like I saw how his head's all bald . . . meanin' the middle of his head's clean as a whistle, but at the edges there's a few wisps here and there like."

"And was the color of his hair black or not?"

"Why should I lie? To the grave it's ah . . . ah . . . It was all colors. Some strands were white, some black, and some he'd put henna on."

Aziz al-Saltaneh slapped herself across the face. "God strike me dead! My little girl'll curl up and die if she sees a head like that on her pillow."

"Well, ma'am, this Cadet Officer Ghiasabadi's no Rudolf Valentino, but we'll buy him a wig so his head'll be hidden."

Mash Qasem shook his head and said, "I don't think he'll go along with that . . . folks from Ghiasabad are very particular about their dignity."

"Moment, the dignity of people in Ghiasabad's located on their heads?"

"Why should I lie? To the grave it's ah . . . ah . . . it's not on their heads, no, but men don't wear wigs. There was a man in our town who . . ."

"All right, all right, we'll solve the matter of curls and tresses later on. When can you talk to this Mr. Ghiasabadi?"

"Whenever you say . . . I'll go and find him tomorrow . . ."

Dear Uncle Napoleon, who had been sitting there in frowning silence, couldn't bear not to speak and he said severely, "Even a child wouldn't talk like this. Do you realize what you're saying? Mash Qasem is to go off to the office of criminal affairs and find Mr. Ghiasabadi and say to him 'Come and get married to my master's uncle's grandchild!' What was in that wine, Asadollah?"

"Well, in any case we can't ask the cadet officer to marry into the family over the phone."

General discussion and argument ensued, until finally uncle colonel said, "In my opinion it's best if Mrs. Aziz al-Saltaneh phones that head of the department of criminal affairs and says for example that something's been stolen from her house but that she doesn't want to lodge a formal complaint. However she'd like an officer to come, quietly and privately, to question her maid and servants, then she can say that if it's possible they could send that same cadet officer who came last year . . . these things can be done in a friendly way. When he comes she can say that fortunately the thing that she'd missed has been found . . ."

"And say the head of the office sends someone else? . . . just supposing he agrees to it."

Asadollah Mirza laughed and said, "All the better! Because I don't think any of the officers can be uglier than Cadet Officer Ghiasabadi. Whoever they send, we'll proposition him. As soon as he comes we'll slam the door on him and we won't let him go till he's signed the marriage register."

"Asadollah!"

After more discussion and argument this suggestion was agreed upon.

The next morning an extraordinary amount of activity connected with the preparations for an elaborate party to be held that night, to celebrate the return of my uncle's son Puri, was going on in uncle colonel's house.

It was agreed that toward sunset all his close relatives would go to the station in a few horse-drawn carriages, in order to welcome Puri. I was extremely upset. With complete callousness I asked God to delay Puri's recovery from his illness. At the first opportunity that presented itself I told Layli how upset and worried I was. She repeated very calmly that she could not disobey her father but, if it were decided that she was to marry Puri, on the evening of the engagement ceremony she would do away with herself. This statement of hers was no consolation to me at all and I wracked my brains for some way out of our predicament. Unfortunately my one friend and confidant, Asadollah Mirza, wasn't at home to sympathize with me.

I heard from Mash Qasem that Aziz al-Saltaneh had phoned the head of the office of criminal affairs and received a promise from him that he would send Cadet Officer Ghiasabadi to her house before noon.

At the same time Mash Qasem told me that they'd agreed that for now they wouldn't let Qamar set eyes on the cadet officer, and then if he agreed to the marriage, perhaps they would be able to convince him, temporarily, to wear a wig.

"And, I mean, he's every right, m'dear, there's no one like folks from Ghiasabad when it comes to dignity and honor. And even these fellers from Tehran who have a hundred nancy-fancy carryin's on, not one in a thousand of 'em 'll wear a wig on his head like a woman."

"Mash Qasem, what has a wig got to do with dignity and honor?"

"Well, good God, a fine feller like you and been to school and all, what are you sayin' things like this for, m'dear? What's more shameful than for a man to wear a wig like a woman? I saw once with my own eyes . . . a group had come to Ghiasabad to put the plays on for the martyrdom of the blessed Hosayn . . . one of the women in Hosayn's family, she had to snatch the veil off her head and tear her hair out . . . they said some feller'll have to wear a wig to act the part. For twenty days and nights they went round the whole of Ghiasabad and not a man was willin' to do it . . ."

"So do you think Cadet Officer Ghiasabadi won't agree to wear a wig?"

"Well, m'dear, why should I lie? To the grave it's ah . . . ah . . . now he's been in Tehran so many years maybe his nature's changed, and he'll be ready to do these shameful things."

I was busy chatting with Mash Qasem in the garden when I suddenly saw Dear Uncle Napoleon hurrying out of the inner apartments of his house and going in the direction of our house. His complexion was strangely pale, and I was dismayed to see him like this. I ran after him toward our house.

Dear Uncle was looking for my father and went straight to his room. I made my way to behind the door.

"Have you heard? Have you heard?"

"What's happened? Why don't you sit down?"

"I'm asking you if you've heard the radio?"

"No, what's going on? Has something happened?"

"They're here . . . they're here . . . they read out the official announcement . . . they said the English have reached Tehran. People must stay away from them and rubbish like that."

My father tried to sympathize with him. "There's no point in your getting so upset . . . there's no reason at all for you to be so worried . . . you know the English better than me, they never attack openly and from the front . . ."

His voice choking, Dear Uncle interrupted him, "It's because I know this perfidious wolf so well that I'm worried. I know they don't attack you face to face, I've spent my life fighting against them."

"Now there's no need for you to be so worried . . ."

"My good sir, I'm not worried on my own behalf. My future is clear. Wherever I go I can't escape from them. I'm not feeling sorry for myself. May a thousand like me be sacrificed for the nation . . . it's the nation I feel sorry for:

'Alas, Iran will be destroyed, a lair
For leopards and wild lions will flourish there!'"

There was a sobbing catch in his voice. When I looked through the crack in the door I saw he was wiping the corner of one of his eyes with a finger.

My father said, "What can we do, though? As you yourself have said:

'When once a savage lion's cornered you
Accept your fate—what else is there to do?'"

"There's nothing that can be done . . . but . . . but I wanted to ask you that, as there's no wall between our houses, see you have the front door securely locked. And I'll tell Mash Qasem not to open the garden door to any strangers . . . and especially don't let the children go out . . . even though I don't think they'd have any quarrel with your children. I'm their prey, me and my innocent children."

Dear Uncle stayed sunk in thought for a moment, and then left the room. He was still in the same state when he saw me and said gently, "My dear boy, you're a big lad now . . . something is going on around us, the depths of which perhaps you can't understand, but I've one request to make of you, and that is that if any stranger comes asking about me don't answer him, say nothing. And tell your sister too . . . don't open the door to any strangers."

"But what's going on, Uncle?"

"What do you think? The enemy's here . . ."

Dear Uncle put his hand on my shoulder and in a voice filled with emotion said, "Every time you see your Uncle it could be for the last time . . . but then that's one of the rules of war!"

Dear Uncle stared at me distractedly for a few moments, but his thoughts seemed to have wandered off elsewhere. Suddenly he pulled himself together and set off for the garden door.

I quietly followed him.

Dear Uncle strode purposefully toward the garden door, but as soon as he opened it he stood as if rooted to the spot.

I went quietly closer. From a few paces away I could hear his labored breathing. Suddenly he turned and went toward Mash Qasem, who was busy watering the flowers, and in a choked voice said, "Qasem, Qasem, where . . . where is he?"

"Who, sir? Where's who?"

"The shoeshine man!"

"He's right here, sir. Isn't he? When I went to get bread in the mornin' he'd already come." Dear Uncle took Mash Qasem by the shoulders and shook him. "Then where is he? Where's he gone?"

"What d'you mean? . . . If you want your shoes shined give 'em to me and I'll take 'em down the bazaar and have 'em done so you can see your face in 'em. That feller was no good at shinin' shoes."

"Idiot! I'm asking you where he is! Where's he gone?"

"Well sir, why should I lie? To the grave it's ah . . . ah . . . I haven't seen him with my own eyes, I'll have to have a look around and see where the hell he's got to."

"Then what are you waiting for? Run! Get on with it! Find out and come and tell me. And close the door behind you!"

Dear Uncle's hands were shaking; he began angrily pacing up and down. Like a caged leopard he took a few paces in one direction and then back again. Mash Qasem took his time about leaving the garden. Dear Uncle caught sight of me. In a voice charged with emotion he said, "My dear boy, this Qasem's a fool, you go and ask, ask the grocer, ask anyone, see where that shoeshine man's got to."

Then it was as if he suddenly realized that it wasn't right for him to show all this agitation in front of me. He found an excuse: "Off you go, boy . . . he has a new pair of my shoes, from Europe."

I quickly went back home to change out of my slippers into shoes. When I reached the garden door I came face to face with Mash Qasem who was coming back in. I kept pace with him as he went over to Dear Uncle.

"Where's he gone, where's he gone, Qasem?"

Slowly Mash Qasem said, "Well sir, why should I lie? . . ."

"Damn and blast your 'Why should I lie's! Speak man, where's he gone?"

"Well, Ebrahim's just out there and I asked him. Accordin' to him he says a constable came and took him off to the police station . . ."

"The police-station? Why? What's he done?"

"Well sir, why should I lie? To the grave it's ah . . . ah . . . I haven't seen anythin' with my own eyes. But accordin' to what this Ebrahim says, he stole a watch . . . it was obvious from his eyes he was a thievin', furtive kind of feller."

"A watch? Whose watch did he steal?"

"That there Indian brigadier went to the police station and complained . . . he said that yesterday when they was havin' that argy-bargy the shoeshine feller lifted it from his pocket! A gold pocket watch."

The wind was instantly taken out of Dear Uncle's sails. His arms fell lifeless at his sides. For a moment he stood thunderstruck, his mouth hanging open. He reached out and grasped at a tree so as not to fall over. Then he closed his eyes and muttered, "The devils! They've started. The plan is being put into effect. O God, I place myself in your hands!"

SIXTEEN

DEAR UNCLE NAPOLEON was extremely upset on hearing the news that the shoeshine man had been arrested and accused of stealing a watch. His eyes remained shut and his lips were trembling. Mash Qasem anxiously asked, "Who's started, sir?"

His eyes closed, in a weak voice, Dear Uncle said, "Those cunning wolves . . . those English . . . this is an English plot."

Mash Qasem thought for a moment and then said, "You mean they want to pretend that we put this Hushang up to stealin' the Indian brigadier's watch?"

"No, no, you don't understand . . . it's something that you don't understand, Qasem. The mysteries of politics are more complicated than you can understand."

"Well now, why should I lie? To the grave it's ah . . . ah! It's not that I don't understand. But if you want to know the truth we have to . . ."

The entrance of Mrs. Aziz al-Saltaneh into the garden cut Mash Qasem off. "Hasn't the man come yet? Eh, God strike me dead, sir, what are you looking so pale around the gills for?"

"It's nothing, it's nothing . . . a commander has to be able to put up with defeat. As Napoleon said, in the school of war it's more necessary a commander learn the lesson of defeat than the lesson of victory."

"What's happened? Who's upset you? . . . Mash Qasem, who's upset the Master?"

"Well now, why should I lie? To the grave it's ah . . . ah! The shoeshine man what stayed by our door's pinched that Indian's watch. They've arrested him . . ."

Dear Uncle yelled, "Why are you talking nonsense, Qasem? Why are you so naive? You only see the outside of the matter. Because you don't know the English."

Mash Qasem seemed to be offended. In a tone of whining complaint he said, "I don't know 'em? Well, God keep you, sir, but if I don't know 'em, who knows 'em? You could say I've brought up these English . . . I know 'em better than their own moms and dads do . . . all these wars and battles I've had with the English, with you as commander, don't they count? In the Battle of Kazerun, who talked to that there sergeant who came with a white flag to talk to you? Who said to him 'What right have you to talk to the Master?' Who sprang out at 'em like a lion? The English are that thirsty for my blood, and you're sayin' I don't know 'em? God rest his soul, there was a man in our town who always used to say 'If the English get their hands on you, savin' your grace, savin' your grace, savin' . . .'"

Dear Uncle yelled, "Enough, Qasem! Let me think and find some way out of this."

Aziz al-Saltaneh took Dear Uncle's arm and said, "All this fuss and bother's not good for your heart. Please come and rest for a moment or two."

Then she began to lead him toward the inner apartments of his house. Dear Uncle suddenly pulled himself together. He drew himself up to his full height, jerked his arm free of Aziz al-Saltaneh's, and said, "I'm perfectly well. I have no need of your help. A commander leaves the field of battle on his own two feet."

And he turned to Mash Qasem. "Qasem, go and see if Mr. Asadollah Mirza is at home and tell him to come here as soon as he can . . . I don't think he's gone to his office today."

Then he went into the inner apartments; his stride was as firm and forceful as he could make it. Aziz al-Saltaneh came over to me and Mash Qasem and said, "God strike me dead but the master was so pale! What's an Indian's watch and the shoeshine man being arrested got to do with the Master?"

Mash Qasem immediately said, "Well now, why should I lie? To the grave it's ah . . . ah! You don't know these English. That woman who had a baby in her house, the English had a hand in that too . . . there was a man in our town who . . ."

I interrupted him, "You don't realize what's going on, Mrs. Aziz. That Indian was sulking because Dear Uncle had said the poor shoeshine man could work in our street, so he went and made this accusation against him. Dear Uncle's angry because the brigadier's been so mean and sneaky."

Then I said to Mash Qasem, "Mash Qasem, didn't Dear Uncle say you should go and see Asadollah Mirza?"

Mash Qasem went over to the door to the inner apartments. He called old Naneh Bilqis, Dear Uncle's maid, and sent her after Asadollah Mirza. It seemed that he didn't want to be away from what was going on for a moment. Then he made his way over to Aziz al-Saltaneh who was expectantly pacing back and forth.

"Missus, not meanin' to be rude like, I wanted to ask you that when this feller from our town comes you leave him to me to convince him. We folks from Ghiasabad understand one another."

"Eh! Damn your cheek! You talk about convincing this stinking baldy to accept my lovely girl . . . God, that girl, she's ruined my life she has, I hope she never sees another happy day."

"Did you tell Miss Qamar she's not to suddenly start talkin'?"

"I've worn my tongue out talking to her, but she still can't shut up about his thick black hair."

"I'll manage all that about his hair. You don't know these folks from Ghiasabad, if he gets wind that somethin' like this is goin' on, it's impossible he'll agree to it . . . Why, that's nothin', once I saw there was a man in our town who . . ."

A noise at the door cut Mash Qasem's story short, "'S like that's him, from our town. Now you say nothin', leave it to me."

As soon as he opened the door Mash Qasem stepped back in astonishment. "Eh? What? It's you? . . . But . . ."

"Yes, yes, it is I . . . I myself . . . Out of my way! Silence!"

A hand landed on Mash Qasem's chest and thrust him aside. Aziz al-Saltaneh and I stood stock-still with astonishment.

Deputy Taymur Khan, the detective from the criminal affairs office and Cadet Officer Ghiasabadi's superior, who had come to our house last year in order to investigate the disappearance of Dustali Khan, came through the doorway.

Two paces behind him Cadet Officer Ghiasabadi, with his ancient porkpie hat pulled down over his eyes, set foot in the garden.

Involuntarily Aziz al-Saltaneh said, "Deputy, sir . . . you?"

"Good day, ma'am . . . Yes, it is I, you are surprised? It seems you were not expecting me! . . . Silence!"

"But . . . but . . . why . . . but we didn't imagine that . . . we didn't think of troubling you . . ."

"Silence! Time is golden . . . explain what article of yours has been stolen! . . . Your answer? Quick, now, immediately, at the double!"

Deputy Taymur Khan said these words in such a curt way that Aziz al-Saltaneh was thoroughly confused, and started to stammer, "I . . . it was . . . I mean . . ."

"What? What about you? . . . What has been stolen? Explain! Quick, immediately, without any hesitation! Yes? What?"

"It was . . . I mean . . . it was . . . a watch belonging to my late father. . . ."

"Gold?"

"Well . . . of course . . . yes, yes."

"With a chain? Quick, now, immediately, at the double!"

"Yes . . . I mean, its chain was . . . yes, with a chain . . ."

"Silence! . . . Don't you suspect anyone? Yes? Well? Silence!"

Mash Qasem was so taken by surprise by Deputy Taymur Khan's unexpected arrival that he was staring at him, thunderstruck and with his mouth wide open. The deputy leapt toward him. "What's your name? What?"

"Well now, why should I lie . . . lie . . ."

"You told a lie? Why did you tell a lie? . . . Confess! Quick, now, immediately, at the double."

"I didn't tell no lie. And why should I lie? To the grave it's ah . . . ah . . . My name, at your service, is Mash Qasem."

"Aha! Aha! I remember . . . suspect number two in last year's crime . . . silence!"

I attempted to shift my position slightly. Deputy Taymur Khan's voice rang out, "Halt! Who gave you permission to leave? Stay precisely here!"

Mash Qasem started to exchange greetings with Cadet Officer Ghiasabadi. The deputy interrupted him, "Silence! You wish to suborn my second in command? . . . For what purpose? Yes? Answer! Quick, immediately! Silence!"

And then he brought his enormous face close to Mash Qasem's face, "So, Mr. Mash Qasem, you said that . . . You are well?"

"Thanks be to God, thank the lord, very kind of you, I'm sure."

"Let me see, Mr. Mash Qasem, have you eaten lunch?"

Mash Qasem laughed, "What things you're sayin', sir, it's still two hours till noon . . ."

The deputy screamed, "How do you know it is two hours till noon? You've looked at a watch? Which watch? A gold watch with a chain belonging to her late father? Well? Yes? Answer! Quick, now, immediately . . . Where have you hidden it? At the double, quick, quick. Answer! Silence!"

At first Mash Qasem laughed. Then he suddenly realized what the deputy was implying and he expostulated, "'Slike you're wantin' to say that, God forbid, that I . . ."

For the first time Aziz al-Saltaneh exploded, "Why are you talking such nonsense, sir? All these people of ours have been with us for twenty or thirty years. They're pure as the driven snow. And who told you to come here anyway? Mr. Ghiasabadi was supposed to come."

At this moment Dear Uncle, who must have heard the noise, came out of the inner apartments. "What's happened, madam? Who's this . . ."

Aziz al-Saltaneh shouted, "I don't know what all this crazy ruckus is all about. I asked the director to send Mr. Ghiasabadi here . . . now this gentleman comes and starts his caterwauling."

Deputy Taymur Khan flew at her. "What's this? I can't believe my ears! Insulting a representative of the state while fulfilling his duty?"

Dear Uncle tried to calm him down. "Don't upset yourself, sir. No insult was intended. The lady has lost something and thought that . . ."

"You be quiet! A man's watch is not something that the lady would put in her purse and lose. I am certain that this watch has been stolen. Theft, stealing, and treachery."

"How can you be so sure? Who has told you?"

"My instinct! The instinct of Deputy Taymur Khan, originator of the international system of surprise attack!"

For a moment Dear Uncle stared uncertainly at Aziz al-Saltaneh. It seemed they had made no decision as to what they were to say had been stolen. And they couldn't really be blamed for this since they'd had no thought of Deputy Taymur Khan's coming and it had also been agreed that when Cadet Officer Ghiasabadi arrived Aziz al-Saltaneh would tell him that the stolen object had been found. But Deputy Taymur Khan's famous system of surprise attack had forced Aziz al-Saltaneh to say, without any hesitation or opportunity for thought, the first thing that came into her head. In any case the deputy's involvement was not to be taken lightly, and they had somehow or other to get rid of him. But the deputy was not someone who would easily give up once he had started his investigations.

At this moment our servant walked past us, with a basket in his hand. The deputy saw him. He shouted, "Halt! . . . Well, well! Who gave you permission to go outside? Who? Eh? Answer! Quick, now, immediately, at the double!"

Our servant was startled and, with his mouth wide open, he stared at the deputy.

Mash Qasem pushed in, "Don't be scared, mate, this Mr. Deputy's character's that way . . . he's come from the criminal office to see who's stolen the watch."

The deputy shouted, "Mash Qasem, silence!"

Then he turned to our servant again. He brought his huge face almost into contact with the servant's face and said, "You! You! If you confess immediately your sentence will be reduced. Confess! Quick, now, immediately, at the double! Confess! Tell us where you have put the watch!"

Our servant's body began visibly to tremble, and he stammered out, "I swear by the blessed Morteza Ali I found it. I didn't steal it. I found it."

We all froze as if we'd been electrocuted. No one could understand what had happened. The sound of the deputy's smug laughter, which was terrifying, rang out, "Ha, ha! Cadet Officer Ghiasabadi, the handcuffs!"

Our poor servant had turned strangely pale, and he started pleading, "No, don't put me in jail! By Morteza Ali, I swear I didn't steal it, I found it."

"You found it? Where? When? Who with? How? Quick, immediately, now, silence!"

Then he threw us a proud look and muttered, "Deputy Taymur Khan's international system of surprise attack cannot fail."

At this moment the garden door opened and Asadollah Mirza, accompanied by Shamsali Mirza, came in. As soon as the sound of Asadollah Mirza's voice was audible, without looking at the two of them the deputy spread his arms and shouted, "Silence! Interfering with the investigation is forbidden!"

By gesturing with his hands and head, Asadollah Mirza asked what was going on. But everyone seemed more dumbfounded than the next person, and no one could answer him. Once again the deputy brought his head close to our servant's face, and said, "Where is the watch now?"

"In my room . . ."

"Cadet Officer Ghiasabadi! Escort this man to his room so that he can fetch the watch!"

Cadet Officer Ghiasabadi took our servant by the arm and they set off. Dear Uncle, Aziz al-Saltaneh and the rest of those present looked this way and that, wondering what the truth of all this could be. With a couple of phrases spoken in French, Asadollah Mirza asked Dear Uncle what was going on. The deputy shouted, "Aha! Who talked in Russian? Silence!"

Finally Mash Qasem, in a few phrases, gave some sort of an explanation to the two newcomers. But the deputy didn't want to give anyone permission to talk. Our servant and the cadet officer returned.

"Silence! Where did you find it? Quick, now, immediately, answer!"

"In the gutter. By the blessed Morteza Ali . . ."

"Silence! When?"

"Yesterday."

The pocket watch, together with its chain, was transferred from the cadet officer's hand to the deputy's. Suddenly Mash Qasem's shouted at the top of his voice, "Eh m'dears! I bet that's the Indian brigadier's watch, what fell out of his pocket in the fight . . . and then they took that shoeshine feller away for it!"

The deputy leapt toward Mash Qasem, "What? An Indian? A fight? A shoeshine man? What's all this about? Answer! Quick, immediately, at the double!"

"Well now, why should I lie . . ."

"I said now, immediately, at the double!"

"God keep you, sir, it's like you're always in a tearin' hurry, I bet you was born two months premature 'cause you couldn't wait. You won't let me say what I have to say . . ."

"Say it! Now, immediately, at the double!"

"I forget what you asked."

"I said the Indian, the fight, the shoeshine man, what was all that about?"

"Well now, why should I lie? To the grave it's ah . . . ah . . . This neighbor of ours, Brigadier Maharat Khan, yesterday he had a fight with the shoeshine man who works round here. Today he went and lodged a complaint that the shoeshine man had pinched his watch . . . but, it looks like it dropped out of his pocket into the gutter, when they was fightin'. This lad here found it."

Mash Qasem's explanation clarified the matter for everyone. It was as if a cloud were lifted from Dear Uncle's face. Hurriedly he said, "Then run and take this watch down to the police station, Qasem, so they'll let the poor devil go."

Deputy Taymur Khan frowned and said, "Just a minute! He's to take the stolen watch down to the police station without so much as a by your leave? And who has enacted such a law? You? Or you? Answer! Quick, now, immediately! Silence!"

For the first time Asadollah Mirza intervened in the conversation. "Moment, moment, Mr. Detective, sir . . ."

Deputy Taymur Khan had not paid any attention to Asadollah Mirza's presence; he turned and looked at him. Suddenly he raised his eyebrows and said, "Just a minute! Aren't you the murderer from last year? Answer! Quick, now, immediately! Silence!"

Asadollah Mirza assumed a mysterious air and said, "That's right, I am that murderer . . ."

And making a circle with his open hands he advanced on the deputy as if about to take him by the throat. "And today I want to take revenge on the officer who discovered my crime. Murder of police detective at the hands of a malignant assassin."

Deputy Taymur Khan took two steps backwards and shouted, "Cadet Officer Ghiasabadi, the handcuffs!"

Shamsali Mirza took his brother by the arm, "Asadollah, this is no time for joking. Let this gentleman do his job and leave."

"You, silence! . . . I'm to leave? Just like that? Just like that? Then what about this lady's stolen watch?"

Aziz al-Saltaneh said, "You know, sir, I really don't want you to find my late father's watch . . . by the way, let me take a look at that watch . . ."

And more or less by force she wrenched the watch from the deputy's hand and gave it to Dear Uncle. Dear Uncle quickly handed it to Shamsali Mirza and said, "Shamsali, please run to the station and hand over the Indian brigadier's watch so they can release that poor shoeshine man."

Shamsali Mirza took the watch and set off. But Deputy Taymur Khan's voice rang out, "Halt! What do you think you're doing with that watch? Give it to me, sir! Quick, immediately, silence! I have to give the orders."

Aziz al-Saltaneh went for him. "Oh yes? And what's it got to do with you?"

"Silence! Madam, you have no right to speak."

Her face glowing with rage, Aziz al-Saltaneh glanced this way and that. She snatched up a dry branch from the ground, took a couple of steps toward the deputy, raised the branch to hit him on the head with it, and said, "Just let me hear you say once more that I've no right to speak!"

With a laugh Asadollah Mirza said, "Mr. Deputy, sir, didn't you hear the lady? She said that you were to repeat once again the words you just said. Politeness is a virtue. Obey the lady's order!"

"Well well, what a splendid scene! Threatening an officer of the state during the performance of his duties . . . intending to strike and injure an officer of the state . . ."

Aziz al-Saltaneh hit the deputy with the branch and said, "Get going, you! Get going, so I can set you straight."

"Where, madam?"

"I want to have a couple of words with your boss."

Deputy Taymur Khan melted. "I never claimed, madam . . . if you yourself . . . if you have no complaint to make, I will be on my way . . . Cadet Officer Ghiasabadi, quick march!"

Asadollah Mirza jumped into the conversation, "What do you mean 'Quick march!' Wait, sir . . . the matter of the watch has to be cleared up . . . someone has to investigate it after all."

And he signalled Aziz al-Saltaneh to carry out her decision, Aziz al-Saltaneh gave the branch to Mash Qasem and said, "Mash Qasem, keep an eye on this gentleman while I make a phone call."

A few moments later Layli came out of the inner apartments of Dear Uncle's house and said, "Mrs. Aziz says the deputy is wanted on the phone."

The deputy hurried off to the inner apartments, followed by Dear Uncle. In a friendly voice Asadollah Mirza started to ask Cadet Officer Ghiasabadi how he was doing. As always, seeing Layli made me forget my sorrows and worries for a few moments, but this didn't last for very long because I started thinking about Puri, uncle colonel's son, who was supposed to turn up that night. For a while we gazed mournfully at one another. I couldn't think of anything to say to her.

A little later Deputy Taymur Khan, followed by Aziz al-Saltaneh and Dear Uncle, came out of the inner apartments. The deputy's face looked very preoccupied. In a curt tone he said, "Cadet Officer Ghiasabadi! You stay here and continue the investigation to find the lady's watch. My superior has recalled me. Silence! For the moment the accused is at liberty."

"Yes sir."

As he passed Asadollah Mirza the deputy said in a choked voice, "I'm leaving, but I shall see you again. For now I have to leave . . . I hope I place the hangman's noose around your neck myself."

"You, sir, if you please, quick, immediately, back where you came from. They need you at your office."

As soon as Taymur Khan had left, Cadet Officer Ghiasabadi assumed his superior's expression and said, "Right, let's begin the investigation . . . Where was this watch, madam? Answer! Quick, immediately, at the double!"

With a smile Asadollah said, "Moment, Cadet Officer, sir, there's no need to be in such a hurry now, why don't you have some tea, and then when the time is right we'll look around and find the watch. I'm quite sure the lady has put it somewhere and she's forgotten where. If by any chance it really has been stolen, then your extraordinary intelligence and sagacity'll find it soon enough. Your face clearly shows what an intelligent person you are."

"Very kind of you, sir."

"No, no, I'm telling the simple truth. I'm an excellent judge of character. I promise you that it'll be your mind that unravels the truth of this criminal affair. Every child knows that you stand head and shoulders above the deputy when it comes to intelligence and sagacity, and the fact that for now you're under his command is another matter all together."

Cadet Officer Ghiasabadi was so pleased and embarrassed that his face turned bright crimson; he said, "Very kind of you to see it that way. Of course, it makes a difference who's got pull and influence and who hasn't."

"If you really want that, it'll be no problem at all. I've a hundred friends and acquaintances, ministers and lawyers and such like, and if I tipped any one of them the wink the business would be as good as done . . . You've been very kind to us, we're very much in your debt."

"You're really too kind . . . you're embarrassing me."

"With your intelligence and sagacity and preeminence it's really a pity that you just sit on your hands and—because you're naturally such a fine, magnanimous person—you don't make any effort to push yourself forward. I'd have thought you would be head of the department by now. Your wife and children haven't committed any sin that they should be held back because of your fine magnanimous nature, Cadet Officer, sir!"

"I'm not married . . . I mean I was but we were divorced . . . I've a child that lives with its mother but of course I pay for its support."

"Incredible! . . . Ah well. Mash Qasem, won't you bring a tea for the cadet officer?"

"Right away, sir . . . why don't you come with me, us bein' from the same town and all . . . come in my room and have a tea, it'll refresh your throat like."

"And so the investigation for the watch . . ."

"There's lots of time for that, let's go off to my room and have some tea."

Mash Qasem and Cadet Officer Ghiasabadi, who had kept his porkpie hat on his head the whole time, went off to Mash Qasem's room.

Asadollah said to Dear Uncle, who had been standing there silent, "It seems we're getting somewhere."

The conversation veered this way and that for a few minutes. Dear Uncle was so anxious to see Shamsali Mirza return from his mission to the police station to free the shoeshine man that he couldn't be separated from the garden door, and Aziz al-Saltaneh was nervously pacing up and down. Asadollah Mirza winked at me and quietly made for the inner apartments of Dear Uncle's house. I followed him.

"Uncle Asadollah, where are you going?"

"I want to find out what's up, to see how far this business of our new son-in-law's progressed. Whether he's said 'I do' yet or not."

Mash Qasem's room was in the basement. With Asadollah in front and me following him, we tiptoed quietly down the corridor that led to the basement. We heard Mash Qasem's voice asking anxiously and incredulously, "Eh, swear on your mom's life you're kiddin'! Swear you hope to die if it ain't so!"

"Eh, die yourself . . . I was hit by a bullet in the war in Lurestan. I was in hospital six months. And that's why my wife divorced me . . ."

"You mean it's all gone? Like it was never there? Not one little bit's left?"

Asadollah threw me an appalled look and whispered, "Of all the rotten luck . . . our castle in the air's about to crumble."

Mash Qasem said, "But come on now, didn't you take some medicine to heal it like?"

"What medicine? There has to be something there for the medicine to heal."

"Eh, it's just our luck, what a place for the pesky bullet to land! And there's me been tellin' tales of how manly the folks in Ghiasabad are!"

It seemed that Mash Qasem had decided to leave Cadet Officer Ghiasabadi alone for a while and to pass on the results of his conversation to the rest of us, because we heard him say, "My friend, you stay here a minute, I've just got to pop my head in the kitchen, by the time you've drunk your tea I'll be back. And have some of these nuts. Don't hold back, make yourself at home . . . eat up!"

Asadollah Mirza and I returned from our hiding place to the yard. Asadollah Mirza was deep in thought. Hearing the voices of Dear Uncle and Aziz al-Saltaneh coming from Dustali Khan's room, he went in that direction. I followed him.

Aziz al-Saltaneh was sitting by Dustali Khan's bed and Dear Uncle was pacing up and down the room.

"What's happened Asadollah? Do you know whether their conversation's over or not?"

"Well now, as Mash Qasem would say, Why should I lie? To the grave it's ah . . . ah . . . It seems as if the matter has come up against a San Franciscan problem." Dustali Khan lifted his head and said, "Even if they put you in the grave, you'd still have to be talking rubbish."

"Moment, moment, as of now our shot-riddled hero is closer to the grave than I am."

There was no opportunity for an argument to develop, because Mash Qasem appeared. He had a very hangdog expression on his face.

Dear Uncle asked, "What's happened, Mash Qasem? Did you talk to him?"

"Yes, sir, I said a lot."

"And what was the result?"

"Well sir, why should I lie? to the grave it's ah . . . ah . . . I haven't dared tell this neighbor of mine yet about Miss Qamar being expectin'. He's agreed to it all the same, but there's a . . . well, the poor devil has a problem, a difficulty like."

"What problem? What difficulty?"

"Well sir, savin' your . . . savin' your . . . savin' your grace, sir, and not to be disrespectful like, I think this man from our town isn't a man from our town."

"What do you mean? How isn't he from your town?"

"His name's Ghiasabadi right enough, but he can't be from Ghiasabad. Because in the war in Lurestan he was hit by a bullet . . ."

"You mean bullets don't hit men from Ghiasabad?"

"They hit 'em, but not where this one hit this poor devil. To cut a long story short, and no disrespect like but this poor feller's got no guts."

Aziz al-Saltaneh asked in a puzzled way, "Mash Qasem, how can he have no guts? . . . And what have guts got to do with . . . ?"

Asadollah Mirza said, "Mrs. al-Saltaneh, Mash Qasem is rather shy, what he means by guts is the famous tower of San Francisco."

Aziz al-Saltaneh slapped herself on the cheek. "God strike me dead! Asadollah, what things you say."

And Dustali Khan followed up her remarks, "When people have no shame or modesty it's better . . ."

Asadollah Mirza angrily cut his words short. "Moment, moment, and you, who are such a paragon of shame and modesty, by what name would you refer to the aforementioned member?"

"A man doesn't use a name . . ."

"Nevertheless, it's a reality that exists. Either one has to call it by its proper name, or one conveys one's meaning by hints and allusions. After all, we can't refer to it as a nose or an ear or an eyebrow . . ."

Dear Uncle interrupted their conversation, "Please, gentlemen, don't argue . . . and in any case whether this particular exists or doesn't exist, what does it matter? You're not expecting them to grow old in one another's arms, are you?"

Aziz al-Saltaneh slapped herself on the cheek. "God strike me dead! God forbid!"

Mash Qasem said, "The bad thing about this is we can't blame the baby on him. We'll have to tell him the truth!"

Dustali Khan said, "At the most ten or fifteen days . . . then there has to be a divorce. That's all we needed, to have this worthless Ghiasabadi for a son-in-law . . . we'll have to explain to him that he takes the money and marries the girl and then a few days later divorces her and goes about his business."

Asadollah Mirza said, "Mash Qasem, go and talk to him. We've no choice now except to tell him the truth. When Cadet Officer Ghiasabadi realizes why we're marrying her off to him he'll also realize that this defect is a mere detail of no importance whatsoever. It makes no difference if a man has legs or if he's completely crippled if he's not going to be running anywhere."

Mash Qasem shook his head and said, "Well sir, to tell the truth, I'm afraid to say this to someone from our town. Sir, if you knew how important their honor is to folks from Ghiasabad, it's impossible you'd dare to . . ."

"Let him know carefully and bit by bit, Mash Qasem!"

"In fact, it's better we tell him all in one go and have hold of his arms and legs so he doesn't start a bloodbath."

After some discussion, it was finally agreed, at Mash Qasem's insistence, that Asadollah Mirza and I would go to assist him; we would sit down on either side of the cadet officer and when Mash Qasem indicated that he was about to broach the subject we would use some excuse to grip the prospective son-in-law's arms, so that he didn't wreak some terrible havoc either on Mash Qasem or on himself.

As we were setting off for the cellar Dustali Khan lifted up the fore part of his body and said in a beseeching voice, "But don't suddenly let him realize that Qamar has her own personal inheritance, or his expectations will really soar."

Asadollah Mirza threw him an angry contemptuous look and muttered, "Don't worry, they won't snatch that morsel from your jaws. Sleep well, great hero!"

In the yard Mash Qasem gave his final orders concerning the precautionary steps that had to be taken, "You be on the watch out. When I give two coughs then you know I'm goin' to tell him the heart of the matter. Then you grab his arms tight while I'm havin' my say. Don't let him go till I tell you."

Dear Uncle Napoleon and Aziz al-Saltaneh both tiptoed over to the cellar window so that they could overhear the crucial exchange.

When we entered the cellar, the cadet officer, who still had his porkpie hat pulled down over his ears, stood up to his full height.

"Please, Cadet Officer, sir, why do you stand on ceremony so much . . . there's no need for any of this between us."

At Asadollah Mirza's insistence, Cadet Officer Ghiasabadi sat on the rug at one end of the room, and Asadollah Mirza and I took up our positions on either side of him.

Mash Qasem looked around the room. He picked up a pair of sugar tongs, and a little hammer for breaking cube sugar, and hid them behind a curtain.

Asadollah Mirza began to speak, "Yes, Cadet Officer, sir, this girl of ours has seen you and likes what she sees . . . her mother and father are both agreeable to it, and you are still young. You can't go on without settling down like this."

The cadet officer hung his head and said, "Whatever you say, sir. But I told Mash Qasem that I . . . I mean I told Mash Qasem my secret."

"Moment, Cadet Officer, sir, that matter's of no importance. There are so many people who've had these problems and been cured. With modern medical methods . . ."

The cadet officer interrupted him and with his head still lowered said, "But sir, I'm not curable. It's my bad luck there's nothing left . . . if you agree to it with me like this, then I've no objections. But the lady's not to say tomorrow that she wasn't told. I'm only doing this, it's the only reason I'm doing it, to be of service to you."

"Her father and mother are happy with it, Cadet Officer, sir."

Mash Qasem confirmed this. "Yes, they're happy. When the girl's happy, then the mother and father'll be happy. So why are you beatin' about the bush?"

"But I want to know why they want me to marry their daughter. Couldn't they find someone more eligible than me in this city?"

Mash Qasem glanced toward me and Asadollah Mirza and coughed a couple of times. From each side I and Asadollah Mirza placed our hands on the cadet officer's arms. Mash Qasem said, "Because the girl is expectin'."

Then he closed his eyes and waited for the cadet officer's reaction. We increased our pressure on his arms. Contrary to our expectations, the cadet officer's face broke into a broad smile. With a laugh he said, "I thought so. So the apple's got a worm in it, and if it weren't for that, she wouldn't be for me at all."

Our worried faces relaxed. We released his arms, and Asadollah Mirza said in mild tones, "Yes, that's the way it is, Cadet Officer, sir . . . it seems that this poor girl went once to the men's public baths and she was unlucky enough to get pregnant . . ."

The cadet officer cut him off with a laugh, "Yes, that men's public bath's a terrible thing!"

Mash Qasem muttered, "God rot you, you've no feelin' of honor at all . . ."

"What did you say, Mash Qasem?"

"Nothin', m'dear . . . to cut a long story short, that's how it is."

"So now the girl has to be married off, and then after a little while there'll be a divorce. Is that what you want?"

Asadollah Mirza answered, "Yes, Cadet Officer, sir, after ten or fifteen days."

"It's not a job for ten or fifteen days. Everyone'll realize, I've my reputation to think of. We'll have to wait at least three months, then invent some excuse . . ."

Asadollah Mirza said, "That'll be no problem . . . Goodness, I forgot, I had to make a phone call. Be so good as to wait here and I'll be straight back." Asadollah Mirza went out. I guessed that he had gone to get Aziz al-Saltaneh's agreement to the length of the marriage, since he came back a few moments later and said, "Right, what were we talking about? . . . Oh yes, about the time . . . yes, that's no problem, three months and then you divorce her."

"But sir, I have to tell you that I've no money for all the expenses."

"My dear Cadet Officer, what are you thinking of . . . you're doing a charitable act, why should you be put to any expense . . . the girl's mother will bear all the expenses . . . you chat with Mash Qasem . . . we'll take care of all the expenses."

Asadollah Mirza signalled to me and we left the basement together. Aziz al-Saltaneh and Dear Uncle both had their ears glued to the basement window. Asadollah Mirza was about to say something but Aziz al-Saltaneh silenced him with a gesture of her hand. She was listening carefully to the conversation between Mash Qasem and the cadet officer and muttering to herself, "The greedy . . . the cheeky devil wants two thousand *tomans* cash."

Asadollah Mirza whispered, "Ma'am, it's worth it . . . you'll never find anyone for less than that."

Aziz al-Saltaneh still had her ear glued to the window pane. Suddenly her face began to glow and she angrily hissed, "The rotten bastard's insulting me . . . when he's sorted out that girl's business I'll show him who's a running sore, who's a shrew . . . God rot his bald head for him."

✤ ✤ ✤

A few minutes later the meeting continued in Dustali Khan's room. Cadet Officer Ghiasabadi was kneeling on the carpet, his head bowed.

Dear Uncle Napoleon said, "Cadet Officer, I hope you realize that you are joining an aristocratic and respected family, and that you should comport yourself during this period of time in a way that will not injure our dignity and reputation."

"I'm at your service. I'll do exactly whatever you say."

Asadollah Mirza said, "What's your opinion concerning a house?"

His question was directed to Dear Uncle. Dear Uncle answered, "Of course we'll have to think about a house so that . . ."

Aziz al-Saltaneh said, "Eh? Do you think I can be separated from my child? The cadet officer will have to come to our house . . . there are empty rooms upstairs, I'll fix them up for them."

Without raising his head the cadet officer said, "Well sir, I've a mother who's getting on and I can't leave her alone."

Asadollah Mirza said, "Fine, bring the aged parent along too."

Dustali Khan jerked himself upright, "Why do you talk such rubbish, Asadollah . . . ? How in our house can . . . ?"

In a palpably mischievous tone Asadollah Mirza said, "There's no choice Dustali! Mr. Ghiasabadi can't leave his old infirm mother without anyone to look after her."

The cadet officer took up the thread of his talk, "That's right, sir, there's just me in the world and my aged worn out mother . . . and my widowed sister."

Asadollah Mirza's eyes lit up, "You have a sister, too? . . . How old is she? What does she do?"

"Well sir, we married her off two years ago and last year her husband was run over by a car . . . Now she sings in a nightclub."

Dear Uncle and Dustali Khan and Aziz al-Saltaneh all said more or less simultaneously, "What? In a nightclub?"

But Asadollah Mirza gave them no chance to speak. "Splendid, splendid. Wonderful. God keep her . . . Well, it's obvious that you can't just leave a young woman without a husband to fend for herself in a town like this . . . the cadet officer's quite right."

Dustali Khan shouted, "Asadollah, can you just shut that filthy mouth of yours!"

"Moment, moment, do you mean that the cadet officer should abandon his mother and sister and come and live as son-in-law in your house? If he can, so much the better . . . the matter has nothing whatsoever to do with me."

The cadet officer stood up. "No, it seems as though the gentleman isn't very taken with me . . . I can't just leave an old infirm woman and a young woman without any support to fend for themselves just like that . . . I'll be on my way."

Mash Qasem and Asadollah Mirza ran toward him. "Where're you goin'? Sit down! What that gentleman says doesn't matter, it's what his wife wants."

Aziz al-Saltaneh had been making a show of crying, "I'm ready to do anything for this poor wretched child . . ."

Dustali Khan shouted, "Woman, do you understand what you're saying? . . . The cadet officer and his old mother and his nightclub singer sister in our house!"

Once again the cadet officer prepared to leave. "With your permission, gentlemen, I'll be on my way . . . I can't listen to people insulting my mother and sister."

Once again they sat him down in his place. Asadollah Mirza shouted, "Dustali, control your tongue, otherwise we'll renew our investigations into who the child's father is; we'll bring him here and force him to marry the girl."

Dustali Khan gritted his teeth in fury and muttered, "Whatever you think is best."

The marriage ceremony was fixed for Thursday night. But the cadet officer insisted that out of respect for his mother he should bring her to ask formally for the girl's hand.

Asadollah Mirza said, "Yes, that's certainly necessary. She can honor us with her presence today. And bring your sister, too. From now on we're all one big happy family."

The cadet officer made as if to leave, but after a few steps turned round. "But, sir, I have to beg you that that matter we mentioned about the war in Lurestan remains just between us. No one in the world knows about this problem of mine. If this leaks out, your daughter's reputation will be gone and so will mine . . . and don't say anything about the lady being pregnant in front of my mother, because if my mother realizes, she'll never agree to it."

After solemn promises had been made concerning the cadet officer's demands, he went on his way.

Asadollah Mirza and Mash Qasem escorted him to the garden door. After a few minutes Asadollah Mirza came back and said cheerfully, "The wig problem's solved too. It's agreed that he'll come this afternoon and I'll take him to Lalehzar Avenue and fix him up with a nice wig so that he won't make Qamar feel sick to her stomach . . . Better give a thought to his clothes as well. For now, Dustali, give me the money for the wig!"

"I have to give the money for the wig, too?"

"Don't if you don't want to . . . then Qamar won't agree to marry the cadet officer. Once again we'll have to start from square one to try and find the baby's real father and bring him here to marry his baby's mother."

Trembling with rage Dustali Khan shouted, "Asadollah I swear on the soul of my father that if you say that rubbish once more I'll murder you!"

"Moment, moment, I don't know why it upsets you so much. I said we'll go and find the shameless, conscienceless, everything-less father of the baby. So why should you get so hot and bothered? God forbid that . . ."

There was a general uproar of people objecting to Asadollah's remarks; Dustali Khan picked up a bottle of medicine that was next to him and flung it at Asadollah's head; it shattered loudly against the wall. With a peal of laughter Asadollah Mirza fled the scene.

⚜ ⚜ ⚜

When I got back home my father, who had been out since morning, had returned and was pacing about in the yard. He called me over and took me to the room next to the front door.

"What was all that fuss about today? They said when I wasn't here Deputy Taymur Khan came."

I told my father the whole story. When he heard that Cadet Officer Ghiasabadi had agreed to marry Qamar he guffawed with laughter and said, "That's really beautiful! A scion of the nation's aristocracy in the arms of Cadet Officer Ghiasabadi! Thank God they've found someone less aristocratic than me, and good luck to them!"

There was bitter poison in my father's laugh.

He was relishing the taste of revenge after years of being treated with disdain, the revenge that nature was taking on Dear Uncle Napoleon and his family. And then staring off into space he muttered, "This marriage mustn't go forward without anyone knowing . . . all the pillars of the community, all the aristocracy must be invited."

Then catching sight of my astonished stare, he started running around the room like a little child. "Read all about it! Read all about it! Latest news . . . aristocracy drags its skirts through filth . . ."

He thought for a few moments. Then he seemed to come to a sudden decision. Paying no attention to me he left the room and went toward the garden door.

"Where are you going, dad?"

"I'll be right back."

I anxiously followed him for a few steps. Then I watched him go as far as the corner of the alleyway. A few minutes later Shamsali Mirza and the shoeshine man came back from the police-station. The shoeshine man set about his work again.

Dear Uncle went over to him with a big smile on his face. "We're very pleased that the misunderstanding has been cleared up."

"God keep you, sir, that bastard Indian accused me of stealing. That lot have no faith or religion."

"Don't worry, God sees to it that justice is done."

Spreading out the cloth he worked on, the shoeshine man continued, "And I'll see he gets what's coming to him, too. Just you wait. When the time comes I know what I've in store for him."

Dear Uncle's eyes shone. Under his breath he repeated the shoe-shine man's words, "When the time comes . . . when the time comes . . ."

Then after a moment's silence he said in a would-be meaningful tone, "Pay no attention to such people. You've other tasks to fulfill. Attend to your own business."

Without understanding what was being implied, the shoeshine man said, "Yes sir, I'll be attending to my own business."

Dear Uncle nodded his head in a satisfied manner and said, "Attend to your own business. It's natural that problems like this will arise."

Without raising his head the shoeshine man said, "Yes, sir, if I can't handle this Indian I'm in a really bad way; those other bas-tards'll eat me alive."

With a satisfied smile Dear Uncle repeated, "Yes those other bastards . . . they're important . . . Ah, Mash Qasem! Fetch a glass of cordial for our friend Hushang, to refresh his throat!"

Mash Qasem was near me. I heard him mutter, "And I hope it's the last he ever drinks!"

SEVENTEEN

AT SUNSET THAT DAY uncle colonel and a few relatives went by horse drawn carriage to welcome Puri, who was supposed to arrive at about nine o'clock at the railroad station. Uncle colonel was upset that the whole family hadn't gone to welcome him, but this was unavoidable. Dear Uncle Napoleon and Asadollah Mirza, and especially Aziz al-Saltaneh, had no alternative but to stay and entertain the cadet officer and his mother and sister who were coming to ask for Qamar's hand.

Asadollah Mirza came a little after uncle colonel had set off. He was very cheerful. As soon as he arrived he said, "I went with the cadet officer and bought him a really beautiful wig. He looks just like Rudolph Valentino . . . he's coming now and you'll see."

Aziz al-Saltaneh was giving her final instructions to Qamar, "God, my dear, what I wouldn't do for you, you're such a lovely girl . . . sit properly like a lady. Don't say a word . . . whatever they ask I'll answer for you."

Asadollah Mirza pinched Qamar's cheek and said, "That's right, my girl, don't say a word. People like it when a girl doesn't say anything. They like shy girls better. If you talk then your husband will go, and then your baby won't have a daddy. Have you got that, my dear?"

Qamar was wearing a pretty green dress; with an innocent smile she said, "Yes, I've got it. I really love my baby. I want to knit him a jacket."

"But my dear if you talk about your baby in front of the people who are coming, they'll go. Then you'll have to stay by yourself . . . don't say a word about your baby. They mustn't realize you're going to have a baby. Now you've really got that?"

"Yes, I've got it, Uncle Asadollah. I won't say anything at all about my baby in front of them."

Then Qamar, Aziz al-Saltaneh and Dear Uncle went into the sitting room. Dustali Khan also hobbled in and lay down on his side on a sofa. Asadollah Mirza and I were in the yard when suddenly Mash Qasem ran toward Asadollah Mirza and said, "Eh m'dears, they're comin'. But my neighbor's not wearin' his wig."

"What? He's not wearing his wig? Then what's on his head?"

"That same old porkpie hat thing."

"What a donkey he is! Mash Qasem, run and keep the women occupied for a minute and send the cadet officer on ahead so I can see what the hell he thinks he's doing."

"His mom's really a fright. I'm afraid she'll scare Qamar!"

"What do you mean? She doesn't look too good?"

"She's got her veil on. . . . But she's fearsome all right . . ."

"How fearsome?"

"Well now, why should I lie? To the grave it's ah . . . ah . . . what I've seen with my own eyes, savin' your grace, savin' your grace, is that she's got a beard and mustache as long as preacher Seyed Abolqasem has."

Asadollah Mirza struck his fist against his forehead and said, "And I suppose it couldn't have been managed if he hadn't brought this beauty queen along . . . Mash Qasem, run and send the donkey here so I can see why the hell he hasn't covered his bald head up."

Mash Qasem ran outside and a moment later the cadet officer entered. His hat was pulled down over his ears. Asadollah glanced toward the sitting room window. He took the cadet officer by the arm, led him into a hallway, and said, "Officer, what kind of a turn-out is this? Where's the wig?"

The cadet officer hung his head and said, "Sir, you'll really have to forgive me. My mom said that if I wore the wig she'd disown me."

"And now this one will disown you. Where's the wig?"

The cadet officer gestured toward his inside jacket pocket and said, "It's here."

Asadollah Mirza thought for a moment and then said, "Cadet Officer, sir, if you could keep your mother and sister busy in the garden for a moment, I'll be with you in just a moment."

Then he turned to Mash Qasem, "Mash Qasem, bring some sweet tea for the ladies . . . have them sit in the arbor till I come."

As soon as the cadet officer and Mash Qasem had left the house Asadollah Mirza signalled Aziz al-Saltaneh to come into the yard; anxiously he said to her, "Ma'am, a new problem's turned up; the bridegroom's mother has told him that if he wears a wig she'll disown him. Do you think if he comes in without a wig on Qamar will be very . . . ?"

Aziz al-Saltaneh cut him off, "God, Asadollah, I'd die for you but think of something! The poor wretch has talked ten times about her husband's head of hair . . . convince him any way you can at least for today to put the wig on that rotten ugly head of his."

"I'll do my utmost . . . God willing, I'll get him to agree."

"Well, you're a fine man and what I wouldn't do for you's no-body's business, but do something. You know how to talk to a woman. There's no woman alive who won't listen to you. Do something."

"But from what Mash Qasem says our groom's mother isn't a woman at all, she's got as long a beard and mustache as the preacher Seyed Abolqasem has."

"I'll drop down dead for you, Asadollah, but do something. You know how to twist old women round your little finger. You can corrupt a saint if you want to."

"Moment, moment, up to now I've never twisted a bearded lady round my little finger. Well, let's go and see what'll happen . . . but remember not to let Qamar stay in the room for long. When she's been sitting there for two minutes have someone call her out and then don't let her back in again. My main worry is that she'll say one word too much."

Asadollah Mirza set off for the garden. I followed him. When he saw me behind him he said, "Dear boy, you come too and help . . . if my razor won't shave her you must try with yours . . . usually these bearded women like young boys."

"What can I do, Uncle Asadollah?"

"Make up to her a bit . . . say nice things about the delicacy of her skin."

"Uncle Asadollah, I'm to say nice things about the delicacy of a bearded woman's skin? She'll think I'm making fun of her."

"Moment, really moment, why are you so naive? So open your eyes and at least you'll learn something."

When we caught sight of the cadet officer's mother in the distance, for a moment the two of us stood rooted to the spot. Asadollah Mirza involuntarily muttered, "Eh, blessed Morteza Ali, where's this seahorse sprung from? I've never seen such a creature in any zoo."

Although we could only see half her face from under her black veil, the two of us were horrified. He was telling the truth. We really couldn't remember any creature as ugly as this one. Even calling her a seahorse was flattering her. The blackness of her mustache and beard were obvious from a distance, and her breathing, which sounded like an old-fashioned steam press, could be heard from a long way off. Despite all this Asadollah Mirza threw caution to the winds and went forward, "Good day to you, madam . . . you are very, very welcome."

Cadet Officer Ghiasabadi made the introductions, "This is my mother Naneh Rajab . . . and this is Akhtar, my sister."

Asadollah Mirza's eyes glittered. The cadet officer's sister was olive-skinned and had a pretty face. She was somewhat stout, had a very prominent bosom, and was wearing violently red lipstick.

As soon as we sat down on the benches in the arbor, the groom's mother Naneh Rajab drained her glass of sherbet and said in a deep voice, "I have to tell you that I don't at all approve of these games. I've brought my son up and he's like a nosegay, he is, there's not a fault or blemish in him, he has a profession, he has his dignity, he's had six years of schooling, and now if his hair's fallen out, that's no fault or blemish . . . he has a hundred girls after him . . . so you can just forget about these wigs and such like silly games."

Her tone was so violent and emphatic that for a moment I thought the transaction was over and done with. But Asadollah Mirza mildly said, "Moment, madam. When you say 'I brought my son up,' it makes one laugh. I swear on your own soul, on my own soul, that I still can't believe you're the cadet officer's mother . . . if you want to make a joke that's another matter, of course."

Perhaps because this bearded woman had somewhat of a complex, owing to her masculine appearance, she rolled her eyes in their sockets and said violently, "What do you mean? Do you think I'm a freak with six fingers and shouldn't have a son?"

"My dear lady, of course you should have a son, but not a son as old as this . . . however is it possible that you, at such a young age, can have such a grown up son?"

The old woman's few yellowing teeth showed in among the hair of her mustache and beard. She fluttered her eyes and turned her head.

"Well now, what things you men say . . . Of course I was very young when I married. I was thirteen or fourteen when I had Rajabali. And this poor boy Rajabali isn't so old, he's had so many worries that it's aged him, as you can see . . ."

"Even so . . . even if the cadet officer is twenty, still it's very hard to believe . . . And you don't even use face-powder or lipstick."

The old woman had opened up like a blossom in springtime; she gave Asadollah Mirza a push in the chest and said, "Eh, what a sweet-talking tongue you've got in your head . . . by the way, what relation are you to the bride?"

Without taking his eyes off the cadet officer's sister's breasts, Asadollah Mirza said, "We're cousins."

A few minutes later the situation had totally changed. We entered the inner apartments with Naneh Rajab in front, followed by her son and daughter, and with Asadollah Mirza and myself bringing up the rear. The cadet officer had his wig on his head and was holding his porkpie hat in his hand.

When the suitor's family entered the sitting room Dear Uncle, and more especially Dustali Khan, remained motionless for a moment. Dustali Khan closed his eyes. The old woman's ugliness was more than they could tolerate.

But Qamar stared at the cadet officer's face and didn't pay much attention to his mother and sister.

Hardly had the guests sat down when my father and mother came in; it was clear that Dear Uncle had sent for them to come.

In response to the cadet officer's mother's first question concerning Qamar, Aziz al-Saltaneh began a long speech about her daughter's good qualities. Dear Uncle and Dustali Khan were silent. Dustali Khan's eyes were staring at the cadet officer's sister's body. He seemed to be weighing in his mind on the one side the horrors of living with the mother and on the other side the pleasures of the sister's company. But for her part the mother didn't take her hungry eyes for one minute from his form, which was stretched out on the sofa.

Then Dear Uncle began to talk about the special and quite exceptional status of his family as far as its social rank was concerned. But he had only uttered a few sentences when Mash Qasem ran in panting and said, "Sir, that Mrs. Farrokh Laqa lady's comin' here."

The complexions of those present—especially Dear Uncle and Aziz al-Saltaneh—noticeably paled. The unexpected appearance of this bad-mouthed gossip, who always wore black, left them paralyzed with shock for a moment. In a voice that he tried to keep calm, so that the guests would not suspect anything, Dear Uncle said, "Qasem, we have guests . . . say there's no one at home."

My father said, "This woman can't keep her mouth shut. To come visiting at such a time when we're discussing private family matters like this . . . however did she get wind of it?"

This bluster showed me my father's hand. I was certain that he himself had told Mrs. Farrokh Laqa. In this way my father could be sure that within twenty-four hours the whole town would know about both the details of the wedding and the particulars of the groom's family.

Dear Uncle turned to the cadet officer, "She's a relative of ours, but she always brings bad luck wherever she goes."

At this moment we could hear Mash Qasem's voice coming from the door to the inner apartments, "Missus, why should I lie? To the grave it's ah . . . ah . . . They've all gone to meet Mr. Puri . . . it wouldn't be a bad idea for you to go down to the station, too . . ."

This was immediately followed by the sound of Mrs. Farrokh Laqa's voice, "Out of my way and let me see . . . I just heard them talking . . ."

I looked out of the window at the door to the inner apartments. Mash Qasem was flung aside and Mrs. Farrokh Laqa, her face glowing and dressed in her usual black clothes and with a black scarf over her head, marched in.

As she entered the sitting room a deathly silence prevailed. Mrs. Farrokh Laqa popped a wedding candy into her mouth and said, "God willing, I hope they'll be very happy. I've heard that we've a joyful event in the near future . . . this lady must be the mother of the groom?"

Dear Uncle had no choice but to reply, "Yes, yes, the lady is his mother. How fortunate that you should come as well; these ladies and the groom turned up unexpectedly. And we said to Mash Qasem that . . . I mean, we thought it was a stranger . . . we told Mash Qasem that if it was a stranger . . ."

Mrs. Farrokh Laqa interrupted him, "It doesn't matter now."

Then she turned to the cadet officer's mother and said, "I wish you luck, dear. You couldn't find another girl as good as this one in the whole city. Pretty, proper, a good housewife, serious . . . by the way, what does your son do?"

Dear Uncle answered for the old lady, "The gentleman's one of the directors of the police department."

"Very nice, too, I wish you luck . . . his face seems familiar to me . . . So, what's his salary?"

Dear Uncle said in a violent tone, "Ma'am, such talk is unworthy of us . . ."

To change the subject of our conversation Asadollah Mirza said, "By the way, Mrs. Farrokh Laqa, I heard that that poor what's-his-name . . . passed away . . ."

He had found a good topic, since the one thing that interested this woman-in-black was the subject of deaths and funerals and the ceremonies that went with them. She assumed a mournful expression and said, "You don't mean his excellency, do you? . . . Yes, he had a heart attack . . . You know he was a distant relative of ours . . . the ceremony's tomorrow . . . it wouldn't do any harm if you came yourself . . . and it wouldn't do any harm if the Master came, too."

Everyone breathed a sigh of relief. But Mrs. Farrokh Laqa immediately went back to the subject of the marriage, and turning to the cadet officer's mother said, "The groom's father is no longer living?"

"No, dear lady, they were still small when he passed away."

"What was his profession?"

Dear Uncle answered for the old woman, "He was one of the landowners of Qom. He owned land in Ghiasabad . . ."

But the cadet officer's mother brusquely interrupted him, "No sir, I'll tell the truth so that tomorrow there'll be no argument about it. His dad—God rest his soul—used to cook sheep's heads and sell them from a barrow . . ."

Dear Uncle closed his eyes and put his head in his hands. Aziz al-Saltaneh snapped her jaws shut and an unintelligible noise issued from her throat.

I stole a look at my father. A strange light was shining in his eyes. I felt that he was experiencing a boundless happiness, but he gave no sign of it.

No one had any idea what to do. They were looking for some remark that would shut Mrs. Farrokh Laqa's mouth.

But Mrs. Farrokh Laqa, having landed the first blow so expeditiously, wasn't going to give them any respite. She nodded her head and said, "So he was a tradesman, not a bad profession . . . Why don't you tell the truth? It's not as though he was a thief!"

Aziz al-Saltaneh threw Asadollah Mirza an imploring look. It seemed that with this look she was asking him to get rid of Farrokh Laqa in any way possible. But Mrs. Farrokh Laqa wasn't giving any quarter. Cadet Officer Ghiasabadi was sitting quietly in a corner; she looked him up and down from head to toe and said, "I'm sure I've seen you somewhere before."

The cadet officer was about to open his mouth but caught sight of Dear Uncle and Dustali Khan gesturing to him, and was silent again. But Mrs. Farrokh Laqa suddenly shouted, "Eh, just a minute, wasn't it you that . . ."

At this moment Asadollah Mirza suddenly threw himself on Mrs. Farrokh Laqa, and slapping her violently on the back with the palm of his hand yelled, "Mouse . . . mouse . . . the little devil . . ."

Mrs. Farrokh Laqa screamed at the top of her voice, jumped up, and ran yelling into the hallway. Everyone started up. Aziz al-Saltaneh and the cadet officer's sister ran out.

And in this way the meeting broke up.

While everyone was standing about and Mash Qasem was hunting for the mouse with a broom, Asadollah Mirza went into the hallway, took Mrs. Farrokh Laqa by the arm and whispered, "My dear lady, come this way please, I've something very urgent to say to you."

And he virtually pulled her into one of the ground floor rooms near the door out to the yard. I followed them. I was surprised to hear Asadollah Mirza violently protesting his devotion to various parts of Farrokh Laqa's body and it seemed that he had placed his hand over the woman-in-black's face because her cries could hardly escape from her throat, "You shameless, dirty . . . I'm old enough to be your mother! Help! . . . You wretch . . . Help! . . . Stop it! I hope I see the grave diggers get their hands on that gut of yours!"

Then the door sprang violently open and Mrs. Farrokh Laqa, trembling with fury and her face white as chalk, flung herself out of the room; she ran screaming toward the door to the street, "The shameless wretch . . . with those lecherous eyes . . ."

A moment later Asadollah Mirza came out of the room after her, still protesting his undying devotion. Once Mrs. Farrokh Laqa had fled from the inner apartments, Asadollah Mirza closed the door and came back. He straightened his tie and clothes and said with a smile, "I'd no choice . . . I had to get rid of her."

"Well, Uncle Asadollah, if she'd go along with all your promises of devotion then what would you have done?"

"Nothing; a trip to San Francisco."

"With that old woman?"

With a smile on his lips Asadollah Mirza nodded his head and said, "She's not bad. . . . I hadn't touched her before, she's got a nice firm chubby body."

When we went back to the sitting room everyone was still on their feet looking for the mouse. Asadollah Mirza suddenly threw himself to the floor in the hallway, placed his handkerchief over an imaginary mouse and shouted, "I've got it!"

And he ran toward the outer door and pretended to throw the mouse into the garden.

The meeting calmed down again. Dear Uncle Napoleon started to smooth things over. "You'll have to excuse us, ma'am, as you can see this woman isn't quite right in the head, she's always such a nuisance."

Asadollah Mirza took up the theme, "An old girl left on the shelf like that . . . the frustration's got to her . . . it's addled her brains."

The cadet officer's mother said mildly, "It doesn't matter, sir, there are these crazies in every family."

Then she fixed her greedy eyes on Dustali Khan and went on, "Among a hundred flowers it doesn't matter if there's one thorn."

I was sitting on a big sofa next to Asadollah Mirza and Dustali Khan. I heard Dustali Khan whisper to Asadollah Mirza, "Asadollah, you remember that double-barreled Belgian gun of mine that you really liked? I'll give it to you on condition that you fix things so that the cadet officer rents a room somewhere else for his mother. I'll give the rent for the room, too, so she doesn't come to our house . . . I mean what's the point of him giving up his house and family for a couple of months and moving his wife and sister from one place to another?"

Asadollah Mirza whispered back in answer, "Moment, moment, you seem to be implying that the cadet officer and his sister should stay in your house, while his mother buries herself somewhere as far away as possible."

"She can take the sister, too. Just think of it—if I see that bearded woman every morning for three months, I'll curl up and die. You can go through the whole city and you won't find another gun like that."

"I'll do my best but it'll be hard to persuade her. This Jeanette McDonald is even now in her imagination seeing you in her arms."

Asadollah Mirza signalled the cadet officer to go outside with him, but after a couple of minutes they both came back.

When the others had begun chatting again, he whispered to Dustali Khan, "I'm very sorry Dustali, he will not agree under any circumstances to be separated from his mother. However much I said it wasn't worth moving his mother for two or three months, it wouldn't penetrate his skull. He says they were ready to move anyway and that they were looking for a house."

"Asadollah, you didn't talk to him the way you should have done. I know what a malicious person you are."

"Moment, however malicious I might be, I wouldn't mind having your Belgian gun, but he really wouldn't agree to it . . . don't take it so badly, she's got a beard but it's a very soft and delicate beard. And then for New Year I've a mind to buy her a razor and shaving brush, so you can put your mind completely at rest."

Dustali Khan growled under his breath, "God rot your lordship's ugly face."

"Moment, Dustali, you're resorting to abuse? If you say too much I'll tell the cadet officer to bring the child he's left with his other wife with him too!"

The cadet officer's mother was warming to her theme, "Believe me, sir, I wanted to see Rajabali married before I died. The other time he got married without me knowing. God strike me dumb for it but I cursed him. And in the war he was hit by a bullet and God strike me dumb but it was touch and go whether he'd live or not. God knows how I prayed and the vows I made . . . thank God and—knock on wood—after the four months when he was lying in hospital, God gave him back to me."

Asadollah Mirza said, "Thank God a hundred thousand times . . . God keep him for you."

The old woman said, "And his heart's so pure and clean, God's always kept him safe . . . and now, praise God, he's going to come into a bit of money and a nice life . . . God willing, he'll marry and with Mr. Dustali Khan to look out for him he'll get rid of that one bad habit he has . . ."

At this hint of his mother's, Cadet Officer Ghiasabadi struggled hard to get her to be quiet, but the old woman paid no attention to his objections, "I know that Rajabali doesn't like me to say this, but I'm a straightforward person. You're giving your daughter to him, and I want you to know everything . . ."

With a smile Asadollah Mirza said, "Let's hope it's all for the best. Now what's this habit he has? He plays with himself too much?"

The old woman let out a hideous laugh and said, "Eh, you'll be the death of me, the things you say!"

And after laughing for a long time she went on, "No, he hasn't got any of those bad habits. But for two or three years now he's had some bad friends, and as a joke they got him hooked . . ."

Dear Uncle and Dustali Khan said together, "Hooked?"

"Yes, but he doesn't smoke that much, half a *mesqal* of opium a day . . . at the most one *mesqal* . . . I took him to the doctor once to get him to quit, but he started again."

With a laugh Asadollah Mirza said, "This isn't a fault ma'am, Mr. Dustali Khan smokes a bit himself occasionally . . . now he's found a nice companion to sit at the opium brazier with."

Dustali Khan was lying back on the sofa and he pulled himself upright so violently that he cried out from the pain, "Ow . . . Asadollah, why are you talking such rubbish? When have I ever smoked opium?"

At the beginning of this conversation Aziz al-Saltaneh had taken Qamar out of the room, and now she returned alone. Once again I saw happiness shining in my father's eyes. Little by little he was getting to know the groom's faults and his heart was overflowing with joy. His face all innocence he asked a few questions about the cadet officer's child from his first marriage.

The cadet officer's mother glanced this way and that and said, "Eh, where's my daughter-in-law. . . .? Miss Qamar, come here my dear."

With an innocent look on her face Qamar came back into the room. The old woman sat her down next to herself and kissed her on the face. "My, what a lovely looking bride you are, and what I wouldn't do for you's nobody's business!"

Qamar got up, went over to her mother, and whispered something which virtually everyone there heard, "Mummy, her beard hurt my face."

To cover up the sound of her voice Asadollah Mirza began speaking very loudly, "God willing, after this wedding we'll be able to eat candies at Miss Akhtar's wedding too."

The cadet officer's mother's face broke into a broad smile, "Akhtar's your devoted servant, sir . . . God willing, with your help we'll find her a husband too."

"Yes, in any case there are lots of eligible young men in this family . . . God willing, we'll be dancing at Akhtar's wedding, too . . . no, you can count on us, we won't leave Miss Akhtar alone."

After some time spent discussing the details of the marriage ceremony it was agreed that the cadet officer's mother would go to Aziz al-Saltaneh's house the next day in order to discuss moving in their furniture and how the rooms were to be arranged.

After the groom and his family had left, silence reigned in the sitting room for a few moments. Dustali Khan especially was like a wounded animal, writhing silently.

Mash Qasem, who had been standing motionless in a corner, broke the silence. "Well, why should I lie? To the grave it's ah . . . ah . . . This neighbor of mine's a good feller, but if you want the truth I'm really scared of his mom. Savin' your grace, did you hear them snorin' noises she made?"

A sign from Asadollah Mirza quieted him.

Then his lordship turned to Qamar, who was sitting quietly and innocently in a corner, and said, "My dear, did you take a good look at him? Did you like the look of your husband?"

"Yes, Uncle Asadollah."

"And you like him?"

"Yes uncle, I like him a lot . . . now can I talk about my baby?"

"Yes dear, say whatever you want . . . well done, girl, for not talking about your baby in front of them."

"I like my baby even more than my husband. I want to knit baby a red jacket."

"Did you like his mother and sister too?"

"Yes, Uncle Asadollah, but his mother had a beard that hurt my face."

"That doesn't matter, dear. Next time I'll tell her to shave her beard . . . Daddy Dustali's agreed to buy her a shaving set."

The sound of someone knocking at the door came from the direction of the garden. Mash Qasem shouted, "I bet that's master Puri . . . Sir, give me my tip for bringin' the good news!"

And he ran toward the door.

Layli and I stared helplessly at one another. Fortunately it wasn't Puri . . . Mash Qasem returned with the evening paper. My father, who was sitting closer to the door than anyone else, took the paper from his hand and in a loud voice read out the headlines on the first page. The Allies had entered Tehran and taken over the railroad system.

Dear Uncle started up and in a choked voice said, "The railroad system? Why the railroad system before everywhere else? God help my brother the colonel!"

To dispel Dear Uncle's anxiety Asadollah Mirza said, "Well, they have to start from somewhere . . ."

Dear Uncle shook his head and said, "Asadollah, you might be a diplomat but you've a very long way to go before you understand the ins and outs of British political maneuverings."

"Moment, moment, are you implying that because your brother has gone to the railroad station tonight the English are taking over the railroad system before anywhere else?"

Dear Uncle muttered, "It wasn't solely for that, but it's not unrelated either . . ."

And then he seemed to start talking to himself, "I'm worried about this innocent family . . . my poor brother the colonel has never put a foot wrong in his whole life and now he has to suffer because of my efforts."

Trying to keep a straight face Asadollah Mirza said, "Just supposing they want to make him suffer for your efforts, how are they to know that the colonel was going to the railroad station tonight?"

With a contemptuous sneer Dear Uncle said, "It's better we just don't talk about it! Do you think they don't know who Puri is? Do you think they don't know he's my nephew? . . . You're really wet behind the ears! I promise you that the dossier on Cadet Officer Ghiasabadi and the subject of Qamar's marriage is on the head of MI5's desk right now! Do you think that Indian and the thousands of other agents they have are just sitting twiddling their thumbs?"

Mash Qasem saw a suitable chance to speak. He nodded his head and said, "Mr. Asadollah Mirza doesn't know them English. Even me and the Master who've been thrashin' them English for thirty years don't know them very well, so how can anyone else . . . there was a man in our town who . . ."

Dear Uncle interrupted him, "If I told you the things I've seen from the English, you'd never believe it. In the Battle of Kazerun, when the British commander threw his sword on the ground in front of me, it's like it was yesterday, he said 'Congratulations, you have overcome whole regiments of the English army with one thousand and fourteen men, and this will be inscribed in gold lettering in the annals of warfare . . .' Believe me my mouth dropped open . . . because the day before I'd counted my men and there were exactly one thousand and fourteen . . ."

Mash Qasem jumped into the middle of his speech, "One thousand and fifteen men."

"Why are you talking rubbish, Qasem? I remember very well, the English colonel said one thousand and fourteen men and it so happened that we were exactly one thousand and fourteen."

"Well, why should I lie? To the grave it's ah . . . ah . . . It's clear in my mind . . ."

"Will you shut up or not, Qasem?"

"But sir, I'm not contradictin' you. That English feller said a thousand and fourteen and he said right too, you'd counted and we was a thousand and fifteen and you'd counted right . . ."

"Qasem, why are you talking such nonsense?"

"But sir, you won't let me talk. The missin' one was Soltanali Khan, God rest his soul, who was shot exactly on that day."

"Yes, yes, you're right . . . to cut a long story short what I meant was that in the middle of all the noise and confusion of the battle they knew exactly how many men we had."

Mash Qasem sighed and said, "May God destroy 'em, for the sake of the Prophet and his family. Poor Soltanali Khan . . . I mean if it hadn't been for the Master I'd have been in my shroud seven times by now . . . God keep the master the gentleman he is . . . for me, rotten no-good me, he leapt into the middle of that hail of bullets like a lion, flung me over his shoulder and carried me off the battlefield . . . the English were left there with their fingers in their mouths dumbfounded, wonderin' what kind of a man this was. With my own eyes I saw tears gatherin' in them English squint eyes . . .'cause most of these English have squint eyes . . ."

Dear Uncle nodded and muttered, "But Qasem do you see how fate has worked out? They've waited for so long, until they got their second chance. Today we have to pay the debt of that magnanimity, that friendship . . ."

Dear Uncle was suddenly gripped by emotion and burst out, "Inhuman devils! Come and take your revenge on me! What do you want from my poor innocent brother?"

With a straight face Asadollah Mirza said, "Now, don't see everything in such a bad light. Just suppose that they've taken over the railroad partly on account of your brother, it's not at all clear that in all that crush they'll be able to find him. And the colonel's not a child to put himself in harm's way . . ."

And to change the subject he said, "Now for the Thursday night, have you invited anyone or not? After all, close family will have to be there."

Dustali Khan jumped into the conversation, "This marriage ceremony has to be carried out with as little fuss as possible."

"That will only cause more of a fuss. Everyone will say there must have been some problem that they made so little of the ceremony."

Aziz al-Saltaneh sent Qamar into another room. After her daughter had left, she said, "We can use the excuse that someone has died and we're in mourning and that's why we're doing it with no fuss."

"But who? Thanks be to God, these days every member of the family's enjoying perfect health."

"Knock on wood, Asadollah . . . God willing, everyone will stay well."

"Moment, that his excellency fellow that Farrokh Laqa was saying had died, what relation was he to us?"

Dear Uncle said, "Don't even consider him. He was some distant relation of Farrokh Laqa's late stepfather . . . and anyway, with those connections he had with the English . . ."

Asadollah Mirza said, "Well, in any case we have to find someone. By the way, Dustali, how's your uncle Mansur al-Saltaneh keeping?"

At the top of his voice Dustali yelled, "God strike you dumb! What bad turn did my poor uncle ever do to you that you're hoping he'll die?"

"Moment, when did I ever hope he'd die? I suddenly remembered I hadn't heard how Uncle Mansur al-Saltaneh was for a while, and I just asked how he's getting on. He's lived for ninety-five years, and God willing, in spite of all his pulmonary and renal and gastric illnesses, he'll live for another ninety-five, I'm not jealous . . . and it's your fault you annoyed Farrokh Laqa, because if you hadn't, she'd have been able to help us now. She'd have left no stone unturned to find a corpse for us."

My father said, "Rest assured that if there had been any funeral in the offing Farrokh Laqa would have told us about it in the few minutes she was here."

Asadollah Mirza laughed and said, "How would it be if we asked Ghiasabadi's mother to go and stand at Uncle Mansur al-Saltaneh's bedside in the middle of the night? Maybe he'd be so terrified that . . ."

Dustali Khan started to shout but Aziz al-Saltaneh cut him off, "Why are we all being so stupid? We can just say that there's been a death in the groom's family."

This was a good idea and everyone supported it.

That night everybody stayed up till late, waiting for uncle colonel to come back with Puri. At about midnight uncle colonel and his wife arrived back at the house. My uncle looked extremely worried and his wife's eyes showed signs of crying. The train had arrived, but Puri hadn't been on it.

Dear Uncle Napoleon tried to comfort his brother and said that it must surely have been because unusual circumstances had prevented him from leaving, but he himself had other ideas.

When I saw Mash Qasem in the morning he said, "The Master was pacin' up and down till mornin'. And he's right, too. The English must've done somethin' to that poor young man . . . when the English take against someone they won't leave the poor devil in peace nor seven generations after him neither . . . God strike their squinty eyes blind!"

"Mash Qasem, what would the English want with a creepy drip like him?"

"Eh m'dear, it'll be a long time till you understand them English . . . we haven't had any news yet . . . but you should hear what terrible things they did to the folks in Ghiasabad . . . There was a man in our town who'd said bad things about the English. They got hold of the apprentice who worked in his brother-in-law's shop in Kazemin; they tied him to a horse's tail and let the horse go in the middle of the desert . . . What do you know about what the English have done? . . . God help me and the Master . . . and may he have mercy on you, too, seein' as you're part of his family!"

Uncle colonel had gone early that morning to the telegraph office and returned in a good mood, bringing the news that although Puri and Khan Babakhan had purchased train tickets, they hadn't been able to find places on the train due to the unusual circumstances prevailing at that time, and they were going to come on the earliest train they could.

EIGHTEEN

UNFORTUNATELY I don't have a clear memory of the evening when Qamar was married: an unpleasant incident so distracted me that I couldn't pay attention to anything except my own concerns. All I remember is that there were about twenty people present from the bride's family, and from the groom's side, apart from his mother and sister, the famous detective Deputy Taymur Khan was there. The thing which I remember more than anything else is Cadet Officer Ghiasabadi's appearance; in a rather loosely fitting off-the-rack suit that Aziz al-Saltaneh had bought for him, and with a bow tie that Asadollah Mirza had tied round his neck, he looked at one and the same time very neat and tidy and rather ridiculous. Apart from our close family, Shir Ali the butcher and his wife came to pay their respects.

But the unpleasant occurrence that happened to me that night was as follows. In Dear Uncle Napoleon's house, where the marriage was to take place, I came face to face with Puri, who had arrived the previous evening with Khan Babakhan. He was sitting on the steps, with that long horse-like face of his. He beckoned me to follow him into the garden and whispered, "I want to have a few words with you."

He took a folded piece of paper out of his inside pocket, and opened it, all the while trying to keep the paper out of my grasp. My heart nearly stood still. It was a letter I had written to Layli a few days previously, and given to her placed between the pages of a book.

Puri spluttered, "So sir, how long have you been in love, then?"

"I . . . I . . . I . . ."

"Yes, you."

Without knowing what I was saying I said, "I have never written any letters. I really . . ."

"Extraordinary! The gentleman's never written any letters!"

And then, keeping the letter carefully out of my reach, he began quietly to read it, "Dear Layli, you know how much I love you. You know that for me life without you has no meaning . . ."

I whispered, "Puri, I swear on the Quran . . ."

"Just a minute, listen to the rest of it: '. . . Since I heard that that slobbering Arab horse is coming back . . .'"

Puri raised his head and said, "If it wasn't for the wedding, this slobbering Arab horse would knock your teeth down your throat. I'll give you slobbering Arab horse, so that you won't forget it for the rest of your life."

"Puri, I swear on my father's soul . . ."

"Shut up! Your father's just like you—a good-for-nothing beggar!"

I couldn't put up with any more. I punched him on the neck with all the force I could muster and tried to snatch the letter from him; but my strength wasn't equal to his and he slapped me hard over the ear. I saw red and sprang at him like a wounded leopard; but I met with a second slap. Desperate, I kicked him violently in the groin and then ran like the wind toward my own house. From the way he screamed and the noise that started up, I knew that he'd been seriously hurt.

I took refuge in the space beneath the roof, where I'd hidden many times as a child, and stayed there motionless. Various people came looking for me, one after another, and didn't find me. My mother and father, in turn threatening me and pleading with me, came searching for me, but I stayed still and silent in my refuge. I heard them saying, "He's hidden somewhere, he'll be found in the end." When the fuss had quieted down I suddenly heard Asadollah Mirza's voice; he was going from room to room calling for me. When he got close I whispered, "Uncle Asadollah, I'm here."

"How did you get up there . . . well now . . . don't be afraid, come on down, there's only me."

When I had come down he said with a laugh, "Here's a fine old mess . . . you've given the lad a rupture. Not that that's so bad. As you're not going to San Francisco yourself, you've stopped that milksop from going to San Francisco, too!"

"How's Puri now?"

"Nothing much wrong, he fell down in the middle of the yard in a faint. They brought Dr. Naser al-Hokama. Now he's feeling a bit better . . . what were you arguing about?"

"He'd stolen a letter I wrote to Layli, and he insulted my dad, too . . . By the way, has he said anything to Dear Uncle?"

"No, but he was talking to your father for a while."

"Now what should I do?"

"For now keep out of sight, till the fuss has died down. The colonel has detailed plans as to what he's got in store for you! Now you're gradually realizing that the road I pointed out to you was the easiest of them all."

"What road, Uncle Asadollah?"

"The San Francisco road."

This event is the reason I was unable to attend the reception for Qamar's wedding. Late that night, when my father and mother came back, I was in my room. As a precaution I had locked myself in. My father came and knocked on the door and ordered me to open it. His voice was harsh and angry. Fearful and trembling, I opened the door. My father came in and sat on the edge of the iron bedstead. I hung my head. After a few moments silence my father said, "I hear that you and Layli have had something going on between you?"

"He's lying. Believe me . . ."

"Don't talk nonsense, Puri showed me the letter you'd written to Layli."

I'd no choice but to be silent. My father was silent for a few moments, too. Then in a mild tone, which was quite contrary to my expectations, he said, "Look, lad, did you never think that if your uncle got wind of this he'd destroy your family?"

I plucked up my courage a little. I said quietly, "I'm in love with Layli."

"Since when?"

"Since the thirteenth of August last year."

"Well done! What a precise date. I bet you know the hour, too!"

"Yes, from a quarter to three."

My father put his hand on my shoulder and in a quiet voice said, "Well now, there hasn't been any monkey business, has there?"

I didn't immediately understand what he was driving at and I said, "I've written her a few letters . . ."

"She likes you, too?"

"Yes, dad, Layli loves me, too."

"I see . . . tell me the truth now, what have you two been up to?"

"You mean what promises have we made . . ."

Impatiently my father said, "No, you goose. I want to know whether, as Asadollah Mirza would say, there's been any San Francisco or not."

My mouth dropped open. Hearing such a remark from my father, who never made jokes of this nature and who'd always been serious and distant with me, quite took my breath away. After a few moments of astonished silence I felt embarrassed once again; I hung my head and said, "Dad, what kind of a remark is that?"

"Don't beat about the bush; I asked you if anything's happened or not."

My father's tone was not that of someone who was joking. Forcefully I said, "Dad, I'm in love with Layli. Dirty thoughts like that have never entered my head!"

I was slowly beginning to realize what was going on. My father had found another possible way of getting at Dear Uncle. I had the feeling that if my reply had been positive he would not have found this so very upsetting. He was silent for a few moments. Since I had disappointed him, he tried to save appearances. "I was just joking. But my dear boy, this girl has been promised to her uncle's son, they won't let her marry you. For now, you have to concentrate on finishing your studies . . . of course if something had happened, the situation would have been different . . . Get these childish thoughts out of your head . . . now that, thank goodness, nothing's happened, concentrate on school and your studies! Off you go and sleep, lad!"

My father left and I was alone. Although I was well aware of his spitefulness and desire for revenge, for the first time a new train of thought was forming in my mind.

It was late when Asadollah's voice was heard in our house. He had come to look for me. I heard him talking to my mother in the hall. "The boy didn't come to the wedding tonight. God forbid, he didn't feel up to it."

He came into my room a moment later and said, "Don't worry, lad, I've talked the colonel round . . . and Layli was very upset, too, poor thing . . . it's obvious she can't stand that boy."

"Uncle Asadollah, Puri hasn't said anything to Dear Uncle, has he?"

"It seems he was able to explain away what had happened without any trouble. I don't think he's said anything to the Master."

I was silent for a moment. Asadollah Mirza laughed and said, "But I don't think they'll be thinking about getting him engaged any time soon, you really did some damage to his private prospects . . . for two or three weeks he's going to have to wear a poultice on the San Francisco area."

Without raising my head I said in a quiet voice, "Uncle Asadollah, I want to ask you something."

"Say on, lad."

"I mean . . . I . . . if I . . . that thing you used to say . . . if Layli and I . . ."

"If you what? If you marry Layli?"

"No, I mean, what do I have to do so I'll marry Layli? What should I do so they won't give her to Puri?"

"I've told you a hundred times: San Francisco."

"If I . . . if San Francisco . . ."

Asadollah Mirza let out a cheerful guffaw, "Bravo! . . . Bravo! . . . you're finally becoming a real man."

"No, Uncle Asadollah, I mean to say . . ."

"Moment, you've got cold feet again?"

"No, but . . . but how?"

"Aha! How you manage it, I'll teach you. Sit down while I draw you a picture. Give me a purple-colored pencil and a bright pink one and I'll draw you a picture of it."

I had no opportunity to object because just at that moment a tumultuous noise started up in the garden, "Run . . . bring that spade . . . that bucket . . . no, go that way. . . ."

With Asadollah in front and me following him we ran into the garden; Asadollah bumped into Mash Qasem who was running full tilt. He asked, "What's happened? What's going on, Mash Qasem?"

"Well sir, why should I lie? To the grave it's ah . . . ah . . . The English have attacked . . . God strike them squinty eyes of theirs blind!"

Mash Qasem explained to Asadollah the cause of the commotion that had brought us out into the garden. Apparently while everyone had been occupied with the coming and going of their guests, some unknown person had removed the wadding used to block the channel from Dear Uncle's water-storage tank and the water had overflowed and flooded three of the cellars one after another.

Asadollah Mirza asked, "You didn't realize who'd taken the wadding out of the channel?"

"The Master says the English've done it. But I don't think the English would come after our water channel before the sweat's even dry from their march . . . besides, if they want to be openin' our water channel, because they're so squinty-eyed they might muddle it up with that brigadier's water channel."

At this moment Mash Qasem caught sight of me; he lowered his voice and said, "Eh lad, but you've the heart of a lion to be seen round here . . . if the Master or the colonel get their hands on you, they'll tear you into eighty pieces."

"Are they really so angry, Mash Qasem?"

"Why should I lie? To the grave it's ah . . . ah . . . If that lad escapes whole and in one piece after that kick you gave him in his privates, he's a really lucky feller. If I'm not mistaken one of the pair of his private equipment's completely ruined . . . when he showed the doctor I saw it; savin' your reverence, it had swollen up like a pumpkin."

And Asadollah Mirza pushed me into a corner and said, "That's right, lad, hide yourself away till things have quieted down. His private parts are no joke!"

Mash Qasem went on, "Dr. Naser al-Hokama's put a poultice on it for now, he said in the mornin' they'll have to take him to the hospital . . . you hit him so hard it's like his privates and his lungs are all muddled up with each other."

I'd no choice but to hide myself among the box trees as Asadollah Mirza went over to Dear Uncle, who was emerging from his private apartments with a rifle sloped over his shoulder.

Dear Uncle shouted, "Qasem, what are you standing about for? Run and help get the water out."

"Well sir, I was just gettin' the lady's bucket."

Dear Uncle said, "It's good the guests had left."

Asadollah Mirza asked, "The groom's gone, too?"

"Yes, damn him, he's gone, too, so that he can move to Dustali's house tomorrow, along with his mother and sister. If Deputy Taymur Khan had been here perhaps he'd have been able to solve the riddle of this crime."

Uncle colonel and my father joined them.

My father said, "But this is really strange! What shameless, unprincipled wretch has done this?"

Dear Uncle Napoleon interrupted him, "Your question's childish . . . I know the strategy of the English . . . this isn't the first time they've employed this battlefield trick. In the south, too, on one occasion they diverted the waters of a river beneath our tents and attacked a few hours later."

Mash Qasem had been leaving but on hearing these words he came back and said, "God sweep 'em from off the face of the earth! D'you remember, sir, how much water they let loose under our feet? This is like what the evil Shemr did at Karbela; Shemr kept the water back, the English let the water go. Thank God we were first class swimmers and divers, because if we hadn't been we'd all have been drownded."

To calm Dear Uncle down Asadollah Mirza said, "But sir, consider the circumstances. The English have entered this city with their tanks and artillery; if they want to do you some kind of an injury, are they going to come and open your water-storage tank?"

"Asadollah, Asadollah, please do not give me instructions on the secrets of British tactics."

"Moment, moment . . ."

"Dear Uncle shouted, "Damn and blast your moment . . . all right so the English are absolutely wonderful people . . . so they're completely in love with me and my family . . . so Shakespeare wrote his *Romeo and Juliet* to describe how things are between me and the English . . ."

Mash Qasem hadn't understood properly and said, "May you never see the day . . . God forbid them English fall in love . . . I mean, with them squinty eyes of theirs, can they be sweet on someone? There was a man in our town who said, savin' your reverence, that the English aren't men at all . . . and them that are are that squinty-eyed they go after their neighbors' wives."

"Qasem, instead of spouting this rubbish go down to the coffee-house and tell that shoeshine lad to come here, I need to see him . . . perhaps he saw who opened the water channel."

"The shoeshine man wasn't by our door during the night."

"Don't talk rubbish! Just do whatever I tell you to!"

Mash Qasem hurried out of the garden. Our servant and uncle colonel's and the rest of our people were busy with buckets emptying the water from the cellars.

At this moment I heard my father say to uncle colonel, "I hope Puri's injury is better?"

Uncle colonel answered coldly, "We have to take him to the hospital in the morning. For now the doctor's given him an injection of morphine to take away the pain."

"I'm very sorry this has happened. I'll punish that boy in such a way that he'll remember it for the rest of his life."

With unexpected mildness Dear Uncle Napoleon said, "No need to punish him too severely. He's just a child, he doesn't understand these things."

I realized from his tone that he wanted to avoid all subjects except that of the attack by the English. Just then Mash Qasem hurried into the garden and made straight for Dear Uncle.

"Sir, the coffee-shop owner said the shoeshine man hasn't been to the shop all night."

For a moment Dear Uncle stared at him dumbfounded and with his mouth hanging open. Then he put his hand to his forehead and said, "The plan is complete! They've done away with that poor boy, too!"

Asadollah Mirza asked, "Who's done away with him?"

"Nothing, nothing . . . in any case we have to stay awake and on guard until morning."

My father backed him up, "Yes, there are wheels within wheels here."

Mash Qasem said, "And what wheels they are . . . to tell the truth, I didn't believe the Master and then I realized that he really is a very wise man. The Master knows them English and that's all there is to it."

"How's that, Mash Qasem?"

"Well, why should I lie? To the grave it's ah . . . ah . . . The Master said the English had done it, I didn't believe him. But now I'm certain them blind devils did it . . . I asked the coffeeshop owner if he hadn't seen someone blond with squinty eyes in these parts today; he said that in the evenin' he'd seen a fish-seller goin' past the coffeeshop and his eyes and hair had a wild fierce look, and his eyes had a bit of a squint in them."

Trying to suppress his laughter Asadollah Mirza said, "The description exactly fits the English General Wavell."

In a stern tone Dear Uncle said, "For now, good night until the morning."

✤ ✤ ✤

On the morning of the next day, which was a Friday, I didn't dare come out of my room; my father didn't come looking for me. But my mother brought me breakfast. From her I heard that the whole family had gone to the hospital with Puri. An hour later Asadollah turned up. I'd spent the whole night afraid and worrying, and I calmed down somewhat when I heard his voice. He came up to see me and said, "The situation's not good; I've talked with your father and we've agreed to send you to stay with Rahim Khan's family in Dezashib, until things quiet down."

Anxiously I asked, "How's that, Uncle Asadollah?"

"The colonel has sworn that he'll empty a couple of bullets into your skull . . . because they have to operate on Puri and take out one of his what's-its-names."

"One of his what?"

"How thick you are! How can I say . . . one of the foundation stones of his tower of San Francisco . . . or, as Mash Qasem would say, one of the pair of his private equipment."

"Did you say uncle colonel wanted to empty a couple of bullets into my skull?"

"Well, do you expect him to empty them into my skull?"

Having no idea what to say I said, "Two handgun bullets . . ."

"That was what surprised me, seeing as how they're only going to take one of the foundation stones of his tower of San Francisco out, why two bullets . . ."

At this point the entry of my father cut our conversation short. "You're a really stupid fool, my boy!"

Asadollah Mirza coolly said, "There's no point in arguing . . . if it'd been you and someone had insulted your father, you'd have got angry, too. And for now, just as I suggested before, it's better we send him to Rahim Khan's house for a few days until things have quieted down."

"I've just phoned them; Rahim Khan said he'll be happy to have him."

I pleaded with them, "No, let me stay . . . I want to stay near Layli."

My father lunged toward me and said in a tone of violent contempt, "Just shut up, will you? God damn you and your silly lovesick carrying-on!"

Fortunately Asadollah Mirza was between us, otherwise I'd have suffered a blow or a kick.

Asadollah Mirza said, "It so happens I'm invited out for lunch in Shemiran; I'll just go and change my clothes and I'll take him."

Then he turned to me, "Listen to what's said, boy! We know how to manage this business of yours better than you do."

They were so heartless they wouldn't even let me wait for Layli to get back from the hospital. An hour later I was in a bus with Asadollah Mirza, going toward Shemiran. After being silent for a while I said, "Uncle Asadollah, how do you think things will turn out now?"

"How will what turn out now?"

"With Puri."

"His body's equilibrium will be upset."

"Why?"

"Because when they take one of them out, one side of his body will be lighter and the other heavier."

"Please don't joke about it. I'm very worried."

"Moment, really moment . . . why are you worried? That horse-faced creep should be worried that he's been barred from *al-San Francisco* for life."

"Then is it true that he'll never again be able to . . . ?"

"To what?"

"To . . . I mean . . . to San Francisco . . ."

"Bravo, bravo, that's the first time I've heard the name San Francisco from your lips. You get 100 percent in Geography. As to whether he'll be able to travel to San Francisco or not, the various doctors and physicians are divided on the matter. Some are of the belief that . . ."

"Uncle Asadollah! Please don't joke about it. Last night I was so worried I didn't sleep till morning."

"You mean you were that worried that Puri wouldn't be able to go to San Francisco?"

"No, but I'm worried that he's been done a permanent injury, and then my conscience will say I'm responsible."

"It's not just your conscience that'll say you're responsible, the law will say so, too . . . but don't think about it. They're not the people to lodge a complaint. An aristocratic family never sets foot in the law courts."

"What will happen to Layli, Uncle Asadollah?"

"For the moment Layli's safe, but when old slobber-chops comes out of the hospital, after three or four months the subject's going to come up again."

"How many months from now?"

Asadollah Mirza interrupted me, "How many months from now do you imagine they're going to give Layli to you? If Puri's only just been barred from *al-San Francisco*, you were born barred!"

"Finally it'll work out in some way or other. I want to ask you to tell Layli that I had to leave her. Tell her if she can to phone me at two o'clock in the afternoon, when Dear Uncle's asleep; and you'll let me know everything that happens. Do you promise?"

"Solemn promise."

Asadollah Mirza gave me his office telephone number and said, "But don't talk too much on the phone, all right?"

An hour later I said goodbye to Asadollah Mirza and so began my first period of absence from Layli.

I was friends with Rahim Khan's son; my stay in their house lasted nearly two weeks. During this period I regularly telephoned Asadollah Mirza and asked him for news. Puri had been operated on. They had taken out one of the two relevant organs, and they were worried they might have to take out the second. When I telephoned Asadollah Mirza on about the tenth day he said, "You owe me something for the good news I'm to give you. The matter rests at the two bullets the colonel's supposed to empty into your skull, and it's not been increased to four."

"What, Uncle Asadollah?"

"It seems that San Francisco's second foundation stone is out of danger. Now on condition that the city can survive on this one foundation, we can start work on getting them to let bygones be bygones and forgive you."

"Can he get married now?"

"Not now, but perhaps in a few months, and even then it'll be, as the Indian Brigadier would say, with his natural forces *bahot* wilted . . . for now, you stay where you are . . . and Layli is fine. Don't worry about her."

On the Friday evening fifteen days after Puri's injury I was forgiven, on the occasion of a celebratory party for Qamar and Cadet

Officer Ghiasabadi held by my father, and Asadollah Mirza personally came to fetch me.

In the bus he gave me some fresh news, "I think it's going to be a
very noisy party tonight. Because apparently either last night or this
morning Dustali Khan and Aziz al-Saltaneh realized that when Cadet
Officer Ghiasabadi said he'd lost his noble member in the wars and
that he'd no worldly goods to his name, he was lying through his
teeth, and as far as I can tell from the women's gossip, he's very well
off. Noticeably well off."

"And so why did he say . . . ?"

"It seems that he'd reckoned that if he said he wasn't in any trouble they wouldn't pay him as much."

"What a sly old so-and-so."

"He's not so sly at all, he's bit of a fool. But I see the hidden hand
of We-All-Know-Who in all this."

"You mean . . ."

"Yes, I mean your father . . . I realized he had a hand in it from
the way it looked."

"What does Qamar say about all this?"

"She seems very cheerful. She wanted a baby and she's got one.
She'd no expectations of wealth or money and God's given her someone who's wealthy, very wealthy at that. So, in short, tonight we
should have a good laugh . . . that's if the night doesn't end in fights
and recriminations, of course."

"Uncle Asadollah, what's Dear Uncle doing?"

"It seems that so far Puri hasn't said anything to him about your
writing letters to Layli . . . or if he has said anything Dear Uncle's so
preoccupied with the English that he hasn't given it a thought."

"Still the English?"

"Yes, the shoeshine man's completely disappeared. Dear Uncle
says the English have killed him and he's wearing his revolver in his
belt again; at night Mash Qasem sleeps outside his door with a rifle.
And your father keeps piling kindling on the fire."

"What does my father say?"

"Every day he fabricates some story about the disappearance of
someone he says was an enemy of the English, and tells it to the
poor old man . . . fortunately the Indian brigadier went away on a
trip a few days ago."

"Uncle Asadollah, you have to try and convince Dear Uncle that the English have no interest in him."

"Moment, as if it would be any use. Everyone who says that the English have better things to do than come after him, he says have been his family's enemies for seven generations back. My poor brother Shamsali came a few days ago to have a chat with him, and he flew at him like nobody's business . . . And Mash Qasem is constantly making up stories about English murders and atrocities."

"Then things are really in a mess, Uncle Asadollah?"

"Really . . . but the most important thing of all is the matter of Cadet Officer Ghiasabadi, the liar, who not only lost nothing whatsoever in the war but seems to have managed to pass himself off as the owner of the wealth of two or three people who were killed then, and now he's busy disguising where it came from."

"What's Dustali Khan doing?"

"He's having a heart attack. Because Cadet Officer Ghiasabadi, for all his bald head, has stolen Qamar's heart away, and now Dustali is terrified that Qamar's property will slip out of his hands. And then, on the other hand, there's the cadet officer's sister, who Dustali really fancies, and she has a friend who considers himself a big-shot and goes by the name of Asghar the Diesel and he's the spitting image of Shir Ali the butcher."

"Has she brought her friend to Dustali Khan's house?"

"No, but every other night he gets drunk and comes and shouts that if they don't open the door to him he'll batter the walls down."

"Uncle Asadollah, you seem to be really enjoying what's going on."

"I haven't been this happy in my whole life. Let their noses be rubbed in the dirt a bit. These aristocratic grandchildren of his excellency the royal leopard and his highness the tiger of the state would say to their own shadows 'Don't come near me, you stink' — now they're going to have to rub shoulders with the likes of Asghar the Diesel and Cadet Officer Ghiasabadi."

"Will there be a lot of people at our house tonight?"

"Yes, your father's laid on a regular feast . . . all in all, I think your father's the director of the whole show. Because last night I heard him saying to the cadet officer that if his sister wanted to invite a friend along she would be very welcome and she was to treat it like her own house. It's a good guess that if the sister invites anyone it'll be Asghar the Diesel . . . and so, in short, your father's not going to forget Puri's insult in a hurry."

"You couldn't manage things so that Asghar the Diesel doesn't come?"

"Moment, moment, it so happens that I'm thinking of giving the cadet officer's sister every encouragement to bring Mr. Asghar along. Dustali owes me much more than this, and if I torment him till the Last Judgment dawns it's no more than he deserves."

When we reached the house Asadollah Mirza left me and said with a laugh, "See you tonight, God willing . . . now I have to go and find the cadet officer and his sister . . . without Asghar the Diesel our gathering will be quite joyless."

My mother took me to uncle colonel. I kissed his hand and asked his pardon. Then she told me I absolutely had to go and pay my respects to Dear Uncle Napoleon.

I went to Dear Uncle's house, my heart thumping as if it would tear my chest apart. I came face to face with Layli in the yard. I finally saw her, after those days of separation that had seemed to last a lifetime. The excitement and inner turmoil I felt as I set eyes on her rendered me speechless; I just said "Hello." For a few moments Layli stared at me without moving and then, her eyes filled with tears, ran off to her room. I didn't dare follow her.

Dear Uncle sat me down next to himself and gave me a moral lecture for a while. Most of his lecture revolved around the notion that the older generation had lived their lives out and that now it was up to us young folk to preserve the sacred unity and harmony of the family. Then he said that, God be praised, Puri was out of danger and that they would be bringing him home from the hospital in a few days; he instructed me to go and see him in the hospital on the following day and ask his pardon.

NINETEEN

THERE WAS AN EXTRAORDINARY amount of activity going on in our house. Chairs and tables had been arranged all around the yard. Although it still wasn't dark, incandescent lamps lit up the whole of our yard and a large part of the main garden. The school teacher, Ahmad Khan, with his *tar* and accompanied by the blind drummer, had come before the guests arrived and the two of them were busy consuming vodka and little snacks.

Suddenly I caught sight of Asadollah, who had entered dressed in a well-cut multicolored suit and a red bow tie. His eyes were glittering. I ran toward him. As soon as he saw me he lowered his voice and said, "Moment, moment, *momentissimo!* . . . rejoice, for tonight our happiness is complete. The cadet officer's sister is not only bringing along Asghar the Diesel but she's also invited Asghar the Diesel's brother, his excellency Akbar the Brains; I wish there were a camera here so I could take a photo of Dustali."

Not many moments passed before Dustali Khan put in an appearance. His face was frowning and preoccupied.

He looked round for my father and went straight over to him. Asadollah Mirza busied himself eating little red grapes and murmured, "I think he's realized what's going on . . . see if you can't overhear what he's saying."

Dustali Khan had found my father in the hallway and was saying to him in a choked, trembling voice, "What kind of a party is this, my good sir? I've just heard that that good-for-nothing bitch has invited her ogre of a friend over here."

My father coolly answered, "And what do you suggest I do, Mr. Dustali Khan?"

"You mustn't allow such trash, such louts, to come to your party."

"Just consider now, I can't stop a friend of a relative of yours from coming. If your son-in-law's sister's friend comes here, can I shut the door in his face? Just think about it for a moment."

With anger in his voice Dustali Khan said, "Then shall I go and invite every passing Tom, Dick and Harry to your party? Would you like that?"

In the same unruffled tone my father replied, "They'd be very welcome . . . no human being is worth less than another. As the Prophet has said, 'The most honorable of you in the sight of God is the most pious of you.'"

"All right then! All right then! I'll bring one of those honorable pious types along to you, then . . . Why shouldn't I invite someone any place that Asghar the Diesel goes?"

I went back to Asadollah and told him about Dustali Khan's quarrel with my father. Then I asked, "What do you think Dustali Khan meant when he said 'I can invite anyone I want'? Who does he want to invite now?"

Busily eating the little red grapes, Asadollah Mirza shook his head and said, "I've no idea. Anything you say about shameless fellows like him is going to fall short. We'll just have to wait and see how he tries to pay your father back."

"What do you mean, 'pay him back'?"

"Moment! It's clear you haven't understood the reason for this party tonight!"

"You mean there's a special reason for it, Uncle Asadollah?"

"So you're so naive that you think your father's put on an elaborate spread like this just out of love for Cadet Officer Ghiasabadi's beautiful hairdo? Just think, when not a single one of the closest relatives, not even your Dear Uncle, who's head of the family, has arranged to have a party for them, why should your father throw a party?"

"Well, so many different weird things have been going on and my head's been so full of it all that I can't think. You tell me what he's aiming at."

"Why doesn't your father get on with Dear Uncle?"

"Because he's always putting him down and saying he's not from a noble family."

"Bravo! And now your father wants to bring Cadet Officer Rajab-ali, son of a man who sold sheep's heads and brother of Akhtar who dances in a nightclub, in front of his face and the faces of all the others who say they're so high and mighty, and make them suffer. He wanted to do this at Qamar's wedding, but he was unsuccessful, now . . ."

"But the whole family knows that Qamar's become the wife of Cadet Officer Ghiasabadi."

"But tonight, as well as the family, he's invited some of the city's most prominent citizens. For example, he's invited Mr. Salar."

"Mr. Salar?"

"Yes, this gentleman is one of the city's real bigwigs. He's a man with unequalled power and influence . . . by having Salar as a guest he's killed two birds with one stone. First, Dear Uncle and Dustali Khan and the family will go right down in Salar's estimation, and second, he'll terrify the wits out of Dear Uncle because Salar is famous for supporting the English."

"So there's also the danger of a fight between my father and Dear Uncle breaking out?"

"Yes, that's my only worry. I feel sorry for you, and if I didn't, I'd have gone straight over to your father's side and given this family the fright of its life . . . And now we've the chance, tell me what you want to do finally."

"Meaning what? I don't understand what you're driving at, Uncle Asadollah?"

"What I'm driving at is this: first, Dear Uncle's not going to let you have Layli, because he doesn't get on with your father. Second, even if he wanted to let you, you'd have to wait at least six or seven years till you could get married. Third, what's that boy who's laid up in the hospital going to be doing? To cut a long story short, there are a thousand problems involved. And you aren't up to San Francisco, either . . . when I think about it properly I see that that Cadet Officer Ghiasabadi . . ."

"Uncle Asadollah . . ."

"Oh damn your Uncle Asadollahs . . . just look how Cadet Officer Ghiasabadi pulled the wool over their eyes . . . he was supposed to take his fee, marry Qamar and then divorce her. Now he's so well dug in that he'd throw Dustali out of the house a hundred times over before he'd go himself . . . and he's so stolen Qamar's heart away that the girl's ready to leave her mother for his sake."

"Wow! Look, Uncle Asadollah, Cadet Officer Ghiasabadi and Qamar have arrived."

Cadet Officer Ghiasabadi, his hand supporting Qamar's arm, entered ahead of Aziz al-Saltaneh. He was turned out very neatly and nicely, so that there was no comparison between how he looked now and the wretched figure he had cut before. Qamar was clinging to him in a very loving way.

"Uncle Asadollah, so what happened about the wig?"

"The wig problem's solved . . . he told Qamar about it, and it seems as far as Qamar's concerned she's always loved a bald head. Every evening she lights his little opium brazier for him . . . really, the San Francisco cure has put her mind to rights. There's no denying that for psychological illnesses, San Francisco's the best medicine!"

Asadollah Mirza went forward a few paces to welcome the cadet officer, "Hello, officer . . . how are you keeping?"

The cadet officer greeted Asadollah with great pomp and ceremony, "Your servant, sir, at your service . . . thanks to your gracious kindness . . . just today I was saying to Qamar, 'We haven't called on his excellency for a while, we must ask him to do us the honor of a visit one evening.'"

Asadollah Mirza said, "Officer, sir, why hasn't your esteemed parent honored us with her presence?"

"She will be coming, she's waiting for Akhtar, so that they can come together."

Asadollah Mirza kissed Qamar on the cheek. "Well, well, what a pretty lady you've turned out to be . . . what a lovely girl!"

Qamar looked at him kindly. "Look what a beautiful dress I have, Uncle Asadollah. Mother sewed it for me."

"Extraordinary, Mrs. Aziz al-Saltaneh is artistic to her fingertips."

"No, Uncle Asadollah, dear Aziz didn't sew this for me . . . my mother-in-law sewed it, Rajab's mother . . ."

Aziz al-Saltaneh frowned, but Asadollah Mirza heaped such praises on her appearance and fine qualities that the frown disappeared.

The guests went over to my father. Just then uncle colonel's servant came up to us holding a tray of glasses of cordial. Asadollah Mirza glanced at the glasses and said, "Thanks, my good man, I won't drink any of this. Tell Mash Qasem to bring me a glass of that special cordial."

Uncle colonel's servant murmured, "Mash Qasem? . . . Haven't you heard, sir? . . . An hour ago they took Mash Qasem off to the police station."

"What? The police station? Whatever has he done?"

Uncle's servant looked this way and that and said, "Well, you didn't hear it from me because the Master told me no one's to know . . . but when evening came he threw a brick from off the roof at an Englishman's head."

"You're kidding? A brick at an Englishman's head?"

"No sir, it's the truth I'm telling you . . . the fellow's head was all covered in blood . . . now the Master's gone to the police station too."

Asadollah Mirza sprang up and said to me, "Come on, let's drop by there and see what's going on . . . I'm worried this might be another of your father's tricks."

In the office belonging to the head of the guard at the station, the first thing we saw was a fairly young man, with a bloodstained face and a handkerchief wound round his head, sitting on a bench. Strands of his curly blond hair were matted with dried blood.

Mash Qasem was standing near the entrance, his head down, opposite Dear Uncle and the head of the guard. An officer was standing to attention next to Mash Qasem.

In a choked voice Dear Uncle Napoleon was saying, "I shall punish him myself. And besides, I've no doubt at all that he didn't do this on purpose."

The man with the broken head, who had slightly squinting eyes, said in the thick accent of someone from the province of Gilan, "What do you mean, 'not on purpose'? We're supposed to believe that, just like that, the brick flew out of his hand and hit me on the head . . . and all those dirty swear words he said came out of his mouth, just like that, too?"

The head of the guard said, "You've been given some money and agreed to it. If the gentleman wants to punish his servant himself what's it got to do with you? Get up and be off with you, attend to your business."

"Whatever you say, sir."

The injured man picked up a basket of smoked fish and set off, and we returned with Mash Qasem to our house. As soon as we left the police station a flood of curses and swear words from Dear

Uncle's mouth broke over Mash Qasem's head. Mash Qasem kept his head down and muttered, "You say whatever you want . . . I'm stickin' to my story. Even if the rogue wasn't English himself, he was one of their spies . . . I've been livin' here for thirty years, how come I've never seen the rotten bastard before? And besides, after thirty years of run-ins with these English, don't I know 'em yet?"

In a voice trembling with rage Dear Uncle shouted, "Mash Qasem! Shut up, because if you don't I'll shut you up with my own hands!"

"I'll shut up. But that poor shoeshine feller whose innocent blood was unjustly shed, on Judgment Day he'll be pluckin' at your elbow . . . right now that poor devil's up in the other world waitin' for you to take revenge on the English for his unjustly shed blood."

We returned to the party, which was by now thoroughly under way. Many of the guests had arrived, and the sound of the teacher Ahmad's *tar* could be heard loudly ringing out. Everyone was being extremely respectful to Mr. Salar, and the place where he was sitting had become the most honored focal point of the gathering. Even Dear Uncle Napoleon, for all his hatred and terror of the English, sat himself down very politely next to him.

My father kept a constant eye on the main entrance. I whispered in Asadollah Mirza's ear, "Uncle Asadollah, do you see how worried my father is? I think he's waiting for some more important guests."

Asadollah took another sip of wine and said with a quiet chuckle, "He's waiting for His Excellency Asghar the Diesel and Lady Akhtar."

Out of fear of my uncles, especially uncle colonel who was still giving me angry looks, I didn't dare get anywhere near Layli, but all the same, whoever I talked to, my wistful gaze was aware of her; and poor child she, too, after my quarrel with Puri, didn't dare come near me. It was as if we both felt guilty.

A few minutes later my father's waiting came to an end. Cadet Officer Ghiasabadi's sister Akhtar entered, accompanied by her mother Naneh Rajab and Asghar the Diesel; Akhtar was wearing a dress of ox-blood red, with a low neckline that revealed her prominent breasts. Even more than her too thickly applied makeup, what drew everyone's attention was the appearance of Asghar the Diesel. He had a thickset body, and a few knife scars shone on his shaved head. He was wearing a green tie (a good guess would be that it was one of Dustali Khan's) which he was finding difficult to tolerate. His accent as he greeted people and asked them how they were doing immediately revealed his social class.

With their entry my father's spirits opened like a flower in springtime, and to the same degree the faces of Dear Uncle Napoleon and uncle colonel closed in on themselves.

As soon as the piece of *tar* music that was being played ended, my father began being elaborately hospitable. "What would you like, Mr. Asghar, sir? Tea, cordial, wine? This is your own house, please don't stand on ceremony."

Asghar seemed to be uncomfortable in such company and murmured, "Very kind of you, thanks very much, I've eaten."

Asadollah Mirza said, "Don't hesitate to say what you'd like . . . there's beer, too."

"'S very good of you . . . if there was . . ."

The cadet officer's sister Akhtar said with a loud laugh, "Your excellency, this Asghar of mine's a bit shy . . . he'll drink whatever you're good enough to give him."

"Moment, moment, we don't have any of that kind of talk with each other here. Now please, on the soul of Miss Akhtar here, don't hesitate."

With his head bowed Asghar the Diesel said, "Well, seeing as 'ow you insist, if there was a nice drop of vodka . . . but if there isn't any it doesn't matter . . . the beer'll be fine."

As he stood up Asadollah Mirza said, "But of course there's some . . . hey, Mash Qasem, bring that bottle of vodka over here."

Sour faced and frowning, Mash Qasem brought the bottle of vodka and a few glasses and put them down on the table next to some bowls of fruit.

"Cheers."

"Cheers. Down the hatch!"

Asghar tossed off the glass of vodka in a single gulp. Asadollah Mirza offered some to the cadet officer's mother.

"Ma'am, won't you wet your whistle, too?"

The bearded woman, with her black teeth—half of which were missing—gave a hearty guffaw and said, "Eh, God keep you your lordship . . . me drink alcohol?"

"What's to stop you, on an evening like this . . . such a fine son you have and now you've got him married . . ." And he insisted on placing a small glass in the bearded woman's hand.

Mash Qasem murmured in my ear, "God save us all . . . they were right to say the devil's a bearded woman"

All the while this hospitality was going on Dear Uncle Napoleon was quivering like a volcano about to overflow with lava. Those who were sitting around Mr. Salar were listening to the conversation in astonished silence. Only Mr. Salar himself was happily staring with smiling eyes at the cadet officer's sister's breasts. Asadollah Mirza also offered her a glass.

My father considered this a suitable moment to say in measured tones, "Mr. Salar, tonight we are truly happy, from the bottom of our hearts . . . our dear son-in-law Mr. Ghiasabadi is a high-ranking official in the security service!"

Dear Uncle had a good idea of what my father was thinking; he squirmed in silence.

Mr. Salar had drunk a couple of glasses of cognac and was in a very pleasant mood; he said, "Well, well, and I'm very happy, too . . . I wish the couple all good luck."

Then he turned to the cadet officer, "Mr. Ghiasabadi, which department of the security service do you work in?"

"The criminal investigation branch, sir."

"Who do you work with? I mean your superior would be . . . ?"

"Well sir, my superior's Mr. Taymur Khan, who was supposed to come here tonight; I don't know why he's late."

"Which Taymur Khan, the one who used to be in charge of security in Khorasan?"

"No sir, he was never in charge of . . ."

Dear Uncle Napoleon caught sight of Dr. Naser al-Hokama, who had just come in, and found an opportunity to cut the conversation short, "Well, well, hello doctor . . . do sit down, sit down. Why have you come so late, doctor? Mr. Salar, I don't know if you're acquainted with Dr. Naser al-Hokama or not?"

Apparently Mr. Salar and the doctor already knew each other and their greetings and inquiries after each other's health went on for some time. Asadollah Mirza murmured, "I don't know where that donkey Dustali's got to . . . eh! Look, talk of the devil! Mr. Dustali Khan . . . come on in. Where have you been till now, Dustali Khan?"

There was a deep frown on Dustali Khan's face. I was able to guess that his plan had not been successful. Trying to pretend he was perfectly happy he said, "I went to find a couple of entertainers."

And then, stressing each word, he went on, "In the Abbas Khan group of entertainers there's a man called Abdollah who does black-face parts; when he plays that low-life character Kakasiah it's enough to make you burst your sides laughing."

I realized what his whole plan had been. The Abdollah he was talking about, who played black-face parts in cheap entertainments, was the grandson of my father's half-sister. From childhood he had been a lazy good-for-nothing kind of person; when he was a young man he had become addicted to opium and had disappeared from our lives. A year before the party we had seen Abdollah playing the black-face role of Kakasiah at a wedding reception for which a group of entertainers had been engaged.

Dustali Khan had turned the whole city upside down trying to find this black-face actor Abdollah in order to bring him to the party and pay my father back for what he'd done, but as luck would have it he couldn't find Abdollah anywhere, and he couldn't put his plan into effect; all the same he had decided that at least he would add his measure of poison to my father's scheme.

He tossed off a glass of vodka and went on, "Yes, he makes a very funny black-face . . . of course, he's a drug addict and a really good-for-nothing character. But very funny . . . it's a pity I couldn't find him."

Mr. Salar jumped into the conversation, "I wish you'd been able to find him. I love those Kakasiah parts. If you know where he might be found, my chauffeur can take the car and go and look for him."

Asghar the Diesel had just tossed off a glass of vodka and was feeling very merry. With a loud laugh he said, "I swear on the soul of Mr. Salar here that I really get a kick out of those Kakasiah turns, too. If I knew where he was I'd go and fetch him myself."

Dustali Khan scratched the back of his ear and turned to my father, "You don't know where we might be able to find him . . . ? Because . . . it seems as though . . . he's some relation of yours. Isn't he your sister's grandson?"

My father snapped his jaws together so violently that the sound was audible. He opened his mouth to say something but it seemed that he was unable to.

Asadollah Mirza jumped into the middle of this cold war. "Since we have the gramophone here, why don't we put a record on? . . . Although Ahmad Khan's here, too . . . Ahmad Khan, why are you sitting there doing nothing? Play something, man!"

And to put an end to the quarrel, the poor fellow jumped up and started swaying his hips and singing, "What a night tonight is—these two get wed tonight. The bride with her groom—under the blanket in bed tonight . . . Good luck go with them now, God willing, good luck . . ."

The teacher Ahmad Khan started to accompany him on the *tar* and, with his mouth full, sang along. The cheerful sound of singing and fingers being snapped filled the air and the party took on a different aspect; this would have been an ideal opportunity for my father to suppress his anger.

Finally Asadollah sank back into his chair, exhausted and with his forehead shiny with sweat, and the noise quieted down again. My father—who had gathered his forces in the interval and prepared a new line of attack—turned toward the cadet officer's mother, as he was refilling Asghar the Diesel's empty glass, and said, "The cadet officer's late father, God rest his soul . . . now his soul's in heaven looking down on us. Every father wants to attend his son's wedding."

The cadet officer's mother had drunk two or three glasses of vodka at Asadollah's insistence and her flushed face showed, in spite of the dark hair on it, how merry she was feeling; after a loud burst of laughter she said, "God rest his soul . . . one day toward the end of his life he was in his shop near the stove and he was overcome by the heat; he came home and collapsed and we brought the doctor to him. He said to me, 'Naneh Rajab, you know I've only one wish in all the world, and that's to see our Rajab married 'fore I die' . . . but this lad was so pigheaded that, God rest his soul, he took that wish to the grave."

To stop anyone from interrupting and the breaking thread of the conversation, my father immediately asked, "Near the stove? But, God rest his soul, what was your husband's profession?"

"God rest his soul. At the end of his life he cooked sheeps' heads . . . mind you, when he was young he was a laborer and used to dig wells, then . . ."

Suddenly Naneh Rajab seemed to realize that perhaps she shouldn't be talking in this fashion and she stroked her beard and said in a contrite tone, "You really must excuse me . . . I mean, it's his lord-ship here's fault who's been giving me all this vodka . . . I'm really ashamed of myself . . . my lips haven't touched a drop for years."

My father wasn't going to let a good opportunity slip and said, "What's this I hear, ma'am, you mean to say that you're ashamed be-cause your late husband used to cook sheeps' heads? . . . In these times now such words have no meaning at all. Didn't the Prophet say that it's the most pious who are the dearest to God? A profession's no way to decide on someone's worth . . . isn't that so, Mr. Dustali Khan?"

My father spoke to Dustali Khan but in reality his words were di-rected at Dear Uncle Napoleon, who had turned as pale as a corpse and the muscles of whose face had contracted in a terrifying manner.

Dustali Khan quivered with rage and the veins on his neck were visibly swollen; he glanced at Dear Uncle. Dear Uncle's answering glance signalled him to keep quiet. Having delivered his blow my fa-ther was busy peeling a cucumber. Asadollah Mirza wanted to change the subject, but Dustali Khan started in on the attack, "As you have such fraternal and egalitarian sentiments, how is it you never let your own sister's grandson set foot in your house? Do you recall how that time when he came to the door, asking you to help him, you had a police officer get rid of him?"

Trying to remain calm and collected my father said, "That wasn't because of his profession. It was because he had trampled on every human value and virtue . . . because he'd become a drug addict . . . because he couldn't leave opium alone. He'd damaged our family's good standing."

Dustali Khan was so furious that he lost all self control and yelled, "How is it that your good standing's so important but the good stand-ing of one of the highest noble families in this country isn't important?"

Dear Uncle wanted to get him to be quiet but he was so angry that he couldn't utter a sound. Besides, my father wouldn't let up. "You mean you're trying to say that the honored and respected Mr. Ghiasabadi is just like that fool of a drug addict?"

Without at all realizing what he was saying Dustali Khan yelled, "And isn't the man an opium addict then?"

The guests watched this argument dumbfounded, unable to find an opportunity to intervene. Suddenly Naneh Rajab, the cadet officer's mother, overturned a bowl of fruit and let out a terrifying scream, "Do you understand what you're saying . . . you and your family aren't good enough to be my Rajab's servants . . . you say another word like that and I'll ram your teeth down your throat . . . God damn your shameless dirty mouths! Get up, Rajab! This is no place for us!"

Dustali Khan, who was quite beside himself with fury, yelled, "Shut up, you old witch, and may the gravediggers get their hands on that beard and mustache of yours in good time!"

Naneh Rajab leapt from her seat like a firecracker and before anyone could intervene gave Dustali Khan a resounding slap across the face. Dustali Khan tried to kick the old woman in the stomach but his foot hit her shin and she screamed with pain.

The cadet officer's sister began shouting and wailing and cursing, "You've killed my mother, you shameless son of a bitch!"

And she went for Dustali. An extraordinary fight started. And then the cadet officer's sister's friend, Asghar the Diesel, who had controlled his anger up to this moment, in one leap got himself behind Dustali Khan, picked him up and ran quickly toward the pool in the middle of the yard. He threw Dustali Khan into the pool with such force that all the guests were soaked from head to toe.

I am unable to describe the noise and confusion and turmoil that ensued.

Half an hour later our house was completely quiet. All the tables and chairs and bowls of fruit and little cakes were scattered haphazardly on the ground. My mother was weeping soundlessly in a corner and my father was striding angrily and purposefully up and down the yard, his hands clasped behind his back; occasionally he would halt near the main garden and say something unintelligible.

I had passed one of the saddest and most unpleasant evenings of my life, and early the next morning I begged my mother to let me go and stay as a guest with a relative who lived on the other side of the city.

I needed to get away from that environment for a while.

When I came back to the house two days later I saw with utter astonishment that the whole garden between our house and Dear Uncle Napoleon's had been divided by four rows of barbed wire that were a meter and a half high and so closely laid that not even a cat could have managed to pass gingerly from one side to the other.

PART THREE

PART THREE CONTENTS

TWENTY

"HELLO, MASH QASEM. Good morning!"

"Hello my lad! How come you're up so early again . . . ? Eh lad, if you can get up so early every mornin', go and say your mornin' prayers through a couple of times. It's not this world that counts after all, you should be thinkin' of the next world!"

"You're right, Mash Qasem . . . I've told myself that when I'm bigger . . . I mean when my studies are over, I'll certainly say my prayers."

"Eh lad, prayer's got nothin' to do with bein' big or little . . . there was a man in our town who . . ."

If I let him start on his story I'd have lost my chance and I cut him off, "Mash Qasem, can I ask you to give this note to Layli?"

"Last night still thinkin' of love and bein' in love, were we? . . . There's sin involved in this, too, you know . . . stirrin' up a girl who's ready to be married like this, and anyway it's useless . . . there was somethin' I wanted to tell you, but I don't rightly know how . . ."

Mash Qasem thought for a moment. I guessed from his face that something new had happened, and I animatedly asked, "Is it about me and Layli?"

"No, no, it's nothin' at all . . . just think it was a . . ."

"Please, Mash Qasem! Please tell me!"

"Eh, God in heaven . . . I'll bite my tongue out . . . I mean why should I lie? To the grave it's ah . . . ah . . . It wasn't anythin' at all."

I started pleading. Either Mash Qasem felt sorry for me or he couldn't control his own love of chattering. He shook his head and said, "If you want to know, the marriage between Miss Layli and Mr. Puri's goin' ahead."

"What? The marriage? How, Mash Qasem? Please don't hide anything from me. Please, on the soul of everyone you love, tell me whatever you know."

Mash Qasem lifted up his cap a little, scratched his forehead, and said, "It seems like Mr. Puri's ailment's all cleared up . . . meanin' that Dr. Naser al-Hokama's medicines have done the job."

"Mash Qasem, please tell the truth. What's happened? What is it you know about?"

"Well lad, look, why should I lie? To the grave it's ah . . . ah . . . it looks like that electric current that Dr. Naser al-Hokama's been pumpin' into his guts has done the job . . . now they want to put him to the test . . ."

"How are they going to put him to the test? I mean, is it possible that . . ."

"That's it, lad . . . they've found a woman to . . . but you have to swear that you never heard what I'm sayin' from me."

"I swear, Mash Qasem, on my father's soul . . . on the holy Quran . . . on Layli's soul . . ."

"Well, this lad who wasn't a man anymore due to losin' his . . . now it's like . . . meanin' . . . well, to cut a long story short he's all right again . . . they're goin' to send a woman in to him to test him. And if he doesn't flunk this test, the next day they're goin' to marry him to Miss Layli."

Although I hadn't really taken the matter in, I was unable to breathe. I stared wildly at Mash Qasem, with my mouth open. I was waiting for further explanations from him. He set off and said, "Lad, you wait while I go and buy the milk and come back, and then I'll tell you all about it." Mash Qasem went out of the garden door and I stood where I was, motionless and dumbfounded.

It was a Friday morning in the spring of 1942. Mash Qasem had long since heard about my secret from my own mouth.

A few months had passed since my father's party in honor of Cadet Officer Ghiasabadi, and I had experienced a great feeling of pain and loss in the meantime. After that famous evening which had ended in such a tumultuous argument, and was the cause of Layli and I being separated by rows of barbed wire, all means of access were closed to me for three or four months.

Having divided his house from ours by barbed wire, Dear Uncle not only forbade all communication between me and Layli, but declared that the rest of the members of his family had no right to speak to any member of my father's family.

And further, since he was utterly convinced that the English were not going to spare his family the horrors of their revenge, he had asked uncle colonel to procure a personal orderly for him. This orderly, who spoke Turkish and didn't know more than a few words of Persian, was a man of imposing bulk who looked very severe. Each morning he accompanied Layli to the door of her school, and at noon he brought her home; the same thing happened in the evenings, and there was no possibility of my being able to speak to Layli when she was on her way to and from school, as I had planned. The couple of times that I followed her in the hope that we might be able to exchange a few words, the orderly whipped off his thick menacing belt from his waist and came after me in such a way that, if I hadn't taken to my heels as fast as I was able to, I'd have been killed by him.

The telephone was also placed under strict watch. After a period spent in fruitless attempts to see and talk to Layli, I finally realized that my one hope of salvation lay in openly confessing my secret to Mash Qasem (it was clear that he had guessed what was going on, anyway) and asking for his help. Mash Qasem listened carefully and patiently, and with his head lowered said, "Eh lad, God have mercy on you. The Master's feelin' for family honor's unique in this town. If the Master found out that someone was sweet on one of his neighbor's girls, he'd split his belly open, so what would he do if it was his own girl!"

"Mash Qasem, Dear Uncle must know. Because it's impossible that Puri or uncle colonel haven't managed to let him know."

"Eh, are you out of your mind, lad? Do you think the colonel and Mr. Puri are tired of life that they'd be tellin' the Master somethin' like that?"

That day Mash Qasem related to me various horrific stories about the disasters that Dear Uncle had visited upon the heads of people who had fallen in love with girls connected with his family, but my situation was beyond being influenced by such stories, and love for Layli had so filled my heart that no thought of such dangers could have removed it. Somehow I finally persuaded Mash Qasem to agree occasionally to take notes from me to Layli. And he agreed, provided there was to be nothing 'unsuitable' in the notes. Even so, every time I gave him a note to take to Layli he would say, "Lad, there's nothin' unsuitable in here, is there?"

"Mash Qasem, I promise you I haven't written anything bad."

For a long time our relationship was confined to these notes, which Mash Qasem refused to pass on more than once a week, and to the two or three times when I accidentally caught sight of Layli; I suffered inexpressible torments.

Fortunately this most recent war between my father and Dear Uncle lasted no more than four months and, through the family's unceasing efforts, ended in peace. Now I can guess the reason why they made it up between them.

From the beginning of the quarrel, Dear Uncle's terror of the English and their desire for revenge increased from one day to the next, to such an extent that he had made himself a virtual prisoner in his own room. Even when he slept he wouldn't be parted from his revolver. Every night Mash Qasem slept with a rifle in the corridor outside his bedroom. He had had iron bars fixed to his bedroom window. His wife found this way of living intolerable, both for herself and for her children, and at her insistence various restricted family councils were called, consisting of uncle colonel, Asadollah Mirza, Shamsali Mirza and one or two other people. I heard about all this from Asadollah Mirza. Each of these individuals had talked separately with Dear Uncle. Dear Uncle had got a new notion into his head, which was that the English and Hitler's agents had come to an agreement concerning his case. The idea was that the English would make concessions to Hitler in other areas on condition that they could pursue their vendetta against Dear Uncle unhindered, and it was for this reason that Hitler had withdrawn his undercover agent, meaning Hushang the shoeshine man.

On his own initiative and without letting the others know, Asadollah Mirza had two or three times telephoned Dear Uncle, using his disguised voice, as if relaying a message from Hitler, and by saying the special password had tried to convince him that the reason the shoeshine man had been withdrawn was that Hitler was now sure that the danger was over and that the shoeshine man had been sent on another important mission; but Dear Uncle hadn't believed him and had responded with various angry messages for Hitler and Goering. He had called even Hitler a lackey of the English, someone colluding with them against him, and said he could only have faith in them if they made the shoeshine man the agent responsible for his safety again.

As a result Asadollah Mirza made desperate efforts to find the shoeshine man. After extensive investigations he realized that the shoeshine man had run away from our area out of fear of Shir Ali the butcher; apparently there had been a skirmish between him and Shir Ali on the same day he had disappeared. What had happened was that the shoeshine man had made a flirtatious remark to Tahereh, Shir Ali's wife, and as luck would have it, Shir Ali had heard about this. He had struck the shoeshine man a blow on the head with a leg of mutton, and then, rumbling like a volcano, had run back to his house and reappeared with a cleaver in his hand. This attack was sufficient to make the shoeshine man flee from the area, without once looking back, with all the strength his young legs could muster.

Asadollah Mirza managed, with a great deal of difficulty, to persuade Shir Ali to forgive the shoeshine man. And then after an incessant search he finally found the shoeshine man in Amirieh Avenue, which was a considerable distance from our house.

After his three-month absence the shoeshine man returned to his former spot opposite the door to our garden, and for a few days Dear Uncle Napoleon was fairly calm. But ten to fifteen days later he was playing the same old tune again; whatever happened, the English wouldn't forgive him for what he'd done.

Today I can analyze and understand the reasons why Dear Uncle and my father agreed to bury the hatchet. Everyone in the family was trying to convince Dear Uncle that, for a thousand reasons, the English had no further interest in what he had done to them. But Dear Uncle could not allow such an idea to lodge within his mind and heart. Among such people, not one of whom was ready to appreciate the danger he was in, he needed the existence of someone who, like himself, believed that the English would not forgive someone's wrongdoings (and such wrongdoings at that, involving the destruction of whole regiments and armies) and that they would not rest until they had laid low the author of their defeats—and this person was none other than my father.

As a result of this psychological state, the person who took the first step along the road to peace was in fact Dear Uncle. Even so, Asadollah Mirza's efforts, at my insistent pleading, played an important role.

To cut a long story short, after about four months of hostilities, they buried the hatchet; part of the barbed wire was taken away and once again I was able to see Layli. Of course, it wasn't with the old freedom, since now Puri kept a very watchful eye on us.

Puri had threatened that if he saw me hanging around Layli once more he would show the love letters I had written to Layli, and which he had kept, to Dear Uncle Napoleon. To satisfy his suspicions I pretended, with Layli's collaboration, that everything was over between us and that I wouldn't think of her anymore; fortunately Puri hadn't taken any steps toward their marriage either. Mind you, the reason for this was nothing to do with his being considerate of the state I was in. Later I found out that because of the psychological shocks he'd suffered, both from hearing the rifle shot and from his anxiety at losing one of his testicles, he'd lost interest in marriage, and that he was in the process of being treated, very discreetly, by Dr. Naser al-Hokama.

Mash Qasem's return broke the thread of my thoughts. "Just wait till I put this bowl of milk in the kitchen, lad, and I'll be back."

Mash Qasem came back into the garden, hitching up his trousers as he did so, so that he could water the flowers, and said, "Just you remember, lad, you swore you never heard it from me!"

"Mash Qasem, I'm ready to swear a hundred times more. I promise on my honor I won't say I heard it from you, not if they tear me limb from limb. Why don't you tell me? I'm dying with all this waiting. What's happened? What's all this about a test?"

"Well now, lad, why should I lie? To the grave it's ah . . . ah . . . What I heard with my own ears . . ."

Mash Qasem looked around and went on in a lowered voice, "Yesterday the colonel went to see the Master . . . they went into a room and shut the door. It just so happened my ear happened to be at the keyhole and I heard what they said. They were talkin' about Puri . . ."

"What were they saying, Mash Qasem?"

"Well now why should I lie? To the grave it's ah . . . ah . . . You know that Puri's not been feelin' too good ever since they took out one of the pair of his private equipment. It's like his privates have lost all their spirit . . . Dr. Naser al-Hokama's treatin' him with that electric current thing . . ."

"I know, Mash Qasem."

"Eh? How do you know?"

"The doctor's son told me, in confidence . . . Puri goes to the doctor every other day. They pass an electric massager over his groin."

"Eh! More fool me! I thought that, except for the colonel and the Master and me, no one knew. Anyways, however much the doctor tries to tell master Puri that he's all right now, the lad won't believe him. It's like all the fight's been knocked out of him. Now the doctor's told the colonel that the way to do it is to marry him off to someone, temporary like, so that, savin' your reverence, they can put his privates to the test. But master Puri says that either he won't marry anyone at all or he'll marry Miss Layli."

I stared at him with my mouth open. He went on, "And now the colonel's found a way . . . they've made an agreement with that Miss Akhtar, Ghiasabadi's sister, that they'll give her a nice bit of money for her to give master Puri his test."

"What? With Cadet Officer Ghiasabadi's sister? But is that possible? I mean, can things like that . . . ?"

"Oh yes, lad. And that slut of a woman didn't say no, neither."

"What did Dear Uncle say, Mash Qasem?"

"At first he said no, no, impossible, but finally he agreed to it."

"What about Cadet Officer Ghiasabadi? Does he know about all this?"

"Well now, why should I lie? To the grave it's ah . . . ah . . . This man from our town, ever since Mrs. Qamar's had her baby, and as luck would have it it came out lookin' just like his sister, there's no talkin' to him . . . he's no notion of how to be civil or decent . . . did you see how they threw Dustali Khan and Mrs. Aziz out of the house?"

"And so when do they want to do all this?"

"Well now, why should I lie? To the grave it's ah . . . ah . . . They said that bit very quiet and I couldn't hear properly. It seems like today or tomorrow the colonel and his wife will go out of the house and leave master Puri there . . . they'll find an excuse not to take Puri. Because he's not to know . . . And then this Akhtar's to find some excuse to go there and do the job."

"Mash Qasem, do you suppose . . . I mean, do you think that this test . . . do you think it'll work?"

"Well, m'dear, if it's that slut she can manage anythin' . . . savin' your reverence, savin' your reverence, savin' your reverence, she could make the family's late grandfather rise up in his grave . . . if I was to give her an inch, savin' your reverence, she'd lead even me into sin."

Without knowing what I was saying I said, "Mash Qasem, how about if we watch out and don't let her be alone with Puri?"

"But as soon as you're not lookin' for a moment she'll be there . . . we must think of somethin' else . . . some way so it's not obvious you know anythin' . . . except for the Master and the colonel and that slut Akhtar, no one knows . . . if there's a fuss and it comes out, the Master'll empty a bullet into my brain . . . the Master says if the English find out such a thing has happened they'll destroy his reputation throughout the whole town . . . and that's the truth too. You've seen them English!"

"Mash Qasem, I don't know what I should do . . . finally we have to come up with something. But for God's sake, if you find out when they're going to do this, let me know."

"Never you worry, I'll tell you . . . but you're not to do somethin' that'll leave me in the lurch . . . I want to put a stop to this even more than you do. The virtue of a girl from Ghiasabad's like my own virtue . . . if you go round this whole country you won't find one place where they care as much about their virtue as Ghiasabad."

Mash Qasem made me swear once more that I would keep this secret to myself, and that I wouldn't act in any way that would make it apparent that he had told me something; in particular he impressed on me the danger of the English interfering in the matter.

Bewildered and depressed, I went back to my room. I thought for a long while but no solution occurred to me. Each solution I thought of had some major problem involved with it.

Hopelessly I set off to call in at Asadollah Mirza's house. I knew that he had gone away on a trip. When I reached the front of his house it was as if God had opened the gates of heaven before me, because I could hear the noise of his gramophone.

"Thank God you're here, Uncle Asadollah. When did you get back?"

"Last night, lad . . . what's happened now then, why are you so pale? Have Dear Uncle and your father quarreled again, or has general Wavell attacked Dear Uncle's house?"

"Worse than that, Uncle Asadollah . . . much worse!"

Asadollah Mirza lifted the needle from the record that was playing on the gramophone and said, "Moment, moment . . . do you want me to guess? You've paid a visit to San Francisco with Layli and you've left her a present in her suitcase?"

"No, Uncle Asadollah. Don't make jokes about it. It's something much more important."

"Oh, shut up with you, man, so it's nothing to do with San Francisco? Los Angeles is in those parts, round the back, and if that's the problem that's not so bad, either."

"No, Uncle Asadollah. But you have to swear that what I'm going to tell you stays just between us . . ."

"Moment, so it has nothing whatsoever to do with San Francisco?"

Impatiently I answered, "As a matter of a fact it does have to do with that. But it's to do with Puri."

"Shame on you, lad! You mean you've been so wishy-washy for so long that Puri's taken Layli to San Francisco?"

"No, no, no . . . you aren't listening at all. Puri's going to San Francisco with someone else . . ."

"Then what are you going around with such a long face for? You want the gates to all of San Francisco to be closed? San Francisco's to be a forbidden city?"

Asadollah Mirza was in such a cheerful mood that there was no talking to him. I shouted, "Just listen to me for one minute, will you!"

"All right, all right . . . I'm all ears, head to toe . . . say what you have to say."

After I had got Asadollah Mirza to swear by all his ancestors and by the prophets and saints that the matter would remain strictly between us, I explained to him what the situation was. He was so overcome by gales of laughter that he fell off his bed onto the floor. After some time his laughter quieted down, he wiped away his tears, and said in a voice still interrupted by laughter, "And so to test the effect of his treatment the doctor's recommending a trip to San Francisco . . . What a splendid doctor! Right from the first I said that Naser al-Hokama's a genius. I wish I were his patient. Mind you, if I were his patient I'd buy my medicine from a different pharmacy."

Although I had neither the spirit nor the patience for all this I started to laugh and said, "Because you've used that pharmacy's medicine before?"

"No, as God's my witness, I've never laid a finger on the cadet officer's sister Akhtar." He swore so many oaths that I was convinced he was lying. After a moment's silence I said, "What do you think we should do now? If he passes this test he's sure to be asking for her hand the following week and the week after that they'll have the wedding . . . at all costs I have to see that he doesn't pass."

"Moment, how do you know he'll pass . . . a stupid student like him."

"Uncle Asadollah, I've heard that this Akhtar is very . . ."

He interrupted me, "Yes, and you've heard right, too. She's a very good examiner. No one fails her tests. Shame on me for not thinking to have her test you first, your geography's terrible, you don't know San Francisco from Los Angeles!"

"Uncle Asadollah, please don't make jokes! I've come to you for help, so that you can think of something to do about all this."

"No problem. You gave him a kick and one of . . . what's that expression Mash Qasem used? You destroyed one of the pair of his private equipment, now give him another kick and destroy the other one of the pair. Then he'll be Sir Puri the Eunuch and you'll have nothing to worry about for good."

"Uncle Asadollah!"

"Although the next day another suitor will come. And the day after that a third suitor and you'll have to put your life on hold while you go around kicking people in the privates from morning till night."

"Uncle Asadollah, I thought that if we let Asghar the Diesel, Akhtar's friend . . ."

"Splendid, splendid, congratulations on this stroke of genius of yours! That's all we need, to set that intoxicated idiot against his mistress, to start a nice bit of bloodshed . . . you can do something much simpler than that, you can take Layli by the hand and at the crucial moment lead her to the room where the exam's taking place."

"I can't do that. Because I've promised on my honor that I won't let who told me all this out of the bag . . . and anyway, how could Layli . . ."

"You've a strange way of living up to your promise!"

"I didn't tell you who told me."

"You think I don't realize who told you? Who told you's written all over it."

"Who do you think told me, Uncle Asadollah?"

Asadollah Mirza held up the four fingers of his right hand and said, "Why should I lie? To the grave it's ah . . . ah . . . no more than four fingers!"

"No, Uncle Asadollah, believe me, Mash Qasem knows nothing about this."

"All right, all right . . . you don't have to swear an oath . . . as far as I can see, either you have to tell Layli and set the cat among the pigeons, or you have to tell Asghar the Diesel and be responsible for shedding the examiner's and her student's blood . . . or you have to keep a close eye on Puri and Akhtar from now until the time of the test and, as soon as they're ready to start, you start screaming at the top of your lungs."

I talked with Asadollah Mirza for a while. Part of the time he was seriously trying to help me, and part of the time he was joking around. We reached the conclusion that, even if we got Akhtar out of the way, others would turn up. Finally, as he lit a cigarette, Asadollah Mirza said to me, "In my opinion you should let the test go ahead. And at that moment you should make such a racket that once again the student will put all such thoughts out of his mind for a while, and for another six or seven months they'll go back to Dr. Naser al-Hokama's electric groin massager, and after that, trust in the Lord . . . perhaps during that time the English will get hold of Dear Uncle . . . or they'll do away with Puri in revenge for all they've suffered at Dear Uncle's hands."

A thought suddenly occurred to me. I shouted out triumphantly, "Uncle Asadollah, I've got it. If we can find out when the test is to be, at the crucial moment we can have a gun go off, or a firecracker, to terrify Puri . . . because you know that Dr. Naser al-Hokama has said to Dear Uncle that this problem of Puri's isn't just from the kick I gave him. The psychological disturbance he suffered when the Allies attacked has also had an influence . . . he heard a gun go off and went into shock."

"But be careful the firecracker doesn't blind him in one eye . . . you've ruined the equilibrium in the lower part of his body, don't ruin it in the upper part . . . the country will need this great genius in the future. Especially now that he's gone into the income tax office and found himself a profession."

"No, don't worry about that. I know what I'm going to do."

"But please take every precaution, and when the unidentified spy tells you that the date for the test has been fixed let me know."

"Of course, Uncle Asadollah."

Asadollah Mirza said with a laugh, "And please don't make the examiner angry with you . . . I want to ask her to give you a graduation test, now you're a grown man, and then she can teach you that

San Francisco's a very fine place with a wonderful climate and that Los Angeles is even nicer than that."

"Goodbye, Uncle Asadollah!"

"Goodbye; *al-San Francisco's* to be a forbidden city!"

❖ ❖ ❖

"Can I come in? . . . In I come then . . . a good mornin' to you."

The classroom door opened wide and Mash Qasem entered. My astonished stare, and the stares of the other pupils, turned from Mash Qasem to the teacher.

Our algebra teacher was an extremely strict and ill-tempered person. Even the principal was not allowed to come into our class while a lesson was in progress. The teacher's facial muscles became taut and he peered at the newcomer from behind his thick black-framed glasses. The children, who all went in terror of him, were appalled. It's easy to guess how I felt in this situation.

Mash Qasem very coolly surveyed the pupils and then turned back to the teacher, "I said good mornin' . . . they've always said that it's good to say good mornin', but if someone says it to you, you *have* to answer. There are fifty people in this room, and your good self . . . I come in and say good mornin' and not one of you says it back."

In a strangled voice the teacher said, "And who might you be?"

"I'm your humble servant Mash Qasem. I said 'Good mornin'.'"

"Who gave you permission to come into the classroom during a lesson?"

"Well now, why should I lie? To the grave it's ah . . . ah . . . I said 'Can I come in?' You didn't say 'No, you can't.' So I came in. And I said 'Good mornin',' too, but you couldn't be bothered to give me one little 'Good mornin'' back."

"A very good morning to you . . . and just who are you? What are you doing here?"

Mash Qasem pointed to where I was sitting,, mute with fear, in the second row, and said, "I'm that boy's uncle's servant . . . his dad's been taken very poorly and they've sent me to fetch the boy home . . ." As he was saying this Mash Qasem winked at me, and fortunately, although the other children saw this, it was not visible to the teacher.

The ill-tempered teacher's facial muscles relaxed for a moment. He motioned me to stand up, "Your father's been unwell?"

"My father . . . I mean . . . no sir . . . I mean . . ."

He turned to Mash Qasem, "Then how has he suddenly become ill?"

"Well sir, I didn't understand that neither . . . the poor feller was just sittin' there puffin' away on his water-pipe and then all of a sudden it was like his breath had got all twisted in his guts . . . he doubled up and gave a yell and fell on the floor . . ." Once again Mash Qasem gave me a wink that he made no attempt to conceal; fortunately the teacher didn't see it this time either.

"Very well, very well, off you go home . . . and next time, my good sir, don't come barging into the classroom like this."

I quickly gathered up my books, but as I was going toward the door with my school bag in my hand the teacher shouted, "Just a minute . . . on Wednesday someone's mother was taken ill and they came to the school for him . . . it wouldn't be, would it, that you don't know your lesson and you're trying to fool me? Go over to the blackboard and let's see how you do."

Mash Qasem wanted to object, but I motioned him to be silent. The teacher gave me an equation to solve on the board, but my mind was incapable of functioning. I was certain that Mash Qasem had brought fresh news about Puri's "test," because I had begged him that if anything happened while I wasn't there to invent some excuse and come after me at school, if that proved necessary.

Naturally I was unable to solve the equation. The teacher shouted, "Just as I'd supposed . . . my dear idiot child, write on the board as follows: 'A plus B squared is equal to A squared plus B squared, plus twice AB' . . . now solve the equation!"

"I'm sorry, sir . . . I . . . I mean I can't think . . . I'm worried about my father and I can't concentrate."

"Amazing! Come here . . . come here . . . closer . . . I will help you to concentrate."

Afraid and trembling, I went toward him. He gave me such a slap across the face that my ears rang with it. I put my hand up to my face and hung my head, but Mash Qasem suddenly came forward and shouted, "Why did you hit the poor lad? If, God forbid, your dad was sick, would you be able to think about your lessons?"

"It has nothing to do with you. Leave the room."

"What d'you mean, it has nothin' to do with me? What I want to know is, is this a classroom or Shir Ali the butcher's shop? Why don't you bring a cleaver here like Shir Ali some time and . . ."

I wanted to shout at Mash Qasem and make him be quiet but no sound came from my throat. The teacher had turned pale with anger; his shoulders shook as he shouted, "Someone go and get Haj Esmail to throw this peasant out!"

His face flushed, Mash Qasem shouted, "I'm goin' under my own steam, don't you worry about that, I'm not stoppin' here . . . thank God I never had no schoolin' and never learnt any of this behavior. God rest his soul, there was a man in our Ghiasabad . . ."

The teacher yelled so that the windows shook, "Out!"

I grabbed Mash Qasem by the arm and pulled him out of the classroom with all the strength I could muster. A few moments later I was pedaling home with Mash Qasem balanced on the panniers of my bicycle.

"Mash Qasem, you've really landed me in it now. That teacher is going to do something awful to me . . . but tell me quickly what's happened . . ."

Holding tightly onto the bicycle saddle Mash Qasem said, "It's these teachers that are the cause of all them little bastard kids bein' in the streets bangin' each other round the head from mornin' till night."

"Tell me what's happened, Mash Qasem!"

"Well, my lad . . . after lunch I saw that the colonel was outside the house whisperin' to that Akhtar woman . . . an hour later when I saw the colonel and his wife goin' out and gettin' rid of everyone from the house I realized something was up . . . half an hour ago I saw the little slut all dolled up like a dog's dinner. I says to myself, today there's something goin' on. So straightaway I came runnin' for you. Because I'd promised I'd come. But on your father's soul . . . on Miss Layli's soul, if you do somethin' so that I get in trouble . . ."

"Mash Qasem, I promise you on my honor . . . whatever happens, it's impossible that I'll say I heard anything from you . . ."

"But lad, don't you be kickin' him again . . . because then your family won't calm down till they've spilt your blood."

"No, you can be sure of that. I promise I won't lay a finger on Puri . . . But Mash Qasem, why have they done this now?"

"Because the house is quiet now . . . the children are at school . . . the pencil-pushers are all in their offices . . ."

"Puri goes to his office, too . . ."

"Well, I don't know how it's happened but the colonel didn't let him go to the office today. And that made me more sure somethin' was up."

Fortunately it was not far from the school to our house and we were there very quickly. I had pedaled so hard I was panting with the effort. I set Mash Qasem down at the end of the street and said, "Mash Qasem, first we have to know whether Akhtar's gone to uncle colonel's house or not."

"But lad, tell me what you want to do . . . I'm really worried."

"Mash Qasem, I promise you I'm not going to harm Puri. If I see things getting to a critical point I'm just going to make a racket so he won't be able to do his dirty work . . ."

"Good for you, lad . . . I like it that you're a clean thinkin' lad. In all the world there's nothin' finer than clean thinkin'. There was a man in our town who . . ."

"Mash Qasem, tell me about it later . . . for now go and see what's happening . . . and I'll go up to the roof and see what's going on in uncle colonel's house."

TWENTY-ONE

AS I ENTERED the house my father and mother were just about to leave.

"Why are you back so early?"

"Our teacher was sick today and we didn't have any class. Where are you going?"

My mother said, "Mrs. Farrokh Laqa is ill and we're going to see how she's getting on; if you want to, you come, too."

"No, I've a lot of studying to do."

"I've put some grapes in the larder; have some if you like."

My father and mother went out, which was lucky for me. From the window of my room I could get onto the roof of the bathroom, and from there, by going along a narrow ledge, I could get to where I could see the yard to uncle colonel's house.

Contrary to my expectations I couldn't see Akhtar there. Puri was in the pool with a towel around his waist, splashing himself. I went back to my room.

On the previous day I had procured four firecrackers from one of my classmates. These firecrackers were the size of walnuts. I don't know what they were made with; to make them explode you had to fling them down hard on the ground. So that it would make more of a noise I wrapped all four of the firecrackers in one piece of cloth and wound thread around them; then I set off for the garden. I could hear Mash Qasem calling me through the trees. When I got closer he said quietly, "Eh lad, I was comin' to tell you. I was just by the door, near the shoe-shine feller, keepin' an eye on that door down at the end. Akhtar went into the garden, smothered in makeup and wearin' her prayer veil . . . I went after her and I saw her go over to the colonel's house . . ."

"Thanks, Mash Qasem . . . thanks . . ."

I wanted to go back to my room but Mash Qasem kept hold of my arm and said, "Lad, you be real careful now; if the colonel realizes, he'll be out for your blood."

"I'm being careful, Mash Qasem. I've one thing to ask you, though; go to Asadollah Mirza's house and get him to come here so that if there's a fuss he can look out for me."

"I don't think he'll have got back from the office."

"When he gets back."

Having said this I hurried back to my room. I put the firecrackers in my pocket and went back to my hiding place by the same route.

Akhtar was wearing a green dress with a low neckline. Her white veil, which had a pattern of roses on it, had slipped back from her head. She was sitting on a chair in the space between the separate gardens of each household. Puri was wearing striped flannel pajamas, and the striped material made his face and body look even more lanky and horselike. Their conversation was still at the formal stage.

"I shall be very grateful, Mr. Puri, sir, if you could do this for me."

Puri spluttered and asked, "And what about last year? Did they take the same amount of tax from him last year?"

"Oh no. Last year he had a friend who fixed it for him. He paid much less tax than this."

"Well, if you could come to me at the office, tomorrow or the day after, I'll see what can be done. I'll have to see his file."

Akhtar's veil was on her shoulders; she grasped its edges in both hands and fanned herself with it, saying, "But it's incredible the weather's so hot."

It was obvious that she was trying to attract Puri's attention to her bare arms and ample breasts.

But Puri paid no attention and said, "Would you like me to bring you a glass of chilled cherry cordial?"

"I really fancy a glass of beer or chilled wine . . . some of that wine of your father's that we drank the other time."

"Unfortunately my dad puts the wine in storage and locks the door."

"I bet it's because he's afraid you'll go and drink it all!"

"Oh no, I never drink alcohol."

Akhtar laughed and said, "Well, if you say so I'll have to believe you . . . and when you have little rendezvous with girls in cafés, I suppose you order cold melon juice?"

Puri blushed. He gave an embarrassed laugh and hung his head, "I don't do that kind of thing."

"Oh, get along with you, don't tell such lies. A young man all tall and handsome like you not do such things? Even if you didn't want to yourself, the girls wouldn't leave you alone."

"You're very kind."

"Now get up and see if some of your father's wine hasn't been left out."

Puri got up and as he was going toward the house said, "I know there won't be any left out."

As soon as Puri left, Akhtar undid a button on the bodice of her dress. Mash Qasem had told the truth. She was a very seductive woman. Even in my dangerous situation perched on top of a wall I felt the saliva in my mouth dry up. I remembered what Asadollah Mirza had said and I thanked God it wasn't me who was being tested. I forced myself to put all such thoughts from my mind. My hand was in my pocket, playing with the package of firecrackers, which was about the size of a tangerine. I'd no idea when I'd have to throw it down on the ground. Puri's voice rang out, "It's really strange but there happens to be a bottle of wine on the table."

Akhtar said with a laugh, "I knew it . . . so why don't you come back here?"

"I'm looking for the corkscrew . . . aha, I've found it."

Puri came back to Akhtar carrying a little tray on which there was a bottle of wine and one glass.

"Eh? Well, God strike me dead! Why just the one glass?"

"I told you I don't drink alcohol."

Akhtar poured some wine in the glass. She tasted a little and said, "Mmm . . . mmm . . . what lovely wine . . . how can you bear not to drink this wine? Just have a sip and see how it tastes!"

"I can't . . . I mean, once I tasted some . . . it's not good for me . . . I get headaches."

"Just for me! Just for Akhtar!"

She pushed the glass against Puri's lips. Puri swallowed some and screwed up his equine face, "It tastes bad!"

"You get the real taste later . . . have another swallow . . . just for Akhtar!"

She forced virtually the whole glass down Puri's throat then suddenly screamed, "Eh! God strike me dead! It's spilt on my dress . . ."

And she lifted up her skirt so that her white plump thighs were completely visible.

Puri started to laugh, "Didn't I say don't insist! Now God's paid you back!"

He was such a feeble mama's boy, such an idiot that—leaving all our personal quarrel aside—I was ready to set the firecrackers off on his head. He took a handkerchief out of his pajama pocket, soaked it in the pool and stretched out his hand with it to Akhtar, "Take this and clean it!"

"The material's georgette, it'll spoil. I'll hold it smooth and you sponge it down."

Akhtar was holding the two sides of her skirt in such a way that most of her thighs remained uncovered. And Puri's horselike face was almost buried in her breasts. I could guess that inside his lanky frame he could feel a revolution going on.

Akhtar tried to fan the flames. She said flirtatiously, "Now if I were to say that Mr. Puri had stained my skirt I wouldn't be lying."

Puri gave a repulsive laugh that bore no resemblance whatsoever to an ordinary laugh. Then he said, "It's good my father isn't here, otherwise it would look really bad."

"And if it wasn't that your father's away, I wouldn't have been alone with his handsome son . . . Ouch! Ouch! What mosquitoes there are round here. Behind my knee's really swollen up . . . what a big lump it's made . . . put your hand there, see what a lump it's made!"

Akhtar took Puri's hand, placed it behind her naked knee, and immediately said, "Don't you have any eau de cologne in the house?"

"We do. Wait and I'll bring it."

Puri set off for the house. Akhtar followed him. I couldn't see them anymore, but as the window was open I could hear their voices coming from a ground-floor room.

Akhtar was saying, "Ouch. It really stings. Rub it in a bit more but don't give me those naughty looks . . . now just a minute, was it you that was saying you don't make rendezvous with girls?"

"Hey! Don't do that . . . my father and mama might come back."

"No, they won't come for ages yet. I saw the colonel by the door and he said they wouldn't be back till tonight."

"But our servant might suddenly . . ."

"Don't talk so much, darling . . . no one's going to come."

From Puri's sudden silence, which was followed by a sentence that was incomprehensible because his mouth was closed, I guessed that Akhtar had stopped his mouth in the appropriate manner. O God, should I set the firecrackers off or not? I wished that Asadollah Mirza had been there and could give me the order to fire! . . . From the sound of the bedsprings I guessed that they had flung themselves on the bed together. One, two three . . . I hurled the firecrackers with all my strength at the closest spot I could manage to the door to the room.

The noise of the explosion much exceeded what I had imagined or expected. And it wasn't just the noise of the firecrackers. It was as if someone had thrown a huge rock into the middle of a storeroom filled with glass. I was so terrified by the glittering fragments of glass that rose high into the air that I lost my balance and my legs slipped from the edge of the bricks where I was standing. But I didn't fall to the ground because I made an instinctive grab at the ledge and managed to hang on. Fortunately I had turned my face toward the wall in order to set the firecrackers off, otherwise I'd have fallen and at least broken both my legs that day. I hung there for a moment until I was able to find a toehold for my feet, too. Even so there was about a six-foot drop from my feet to the ground.

Akhtar's scream was mingled with a weird sound that issued from Puri's throat. "Puri Khan . . . Puri Khan . . . how are you? What was that? For God's sake, say something!"

Puri spoke through clenched teeth in a trembling, stuttering voice, "No . . . I'm . . . I'm . . . I'm all right . . . that noise . . . the noise . . . artillery . . . a rifle . . ."

Akhtar screamed, "I'm out of here!"

And she pulled her veil over her head and dashed toward the side door. The sound of fists pounding on the main door and various people shouting could be heard. But Puri seemed not to have the strength to get up, because he called out in the same choked, stuttering voice, "I . . . I'm . . . I'm coming . . . I . . ."

I was in a tricky situation. My feet had no firm hold and my arms could no longer support the weight of my body, but before I could lift my hands from the ledge one of the bricks came away and I fell to the ground. I felt a severe pain go through me, but I managed to stand up.

But before I could think of escape, I saw Puri's lanky form emerging from the room; he was as pallid as a corpse. When he saw me perhaps his anger somewhat overcame his terror. He seemed to find his tongue to some extent, and he yelled, "So it was you that did it . . . that noise . . . you caused that noise?"

"No, no, Puri, I swear on my father's soul . . . God strike uncle dead if I did it."

But my confusion and anxiety were sufficient to stop him believing my oaths of innocence. I took advantage of his momentary hesitation to look over at the corner of the yard where I had thrown the firecrackers; it seemed that they had landed in the midst of a very large wide-mouthed glass carboy, that happened to be in the yard, and shattered it. Half of its rounded base was still there but fragments of glass had carpeted the whole yard. In the midst of the racket that was coming from outside Puri ran at me and began hitting me. For a moment my instinct for self-preservation overcame me and my leg was about to launch a kick at his leg, but then it was as if the promises I had made to Asadollah Mirza and Mash Qasem that I would not hurt Puri froze me to the spot. The pressure on the door from the street became so intense that the latch gave way. Uncle colonel came into the yard, followed by various members of our family.

Uncle colonel's yelling rose above all other sounds, "What's happened, Puri? . . . What was that noise?"

"This son of a bitch threw a hand-grenade into our house."

I kept doing my utmost to exonerate myself, "I swear by my father . . . uncle, I swear by your soul that I didn't do it."

Uncle colonel released my collar from Puri's grasp and began squeezing my neck, "Confess, you miserable little bastard!"

"I swear, on your own death . . . on my father's soul . . . I heard the noise, too, and went up on the roof to see what was going on . . . then my foot slipped."

I looked despairingly toward the door to the street. I hoped Mash Qasem or Asadollah Mirza would arrive and save me, but there was no sign of them. Uncle colonel kept up the pressure on my neck and yelled, "And I'll tie your feet to a pole and beat them so hard your toenails will drop out and then I'll fling you in jail . . . Puri, get me a switch!"

Puri quickly broke a switch off from a tree and put it into his hand. I kept struggling to save myself. Before the first blow from the switch could strike me a voice rang out from the direction of the door, "Hold your hand!"

Everyone froze, but I was petrified with terror. Dear Uncle Napoleon appeared on the threshold. Among the folds of his cloak I saw a glitter from the drawn revolver he was holding. Fortunately Mash Qasem's calm face could be seen beside him; he had the double-barreled shotgun sloped over his shoulder.

Uncle colonel and Puri were about to open their mouths but Dear Uncle Napoleon's shout cut them off, "Have you taken leave of your senses? At such a dangerous moment, instead of seeing to our defenses, you pounce on this boy!"

"Uncle, this good-for-nothing guttersnipe has blown the house apart, he threw a hand grenade . . . he wanted to kill us!"

"Silence! Even stupidity has its limits! You've wasted so much time that the real perpetrator of this attack has got back to his house by now!"

During all this Mash Qasem was striding back and forth with the shotgun on his shoulder, keeping a sharp eye on the wall that ran past uncle colonel's house, on the other side of which there was a narrow alleyway. "God blind 'em, they either attacked from that there alleyway . . . or it was from a balloon . . ."

All heads turned in his direction. Mash Qasem went on in a loud voice, as if talking to himself, "Seems like I did hear the noise of a balloon . . . may God ruin them English . . ."

Everyone voiced objections simultaneously, but especially uncle colonel and Puri, "So it's the English again? Mash Qasem's started talking rubbish again . . ."

For a moment Dear Uncle Napoleon was silent. It was intolerable to him that something the English had done should be attributed to someone else. He exploded like a volcano, "Yes, the English . . . the English . . . you think the hostility of the English against me is a joke . . . so I'm crazy . . . so all this talk is just a fantasy . . . so I talk rubbish . . . I'm sick to death of all of you . . . morning, noon and night I stay awake to save you from the evils of the English, I'm here risking my life, my honor and my reputation. Could there be any better evidence? Isn't it enough that they throw a bomb into our house from the alleyway or from a plane or from God knows what damned place? How can I explain it to you idiots? God strike me dead so I'll be free of such relatives."

Dear Uncle's appearance had become quite terrifying. His whole body began to shake. He brought his hand up to his forehead, leant against the wall, and then slid slowly and gently to the ground. His eyes were closed and the revolver fell from his hand.

Mash Qasem ran to his side. Perhaps mainly to distract people's attention so they'd leave me in peace he shouted out, "Eh God in heaven, you've killed the Master! With relatives like this, why should the English take the trouble to do the job themselves!"

Puri said, "I am absolutely convinced that it was done by this little son of a bitch. I'll prove it."

Mash Qasem was busy massaging Dear Uncle Napoleon's shoulders; in one violent movement he drew himself up to his full height. He pointed the barrels of the double-barreled shotgun at Puri and shouted, "You killed the Master . . . now I'm goin' to kill the lot of you. God forgive me but I've no choice! . . . Say your prayers!"

Puri, uncle colonel and everyone else present turned pale; going backwards step by step, never taking their eyes off the barrels of the gun, they started stammering, "Mash . . . Mash . . . Mash Qasem, dear . . . now don't . . . now don't do anything crazy."

Although I knew that Mash Qasem wasn't even aware that to shoot the gun he had to pull the trigger, and although I was virtually certain that his gun was not loaded, nevertheless I felt a little anxious. Just at this moment a voice suddenly came from the door leading to the street, "Moment, moment, moment, *momentissimo!*"

Asadollah Mirza entered, his eyebrows raised in an expression of amazement. Puri started whining, "You're our one hope, Uncle Asadollah . . . this Mash Qasem wants to kill us."

Laughing, Asadollah Mirza said, "Good for Mash Qasem! I didn't know he was also a hunter of domestic livestock!"

But Mash Qasem interrupted him and shouted, "They've killed my Master and I have to take revenge for the Master . . . each of these bullets is for one of them and the last's for me!"

Asadollah Mirza quickly started counting those present, "One, two, three, four, five, six, seven, with me makes eight . . . Mash Qasem, how many bullets does that double barreled gun have that you want to kill all this crowd? And then you've got to have one left over for yourself . . . Well, that's enough joking, let's see now, what exactly has been going on? Who wanted to kill your master?"

Mash Qasem said in a loud voice, "Well now, why should I lie? To the grave it's ah . . . ah . . . I have to kill the lot of them, 'cause they've killed my Master."

"Forgive him for now . . . this boy's an ass, a fool. He made a mistake . . . what was that you said? They've killed the Master? Where's the Master? What's happened to the Master?"

And he finally caught sight of Dear Uncle Napoleon's motionless body. He ran to him and shouted, "And you're trying to take revenge instead of bringing a doctor and medicine . . . what's happened? Sir! Sir! How are you feeling, sir?"

Asadollah Mirza sat on the ground and began massaging Dear Uncle's shoulders; Mash Qasem hoisted the gun up on his shoulder and ran to help him.

Asadollah Mirza said anxiously, "What happened? . . . Mash Qasem, bring that rug over here, we can lay the Master down on it . . . and you, lad, run into the other yard and bring the bottle of ammonia . . . run, lad!"

Asadollah's emotion had an effect on everyone and a general running hither and thither began. Asadollah Mirza went on massaging Dear Uncle's hands and feet and shouted, "Isn't there anyone to tell me what happened? . . . Why has the master fainted?"

Pointing at me with his long finger, Puri spluttered out, "The whole thing's the fault of that little bastard there . . . he threw a bomb in our house . . . he wanted to kill us . . ."

"Moment, the bomb hit the Master?"

"No, it just made a noise like you'd never believe . . . the glass in the windows smashed, but I wasn't hit."

"And then the Master fainted at the noise?"

Puri shook his long face and said, "No, uncle dear, he came later. I said this good-for-nothing had thrown the bomb and he said the English had done it."

"Now whether he did it or the English did, it's not something to faint about. It must be that . . ."

Puri interrupted him, "But he got really angry."

As he was lightly slapping Dear Uncle's face Asadollah Mirza said, "It's not at all unlikely that the English did it. I mean, where is this innocent child going to get a bomb from?"

"Uncle Asadollah, don't look at his butter-wouldn't-melt-in-my-mouth appearance. He's more of a little son of a bitch than you'll ever know; wasn't it him last year who . . ." It seemed that Puri suddenly realized he had said too much, and that bringing up the incident of last year's kick would not be to his benefit.

He fell silent and I took advantage of the opportunity, "Believe me, Uncle Asadollah, I have no idea what happened. You can ask Miss Akhtar, she was here."

Once again Asadollah Mirza raised his eyebrows, "Moment, moment, what was Miss Akhtar doing in the midst of all this?"

Mash Qasem saw a good opportunity to interfere, "Why should I lie? I didn't understand what the lass was doin' here neither. When the bomb went off I saw her dash out the door and go off to her own house . . ."

Uncle colonel jumped into the conversation, "The cadet officer's sister Akhtar had come to get some advice from young Puri about one of her relatives who had a tax problem . . ."

Mash Qasem shook his head and said, "If I was you I wouldn't let that lass be alone with young Puri . . . they use these things as an excuse to lead young men away from the straight and narrow."

I saw my chance and said, "Besides, if Asghar the Diesel realizes that Miss Akhtar has come to see Puri, he'll split his stomach open . . . he'll chop Puri into a hundred little bits."

It was clear that uncle colonel and Puri were troubled by my remark. Uncle put his hand on my shoulder and said, "Look, lad, don't repeat all this . . . if it should get back to that clod, that lout, he'll be thinking that . . ."

The bottle of ammonia was brought and Asadollah Mirza took the top off and passed it under Dear Uncle Napoleon's nose; at this moment Layli arrived. When she saw her father in such a state she immediately burst into tears, "Daddy, daddy dear . . . daddy!"

Seeing her tears and hearing her sobs, my tears were on the point of spilling over, too. Fortunately Dear Uncle opened his eyes. Asadollah Mirza's voice rang out, "Didn't I tell you? . . . Praise the

Lord, nothing serious has happened . . . he was just a little over-come by the heat . . . sir . . . sir . . . how are you feeling?"

Dear Uncle Napoleon raised his hand to his forehead and said in a weak voice, "Why am I . . . why . . . I seem to have collapsed . . ."

For a few moments Dear Uncle stared blankly around, until he remembered what had been going on. He turned his head toward where the scattered fragments of the glass carboy were lying; sud-denly his eyes widened and he shouted, "Idiot, don't touch it! . . . Who told you to sweep it up? . . . Somebody take the broom away from that fool."

The servant who'd been about to sweep up the bits of glass froze on the spot. I ran forward and took the broom from his hand. At the same time I bent down and snatched up a bit of blackened fire-cracker and hid it in my fist.

Dear Uncle, who had with difficulty raised himself into a half sit-ting position, said, "Someone go and fetch Cadet Officer Ghiasabadi!"

Once again signs of anxiety were plain on uncle colonel's and his son's faces. Quickly uncle colonel said, "My dear brother, what do you want with the cadet officer? You don't want to be listening to his rubbish . . . and in fact it's been established to our satisfaction that this boy was quite innocent . . ."

Dear Uncle Napoleon interrupted him, "I want to ask the cadet officer his opinion, in his capacity as an expert."

"But why the cadet officer? . . . I myself know much better than him . . ."

Once again Dear Uncle interrupted him and said in a weak voice, "Don't talk rubbish! You spent your whole life in the commis-sariat. You don't know a thing about these matters."

And Mash Qasem took advantage of Dear Uncle's weakness and continued the tale, "Besides the Master knows better than everyone . . . me and the Master grew up among artillery and rifles and gunpowder . . . God bless them times! The English themselves, if they got somethin' stuck in the barrels of their artillery, they'd send for the Master . . . eh, what times they were and no mistake . . . it's like it was yesterday . . . I remember in the Battle of Mamasani we had a gunner and if you said to him hit Kahrizak he'd hit Ghiasabad . . . he'd wasted all the shells and there was just one shell left . . . the Master, God pre-serve him, came down like a lion behind that gun . . . he took aim himself . . . and all at once all the tents and flags and banners of the English went up like smoke . . . then when we went forward we saw how the shell had landed smack in the middle of the English tablecloth . . . their bowl of stew and the chicken and rice was all in tiny bits . . ."

His voice choking with anger, uncle colonel said, "Mash Qasem, there's a limit to how much rubbish one can talk . . ."

Mash Qasem was very cheeky when it came to defending his master, and he yelled, "You mean the Master don't know how to fire artillery . . . you mean he don't know nothin' at all . . . you mean the Master's war with the English is all a lot of hot air?"

Uncle colonel said, emphasizing each word, "When did I say such a thing? . . . I meant that now is not the time for such talk . . ."

Fortunately this argument did not have time to develop. Holding their baby, Cadet Officer Ghiasabadi entered, followed by Qamar.

The cadet officer no longer bore any resemblance to the palsied functionary of a year ago. Although he continued to smoke opium as before, his complexion and appearance and spirits had improved a great deal. He was wearing a purple striped suit. The starched collar on his shirt shone. He had trained long strands of hair from his temples over his scalp so that his baldness was no longer so obvious. Qamar, too, looked better than before. She had lost a little weight. In her eyes there was a glitter of happiness, the enjoyment of good fortune.

Asadollah Mirza shook Dear Uncle Napoleon and said, "Sir, sir . . . the cadet officer's come. Open your eyes."

Dear Uncle opened his eyes a little and said in a weak voice, "Cadet Officer, today there was an explosion in this house . . . perhaps the noise of it could be heard in your house . . . as you're an expert in these matters I want to you to examine the area and tell me what kind of explosives were used."

"Very strange I didn't hear the noise . . . though our house is quite a distance from here and I was taking a nap . . ."

Mash Qasem said, "God blind their squinty eyes . . . and save us from them there English . . ."

It seemed that he wanted in this way to give the cadet officer a hint as to how he was to proceed, but the cadet officer said in stern tones, "Silence! . . . it's a condition that you do not interfere with my work . . . Qamar dear, take Ali and I'll get down to work."

The cadet officer put the baby in Qamar's arms, took a magnifying glass out of his pocket and started examining the fragments of glass. Qamar's son was a really beautiful child. Although the whole family insisted for one reason or another that he looked just like the cadet officer's sister, on account of the roundness of his face, he bore a striking resemblance to Dustali Khan.

Dustali Khan's absence from the group was noticeable. Two or three months after Qamar's marriage to Cadet Officer Ghiasabadi, the poor fool had used every means he could think of to get the cadet officer to honor his promise and divorce Qamar. But the cadet officer had so stolen Qamar's heart away that the strongest swordsman in the land could not have separated them, especially since the cadet officer had got wind of the extent of Qamar's inheritance and he wasn't going to let such a juicy morsel as that get away.

Despite the fact that they had once given him a considerable amount of money to persuade him to stick to his promise, at the last moment Qamar had made such a fuss that the whole plan had collapsed. The poor child had fallen deeply in love with the cadet officer. Under the influence of all Qamar's kindness the cadet officer too had gradually become very fond of her. And then there was the fact that the cadet officer's mother and sister had been the reason why Dustali Khan and Aziz al-Saltaneh had quit their house and set up home in another house which they owned in the same area. Aziz al-Saltaneh had felt obliged to keep up her relationship with her daughter and son-in-law, but Dustali Khan was out for the blood of the cadet officer and his family. This was especially so because, contrary to the cadet officer's initial pretence of impotence due to his loss of the relevant member, he had clearly demonstrated that he was sexually wholly potent. Not only did Qamar appear to be satisfied with him, but certain of the neighboring women who had normally been part of Dustali Khan's entourage also seemed to be satisfied with him. It was even whispered about that the cadet officer enjoyed a special relationship with Tahereh, the wife of Shir Ali.

The cadet officer suddenly paused and raised his head, "Let me see now! . . . Who heard the explosion before everyone else?"

Uncle colonel, who was like a wounded bear sitting silent on the steps, said, "What has that got to do with it?"

"I asked who was closer than everyone else to the site of the explosion and heard the noise before everyone else?"

Mash Qasem answered for him, "Well now, why should I lie? To the grave it's ah . . . ah . . ."

And then, pointing at Puri and me, he went on, "With my own eyes I didn't see nothin' but I heard the noise . . . seems like these two young masters here heard it before me . . ."

The cadet officer turned to Puri. "What was the noise you heard? Was it like the sound of an ordinary firecracker or like something else . . ."

"Like the noise of an ordinary firecracker but . . ."

I hurriedly interrupted him, "No, it was nothing like the noise of a firecracker . . . it was just like the noise of a bomb."

The cadet officer whirled round to me. "Where have you heard the noise of a bomb? . . . Answer, quick, now, immediately, at the double!"

"In those war films they show in the cinema . . . you know, newsreels of the war."

Puri said angrily, "He's talking nonsense, it was nothing like the noise of . . ."

I didn't let him finish, "No, he doesn't know what he's talking about. You can ask whatsaname who was here . . . ask whatsaname . . ."

"Ask who? Answer! Quick, now, at the double!"

Puri realized who I was referring to, and to shut me up he said in a flustered way, "Well, it was a bit like the noise of a bomb . . . like this Boom! Boom! . . ."

But the cadet officer wouldn't let go. "Speak! You said we could ask who? Who? Quick, now, at the double!"

I'd no choice but to prevaricate and said, "Ask Mash Qasem . . . he was very close by . . ."

Uncle colonel yelled, "Sir, how long is this ridiculous spectacle going to go on for? Leave us to go about our business."

In imitation of his former superior, Deputy Taymur Khan, the cadet officer shouted, "Silence! Speaking is forbidden during the period of the investigation! . . . I mean till I've asked a question . . . Mash Qasem! Speak! What kind of a noise did you hear?"

Mash Qasem raised his eyebrows and answered, "Well now, why should I lie? To the grave it's ah . . . ah . . . What I heard with my own ears was a noise that . . . you'd think it was artillery and a rifle and a bomb all mixed up together . . . it was somethin' between a rifle and a bomb and the roar of a leopard . . . there was the noise of a balloon mixed up in there too, like it was . . ."

Asadollah cut him off with a laugh, "Moment, wasn't there also a bit of a folk song with a Persian fiddle mixed in as well?"

The cadet officer threw an angry look at him. But the goodwill he felt because of Asadollah Mirza's friendly behavior toward him stopped him from shouting. In a mild tone he said, "Your excellency, would you allow your humble servant to continue his investigations?"

And after once more bending over the ground with his magnifying glass he said in measured tones, "It is very clear . . . this bomb was of the kind that they refer to as a 'grenade' . . ."

Wide-eyed, Dear Uncle Napoleon half sat up and asked violently, "Made where?"

The cadet officer scratched his head and said, "Well now . . . that's a bit . . . I mean it was either made in Belgium or made in England . . . I mean there was a time when the English had a lot of these . . ."

Dear Uncle Napoleon once again fell back on the cushion that had been placed beneath his head and said, "Now do you see? . . . Now do you understand . . . ? Now has it been proved to you who are so certain that I don't understand anything? Are you still unsure? Is the English hostility toward me still all a fantasy? As Napoleon once said, 'The one thing that is limitless is stupidity.'"

Dear Uncle's voice was getting gradually louder and louder. Her voice trembling, Layli cried out, "Daddy, don't get angry, it's not good for you . . . please, for my sake, don't get angry!"

But Dear Uncle's emotion was not to be calmed down. "When I, poor devil that I am, say something, shout something, scream something, not one person bothers to listen. Not one person wants to understand the truth, not one person pays attention . . ."

The door and windows shook with Dear Uncle's yells, foam appeared at the corner of his lips. "But . . . but . . . the English will not get me . . . I shall smash them into pieces . . . I shall consume them with fire . . . let them throw bombs, let them throw grenades . . . ach." Dear Uncle's eyes closed; his body shook with spasms for a few moments and then he fainted again.

General confusion ensued. Voices were raised on every side, and Asadollah Mirza's rang out over them all, "What the hell do you think you're doing? Do you want to kill the old man? . . . Mash Qasem, run and fetch Dr. Naser al-Hokama."

As he was running toward the door to the street Mash Qasem said, "Didn't I say your excellency should've let me do away with 'em . . . this lot are the Master's enemies . . ."

A few minutes passed with the confused voices of everyone present and the sound of Layli's sobs, until Dr. Naser al-Hokama entered carrying his bag. "Your good health, your good health, what has happened?"

The doctor's examination took a few minutes Everyone stared silently at his mouth. Finally he lifted his head and said, "Your good health, his heartbeat is irregular and we must immediately get the Master to the hospital . . ."

"Isn't it dangerous to move him in this state?"

"At any rate, the danger is less than if we just sit on our hands and stare at him. I'll give him an injection now, and then we can take him . . . get a car ready."

Two people went for the car and the doctor busied himself sterilizing a syringe. Layli went on crying. Dear Uncle's wife, who had arrived home a few moments earlier, was beating herself on the head and chest.

Asadollah came over to where I was standing to one side, silently hanging my head and feeling guilty; he muttered, "Damn you, lad! Because you aren't up to one unimportant little trip to San Francisco, you see what a fine mess you've made!"

"Uncle Asadollah, how was I to know that . . . ?"

A smile played about Asadollah Mirza's lips; he said quietly, "Go and get a whole chest of grenades together . . . because in three months time that Arab horse is going to be well again and you'll have to explode another grenade . . . and three months after that another, and gradually you'll have to increase their force and throw three or four together."

I hung my head again and said, "Uncle Asadollah, I've made a firm decision to . . ."

"To take a little trip to San Francisco? Bravo, well done, congratulations . . . couldn't you have made this decision two days earlier so that you wouldn't have brought that old man to this sorry state?"

"No, Uncle Asadollah, I . . ."

"You mean two days ago your luggage wasn't ready and now it's ready? That's still something to be thankful for."

"No, no, no, why do you keep joking? It's another decision. It's not San Francisco . . ."

"Los Angeles?"

I was ready to scream. With difficulty I controlled myself and said in a choked voice, "I've decided to kill myself."

Asadollah Mirza glanced at me and smiled, "Bravo, well done, this is an excellent decision. And when will this auspicious event take place?"

"I mean it, Uncle Asadollah."

"Moment, moment, so you've chosen to take the easy way out . . . people always go after the easy way . . . there are many for whom it's easier to go on a little pilgrimage to the cemetery than to go to San Francisco. . . . Well, that's how people are. There's nothing you can do when as the brigadier says your nature's all *bahot* wilted and there is being no San Francisco . . . so the pilgrimage to the cemetery it is."

"Uncle Asadollah, you are standing in front of someone whose mind is completely made up. Don't make a joke out of it."

"Right, so, let's see, have you chosen how you're going to do it?"

"Not yet, but I'll find a way."

"Drop by and see me tonight, I'll find some method in the house for you that won't be too much trouble or too painful."

And then with a serious and sad expression he added, "God rest your soul! You were a nice young man! Have them write on your tombstone: 'Oh good people now in this world, or yet to come to this world—he who lies here in this earth is I, who never made it to San Francisco . . . ' Perhaps in the other world they'll look out for you and send you to San Francisco there."

At this moment Dr. Naser al-Hokama's voice could be heard, "If the car had come earlier we could have moved him by now . . . the injection has brought him round a bit but we have to think of something more fundamental."

A few moments later they announced that a rented car was ready by the door. On the doctor's orders they had got a travelling cot ready. They carefully laid Dear Uncle down on it. Mash Qasem and two of the servants lifted it up from underneath.

In this way they carried Dear Uncle close to the door leading from the garden; when they put the bed down so that they could raise the patient's body and place him in the car, he suddenly opened his eyes. He stared around with an uncomprehending look and then said in a weak voice, "Where am I? . . . What's happened? . . . Where are you taking me?"

Uncle colonel bent his head down to him and said, "My dear brother, you collapsed. The doctor said we're to take you to the hospital."

"The hospital? Take me to the hospital?"

"Your good health, your good health, it's nothing serious but it's possible that some equipment we don't have here might be necessary. Perhaps you might need some oxygen . . ."

Dear Uncle was quiet for a moment; then he yelled, "Well, you can think again about taking me to the hospital! Who told you to take me to the hospital? You want to hand the sheep over to the wolf, do you? You want to deliver me into the hands of the English, do you?"

Dear Uncle's voice became mixed in with those of his relatives. Virtually everyone thought that despite Dear Uncle's objections they should take him to the hospital, by force if necessary. In the middle of this confused to-ing and fro-ing my father and mother suddenly came in from the street. My mother screamed, "God strike me dead, what's going on, brother?"

Once again a confusion of voices was raised in explanation; as soon as Dear Uncle Napoleon, who was still lying on the bed, saw my father he shouted, "Help me, brother . . . these idiots want to kill me. In this town where the English are waiting like wolves to get their hands on me, they want to take me to the hospital."

In a firm voice my father said, "Then they should think again! With the English here in the city it's quite inadvisable to take the Master to the hospital. Have the doctor come to the house."

Doctor Naser al-Hokama said, "Your good health, but it's possible some medical equipment that we don't have here might be necessary."

In the same decisive tones my father said, "Bring all the equipment to the house and I'll pay for it."

Infinite gratitude welled up in Dear Uncle's gaze. Calmly he closed his eyes.

TWENTY-TWO

"Hello."

"Hello, Layli. How are you?"

"Come, come over here, I've something to tell you."

Layli was speaking very quickly. She had turned pale, and an unusual degree of anxiety was visible in her black eyes.

I hurried after her. We reached the sweetbrier arbor.

"Tell me, Layli, what's happened? How's Dear Uncle . . . ?"

"Mash Qasem has sent you a message."

"Mash Qasem?"

"Yes! It seems that, God forbid, daddy's losing his mind . . . this morning he suddenly went after Mash Qasem with the shotgun and wanted to kill the poor thing . . ."

My eyes wide with astonishment, I interrupted her, "Kill him? Why? Whatever has Mash Qasem done?"

"Daddy says he's an English spy."

I nearly burst out laughing. But Layli's worried face stopped the breath in my throat. "What? . . . Mash Qasem's an English spy? You're joking?"

"No, it's very serious . . . he went after him with the shotgun. If the poor thing hadn't taken to his heels he might have been killed."

"Now what's happening?"

"Mash Qasem's run away from daddy . . . for now he's gone into the kitchen and locked the door on himself, but he's so afraid of daddy he daren't come out . . . he asked me in secret from behind the door to tell you to go straight to your father and to Asadollah Mirza to tell them to come and help him . . ."

"You didn't say anything?"

"I wanted to say something but daddy shouted at me so violently I was terrified . . . he's pacing up and down in the yard with the shotgun, saying things I've no idea what they mean."

"All right, you go and watch out till I can tell them."

It was a Friday morning. My father had left the house before the rest of us had woken up. I hurried off toward Asadollah Mirza's house.

About two weeks had passed since the day I had set off the firecrackers in uncle colonel's yard. Since that time Dear Uncle Napoleon had been confined to his bed for a few days. A heart specialist and a nerve specialist were keeping him under observation in the house. The heart specialist was of the sincere belief that the cause of Dear Uncle's illness was a heart problem, and the nerve specialist said that the heart specialist didn't understand anything and the cause of the illness was a nervous problem. After a week the various tranquilizing drugs and medicines he was being given began to take effect and brought Dear Uncle gradually back to health, but, apart from my father and occasionally Asadollah Mirza, he wouldn't let anyone near him, and whichever of his relatives went to see him, he pretended to be asleep.

Usually while he was under the influence of the tranquilizing drugs he was calm, but later he would start shouting and screaming. He saw lackeys of the English everywhere.

More than my feeling of sympathy for Dear Uncle, I was upset on Layli's behalf, because every time I saw her her eyes were filled with tears. Layli had a limitless love for her father. Layli's emotional turmoil had made me forget my own difficulties and troubles.

Asadollah Mirza was asleep and his old servant didn't want to let me in the house. But I begged and pleaded so much that she let me in.

When Asadollah Mirza heard my voice he called out from within his bedroom, "Sit down in the living room for a minute till I come."

"Uncle Asadollah, open the door. It's about something very important."

"Moment, I'm not in a suitable state, just wait till . . ."

I interrupted him, "Someone's life's in danger. It doesn't matter. Open the door and let me in."

"I said sit down in the living room till I come . . . by the time you've got the stuff together to kill yourself I'll be there."

Asadollah Mirza was referring to what I had said to him a few days before . . . I'd no choice but to obey, especially since I heard him whispering and realized he wasn't alone. I sat in the living room and waited for him; during those few days I had been so taken up with worrying about Layli's state that I had forgotten the suggestion I'd made to Asadollah Mirza that day—that I'd kill myself.

A few minutes later Asadollah Mirza came into the living room wearing a red silk dressing-gown. He didn't give me a chance to speak.

"God willing, the auspicious event will be today? I thought that you'd finally been to San Francisco and changed your mind! You're completely right! When a man doesn't go to San Francisco he's got no business being in this world. The sooner he gets out of it, the better."

"No, Uncle Asadollah, Layli is really upset and I haven't been able to think about my . . ."

"Well, that's obvious. The girl has her expectations . . . a bit of San Francisco, a bit of Los Angeles . . . she's suffocating in this town."

"Uncle Asadollah, it's about a problem of Mash Qasem's. Poor Mash Qasem . . ."

"Moment, moment . . . Mash Qasem and San Francisco? That fellow from Ghiasabad's stolen a march on you too?"

"No, Dear Uncle wants to kill Mash Qasem."

"Because he went to San Francisco?"

"No, because he says he's an English spy."

Asadollah Mirza gave a great guffaw of laughter, "He must have found a telegram that Churchill had sent from London to Ghiasabad in Mash Qasem's pocket."

"I don't know how it happened, but today Dear Uncle suddenly went after him with a shotgun. And he was so afraid he hid himself in the kitchen and locked himself in. He pleaded with Layli from behind the door that I go and fetch you and my father . . . because Dear Uncle is waiting for him in the yard, with the shotgun."

"All right, all right, off you go and I'll be there in an hour."

"Uncle Asadollah, will you let me stay so that we can go together, because my father's gone out of the house, too? It might be too late."

Asadollah Mirza scratched his head and said, "Well, I can't really . . . they're supposed to . . . I mean the builder's supposed to come, the kitchen ceiling's beginning to collapse . . ."

"Uncle Asadollah, say that the builder should wait till you get back. It's a matter of life and death."

At this moment I heard a woman's high-pitched voice coming from the direction of the bedroom, "Asi . . . Asi . . . where have you gone?"

I said, "Uncle Asadollah, the builder seems to have arrived . . . to be honest, I think I recognize the sound of that builder's voice."

Asadollah Mirza pushed me toward the living room door and said, "Don't talk nonsense! This builder's not from this town . . . go in the yard while I put some clothes on."

It seemed he was worried lest I hear the builder's voice again. I walked anxiously up and down in the yard for a few minutes, until Asadollah Mirza was ready and we set off together for the house.

"By the way, what news of the Arab horse? Did your firecrackers have any effect on him or not?"

"I don't know, Uncle Asadollah . . . all I know is that he's going regularly to Dr. Naser al-Hokama again."

"For as long as Dr. Naser al-Hokama's treating him, you can be sure that Layli's safe. Because Dr. Naser al-Hokama's been treating himself for forty years and there's still no sign of life . . . his first two wives divorced him. And if it wasn't for that donkey Dustali Khan, his present wife would've divorced him too."

"Uncle Asadollah, the doctor has a child by this wife."

"Moment, moment, he didn't give birth to it himself, did he?"

When we reached the door to the garden I saw Layli through the opening; she was waiting anxiously in the garden for our arrival. Asadollah Mirza said to me, "Wait, I'll go first and you come after me, so it won't be obvious why we've come."

Asadollah Mirza went into the inner apartments. Layli and I waited for a moment in the doorway. Dear Uncle Napoleon had his cloak on, and the double-barreled shot gun was in his hand.

Asadollah Mirza made a boisterous entrance, laughing as he did so, "Well, well. You're going hunting are you? The best of luck! Which way are you going?"

Dear Uncle Napoleon turned round and for a moment stared blankly at the newcomer. Asadollah Mirza stopped laughing, "Although I don't recall that this is the hunting season."

Dear Uncle narrowed his eyes and said in a voice quite unlike his normal voice, "It so happens it is the hunting season . . . the season for hunting the spies and lackeys of the English."

Asadollah Mirza pretended to be surprised. "Are you referring to me?"

"No, I'm not saying you are . . . although perhaps . . . one day it might turn out that you're a lackey of theirs, too!"

For a moment he went on staring at him, then he shouted, "But who ever would have thought that the English had bought Qasem? Who'd have thought that Qasem would plunge a dagger in my back?"

"Moment, moment . . . Mash Qasem has betrayed you?"

"And what a betrayal! . . . a hundred times worse than Marshal Grouchy's betrayal of Napoleon . . . all Grouchy did was that he could have gone to help his benefactor at Waterloo and he didn't. But he didn't then plunge a dagger in his back."

"But sir, just think for a moment . . ."

Asadollah Mirza was about to say something but changed his mind. He seemed to guess that he had to try another tack. "It's very strange. Really, I'd have thought it of anyone except Mash Qasem, to whom you've been so kind."

Asadollah Mirza's sympathy calmed him somewhat, and in a whining tone he said, "O Asadollah, you tell me . . . I feed him and he bites my hand; why? . . . In the wars I risked my own life so many times to save his dirty little life—should someone like that betray me in this way? . . . Why did he have to sell himself to the English?"

"How did you discover his treachery?"

"I'd suspected him . . . this morning I caught him red-handed and he confessed . . . Do you hear me? In his own stuttering voice he confessed that he's a lackey of the English."

At this moment Mash Qasem's voice rang out from behind the solid kitchen door, "The master'd put the shotgun against my heart; he said 'Confess or I'll kill you,' so I did."

When he heard his voice, Dear Uncle began to tremble. He wanted to shout but no sound came from his throat. Asadollah Mirza sat him down on the steps, and Layli called out through her tears, "Daddy dear, don't get angry; it's not good for your heart."

"Run, dear, and get your daddy a glass of water."

The kitchen in Dear Uncle's house, where Mash Qasem had taken refuge, was constructed in a particular way. After you went through the door from the yard you had to go down a few steps. At the bottom of the steps on the right there was the lavatory, on the left was the faucet to the water-storage tank, and straight ahead was the kitchen. In fact, by shutting the door to the yard Mash Qasem had cut off access to the lavatory, the water-storage tank and the kitchen, and I was hopeful that, as the people in the house would need these three places, some way of saving Mash Qasem would be found.

Dear Uncle Napoleon drank the water, and his condition improved a little.

Asadollah Mirza went over to the kitchen door, behind which Mash Qasem was hiding, and called out, "Mash Qasem, Mash Qasem, come out and kiss the master's hand and say you're sorry!"

"I've no objection, you tell the master to promise I'll be safe! I'm the master's servant . . . I'm his to command . . ."

Dear Uncle yelled, "Thieving spy! Say your prayers, either you'll have to die of hunger in there or I'll fill your empty head with lead."

Mash Qasem's voice was heard again, "Master, I swear by the blessed Qamar-e bani Hashem. I've never seen the English in all my life . . . I mean me who's been fightin' with the English for a hundred years, as you yourself have witnessed, how would I . . ."

Asadollah Mirza said, "Mash Qasem, it's no good denying it. The Master's understood everything. You'd do better to ask for forgiveness for your sins."

"But sir, why should I lie? . . . I haven't done nothin'."

Quietly, so that Dear Uncle wouldn't hear, Asadollah Mirza said, "Mash Qasem, don't be so stubborn, just say you were wrong and you're sorry."

"I've spent a lifetime fightin' against the English and now I'm to come and say I've turned into one of their spies? Will God like that? . . . and then how am I to look the folks in Ghiasabad in the eye? The folks in Ghiasabad, who are thirsty for the blood of the English . . . !"

All Asadollah Mirza's good offices in the cause of solving the dispute were in vain. My father, and then uncle colonel and lots of other people, came and conducted lengthy negotiations but no conclusion was reached. The spy continued to claim sanctuary in the kitchen and Dear Uncle continued to be unforgiving and to pace up and down in front of the kitchen, with the shotgun in his hand, cursing him.

I was going back and forth at my wits' end. I heard Asadollah Mirza and my father talking in the garden, "I'm afraid that poor devil Mash Qasem will pass out from fear . . . if he can keep going for another one or two hours perhaps there'll be a way out of all this . . ."

"What way out, your excellency . . . ? The Master's taken complete leave of his senses . . . if you're thinking that because Mash Qasem is in the kitchen and they're going to need the kitchen, then think again! The Master's sent out for *chelo kebab* for everyone."

"Moment, moment, apart from the kitchen, the lavatory's there as well . . . he's sending the people in his house over to your place to do their business. And when he needs to go himself he's going to have to go to your place, and then we can let Mash Qasem get away."

"I don't think that'll work either. He's so obsessed with the English that . . ."

Asadollah Mirza interrupted him, "Since this morning, using as an excuse that he's not very well, I've given him four or five glasses of water to drink; we must await the outcome."

More time passed. Everyone was waiting for the water to have its necessary effect on Dear Uncle's constitution, but Dear Uncle went right on sitting on the steps with the shotgun in his hand, never taking his eyes off the kitchen door. It was around noon that I once more stuck my head round the door to the private apartments; Dear Uncle had stood up and was walking about. I felt I could sense his discomfort; I wanted to run and tell the good news to Asadollah Mirza, who was in our house with my father, but first I had to be sure.

A few minutes passed in this way and then I suddenly heard Dear Uncle's voice, "Naneh Bilqis, bring me that flower-vase of mine."

All my hopes turned to despair. When he heard the news Asadollah Mirza shook his head and said, "We'll have to think of something else . . . the prison warder has seen to his needs on the spot . . . another way occurs to me. It wouldn't be a bad idea to try it . . . you come, too, we'll go together."

My father asked, "And what's my role in this?"

"In fact, your role's the crucial one. Because you're the only person he isn't disgusted with. At the moment the Master needs the whole world to know that the British Empire has nothing else on its mind except destroying him, and no one's as essential as you are for keeping up his morale . . . and anyway, I can't deal with this lunatic alone."

Asadollah Mirza and my father went to find Dear Uncle and I stuck to them like a shadow.

Asadollah Mirza opened the conversation, "You're of course aware that treachery is not a new phenomenon in the world . . . didn't Marshal Ney betray Napoleon?"

Dear Uncle threw Asadollah Mirza an angry look from behind his sunglasses and said, "If Marshall Ney was a traitor, he later washed away all his sins . . . when Napoleon came back from the island of Elba and they sent Ney to fight against him, as soon as he set eyes on his benefactor he dismounted from his horse and kissed Napoleon's hand . . . he placed his sword at his service."

"And then did he serve Napoleon well?"

"Yes, he served him very well . . . he proved his loyalty by his own death."

My father interposed, "In fact this kind of person, the people who are sorry for their treachery, are much more ready to serve and are much more sincere than many others."

Asadollah Mirza said, "Of course it was Napoleon's magnanimity that induced Marshall Ney to sacrifice himself in this way." A calm gradually spread over Dear Uncle's face.

With a faraway gaze in his eyes he said in mild tones, "Yes, I've proved this many times in the wars myself . . . when I used to give an enemy commander quarter, an enemy would suddenly become a sincere friend . . ."

Asadollah Mirza winked at my father and said, "Now, in my opinion this man, too, well, he was mortal . . . he was weak . . . they tricked him . . . It needs a lot of strength for a man to save himself from their snares . . . you yourself, if it hadn't been for your strength and personality, do you think they wouldn't have tricked you?"

"How many times they tried . . . what promises, what stratagems . . . they promised money, they sent women . . . what things they did!"

"Moment, now I've a question. Do you think if it had been anyone else but you he wouldn't have given in? He wouldn't have been tricked?"

"Well, of course, he'd have been tricked . . . without any doubt he'd have been corrupted."

"In that case, what can you expect from a simple villager turned servant? . . . They fooled the poor devil, they tricked him."

In an annoyed tone Dear Uncle said, "But this good-for-nothing isn't prepared honestly and sincerely to confess, to ask for forgiveness, to show that he's sorry."

"What do you mean, sir? . . . The poor devil's imprisoned in the kitchen, you're waiting behind the door with a shotgun in your hand. What do you expect? You give him permission to come out, I'll say a couple of words to him, and you'll see that he's really sorry."

After a few moments' silence Dear Uncle raised his head and muttered, "Very well then; we'll try it."

Everyone breathed a sigh of relief. They took the shotgun into a room, and after Mash Qasem had been assured that the situation was safe he drew back the bolts on the door. Asadollah Mirza went into the kitchen. After a few minutes Mash Qasem emerged from the kitchen with his head bowed, and Asadollah Mirza followed him out.

Dear Uncle stood up and stared motionless into midair.

Asadollah Mirza said, "Sir, will you give him permission to kiss your hand and ask for forgiveness?"

Dear Uncle was silent for a few moments; then he answered without looking at him, "First he has to answer my questions."

"He'll answer whatever questions you ask."

Dear Uncle was only talking to Asadollah Mirza, "First he has to say where the English contacted him."

"Did you hear, Mash Qasem? Where did the English contact you?"

Without raising his head Mash Qasem said, "Well sir, why should I lie? To the grave it's ah . . . ah . . . in the . . . I mean . . . the truth is, in the baker's."

"At what time?"

"Well . . . I mean . . . last Tuesday . . . no, no, good heavens, it was Wednesday."

"How did they contact you?"

Asadollah Mirza repeated Dear Uncle's question for Mash Qasem. For a moment Mash Qasem gazed helplessly at Dear Uncle's immobile form, then he said, "Well now, why should I lie? To the grave it's ah . . . ah . . . I was buyin' bread. All of a sudden I sees an Englishman in the alleyway lookin' at me out of the corner of his eye . . . every now and then he winked at me . . . to tell the truth at first I thought, God strike me dumb, that he fancied me . . . 'cause accordin' to a man in our town, he used to say that . . ."

Without looking at him Dear Uncle said sternly, "Stick to the point!"

Asadollah Mirza slapped Mash Qasem on the back and said, "Stick to the point, Mash Qasem! Say how they got in touch with you."

"Well, they just did . . . before I could turn round they'd done it."

"How much money did they promise you for killing me?"

"God in heaven! Me kill the Master? God cripple my arm if it crossed my mind!"

Asadollah Mirza hurriedly interrupted him, "No, no sir, for the time being there was no mention of killing. He just had to pass them information about you . . ."

"And what has he decided now?"

"Well now, sir . . ."

Asadollah Mirza signalled to him and said, "The Master means are you sorry or are you going to work for the English?"

"Well now, sir, why should I lie? I'm damned if I'll work for them English . . . I'll give 'em two good cuss words and send 'em packin' off to their ancestors . . . I'll tell 'em I've eaten the Master's bread, that I'm the Master's humble servant . . ."

"When will you give them this answer?"

Mash Qasem suddenly exploded, "I swear by the blessed Qamar-e bani Hashem that if I . . ."

Asadollah Mirza interrupted him and shouted, "Answer, Mash Qasem! When will you give them their answer? Today or later?"

"Well sir . . . I mean to say . . . today, then . . . right now."

"Now go and kiss the Master's hand."

Dear Uncle was gazing into space and his tall form continued to stand motionless on the same spot. I'm quite sure that he saw himself as being in Napoleon's clothes and situation when Napoleon's army came face to face with Marshall Ney's.

Mash Qasem hesitantly went toward him. He bent over and kissed his hand. Dear Uncle opened his arms and pressed him to his chest. "I forgive you because of your past service . . . of course, on condition that you are really sorry for what you have done, and that you will devote your remaining strength to the service of your benefactor!"

A teardrop glittered in each of Dear Uncle Napoleon's eyes.

⚜ ⚜ ⚜

An hour later my father and Asadollah Mirza were busy chatting in the sitting room of our house.

"I am very worried about the Master . . . little by little his behavior's becoming quite crazy. We really have to think of something."

"Well, your excellency, I'm just astonished that someone with his wits about him should get to the state where he behaves in this way."

"Moment, it's very strange that you shouldn't know why he's got into this state! But all the same it's happened and we have to think of something . . . it seems as though the hostility of the English has become an absolute necessity for him."

"And the existence of spies and traitors, too . . ."

"I think the only way he can be cured now is for the English to arrest him and imprison him for a while."

"But how can we make them . . . as if we could force the English to arrest a retired officer from Liakhoff's Cossack regiment. Don't they have anything better to do?"

Asadollah Mirza shifted his position on the sofa and said, "I've thought of a good idea which I'll put to you now . . . get up, lad, and shut the living room door."

My father said to me, "And leave the room."

"No, let him stay. Your son's not a stranger. Perhaps he'll even be able to help us. But of course he mustn't talk about it to anyone."

This was the first time that a serious exchange of views was to be held in my presence. Asadollah Mirza said, "In my opinion something must be done as soon as possible. The old man's going crazy. Today poor old Mash Qasem very nearly lost his life because of his master's fantasies."

My father said, "I've already said two or three times to the colonel that he should arrange for a consultation with psychiatric specialists, and if not . . ."

Asadollah Mirza interrupted him, "Moment, don't even think of it; if the Master went and stood stark naked blowing a trumpet in the middle of Tupkhaneh Square, it's out of the question that the colonel and the rest of the family would agree to consult a psychiatrist. Is it thinkable that the Master, who's the son of the late lamented Master and the grandson of the family's Grandfather, should go crazy? God forbid, don't even mention it!"

"Then we'll have to wait until he kills someone for being an English spy, and they take him off to jail . . . Just think of it, if Mash Qasem had been a bit less quick off the mark today his corpse would now be in the public mortuary and the Master would be in jail . . . the government takes no account of late lamented grandfathers and so forth. They throw murderers in jail."

Asadollah Mirza shook his head and said, "In any case it's as I said. Forget all thoughts of psychiatrists. If we want to help him we have to think of something else."

"Yes but what else, your excellency? If you're thinking that Churchill should come and ask the Master's pardon, I don't think there's a chance of that at the moment."

"Not Churchill, but if a representative of the English came . . ."

My father interrupted him, "The commander of the British army in Iran, for example, or the minister for the navy?"

"No. If you'll let me finish. If we can arrange it so that, for example, someone comes on behalf of the English to negotiate with him, maybe . . ."

Once again my father interrupted him, "You're joking, aren't you, your excellency? It's true the Master's losing his wits but he's not such a child that he'd fall for something like that."

"A person who's ready to write a letter promising to give his life for Hitler wouldn't be such a child?"

My father's mouth dropped open. Asadollah Mirza went on with a smile, "When the late Grandfather is eating *ab-gusht* with Jeanette McDonald, can't Churchill's representative come and see the Master?"

My father began stammering, "You mean . . . you . . . what I mean is . . . but in fact . . ."

Asadollah Mirza laughed and said, "Yes, I too am in the know . . ."

"Who told you?"

"The Master himself mentioned it once. But never mind all that."

My father gave a forced laugh and said, "So we had a little joke once . . . the Master didn't believe in it . . ."

"Oh yes, he did, he believed it all too well . . . but we'll leave that aside for now. The important point is this: are your really ready for us to help this old man, to lessen the trials and tribulations of the four or five days of life that he still has left to him?"

My father said, in accents of heartfelt sincerity, "On the souls of my children . . . on the soul of my father, I have no animosity toward him left in me, and I sincerely hope that his health will return to normal."

"Good, in that case I think we can do something. The colonel wasn't at home but I left a message that he's to come here when he gets back, and we can discuss the matter together. I've thought that if we could arrange things so that an Englishman would come and negotiate with the Master, and assure him that the English have forgiven him his sins, then the situation would change completely."

My father shook his head and said, "I don't think that even if Churchill himself came and handed him a signed affidavit it would penetrate the Master's head that the English have forgotten about their hostility toward him. Never mind the reality of the situation. Imagine someone who in countless lengthy wars has destroyed thousands of English individuals, dragging them through blood and filth . . . who has ruined all their colonial ambitions . . . and then this person is to believe that all of a sudden the English are going to overlook his sins against them?"

"Moment, moment, but if the English have another major enemy it's possible that for a while, until the end of the war, for example, even if it's not sincerely and from the heart, they'd announce a ceasefire. At all events it'll do no harm to try."

"But your excellency, where are you going to find a representative of the English?"

"Through that Brigadier Maharat Khan, the Indian . . . I've heard he's supposed to come back from the south in the next two or three days. I can somehow or other get him to agree to provide us with a representative of the English."

A light went on in my brain. The familiar voice I had heard that morning in Asadollah Mirza's house rang in my ears once again. I murmured, "Uncle Asadollah, did you hear that from the builder?"

Asadollah Mirza gave me a furious look and hurriedly went on with what he had been saying, "This brigadier has business dealings with the English and that's why he makes regular trips down south . . ."

At this moment uncle colonel came in. When he had heard what had happened that day and Asadollah Mirza had put his plan before him, he said angrily, "But do we have to discuss the matter in front of the children?"

Asadollah Mirza slapped me on the back and said, "Moment, colonel sir, first of all, this lad isn't a child anymore. He's a clever young man. Secondly, if we prevented a calamity from happening today, it was through this young man's good offices. In any case he's a trustworthy person, and we need him."

Uncle colonel said nothing further on this subject, but he began to object to Asadollah Mirza's plan. He was of the opinion that such an important personage from such a prominent family should not be played with in this way. Asadollah Mirza said, "Moment, colonel, you weren't here today and you didn't see what a close shave with danger the Master had. Either we have to have the Master confined to a psychiatric hospital, or we . . ."

Uncle colonel angrily interrupted him, "Don't talk nonsense, Asadollah. I'd rather empty a bullet into my brain than agree that we take my older brother to a psychiatric hospital. The reputation of a hundred-year-old noble family is no joke. I'm ready to give my life for my brother's health, but think of something reasonable!"

After a great deal of discussion and argument uncle colonel began gradually to soften. But he said in despairing tones, "The point is that I don't think my older brother will believe that the English have suddenly and so easily forgiven him for what he's done to them."

"Moment, moment, we'll go into every aspect of the matter, of course, if we can find someone to do it. First he'll lay down strict conditions, and then through our intervention he'll gradually become more accommodating and then finally he'll agree that if the Master doesn't oppose the English, or sabotage their efforts, until the end of the war, he'll pass the Master's file up to a higher level with a positive recommendation."

Uncle colonel thought about it, then said, "What excuse are you going to use to my brother to start all this? Are you just going to say that the English have suddenly decided to get in touch with him?"

"We'll say that since the war's been going badly for them, the English have decided to come to an accord with their enemies in every country. Leave it to me to satisfy the Master on that point."

At this moment Puri arrived looking for uncle colonel and said that a guest had come for him. After uncle had left my father said, "Your excellency, I will spare no efforts, but I still have to say that I've no faith in this scheme of yours. The Master I see before me now has decided on his own fate. The English have to persecute him, and finally they have to destroy him, as they did Napoleon; I can assure you that even now he can clearly see the hills and plains of the island of St. Helena."

I accompanied Asadollah Mirza to the door. When we reached the street he took hold of my ear and said, "You little devil, what was all that about the builder? Is this a time to be gossiping in front of people?"

"I swear to God I didn't mean anything, Uncle Asadollah, I just . . ."

"Damn you and your 'I just' . . . Brigadier Maharat Khan is a very good friend of mine . . ."

"But I've never seen you with the brigadier . . ."

"That's because I'm afraid that Dear Uncle of yours will say I'm an English spy, too."

"But that night you took Lady Maharat Khan home in the carriage . . ."

"Moment, the brigadier had gone on a trip and he entrusted his wife to me . . . and I'm supposed to leave her to rot in her house? I took her to a restaurant and gave her an ice cream."

"Just an ice cream, Uncle Asadollah?"

"Yes, just an ice cream. Impossible that the notion of San Francisco with a woman who has a home and a husband would even cross my mind. Do you understand what I'm saying? It's impossible and it's out of the question! Praise God I can't be accused of things like that!"

"Uncle Asadollah, wasn't the seventeenth lesson you gave me that when there's a chance of San Francisco, you set out first and then you see who your travelling companion is?"

"You're a really cheeky child, you know! I say something, so you have to repeat it . . . ? All your strength is in your jaw. As the brigadier would say, your virility's *bahot* wilted but your jaw is being *bahot* powerful!"

"Uncle Asadollah, do you think the scheme you've worked out for Dear Uncle will come to anything?"

"You should pray for a good result, because you and your father are the sole basic cause of all this trouble. Your father's sent the old man crazy because they told him he was a country bumpkin with no background, and you've gone around setting off firecrackers and gunpowder because you're not up to a trip to San Francisco. Between you you've really driven the poor devil out of his mind."

❖ ❖ ❖

One evening three or four days later Asadollah Mirza, accompanied by uncle colonel, came to see my father. He took me by the arm and had me come into the living room with them.

"It looks as though we're about to get the show on the road. I had a long conversation with the brigadier. Poor devil, he's full of goodwill but he says he can't find an Englishman. All he has is an Indian friend who's a corporal in the British army and he can convince him to be part of our scheme. For a consideration, of course!"

Uncle colonel said nothing.

My father shook his head and said, "It seems very unlikely to me that the Master would be ready to negotiate with a corporal, and an Indian at that. What does this Indian look like? Would it be possible to pass him off as an Englishman?"

"It wouldn't be possible to pass him off as a Baluchi tribesman, never mind as an Englishman. From what I heard he's a dyed-in-the-wool milky-coffee-colored Sikh."

"But your excellency, even supposing we can get the Master to meet with an Indian, what about his rank? The Master's not going to accept anyone less than a general."

"That doesn't matter. The Master doesn't know the ranks in the British army, we'll say he's a colonel."

"Have you talked to the Master at all, your excellency?"

"I've prepared the ground in his mind. I've seen him a couple of times and said that in every country—friendly, neutral and occupied—the English are making every effort to get their enemies on their side."

"What reaction did he show?"

"Of course he made a great fuss and said that if they got in touch with him, he'd never go along with them. But when it gets to the point, I think he'll agree."

"Then you haven't talked about the Master himself yet?"

Asadollah Mirza said, "I've made hints. He said that he would never trust the English and their promises and that if they were supposed to send a representative to him one day, first he'd give orders that the man be disarmed and then he'd hide Mash Qasem behind the curtain with the shotgun so that if the representative were about to try anything he could jump out and send him packing."

"Now would you just consider, your excellency? I'm afraid that this is going to mean trouble for all of us. If this is how it's going to be, suppose the Indian puts his hand in his pocket to get his handkerchief out to blow his nose on, and the Master orders Mash Qasem to fire. Do you know what kind of hell will break loose for us then?"

Asadollah Mirza thought for a moment and said, "In my opinion we'll have to put Mash Qasem in the picture, too."

After a few minutes of discussion Asadollah Mirza asked me to go and find Mash Qasem.

"Good evenin' to you."

"Good evening, Mash Qasem. How are you? No illnesses, God willing?"

Asadollah Mirza insisted that he sit down. After a great deal of protest, Mash Qasem finally knelt on the ground in a corner of the living room. "Listen, Mash Qasem. I know you love the Master very much and I know you're very upset about this illness of his."

"Well sir, I don't believe in them doctors' medicines. It's like the Master's insides are overheated somehow. There was a man in our town who . . ."

"Listen, Mash Qasem! For some time now the Master's been really living in a fantasy world. That day, just because of some silly fancy of his, he nearly killed you, God forbid! Just think of it, someone in their right mind would never go and make such an accusation against you, that you had agreed with the English that you'd spy on the Master . . . and so in this case it's clear that the Master is not at all well. Don't you agree?"

"Well sir, why should I lie? To the grave it's ah . . . ah . . . I don't want to go against what you're sayin', but you can't be too careful with them English."

Asadollah Mirza looked at him in astonishment and said, "Mash Qasem, you at least know that all that kind of talk is nonsense."

"How would I know that, sir?"

Impatiently Asadollah Mirza said, "But Mash Qasem, all right, so the English are bad, vicious, evil—but is it true what he said about you, that you were cozying up to the English?"

With his head bowed, Mash Qasem answered, "Well sir, that's not too far from the truth neither."

My father broke into the conversation and said angrily, "So the English did contact you?"

"Well sir, why should I lie? To the grave it's ah . . . ah . . . If you want the truth, yes."

Uncle colonel joined in for the first time. In a voice clearly affected by anger he said, "Qasem, we didn't come together here to make jokes. Don't talk rubbish!"

"Right sir, if you think I'm talkin' rubbish, then it's better I don't talk at all . . . now can I go and water the flowers?"

"Moment, moment, colonel sir, let him have his say."

Then he turned to Mash Qasem and said mildly, "Say what you have to say, but make it quick because we've a lot of business to get through."

"Well sir, I've not got nothin' to say. You asked somethin' and I gave you the answer."

Asadollah Mirza was ready to explode but he tried to control himself. "But Mash Qasem, how is it possible the English contacted you? The Master got some crazy notion into his head, he mentioned it and you swore it was a lie . . ."

"Well now, why should I lie? To the grave it's ah . . . ah . . . The lie wasn't a lie neither."

"What? But Mash Qasem, didn't I myself tell you to confess! In the kitchen, didn't I tell you what to say? And now you're telling me that . . ."

Mash Qasem interrupted him again, "Well sir, the truth is, you told me but I didn't tell a lie neither."

"You mean the English really got in touch with you? But Mash Qasem, just think about it for a moment. Why are you saying such senseless things? Where did they get in touch? Who got in touch? Whatever did they get in touch for!"

"You won't let me talk, sir!"

Uncle colonel yelled, "For goodness sake, say what you have to say and we'll shut up. How did they get in touch?"

Mash Qasem took one of his knees in his arms and said, "Well now, sir, why should I lie? To the grave it's ah . . . ah . . . They've tried a hundred times till now to get me on their side . . . I remember in Ghiasabad one time an Englishman came . . ."

Asadollah Mirza said in a voice which he tried to keep calm, "Mash Qasem, please leave the time in Ghiasabad aside and tell us about this time."

"Right you are then . . . this time . . . meanin' a few days ago, well, one day I'd gone to the baker's, and I saw an Englishman walkin' up and down two or three times outside the shop. He was lookin' at me with them blind squinty eyes of his like you'd think I was a fourteen-year-old girl . . . At first I says to myself it's because he's squinty-eyed and he's lookin' at someone else, then he came into the baker's and he asked the feller behind the scales somethin'. When I came out he kept pace with me . . . it was like, savin' your reverence, savin' your reverence, he was after me. Then when we got to our house he said in a voice that . . . may you never see such a day, sir, his voice was like you'd think it was a leopard snorin' . . . and such language he used, his language was like between Turkish and Rashti and Khorasani . . . he asked me 'Are you from this place?' . . . I didn't answer but in my heart I said God strike all them English blind . . . I dashed in the house . . . But I watched him through the crack in the door . . . I saw he went this way and that a bit . . . he looked at the doors to the houses and then knocked at the door of that Indian and went into his house."

"And that was all, Mash Qasem?"

"No sir, that was just the beginnin' . . . I saw him twice later on. He gave me such a look I felt my heart give way . . ."

Asadollah Mirza threw a despairing glance at my father and said, "Of course, of course, they made those contacts with you . . . and it's exactly because of those contacts that we've brought the matter up."

And after winking at my father he turned to Mash Qasem and said, "Mash Qasem, tell us the rest of the story later . . . we see that you have well understood what dangerous plans the English have for the Master."

Mash Qasem interrupted him, "And the same for me, too . . ."

"Of course, certainly . . . now we've learned that the English wish formally to get in touch with the Master himself, so that they can clear up the differences between them, and that, God willing, the whole affair will end in peace and concord."

"But sir, you've got be on the lookout for the tricks these English get up to."

"Completely correct . . . but what we are asking is that you help us . . . of course, when the representative of the English sees the

Master, certainly the Master will ask you to stand guard and see that he doesn't try anything . . ."

Mash Qasem said with a sneer, "The English try anythin' with me? . . . one time, and what a time it was, too, I remember ten Englishmen went for me in Ghiasabad . . . from evenin' till the next mornin' I kept swingin' my spade around my head and none of 'em dared come forward . . . finally their boss, who was from the village further down, said to his mates, 'Let's go, I know this Mash Qasem. He's not one of those we took him for' . . . and they put their heads down and went. And I shouted after 'em, 'You bastards, go tell your masters Mash Qasem's not one of those, over my dead body you'll be takin' the water' . . . 'cause the quarrel was over water . . ."

Uncle colonel yelled, "Mash Qasem, what has the water in Ghiasabad got to do with the English?"

Mash Qasem shook his head and said, "You've a long way to go before you know the English . . . there's no place in all this world the English hate so much as Ghiasabad. They wanted to take the water so that Ghiasabad would be ruined and wrecked and crushed . . ."

Asadollah Mirza interrupted, "Colonel, Mash Qasem is not saying anything illogical. Naturally when a town or citadel has its water supply cut off, the people in the town surrender."

"Really? What wisdom issues from your mouth, I'm quite overcome."

"Now Mash Qasem, what we are asking is this: say the representative of the English comes to see the Master, then you should be careful that if it happens that the conversation doesn't lead to any conclusion, no harm comes to the representative, because the British army's here. If one of their men is harmed, all our people will be blown to kingdom-come . . . The representative's coming to talk, if the conversation leads somewhere, all well and good, but if it doesn't lead anywhere . . . Well, even if the Master gives some order or other because he's angry, you have to see to it that the representative leaves the house safely."

After bringing forward various objections, Mash Qasem was finally convinced that whatever happened he had to watch out for the representative's safety.

After Mash Qasem had been dismissed, Asadollah Mirza said, "I feel quite delirious . . . there's no doubt that Mash Qasem sees himself as Talleyrand . . . now the second problem is that Brigadier Maharat Khan says that this corporal friend of his will only agree to play his part if we give him an Esfahani rug. Now I myself only have two rugs in the house. Perhaps the colonel . . ."

"My older brother has some Esfahani rugs, perhaps one of those could be . . ."

"Moment, moment, colonel sir, do you want to tell the Master that if they're to overlook his sins he has to give a colonel in the British army, who's also Churchill's personal representative, a rug?"

"No, but there's no other choice."

My father, who had been deep in thought, joined in, "No colonel, you have to make this concession, compared with getting rid of the Master's illness, what's one rug worth?"

"I'm ready to die to get rid of my brother's illness but hang it all, those rugs of mine are a pair, one won't be right by itself."

It took some time before my uncle agreed to hand over a rug to Brigadier Maharat Khan, as payment for the Indian corporal.

The result of these discussions was reviewed the next day. Asadollah Mirza, helped by my father and uncle colonel, convinced Dear Uncle Napoleon to submit to a meeting with a representative of the British army. However, they didn't dare tell him that this representative was an Indian, because it had taken an immense amount of trouble to get him to accept that a colonel was coming to see him and not a general. Discussions as to the site of the meeting also took a very long time. Dear Uncle insisted that the representative of the English should come to his house, and Asadollah Mirza and his accomplices said that Dear Uncle should go to the General Staff headquarters of the British army. Finally it was agreed that the meeting should take place at a third location, i.e., our house. Uncle colonel's rug was sent to the Indian corporal by means of Brigadier Maharat Khan. It was agreed that on Wednesday evening Asadollah Mirza and my father would meet the Indian corporal in the Brigadier's house, and there they would set out the details of the scheme for him. Dear Uncle Napoleon, who appeared to consider himself as being in the same situation as Napoleon at Fontainebleu before the representatives of the Allied armies arrived, did not set foot outside of his room as he awaited the moment of the encounter.

TWENTY-THREE

THE APPOINTED WEDNESDAY, when the English representative was to begin his negotiations with Dear Uncle Napoleon, arrived.

Using as an excuse that he was having some men friends over, my father had before noon sent everyone in the house, including our servant, over to one of my aunts who had a house in Tajrish; by insisting and pleading, I had persuaded him to allow me not to go to this gathering and to stay in the house. The meeting had been arranged for four in the afternoon. From two onwards my father and Asadollah Mirza were coming and going from the Indian brigadier's house, their faces alternately open and shining and then closed and gloomy. It seemed they were settling various issues and problems. Then uncle colonel came over to our house, too. From their whispering and the muttered words they exchanged I realized that the only awkward problem still remaining was the fact that the representative was an Indian. Asadollah Mirza was more optimistic than everyone else and kept repeating, "God willing, that'll be all right, too." A little after three o'clock they sent uncle colonel to fetch Dear Uncle Napoleon.

For two days I had held back from going anywhere near Layli or talking to her, because I didn't know what to say to her. If by any chance she had got wind of this meeting and were to ask me about it, I didn't know how I should answer. Since I was certain that Dear Uncle would not permit me to be present during the negotiations, I had prepared myself a nice little hiding place behind one of the living room doors, which gave onto a small side room. Fortunately this side room behind the living room had a door to the hallway so that I would not be imprisoned in my hiding place. Asadollah Mirza had told me that wherever I might be I should be ready to come and help the proceedings along if that proved necessary.

When Dear Uncle Napoleon set foot in the yard to our house I was at an upstairs window, watching. Dear Uncle was wearing a dark suit with the ribbon of an order which, according to him, he had been awarded by King Mohammad Ali Shah pinned to the lapel. He was wearing a black and white striped tie over his white shirt. His face reminded me of the newsreel images of Daladier, the French president before the Second World War, as he went into the conference room at Munich. Mash Qasem was following him. He seemed to be wearing one of Dear Uncle's suits because the sleeves and legs were far too long for him.

My father and Asadollah Mirza went out to welcome Dear Uncle. In response to their warm and friendly greetings, Dear Uncle's answers were very dry and clipped.

I ran to my hiding place. As soon as Dear Uncle entered the living room he started drawing up a plan of where various people were to stand. "My brother the colonel will stand here . . . and you here Asadollah . . ."

"Moment, I should be to the right of the English representative . . ."

Dear Uncle cut him off, "Who has made such a decision . . . ? Not at all; just as I said, you stand here!"

"But take into account the fact that I have to act as interpreter and I can't from over there . . . I must be at a certain distance between you and the representative."

"But isn't that Brigadier Maharat Khan coming?"

"But you yourself wouldn't agree to his coming."

"Yes, it would not be right for a stranger to be present at such important negotiations, and an Indian at that."

Asadollah Mirza and my father and uncle colonel exchanged despairing glances. Dear Uncle Napoleon went on, "In that case you stand where you were saying. And Mash Qasem is to stand two paces behind me on the left-hand side."

"I'm very pleased you changed your mind about Mash Qasem. It's really not necessary for him to be on the lookout from behind a curtain."

Mash Qasem, who was having difficulty moving in his ill-fitting clothes, said, "God keep you, sir . . . I've killed that many English in the wars it'll be enough for seven generations . . . God wouldn't want me to be dirtyin' my hands with the blood of no more English. I remember there was a man in our town who . . ."

Dear Uncle cut him off with an angry look and said, "For this job we need someone who is completely reliable."

Asadollah Mirza and my father exchanged puzzled looks, but they had no opportunity to say anything because the door to the living room opened and Puri, uncle colonel's son, entered with a double-barreled shotgun in his hand.

Dear Uncle said in a stern voice, "Puri, according to my orders to you, you're to stay on guard behind the hallway door the whole time; keep your finger on the trigger and, as soon as I give the command, fire!"

Asadollah Mirza, who was staring at Puri in astonishment, involuntarily said, "Oh, my sainted aunt!"

Then he turned to Dear Uncle, "But sir . . . in our negotiations it was agreed that the representative was to come unarmed. This is against all custom and decency and ethical principles, and even against the rules of war."

Staring into midair from behind his dark glasses Dear Uncle said calmly, "I know the rules of war better than you do. But one must not ignore the malicious nature of the enemy. Puri! Carry out your commander's orders!"

Uncle colonel, who had been watching this exchange in stunned surprise, joined the conversation, "Brother, this boy has no idea how to fire a gun. If, God forbid, he should suddenly . . ."

"He has no idea? . . . Then what was he playing at during his military service?"

"Well he was working in the commissariat . . . I mean, of course he did some shooting, too, but not with a shotgun!"

Puri was listening to this conversation with an idiotic expression on his pale, equine face. Dear Uncle turned to him, "Puri, if you are really not capable of this, then honestly say so before you accept the post . . . as Napoleon said, 'To confess one's inability is a kind of ability.'"

Stammering and spluttering, Puri said, "I . . . uncle . . . whatever your orders are . . . I'm ready to sacrifice my life for you."

"Then report to your post . . . your commander is giving you your orders!"

Asadollah Mirza jumped into the conversation, "Moment, moment, firing a military rifle and firing a double-barreled shotgun are very different things. If you'll allow me, I'll explain the details to Puri . . ."

And before Dear Uncle had an opportunity to answer, he dragged Puri out into the hall and shut the door. I peeped out into the hall.

Asadollah Mirza took the gun from Puri and said, "Let's see, lad . . . What! This gun's really loaded . . ."

Puri spluttered, "That's what I'm afraid of . . . but Dear Uncle ordered me to . . ."

"Moment, moment . . . Now, you're no fool; we've taken a thousand pains and finally succeeded in getting a representative of the English to come here to solve the existing differences between them and your uncle, and God willing your uncle's health will improve then . . . Now just imagine the negotiations don't get anywhere or there's some kind of argument . . . do you have to shoot the representative in the belly? . . . Don't you realize they'll arrest you and hang you for murder?"

"I won't really fire it, Uncle Asadollah."

"But if there's a cartridge in the barrel and, God forbid, your finger touches the trigger, it'll fire."

Puri started spluttering, "But doesn't it have a safety catch?"

"Where the hell would a decrepit old gun like this have a safety catch? . . . And besides, can't you remember how you went into shock when you heard that bomb go off? And God forbid the barrel should explode in your hands . . . in the last two or three months four of these guns have exploded in people's hands."

"Uncle Asadollah, I'm really afraid . . ."

"And you're quite right to be afraid . . . Now I'll just fix it like this . . . Aha, aha!"

"You've taken the cartridges out!"

"Ssshhh! Don't say a word; stay right here and walk up and down with the gun, I promise you there'll be no need for any firing . . . these old guns are no joke. Fifty times out of a hundred they explode, and they explode under the barrel so that all the pellets go into the belly of the person holding the gun . . . Would it be right for you to be mutilated at your age? To lose your virility, say? Do you still have any hopes of San Francisco?" Puri was so terrified he had begun to tremble. His mouth hung open but he couldn't say anything else.

When Asadollah Mirza returned to the living room Dear Uncle Napoleon was sitting on the sofa and the others were standing. Asadollah Mirza signalled a few times to uncle colonel. Uncle colonel twisted his mouth and jaw this way and that for a while, and finally started to speak, "You know, brother, there's one thing I have to mention to you."

With a sudden movement Dear Uncle Napoleon swivelled his head round toward him. In a voice filled with anxiety and uncertainty uncle colonel went on, "In each country, for negotiations with their opponents, the English make use of their people who are in that country, or in that area . . . and, er, how can I put it . . . in fact they feel that a person from the area will be more familiar with the . . . particular spiritual quality of the place . . ."

"I don't understand what you're driving at."

"Meaning . . . I mean to say . . . this colonel that's coming to see you now . . . he's an extremely important personage in the British army . . ."

Dear Uncle Napoleon said dryly, "Isn't that what was agreed upon? They should thank God that I've agreed to talk to a colonel instead of a general."

Uncle colonel gave Asadollah Mirza and my father an agitated look and went on, "Meaning that this colonel . . . who's very close indeed to Churchill . . . in fact, you could say he's Churchill's righthand man . . . is the commander in chief of the British army and is an Indian."

Asadollah Mirza closed his eyes.

Dear Uncle Napoleon's lips began to tremble perceptibly. He turned pale and repeated in a voice that seemed to come from the bottom of a well, "An Indian . . . an Indian . . ."

Mash Qasem suddenly slapped one hand on top of the other and said, "Eh, you don't say! . . . God save us from them there Indians!"

Uncle colonel seemed to feel that if he once stopped talking he wouldn't dare start again, and he went on, "But this Colonel Eshtiagh Khan is so important that the viceroy of India won't take a drink of water without consulting with him first."

Fortunately Asadollah Mirza's interruption averted the calamity promised by Dear Uncle's Napoleon's terrifying expression. "Moment, colonel, don't forget that Colonel Eshtiagh Khan bears the title 'Sir'; you should say 'Sir Eshtiagh Khan.'"

This mention of the title "Sir" had a miraculous effect on Dear Uncle Napoleon. It was as if water had been poured on the flames and quenched them. After a few moments' silence he said in a quiet voice, "If the representative has complete authority, delegated by the English, what difference does it make to me?"

Asadollah Mirza and my father and uncle colonel breathed a sigh of relief. At this moment my father, who was near the window, leaned out toward the yard and shouted, "Mr. Shir Ali . . . Mr. Shir Ali, did you want something?"

The sound of Shir Ali the butcher's gruff, harsh voice came up from the yard, "Good day to you . . ."

But before he could answer my father's question, or my father could say anything else, Dear Uncle Napoleon said, "Leave him alone. I told him to come here . . . so that if we wanted tea or anything he could bring it to us."

My father called into the yard, "Make yourself at home, Mr. Shir Ali . . . the folks aren't here yet . . . pour yourself a cup of tea . . . the samovar downstairs is on."

Those present looked at each other and said nothing. There was no doubt at all that Dear Uncle Napoleon had taken every precaution. He had even asked Shir Ali to be in the area, to deal with any possible eventualities.

Dear Uncle continued to sit on the sofa and the four other participants to the meeting continued to stand where they were. Even Asadollah Mirza, whom it was normally impossible to keep quiet for a moment, had closed his mouth. Finally Mash Qasem's voice broke the silence, "Then why hasn't this English Indian come? To be honest, I'm really worried. God rest his soul, there was a man in our town who . . ."

Uncle colonel growled at him, "Mash Qasem!"

But Mash Qasem was not going to be cut short, "Well now, sir, why should I lie? To the grave it's ah . . . ah . . . When I . . ."

Fortunately Shir Ali's harsh voice rang out from the stairs, "Sir, that guest of yours has come!"

Dear Uncle quickly stood up and, after signalling to the others to stay in their assigned places, he placed his hand on the ribbon on his coat collar and stood to attention. Shir Ali opened the door. Officer Eshtiagh Khan made his entrance.

Corporal Eshtiagh Khan, or as they were calling him, Colonel Sir Eshtiagh Khan, was a short, fat Indian. He was wearing a summer uniform consisting of a short-sleeved shirt and shorts. The flap on the revolver holster on his belt had been left open so that it was obvious the holster was empty.

As soon as he entered he clicked his heels together and raised his hand to his turban in a military salute, *"Good afternoon, sir . . . How do you do!"*

Dear Uncle, who was standing to attention with the color drained from his face, snapped his hand up to his eyebrows. Not only Dear Uncle but everyone else present seemed to be affected by the formality of the occasion, since no one answered except Mash Qasem, who said, "Good day to you."

Mash Qasem's interjection jolted Asadollah Mirza into speech, *"Good afternoon, Sir Eshtiagh Khan."*

The Indian said something in English, which I think was an objection to the title "sir" because apparently this had not been part of their agreement, but a gesture from Asadollah Mirza silenced him.

After Dear Uncle had shaken hands with the Indian corporal, an act that was accompanied by his clicking his heels together, everyone apart from Mash Qasem, who stayed on his feet, sat down in the places that had been assigned to them.

Although I did well in my English lessons at school, I didn't understand a word the Indian said, but I could understand what Asadollah Mirza said, and I recognized the mistakes he made, saying masculine pronouns for feminine and vice versa, as he spoke.

After an introductory exchange of polite greetings, Dear Uncle recovered his dry, formal tone. "Asadollah, I must ask you to translate whatever I say word for word . . . Say that I require my life and wealth and honor for the sake of my motherland. If I'm supposed to make some concession to the English, I'd a thousand times rather be killed and my body be eaten by wolves and hyenas . . . Translate!"

Asadollah Mirza started spouting English words at a great rate, and in among these I heard the word *"wolf"* which he said more loudly than the rest. Finally, in order to show that he was translating word for word, he paused and said in Persian, "Hyena . . . What's the English word for hyena?"

Mash Qasem's voice rang out, "Must be 'corpse eater' . . ."

Dear Uncle said, "Well, that's not important for now . . . Say that I myself am aware of the immensity of the damage I have done to the British army . . . In the Battles of Kazerun and Mamasani, and in tens of other battles, I must have destroyed a thousand members of the British army. I have done the utmost damage to their colonial designs, but all this was for the sake of my motherland . . . It was because the English had raped my motherland . . . During his infancy one of our poets put his hand into a bird's nest, and the bird pecked him with its beak in such a way that blood spurted out; he wrote:

> *'My father laughed and said (although I cried),*
> > *Learn from this hen true patriotic pride!'*

Asadollah, if you please, translate, word for word!"

Asadollah Mirza looked helplessly from one side to the other and began spilling out a string of English words, in the midst of which he twice repeated the word *"chicken"* (I knew what that meant) very loudly. The Indian, who seemed to have understood nothing whatsoever of the translator's speech, kept nodding his head and saying in a confirmatory way, *"Yes, yes, chicken . . . yes, chicken . . . delicious . . . very delicious . . ."*

As it happened our English teacher had taught us the meaning of the word "delicious" two weeks previously.

Asadollah Mirza turned to Dear Uncle, "Colonel Sir Eshtiagh Khan says that: 'Yes, yes, we possess exhaustive information concerning all the details of these struggles, and we feel the greatest respect for him as a patriot, however . . .'"

A frown spread over Dear Uncle's face and he said darkly, "Asadollah Mirza, this individual didn't say more than a few words . . . was all this in those few words? You're not embellishing his remarks are you?"

Asadollah Mirza hurriedly said, "Come now, sir! Do I know English or do you? As everyone knows, English is a language of brevity and economy. . . . There are some words that if we wanted to translate them into Persian we'd have to talk for half an hour. . . . Didn't you hear Churchill's last speech? He spoke for a quarter of an hour in the House of Commons, and the Persian, French and Arabic translations were so long that everyone fell asleep."

Mash Qasem had been silent for a while and could contain himself no longer, "If you're askin' me, that's not too far from the truth neither . . . whatever you say about the English could be true. That time that English sergeant came to ask for quarter from me, he just said *'falasakh,'* and then the interpreter fellow talked for an hour describin' to us what he wanted to say."

Uncle colonel gave him a contemptuous look and said quietly, "Be quiet, Mash Qasem! So you know English, too, do you now?"

"Well now, sir, why should I lie? To the grave it's ah . . . ah . . . I know the English better than they knows themselves. You mean you want to say that me who's been fightin' with the English for these forty years, that I don't understand their language? I remember, and a good feller he was, too, there was a man in our town who . . ."

Dear Uncle Napoleon said violently, but in a quiet voice, "Qasem, shut up! . . . Asadollah get on with explaining the situation more quickly . . . Ask him what the message he has for me is . . . And by the way, tell him that it's in my blood to fight against foreigners. In fact, my late grandfather gave his life in the struggle against foreigners."

Asadollah Mirza quietly answered, "Moment, moment, if you remember your late grandfather passed away from cholera during the year of the epidemic."

"Don't talk nonsense, Asadollah! Translate exactly what I said."

Asadollah Mirza started saying meaningless words in English again, except that this time he repeated the words *"last great gentleman"* two or three times. Apart from these words I didn't understand anything of what he was saying and apparently the Indian didn't either, because in answer he simply came out with a few words that clearly had no rhyme or reason to them. Asadollah Mirza turned to Dear Uncle. "Colonel Sir Eshtiagh Khan says that the government he serves is aware of the brave acts committed by your family, but that on condition that today you formally undertake not to sabotage their operations, after the war your file will be transferred, with a positive recommendation, to a higher . . ."

At this moment an extraordinary noise coming from the yard cut his speech short. A number of people seemed to be grappling with one another. Everyone in the room froze to the spot in astonishment. Finally Shir Ali's gruff voice could be made out in the general racket, "I said that the Master's got a foreign visitor."

And a voice which I recognized a moment later as belonging to Dustali Khan yelled, "So he's got a foreign visitor. And I've got urgent business with him."

The noise of the quarrel was closer now, and came from the direction of the stairs. Suddenly the living room door burst open.

Dustali Khan dragged Cadet Officer Ghiasabadi into the room by the collar; the cadet officer was wearing striped pajamas.

"I'll give you hell for this, you shameless good-for-nothing . . . today I am going to make very plain to you just where you and I stand."

Dear Uncle Napoleon sprang to his feet and shouted, "Dustali Khan, what is going on? What kind of impudent behavior do you think this is? Can't you see that . . . ?"

Without paying attention to anyone else in the room, Dustali Khan dragged the cadet officer over to Dear Uncle and shouted, "This shameless bastard was supposed to marry the poor girl and divorce her two months later. Not only he didn't divorce her, now he's made her pregnant . . . and he's selling Akbar Abad so that he can pocket the money."

The friendly warmth with which Mash Qasem and Cadet Officer Ghiasabadi greeted one another decreased the violence and vehemence of the encounter. "How are you keepin', Rajabali Khan? . . . By the way, yesterday Mash Karim came over from Ghiasabad and he was askin' after you. I says, well, we're neighbors now but I never see Mr. Ghiasabadi . . ."

Cadet Officer Ghiasabadi freed his collar from Dustali Khan's clutches and began to return Mash Qasem's greeting; then he became aware of the others present. "Good day to you . . . you'll have to excuse us. This fellow's got some notion in his head . . . I don't understand why, with his own wife, a man doesn't have the right to . . ."

But he didn't have the opportunity to finish his sentence. Dustali Khan's voice cut him off, "Well, well, and good day to you, Mr. Eshtiagh Khan . . . Whatever are you doing here? By chance I was asking Brigadier Maharat Khan about you a few days ago . . ."

Dear Uncle Napoleon froze as if he'd been electrocuted. "Dustali Khan, do you know Colonel Eshtiagh Khan?"

For a moment Dustali Khan's surprised glance wavered between Dear Uncle's face and the Indian's, and before he could become aware of Asadollah Mirza's and uncle colonel's signals he burst out laughing. "Since when has Corporal Eshtiagh Khan become a colonel? . . . Let me congratulate you, Mr. Eshtiagh Khan. That time we went up to Pas Ghaleh with the brigadier you were still a corporal . . ."

Everyone paused, as if transfixed. Eshtiagh Khan had not foreseen such an unlikely encounter and he stared dumbfounded at

Asadollah Mirza and my father and uncle colonel, but they were so taken aback that no one came to his assistance, and Dustali Khan went on pressing him to speak. "Eshtiagh Khan, what are you being so quiet for . . . what's happened?"

With concern, astonishment and anxiety all over his face, the Indian opened his mouth and said in an Indian accent but in Persian, "How can I put it . . . today I am paying a visit to this gentleman . . ."

Dear Uncle placed his hands on the arms of the sofa. His whole body began to shake, his face had turned frighteningly pale; he shook, and shook, and then fell back helplessly against the sofa repeating, "Treachery . . . treachery . . . history is repeating itself . . ."

There was general confusion. Uncle colonel ran anxiously over to him, "Brother . . . brother . . ."

Dear Uncle's eyes were almost closed; in a choked, trembling voice he said, "Treachery, treachery . . . my brother . . . Lucien Bonaparte!"

My father shouted, "Sir . . . sir, how are you?"

"Treachery, treachery . . . my sister's husband . . . Marshal Murat!"

"Moment, moment, who has betrayed you? Why won't you listen to me?"

"Shut up, General Marmont!"

Mash Qasem was about to say something. Asadollah Mirza shouted, "Don't you open your mouth. You're General Grouchy and the file on you's worse than everyone else's!"

Suddenly Dear Uncle's scream echoed around the room, "Treachery . . . Puri! . . . Shir Ali! . . . Attack!"

At this command of "Attack!" everyone seemed to take leave of their senses. Even the Indian, who hadn't yet understood the meaning of Dear Uncle's order, had been very upset by Dear Uncle's reaction, which he had not at all expected, and was making signals with his hands and head asking Asadollah Mirza and my father what he should do now. I considered there was no longer any reason for me to stay hidden and made my way into the room. I stood dithering in the doorway. I heard Asadollah Mirza say quietly to the Indian corporal, "Officer, beat it! Things are really heating up, oh yes!"

And he dragged him toward the door. In the hallway he found himself face to face with Shir Ali who had come up the stairs and said, "Wait a minute, sir, I'll deal with him."

And, as if it were a club, he raised the leg of mutton he had in his hand. The previous year Shir Ali had made the pilgrimage to Mashhad, and since then he had repented his sins and sworn he wouldn't go after anyone with a cleaver.

Asadollah Mirza took him by the arm and quietly said, "Moment, Shir Ali, have you gone crazy . . . a guest is favored by God."

"Well sir, the master said 'Whenever I call out, you run and deal with them who are against me.'"

"Shir Ali, what are you thinking of . . . this officer is a friend of the Master's."

The Indian had turned extremely pale; to address Shir Ali he had to crick his neck and stare into the sky; in a terrified voice he said, "On your soul I swear I am without hostilities . . . the Master is my very kind friend . . . the Master is the beloved of my heart . . ."

Shir Ali stood to one side. At this moment Puri's face showed up over my shoulder; I think he had been so anxious that he had been caught short and gone to the lavatory. He spluttered out, "Uncle Asadollah, let me deal with this Indian."

Asadollah Mirza leapt at him, "Oh, shut up with you! Now you're to be our General Rommel, are you?"

And as he saw that Puri was still threatening the Indian, he said to Shir Ali, "Shir Ali, keep ahold of this lad for me till I get back."

While Shir Ali's arms were around Puri's long skinny body, Asadollah Mirza descended the stairs with the Indian two steps at a time. As he went down he kept swearing at the Indian in a loud voice and clapping his hands violently together. "You little bastard, you thought you could trick us! . . . I'll show you what's what! I'll give you a lesson you'll never forget!"

When he had ejected the Indian from the yard and returned, he turned to Puri, who was still struggling in Shir Ali's arms. "Idiot child, if you had raised your hand against that Indian, tomorrow they'd have had you in the British army camp and emptied two bullets into your empty head."

"Uncle Asadollah, I wasn't really going to hit him . . . I wanted Dear Uncle to hear my voice . . . so you answer Dear Uncle when he asks."

"All right, answering Dear Uncle's up to me . . . Let him go now, Shir Ali . . . and you go into the yard."

I'd gone with Asadollah Mirza every step of the way and now I followed him back into the living room. My father and uncle colonel, helped by Mash Qasem, were supporting Dear Uncle's upper body and getting him to take sips of brandy.

When he heard Asadollah Mirza's voice, Dear Uncle opened his eyelids. "Asadollah, what's happened? . . . What did you do?"

"You wouldn't believe how quickly he dashed off . . . a really primitive little wretch . . . I taught him a lesson . . . I pounded him into bits."

Suddenly Dear Uncle seemed to recall the treachery of those who were near him; his eyes grew completely round, his lips began trembling again and with his remaining strength he yelled, "I don't want to see your traitors' faces."

Uncle colonel was about to say something, but Asadollah Mirza didn't give him the chance, "Sir, by your own soul . . . by the soul of our late grandfather, we too were deceived."

"You mean you're that stupid? . . . You mean you . . ."

Asadollah Mirza hurriedly interrupted him, "Moment, moment . . . do we have to tell you about the tricks and hoaxes the English get up to . . . They could trick heaven itself . . . when they can trick Hitler, do you think they can't fool us?"

Such remarks were of the kind that Dear Uncle himself made, and they worked on him in the best possible way. "You poor wretches! When I say beware of the tricks and hoaxes that old fox gets up to, you laugh at me!"

Everyone breathed a sigh of relief. Mash Qasem's throat seemed to have dried up in the face of these strange and unexpected events; now his tongue had loosened. "Sir, how long will it take till these gentlemen to understand what you tell 'em . . . I swear to God that if I was in Hitler's place, I'd have taken the Master as my right-hand man to catch them English red-handed and force 'em to show us what they'd got up their sleeves."

Luckily this time Mash Qasem's interference was just what was needed; a calm expression began to spread over Dear Uncle's features. But Mash Qasem was not going to give up. "Well now, why should I lie? . . . To the grave it's ah . . . ah . . . In all my life I never saw such a disgustin' thing as sendin' an Indian corporal to pass himself off as the British commander-in-chief."

Dear Uncle had closed his eyes for a moment; he opened them and said in a choked voice, "They did it deliberately . . . deliberately . . ."

And, gradually raising his voice, he continued, "They wanted to persuade me to negotiate with a corporal so that my and my family's honor and dignity would be destroyed. They wanted to humiliate me . . . this was a plan of revenge for them."

Uncle colonel anxiously said, "Brother . . . brother . . . Calm down! Don't upset yourself, you'll collapse again."

Dear Uncle yelled, "How can I not be upset? . . . How can I stay calm faced with this huge conspiracy? . . . They send an Indian corporal to me so that tomorrow they can write in their histories that a great fighter disgracefully surrendered his sword to an Indian corporal."

My father said, "Well, God be praised, their plot's dissolved and gone now."

In a quieter voice Dear Uncle said, "It was the hand of fate . . . Mars, the god of war, did not want an old fighter to be dragged down to the lowest level . . . If Dustali hadn't arrived . . ."

Mash Qasem jumped into the conversation, "It's true, it's true, if that neighbor of mine hadn't arrived, whatever would have happened to us! Once again it's Ghiasabad and the folks from Ghiasabad to the rescue!"

Dear Uncle glanced at Dustali Khan and said, "Dustali, come closer . . . come and sit down . . . If God closed these fools' eyes, at least he put it in your heart to come and help me in this terrible whirlpool! . . . You are my commander!"

Asadollah Mirza, who had been watching this scene with some astonishment, said quietly to my father, "Do you see that? Now we've become the baddies . . . and that donkey Dustali has become the merciful agent of the god of war."

And my father quietly replied, "Never mind . . . let the Master calm down . . . and Dustali Khan can be the god of war himself for all I care."

Asadollah Mirza quickly poured Dear Uncle another glass of brandy. After the storm a pleasant calm reigned. At this moment Puri appeared in the doorway but before Dear Uncle could catch sight of him Asadollah Mirza dashed over to him and said quietly, "Get out of here . . . If the Master catches sight of you he'll remember again. Stay outside for a minute!"

And he shut the door. I was standing in another doorway out of sight of Dear Uncle; Asadollah Mirza signalled me to stay there. Uncle colonel went over to Asadollah Mirza and said quietly, "Asadollah, in the midst of all this, what's going to happen about my rug?"

"Moment, moment, colonel sir! Do you want to start another row? You who's always saying you're ready to die for the sake of the Master?"

"But look here, that wretched little charlatan didn't do anything. I mean, it's not as if I'd sworn before God I'd give an Esfahani rug to Corporal Eshtiagh Khan."

Asadollah Mirza raised his eyebrows and said quietly, "All right, you'll get it back from him. Don't worry so much!"

"And where am I going to lay hands on the man?"

"Well, I'd say to your luminous lordship that . . . but of course the corporal agreed to our game because he's being transferred to-night. But don't worry, he gave me his address. Tomorrow send him a card addressed to Officer Eshtiagh Khan, the Front at El-Alamein, tank number 238."

Uncle colonel muttered furiously, "God rot you and your ugly aristocratic face . . ."

"Moment, of course, that's if he hasn't been killed by the time the card arrives . . . ! Of course, there's another way and that's that you tell the Master to give you an Esfahani rug in exchange."

"Oh really! That's all we need, for me to tell my brother that we gave the Indian corporal a rug as a bribe so that he'd come and negoti-ate as a representative of the English! Do you think I'm tired of life?"

"Colonel sir, the world has its ups and its downs . . . its winners and its losers."

Uncle colonel gave him a furious look and went over to the rest of those present, who were gathered around Dear Uncle Napoleon and talking in undertones.

TWENTY-FOUR

DEAR UNCLE had closed his eyes; he now opened them. His face had become calm and in a calm voice he said, "I've seen many things like this . . . even Napoleon, who had to swallow poison from the English throughout his whole life, was tricked again by them when he surrendered after Waterloo and placed his fate in their hands . . . they had made him promises . . . but the poor wretch was finally exiled to St. Helena. My blood's not thicker than his."

And then, as if he wished to change the subject entirely, he turned to Dustali Khan and said, "Now, Dustali Khan, what was the argument you had with Cadet Officer Ghiasabadi about?"

Striking a finger against the table as he spoke, Dustali Khan said in a menacing voice, "You are the head of this family . . . either you must make it plain where I stand with this stupid donkey . . . or you must allow me to have the law restrain him from looting our lives and property and honor."

Cadet Officer Ghiasabadi seemed to have smoked a great deal of opium and to be in a state of complete mental serenity; he said tranquilly, "First, the stupid donkey is the person who says it; second, when have I ever disturbed the Master's life and property and honor?"

Mash Qasem jumped into the conversation, "Well, God strike me dumb if I lie, till now no one's ever heard of a man from Ghiasabad hurtin' anyone's honor . . . Really, why should I lie? In all this country you won't find any place comes near Ghiasabad when it comes to honor."

Although Dustali Khan was trying to control himself, he completely exploded and lashed out at Mash Qasem, "You just shut up! God damn everyone from Ghiasabad and their honor, too."

Mash Qasem rarely became angry but he said aggressively, "Sir, keep a civil tongue in your head! Say whatever you want to me, but the honor of folks from Ghiasabad is not for jokin' about!"

I glanced at Asadollah Mirza. His gloomy expression had completely opened up and the usual mischievous smile had returned to his face. "Moment, moment, Mr. Dustali Khan, Mash Qasem is quite right. Leave the honor of Ghiasabad alone; since you yourself are the great champion of honorable behavior, you shouldn't . . ."

Dear Uncle Napoleon's peremptory voice rang out, "Silence! . . . Two people have a difference of opinion. They have presented the matter to the older members of the family. Their problem must be dealt with in a just fashion. Please allow the plaintiffs to state their case. Continue, Dustali Khan, and stick to the point."

Dear Uncle Napoleon's severity put everyone's mind at rest, because it was clear that temporarily he had forgotten about the English. Trying to keep calm, Dustali Khan said, "In order to save the family's good name I said that this individual should come and marry the girl, a month later he should divorce her, and he would be given two thousand *tomans* . . . and that's what happened . . . now leaving aside the fact that . . ."

Cadet Officer Ghiasabadi, who was eating a kind of nougat called *gaz*, jumped into the conversation, "You handed over two thousand *tomans*, and then I worked it out . . . now there's still . . ."

"What nonsense are you talking, you rotten, shameless little . . . What did you work out?"

The cadet officer said tranquilly, "You lived for five years in my wife's house at a hundred *tomans* a month rent . . . now, let's say fifty *tomans* . . . in five years that'll come to three thousand *tomans*. You still owe me a thousand *tomans*."

Dustali was so furious his voice seemed to stick in his throat. Asadollah Mirza murmured, "Oh no, sir, the rent would be at least a hundred *tomans* . . . You worked it out very generously! It'd be at least six thousand *tomans*."

Dustali Khan's fury turned on Asadollah Mirza. "You just shut up, Asadollah!"

"Moment, I didn't say anything. The cadet officer had made a mistake in his arithmetic, I pointed it out."

Dear Uncle said sternly, "Asadollah, be quiet!"

But Mash Qasem opened his mouth, "These days, if you please, it's even more than two hundred *tomans*. I remember myself there was a man in our town who . . ."

Asadollah Mirza said, "Mash Qasem, let Mr. Dustali Khan have his say . . . he was talking about the violation of honor."

Gently sawing at a piece of *gaz* with a penknife, so that he could then break it, the cadet officer tranquilly said, "Yes, please tell me whose honor I've violated."

Shaking with rage, Dustali Khan said, "Sir, you see how impudent he is! That sick, innocent girl . . ."

The cadet officer cut him short, "Sick, innocent yourself! If you're referring to my spouse . . ."

Dear Uncle Napoleon shouted, "Cadet Officer, you work in the security ministry and you must know the rules and customs of the courts. This is in reality a family court. Until I give permission to speak, you have no right to interrupt. You will have your say at the appropriate time . . . Continue, Dustali."

"Take into account how some good-for-nothing stranger had deceived this sick innocent girl . . ."

Once again the cadet officer interrupted, "Sir, take into account how he's talking drivel."

And he immediately fixed his gaze on the ceiling and went on, "First, the good-for-nothing is the person who says it; second, he wasn't a stranger at all."

Dustali Khan half rose from his chair in a threatening way. "He wasn't a stranger? You know him . . . You know who planted the child in this innocent girl's belly?"

Popping a piece of *gaz* into his mouth, the cadet officer said tranquilly, "Certainly I know. It was me."

"You? You shameless liar!"

"I'm speaking the absolute truth."

Laughter and happiness fairly burst from Asadollah Mirza's face; he said, "Moment, Mr. Dustali Khan, reason and logic are not to be ignored! The cadet officer himself says that the child is his and you're saying it's the child of a stranger? Either you know the child's father or you must take the cadet officer's word for it!'

Dustali Khan had turned as red as a tomato. He was so angry that his voice could hardly emerge from his throat, "But when? Where? . . . This man never even knew Qamar. Where did this happen without our realizing?"

The cadet officer answered in the same tranquil manner, "Where have you been all your life, brother? Since last year, when I came with Deputy Taymur Khan looking for your corpse, my heart's belonged to Qamar . . . we fell for each other . . . Oh, what nights they were . . . what moonlit nights!"

Hardly able to keep from laughing, Asadollah Mirza said, "And you're asking when and where? They're not going to go to San Francisco in front of you! . . . San Francisco's altogether a town for just two people. If there are three of you, you have to go to Los Angeles."

Dustali Khan, who was so furious he was on the point of collapse, yelled, "But Asadollah, wasn't it in front of you that he said he wasn't capable of anything? That in the war a bullet had hit his goddamned filthy member?"

With his mouth full the cadet officer said, "The gentleman's member is the goddamned filthy one."

"Moment, the jury must now vote on which of the two plaintiffs in the case has the cleaner member; I vote for the cadet officer."

Dear Uncle Napoleon ground his teeth together. He wanted to cut off their talk with dignity and firmness but he couldn't find an opportunity to do so. Asadollah Mirza, who was in heaven he felt so happy, turned to the cadet officer with pretended surprise and said, "Moment, Cadet Officer, did you say such a thing? . . . I don't remember your saying that a bullet had hit your member."

With a chuckle the cadet officer said, "It happens he's telling the truth . . . I said that myself."

Dustali Khan yelled at Dear Uncle, "You see that? You see that? He confesses it himself!"

But before Dear Uncle could question him, the cadet officer said tranquilly, "Well, the truth of the matter is that that day you had me over to the house with Deputy Taymur Khan, with the excuse a watch had been lost . . . I thought you'd realized that Qamar was having my baby and you wanted to catch me out and send me off to the courts and jail . . . I mean, I do this all the time, it's my job . . . I've nabbed thousands of criminals . . . I said I'd been hit by a bullet so you'd leave me alone and not send me to the courts and the police . . ."

Mash Qasem, who'd been silent for a while, jumped into the conversation, "Eh, can you beat that! . . . What a brain . . . Well done,

Ghiasabad! I mean I kept sayin' there's no one like the folks from Ghiasabad when it comes to bein' manly, to bein' real men . . ."

Asadollah Mirza could not control himself any longer and burst into a loud guffaw of laughter; with his words broken by peals of laughter he said, "Congratulations . . . Cadet Officer Ghiasabadi . . . from today I welcome you as an honorary citizen of San Francisco!"

The cadet officer laughed along with him and said, "Very kind of you, your excellency . . . you're really very good to me."

Dear Uncle shouted, "Gentlemen! The meeting is degenerating into laughter and jokes . . . Asadollah! . . . Cadet Officer! Silence!"

Then he turned to Dustali Khan and said, "Continue, Dustali!"

But Dustali Khan was as silent as if he'd been electrocuted; his complexion had turned the color of lead. Uncle colonel sat completely silent, with his head bowed. I could guess that thoughts of his Esfahani rug prevented him from following what was going on at the meeting. My father's face was bright and cheerful.

Cadet Officer Ghiasabadi began a furious counterattack. "I'm very fond of my wife. My wife's very fond of me. We have a lovely little child . . . and there's another on the way. In Mr. Dustali Khan's eyes this is dishonorable, but when he himself went on Wednesday into a married woman's house while her husband was away, that was perfectly all right."

Dustali Khan emerged from his catatonic state and yelled, "Me . . . in a married woman's house?"

The cadet officer mildly answered, "Will you let me call Fati here? . . . Fati, the daughter of Mrs. Khanomha, who's Qamar's aunt . . . so that we can ask her who it was sneaked out of Shir Ali the butcher's house on Wednesday?"

Once again Dustali Khan froze. A wide grin split Asadollah's face from ear to ear. He took his glasses from his pocket and put them on. Staring at Dustali Khan's face he said with a mischievous laugh, "Dustali? . . . Really? . . . You finally got to San Francisco with Tahereh, Shir Ali's wife . . . Right into the city?"

"Asadollah, shut up!"

"Moment, Dustali! The truth will set you free! . . . Confess, because if you don't the cadet officer's going to send for Fati!"

"Asadollah, just don't complain if I do something terrible to you!"

"Moment, moment, *momentissimo* . . . Good luck to you! . . . Shir Ali's wife wasn't enough, then; now you want to do something terrible to me, too? What kind of a pill have you swallowed to make you so evil minded?"

Dear Uncle's voice rang out, "Asadollah! Asadollah!"

At that moment Dustali Khan snatched up the tin of *gaz* and, making as if to throw it at Asadollah, said, "I'll knock your brains out if you're not careful!"

Asadollah Mirza stopped laughing and said, "What's this, what's this for?"

Then he suddenly jumped up from his place and dashed over to the window. He bent down toward the yard and shouted, "Mr. Shir Ali . . . Shir Ali . . ."

Dear Uncle Napoleon and everyone else shouted virtually in chorus, "Asadollah . . . stop it!"

Asadollah went on with what he had been saying, "Shir Ali, if it's not too much trouble, bring up a few teas . . ."

For a moment silence reigned in the room. Mash Qasem made use of the opportunity, "Well now, why should I lie? To the grave it's ah . . . ah . . . In forty years I haven't seen such shameless behavior. God help us if Shir Ali gets wind of it . . . You know, Mr. Dustali Khan, that today Shir Ali's brought a leg of mutton along . . . ?"

A moment later Shir Ali's formidable and gigantic form, bearing a tray of tea glasses, came into the room. "Good day to you."

While everyone was silently taking glasses of tea and putting sugar in them, Asadollah Mirza, with a serious expression and a smile in his eyes, said as if he were continuing a conversation, "Yes, just as I was saying, these things can get very bad . . . Well, people who have any interest in their family's honor and respectability become upset . . . It doesn't matter if they're upper class or lower class, whether they're rich or tradesmen . . . take, for example, Mr. Shir Ali here . . ."

And after pausing for a moment he turned to Shir Ali. "You, Mr. Shir Ali . . . I'd like to ask you . . . suppose you have a friend, someone you feel close to . . . and you see a strange man go into his house when he isn't there . . . How would you feel?"

Shir Ali muttered forcefully, "Your excellency, on the Master's soul, don't be saying those things . . . you just have to say those things and I come over all funny, saving your reverence, I want to crush these walls in my fists, I want to tear this door and these windows from their hinges . . ."

Without realizing that he was still holding a tray with a glass of tea on it, Shir Ali clenched his fists; the glass of tea spilled on uncle colonel's head, and a scream of "I'm scalded!" went up to the heavens. Dear Uncle Napoleon's lips began to quiver. He turned pale, and as he tried to stand up he let out a terrifying scream, "I said, Enough! No more! . . . This is a plot of theirs, too . . . This is another blow . . . They want to smash my family into pieces . . . They're afraid of me and they strike at my family . . . God, is there no end to their cruelty, to their lack of decency?"

And in the midst of the general racket and uproar of the meeting coming to an end, Dear Uncle Napoleon once again fell back motionless on the sofa.

His father's cry had brought Puri into the room; he kept repeating, "Who did this . . . Who scalded my dad?"

Finally Asadollah Mirza shouted, "You stupid donkey, instead of going for a doctor, you stand there screaming! Whoever did it, what do you want to do to him? It wasn't done on purpose . . . The tea slipped from Shir Ali's hand and spilt on your father's head. And now you want to go and get a pin and stick it into him 'cause he's been a naughty boy?"

"So should I go for a doctor?"

"Yes, go . . . it'll be enough if you're not here screaming, the patients'll get better by themselves." ·

Puri went for a doctor.

Asadollah Mirza and Mash Qasem were massaging Dear Uncle Napoleon's hands and feet; no one was paying much attention to uncle colonel's scald. Except that, with his face flushed with rage, Dustali Khan said, "It's all the fault of that good-for-nothing little swine. Besides being a thief and a crook, the disgusting little swine's a murderer . . . can't you see how he's blinded the colonel?"

Cadet Officer Ghiasabadi tranquilly answered, "Did I have any thing to do with this, sir? Do you consider that I . . ."

Dustali Khan's yell interrupted him, "I'll show you who you're dealing with! You think you can scald the colonel's face, do you?"

"I'm waiting for you to show me."

And then he went on under his breath, "This is very peculiar. What has my wife getting pregnant got to do with the colonel's head being scalded? It's not as if I've the faucet on a samovar instead of . . ."

Asadollah Mirza had caught his words in passing and said, "The cadet officer's quite right. It's not as if he has the faucet on a samovar to do his business with. And even if he did, it wouldn't scald the colonel's face and head. Unless of course, God forbid, we're to imagine that . . ."

Dustali Khan screamed, "Just shut up, Asadollah."

Instead of answering, Asadollah Mirza turned to Shir Ali. "Shir Ali, you won't suddenly go off and leave, will you . . . I've a couple of words to say to you; if it's not too much trouble, wait downstairs till I call you."

Dustali was so furious he had forgotten Shir Ali was there; he turned pale again and said in a mild voice, "Asadollah, this is no time for joking. Can't you see that the Master has fainted . . . that the colonel's been scalded!"

Shir Ali left the room while uncle colonel was moaning and groaning, "Who feels sorry for me? . . . Who cares about me being scalded?"

"Come, come, my dear colonel, we all care about you, but the Master's not well . . . we have to make him all right first."

Uncle colonel whined, "You mean I'm all right? . . . My whole face feels as though it's been put in a baker's oven."

"Take your hand away and let's see how it is . . ."

At this moment Puri came back panting and said that Dr. Naser al-Hokama was not at home. While my father and Mash Qasem were busy pouring a cordial down Dear Uncle Napoleon's throat, Asadollah Mirza more or less dragged uncle colonel's hand away from his face. His cheek and chin were just a little red.

In a scornful, mocking voice Asadollah Mirza said, "Dear, dear . . . look, a layer of skin and flesh has come away!"

Mash Qasem took his words seriously and before he had even looked properly said, "Eh, can you beat that! . . . Savin' your reverence, the colonel's face is like. . . ."

Asadollah Mirza guessed that Mash Qasem was about to compare the colonel's face to something and interrupted him, "Mash Qasem, why are you stirring things up? . . . I was joking. Look, it's just turned a bit red."

But Mash Qasem was not going to give up, "Well sir, why should I lie? To the grave it's ah . . . ah . . . In this business of burns and scalds I'm a bit of a doctor myself . . . There's only one thing for a burn like this."

Anxiously uncle colonel said, "What thing? What do we have to do?"

"Well sir, why should I lie? To the grave it's ah . . . ah . . . Savin' your reverence, savin' your reverence, if you'll excuse me like, what you have to do is rub a little boy's pee on it."

Asadollah Mirza was about to object but he suppressed what he'd been going to say and, after a moment's pause, said, "I've heard that, too. But where are we going to get a little boy from now?"

"I think if he's a big boy it don't matter. Just so long as he isn't too old. If you ask me, I mean as far as I can tell, if it was Mr. Puri's it'd be sure to work."

Uncle colonel's objections shook the heavens, "Drop dead, will you! . . . Now you're wanting to rub any bit of filth you can lay your hands on on my face ? . . . Instead of talking such rubbish, go and get a little oil. Almond oil, castor oil . . . bring me some kind of oil."

As Mash Qasem was leaving the room he said, "All right then I'll go . . . but it's not nearly as good as the medicine I said."

Asadollah Mirza said, "Now, it'll do no harm to try."

Puri spluttered his objections, "Don't talk such nonsense . . . and anyway I can't go now . . ."

Uncle colonel was close to screaming again but Mash Qasem came back with a spoonful of something greasy. "Well sir, we didn't have no almond oil nor no castor oil . . . so in the kitchen I got a bit of Kermanshah cooking oil and brought it."

After they had rubbed the Kermanshah oil, for lack of anything better, on uncle colonel's skin, he calmed down somewhat and said, "Well, never mind about me . . . Think of something for my brother!"

My father's voice responded, "Don't worry too much . . . his breathing's become regular . . . now he's coming round . . . just that it would be better if you went in the next room so the Master can rest here a little, so that he gets completely better."

Asadollah Mirza said, "I agree it would be better if we went in the other room so that there's less noise in here . . . Come on, Puri . . . Off you go, Dustali!"

Dustali Khan sat down on a chair and said, "I swear that until I know how I stand with this man, I will not set foot outside this room. I'll stay until the Master feels better and he clears up for me where I stand with this esteemed in-law of his!"

Cadet Officer Ghiasabadi's voice joined in, "The same goes for me . . . I'll stay here till the Master stops this esteemed relative of his from being such a nuisance."

In a peremptory tone Asadollah Mirza said, "Dustali, out!"

"I said I'm not moving from here."

"You're not moving, aren't you? . . . Moment, moment, Mr. Shir Ali!"

"Don't you come all high and mighty with me . . . Call him and we'll see if you dare mention his wife's name."

Mash Qasem jumped in, "I beg you, your excellency . . . if this Shir Ali hasn't been able to control his wife up to now, it's because no one dares tell him what she's been up to! You remember master Gholam? . . . Have you forgotten about the dough-kneader at the baker's? And as for those who pass the news on to him . . . he burns their houses down!"

Before Asadollah Mirza could reply, a groan came from Dear Uncle Napoleon's closed mouth. Everyone gathered round him.

A few moments later Dear Uncle opened his eyes. For a while he stared around in a bewildered fashion, then said in a weak voice, "I don't know why I should be like this!"

Then he seemed to remember what had been going on. "A corporal . . . an Indian corporal instead of a colonel!"

Asadollah Mirza quickly said, "Moment, sir . . . that matter's all over and done with . . . I dealt with him very severely, and I sent him packing from the house . . . so now forget about him!"

Dear Uncle stayed silent for a few moments, gazing bewilderedly about; then he repeated under his breath, "You sent him packing . . . sent him packing . . . you did well . . . you did a good thing . . . I . . . I'm past it now, but you won't agree to be shamed by them. We've fought together, shoulder to shoulder, back to back . . . and now we'll be captured together."

Uncle colonel shouted anxiously, "My brother . . . brother!"

But it was as if Dear Uncle Napoleon didn't hear his voice. With the same bewildered look, and in the same tone he went on, "We'll be captured together, but with honor . . . respected and with dignity! In the histories they'll write 'The great commander held out to the last of his strength . . . '"

"Brother . . . brother . . . !"

Dear Uncle Napoleon turned toward him. He looked at him for a moment and then mildly asked, "Why have you smeared oil on your head and face?"

"Well, my face was scalded, brother."

"Scalded? . . . scalded? . . . Good for you! Scalded with honor, not with shame and disgrace."

Then his gaze travelled from one face to another of those present, "Did you see, Dustali? . . . Did you see how a great commander lives? . . . You too will go into captivity with me, but with honor!"

For a moment Dear Uncle was quiet. Everyone exchanged anxious looks. Dustali Khan's voice broke the silence, "Sir, I'm a captive right now, sir! A captive to this human devil . . . I've stayed here to know where I stand with this man! With this esteemed Cadet Officer Ghiasabadi!"

"Cadet Officer Ghiasabadi? . . . the cadet officer's in captivity with us, too? My dear Cadet Officer!"

Cadet Officer Ghiasabadi, who was staring at Dear Uncle in astonishment, muttered, "No, he's completely off his head."

At this Dustali Khan hit him smartly on the head and said, "You're dad's off his head, you rotten little good-for-nothing."

The cadet officer gave Dustali Khan a good slap on the neck and the two went for each other, but the simultaneous cries of my father and uncle colonel separated them. Just then Dear Uncle Napoleon raised himself with difficulty, as if he could hear nothing of their row, and began to stagger toward the door.

"Let us go and prepare for our departure!"

Everyone ran to his side. "Moment, moment, the Master's leaving . . . sir, allow us to help you!"

Without turning his head Dear Uncle Napoleon said in the same mild, calm tone, "Asadollah, is that you? . . . We'll go and get the luggage ready, but with honor, Asadollah! Captivity is our inheritance . . . but captivity with honor!"

With Asadollah Mirza and Mash Qasem supporting his arms, Dear Uncle Napoleon set off. Everyone followed after him; they looked like people escorting a corpse to the grave. After getting Dear Uncle to his house, Asadollah Mirza came back to my father's. He was sad and silent.

My father began the conversation, "It's all the fault of that stupid fool Dustali Khan who upset our plans."

"Moment, moment, you can be sure that the Master, perhaps even without realizing it himself, actually wants to be taken into captivity . . . He's made up his mind that destiny is going to give him the same fate as was given to Napoleon . . . You could even say thank goodness Dustali Khan came when he did and brought the matter to a conclusion in this way . . . I'm certain that if the Indian had made every possible concession to him, still at the last minute he'd have found some excuse to set Shir Ali the butcher on him so that the negotiations would collapse."

"What do you think we should do now?"

"God knows, my mind isn't capable of thinking up anything else. We'll have to wait and see what happens."

Three days after Dear Uncle's meeting with the Indian corporal, very early in the morning, Mash Qasem signalled me to come into the garden, and said that Layli wanted to see me.

I saw Layli in the sweetbrier arbor. She was wearing the grey dress of her school uniform. What made me catch my breath was that her eyes were red and swollen. She seemed to have been crying all night until the morning, and when I knew the reason for her emotional distress I felt even more breathless. The previous night her father had called her and Puri to him and told them he was certain that in the next two days the English would arrest him. They would take him to a place from which there was virtually no hope he would ever return, and his last request of them was that they be ready to be married, so that as soon as the English appeared the marriage ceremony could take place in the presence of their doomed commander.

It was difficult for me to speak, "What did you say, Layli?"

The poor child burst into tears again; sobbing, she said, "What could I say? Daddy's sick; if I'd said no, I'm sure that with his bad heart his life would've been in danger."

"But Layli, if they're going to leave your wedding until the English officials come for him, I'm not worried. Because you're a grown girl and you know that's all just a fantasy. The English have no interest in Dear Uncle at all."

"I know . . . if he was going to wait till the English officials came, that would be all right. But he said that next month it's the birth of one of the Imams, and they should get on with the wedding by then. But he said that we should be ready so that if the English came to take him away before the month was up, they could send for the Seyed straightaway and have the ceremony . . . you tell me what I should do."

"Layli, if you get married, I won't stay alive after that . . . tell your dad that you want to wait and marry me!"

With tears pouring down her face, Layli said, "If he was well, if he wasn't ill, I'd tell him; but I'm really afraid. I'm sure that if I contradict him, God strike me dumb for saying it, it'll all be over . . . You think of something!"

Bewildered and upset, and feeling as if my heart would burst from my chest, I promised her I would think of something.

But what could I think of?

Once again I thought of the only person in the family whose clear-sightedness and human sympathy I trusted, Asadollah Mirza. Without realizing what I was doing, instead of going to school I set off for his house. I was sure that he would repeat the same old jokes and not give me a straight answer, but I had no other recourse.

I imagined how my conversation with him would go: "Uncle Asadollah, I don't know what to do."

"Why can't you get it into your silly head? I've said over and over, don't forget San Francisco . . ."

This was the only road Asadollah Mirza ever suggested to me. But I loved Layli so much that, even if at his promptings I occasionally imagined such things, I hated myself for it and drove the thought of them furiously from my mind.

Asadollah Mirza was preparing to leave for the office. I had guessed correctly. As he was shaving in front of the mirror he said, "Oh, get away with you . . . I've told you over and over, take a trip to San Francisco . . ."

The noise of my objections couldn't stop his talking. "I've told you a thousand times, don't forget San Francisco . . . if you're not going to go to San Francisco, try Los Angeles . . . that's a very nice little trip . . . these days I myself am supposed to go on a trip . . . but I have bad luck. Instead of San Francisco I'm supposed to go to Beirut . . . don't forget to take a trip . . . as the poet of Shiraz, Sheikh Sa'di, says:

'Why suffer like a barnyard fowl at home
When you can fly on journeys like a dove?'

Have you read it or not? It's a famous poem by Sa'di:

'Don't give your heart to any friend, to any place,
For lands and seas are broad, and vast the human race.'"

Asadollah Mirza suddenly fell silent and looked at me,."Moment, moment, moment, let me see . . . Look at me, let me see . . . Are you really crying? . . . You great big silly donkey! Instead of packing your bags and setting off tonight for San Francisco, you're crying like a little girl."

Asadollah Mirza tried not to show it, but it was clear he was very moved . . . he wiped the soap from his face with a face-cloth and sat down next to me. In a serious, concerned voice he said, "My dear boy, don't be upset. I'll think of something for you . . ."

Then he went over to a sideboard, filled two small glasses from a bottle, and came back to me. "Drink this first, before we talk! . . . I said, Drink it! . . . For goodness sake, are you going to or not?"

Without thinking I took the glass from his hand and drank. I felt a burning sensation down to the pit of my stomach.

"And take this cigarette as well! . . . I'm warning you! . . . Take it! . . . Bravo!"

Asadollah Mirza lit a cigarette for himself too. He leant back in an easy chair. After a few moments' silence he said, "Please, listen to what I'm going to say very seriously . . . I'm not joking, not at all. Since, my good man, you've shown again and again that you're not up to San Francisco, and since the only way of solving the problem revolves around San Francisco . . . I think that you should at least agree to pretend to go to San Francisco! Or pretend to go to Los Angeles . . . though, no . . . that's no good."

"Uncle Asadollah . . ."

"Moment, don't talk when I'm talking! . . . Imagine a university or some educational institution where the conditions of success are that you are literate and that you study . . . now someone turns up who wants to be successful there, but he can't be bothered to study. He has to pretend to study, to be a serious student. And in my opinion, if Layli is to be successful without you two making a trip to San Francisco, she has to assume the face of a tired traveller who has just come back from San Francisco . . . and then Dear Uncle will be forced either to marry you off right now, or to wait two or three years and then give you to one another."

"Uncle Asadollah, this is a really hard task. Even if I agree to it, I don't think Layli will."

"Then she'll go and become the wife of that spluttering Arab horse."

"Doesn't any other way occur to you now?"

"Well, maybe the only other way is for you to marry me . . . In any case you'd better hurry up because something else has happened which I told your father about yesterday. And now I'll tell you about it; if Dear Uncle hears of this event he'll call Seyed Abolqasem over this very night and marry Layli off to Puri."

"What event, Uncle Asadollah?"

"Of course the news hasn't been officially announced yet, but it's true. The Allies have arrested a large number of people who they believe to be against the English and supporters of the Germans, and sent them off to Arak . . . if Dear Uncle gets wind of this, he'll pack his bags and the first thing he'll do will be to send Layli over to her husband's house."

"Uncle Asadollah, do you think you could give me another glass of cognac?"

"Bravo! Bit by bit you're becoming a man! . . . These are the signs of reaching puberty . . . cigarettes, cognac and San Francisco . . . God willing, you'll get to the third yet!"

"Uncle Asadollah, couldn't you talk to Dear Uncle and tell him about our situation?"

"Moment, moment, *momentissimo* . . . You can be sure that if Dear Uncle realizes that something like this is going on, he'll have Seyed Abolqasem round here in five minutes to marry Layli off to Puri, even if he has to drag him down from the pulpit to do so."

Since I knew I wasn't able to carry out Asadollah Mirza's advice, and even, as he would put it, pretending to have gone to San Francisco was beyond me, I started pleading with him. Finally he softened and said gently, "Like a doctor who knows that water is bad for a patient that's just had an operation, but who gives way when confronted with his begging and pleading, I too—although it will make the situation worse . . . although maybe . . . just wait while I think about it today, I'll see if something can't be done."

That evening Asadollah Mirza came to find me.

"Did you think about it, Uncle Asadollah? Did a way occur to you?"

"Unfortunately it's impossible to talk to Dear Uncle about you and Layli. As I said, if he gets wind of this, it's all over . . . I went to see him especially, and found an excuse to mention you, and I saw that the situation is very bad indeed."

"What did he say, Uncle Asadollah? Tell me . . . please!"

Asadollah Mirza hesitated for a few moments and then said, "It's not a bad idea for you to hear what he said, so that you'll give up all hopes in that direction. When you were mentioned he only said:

'A wolf is what a wolf-cub grows to finally
     Although it might grow up in human company.'"

"What did you say?"

"Moment, after he'd shown what he felt, did you expect me to say 'I came to ask for your daughter's hand for the wolf-cub'? . . . And now I'm afraid of something else. As he was saying those verses that donkey Dustali arrived and heard him. I'm afraid he'll pass what he heard on to your father and there'll be another problem to add to those we already have. In short, be prepared for things to get very much worse."

"But is it possible for things to get worse than this, Uncle Asadollah?"

"You bet it is! . . . If that remark reaches your father's ears, within two hours he'll find some way to see that Dear Uncle hears about people being sent off to Arak . . . And then he'll immediately start the 'Here comes the bride' proceedings!"

"Tell Dustali Khan not to make any fuss."

"Either you're still a child or you don't know what a malicious nature that donkey Dustali has . . . if I were to say such a thing it would make matters worse; as things stand, perhaps God will put it into his mind to guard his disgusting tongue . . . In any case you study how to pretend you've been to San Francisco till I see how things are turning out."

I parted from Asadollah Mirza in a very distressed and confused state of mind. The new terror he had planted in my thoughts was an unbearable torment to me. If Dear Uncle's remark were really to reach my father's ears, and my father saw to it that Dear Uncle heard about people being arrested and sent off to Arak, then what would happen?

My terror was not groundless. I think Dustali Khan took it upon himself to gossip, because on the following evening, in uncle colonel's house, where Dear Uncle Napoleon and a few relatives had gathered for supper, Farrokh Laqa suddenly turned up quite unexpectedly. As usual she was dressed in black from head to toe. "Very nice to see you all . . . well, well, what a party! . . . In the afternoon I went to the funeral ceremony for Monir's husband . . . I was coming back this way, and I said to myself, I'll just say hello."

A profound silence settled on the group. Shamsali Mirza had just come back from a trip to Hamadan and, simply to make his presence known, asked, "Which Monir?"

"Monir who's Etemad al-Mamalek's daughter . . . the poor thing's had a lot of bad luck recently . . . her husband was no age at all, he came home from the office at noon and went to wash his hands and face and had a heart attack in the outhouse . . . by the time they'd got a doctor it was all over with him, God rest his soul . . . today at the ceremony they said he'd had the heart attack because he was so upset about his sister's husband . . ."

"What's happened to his sister's husband, then?"

"But you must have heard . . . the English arrested his sister's husband a few days ago, along with some other people, and had them all sent off . . . people say they sent them to Arak . . ."

Suddenly Dear Uncle Napoleon's choked voice broke in, "The English? Why?"

Asadollah Mirza tried to change the subject by making noise and generally stirring up the meeting, but Dear Uncle shouted, "Wait, Asadollah, I need to know! Ma'am, you said the English have arrested some people?"

"Yes, and Etemad's sister's husband was one of them, the poor thing . . . poor thing, he had no idea of what was going on."

Terrified, I looked at Dear Uncle's pallid face. Perhaps many there did not know why Dear Uncle was so worried, but at least two or three people were well aware of the reason and a few others guessed.

There were a few moments of silence. Dear Uncle muttered, "The English . . . the English . . . they've set to work."

Suddenly he stood up and yelled, "Qasem . . . Qasem . . . we're going home."

And he left the room, paying no attention to the guests' noisy protests.

TWENTY-FIVE

AFTER DEAR UNCLE NAPOLEON had left the room, uncle colonel ran after him. Everyone exchanged puzzled looks. Asadollah Mirza stared pointedly at my father, but my father avoided his eye.

Finally Farrokh Laqa said, "I don't understand why the Master was so upset. The Master isn't any relation of Monir's husband, or of his sister's husband!"

Asadollah Mirza gave her an angry look. Trying to maintain an outward calm, he said, "No, the Master's upset about poor Mansur al-Saltaneh . . . you know, that uncle of Dustali's . . ."

"But what's happened to Dustali's uncle?"

"You mean you haven't heard, ma'am? . . . God rest his soul, he suffered so much . . ."

Farrokh Laqa suddenly smelt the possibility of another funeral ceremony and her eyes shone. "God strike me dead! Then why haven't I heard about it? When did this happen? Where's the funeral ceremony?"

"Oh, it's not clear yet where they'll hold the ceremony, because it only happened today . . ."

"Well, see me in the grave, but I never heard about it!"

"Moment, I think it wouldn't be a bad idea for you to go and drop in on Dustali."

"It's a pity it's so late, otherwise . . ."

Asadollah Mirza interrupted her, "No, it's not so late . . . as it happens when I was on my way here I saw Dustali was just going home."

Mrs. Farrokh Laqa was of two minds. Asadollah Mirza continued, "What with the relationship your mother had with them, I'd imagine that it'll be you yourself who binds up the late lamented's jaw."

Farrokh Laqa stood up and said, "You're right, this is terrible. I'll go now and pay Dustali Khan and Aziz al-Saltaneh a visit . . ."

When Farrokh Laqa had gone, everyone present who understood why Asadollah Mirza had invented this piece of news breathed a sigh of relief. Asadollah Mirza turned to uncle colonel. "The important thing was to get that old owl to go back to the ruin where she belongs . . . now, please tell us how the Master is."

Uncle colonel said with a gloomy face, "My brother threw me out, very angrily. He said he wanted to be alone."

An hour later only Asadollah Mirza, uncle colonel and my father were still there. And I was sitting hunched in a corner listening to their conversation.

My father said, "To be honest, I'm afraid that—God forbid—the Master will do himself an injury . . . do you remember that day he was talking about when Napoleon took poison after the defeat inflicted by the Allied armies?"

Asadollah Mirza took a sip of wine and said, "I'm not worried about that. If you remember the first time that Napoleon had to surrender he took poison, but after Waterloo he waited until they came and took him off to St. Helena."

"But, after all, we shouldn't expect him to follow exactly in Napoleon's footsteps . . ."

Uncle colonel, who had been deep in thought, said, "Asadollah Mirza, I've had an idea. How would it be if I personally had a talk with the Indian, Brigadier Maharat Khan?"

"You want to talk about the Master with Brigadier Maharat Khan? But the Brigadier . . ."

"No, about myself . . . about the rug that rotten little charlatan of an Indian walked off with without so much as a by-your-leave . . . I mean just think of it . . . there never was such a shameless thief . . ."

"God keep you, colonel, your brother's slipping away and you're still thinking about your rug?"

"No, I'm not worried about my older brother . . . he's not a willow tree to tremble in a wind like this . . . A man who's spent his whole existence fighting and struggling knows how to put up with the ups and downs of life."

Asadollah Mirza gave my father a hopeless look and said, "Then in that case, I'm going to go and have a good sleep, too. Charity begins at home, they say."

As I was returning home along with my father and Asadollah Mirza, I heard Asadollah Mirza ask my father quietly and sarcastically, "Can you guess who told Farrokh Laqa about the English rounding people up and sending them off to Arak?"

My father stopped in his tracks and took him by the arm. "Now, your excellency, are you implying . . . ?"

"Moment, moment, I'm not implying anything; just asking."

"No, no, it seemed to me your were hinting at something . . . If you're thinking I had anything to do with this, you're mistaken. I swear on my father's soul I had nothing to do with the matter."

It wasn't just that I doubted him because I knew my father swore things very easily on the soul of his father, but it was clear that Asadollah Mirza too had gathered what he wanted to know because as I was accompanying him to the door after we'd got home he said, "No, there's no doubt at all, that filthy Dustali Khan has been gossiping to your father."

"What do you think we should do now, Uncle Asadollah?"

"Well, I can't think of anything else . . . I'm a local doctor, and when someone's caught a cold or feels under the weather I can prescribe a herb tea or an aspirin, but when it's a serious illness and it takes root, they have to call in a professional . . . on the first day I prescribed a touch of San Francisco, because I'm only a specialist in San Francisco. The patient didn't act on my prescription . . . and now things have gone way beyond San Francisco and Los Angeles and such like matters, so they'd better take this patient's family to a professional who'll prescribe another city for them!"

"You mean you want to give up on us?"

"No, lad, but for now there's nothing I can do . . . we'll have to wait and see first what happens about sending Dear Uncle off to Saint Helena, then we'll think again . . ."

By this time we had reached the alleyway. Suddenly I saw someone in the distance running toward us. It was the shoeshine man. After the customary greetings he said to Asadollah Mirza, "Sir, I need you to do something for me."

"Moment, I have to do something for you, too? . . . It's very strange that I can't manage my own affairs but at the same time I've turned into the area's general problem-solver . . . What's going on now? What's happened?"

"Well, two or three days ago the Master started pestering me to pack up the tools of my trade and leave. Till now Mash Qasem's

brought me three or four messages that the Master doesn't want me
to have my stall here."

"What did you say?"

"But sir, just consider. I've been here so long now I've found a
nice group of customers, and where am I to go? You can't run a business gadding about from one place to another."

"No. I want to know, when Mash Qasem brought the message,
what exactly did you say?"

"I said 'Tell the master that I'm stopping here . . . I mean, I can't
go anywhere else.'"

Asadollah Mirza ground his teeth together and muttered, "You
gave the worst possible answer! Now you'll really have to go!"

Then he started advising the shoeshine man that he shouldn't be
too stubborn and said that it would be best to listen to what he was
told and to set his stall up a couple of streets further down. But the
shoeshine man begged and pleaded with him to speak on his behalf.

"Moment, moment, God forbid it's not true what people are saying, is it? That you've got yourself mixed up with one of the women
around here?"

After the shoeshine man had spent some time swearing that
nothing like that was going on, Asadollah Mirza promised that he
would do what he could for him, and when the shoeshine man had
left, he burst out with a great guffaw of laughter. "It's just one damn
thing after another . . . as if we didn't have enough troubles, here's
another . . . On the one side, this fellow's got himself mixed up with
Shir Ali's wife and doesn't want to go; on the other side, your Dear
Uncle's waiting for the English officers to turn up to take him off to
Arak, and he doesn't want this fellow to be here in case, God forbid,
he scares them off . . . this is turning into a real madhouse."

"Uncle Asadollah, do you mean you think Dear Uncle still believes this shoeshine man is working for the Germans?"

"Perhaps he's no longer so sure, but there's still a doubt in his
heart . . . and however things stand, he wants to smooth the way of
the English into this neighborhood."

"Uncle Asadollah, I've made so many problems for you I'm embarrassed to talk anymore about . . ."

With a laugh Asadollah Mirza interrupted what I was saying, "No,
don't be embarrassed, say on . . . but instead I'll read your thoughts.

You want to say that now Dear Uncle is really waiting for the English to come, that means your and Layli's situation is in danger . . . It's not all unlikely, but don't ask me any more questions, give me till the morning to think and see what occurs to me."

Once again, I passed one of the worst nights of my life. During the short time sleep did close my eyes I had nightmares in which all my surroundings were muddled together:

Wearing a wedding dress, Layli was going toward the door to a castle; she was arm-in-arm with her husband and walking between two rows of English soldiers who were holding their swords above the couple's heads; Layli's husband was none other than Shir Ali the butcher. The commander of the English troops was Mash Qasem, and he was wearing a Scottish military uniform that included a kilt instead of trousers. I was shouting. Puri was walking behind the bridal couple, looking at me with that equine face of his, and cackling in a terrifying manner.

Carrying a rug, uncle colonel came after the bride and groom. Wearing a doorman's uniform and a blond wig, and with a thick staff in his hand, Cadet Officer Ghiasabadi was announcing, "The bride and groom!" Dr. Naser al-Hokama was playing the saxophone. My father and Asadollah Mirza had linked hands and were circling around me singing a folksong from the American west, in which the name San Francisco came again and again, and the repetitions rang in my ears . . . San Francisco . . . San Francisco . . . Once again I'd started to shout and to run; Mash Qasem came toward me in his Scottish soldier's uniform and said, speaking Persian but with an English accent, "Lad, get out of here, it's all over with you." And I was shouting, "Mash Qasem, do something! Weren't you my friend?" And he was answering in that same English accent, "Well lad, why should I lie? To the grave it's ah . . . ah . . . It's not my fault, ask that gentleman there." And I looked to where his outstretched finger was pointing: Dear Uncle Napoleon was wearing the hat and uniform of Napoleon and was seated on a white horse; he had a leg of mutton in his hand and was shouting out "Attack! Forward!" and his cavalry trampled me beneath their horses' hooves . . . and Farrokh Laqa, dressed in black from head to toe, was saying the prayers for the dying over me.

When I wanted to get up in the morning I was unable to. My whole body ached. I lay there so weak that the time to go to school came and went. When my mother came to find me she struck herself on the head and chest. I was burning with a high fever. When I tried to get up, my head began to turn and I fell back motionless into the bedclothes.

I realized that I was ill more from my mother's and father's concern and from their constant coming and going, than from how I actually felt. They brought Dr. Naser al-Hokama. In among his whispered words I heard the word "typhoid." Although my brain wasn't functioning properly because of my high fever and my illness, I was certain that it was the terrible night I had passed that had caused my fever and that the doctor was mistaken. I passed the whole day in this wretched state. Then I realized that I'd been delirious a few times. Toward evening I began to get a little better. I recognized Asadollah Mirza's smiling face. But I couldn't speak.

On the following morning I had another reason to be sure of Dr. Naser al-Hokama's ignorance and lack of knowledge of the nature of things. My fever had quite gone and I was almost back to health again but I felt extremely weak. When I wanted to get up my mother noisily protested, but I assured her that I was well and made my way to the garden.

Mash Qasem was busy watering the flowers. But unusually he had on the clothes he wore for going out; he had rolled the legs of his trousers up above his knees, and he was handling his watering-can very carefully so as not to wet his clothes.

Without raising his head he said, "Thank God your feelin' poorly wasn't anythin' serious, lad. I was really worried. Yesterday I came to ask about you, in the afternoon . . . you was delirious . . . I wish that doctor could see you today . . . The heathen was sayin' yesterday how you'd surely got typhoid . . . that crowd don't know a buffalo from a fiddle, and that's God's truth!"

"Mash Qasem, praise God, I'm all right now. But why are you wearing your clothes for going out? Are you going anywhere?"

Mash Qasem gave me a sorrowful look and answered, "Well lad, why should I lie? To the grave it's ah . . . ah . . . We'll be leavin' today or tomorrow. Maybe this is the last time I'll be waterin' the flowers; likely enough the English are on their way right now. Whatever bad or good you've seen from me, forgive me!"

"Mash Qasem, what's Dear Uncle doing?"

"Eh, eh, don't ask, lad. May God put no Moslem through what he's been through! From the night before last to now you'd think the Master'd aged twenty years . . . The night before last he didn't sleep till mornin'. Poor feller, it's like he was writin' his will."

"How is he today?"

"Today, thanks be to God, you could say he was calm . . . All his wildness went yesterday."

"Mash Qasem, has Layli gone to school or is she still in the house? . . . I want to have a word with her."

"Eh, where've you been, lad? Crack of dawn this mornin' the Master sent all the children with the colonel to Abali, to where the colonel's orchard is . . . And he's right, too. When the English come he doesn't want the children to see 'em shackle the Master and take him off . . . And maybe they'd be doin' somethin' terrible to the children. Whatever you can say about the English is true . . ."

"How long will they stay there, Mash Qasem?"

"Well lad, till the English come and take us."

"And if they don't come, what then?"

Mash Qasem sneered, "You're such a child, lad, you don't know the English yet . . . since the night before last me and the Master haven't taken our clothes off. Twice we've packed up the saucepans so's we wouldn't die of hunger on the way to Arak . . . because the English only give their prisoners stew made with brick dust and snake oil. There was a man in our town once who fell into the hands of the English . . ."

It was impossible to get anything out of Mash Qasem. I decided to go and find Asadollah Mirza, but he turned up before I'd left the house. He had come to ask how I was doing. When he saw me on my feet he was extremely pleased. "Just think of it . . . that stupid Naser al-Hokama was quite sure it was typhoid . . . at least we can be thankful he didn't say the child had caught syphilis . . . !"

I tried to get a moment alone with him, but I guessed that he was very preoccupied with something, or perhaps, with all the family problems that were going on, he didn't have the patience to listen to my lovesick moanings.

He was soon busy talking to my father. "What's new, then? Has General Wellington come to take the Master yet?"

"Well, I haven't seen him yet, but this morning I asked Mash Qasem and he said that after he'd sent the family off he seemed to calm down . . . mind you, last night he slept in his clothes again."

"Shall we go and ask him how he's getting on?"

My father and Asadollah Mirza set off for Dear Uncle's house. Without thinking, I followed them. Dear Uncle didn't even glance at me. It seemed that either he hadn't heard or hadn't understood that I'd been ill. He was wearing a dark suit. Mohammad Ali Shah's insignia was on the lapel. What frightened me was his extreme pallor, and his sunken eyes. He was sitting calmly on the sofa. He wanted to get up to greet my father and Asadollah Mirza but was unable to. Asadollah Mirza was about to begin joking and laughing, but confronted by Dear Uncle's shattered face, he became silent.

However mentally calm Dear Uncle appeared to be, physically he was wasting away.

My father said, "You're a little pale. It seems you didn't sleep well. You'd better lie down."

Dear Uncle said in a calm voice, "I have rested. Now is the time for vigilance."

I looked out at the yard and the rooms that gave on to it. The house was completely empty and forlorn. Apart from Dear Uncle and Mash Qasem, there was no one there. Big padlocks were visible on the doors to most of the rooms.

Asadollah Mirza was worried about the state Dear Uncle was in and said, "I think it wouldn't be a bad idea for you to rest a little, and then if it happened . . ."

Dear Uncle suddenly became angry. "Asadollah, fatigue may have made me weak, but I want them to know that a warrior is still a warrior at the moment he is taken prisoner . . . they must not see my weakness."

"Moment, moment, you mean a warrior can't lie down? We read about it thousands of times in history; when he was waiting for the representatives to come from the allied armies, even Napoleon slept and rested as usual."

"Asadollah, what they want is for me to be worn down, to be broken, and then to arrest me, so that tomorrow they can besmirch my name in the history books."

"But sir . . ."

Asadollah had no chance to finish his sentence because the noise of some kind of uproar came in from the alleyway. Dear Uncle Napoleon's eyes stared fixedly at the door. His voice filled with emotion, he said, "What's happening? It seems they've come."

Asadollah Mirza stood up to go out, but Mash Qasem entered. "What was that noise, Mash Qasem?"

"Well sir, Shir Ali's havin' a word with that shoeshine feller."

Dear Uncle had leaned forward; he fell back again and asked mildly, "What happened finally? Has the shoeshine man gone or not?"

"What d'you mean, gone? As soon as Shir Ali lifted the leg of mutton in his hand, the poor feller flew off . . . he left his tools and stall and took off."

Calmly, Dear Uncle turned his face toward Asadollah Mirza. "Nothing important. A young lout who carried on his business here and at the same time had designs on people's wives and daughters."

Mash Qasem let everyone in on Dear Uncle's thoughts. "God keep you, sir. I wish you'd done this on the first day. On that first day I said this lad was a shameless feller."

There was sweat on Dear Uncle's forehead. He kept his hand on his heart, but continued to sit stiffly upright. A few moments passed in silence. Dear Uncle turned to Mash Qasem, "Qasem, have you put my gaiters in the suitcase?"

"Them as you tie on your shoes?"

"Yes, those."

"I've put both pairs in."

My father and Asadollah Mirza exchanged occasional glances, but they seemed unable to find anything to say. The silence was becoming uncomfortable. Mash Qasem quietly left the room.

Mildly, Dear Uncle said, "Asadollah, I've seen to everything. I'm leaving at peace with myself. But there's one thing I want to ask you . . ." Dear Uncle had no opportunity to finish what he was saying. Once again a commotion could be heard, this time coming from the garden.

Dear Uncle sat bolt upright on the sofa and listened. In amongst the uproar Mash Qasem's voice could be heard shouting that they mustn't disturb the Master. After listening for a moment Dear Uncle said in a choked voice, "Apparently they've come . . . Asadollah, go and see what that idiot Qasem is doing. It seems he's putting up a resistance, though I ordered him not to resist."

Asadollah Mirza had no chance to leave. The door burst open and Dustali Khan came in; his face was glowing and his head was swathed in bandages.

He was screaming and yelling so hard that it was impossible to make out what he was saying. Finally Dear Uncle said in peremptory tones, "Dustali, calm down! What's happened?"

Dustali Khan went on screaming and yelling. Asadollah Mirza shouted, "Dustali, shut up! Can't you see the Master isn't well?"

Dustali Khan seemed not to have been aware of Asadollah's presence until this moment; he stared at him wildly for a moment, then suddenly yelled, "And you, you shameless good-for-nothing little . . . you shut up! It's a pity for this family that you're part of it!"

"Moment, moment, Dustali what's happened? It's clear that whoever's knocked you on the head has made a good job of it because you've lost even that bit of common sense you once had! Why are you going for me like this?"

"What shameless bastard was it who sent Farrokh Laqa the night before last to say prayers for the dead for my uncle Mansur al-Saltaneh? Whatever has my poor uncle done to you that you should be so keen to see him dead?"

Dear Uncle angrily said, "Dustali, don't argue! This is no time for arguments! What's happened?"

Dustali Khan pulled himself together somewhat. He had two or three pieces of paper in his hand. He slammed his fist down on the table and said, "Either everyone in the family signs this document, or I will not bear the name of this family any longer."

"What document is this, Dustali? And why is your head all bandaged up?"

"Ask that lout, that scum you gave my daughter to. That shameless, lousy drug-addict broke my head with a stone . . . ask that Mr. Ghiasabadi from Qom!"

Asadollah Mirza burst into a guffaw of laughter, "Bravo, Mr. Ghiasabadi! This was very nicely done!"

Once again Dear Uncle mildly asked, "And what's this document for now?"

"If you'll be so kind as to take a look . . . this is from Dr. Naser al-Hokama and it certifies that Qamar has a psychological illness . . . it's a document that various people in the area have signed their agreement to. Sir, the girl is crazy. That rotten little charlatan Ghiasabadi is using up all her property and wealth . . . just think of it, he's selling Akbar Abad . . . if you'll allow me, I'll read the document: 'On behalf of all those distinguished gentlemen who are aware . . . '"

At this moment the noise of shouting came up from the garden. Dear Uncle yelled, "Silence, Dustali!" Then he muttered calmly, "It seems that this time they really have come."

And he tried to stand, but large drops of sweat stood on his forehead and he fell back where he was sitting.

Later on, whenever I read the story of Tristan and Isolde or heard people mention it, I thought of Dear Uncle waiting during that moment, because the emotion and anxiety with which he waited was in every way equal to the emotion and anxiety with which Tristan waited for the arrival of the golden-haired Isolde.

A moment later the door opened. Cadet Officer Ghiasabadi and his mother, and behind them Aziz al-Saltaneh, entered the room. Dear Uncle had been staring expectantly and agitatedly at the door; a sudden wave of despair welled up in his eyes. With a curse he turned his head away. The newcomers were all screaming and yelling and swearing together. Finally the sound of Aziz al-Saltaneh's yells drowned out the others' voices, "Dustali, I'll give you what for so it'll go down in history! Get going and get lost and get back to the house, you should be ashamed to look your son-in-law in the face!"

"I hope the gravediggers get hold of my son-in-law in double quick time! I'd rather have seventy years of bad luck than have such a crook of a son-in-law. The good-for-nothing's taking advantage of that girl's craziness . . ."

At this moment the cadet officer's mother gave such a scream that the window panes shook. "What a hell of a cheek you've got . . . never mind you, your father and grandfather should be proud to have such a son-in-law in the family . . . If you don't watch it, I'll smash your head and teeth in. Don't you make such remarks about my daughter-in-law! And she's got more brains than a hundred like you!"

At this moment, as Cadet Officer Ghiasabadi and his mother and Aziz al-Saltaneh were all cursing Dustali Khan, Aziz al-Saltaneh hit

Dustali Khan such a blow on his broken head, with her handbag, that his cries and moans went up to the heavens, and Dear Uncle's faint shouts, too, could be heard, "Stop it! Leave him alone! . . . At such a time . . . at a moment like this you can find time to . . . O God, send the English to free me from this crowd!"

And then there was a kick at the door. Mash Qasem came into the room; his eyes were red with anger and his lips were trembling; he let out a terrifying yell, "Shir Ali, throw all this lot out . . . these devils are killin' the Master, they are!"

Shir Ali, who had come in after Mash Qasem, glanced at Asadollah Mirza. As soon as he saw him give a signal of agreement, without any more hesitation he picked up Dustali from behind and began to swing him around in such a way that his legs were like a club banging against the bodies of the cadet officer and his mother and Aziz al-Saltaneh.

"Get lost, all of you . . . come on, out, before I crush you to pulp."

Screaming and shouting, the cadet officer and his mother and Aziz al-Saltaneh fled from the dangerous blows dealt by the legs of Dustali Khan, who was struggling in Shir Ali's embrace. When the room had been cleared, Dear Uncle, whose complexion had turned even paler and whose lips were trembling, moaned, "The English . . . the English . . . what are they waiting for?"

Asadollah Mirza was staring in consternation at Dear Uncle's pallid face; he shouted, "Mash Qasem, run and fetch Dr. Naser al-Hokama! Run, man!"

And he himself ran into the hall and picked up the telephone receiver. He dialled a number and said, "Doctor, send that medicine over to the house . . . I couldn't come myself, but send it quickly . . . the patient's not at all well."

Then with my father's help he laid Dear Uncle on his bed and took his pulse. "His pulse is very weak . . . I hope to God that idiot of a doctor is at home!"

Dear Uncle had turned completely white. Big drops of sweat were visible on his forehead and nose. Asadollah Mirza removed Dear Uncle's dark glasses and put them aside. My father was anxiously running back and forth. Without opening his eyes, Dear Uncle started to talk. "You come . . . you have to come with me . . . I've a lot to say . . .

they're certainly coming . . . they'll get here any minute . . . God give me strength to stand face to face with them . . ."

When the sound of Mash Qasem's footsteps could be heard in the yard, Dear Uncle opened his eyes a little and asked in a quavering voice, "Have they come? . . . Have they come?"

But when he saw Mash Qasem he was disappointed once again, and his head fell to one side. Dr. Naser al-Hokama had gone out of the house. My father sent Mash Qasem after the heart doctor who had looked after him for a while.

Asadollah Mirza was looking at Dear Uncle with fear and obvious anxiety and was massaging his hands and feet.

After a few minutes the sound of firm, regular footsteps came in from the yard. Dear Uncle seemed to collect the last remnants of his strength together to lift his head up and ask in a weak voice, "Have they come? . . . Have they come? . . . Lift me up . . . surely they've come."

Asadollah Mirza put his arm beneath Dear Uncle's shoulders and lifted him into a sitting position. The door to the room opened and I stood stock-still with astonishment.

An English soldier, holding the Union Jack in his left hand, stepped into the room. He clicked his heels together, brought his hand up to the brim of his cap in a military salute and in broken Persian announced to Dear Uncle, "Excuse me. You must forgive me . . . but I is representative . . . I must arresting you . . . I ask you did not resist!"

Dear Uncle's faint, lifeless eyes glittered. With difficulty he raised his right hand to his forehead in a military salute, and said in a barely audible voice, "I gave orders . . . I . . . I gave orders . . . that they shouldn't resist . . . great commander . . . a great commander is at your service."

And with celestial serenity he closed his eyes.

Asadollah Mirza laid him back on the bed and said, "I think you'd better rest now."

My father took Dear Uncle's pulse and said anxiously, "His pulse is weak and irregular . . . God, what's keeping that doctor . . . it wouldn't be a bad idea if I phoned Dr. Seyed Taqi Khan . . ." And he went off to the telephone.

I was staring dumbfounded at the English soldier when I realized that Asadollah Mirza had signalled to him with his eyes that he leave the room; as he left, Asadollah Mirza went after him.

I had understood nothing of what was going on. I peeped into the hallway and heard Asadollah Mirza's and the English soldier's conversation. Asadollah Mirza was trying to put a bank note into his hand but the Englishman was protesting in a thick Armenian accent, "Your excellency, I can't do it . . . you've been really good to me . . . you gave me the money for this shirt and trousers and the cap . . ."

"Please, Mr. Ardavas, I insist. It's nothing . . . this is the money for the English flag. Don't be so difficult!"

"I painted the flag on a bit of cloth myself. I really can't take it, on your brother's soul."

"For my sake, Barun Ardavas!"

"On your own soul, it's not possible . . . you want me to do you a little favor and I'm to take money for it?"

"I said for my sake! . . . So you aren't my friend?"

"What do you mean, you've been really good to me . . . I didn't do anything. I just put this shirt and trousers on in the yard and came up and said a couple of words!"

"Ardavas, I'll get angry, you know."

"Well, if you're ordering me to, all right. But really I'm ashamed to . . ."

"Bravo! . . . but this matter's to stay between us, all right? Put your own clothes on and be off till, God willing, we meet again!"

"Very good of you, your excellency . . . goodbye."

My father appeared in the doorway at this moment and stood there listening to them. The Armenian quickly changed his khaki shirt and trousers for civilian clothes, picked up the uniform and the English flag, and went on his way.

My father shook his head and said, "Well done, your highness! . . . And wherever did you find him? He looked so English I thought you'd hired a real Englishman."

"This Ardavas works in a café on Lalehzar Avenue . . . for years people have called him Ardavas the Englishman . . . his house is near here. The day before yesterday I thought I'd prepare this last present for the Master . . . How is he?"

"Well, it looks as though he's sleeping, but his complexion's not good at all."

"Anyway, it's better he should rest a little. Any news of the doctor?"

"There is. I talked to Dr. Seyed Taqi Khan and he said he'll come right away."

A few moments later the heart doctor came in with Mash Qasem, and almost immediately Dr. Seyed Taqi Khan also arrived. Dear Uncle was lying unconscious and motionless; when they examined him he showed no reaction. Both doctors gave their opinion that he should be taken immediately to the hospital.

Mash Qasem was more anxious than anyone else. "By all the saints, may God destroy 'em, everythin' the master's suffered's been because of them."

Asadollah Mirza angrily said, "Moment, Mash Qasem, don't start that old song and dance again."

"No sir, why should I lie? To the grave it's ah . . . ah . . . If you ask me, I guarantee you they slipped him something that didn't agree with him."

Dr. Seyed Taqi Khan was busy closing his medical bag; suddenly he pricked up his ears and said in a thick Tabrizi accent, "What? . . . You said they'd given him something that didn't agree with him?"

"Well why should I lie? To the grave it's . . ."

Asadollah Mirza and my father cut him off, "Really, Mash Qasem . . . this is nonsense . . ."

Dr. Seyed Taqi Khan shouted, "Let him say what he has to say! It so happens that I can see symptoms of poisoning in this patient."

The heart doctor laughed and said, "My dear doctor . . . this patient has been under my supervision for a considerable time . . . he had these same symptoms during all his past heart problems . . ."

Dr. Seyed Taqi Khan was a bad-tempered individual and he said sharply, "It is possible that you know the patient better than I do, but I am a coroner and from morning till night I see a hundred poisonings just like this."

"You can see a thousand and I would still maintain that such symptoms are normal for a patient suffering from cardiac arrest."

"I would ask you not to give me lessons in medical science . . . if I see the symptoms of poisoning in a patient I have a duty to report the matter to the relevant authorities, and this I shall do."

Asadollah Mirza and my father started to protest noisily but Dr. Seyed Taqi Khan would not take back what he had said.

Trying not to lose his self-control, Asadollah Mirza said, "Doctor, how is it that you thought of it just when this simple minded servant here said something? Why hadn't you noticed the signs of poisoning beforehand? Besides, listen to the rest of what Mash Qasem has to say."

Then he turned to Mash Qasem. "Mash Qasem, in your opinion, who gave something to the Master that didn't agree with him?"

"Well now, why should I lie? To the grave it's ah . . . ah . . . With my own eyes I never saw it. But I'm certain the English slipped the Master something that didn't agree with him."

Asadollah Mirza turned to the doctor. "Did you hear that, doctor? Mash Qasem believes that the British Empire has poisoned the Master."

"Who? . . . the British Empire . . . at all events, this is something that will be clarified in the hospital."

The heart doctor sneered, "They'll have to get the opium out of the patient's stomach and do a medicolegal analysis of it. Of course if it's English opium, then the English did it and they'll have to send an executive officer after Churchill!"

Dr. Seyed Taqi Khan gave his colleague a furious look, and if Asadollah Mirza had not started noisily protesting, he would certainly have let loose a flood of curses against him.

"Moment, moment . . . gentlemen, human decency and your profession require you to consider the patient, and not to quarrel about some trivial matter . . . Mash Qasem! Run and find a taxi so that we can take the Master to the hospital."

Half an hour later, despite the injection he had been given, Dear Uncle was still unconscious. They transferred him to the car. It was agreed that Mash Qasem immediately go and see uncle colonel in another taxi, and that he ask the colonel to leave the children where they were while he himself came back to town.

Asadollah Mirza gave Mash Qasem his last instructions. "But Mash Qasem, tell him in such a way that he won't be too worried; tell the colonel that the Master himself has requested that he come back to town. If the colonel's wife wants to come she can, but it's not necessary to bring the children."

The heart doctor set off for the hospital in his own car; the rest of us (including Dr. Seyed Taqi Khan) went in the car in which we had placed Dear Uncle.

❧   ❧   ❧

It was about noon. I was sitting on a bench in a hallway of the hospital, watching the gradually increasing number of our relatives who were going back and forth there.

They had placed Dear Uncle in an oxygen tent and were allowing no one into his room. The matter of Dear Uncle's being poisoned, in which Dr. Seyed Taqi Khan had been so interested, had been ruled out at the first examination, and Dr. Seyed Taqi Khan had left the hospital in a sulk.

I thought about Layli, and sometimes the thread of my thoughts led me to hate myself:

If Dear Uncle . . . if, God forbid, Dear Uncle were not to get better . . . How old is Dear Uncle? He himself says a little over sixty but my father says he's seventy if he's a day. A seventy-year-old's an old man! . . . But God forbid . . . God willing, he'll live a hundred years! . . . But . . . but . . . if he gets better he'll certainly marry Layli off to Puri . . . I'll be ruined, and so will Layli! . . . What kind of a thought is this that's found its way into my brain? Do I want Dear Uncle not to get well? . . . No, no, God forbid . . . O God, may they make Dear Uncle well again . . . but however could I interfere in what God's doing? . . . Whatever He wills . . . I'd better think of something else . . . By the way, why did Asadollah Mirza tell Mash Qasem not to bring the children? . . . Layli might want to see her father for the last time . . . There I go with that 'last time' again! I'm sorry, God, really sorry!

The relatives were all gathered together speaking to one another in low voices. My mother and aunts were very on edge, and the men were trying to calm them down. I went closer to see if there was anything new to be learned.

The latest news was that the doctors had said if he lasted until the evening it might be possible to save him. One of the doctors said in a puzzled way that during the one period in which he had regained consciousness for a few moments, he had repeated the names "St. Helena" and "Les Invalides" a few times, in among other words that were incomprehensible.

Finally I saw Asadollah Mirza in a corner by himself. I went over to him. "Uncle Asadollah, how do you think it'll turn out? I mean the doctors said that if by evening . . ."

Asadollah Mirza said in a low voice, "Yes, that's how it is . . . you're quite right . . . you've put your finger on it."

"I've put my finger on it?"

At that moment I realized, from the faint smile on his face and from his gaze which looked past my ear at something, that he was not paying any attention to me. I looked in the direction he was looking. A young nurse, who was making a show of arranging drugs and medicines on a table, was busy exchanging smiles and glances with him; she had entirely captured his lordship's attention.

I waited for a moment until the nurse went into a room. Asadollah Mirza was at liberty again and I could talk to him. "Uncle Asadollah, do you think Dear Uncle's in any danger?"

"It's with God now, lad. There's nothing we can do except pray."

"Uncle Asadollah, do you think . . . I mean, I want to ask you something . . ."

"Say on, lad. Ask away."

"I want to ask . . . when you said to Mash Qasem to bring uncle colonel but not to bring the children, were you thinking of me?"

"Moment, I don't follow. How would I be thinking of you?"

"I thought you didn't want Layli and Puri to be here in case Dear Uncle suddenly regained consciousness and sent for the notary, as he'd planned, and had Puri and Layli married."

Asadollah Mirza looked at me for a moment. A strange sadness welled up in his eyes. He pressed my head against his shoulder and after a few moments of silence said, "Everyone's here, nothing's going to be done by you and me staying here . . . let's go and have lunch at my house."

"I can't come . . . I have to stay here."

"Why should you be here? . . . Are you a physician, or an expert on oxygen?" Then he suddenly stared at the end of the hospital corridor. He seized my hand and pulled me up. "Let's get out of here . . . there's a bad smell spreading . . . look, Mrs. Farrokh Laqa's coming." Then, dragging me behind him, he said to my father as we passed, "I'm taking this boy home . . . what's the point of his staying here? We'll go and come back in the afternoon."

My father and mother welcomed the suggestion.

For the whole way home Asadollah Mirza talked of one thing and another. It was obvious he wanted to distract me from thinking about Dear Uncle and the things that had happened that day.

When we entered the living room of his house he went straight to the sideboard and brought out a bottle of wine and two glasses.

"Have a glass . . . we're really tired and worn out today. We deserve this glass."

Then, by insisting, he made me drink a second glass.

"But that was a really nice hospital . . . the next time I'm feeling sick I'm certainly going there . . . Did you see what nice pretty cuddly nurses they have . . . you know that line by Sa'di:

'*There was a doctor once in Merv whose slender height*
Shone like a cypress in the gardens of delight.'

Do you know it or not?"

"Uncle Asadollah, to be honest I don't feel like this kind of talk."

"Then drink another glass till you do feel like it . . . For goodness sake! . . . I said drink! . . . Bravo!"

Then he threw himself down on the sofa and went on with what he had been saying, "Once upon a time I was like you, too . . . very sensitive . . . very melancholy . . . but time changed me . . . a person's body is formed in the workshop of his mother's body, but a person's soul in the workshop of the world . . . have you heard about my former wife?"

"No, Uncle Asadollah . . . I mean, I knew you had married someone and then later divorced her."

"As simple as that, was it? I married a woman and then divorced her? Well, sit down and I'll tell you about it."

"Not now, Uncle Asadollah."

"Moment, then you have to drink another glass."

"No. I'm not feeling too good . . . just tell me about it."

"I was seventeen or eighteen when I fell in love . . . I fell in love with a distant relative . . . in fact she was the granddaughter of the uncle of that Farrokh Laqa who's always dressed in black . . . the girl wanted me, too . . . you know how you've no control over who you fall in love with when you're a child, when you're young . . . mothers and fathers make their children fall in love . . . from the first day they're always joking and drumming into the children's ears 'you're my little son-in-law,' 'you're my little daughter-in-law' . . . until one day you get to the age when you fall in love and you find you've fallen for your father's 'little daughter-in-law!' . . . and I fell for my father's little daughter-in-law. But when the fathers found out they gave us a very hard time. Her father had found her a richer husband than I was. And my father had found a richer bride . . . not that she was really rich. By the standards of that time the difference in income from land rent between us was about two hundred *tomans* a year. We put up with so many blows and curses that finally they let us marry one another. That day I felt I had set foot in heaven . . . for all of two years not even the thought of another woman crossed my mind. It was as if in all the world there were no other woman except my wife . . . this world and the next and sleeping and waking and the past and the future and everything were contained in this one woman . . . And apparently my wife felt this way about me, for a year; but gradually I changed in her eyes . . . I can't be bothered to describe the process of transformation, but in the second year, when I hurried home from the office, the reason as far as she could see was that I didn't have anywhere else to go. If I didn't look at other women it was because I didn't have the guts to . . ."

Asadollah Mirza poured himself another glass of wine and went on, "Tell me, do you remember asking me at various times who this photograph is of?" Asadollah Mirza pointed at a photograph, which had been for years on the stove in his living room, of an Arab wearing a kaffiyeh on his head.

"Yes, I remember. You mean that friend of yours, Uncle Asadollah?"

"Moment, moment. I always told you he was one of my old friends, but in fact he's not my friend, he's my savior."

"Your savior?"

"Yes, because one fine morning my wife ran off with this lout of an Arab. Then I divorced her and she became the wife of this Mr. Abdolqader Baghdadi."

"Uncle Asadollah, this Arab stole your wife and then you framed his photograph and put it on top of the stove in your house?"

"You're still a child, you don't understand. If you were drowning in the ocean and then at the last minute—when you were suffering unspeakable torments and your soul was being torn from your body— a whale were to save you, in your eyes that whale would be as beautiful as Jeanette McDonald. And this ugly Abdolqader is the whale who became Jeanette McDonald in my eyes."

"Uncle Asadollah, in my opinion putting his picture on the stove is a bit . . ."

Asadollah Mirza interrupted me, "Moment, wait for a few years and then tell me your opinion . . . let me just explain what Abdolqader was like. The difference between me and Abdolqader was that I spoke to my wife with refinement and he spoke to her coarsely and violently, I took a shower once a day and he took one once a month, I didn't even eat spring onions and he ate onions and garlic and radishes by the kilo, I read her poetry by Sa'di and he belched at her . . . and so in my wife's eyes I was stupid and he was clever, I was an idiot and he was intelligent. I was coarse and he was refined . . . But apparently he was a very good traveller . . . he was certainly good at travelling . . . he always had one foot here and one foot in San Francisco or Los Angeles."

I stared at the framed picture of the Arab on the stove and Asadollah Mirza went on talking. I no longer heard what he was saying or understood what he was driving at. Eventually I interrupted him, "Uncle Asadollah, why are you telling me this?"

"To make you see things a little more clearly. To make you understand a little sooner things that eventually you're going to have to understand whether you want to or not."

"You mean you want to say that Layli . . ."

He cut me off, "No, I've no such intention, but I want to say that if it happens that one day they give Layli to Puri, you haven't lost so much . . . if one fine day she's going to leave you for the sake of some Abdolkhaleq Mosuli or other, then it's all the better that they give her to Puri in the first place."

"Uncle Asadollah, Uncle Asadollah . . . you don't know how much I love Layli! You were in love, too, but my love . . ."

"Your love is greater than all other loves . . . of course, there's no doubt of that . . ."

"But if Dear Uncle's plan is put into practice, or if he gets better and they want to . . ."

Asadollah Mirza interrupted me, "They want to send for the notary, then you'll do away with yourself . . . I know that . . . The plan was nearly put into practice when they brought the notary over."

"What, Uncle Asadollah? Dear Uncle had the notary over?"

"Yes, but it was for something else . . . yesterday evening, when you were sick, they brought the notary to the house . . . the notary and Seyed Abolqasem . . . Dear Uncle was looking after five thousand *tomans* Mash Qasem had saved and for that they've sold Mash Qasem forty or fifty thousand meters of land out in the middle of God-knows-where, land which isn't worth one tenth of a *qeran* a meter and they've sold it to him for one *qeran* a meter . . . I only learned about all this last night. Mash Qasem came by and he was like a stuck pig he was so angry. But the poor devil was so afraid that Dear Uncle would get annoyed and his health would deteriorate that he'd agreed to it, and then . . . ."

"Uncle Asadollah, if he had brought the notary to the house, then why didn't he settle the matter of Layli and Puri as well?"

Asadollah Mirza was silent for some moments. I stared uneasily at his mouth. He muttered, "He settled that matter, too."

And he placed his hand over mine.

I don't know for how long I stayed there, bewildered and unable to move. My mind wasn't working properly. As if a needle were stuck in a record his words repeated themselves in my ears, without my properly understanding what they meant.

Later, I went over those moments for many long nights and days and was able to reconstruct the scene for myself.

Asadollah Mirza described to me how, the previous night, Dear Uncle had secretly summoned Layli and Puri and uncle colonel, and how, after making tragic and terrible speeches, he had persuaded them to agree to honor the last wish of a condemned and dying man.

The result of this was that that night Layli and Puri, before God and before the law, had formally become husband and wife.

In all the many times I have gone over this scene in my mind, what is not clear to me is my own reaction to this news. The one thing that has stayed in my mind is that for a moment my eyes stared at the hands of Asadollah Mirza's old clock, which was on the stove next to the picture of Abdolqader Baghdadi. It was a quarter to three in the afternoon. And this time made me remember the beginning of my love, which had started at a quarter to three one Friday the thirteenth of August.

On the evening of that day I once again succumbed to a violent fever. This time my high fever lasted for a few days and was so extreme that I have no proper memory of that period. Even the weeping and mourning for Dear Uncle's death, which happened the evening of that same day, left no clear impression on me. On the third day of my illness, at Asadollah Mirza's insistence, they took me to the hospital. No doctor was able to diagnose my illness. Dr. Naser al-Hokama stood by his original diagnosis of typhoid; the doctors in the hospital didn't agree with this diagnosis, but they themselves couldn't give a correct diagnosis either. More than anyone else it was Asadollah Mirza who cared about me. Later I also learned that when I was ready to go home from the hospital, he persuaded Dear Uncle's wife to take the children to her brother's house in Esfahan, and since he had been given a government posting in Beirut, he also persuaded my father to agree that I should go to Beirut with him and that after I had convalesced I should continue my education there.

It was the middle of summer when I went to Beirut with Asadollah Mirza. I was there until the end of the war. After the war I went from Beirut to France. And after many long years, during which I continued to bear the burden of my disappointed love, I returned to Tehran.

EPILOGUE

THE STORY OF MY LOVE, and what love put me through, has come to an end, but perhaps I should make some further mention of the people in my family and the heroes of this tale.

Later I realized that Layli accepted the disappointment much more easily than I had done. Of course it took some time before she and Puri began their life together. Apparently Dr. Naser al-Hokama's cure went forward at a slow pace. But when I returned they were the proud parents of three girls, all of whom, fortunately for Puri's reputation, were the image of their father. They lived in the house in the garden with uncle colonel, who had retired with the rank of major; they were the last inhabitants of the remaining part of the garden.

Of this story's other heroes I'll mention first what happened to the most fortunate of them, Cadet Officer Ghiasabadi and Qamar. The cadet officer managed Qamar's inheritance so shrewdly that he gradually became a rich man. Four or five years after I returned from abroad, he took his children to America to continue their education there. After Aziz al-Saltaneh had died, since Qamar couldn't bear to be so far away from her children, she and her husband went to America and I think they are now living in California.

After Aziz al-Saltaneh's death, Dustali Khan married again, and from what I have heard his new wife leads him such a dance that every day he blesses the memory of Aziz al-Saltaneh a thousand times over.

One day a few years ago, in among my late father's papers, I found Dear Uncle Napoleon's letter to Adolf Hitler, on which my father had written as a joking footnote, "Filed due to the death of the recipient." I saw Asadollah Mirza for the last time at Dr. Naser al-Hokama's funeral, and, though he was by then more than sixty years old, he looked no more than fifty. He had insinuated himself into the midst of the group of women who were there and was enjoying himself so thoroughly with the young females of the family that he didn't pay much attention to me; he merely said, "Poor Mrs. Farrokh Laqa, how desperately she wanted to be present at Dr. Naser al-Hokama's funeral, but she didn't last long enough."

"Uncle Asadollah, I wanted to say something to you."

"Moment, if it's not urgent can we talk about it later . . . if you get the chance drop by my house and we'll sit and drink a glass together . . ."

Then he ran over to a middle-aged woman and her daughter. "Wonderful to see you . . . I've missed you so much . . . Good heavens, Shahla my dear, how you've grown. Please fix an evening when you can come to my house with dear Shahla . . . will you come and see your uncle, Shahla? . . . What a lovely girl she is and no mistake."

Out of all this group, each of whom in turn had been accused of being a lackey and a spy of the English, there was only one real spy and that was the Indian Brigadier Maharat Khan, who had passed on news of the movements of the English to the Germans, and who was arrested by the English before the end of the war.

Mash Qasem seemed to have disappeared off the face of the earth, and from a year after Dear Uncle's death no one in the family had any news of him. The event seemed to have affected him so much that he didn't want to see any member of the family, or else, as some in the family said, he had died grieving for Dear Uncle. A long time after Dear Uncle died I learned that on his last day in the hospital he had regained consciousness for only a moment, and when he saw Mash Qasem at his bedside, a faint smile came to his lips. Mash Qasem, and those who were very close to him, heard him say "Bertrand, you will come with me!" and for a while Mash Qasem was upset thinking that "Bertrand" was some kind of a demon. Then, to reassure him, Asadollah Mirza spent hours telling him the story of how Marshal Bertrand had accompanied Napoleon into exile on St. Helena.

I think it must have been in 1966 that I went for a holiday trip to a small provincial town. On the first evening I went in search of a friend I had known abroad when I was at college and who was now a doctor. After our years apart, he showed himself to be extremely pleased to see me. He was dressed in clothes for going out. He said he had been invited to a friend's house, and as there would be a great number of people there, he could take me along with him.

We entered a large and very beautiful garden; on one side the instruments of an Iranian musical ensemble were laid out on the grass, and in another corner a Western band was playing and the young people were dancing. There were about a hundred and fifty guests. The party was being held to say goodbye to a son of the family who was leaving to continue his education in America. It was a very warm, friendly gathering and the family were extremely kind and hospitable. Two or three people stayed with me the whole time so that I wouldn't feel left out.

After supper I was sitting smoking near the pool, on a bench that was by a large sweetbrier arbor. A few of the guests were sitting under the arbor and a *tar* player, whom they referred to as a master musician, was performing pieces for them. Suddenly one of the guests in the arbor stood up and shouted in one direction, "Mr. Salar, come over and see us for a moment."

A dignified old man with a large white mustache and wearing thick glasses entered the arbor. All the guests stood as a sign of respect. The *tar* player bowed to him.

At this moment my friend came over to me. "Hunched up and hiding yourself away again?"

"No, I feel tired. If you don't mind, I'll sit for a minute."

"Then let me fill your glass."

"Thanks . . . tell me, who's the gentleman with the white mustache?"

"What, you haven't seen Mr. Salar . . . ? Mr. Salar's the host."

"What does he do? What's his profession? He seems to be a man of some importance."

"Well, he doesn't do anything, he's a landowner. From what people say, he owned a lot of land in Tehran that he'd bought when it was still desert and later it got to be worth a thousand or two thousand *tomans* a meter . . . to cut a long story short, in a few years he became a millionaire . . . but he's a very nice man, come and I'll introduce you to him . . . you're sure to like him. He's got lots of interesting memories . . . do you know, he was one of the constitutionalists . . . and for years he fought against the English."

"Against the English?"

"Yes, and it seems that the English tried to kill him a few times . . . come on, I'll introduce you to him."

"No, thanks . . . they're talking now. Later on."

Mr. Salar laid his stick aside, sat down and turned to the *tar* player. "Did I put you off playing by coming? Why don't you play?"

"It's very kind of you, sir, I'm a little tired."

The old man laughed and said, "You see these youngsters of to-day? They play a few notes and they're tired . . ."

My friend's mention of his former activities on behalf of the con-stitution, and his fighting against the English, made me prick up my ears. It seemed to me that Mr. Salar's voice sounded somehow famil-iar; the old man went on, "What days they were to be sure, I remember well . . . it was in the thick of the Battle of Kazerun . . . I don't know if I've told you or not. The English had hemmed us in from one side . . . on the other side there was Khodadad Khan who was one of their lackeys, with about a thousand cavalry . . . I saw there was no way out except for me to shoot Khodadad Khan . . . I had a fur hat and I put it on a stick. Khodadad Khan raised his head from be-hind a rock . . . I commended myself to Ali and aimed at the middle of his forehead . . . God rest his soul, I had a private who later on when the English wanted to arrest me, well, the poor devil wasn't very brave and he was so terrified he had a heart attack and died . . . What was I saying . . . oh yes . . . we'll leave aside how when the bullet hit Khodadad Khan his army scattered, and how we attacked the English . . . but we were talking about instruments . . . there was a Dustali Khan I knew who could play the *kamancheh* fiddle very nicely, believe me, sir, he'd play the *kamancheh* from when the sun went down to when it came up . . . again, some of those English we'd captured, their mouths were hanging open they were that amazed, they kept saying in English, Bravo, Well done, Terrific! . . ."

At this moment the host's daughter put her head round the edge of the arbor and said with a laugh, "Daddy, what kind of a time is this you've chosen to be retelling your memories? Let the guests enjoy themselves . . ."

The men all objected together and made many fine compli-ments to the effect that the stories they were hearing could not be bettered, and for their part the women flirted, "Goodness knows you tell the stories so beautifully, Mr. Salar."

I more or less recognized both the voice and the person, but I was still not quite certain. The daughter suddenly sat herself down on her father's lap and said laughing, "Now daddy, do you know any English at all?"

"Well now, why should I lie? To the grave it's ah . . . ah . . ."

Mr. Salar suddenly went silent, as if he had not wanted to say these words, but they had escaped from his mouth all the same; he looked around, then continued with what he had been saying.

Just then my friend came over with a glass of whisky and said, "You're really listening to Mr. Salar's conversation with great interest! Come on and I'll introduce you."

I said, "I'd really like that, from the bottom of my heart, but I don't want to come face to face with Mr. Salar just now. Later on, God willing."

And I didn't get the opportunity to see him after that.

Tonight I was busy writing out the last lines of this narrative. The phone rang. Someone wanted to talk to me from a hotel in Paris.

"Yes, who is it?"

"Hello lad, how are you then? Don't you ever think of me? Don't you recognize my voice?"

"Eh, Uncle Asadollah, where are you?"

"I've been in Paris for a week. . . . tomorrow morning I want to go to the south of France . . . and I'm taking two lovely little mademoiselles along with me, sweet as cooing doves they are. I wanted to know if you'd come for four or five days and we could be together?"

"Uncle Asadollah, I've a thousand things to do . . . If I'd known earlier maybe . . ."

"Moment, you wanted me to book time with you back during *Nowruz* in March for now? I only met these two yesterday, they're from Sweden . . . don't make such a fuss, just come . . . and from there we'll take a little trip to San Francisco."

"Uncle Asadollah, I'm very sorry but I've administrative duties to attend to. And besides, I don't know if I can get myself from Geneva to Paris by tomorrow morning. God willing, we'll do it another time . . ."

Asadollah's shout rang in my ears, deafening me, "Oh, get out of here! Always the same story—when you were a child, when you were a young man, and now—you've never been up to San Francisco and you still aren't . . . so goodbye till we meet in Tehran!"

THE END — GENEVA, AUGUST 1970

MASH QASEM
BY ARDESHIR MOHASSESS

GLOSSARY

AB-GUSHT: A soup made from meat, legumes and potatoes. The boiled meat is then pounded to a paste and eaten separately from the broth, which is eaten with bread.

ALI/ MORTEZA ALI: The son-in-law of the Prophet Mohammad and the father of Hasan and Hosayn (qv). After the prophet himself he is the most revered figure of Shi'i Islam and is considered by the Shi'i to be the paragon of all virtues, as well as being the archetypal victim of others' evil. His name is frequently invoked in oaths, particularly but not exclusively by the very devout and the poor.

AMIR ARSALAN: The hero of a very popular nineteenth-century prose romance probably orally composed by a member of the entourage of the ruling Qajar court named Naqib al-Mamalek and written down by the Qajar princess Fakhr al-Dawla.

ASGHAR THE MURDERER: A serial murderer (his victims were boys whom he raped and then killed) of the 1930s who occupies approximately the place in popular lore that Jack the Ripper does in Britain or Jeffery Dahmer in America.

ASH-RESHTEH: A soup made with herbs and noodles. Often when someone goes on a journey, a relative will make this soup which is then eaten at a party; this is thought to ensure a safe return.

BAHOT: An Urdu and Hindi word meaning "a lot, completely, entirely."

CHELO KABAB: Pieces of meat grilled on skewers and eaten with rice.

COLONEL LIAKHOFF: When Mohammad Ali Shah (qv) succeeded to the throne in 1907 he was determined to crush the forces within the country that had managed to set up a parliament (the *majlis*) and wished to break the monarchical autocracy. Colonel Liakhoff was the commander of a Cossack brigade which, on behalf of the new shah, carried out a coup against the shah's constitutional opponents. Liakhoff's most spectacular feat was the bombardment of the parliament building in 1908, and Dear Uncle Napoleon is supposed to have been present at this event as a member of the Cossack brigade.

CONSTITUTIONAL REVOLUTION: A Persian political movement which grew up in the later years of the nineteenth century. The movement was made up of differing groups, some religious and some secular; its secular aims included a devolution of power from the shah to a representative assembly (the *majlis*) and a drastic decrease in the influence of foreign powers (in particular the British and the Russians) over the government and economy of the country. Because of the latter aim the movement was with hindsight seen as intensely patriotic, and Dear Uncle Napoleon likes to imply that he was a participant in its agitations, though in reality he was involved in the movement's attempted suppression under Colonel Liakhoff (qv).

FERDOWSI: The great epic poet of Iran, who lived from 940 to c.1020. His poem, the *Shahnameh*, is popularly seen as the most patriotic of Iranian literary works and is full of descriptions of battles and individual heroism; it is thus entirely appropriate that many of the fragments of poetry which Dear Uncle Napoleon quotes are by Ferdowsi.

HAFEZ: A fourteenth-century poet, and the most famous of Iran's lyric poets. The poem by him to which Asadollah Mirza alludes, and which he says he quoted to Maharat Khan, is said to refer to a period of exile Hafez spent away from his hometown Shiraz, and hence its relevance to the occasion.

HASAN: The son of Ali (qv) and brother of Hosayn (qv). Believed by the Shi'i to have been martyred by poisoning. The shrine to which Mash Qasem wishes to make a pilgrimage, in Chapter 12, is near Tehran and is the grave of a different and less significant Hasan.

HOSAYN: The son of Ali (qv) and brother of Hasan (qv); martyred at the Battle of Karbela (qv), the commemoration of which is the most emotionally charged mourning ceremony in the Shi'i calendar.

IMAM(S): The vast majority of Iranians belong to the Twelver Shi'i sect of Islam, which recognizes twelve imams. These are Ali (qv), his sons Hasan and Hosayn (qv), and male descendants of Hosayn to the ninth generation. The imams are considered to be sinless, to be particularly dear to God, and to be perfect exemplars of humanity. All are believed to have been martyred except the last, who went into hiding (occultation), still lives, and will emerge from occultation to lead the forces of good during the last days before God's final judgment of the world.

JEANETTE MACDONALD: A 1930s Hollywood movie star and singer.

KAMANCHEH: A small stringed instrument, held vertically and played with a bow. It has a small cylindrical body, a long neck and a long blunt spike or foot which the player usually rests on one knee.

KARBELA: The site (in modern day Iraq) of the battle at which Hosayn was martyred and where he is believed to be buried. A major site of Shi'i pilgrimage.

LAYLI AND MAJNUN: The most famous pair of lovers of Islamic literature. Though the story is originally Arabic, well-known versions of the story exist in both Persian and Turkish. As the lovers belong to antagonistic tribes, and as the tale ends tragically, it is often compared to the story of Romeo and Juliet.

MASUMEH: An epithet (meaning "the chaste") applied particularly to Fatima, daughter of the Imam Musa al-Qasem, who died in 816 at Qom, in central Iran. The shrine erected over her grave is one of the two major sites of Shi'i pilgrimage in Iran, the other being the shrine erected over her brother Imam Reza's grave in Mashhad.

MOHAMMAD ALI SHAH: Shah of Iran from 1907 to 1909; an autocratic opponent of democratic reform, he was forced to abdicate after his attempts to crush the liberal opposition.

MOHAMMAD SHAH: Shah of Iran from 1834 to 1848.

MOSLEM IBN AGHIL: A nephew of Ali (qv) and a cousin and staunch supporter of Hosayn (qv); he was captured while attempting to raise forces on Hosayn's behalf and was killed. His two sons were killed at Karbela (qv). Though he is an important figure for the Shi'i, he is not an imam and the anniversary of his death is not normally commemorated in the way that the deaths of Ali and Hosayn are, so that Dear Uncle Napoleon's last minute arrangement of a mourning ceremony in his name has a rather desperate air to it.

NAIN: A small and very beautiful oasis town in central Iran, famous for its carpets and cloth.

NANEH: An affectionate term for an older woman, meaning "mother" (cf. the French use of *mère*).

NASER AL-DIN SHAH: Shah of Iran from 1848 to 1896.

NOWRUZ: The Persian New Year's festival, which falls precisely on the Spring equinox around March 21.

QAMAR-E BANI HASHEM: A title (meaning "Moon of the Hashemites") given to Abbas, the brother of Hosayn (qv), killed at Karbela (qv).

QERAN: The old name for the low denomination coin now called a *rial*.

QOM: A town in central Iran, famous as a site of Shi'i pilgrimage and for its theological schools.

QURAN: Also transliterated in English as Koran. The holy book of Islam, believed by Moslems to be uncreated and to have been revealed to the Prophet Mohammad in a series of revelations at Medina and Mecca.

QORBAN: The festival of sacrifices, a major event in the Islamic calendar.

SA'DI: A thirteenth-century Iranian poet. He is famous for the elegance, charm and canny worldliness of his writings, so it is entirely appropriate that the canny and would-be charming ladies' man Asadollah Mirza quotes him frequently. Dear Uncle Napoleon also quotes him (the verses about a wolf cub growing up as a wolf no matter how he is raised, which Dear Uncle Napoleon applies to the narrator, are from Sa'di's *Golestan*).

SEYED: A direct descendant of the Prophet Mohammad. Seyeds are accorded particular respect by Shi'a Moslems.

SHA'ABDOLAZIM: A minor place of pilgrimage to the south of Tehran.

SHEMR: Commander of the troops who defeated Hosayn (qv) at Karbela (qv). Before the battle he caused the water supply to

Hosayn's troops to be cut off so that they suffered from extreme thirst; this latter incident is very famous in the lore of Shi'i Islam and it is this to which Mash Qasem refers when Dear Uncle Napoleon's cellars are flooded.

SHIRIN AND FARHAD: A pre-Islamic Persian love story. The lowly stone mason Farhad falls in love with the princess Shirin but his royal rival for her love has him told that she has died, whereupon Farhad himself dies. The story exists in various versions, the most famous being by the poet Nezami (twelfth century).

TAR: A traditional plucked stringed instrument, similar to a slim lute.

TOMAN: A coin equal to ten *rials*. Because of the vagaries of exchange controls and inflation it is difficult to give a precise western equivalent. Before the Islamic Revolution of 1979 there were approximately seven *tomans* to one US$. At the time of writing (1996) one US$ is worth more than 300 *tomans*.

YAZID: The caliph who ordered Shemr (qv) to move against and destroy Hosayn (qv). Together Yazid and Shemr occupy a place in Shi'i lore more or less equivalent to that of Judas in Christian lore.

ZARB: A small drum, held under one arm and played, often with dazzling rhythmic dexterity, with the hands (finger tips, palm, knuckles, ball of the thumb).

ABOUT THE AUTHOR

IRAJ PEZESHKZAD was born in Tehran, Iran, in 1928 and educated in
Iran and France where he received his degree in Law. He served as a
judge in the Iranian Judiciary for five years prior to joining the Iranian
Foreign Service. He was posted to Austria, Czechoslovakia, Switzer-
land, and Algeria before returning to Iran to eventually head the
Cultural Relations Division of the Iranian Foreign Ministry. He began
writing in the early 1950s by translating the works of Voltaire and
Molière into Persian and by writing short stories for magazines. His
novels include: *Haji Mam-ja'far in Paris* and *Mashalah Khan in the
Court of Haroun al-Rashid* (for young adults). He has also written several plays and various articles on the Iranian Constitutional Revolution
of 1905, the French Revolution, and the Russian Revolution. He is
currently living in Paris, where he works as a journalist.

ABOUT THE TRANSLATOR

DICK DAVIS was born in Portsmouth, England, in 1945 and educated
at King's College, Cambridge (B.A. and M.A. in English Literature)
and at the University of Manchester (PhD. in Medieval Persian
Literature). He has taught at the universities of Tehran, Durham,
Newcastle, and California (Santa Barbara) and is currently associate
professor of Persian at Ohio State University. He lived for eight years
(1970-1978) in Iran, as well as for periods in Greece and Italy. He has
published numerous books of poetry (one of which received the Royal
Society of Literature's Heinemann Award, and another the Ingram-
Merrill Award), translations of medieval Persian poetry (including
Ferdowsi's *The Legend of Seyavash*, and with his wife Afkham
Darbandi, *Attar's Conference of the Birds*, both with Penguin Classics),
as well as scholarly works and editions. He is a Fellow of the Royal
Society of Literature.

Colophon

The
text type
is a digitized
version of Janson,
a typeface long thought
to have been made by the Dutchman
Anton Janson,
a   type
founder
practicing
in Leipzig during
the   years   1668-1687.
However, this type is actually the work of Nicholas
Kis (1650-1702), a Hungarian
who probably learned his trade
from the Dutch type founder
Dirk Voskens. The type was
set at Mage by Tony Ross
using FrameMaker 4.0 and
Quark XPress 3.32 on an
Apple Macintosh Quadra
900. The book was printed
and bound by Thomson-Shore
in Dexter, Michigan. The
front cover illus-
tration   is   a
computer
generated
image from
watercolors
by Ardeshir
Mohassess.
The jacket was
designed by
Rohani
Design. The
book was
designed by
Mohammad and Najmieh Batmanglij